Anonymous

A New Theatrical Dictionary

Containing an account of all the dramatic pieces that have appeared from the

commencement of theatrical exhibitions to the present time.

Anonymous

A New Theatrical Dictionary
*Containing an account of all the dramatic pieces that have appeared from the
commencement of theatrical exhibitions to the present time.*

ISBN/EAN: 9783337410926

Printed in Europe, USA, Canada, Australia, Japan

Cover: Foto ©Andreas Hilbeck / pixelio.de

More available books at **www.hansebooks.com**

A NEW

THEATRICAL
DICTIONARY.

CONTAINING

AN ACCOUNT OF ALL THE

DRAMATIC PIECES'

THAT HAVE APPEARED FROM THE COMMENCEMENT
OF THEATRICAL EXHIBITIONS TO THE
PRESENT TIME.

TOGETHER WITH

Their Dates when Written or Printed, where Acted, and Occasional
Remarks on their Merits and Success.

TO WHICH IS ADDED,

AN ALPHABETICAL CATALOGUE

OF

DRAMATIC WRITERS,

WITH

The Titles of all the Pieces they have Written, annexed to each Name.

AND ALSO

A Short Sketch of the Rise and Progress of the

ENGLISH STAGE.

LONDON.

PRINTED FOR S. BLADON, No. 13, PATERNOSTER-ROW.

M.DCC.XCII.

PREFACE.

DRAMATIC Compofitions have ever been ranked among the principal productions of human genius; and the reprefentations of them on the public Stage have been recommended by the wifeft and moft approved men of all ages, as affording the moft ufeful and inftructive leffons in the School of Morality and Virtue. In the theatrical reprefentations of our beft dramatic pieces, Nature is feen in her native colours, and the rifing generation are taught, in this humanizing and inftructing academy, to view the various difpofitions of the human heart, and fee the manners of the world, without encountering thofe dangers, which the different purfuits of life are perpetually throwing in their way.

If then dramatic ftudies be of fo much importance, every attempt to render them

more

more eafy and familiar cannot fail of being acceptable to the public. With this view we offer the following work to their candid perufal ; and, though 'it contains every play of confequence that has ever appeared, yet we have comprifed it in the fize of one moderate volume, without depriving the different articles of their neceffary information.

The name of the author of each piece is given, excepting thofe which are anonymous publications, together with the dates when printed or acted, and occafional remarks on their merit and fuccefs, and other incidental particulars.

At the end of this volume we have given an alphabetical catalogue of the names of all the dramatic writers, and to each name we have annexed the titles of all the pieces they have publifhed or written, fo that the works of each author may be feen at one view. Thofe that have not been printed are thus * marked ; and the time which any author flourifhed may be eafily afcertained, by referring to the defcription of their plays in the preceding part of this volume.

We

We have alfo added a fhort fketch of the Rife and Progrefs of the Englifh Stage, which, we hope, will be confidered as a proper companion to a work of this nature. We are fenfible how much we ftand in need of the candour and indulgence of the public, well knowing that all human productions muft be imperfect, and that works of this nature in particular cannot be free from errors. Where fuch fhall occur to the obfervation of our readers, if they will pleafe to tranfmit their corrections to the publifher, they will be gratefully received, and duly attended to in a future edition.

ADVERTISEMENT.

C O N T E N T S.

ABBREVIATIONS

EXPLAINED.

B.   Burletta
B. O. Ballad Opera
C.   Comedy
C. H. Comical Hiſtory
C. F. Comic Farce
C. O. Comic Opera
C. S. Comical Satire
D. C. Dodſley's Collection of Old Plays
D. E. Dramatic Entertainment
D. N. Dramatic Novel
D. R. Dramatic Romance
D. P. Dramatic Poem
D. S. Dramatic Satire
E.   Entertainment
F.   Farce
F. T. Fairy Tale
F. O. Farcical Opera
H. P. Hiſtorical Play
I.   Interlude
M.   Maſque
M. E. Muſical Entertainment
M. D. Muſical Drama
M. O. Muſical Opera
O.   Opera
P. D. Paſtoral Drama
T.   Tragedy
T. C. Tragi-Com.

NEW THEATRICAL

DICTIONARY.

ABDELAZAR; or, *The Moor's Revenge.* Trag. by Mrs. Aphra Behn. Acted at the duke of York's theatre, 4to. 1677. This play is evidently an alteration of Marloe's *Lascivious Queen.* From this piece, however, Dr. Young took the hint of his admirable tragedy of *The Revenge*; the death of a father, and the loss of a crown, being the prime motives of resentment equally in *Abdelazar* and *Zanga.*

Abdicated Prince; or, *The Adventures of Four Years.* Tragi-Com. Anonym. Acted at Alba Regalis, by several persons of great quality, 4to. 1690. This piece is entirely political, and seems not to have been intended for the stage: it contains, under feigned names, the transactions of the English court and nation during the reign of James II. with the abdication of that

prince, but written with great partiality.

Abel, an Oratorio, performed at Cov. Gard. 1755.

Abradates and Panthea. Trag. Acted by the Scholars of St. Paul's School, 1770. Not printed.

Abraham's Sacrifice. Of this play neither the author nor date is known; but it is supposed to be a translation from Theodore Beza.

Abra-Mule; or, *Love and Empire.* Tragedy, by Dr. Joseph Trapp. Acted at the new theatre in Lincoln's-Inn-Fields, 4to. 1704. The scene lies in Constantinople, and the plot of it may be more fully seen in a book called *Abra-Mule*; or, the true history of the dethronement of *Mahomet* IV. by M. Le Noble; translated by S. P. The incidents in this piece are in themselves so affecting, and the plot so interesting, that it has generally

B

nerally met with applause in the performance.

The Absent Man Farce, by Isaac Bickerstaffe. Acted at Drury-Lane, 8vo. 1768. This piece has some merit, and met with no unfavourable reception. Another piece, of the same name, by Mr. T. Hull. Not printed.

Accolaftus. Comedy, by John Palfgrave, Chaplain to Henry VIII. 4to. 1640. This piece, which is a translation from a Latin play of the same name, was the third dramatic piece ever published in England.

The Accomplished Maid. Com. Op. by Mr. Toms. Acted at Covent-Garden, 8vo. 1766. A translation of *La Buona Figliola.*

Achilles ; or, *Iphigenia in Aulis.* T. by Abel Boyer. Acted at Drury-Lane, 4to. 1700. This is a translation from the *Iphigenia of Racine.* It was acted without success.

Achilles. An Opera, by John Gay, 8vo. This piece, which is in the manner of the *Beggar's Opera,* is a ludicrous relation of the discovery of Achilles by Ulysses. The scene lies in the court of Lycomedes. Achilles is in woman's cloaths through the whole play, and it concludes by his marriage with Deidamia. It was acted in 1733

at Covent-Garden. It has been since abridged and reduced to a Ballad Farce, and as such was acted in 1773 with very indifferent success.

Achilles in Petticoats. An Opera, altered from Gay, by George Colman. Acted at Covent-Garden, 8vo. 1774. This alteration met with little success.

Acis and Galatea. A Masque, by P. Motteux, from *Ovid's Metam.* Book XIII. set to music by John Eccles, and performed at Drury-Lane.

Acis and Galatea. An English Pastoral Opera, in three acts, by John Gay. The story is taken from the 13th Book of *Ovid's Metamorphoses* ; the music composed by Handel, and was performed at the Haymarket, 1732.

Act at Oxford. Com. by Thomas Baker, 4to. 1704. This piece, the scene of which lies in Oxford, was never acted.

Actæon and Diana. An Interlude, by Mr. Robert Cox, 4to. No date. The story is taken from *Ovid's Metamorphoses.*

Adelphi ; or, *The Brothers.* Com. translated from *Terence,* by Richard Bernard, 4to. 1598.

Adelphi. The same play, translated by Laurence Echard, 8vo. 1694.

Adelphi.

A D

Adelphi. Com. tranflated by T. Cook, 12mo. 1734.

Adelphi. Com. tranflated by S. Patrick, 8vo. 1745.

Adelphi. Com. tranflated by Gordon, 12mo. 1752.

Adelphi. Com. tranf-lated by G. Colman, 4to. 1765.

A new tranflation of the *Adelphi* of Terence into blank verfe, 8vo. 1774. None of thefe tranflations were ever intended for, nor are they by any means adapted to, the Englifh ftage.

Adrafta; or, *The Wo-man's Spleen and Love's Con-queft.* Tragi-Com. by John Jones, never acted, but printed in 4to. 1635.

The Adventurer. Farce. Acted at Drury-Lane, 1790. The dialogue of this piece is humourous and fprightly, and the wit is pointed and generally fterling.

Adventures in Madrid. Com. by Mrs. Pix. Act-ed at the Queen's Theatre in the Haymarket, 4to. No date.

Adventures of Five Hours. Tragi-Com. by Sir Samuel Tuke, Bart. 4to. 1664. 4to. 1671. It is tranflated from a Spanifh play, recommend-ed by king Charles II. was acted with great applaufe, and has feveral copies of verfes prefixed to it by Mr. Cowley, and other eminent poets of that time.

A G

Adventures of Half an Hour. F. by Chriftopher Bullock. 12mo. 1716.

The Adventures of a Night. A Farce, acted at Drury-Lane, 1783. This piece, though not a firft-rate per-formance, poffeffes a good fhare of farcical merit.

Aeroftation, or, *The Tem-plar's Stratagem.* Farce, by Mr. Pilon. Acted at Covent-Garden, 1784. The paffion of a lady of fortune for bal-loons furnifhes the plot of this piece.

The Affected Ladies. C. by John Ozell. A literal tranflation of the *Precieufes Ridicules* of Moliere.

Againft Momus's and Zoi-lus's. A Dramatic Piece, by John Bale, bifhop of Offory, the firft Englifh dramatic writer. Of this piece we have no remains but the bare mention of it by himfelf, in his account of the writers of Britain.

Againft thofe who adulte-rate the Word of God. A Dramatic Piece, by the laft-mentioned author; and of which we have exactly the fame kind of knowledge. In all probability, they were written at fome time be-tween 1530 and 1540.

Agamemnon. T. by James Thomfon. Acted at Drury-Lane, 8vo. 1738.

Agamemnon. Tr. tranf-lated from *Seneca* by John Studly,

Studly, in queen Elizabeth's reign.

Agamennon. Trag. translated from *Æfchylus,* by R. Potter, 4to. 1777.

Agis. T. by John Home, performed at Drury-Lane, 1758, 8vo. This play is founded on a story in the Spartan History.

Aglaura. Tragi-Com. by Sir John Suckling; acted at the private house in Black-Fryars, 8vo. 1646. The author has so contrived this play, by means of an alteration in the last Act, that it may be acted either as a tragi-comedy, or a perfect tragedy. The scene lies in *Perfia.*

Agnes de Caftro. Trag. by Mrs. Cath. Trotter, afterwards Cockburne, 4to. acted at the Theatre Royal, 1696. It is built on a French novel of the same name, translated by Mrs Behn, and deservedly met with very good success.

The Agreeable Surprife. Farce, by J. Keefe. Acted at the Haymarket, 1781, but not printed. Very exceptionable for its indecency.

Agrippa, King of Alba ; or, *The Falfe Tiberinus.* Tragi-Com. by John Dancer. This is a translation from M. Quinault ; it is in heroic verse, was performed several times with great applause at the Thea-

tre Royal in Dublin, and was printed at London in 4to. 1675.

Agrippina, Emprefs of Rome, her Tragedy, by Tho. May, Efq. The scene of this play lies in Rome, and the plot is taken from the Roman historians. It was acted in 1628, and printed in 12mo. 1639 and 1654.

Agrippina, a Tragedy in rhime, by John Lord Hervey. Not printed.

King Ahafuerus and Queen Efther. An Interlude, attributed to Robert Cox, comedian, and is published in the second part of *Sport upon Sport,* 1672.

Ajax. Tragedy, 12mo. 1714. This is only a translation from the Greek of *Sophocles,* by one Mr. Jackson, but revised by Mr. Rowe.

Aladin ; or, *The Wonderful Lamp.* Pantomime, taken from the Arabian Nights Entertainment. Acted at Covent-Garden, 1788.

Alaham. Tra. by Fulke Grevile, lord Brook, folio, 1633. The scene of this play is laid at the mouth of the Perfian Gulph, and the plot taken from some incidents in Herbert's travels. The author has followed the model of the ancients ; the Prologue is spoken by a Ghoft, who gives an account of every character, and

fo

fo ftrictly has he adhered to the rules of the drama, that he has not throughout introduced more than two fpeakers at a time, excepting in the choruffes between the Acts.

Alarbas. A Dramatic Opera, written by a gentleman of quality, 4to. 1709. The fcene lies in *Arcadia* in Greece.

Alarum for London; or, *The Siege of Antwerp : with the ventrous Acts and valorous Deeds of the Lame Soldier.* Tragi-Com. Acted by the lord-chamberlain's fervants, 4to. 1602. This play is not divided into acts, the plot is taken from *The Tragical History of the City of Antwerp.*

Albertus Wallenftein, late Duke of Fridland, and General to the Emperor Ferdinand II. Trag. by Henry Glapthorne. It was acted at the Globe, by the Bank Side, 4to. 1634. The fcene lies at *Egers.*

Albina. Trag. by Mrs. Cowley. Acted at the Haymarket 1779, 8vo.

Albion. An Interlude, of which we know nothing more than the name.

Albion; or, *The Court of Neptune.* A Mafque, by T. Cooke, 8vo. 1724. The fcene laid on the Britifh feas.

Albion and Albanius. An

Opera, by J. Dryden. Acted at the Theatre Royal, fol. 1685. Set to mufic by Lewis Grabue, Efq. The fubject of this piece is wholly allegorical, being intended to expofe lord Shaftefbury and his adherents.

Albion Queens. See *Ifland Queens.*

Albion Reftor'd; or, *Time turn'd Oculift.* A Mafque, never acted, 8vo. 1758.

Albion's Triumph, perfonated in a Mafke at Court, by the King's Majefty and his Lords (all whofe names are at the end), *the Sunday after Twelfth Night,* 1631, 4to. The fcene is Albipolis, the chief city of Albion.

Albovine King of the Lombards. Trag. by Sir W. Davenant, 4to. 1629. The fcene lies in Verona.

Albumazar. Comedy, prefented before the King's Majeftie at Cambridge the 9th of March, 1614, by the gentlemen of Trinity College, 4to. 1615. 4to. 1634. This play was written by Mr. Tomkis, of Trinity College ; and acted before king James on the day above-mentioned.

Albumazar. C. by David Garrick. Acted at Drury-Lane, 8vo. 1773. This is an alteration of the above play. Though it had the advantage of the beft performers, yet neither on this, or a former revival

revival of it in 1748, did it meet with much fuccefs.

Alcamenes and Menalippa. Trag. Date and author unknown.

Alceftis. Tragedy, tranflated from Euripides, by R. Potter, 4to. 1781.

Alchymift. C. by Ben. Jonfon. 4to. 1610. This play is too well known and admired to need any comment on or account of it.

Alcibiades. Tragedy, by Thomas Otway. Acted at the Theatre Royal, 4to. 1675. 4to. 1687. The ftory of this play is taken from *Corn. Nepos and Plutarch.* The author has, however, confiderably departed from the hiftory, and without any apparent reafon. This is the worft of Otway's tragedies.

Alexander the Great. By T. Ozell, tranflated from *Racine,* 12mo. 1714.

Alexander the Great. Op. performed at Lincoln's-Inn-Fields, 8vo. 1715.

Alexander and Campafpe. A Com. by John Lyly, played before queen Elizabeth, on Twelfth-Night, by the children of St. Paul's, 4to. 1584. Plot from Pliny's *Nat. Hift.* B. 35. Ch. 10.

The Alexandræan Tragedy; by William Alexander, earl of Stirling, 4to. 1605. The ground-work of this play is laid on the differences which arofe among Alexander's captains, after his deceafe, about the fucceffion. The fcene lies in Babylon, and the plot is to be found in Quintus Curtius, Juftin, and other hiftorians.

Alexas; or, *The Chafte Gallant.* By Philip Maffinger. His bafhful lover feems to be fometimes called by this name.

Alexis's Paradife; or, *A Trip to the Garden of Love at Vauxhall.* Com. by James Newton, Efq. 8vo. 1732.

Alfred. A Mafque; by James Thomfon and David Mallet, 8vo. 1740. The fcene of this play lies in Britain; and the ftory is from the English hiftory at the time of the Danifh Invafion.

Alfred. An Opera, as altered from the above play. Acted at Covent-Garden, 8vo. 1745.

Alfred. A Mafque, by David Mallet. Acted at Drury-lane, 8vo. 1751.

Alfred. Trag. altered from Mallet, by David Garrick. Acted at Drury-lane, 8vo. 1773.

Alfred. Trag. by John Home, 8vo. 1778. Acted only three nights at Covent-Garden.

All Alive and Merry. Comedy, by S. Johnfon, the dancing-mafter. This piece was acted at Lincoln's-coln's-Inn-Fields, about the year 1737, without any fuccefs, and has never been printed.

All Bedevilled ; or, *The Houfe in an Uproar.* Farce, by Mofes Browne, 8vo. 1723.

All Fools. C. by George Chapman, 4to. 1605. D. C. The plot is founded on *Terence's Heautontimorumenos.*

All for Love ; or, *The World well Loft.* Trag. by John Dryden, acted at the Theatre Royal, 4to. 1678. This is generally confidered by the critics as the moft compleat dramatic piece of that juftly admired author. There needs, perhaps, no other reafon to be affigned for its being fo, than that it was the only one (amongft a very large number) which he was permitted to bring to that perfection which leifure and application, added to a moft capital degree of genius, might be expected to attain. The plot and general defign of it is undoubtedly borrowed from Shakfpeare's *Anthony and Cleopatra.* It may perhaps ftand hereafter as a matter of conteft, whether this tragedy is, or is not, to be efteemed as an invincible mafter-piece of the power of Englifh poetry.

All for Money. A moral

and pitiful Comedy. Compiled by Tho. Lupton, 4to. B. L. 1578.

All for the Better ; or, *The Infallible Cure.* C. by F. Manning ; acted at Drury-Lane, 1703, 4to. The fcene lies in Madrid.

All Miftaken ; or, *The Mad Couple.* Com. by the Hon. James Howard, Efq. acted at the Theatre Royal, 4to. 1672. The fcene lies in Italy.

All in the Wrong. Com. by Arthur Murphy, 8vo. 1761. This comedy made its firft appearance at the Theatre Royal in Drury-Lane, under the conduct of Mr. Foote and the author. It met with fuccefs, and defervedly. The intention of it is to bring together into one piece, and reprefent at one view, the various effects of the paffion of jealoufy in domeftic life. The characters are not ill drawn, though perhaps not perfectly finifhed ; on the whole, however, it is a very entertaining comedy.

All's Loft by Luft. Trag. by William Rowley. Acted at the Phœnix, 1633, 4to. This play was well efteemed. Its plot is chiefly from Novel 3, of the *Unfortunate Lovers.*

All up at Stockwell ; or, *The Ghoft no Conjuror.* Interlude. Acted at Drury-Lane,

Lane, as a benefit, 1772. Not printed.

All's Well that Ends Well. C. by Shakſpeare, fol. 1623.

All the World's a Stage. Farce, by Mr. Jackman. Acted at Drury-Lane, 8vo. 1777.

Almanzor and Almahide; or, The Conqueſt of Granada. The ſecond part by John Dryden. Acted at the Theatre Royal, 4to. 1672.

Almena. Op. by Richard Rolt. Acted at Drury-Lane, 8vo. 1764. The muſic by Arne, jun. and Battiſhill.

Almeyda; or, The Rival Kings. Trag. by Gorges Edmund Howard, 12mo. 1769. The ſtory of this play is taken from *Almoran and Hamet*, by Dr. Hawkeſworth, and is not without merit.

Almida. Trag. by Mrs. Celiſia. Acted at Drury-Lane, 8vo. 1771. From the excellent performance of Mrs. Crawford this play had a conſiderable run.

Almyna; or, The Arabian Vow. Tragedy, by Mrs. Manley. Acted at the Theatre Royal in the Haymarket, 1707, 4to. The ſcene lies in the capital of Arabia, and the fable is taken from the life of *Caliph Valid Amanzer*, with ſome hints from the *Arabian Nights Entertainments*.

Alonzo. Trag. by John Home. Acted at Drury-Lane, 8vo. 1773. By the aſſiſtance of excellent acting, this piece obtained a nine nights' hearing, and then ſunk into oblivion.

Alphonſo, King of Naples. Tragedy, by George Powell. Acted at the Theatre Royal, 1691. 4to. The ſcene lies in Naples, and the ſtory is founded on Neapolitan hiſtory.

Alphonſus, Emperor of Germany. Tr. by George Chapman, often acted with great applauſe in Black-Fryars, printed in 4to. 1654. This play ſeems to have been written in honour of the Engliſh nation, in the perſon of Richard earl of Cornwall, ſon to King John, and brother to Henry III. who was choſen king of the Romans in 1257, at the ſame time that Alphonſus, the 10th king of Caſtile, was choſen by other electors.

Alphouſus, King of Arragon. Hiſtor. Play, by R. G. acted with applauſe, and publiſhed in 4to. 1599.

Altemira. Trag. by Benj. Victor, 8vo. 1776.

Altemira. Tragedy, in rhime, by Roger Boyle, earl of Orrery. Acted in Lincoln's-Inn-Fields. The ſcene is Sicily.

Alzira; or, The Spaniſh Inſult repented. T. by Aaron Hill. Acted at Lincoln's-Inn-

AM

Inn-Fields, 8vo. 1736. This play is a translation from Voltaire.

Alzuma. Tragedy, by Arthur Murphy. Acted at Covent-Garden, 8vo. 1778. This play is far inferior to the *Orphan of China, Zenobia,* and the *Grecian Daughter,* by the same hand, and was received with coldness throughout its nine night's existence on the stage.

Amana. Dram. Poem, by Mrs. Elizabeth Griffith, 4to. 1764. The story of this piece is taken from *The Adventurer,* No. 72 and 73. It was never acted.

Amasis, King of Egypt. Trag. by Charles Marsh. Acted one night at the Little Theatre in the Haymarket, 8vo. 1738. Scene Memphis.

Amazonian Queen; or, *The Amours of Thalestris to Alexander the Great.* A Tragi-Com. in heroic verse, by J. Weston, 4to. 1667.

The Ambiguous Lover. A Farce, by Miss Sheridan. Acted at Crow-Street, 1781. Not printed.

The Ambitious Slave; or, *A Generous Revenge.* Tr. by Elkanah Settle. Acted at the Theatre Royal, 4to. 1694. The scene is the frontiers of Persia.

The Ambitious Statesman; or, *The Loyal Favourite.* Tr. by J. Crowne. Acted at

AM

the Theatre Royal, 4to. 1679. This play met with very indifferent success. The scene lies in Paris.

The Ambitious Stepmother. Tr. by Nicholas Rowe, 4to. 1700. Acted at Lincoln's-Inn-Fields. The scene lies in Persepolis, and the characters are made Persian, but the design of the play seems to have been taken from the establishing Solomon on the *Throne of David,* by Bathsheba, Zadock the Priest, and Nathan the Prophet. See 1 Kings, ch. i. from ver. 5.

Amboyna; or, *The Cruelties of the Dutch to the English Merchants.* Trag. by J. Dryden. Acted at the Theatre Royal, 4to. 1673. 4to. 1691. Scene Amboyna. The plot of this play is chiefly founded on history.

Amelia. Opera, after the Italian manner, by Henry Carey, set to music by J. F. Lampe, and performed at the French Theatre in the Haymarket, 8vo. 1732.

Amelia. A Musical Entertainment, by Richard Cumberland. Acted at Covent-Garden, 8vo. 1768. This was taken from *The Summer's Tale* of the same author.

Amelia; or, *The Duke of Foix.* Translated from Voltaire,

Voltaire, in vol. II. of Dr. Franklin's Edition, 12mo. The original play was acted Dec. 1752.

Amends for Ladies; with the merry pranks of *Moll Cut-purse*; or, *The Humours of Roaring*. Com. by Nat. Field, 4to. 1618. 4to. 1639. Scene London. This play was written by our author by way of making the ladies amends for a comedy called *Woman's a Weathercock*, which he had written some years before, and whose very title seemed to be a satire on their sex.

Aminta. The famous Pastoral, by Torquato Tasso, translated by John Dancer, 8vo. 1660.

Amintas. An English Op. performed at Covent-Garden, 8vo. 1769. An alteration of Rolt's *Royal Shepherdess*.

Aminta. A Pastoral, 4to. 1628. Translated from the Italian of Tasso, with Ariadne's complaint, in imitation of *Anguilara*.

Amintas. English Opera, acted at Covent-Garden, 1769. Compiled from the Italian of Metastasio, and the English Opera of the Royal Shepherd.

Amintas. Dramatic Past. translated from Tasso, by William Ayre, 8vo. 1737.

Amorous Bigot, with the second part of *Teague O'Di-*

velly. Com. by Thomas Shadwell.

Amorous Miser; or, *The Younger the Wiser*. Com. by P. Motteux, 4to. 1705. The scene lies in Spain.

Amorous Old Woman; or, *'Tis well if it Take*. Com. attributed by Langbaine to Thomas Duffet. Acted at the Theatre Royal, 4to. 1764. It was afterwards re-published, with a new title-page, by the name of *The Fond Lady*.

Amorous Fantasme. Tragi-Com. by Sir Wm. Lower, 12mo. 1660. This play is translated from the *Fantome Amoureux* of Quinault.

Amorous Prince; or, *The Curious Husband*. Com. by Mrs. Behn. Acted at the Duke's Theatre, 4to. 1671. The plot of this play is built on the Novel of the *Curious Impertinent*, and on Davenport's *City Night-Cap*. Scene the Court of Florence.

Amorous Quarrel. C. by Ozell, translated from Moliere's *Depit Amoureux*.

Amorous War. T. C. by J. Maine, D. D. 4to. 1648.

The Amorous Widow; or, *The Wanton Wife*, by Betterton, 4to. 706. This is no more than a translation, *ad libitum*, of Moliere's *George Dandin*. Exclusive of some little deficiencies in point of delicacy, this may justly juftly be efteemed a very good play.

L'Amour à la Mode; or, *Love à la Mode.* Farce, in three acts, 8vo. 1760. This is merely a tranflation from the French, and faid to be the work of Hugh Kelly.

Amphitryon. Tranflated from Plautus, by Thomas Cooke, 12mo. 1746.

Amphytrion; or, *The Two Socias.* Com. by J. Dryden. Acted at the Theatre Royal, 4to. 1691. This play is founded on the two Amphytrions of Plautus and Moliere. The fcene lies in Thebes, and the mufic of the fongs is compofed by Purcell.

Amphytrion. Com. tranflated from Plautus, by L. Echard, 8vo. 1694.

Amphytrion. Com. tranflated from Moliere, by Ozell.

Amphytrion; or, *The Two Socias.* Com. altered from Dryden, with Moliere's Dialogue-Prologue between Mercury and Night introduced into the firft fcene, and the addition of fome new mufic; acted at Drury-Lane, 8vo. 1756.

Amphytrion. Com. tranflated from Plautus by Bonnel Thornton, 8vo. 1767.

Amyntas. A tranflation in Hexameter verfe, by Abraham Fraunce, 4to. 1591.

Amyntas. The very fame work, by Oldmixon, 4to. 1698.

Amyntas of Taffo. Tranflated from the original Italian, by Percival Stockdale, 8vo. 1770.

Amyntas; or, *The Impoffible Dowry.* Paft. by Thomas Randolph. Acted at Whitehall, 4to. 1638.

The Anatomift; or, *The Sham Doctor.* Com. by Edward Ravenfcroft, 4to. 1697.

Andria. Terens in Englyfh, or the tranflacyon out of Latin into Englyfh of the firft comedy of *Tyrens,* callyd *Andri.* No date. Suppofed to be printed by Raftell.

Andria. Com. by Maurice Kyffin, 4to. 1588. I believe this to be the fecond tranflation in our language of any of Terence's works. It is printed in the old black letter, and has the following full title, viz. *Andria, The firft Comædie of Terence, in Englifh. A Furtherance for the Attainment unto the right Knowledge and true Proprietie of the Latin Tong,* &c.

Andria. Comedy, tranflated from *Terence,* by Richard Bernard, 4to. 1598.

Andria. Comedy, tranflated from *Terence,* by Tho. Newman, 8vo. 1627.

Andria

Andria. Tranflated by Echard, 8vo.

Andria. Tranflated by T. Cooke, 12mo. 1734.

Andria. Tranflated by S. Patrick, 8vo. 1745.

Andria. Comedy, tranflated from Terence, by Mr. Gordon, 12mo. 1752.

Andria. Tranflated by George · Coleman, 4to. 1765.

Andromache. T. by J. Crowne. Acted at the Duke's Theatre, 4to. 1675. This play is only a tranflation of Racine's *Andromaque*, by a young gentleman, chiefly in profe, and publifhed, with fome alteration, by Crowne. It was brought on the ftage without fuccefs.

Andromana ; or, *The Merchant's Wife*. Trag. 4to. 1660. by J. S. (i. e. James Shirley.) The plot is founded on the ftory of Plangus, in Sir P. Sidney's *Arcadia*.

Andronicus Comnenius. Trag. by J. Wilfon, 4to. 1664. Scene Conftantinople.

Andronicus. Trag. Impietie's long Succeffe, or Heaven's late Revenge, 8vo. 1661. Scene Conftantinople. For the plot, fee the Life of Andronicus in Fuller's *Holy State*.

Angelica ; or, *Quixote in Petticoats*. C. in two acts, 8vo. 1758.

Annette and Lubin. Com.

Op. of one act, by C. Dibdin. Acted at Covent-Garden, 8vo. 1778.

The Antigallican. F. by Mr. Mozeen, 8vo. 1762. This piece was performed one night only, for the benefit of the author and Mr. Ackman. It was received with fome approbation.

Animal Magnetifm. Com. of three acts. Performed at Covent-Garden, 1788. This Farce is borrowed from the French.

Antigone, The Thebane Princefs. Tr. by Tho. May, 8vo. 1631. Scene in Thebes.

Antigone. Tragedy, tranflated from Sophocles, by George Adams, 8vo. 1729.

Antigone. Tragedy, tranflated from Sophocles, by T. Franklin, 4to. 1759.

Antiochus. Tragedy, by M. Mottley, 8vo. 1721. Acted at the Theatre Royal in Lincoln's-Inn-Fields. The plot is built on the well-known ftory of Seleucus Nicanor giving up his wife Stratonice, to his fon Antiochus, on being informed by his phyfician that his incurable illnefs was occafioned by his love for her. The fcene lies in Antioch.

Antiochus. Tragedy, on the fame ftory, by Charles Shuckborough, Efq. of Longborough, Gloucefterfhire : never acted, but printed in 8vo. 1740.

Antiochus

Antiochus the Great ; or, *The Fatal Relapse.* Tr. by Mrs. Jane Wiseman. Acted at Lincoln's-Inn-Fields, 4to. 1702.

Antipodes. Comedy, by Richard Brome. The scene London. Acted by the Queen's servants at Salisbury-court, in Fleet-street, 1638. published 4to. 1640.

The Antiquary. Com. by Shakerly Marmion. Acted at the Cockpit, 4to. 1641. This is a very pleasing play, and has much merit.

Antony and Cleopatra. Trag. by Shakspeare, fol. 1623. This is an excellent play, and has been frequently performed with success.

Antony and Cleopatra. Tr. by Sir Charles Sedley, 4to. 1677. Acted at the Duke's Theatre. This play falls greatly short of the merit either of Shakspeare's or Dryden's Tragedy.

Antony and Cleopatra. An historical Play. Acted at Drury-Lane, 8vo. 1758. Altered by Mr. Capell, with the assistance of Mr. Garrick. It was acted with considerable applause.

Antony and Cleopatra. A Tragedy, by Henry Brooke, Esq. 8vo. 1778. Not acted. Printed in the author's works, 4 vols. 8vo.

Antonio and Mellida. An historical Play, 4to. 1602.

Antonio's Revenge ; or,

The Second Part of Antonio and Mellida. Tr. These two plays were written by J. Marston. Both were acted by the children of St. Paul's, and both printed in 4to. 1602.

The Tragedie of Antonie. Done into English from the French, by Mary countess of Pembroke, 12mo. 1595. At the end of the play is this date—At Ramsbury, 26 of Nov. 1590.

Any Thing for a Quiet Life. Com. by Thomas Middleton. Acted at Black-Fryars, printed in 4to. 1662.

Apocryphal Ladies. Com. by Margaret duchess of Newcastle. This play is, as many other of her pieces, irregular and unfinished, and is divided into twenty-three scenes, but not reduced to the form of acts.

Apollo and Daphne ; or, *The Burgo-Master Trick'd.* By Lewis Theobald, 8vo. 1726. This is nothing more than the vocal parts of a Pantomime Entertainment, performed two years before at Lincoln's-Inn-Fields Theatre.

Apollo and Daphne ; or, *Harlequin's Metamorphoses.* A Pantomime, by John Thurmond, 12mo. 1727.

Apollo and Daphne. A Masque, by J. Hughes, 4to. 1716. The scene lies in the valley of Tempe in Thessaly.

AP

Theffaly. It was fet to mufic, and performed at the Theatre Royal in Drury-Lane.

Apollo Shroving. Com. 8vo. 1627. Written by Wm. Hawkins, the fchool-mafter of Hadleigh, in Suffolk, for the ufe of his fcholars, and acted by them on Shrove-Tuefday, Feb. 6, 1626.

The Apothoefis of Punch. A Satirical Mafque, with a Monody on the Death of the late Mafter Punch. Acted at the Paragonian Theatre, Exeter 'Change, 8vo. 1779. This is an attempt to ridicule Mr. Sheridan's Monody on Mr. Garrick's Death.

The Apparition; or, The Sham Wedding. Com. Acted at Drury-lane, 4to. 1714.

The Apparition. Com. tranflated from Plautus, by Richard Warner, 8vo. 1773.

Appearance is againft Them. Farce, by Mrs. Inchbald. Acted at Covent-Garden, 1785. The characters of this piece are fketched with much knowledge of the world, and the dialogue has a great fhare of eafe and vivacity.

Appius. Trag. by John Moncrief. Acted at Covent-Garden, 8vo. 1755, with no fuccefs.

AP

Appius and Virginia. Trag. Com. by R. P. 4to. 1576, in black letter, and not divided into acts, *wherein* (as it is faid in the title-page) *is lively exprcffed a rare example of the vertue of chaftity, in wifhing rather to be flaine at her owne father's hands, than to be defloured of the wicked judge Appius.*

Appius and Virginia. Trag. by J. Webfter, 4to. 1654. The fcene lies in Rome, and the ftory is taken from Livy, Florus, &c.

Appius and Virginia. Trag. by J. Dennis. Acted at Drury-Lane, N. D. 4to. (1709.) The ftory of this is the fame as the preceding one

Apprentice. Farce, of two acts, by Arthur Murphy. Acted at Drury-Lane, 8vo. 1756. The intention of this farce is entirely to expofe the abfurd paffion fo prevalent amongft apprentices and other young people, of what is called Spouting. It met with confiderable applaufe

April Day. A Burletta, of three acts, by Mr. Ohara. Acted at the Haymarket, 8vo. 1777.

The April Fool. Farce, by Mr. M'Nally. Acted at Covent-Garden, 1786, for the benefit of Mrs. Banifter. This Farce was intended

tended for the trick of the day.

The Arab. Tragedy, by Mr. Cumberland. Acted at Drury-Lane, 1785, for the benefit of Mr. Henderson.

Arcades. A kind of Masque, by J. Milton. This is very short and incomplete; though it is the work of that first-rate poet.

Arcadia. Past. by James Shirley. Acted at the Phœnix in Drury-Lane, 4to. 1640. The plot of this play is founded on Sir Ph. Sidney's *Arcadia,* and is itself the foundation of a modern tragedy, called *Philoclea.*

Arcadia ; or, *The Shepherd's Wedding.* A dramatic Past. 8vo. 1761. This little piece is extremely short and simple, being only a compliment to their present majesties on their nuptials. The words are by Mr. Robert Lloyd, and the music composed by Stanley.

Arden of Feversham. Tr. Anonym. 4to. 1592. The plan of this play is formed on a true history, then pretty recent, of one Arden, a gentleman of Feversham, in the reign of Edward IV. who was murthered as he was playing a game at tables with one Mosebie.

Arden of Feversham, Tr. by George Lillo. Acted at Drury-Lane, 1759.

Printed in 12mo. 1762. This was left imperfect by Mr. Lillo, and finished by Dr. John Hoadly.

Argalus and Parthenia. Tragi-Com. by H. Glapthorne. Acted at Drury-Lane, 4to. 1639. The plot of this play is also founded on the story of the two lovers in Sir P. Sidney's *Arcadia.*

Ariadne ; or, *The Marriage of Bacchus.* Opera, by P. P. 1674. 4to. This piece is a translation from the French, and was presented at the Theatre Royal in Covent-Garden, by the gentlemen of the academy of music.

Ariadne ; or, *The Triumphs of Bacchus.* An Op. by Thomas Durfey. 8vo. 1721. Never performed, but printed with a collection of poems in the year 1721.

Aristippus ; or, *The Jovial Philosopher.* By T. Randolph, *demonstrativelie proveing that quaries, points, and pottles, are sometimes necessary authors in a scholar's library ; presented in a private shew ; to which is added,* The Conceited Pedler, *presented in a strange shew ;* 4to. 1635.

Aristomenes ; or, *The Royal Shepherd.* Trag. by Anne countess of Winchelsea, 8vo. 1713. The story of this play

play is founded on the Lacedæmonian hiftory.

Arminiu.. Tr. by Wm. Paterfon, 8vo. 1740. The Lord Chamberlain refufed to licenfe this play.

The Arraignment of Paris. A Dram. Paft. prefented before the Queen's Majefty, by the children of her chapel; and printed in 4to. 1584

Arfafes. Tr. by William Hodfon, 8vo. 1775. Not acted.

Arfinoe; or, The Inceftuous Marriage. Trag. by A Henderfon. No date, 8vo. (1752.) This play was never acted. The ftory is Egyptian; the execution contemptible.

Arfinoe, Queen of Cyprus. An Opera, after the Italian manner, by Peter Motteux, performed at the Theatre Royal in Drury-Lane, 1707. 4to.

Art and Nature. C. by the Rev. Mr. Miller, 8vo. Acted at Drury-Lane, 1738. The principal fcenes in this play are founded on the *Arlequin Sauvage* of M. De l'Ifle, and Le Flateur of Rouffeau; but it met with no fuccefs.

Artaxerxes. Opera, 8vo. 1763. This piece was compofed by Dr. T. A. Arne, and was performed at Covent-Garden Theatre partly by Englifh, and partly

by Italian fingers. It met with good fuccefs.

Artaxerxes. Op. tranflated from *Metaftafio,* by John Hoole, 8vo. 1768.

The Artful Hufband. C. by W. Taverner, 4to. N. D. Acted with great applaufe at the Theatre in Lincoln's-Inn-Fields.

The Artful Wife. Com. alfo by W. Taverner. Acted in the fame place, 8vo. 1718, yet, although it is in every refpect far fuperior to the former, it did not meet with the fame fuccefs.

Artifice. C. by Sufanna Centlivre. Acted at the Theatre Royal in Drurylane, 1723, 8vo.

The Artifice. A Comic Opera, in two acts, by Wm. Auguftus Miles. Acted at Drury-Lane, 8vo. 1780. This piece was acted with little fuccefs, yet full as much as it deferved.

Art of Management; or, Tragedy Expelled, a Dramatic Piece, by Mrs. Charlotte Clarke; performed once at the Concert-room in Yorkbuildings. This piece was intended as a fatire on Charles Fleetwood, Efq; then manager of the Theatre Royal in Drury-Lane; but that gentleman and his party found means to put a ftop to its further progrefs on the ftage. It was printed in 1735, 8vo. with a humourous

A S

moutous dedication to Mr. Fleetwood.

Arviragus and Philicia. Tragi-Com. in two parts, by Lodovick Carlell, 8vo. 1639. The ſtory of this play is founded on the Britiſh Hiſtory, by Geoffrey of Monmouth and others, concerning Arviragus, who reigned in Britain in the time of Claudius Cæſar.

As it ſhould Be. An Entertainment, in one act. Performed at the Haymarket. 1789. This is a lively trifle.

The Aſſembly. Com. by a Scots gentleman, 12mo. 1722. Scene Edinburgh. This piece is no more than a groſs abuſe on the Whig party in Scotland. By Dr. Arch. Pitcairne.

The Aſſembly. Farce, by James Worſdale. This piece had nothing extraordinary in it.

The Aſſignation ; or, *Love in a Nunnery.* Com. by J. Dryden. Acted at the Theatre Royal, 4to. 1673. This play was damned in the repreſentation, and is one of thoſe haſty performances which, at times, threw a cloud over the merit of that prince of poets.

The Aſs-Dealer. Com. tranſlated from Plautus, by Richard Warner, 8vo. 1774.

Aſtrea ; or, *True Love's Mirrour.* By Leonard Wil-

A T

lan, 8vo. 1651. The plot from a romance of the ſame name.

The Aſtrologer. C. This play was taken from *Albumazar.*

As You Find It. Com. by Charles earl of Orrery. Acted at Lincoln's-Inn-Fields, 4to. 1703.

As You Like It. Com. by W. Shakſpeare, fol. 1623. The plot of this play is taken from Lodge's *Roſalynd,* or *Euphues' Golden Legacye,* 4to. 1590, and Shakſpeare has followed it more exactly than is his general cuſtom when he is indebted to ſuch worthleſs originals. The ſcene lies partly at the court of one of the provincial dukes of France, and partly in the foreſt of Arden.

Athaliah. Trag. by W. Duncombe, 8vo. 1724. 12mo. 1726. This is no more than a tranſlation, with very little liberty, of the *Athaliah* of Racine. The ſcene lies in the Temple of Jeruſalem.

The Atheiſt ; or, *The Second Part of the Soldier's Fortune.* C. by Thomas Otway. Acted at the Duke's Theatre, 4to. 1684.

The Atheiſt's Tragedie ; or, *The Honeſt Man's Revenge.* By Cyril Tournuer, 4to. 1612.

Athelſtan. Trag. by Dr. Browne,

AU

Browne. Acted at Drury-Lane, 8vo. 1756. This tragedy is founded on the British History, and has great merit, though it did not meet with success.

Athelwold. Tragedy, by Aaron Hill, Esq. Acted at Drury-Lane, 8vo. 1731. The language is poetical and spirited, the characters chaste and genuine, and the descriptions affecting and picturesque.

The Athenian Coffee-House. Com. It is said to be a satire on the authors of the *Athenian Oracle.*

Aurenge-Zebe; or, *The Great Mogul.* Trag. by J. Dryden. Acted at the Theatre Royal, 4to. 1676. This play is written in rhyme, yet is far from being the worst of the writings of that great poet. The scene lies at Agra, the capital of the Mogul's territories in India.

Aurora's Nuptuals. A Dramatic Performance, occasioned by the nuptuals of William prince of Orange,

AU

and Anne princess royal of England. Acted at Drury-Lane, 4to. 1734.

The Author. Comedy of two acts, 8vo. 1757, by S. Foote, Esq. Acted at Drury-Lane. This piece was written only for the sake of affording to the writer of it an opportunity of exerting his talents of mimickry, at the expence of a gentleman of family and fortune, Mr. Aprice; whose particularities of character, although entirely inoffensive, were rendered the butt of public ridicule in the part of *Cadwallader.*

The Author's Farce. C. of three acts, by H. Fielding, Esq. 8vo. 1732. This comedy was designed principally to ridicule the then prevailing fondness for the Italian singers. It was first acted in the Haymarket with very considerable success. ✱

The Author's Triumph; or, *The Managers Managed.* A Farce. Anonym.

B A

THE BABLER. Com. translated from Voltaire, and printed in Dr. Franklin's Edition, 12mo.

The Bacchæ. Tr. translated from Euripides, by R. Potter, 4to. 1781.

B A

The Banditti; or, *A Lady's Distress.* A Play, by T. Durfey. Acted at the Theatre Royal 4to. 1686. The scene lies in Madrid, and some part of the plot is taken from Shirley's *Sisters.*

The

B A

The Banditti ; or, *Love's Labyrinth*. An Opera, by Mr. O'Keeffe. Acted at Covent-Garden, 1781, and well received.

Banish'd Duke ; or, *The Tragedy of Infortunatus*, 4to. Acted at the Theatre Royal, 1690. The scene lies in a village in Belgium, the character of *Infortunatus* is drawn for the duke of Monmouth, and those of *Romanus* and *Papissa*, for king James II. and his queen.

The Banishment of Cicero. Trag. by Richard Cumberland, Esq. 4to. 1760. This play was never acted, having been refused by Mr. Garrick, to whom it was offered.

The Bankrupt. Com. by Samuel Foote. Acted at the Haymarket 1773, printed 8vo, 1776. This performance, like the rest by the same author, contains little else than detached scenes without any plot.

Of Baptism and Temptation, two Comedies, by bishop Bale. Of these we know no more than the name.

Barbarossa. Tr. by Dr. Browne. Acted at Drury-Lane, 8vo. 1755. This play is by no means so good a one as the *Athelstan* of the same author above-mentioned. The design seems

B A

borrowed from the tragedy of *Merope*.

The Barber of Seville. Com. of four acts, 8vo. 1776. Not acted.

Barataria ; or, *Sancho turned Governor*. Farce, altered from D'Urfey, by Mr. Pilon. Acted at Covent-Garden, 1785. This piece was well received.

Barnaby Brittle. Farce, acted at Covent-Garden, 1781. A paltry piece, taken from the George Dandin of Moliere.

The Baron Kinkvervankotsdorsprakengatchdern. M. Comp. by Miles Peter Andrews. Acted at the Haymarket, 8vo. 1781. Unsuccessful.

Bartholomew Fair. C. by Ben Jonson, 1614. This play has an infinite deal of humour in it, and is, perhaps, the greatest assemblage of characters that ever was brought together within the compass of one single piece.

The Bashful Lover. Tr. Com. by P. Massenger. Acted at the private house in Black-Fryars, 8vo. 1655.

The Basset Table. Com. by Mrs. Centlivre, 4to. 1706. This play contains a great deal of plot and business, without much either of sentiment or delicacy.

The Bastard. Tra. 4to. 1652. Scene in Seville. Mr.

Mr. Coxeter attributes this play to Cofmo Manuche.

The Baftard Child ; or, *A Feaft for the Church-wardens*. A Dramatic Satire of two acts ; acted every day within the bills of mortality. By Daniel Downright, 8vo. 1768.

The Bath ; or, *The Weftern Lafs*. Com. by T. D'Urfey. Acted at Drury-Lane, 4to. 1701.

The Bath Unmafk'd. C. by Mr. Odingfells. Acted at Lincoln's-Inn-Fields, 8vo. 1725.

The Battle of Alcazar, with Captain Stukeley's death. Trag. Anonym. Acted by the lord high admiral's fervants, 1594, 4to. The plot taken from Heylin's *Cofmography*, in the Hiftory of Spain, &c.

The Battle of Augrim ; or, *The Fall of St. Ruth*. Tr. by Robert Afhton. This play is little more than a bombaftic narrative of the tranfactions of the celebrated 11th of July, 1691, when the Irifh rebels met with a thorough defeat from the army belonging to King William. The fcene lies in and before the town of Aughrim.

Battle of Haftings. Tr. by Richard Cumberland, Efq. Acted at Drury-Lane, 8vo. 1778. The coat of Jofeph, and the drefs of

Harlequin, were never compofed of patchwork more general than is the ftyle of this performance.

The Battle of Hexham ; or, *Days of Old*. A Mufical Piece, by Mr. Colman, jun. Acted at the Haymarket, 1789, and well received.

Battle of Sedgmoor. A Farce of one fhort act, faid by Coxeter to have been rehearfed at Whitehall. It was never acted, but injurioufly fathered on the duke of Buckingham, and printed among his works, in 2 vols. 8vo. 1707.

Battle of the Poets ; or, *The Contention for the Laurel*. Acted at the Little Theatre in the Haymarket, 1731, 8vo. The piece contains much fcurrility on Mr. Cibber, and other poets, with very little wit.

Bayes's Opera, by Gab. Odingfells, 8vo. 1730. This is one of the many mufical pieces which the *Beggar's Opera* gave birth to. It was acted at Drury-lane without fuccefs.

The Beau Defeated; or, *The Lucky Younger Brother*. C. Acted at Lincoln's-Inn-Fields, 4to. without a date.

The Beau Merchant. C. 4to. 1714. Written, according to Coxeter, by one Mr. Blanch, a gentleman near Gloucefter, but was

never

B E

never acted. The scene lies in a coffee-house in Stockjobbing Alley.

The Beau's Adventures. Farce, by Phil. Bennet, Esq. 1733, 8vo. Was probably never acted

The Beau's Duel ; or, A Soldier for the Ladies. C. by Mrs. Centlivre, 4to. 1704. This is one of the most indifferent amongst that lady's pieces, and is now never acted.

The Beau's Stratagem. Com. by G. Farquhar. Acted at the Haymarket, 4to. 1707. This play was begun and ended in six weeks, the author labouring all the time under a settled illness, which carried him off during the run of his piece.

Beauty in Distress. Tr. by P. Motteux. Acted at Lincoln's-Inn-Fields, 4to. 1698. There are many fine lines in this drama, and great variety of pleasing incidents.

Beauty the Conqueror ; or, The Death of Marc Anthony. Trag. by Sir Charles Sedley, 1702. This play was never acted.

The Beggar on Horseback. F. by Mr. O'Keefe. Acted at the Haymarket, 1785. Of this farce we may say, its humour, its scenes, its double meanings, and even its faults, make us laugh.

B E

The Beggar's Bush. T. Com. by Beaumont and Fletcher, folio, 1647.

Beggar's Opera, by John Gay. Acted at Lincoln's-Inn-Fields, 4to. 1727. The great success of this piece, which carried it through a run of sixty-three nights, during the first season it was performed, and the frequent repetitions of it since, have rendered its merits so well known, that it is unnecessary to say any thing farther of it in this place.

The Beggar's Pantomime ; or, The Contending Columbines. An Interlude, acted at Lincoln's-Inn-fields, 12mo. 1736.

The Beggar's Wedding. A Ballad Opera of three acts, by Charles Coffey, 8vo. It was first performed at Dublin with but indifferent success, but being afterwards reduced into one act, and played in London under the title of *Phœbe,* in 1729, it pleased so well as to obtain a run of thirty nights.

Believe as you List. Com. by P. Massinger. This play was never in print, but was certainly acted.

Bellamira ; or, The Mistress. Com. by Sir Charles Sedley. Acted by their Majesties' servants, 4to. 1687. The scene of this play lies in London, but the
plot

plot is taken from the *Eunuch of Terence.*

Bellamira her Dream ; or, *The Love of Shadows.* T. Com. in two parts, by Tho. Killigrew. Thefe two plays were printed with the reft of his works, in fol. 1664.

The Belle's Stratagem. Comedy, by Mrs. Cowley. Acted at Covent-Garden 1780. This play has not yet appeared in print, but the fuccefs of it was very great on the ftage during a confiderable run.

The Belle's Stratagem. C. Acted by his Majefty's fervants, 8vo. 1781. A paltry performance in imitation of Mrs. Cowley's play of the fame name.

Bell in Campo. Trag. in two parts ; written by Margaret duchefs of Newcaftle, never acted, but printed among her works, fol. 1662.

Belifarius. Trag. by W. Philips. Acted at Lincoln's-Inn-Fields, 8vo. 1725.

Belphegor ; or, *The Marriage of the Devil.* Tragi-Com. by John Wilfon. Acted at Dorfet-Garden, 4to. 1691.

Belphegor ; or, *The Wifhes.* Com. Op. of two acts, by Miles Peter Andrews, performed at Drury-Lane, 1778. A flimfy performance.

Belteſhazzar ; or, *The*

Heroic Jew. A Dramatic Poem, by Thomas Harrifon. Scene Babylon. Never acted, but printed in 12mo. 1727, and 1729.

The Benefice. C. by Dr. Robert Wild, 4to. 1689.

The Betrayer of his Country. Tragedy, by Henry Brooke, Efq. 1741. Never publifhed.

Better Late than Never. Comedy, by Mr. Andrews. Acted at Drury-Lane, 1790, and well received.

Betty ; or, *The Country Bumpkins.* A Ballad Farce, by H. Carey. This was acted with very little fuccefs at Drury-Lane, 1738.

Bianca. Trag. by R. Shepherd. Not acted. Printed at Oxford, 8vo. 1772.

Bickerftaff's Burying ; or, *Work for the Upholders.* Farce of three long fcenes, by Mrs. Centlivre ; acted at the Haymarket, 4to. no date.

Bickerftaff's Unburied Dead. A Moral Drama. Acted at Lincoln's-Inn-Fields, 1743, 8vo.

The Bird in a Cage. C. by James Shirley. Acted at the Phœnix, Drury-lane, 4to. 1633. Scene in Mantua.

The Birth of Hercules. Mafque, by William Shirley, fet to mufic by Dr. Arne, and intended for reprefentation at Covent-Garden. 4to. 1765.

The

The Birth of Merlin ; or, *The Child has left a Father.* Tragi-Com. by William Rowley. The scene lies in Britain, and the story is taken from Geoffrey of Monmouth. It was frequently acted with great applause, and was published in 4to. 1662.

The Biter. Com. by Mr. Rowe, 1705, 4to. Acted at Lincoln's-inn-Fields. This was the only attempt of our author in the comic way, and met with no success.

The Blackamoor wash'd White. Comic Op. by Henry Bate. Acted at Drury-Lane, 1776. This piece met with an ill reception.

The Black Man. An Interlude, attributed to Cox the comedian, and printed in 4to. 1659.

The Black Prince. Tra. by Roger earl of Orrery. Acted at the duke of York's theatre, fol. 1669 and 1672.

The Blacksmith of Antwerp. Farce, by Mr. O'Keefe. Acted at Covent-Garden, 1785. A piece of no great merit.

The Blazing Comet, The Mad Lovers ; or, *The Beauties of the Poets.* A Play, by Samuel Johnson, author of *Hurlothrumbo.* Acted at the Haymarket, 8vo. 1732.

This is, like his other writings, a farrago of madness, absurdity, and bombast, intermingled with some strokes of genius and imagination.

The Blind Beggar of Alexandria. Com. *Most pleasantly discoursing his various humours in disguised shapes, full of conceit and pleasure.* By George Chapman. It was published in 1598.

The Blind Beggar of Bethnal Green, with the merry Humour of Tom Stroud, the Norfolk Yeoman. Com. by John Day. Acted by the prince's servants, 4to. 1659.

The Blind Beggar of Bethnal Green. A Ballad Farce, by Robert Dodsley. It was acted at Drury-Lane, but without much success, in 1741.

The Blind Lady. Com. by Sir Robert Howard, 8vo. 1661. The scene lies in Poland, and the plot is taken from Heylin's *Cosmography,* lib. 2.

The Bloody Banquet. Tr. printed in 4to. 1620, and is, in some of the old Catalogues, ascribed to Thomas Barker.

The Bloody Duke ; or, *The Adventures for a Crown.* Tragi-Com. Acted at the court of Alba Regalis, by several persons of great quality, 4to. 1690.

The

The Blunderer. Com. tranflated from Moliere, printed in Foote's *Comic Theatre*, vol. IV.

Boadicea Queen of Britain. Trag. by Charles Hopkins. Acted at Lincoln's-Inn-Fields, infcribed to Mr. Congreve, 4to. 1697. *Boadicea* was well received.

Boadicea. Tr. by Richard Glover. Acted at Drury-Lane, 8vo. 1753, but met with no great fuccefs.

A Bold Stroke for a Wife. Com. by Mrs. Centlivre. Acted at Lincoln's-Inn-Fields, 8vo. 1717. - It met with very good fuccefs; and, notwithftanding the abfurdity and impoffibility of the plot, there is much bufinefs and variety in it to keep up the attention of an audience.

A Bold Stroke for a Hufband. A Comedy, by Mrs. Cowley. Acted at Covent-Garden, 1783. The dialogue of this piece is lively, animated, and fenfible, and the plot well managed.

Bon Ton ; or, *High Life above Stairs.* Farce, by David Garrick. Acted at Drury-Lane, 8vo. 1776.

Bon Ton. Com. of three acts, by Gen. Burgoyne. Acted at Drury-Lane, 1775. A lively picture of the manners of the great world, but abounds not in wit or humour.

The Bondman. An an-cient ftory, by P. Maffinger. Acted at the Cock-pit, Drury-Lane, 4to. 1623, 4to. 1638. This is a very excellent tragedy.

The Bond Man. Tragi-Com. altered from Maffinger, by Richard Cumberland. Acted at Covent-Garden, 1779. Not printed.

Bonds without Judgement. Farce. Acted at Covent-Garden, 1787, for the benefit of Mrs. Wells. It is founded on the general cuftom of fending ladies to the India market.

Bonduca. Tragedy, by Beaumont and Fletcher, fol. 1647. This play is upon the ftory of a queen of Britain, who is indifferently ftyled by the hiftorians Boadicea, and Bonduca. It is efteemed a very good play.

Bonduca ; or, *The Britifh Heroine.* Trag. Acted at the Theatre Royal, 4to. 1696.

Bonduca. Trag. altered from Beaumont and Fletcher, by George Colman. Acted at the Haymarket, 8vo. 1778. A judicious alteration from Beaumont and Fletcher's piece with the fame title. We muft do Mr. Colman the juftice to fuppofe, that he would have retained more of the authors, but that he was conftrained to cut

cut them down to the ability of his performers.

The Bow-ftreet Opera, in three acts, 8vo. 1773. Abuse of Sir John Fielding.

Braganza. Tr. by Robert Jephfon, Efq. Acted at Drury-Lane, 8vo. 1775. A fuccefsful tragedy on its original appearance, but has fallen into neglect since the firft feafon. The plot of it too nearly refembles fome parts of *Venice Preferved.*

The Braggadocio; or, *Bawd turn'd Puritan.* C. written by a perfon of quality, 4to. 1691. Scene London.

The Braggard Captain. Com. tranflated from Plautus, by Bonnell Thornton, 8vo. 1767.

Bravo turn'd Bully; or, *The Depredators.* A Dramatic Entertainment, 8vo. 1740.

The Brazen Age. A Hiftory, by Thomas Haywood, in 4to. 1613. It is taken from Ovid's *Metamorphofes.*

Brennoralt ; or, *The Difcontented Colonel.* Tragedy, by Sir John Suckling. This is printed among his works, in 8vo. 1646.

Bridals. Com. by the duchefs of Newcaftle, publifhed among her works, fol.

The Bride. Comedy, by

Thomas Nabbes, 4to. 1640. Acted at Drury-Lane.

Britain's Happinefs. A mufical Interlude, by P. Motteux, performed at both the Theatres, 4to. 1704. The fcene, a profpect of Dover caftle and the fea. This Interlude had long before been intended only for an introduction to an opera, which, if ever finifhed, was to have been called *The Loves of Europe,* every act fhewing the manner of a different nation in their addrefs to the fair fex.

Britannia. A Mafque, by David Ma le , 8vo. 1755. This piece was fet to mufic by Dr. Arne, and performed with fuccefs at the Theatre Royal in Drury-Lane. Prefixed to it is a prologue, in the character of a drunken failor reading a play-bill, written in conjunction by Meffrs. Mallet and Garrick, and fpoken by the latter with univerfal applaufe ; and which, the fubject being extremely popular, as a French war had not been long declared, was called for and infifted on by the audience many nights in the feafon when the piece itfelf was not performed.

Britannia and Batavia. Mafque, by George Lillo, 8vo. 1740.

Britannia.

BR

Britannia. An Englifh Opera, by Mr. Lediard. Acted at the new theatre in the Haymarket, 4to. 1732.

Britannia, or, *The Gods in Council.* Dramatic Poem, by Robert Averay, 4to. 1756.

Britannia Triumphans. A Mafque, by Sir W. Davenant and Inigo Jones. It was prefented at Whitehall, by King Charles I. and his lords, on the Sunday after Twelfth-Night, 1637, and was printed in 4to. 1637.

Britannicus. Trag. by J. Ozell 12mo. 1714. This is only a tranflation of a French play of the fame name by M. Racine.

The Britifh Enchanters; or, *No Magic like Love;* by lord Lanfdowne. It was firft called a Tragedy, and was acted at the Queen's Theatre in the Haymarket, 4to. 1706. The author, who took an early diflike to the French and Italian Operas, feems in this attempt to have aimed at reconciling the variety and magnificence effential to operas, to a more rational model, by introducing fomewhat more fubftantial than the mere gratification of eye and ear. Its fuccefs was great, but was put a ftop to by the divifion of the

BR

theatre and a prohibition of mufical pieces.

The Britifh Stage; or, *The Exploits of Harlequin.* Farce, 8vo. 1724. Performed at both Theatres with great applaufe.

The Briton. Tragedy, by Ambrofe Philips. Acted with confiderable fuccefs at the Theatre Royal, Drury-Lane, 8vo. 1721. Whatever was the reception of this tragedy, fays Dr. Johnfon, it is now neglected; though one of the fcenes, between *Vanoc,* the Britifh Prince and *Valens,* the Roman General, is confeffed to be written with great dramatic fkill, animated by a fpirit truly poetical.

Britons Strike Home; or, *The Sailors Rehearfal.* A Ballad Farce, by Edward Philips, performed, but without fuccefs, at Drury-Lane, 1739. 8vo.

The Broken Heart. Tr. by Mr. John Ford. Acted at Black-Fryars, 4to. 1633.

The Broken Stockjobbers; or, *Work for the Bailiffs.* A Farce, as lately acted in Exchange-Alley, 8vo. 1720.

The Brothers. Com. by J. Shirley. Acted at Black-Fryars, 1652. 8vo. Scene Madrid.

The Brothers. T. by Dr. Young. Acted at Drury-Lane, 8vo. 1752. The fcene

fcene of this play lies in Macedon, and the plot from the Hiftory of Macedonia in the reign of the laft Philip. The two charatters of *Demetrius* and *Perfeus* are admirably drawn, and their conteft, before their father in the third aft, perhaps the fineft pieces of oratory in the Englifh language. But there is one particular circumftance relating to this play, which does as much honour to the heart, as the play itfelf does to the abilities of the author, which is his having not only given up the entire profits of three benefits arifing from it, but alfo even made up the amount of them to the fum of 1000*l*. and generoufly beftowed it to the nobleft of all purpofes, viz. the propagation of the Gofpel in foreign parts.

The Brothers. A Com. by Richard Cumberland, Efq. Acted at Covent-Garden, 8vo. 1769. This play was received with no inconfiderable applaufe.

Brutus. Tra. tranflated from Voltaire; printed in Doctor Franklin's edition of that author's works, 12mo.

Brutus of Alba; or, *The Enchanted Lovers.* Trag. by Nahum Tate. Acted at the Duke's Theatre, 4to 1678.

Brutus of Alba; or, *Augufta's Triumph.* An Op. Acted at the Theatre in Dorfet-Gardens, 4to. 1697, and publifhed by George Powell and John Verbruggen.

Bury Fair. Com. by Thomas Shadwell, 4to. 1689.

Bufiris, King of Egypt. Tragedy, by Dr. Edward Young, 8vo. 1719. It appeared with fuccefs on the ftage at Drury-Lane, but is written in a glaring ambitious ftyle, like that which we probably fhould have met with in the dramas of *Statius*, had any of them efcaped the wreck of Roman literature. The haughty meffage fent by *Bufiris* to the *Perfian Ambaffador* is copied from that returned by the *Æthiopian Prince* to *Cambyfes* in the third book of *Herodotus*. The plot of this play, we believe to be of the author's contrivance. The dialogue contains many ftriking beauties of fentiment and defcription, but is wanting in that power which not only plays with imagination, but feizes on the heart. Dr. Johnfon fomewhere obferves that of Congreve's three comedies, two are ended by means of a wedding in a mafk. With equal juftice we may add,

that

that the three tragedies of Dr. Young are concluded by fuicides in three pairs, *Memnon* and *Mandane*, *A-lonzo* and *Leonora*, *Demetrius* and the *Thracian Princess*.

Buffy d'Ambois. Tr. by G. Chapman, 4to 1607. The plot of it is taken from the French hiftorians in the reign of Henry III. of France.

Buffy d'Ambois, his Revenge. Tra. by the fame. Acted at White Fryars, 4to. 1613 and 1641. This play is neither fo good a one, nor fo ftrictly founded on truth, as the foregoing, nor was it received with fo much applaufe upon the ftage.

The Bufy Body. Com. by Mrs. Centlivre. Acted at the Theatre Royal in Drury-Lane, 4to. 1708. This play met with fo flight a reception from the players, that they even for a time refufed to act it, and when prevailed upon fo to do, which was not till towards the clofe of the feafon, Mr. Wilks fhewed fo much con-

tempt for the part of Sir *George Airy*, as to throw it down on the ftage at rehearfal, with a declaration, that no audience would endure fuch ftuff. The fuccefs the piece met with, however, falfified thefe prognoftications ; and to do juftice to the author, it muft be confeffed, that although the language of it is very indifferent, and the plot mingled with fome improbabilities, yet the amufing fprightlinefs of bufinefs, and the natural impertinence in the character of *Marplot*, make confiderable amends for the above-mentioned deficiencies, and render it even to this hour an entertaining and ftandard performance.

Buthred. Trag. Acted at Covent-Garden, 8vo. 1778. It is an anonymous tragedy, acted four nights to very patient audiences.

Buxom Joan. Burletta, by Mr. Willet. Acted at the Haymarket, 4to. 1778. Taken from the original fong fung in *Love for Love*.

C A

THE *Cady of Bagdad.* Com. Opera, of three acts, by Abraham Portal, performed at Drury-Lane, 1778. This piece had no fuccefs.

C Æ

Cæfar and Pompey. A Roman Trag. By George Chapman, 4to. 1607, 4to. 1631. Acted at Black-Fryars. Scene Rome and Pharfalia.

Cæfar

C A

Cæsar Borgia, Son to Pope Alexander VI. Trag. by Nat. Lee. Acted at the Duke's Theatre, 4to. 1680. The scene lies in Rome, and the plot is built on the histories of *Guicciardini* and *Marina*, and Ricaut's Lives of the Popes. The play, like many others by this author, has great beauties, mingled with many strokes of rant, bombast, and absurdity, and therefore does not now stand in the list of acting dramas. It met, however, with good success at first.

Cæsar in Egypt. Trag. by C. Cibber. Acted at Drury-Lane, 8vo. 1725. Colley Cibber's genius, however pleasing in comedy, is very far from being admired in a tragic cast of writing, nor is this Play even considered as his tragic master-piece. The scene of it lies in Alexandria, and the plan is borrowed from the *Pompée* of P. Corneille.

The History and Fall of Caius Marius. Tra. by T. Otway. Acted at the Duke's Theatre, 4to. 1680. The scene of this play lies at Rome, and the characters of *Marius*, jun. and *Lavinia*, are taken, and that even in many places verbatim, from those of *Romeo* and *Juliet*.

Caligula, Emperor of Rome. Tr. by J. Crowne. Acted at the Theatre Royal, 4to. 1698. The scene lies in the Imperial Palace at Rome, and the plot is taken from Suetonius's Life of that Prince.

Calisto; or, *The Chaste Nymph.* A Masque, by J. Crowne, 4to. 1675. It was written by command of king James II's queen, and was oftentimes performed at court by persons of great quality. It has songs between the acts. The scene lies in Arcadia; the duration of it an *artificial day*; and the plot is founded on Ovid's *Metamorphoses*, Lib. ii. Fab. 5, 6.

Calypso and Telemachus. Opera, by John Hughes, Esq. 8vo. 1712, performed at the Queen's Theatre in the Haymarket. The music composed by Mr. Galliard. The story on which it is founded, is in the adventures of Telemachus by the archbishop of Cambray.

Calypso. An Opera, by Richard Cumberland. Acted at Covent-Garden, 8vo. 1779. The adventures of Telemachus, in different shapes, have already surfeited the world. Opera, masque, and tragedy, have all maintained this hero in a languishing kind of existence. Mr. Cumberland has been more merciful. He contrived to give him as little

C 3

little pain as poſſible, by procuring him almoſt inſtantaneous damnation.

The Camp. Dram. Entertainment, by Richard Brinſley Sheridan. Acted at Drury-Lane, 1778. Though the ſcenery of this after-piece is uncommonly various and characteriſtic, yet the drama itſelf muſt be allowed to poſſeſs a ſtill higher degree of merit. All the ſhifts, impoſitions, diſtreſſes, intrigues, manœuvres, &c. peculiar to a camp, are deſcribed in the dialogue, or exhibited in the dumb ſhow of Mr. Sheridan's performance, which, throughout two ſeaſons, was a conſiderable favourite with the public, being well attended, while the plays of Shakſpeare were acting to almoſt empty benches. Such is the ſucceſs of comic novelty, eſpecially when produced by a hand ſo maſterly as that of our author, aſſiſted by the labours of the firſt ſcene-painter in Europe, the extent of whoſe ſkill was diſplayed in a moſt perfect repreſentation of the late encampment at Cox-Heath.

Cambyſes, King of Perſia. Play in old metre, by Tho. Preſton, 4to. without a date. The ſtory is taken from Herodotus and Juſtin.

Cambyſes, King of Perſia.

Trag. by Elkanah Settle. Acted at the Duke's Theatre, 4to. 1671.

Camilla. An Opera, by Owen Mac Swiny; firſt performed at the Theatre Royal in Drury-Lane, and afterwards in the Haymarket, 4to. 1706.

The Campaigners; or, *Pleaſant Adventures at Bruſſels.* Com. by T. Durfey, 4to. 1698. Part of the plot is taken from a novel called *Female Falſhood.* Scene Bruſſels.

The Campaign; or, *Love in the Eaſt-Indies.* Opera, by Mr. Jephſon. Acted at Covent-Garden, 1785, with ſome degree of applauſe.

The Candidate. Farce, by Mr. Dent, acted at the Haymarket, 1782. This piece, though not one of the moſt capital performances, contains no inconſiderable ſhare of pleaſantry, and afforded much entertainment to the audience.

Candlemas-Day; or, *The Killing of the Children of Iſrael;* by Kan Parfre, written in 1512.

The Canterbury Gueſts; or, *A Bargain Broken.* C. by E. Ravenſcroft. Acted at the Theatre Royal, 4to. 1695. This is a very indifferent play, and met with very indifferent ſucceſs. Scene Canterbury.

The Capricious Lovers. Com.

Com. by Mr. Odingfells. Acted at Lincoln's-Inn-Fields Theatre, 1726, 8vo.

The Capricious Lovers. Comic Opera, by Robert Lloyd. Acted at Drury-Lane, 8vo. 1764.

The Capricious Lady. A Comedy, altered with great judgment from Beaumont and Fletcher, and acted at Covent-Garden, 1783.

The Captain. Com. by Beaumont and Fletcher, fol. 1647. This is far from one of the moft capital pieces of thefe united authors.

Captain O'Blunder ; or, *The brave Irifhman.* Farce, by Tho. Sheridan. Dublin, 12mo. about 1748. It was written by Mr. Sheridan when a mere boy at College ; but the original copy being loft, it was fupplied from the memory of the actors, who added and altered it in fuch a manner, that hardly any part of the original compofition now remains.

The Captive. Com. Op. by Ifaac Bickerftaffe. Acted at the Haymarket, 8vo. 1769. This is taken from the comic fcenes of *Don Sebaftian.* It was fet to mufic by C. Dibdin, and was but coolly received.

The Captives. Trag. by by John Gay. Acted at Drury-Lane, 8vo. 1723. Mr. Victor gives the following anecdote relative to this play : Mr. Gay "had intereft enough with the late queen Caroline, then Princefs of Wales, to excite her royal highnefs's curiofity to hear the author read his play to her at Leicefter-Houfe. The day was fixed, and Mr. Gay was commanded to attend. He waited fome time in a prefence-chamber with his play in his hand ; but being a very modeft man, and unequal to the trial he was going to, when the door of the drawing-room, where the princefs fat with her ladies, was opened for his entrance, he was fo much confufed and concerned about making his proper obeifance, that he did not fee a low footftool that happened to be near him, and ftumbling over it, he fell againft a large fkreen, which he overfet, and threw the ladies into no fmall diforder.

The Captives. A Trag. by Mr. Delap. Acted at Drury-Lane, 1786, and very indifferently received.

The Capuchin. Com. by Samuel Foote. Acted at the Haymarket, 8vo. 1778. very indifferently received. This was an alteration of *The Trip to Calais* and was acted in 1776.

Caractacus. A Dramatic Poem, by Mr. Mafon, 4to: and 8vo. 1759. This piece is

written

written after the manner of the Greek tragedy, with odes and chorufes, and was never intended for the English ftage. In the clofet, however, it muft always give ineffable delight to every mind capable of judgment, as it lays the ftrongeft claim to immortality, and is one among a few inftances that poetical genius is fo far from its decline at this time in thefe realms, that we have writers now living, fome of whofe works no Britifh bard whatfoever, Shakfpeare, Spencer, and Milton not excepted, would have reafon to blufh at being reputed the author of.

Caraſfacus. Dramatic Poem, by W. Mafon. Acted at Covent-Garden, 8vo. 1776. This alteration was made by the author, and was received with applaufe.

The Cardinal. Tra. by James Shirley, 8vo. 1652. Acted in Black-Fryars. Scene Navarre.

The Carelefs Hufband. Com. by C. Cibber. Acted at the Theatre Royal, 4to. 1704. This comedy contains, perhaps, the moft elegant dialogue, and the moft perfect knowledge of the manners of perfons in real high life, extant in any dramatic piece that has yet appeared in any language whatever. Yet fuch is the natural malevolence of mankind, and fuch our unwillingnefs to beftow praife, at leaft on the living, that Mr. Cibber's contemporaries would not allow him to have been the author of it: fome attributing it to the duke of Argyle, to whom it was dedicated, fome to Mr. Defoe, fome to Mr. Maynwaring, &c. As, however, during a long courfe of years, in which it has conftantly been performed with the greateft fuccefs, no claim has been laid to any part of it, we furely may pay the deferved tribute of praife to him who by this prefcription ftands as the undoubted author of the whole, and to whom the Englifh ftage is to this hour greatly obliged for a very confiderable fhare of its comic entertainments during the courfe of every feafon. When Mr. Cibber had written two acts of this play, he fays, he threw them afide in defpair of meeting with a performer capable of doing juftice to the character of Lady *Betty Modifh*, owing to the ill ftate of health of Mrs. Verbruggen, and Mrs. Bracegirdle being engaged at another theatre. In this ftate of fufpence, Mrs. Oldfield, whofe talents the author had but an indifferent opinion of, exhibited excellences

excellences which he had no expectation of seeing, and which encouraged him to complete his work. Near forty years after the representation of this comedy, he says, " Whatever favourable reception it met with, it would be unjust in me not to place a large share of it to the account of Mrs. Oldfield ; not only from the uncommon excellence of her action, but even from her personal manner of conversing. There are many sentiments in the character of Lady *Betty Modish*, that we may almost say were originally her own, or only dressed with a little more care than when they negligently fell from her lively humour : had her birth placed her in a higher rank of life, she had certainly appeared, in reality, what in this play she only excellently acted, an agreeably gay woman of quality, a little too conscious of her natural attractions."

The Careless Lovers. C. by Edward Ravenscroft. This play was written after the time that Dryden had attacked our author's *Mamamouchi*, and therefore in the epistle and prologue he has endeavoured to revenge his cause, by an attack on Dryden's *Almanzor* and his *Love in a Nunnery*. And

retorting back on him the charge of plagiarism, which, notwithstanding what Mr. Ravenscroft says in his prologue, he is far from being clear of in regard to this very piece, as the sham scene in the fourth act is apparently stolen from Moliere's M. de *Pourceaugnac*, Act 2. Scene 7 and 8.

The Careless Shepherd. A Pastoral, without either author's name or date.

The Careless Shepherdess. A Pastoral Tragi-Com. by Thomas Goffe, 4to. 1656. This play was acted before the king and queen at Salisbury-Court. The scene lies in Arcadia.

The Cares of Love; or, *A Night's Adventure.* A Comedy, by A. Caves. Acted at Lincoln's-Inn-Fields, 4to. 1705.

The Carmelite. Tragedy, by Mr. Cumberland. Acted at Drury-Lane, 1784. This play has many marks of invention, pathetic and striking passages, and happy turns of expression.

The Carnival. Com. by Thomas Porter, 4to. 1664. Scene Sevile.

The Carnival of Venice. Com. Op. acted at Drury-Lane, 1781. This piece was well received.

The Carthaginian. Com. translated from Plautus, by Richard Warner, Esq. 8vo.

Cartouche ;

C 5

Cartouche; or, *The Robbers*. Anonym. 8vo. a Comedy. This is a translation from the French, and was acted at the Theatre in Lincoln's-Inn-Fields, 8vo. 1722.

The Case is Alter'd. C. by Ben Jonson, 4to. 1609. This is not one of the most celebrated of this author's works, nor is it at this time ever acted.

The Casket. Comedy, translated from Plautus, by Richard Warner, Esq. 8vo.

Cassandra; or, *The Virgin Prophetess*. Opera. Acted at the Theatre Royal, 4to. 1692.

The Castle of Andalusia. Op. 1782. Covent-Garden.

Cataline, his Conspiracy. Trag. by Ben Jonson, 4to. 1611. This play has great merit, but is too declamatory for the present dramatic taste. Jonson has in this, as in almost all his works, made great use of the Ancients. His *Sylla's* Ghost, at the opening of this play, is an evident copy from that of *Tantalus* at the beginning of Seneca's *Thyestes*, and much is also translated from Sallust through the course of this piece. For the plot, see Sallust. Scene in Rome.

Cataline; or, *Rome Preserved*. Tragedy, translated from Voltaire. Printed in Dr. Franklin's translation, 12mo.

Catharine and Petruchio. Farce, by David Garrick, Esq. Acted at Drury-Lane, 8vo. 1756. This is nothing more than an alteration of Shakspeare's *Taming of the Shrew*, by inverting and transposing different parts of it, rejecting the superfluous scenes, and reducing the whole into a regular piece of three acts. But the judgment wherewith this is executed, and the valuable use that the author has made of Shakspeare, whom he has neither deviated from, nor added to, does great honour to his understanding and knowledge of theatrical conduct, and has rendered a comedy, which, from the many absurdities mingled with its numerous beauties, had long been thrown aside, one of the most entertaining of the *petites pieces* on the present acting list.

Cato. Tr. by J. Addison. Acted at Drury-Lane, 4to. 1712. This play was performed eighteen times during its first run, is ushered into notice by eight complimentary copies of verses to the author, among which, one by Sir Richard Steele leads up the van, besides a prologue by Mr. Pope, and an epilogue by
Doctor

Doctor Garth, and has ever since been fo univerfally admired, that it appeared totally unneceffary to add any thing further in its commendation. As to its faults, if fuch it has, the coutemporary critics have fufficiently endeavoured to point them out. It may not, however, be impertinent to obferve in this place, that the beauties of poetry and the fpirit liberty which fhine through the whole, fcarcely more than compenfate for its want of *pathos*, and the deficiency of dramatic bufinefs. It cannot, however, furely be thought an ill compliment to the author, to confefs, that although as a play it may have many fuperiors, yet it muft ever be allowed to ftand foremoft in the lift of our dramatic poems. The ftory is founded on hiftory, and the fcene lies through the whole piece in the governor's palace at Utica. Of a work fo much read, it is difficult (as Dr. Johnfon obferves) to fay any thing new. About things on which the public thinks long, it commonly attains to think right; and of Cato it has not been unjuftly determined, that it is rather a poem in dialogue than a drama, rather a fucceffion of juft fentiments in elegant language, than a

reprefentation of natural affections, or of any ftate probable or poffible in human life. Nothing here excites or affuages emotion ; here is no magical power of raifing phantaftic terror and wild anxiety. The events are expected without folicitude, and are remembered without joy or forrow. Of the agents we have no care. Cato is a being above our folicitude ; a man of whom the gods take care, and whom we leave to their care with heedlefs confidence. To the reft neither gods nor men can have much attention ; for there is not one amongft them that ftrongly attracts either affection or efteem. But they are made the vehicles of fuch fentiments and fuch expreffion, that there is fcarcely a fcene in the play which the reader does not wifh to imprefs upon his memory. See alfo the remarks of Dennis, as quoted by Dr. Johnfon in his life of Addifon.

Cato of Utica. Tragedy, tranf. from Des Champs, 12mo. 1716. This does not appear to have been acted.

The Cave of Trophonius. Farcical Opera. Acted at Drury-Lane, 1791, for the benefit of Mrs. Crouch.

The Cauldron. Pantomime. Acted at Drury-Lane, 1785.

Celeftina ;

Cileſtina; or, *The Spaniſh Bawd*. Comedy, 1708. This was written originally in Spaniſh, by Don Mateo Aleman, one of the moſt celebrated dramatic authors of that nation, in 21 acts, and was tranſlated above an hundred years ago, at the end of Guſman de Alfarache, *The Spaniſh Rogue*.

Cenia; or, *The Suppos'd Daughter*. Tragedy, 8vo. 1752.

Cephalus and Procris. Dramatic Maſque. With a Pantomime Interlude, called *Harlequin Grand Volgi*. Acted at Drury-Lane, 8vo. 1733.

Chabot (Philip) Admiral of France, by George Chapman and James Shirley. Acted at Drury-Lane, 4to. 1639. The ſtory of it is taken from the French Hiſtorians, in their account of the reign of Francis I.

A Challenge at Tilt at a Marriage. A Maſque, by Ben Jonſon. Fol. 1640.

Challenge for Beauty. Tragi-Com. by Thomas Heywood, 4to. 1636. Acted in Black-Fryars and the Globe. Scene Portugal.

The Chambermaid. Ballad Opera, of one act, by Edward Philips, performed at the Theatre Royal, Drury-Lane, 1730, 8vo.

The Chances. Com. by Beaumont and Fletcher, fol. 1647. The ſcene lies in Bologna.

The Chances. Com. by the duke of Buckingham. Acted at the Theatre Royal, 4to. 1682. This is only the preceding play altered and amended. It has been frequently performed with great applauſe, and indeed the vaſt variety of buſineſs and hurry of intrigue, which is happily produced by the confuſion of miſtaking two characters ſo extremely different as thoſe of the *Conſtantias*, cannot avoid keeping up the attention of an audience, and making the piece appear, if one may ſo term it, entirely alive. Yet notwithſtanding the alterations made in it, firſt by the duke, and ſince that in the preparing it for ſome ſtill later repreſentations, there runs a degree of indelicacy through a few ſcenes, and a libertiniſm through the whole character of *Don John*, which, to the honour of the preſent age be it recorded, have for many years paſt, experienced a very ſingular diſapprobation, whenever they have been attempted to be obtruded on the public.

The Chances. Com. with alterations, by David Garrick, Eſq. Acted at Drury-Lane, 8vo. 1773.

Changes; or, *Love in a Maze*. Comedy, by James Shirley.

Shirley. Acted at the private houfe Salifbury-Court, 4to. 1632. Scene London. This play met with confiderable fuccefs.

The Changeling. Trag. by Thomas Middleton, 4to. 1653. The fcene is Alicant, and the principal foundation of the plot may be found in the ftory .of *Aljemero* and *Beatrice Joanna*, in Reynolds's *God's Revenge againft Murder*, book i. ch. viii.

The Chaplet. A Mufical Entertainment, by Mofes Mendez, 8vo. 1749. Acted at Drury-Lane. This piece, if not great, at leaft deferves the praife of being very pleafing.

The Chapter of Accidents. Com. by Mifs Lee. Acted at the Haymarket, 8vo. 1780. This play poffeffes confiderable merit, and was acted with much applaufe.

Charles VIII. of France ; or, *The Invafion of Naples by the French.* An Hiftorical Play, by J. Crowne. Acted at the duke of York's Theatre, 4to. 1672.

The Charitable Affociation. Com. of two acts, by Henry Brooke, Efq. 8vo. 1778. Not acted. The fcene York.

The Cheat. Com. tranflated from Plautus, by R. Warner, Efq. 8vo.

The Cheats. Comedy, by John Wilfon, written in the year 1662, 4to. 1663. This play met with general approbation.

The Cheats of Scapin. A Farce, by T. Otway, 4to. 1677. It is little more than a tranflation of Moliere's *Fouberies de Scapin.* The fcene Dover.

The Cheats of Scapin. C. by Ozell. This is only the abfolute tranflation of Moliere's play.

The Chelfea Penfioner. C. Opera, by C. Dibden. Acted at Covent-Garden, 8vo. 1779. The hint of this piece is taken from the ftory of Belifarius.

The Chefhire Comics. C. by S. Johnfon, 1730. This piece is full of madnefs and abfurdity, yet it has in it many ftrokes of wonderful imagination.

The Child of Nature. C. by Mrs. Inchbald. Acted at Covent-Garden, 1788. The fentiments are pretty and affecting.

The Chimæra. Comedy, by T. Odell. Acted at Lincoln's-Inn-Fields, 8vo. 1721. The date and title of this piece are fufficient to point out the defign of it, which was to expofe the follies and abfurdities that mankind were drawn into by the epidemical madnefs of the South-Sea bubble.

The Chinefe Feftival. A Ballet or grand Entertainment

ment of Dancing, compos-
ed by Mr. Noverre, 1755.
This piece was unjustly
condemmed, under this idea,
which was propagated by
interested people, that none
but French performers were
engaged therein.

Chit Chat. Com. by T.
Killigrew, Esq. 8vo. N. D.
(1722). This play is little
more than what its title implies, viz. an unconnected
piece, consisting principally
of easy and genteel conversation: yet it met with considerable applause when represented at Drury-Lane
Theatre, and so strongly was
the interest of the author,
who had a place at court,
supported by the duke of
Argyle and others of his
friends, that the profits of
this play were said to have
amounted to upwards of a
thousand pounds.

Chit Chat. Interlude,
Acted at Covent-Garden,
1781. Not printed.

Chloridia; or, *Rites to
Chloris and her Nymphs.*
Masque, by Ben Jonson,
presented at court by the
queen and her ladies at
Shrovetide, 1630, 4to.

The Choice of Harlequin;
or, *The Indian Chief.* A
pleasing Pantomime, acted
at Covent-Garden, 1781.

The Choephorae. Trag.
translated from *Æschylus,*
by R. Potter, 4to. 1777.

The Choloric Father. C.
Opera, by Mr. Holcroft.
Acted at Covent-Garden,
1785. This piece has less
invention, novelty, and interest, than any of Mr.
Holcroft's other productions.

The Choleric Man. C.
by R. Cumberland, Esq.
Acted at Drury-Lane, 8vo.
1775. This play is taken
from *Heautontimorumenos* of
Terence. It succeeded on
the representation.

The Christian Hero. T.
by George Lillo, 8vo. N.
D. (1734). This play was
performed at the Theatre in
Drury-Lane, and with but
very little success.

A Christian turn'd Turk;
or, *The tragical Lives and
Deaths of the two famous
Pirates, Ward and Dansiker.*
Trag. by Robert Daborn,
Gent. not divided into acts,
4to. 1612. The story is
taken from an account of
the overthrow of those two
pirates, by Andrew Barker,
4to. 1609.

Christianetta. A Play by
Richard Brome, in 1640.
Not printed.

Christmas, his Masque, by
Ben Jonson, presented at
court, 1616.

Christmas Ordinary. A
private Shew, wherein is
expressed the jovial freedom
of that festival, acted at a
gentleman's house among
other revels, 4to. 1682.

A

A Chriſtmas Tale, in five parts, by David Garrick, Eſq. Acted at Drury-Lane, 8vo. 1767. A performance yet more contemptible in its compoſition than *Cymon,* which led the way to this childiſh and inſipid ſpecies of entertainment. The ſucceſs of the *Chriſtmas Tale,* though moderate, was chiefly owing to the aſſiſtance of Loutherburgh, who about this period began to exert his talents as a ſcene painter, in the ſervice of Drury-Lane theatre. This piece, after being gradually curtailed, and reprobated in the news-papers, was at laſt hooted and laid aſide.

Chriſt's Paſſion. Trag. by George Sandys, 8vo. 1640. This play was not intended for the ſtage, and is only a tranſlation of the *Chriſtus Patiens* of Hugo Grotius, with annotations.

Of Chriſt when he was twelve years old. Comedy, This is one of the pieces written by Biſhop Bale, of which we know nothing more than the name.

Chrononhotonthologos. A Mock Trag. by Harry Carey, 8vo. 1734. Acted with ſucceſs at the Little Theatre in the Haymarket. This piece, though deſigned as a ridicule on the extravagance of ſuch tragedies as were in favour about the time it was written, would produce no effect on modern audiences, who have beheld *Zingis, Sethona,* and the *Fatal Diſcovery,* which every way exceed it in tumour, meaneſs, and improbability.

Chuck ; or, *The School Boy's Opera,* 1736. This piece is extremely puerile, yet the author has thought proper to put Mr. Cibber's name to it.

The Churl. Com. tranſlated from Plautus, by R. Warner, Eſq. 8vo.

Cicilia and Clorinda ; or, *Love in Arms,* Tragi-Com. by Thomas Killigrew. Fol. 1664. This is formed into two plays, the ſcene of both pieces lie in Lombardy.

The Cid. Tragi-Com. by Joſeph Rutter. Acted at Court, and at the Cock-pit, Drury-Lane. This play is in two parts, both printed in 12mo. the firſt in 1637, the ſecond in 1640. They are tranſlations, with ſome alterations, of the celebrated *Cid,* of Corneille.

The Cid ; or, *The Heroick Daughter.* Tragedy, 12mo. 1714. This is a tranſlation from Corneille, by John Ozell.

Cimene. A ſerious Opera, acted at the Haymarket, 1783. Well received.

Cinna's Conſpiracy. Tr. Anonym. Acted at Drury-Lane,

Lane, 4to. 1713. The scene Rome. Plot frome the Roman History.

Circe. Dram. Opera, by Dr. Charles D'Avenant, 4to. 1677. Acted with considerable applause. Prologue by Dryden, Epilogue by lord Rochester, and the Music by Bannister.

The Citizen. Com. of three acts, by Arthur Murphy, 1761. This piece was brought on the stage in the summer of 1761, at Drury-Lane, under the management of Mr. Foote and its author. It is rather a long Farce than a Comedy, the incidents being all farcical, and the personages *outre*. The character of *Maria*, a girl of wit and sprightliness, who in order to escape a match which she has an aversion to, and at the same time make the refusal come from her intended husband himself, by passing on him for a fool, is evidently borrowed from the character of *Angelique* in the *Fausse Agnée* of *Destouches*; nor has the author been quite clear from plagiarism as to some other of the characters and incidents. It did not meet with so much success, as either the *All in the Wrong*, or the *Old Maid* of the same author, which appeared at the same time; and indeed Mr. Murphy has seemed himself to acquiesce in the

public judgment by not having suffered this piece to appear in print as originally acted. It was, however, remarkable for having given an opportunity of shewing the extraordinary talents of a young actress who had never trod the stage before, viz. Miss Elliot, who was extremely pleasing in every various transition of the character of *Maria*.

The City Heiress ; or, *Sir Timothy Treatall.* Com. by Mrs. Behn. Acted at the Duke's Theatre, 4to. 1682. This play was well received but it is in great measure a plagiarism, part of it being borrowed from Middleton's *Mad World my Masters*, and part from Massinger's *Guardian*.

The City Lady ; or, *Folly Reclaim'd.* Comedy, by Thomas Dilke. Acted at Little Lincoln's-Inn, 4to. 1697. Scene Covent-Garden. It was acted with success.

The City Madam. Com. by Philip Massinger. Acted at Black-Fryars, 4to. 1659. This is an excellent comedy. The plot, the business, the conduct, and the language of the piece, are all admirable.

The City Match. Com. by Jasper Maine, D. D. A good comedy. See *The Schemers*.

The

C L

The City Night Cap; or, *Crede quod habes et habes.* Com. by Robert Davenport. Acted at the Cockpit, Drury-Lane, 4to. 1661. This play met with very good fuccefs.

City Politiques. Com. by J. Crowne, 4to. 1683. This play was a very fevere fatire upon the Whig party then prevailing.

The City Ramble; or, *The Playhoufe Wedding.* Com. by E. Settle. Acted at the Theatre Royal, 4to. N. D. (1712).

A City Ramble; or, *The Humours of the Compter.* Farce, by Charles Knipe. Acted at Lincoln's-Inn-Fields, 12mo. 1715.

The City Shuffler. A Play, probably never printed.

The City Wit; or, *The Woman wears the Breeches.* Com. by Richard Broome, 8vo. 1653.

The Clandeftine Marriage. Com. by George Colman and David Garrick. Acted at Drury-Lane, 8vo. 1766. This is indifputably one of the beft comedies produced in the prefent times. The hint of it came from Hogarth's *Marriage Alamode*, as the prologue confeffes.

Claudius Tiberius Nero, Rome's greateft Tyrant (the Tragedie of) truly reprefented out of the pureft Records of thofe Times. 4to. 1607.

C L

Claricilla. Tragi-Com by Thomas Killigrew. Acted at the Phœnix in Drury-Lane, 12mo. 1641.

Clementina. Trag. by Hugh Kelly. Acted at Covent-Garden, 8vo. 1771. This play is entitled to fome degree of applaufe, if regarded merely as the work of an unlettered man, but would confer no credit on any author of a higher rank.

Cleomenes; or, *The Spartan Hero.* Trag. by John Dryden. Acted at the Theatre Royal, 4to. 1692. This play was acted with great applaufe. The plot of it is profeffedly taken from Plutarch, but improved by the addition of *Caffandra's* love for *Cleomenes*, and the giving him a fecond wife. The fcene lies in Alexandria and the port of that city, and to all the editions is prefixed the life of Cleomenes. Dr. Johnfon obferves, that this tragedy is remarkable, as it occafioned an incident related in the *Guardian*, and allufively mentioned by Dryden in his preface. As he came out from the reprefentation, he was accofted thus by fome airy ftripling: *Had I been left alone with a young beauty, I would not have fpent my time like your Spartan. That, Sir,* faid said Dryden, *perhaps is true; but give me leave to tell you, that you are no hero.*

Cleone. Tragedy, by R. Dodsley. Acted at Covent-Garden, 8vo. 1758. An imperfect hint towards the fable of this tragedy was taken from the *Legend of St. Genevieve,* written originally in French, and translated into English in the last century by Sir William Lower. Mr. Pope had attempted in his very early youth a tragedy on the same subject, which he afterwards destroyed. The circumstance of *Siffroy's* giving his friend directions concerning his wife, seems to favour somewhat of *Posthumus's* orders in *Cymbeline.* The last acts, containing *Cleone's* madness over her murdered infant, are wrought to the highest pitch, and received every advantage they could possibly meet with from the inimitable performance of Miss Bellamy, to whose peculiar merit, in this part, it would be doing injustice not to pay that tribute in this place, which the most judicious audience in the world, viz. that of London, afforded her during a long and crowded run of the piece, though Mr. Garrick (who had refused it because it contained no character in which he could have figured himself) did his utmost to overpower it, by appearing in a new part on the very first night of its representation. Annexed to this tragedy is an ode, intituled *Melpomene,* which does honour to its author.

Cleonice, Princess of Bithynia. Tragedy, by John Hoole. Acted at Covent-Garden, 8vo. 1775. Mr. Hoole's third production. An ill-fated piece, but not more deserving severity than many others that have escaped it. This author's conduct, after the miscarriage of his play, is worth the imitation of other unsuccessful dramatists. Mr. Hoole returned a part of the money he had received for the copy, observing, that he designed it to have been as lucrative to the publisher as to himself, and therefore it was unjust that the chief loss should happen to the former.

Cleopatra. Tragedy, by Samuel Daniel, 8vo. 1595. This play is founded on the story of *Cleopatra,* in Plutarch's Lives of Anthony and Pompey.

Cleopatra, Queen of Egypt, her Tragedy, by Thomas May, 12mo. 1654. This is upon the same story with the foregoing.

Cloacina. A Comi-Tra. Anonymous, 4to. 1775. This piece contains some pleasant satire on the caprice of managers, and the bad taste tafte difplayed by our modern writers of tragedy.

The Clouds. Com. tranflated from Ariftophanes, by T. Stanley, 1656. The fame tranflated by J. White, 1709, and by L. Theobald, 1715.

The Cobler of Prefton. Farce of two acts, by Cha. Johnfon, 8vo. 1716. Acted at Drury-Lane.

The Cobler of Prefton. Farce, by Chriftopher Bullock. Acted at Lincoln's-Inn-Fields, 12mo. 1716. This farce was begun on Friday, finifhed on Saturday, and acted on the Tuefday following. It was hurried in this manner, to get the ftart of Mr. Charles Johnfon's farce of the fame name.

The Cobler; or, *A Wife of Ten Thoufand.* Ballad Opera, by C. Dibdin. Acted at Drury-Lane, 8vo. 1774.

Cœlia; or, *The Perjured Lover.* A Play, by Charles Johnfon. Acted at Drury-Lane, 1733. Unfuccefsful.

Cælum Britannicum. A Mafque, by Thomas Carew, 4to. 1634. This mafque was written at the particular command of the king, and performed by his majefty and the nobles, at the Banquetting-houfe at Whitehall, on Feb. 18, 1633.

The Coffee-Houfe. Com. by the Rev. James Miller.

Acted at Drury-Lane, 8vo. 1737. This piece met with no kind of fuccefs, from a fuppofition, that Mrs. Yarrow and her daughter, who kept Dick's Coffee-Houfe near Temple-Bar, and were at that time celebrated toafts, together with feveral perfons who frequented that houfe, were intended to be ridiculed by the author.

The Coffee-Houfe; or, *The Fair Fugitive.* C. tranflated from Voltaire, 8vo. 1760.

The Coffee-Houfe Politician; or, *The Juftice caught in his own Trap.* Com. by Henry Fielding, 8vo. 1730. This play has no very great fhare of merit, yet was performed with tolerable fuccefs at the Little Theatre in the Haymarket.

Cola's Fury; or, *Lyrenday's Mifery.* Tragedy, by Henry Burkhead, 4to. 1645. The fubject of this play is the Irifh rebellion which broke out in the year 1641, but was never acted.

The Combat of Capps. A Mafque, 1582. This piece is very fcarce.

The Combate of Love and Friendfhip. C. by Robert Mead, 4to. 1654. This play was prefented, during the author's life-time, by the gentlemen of Chrift-Church College, Oxford, but was not publifhed till after his deceafe.

Th

The Comedy of Errors, by William Shakcfpeare, fol. 1623. This play is founded on the *Mænechmi* of Plautus, tranflated by W. W. 4to. 1595. Mr. Stcevens obferves, that we find in it more intricacy of plot than diftinction of character ; and our attention is lefs forcibly engaged, becaufe we can guefs in a great meafure how the *denouement* will be brought about. Yet the poet feems unwilling to part with his fubject, even in the laft and unneceffary fcene, where the fame miftakes are continued till their power of affording entertainment is entirely loft.

The Comedy of Errors, altered from Shakfpeare, by Thomas Hull. Acted at Covent-Carden, 1779. Not printed.

The Comical Gallant, with the Amours of Sir John Falfaff. Com. by J. Dennis. Acted at Drury-Lane, 4to. 1702. The fcene of this play lies in Windfor park and the town of Windfor ; and the piece is no other than a very indifferent alteration of Shakfpeare's *Merry Wives of Windfor*.

The Comical Hafh. Com. by the duchefs of Newcaftle, fol. 1662.

The Comical Lovers. Com. by C. Cibber, 4to. 1712 ;

acted by fubfcription at the Queen's Theatre in the Haymarket. This piece is compofed of the comic Epifodes of Dryden's *Maiden Queen* and *Marriage à la Mode* joined together : the alteration coft the author, as he fays himfelf (Preface to *Double Gallant*), fix days trouble, and met with a very favourable reception. There are but fix characters in it ; and thefe were performed by Mrs. Bracegirdle, Mrs. Oldfield, and Mrs. Porter, Mr. Wilks, Mr. Booth and Mr. Cibber. A tag to the fourth act feems pointed at the parting of *Monefes* and *Arpafia* in *Tamerlane*, and is a humourous picture of many fuch parting fcenes in fome of our love-fick tragedies.

The Comical Revenge; or, *Love in a Tub*. Com. by Sir George Etherege. Acted at the Duke of York's Theatre, 4to. 1669. 4to. 1689. This comedy has generally fucceeded very well upon the ftage, but was laid afide on account of the loofenefs of its characters and expreffions.

The Commiffary. Com. by Samuel Foote. Acted at the Haymarket, 8vo. 1765. It was performed with fuccefs.

The Committee. Com. by Sir Robert Howard, fol. 1665.

1665. This comedy, which has had the fecond title of *The Faithful Irifhman* added to it, was written not long after the Reftoration, and was intended to throw an idea of the utmoft odium on the Round head party and their proceedings. The piece has no great merit as to the writing, yet, from the drollery of the character of *Teague*, and the ftrong picture of abfurd fanaticifm, mingled with indecent pride, drawn in thofe of Mr. Day, Mrs. Day, and Abel, it even now, when every fpark of party fire, as to that part of the Englifh hiftory, is abfolutely extinct, has eftablifhed itfelf as a ftandard acting comedy, and conftantly gives pleafure in the reprefentation.

The Committee Man Curried. Com. in two Parts, by S. Sheppard, 4to. 1647. A piece difcovering the corruption of committee-men and excife-men; the unjuft fufferings of the Royal party; the devilifh hypocrify of the Roundheads; the revolt for gain of fome minifters. Not without pleafant mirth and variety.

A Commonwealth of Women. A Play, by Thomas Durfey. Acted at the Theatre Royal, 4to. 1686. This play is borrowed from Fletcher's *Sea Voyage*, and is very indifferently executed.

The Compromife; or, *Faults on both Sides.* Com. by Mr. Sturmy, 8vo. 1723. Acted at the Theatre Royal in Lincoln's-Inn-Fields.

Comus. A Mafque, by Dr. Dalton. Acted at Drury-Lane, 8vo. 1738. This piece is a very judicious alteration of Milton's Mafque at Ludlow-caftle, wherein it is rendered much more fit for the ftage by the introduction of many additional fongs, moft of them Milton's own, of part of the *Allegro* of the fame author, and other paffages from his different works, fo that he has rather reftored Milton to himfelf than altered him.

Comus. Mafque. Altered from Milton, by George Colman. Acted at Covent-Garden, 8vo. 1772.

The Conceits. A Play, by R. Marriot, 1653. Not printed.

The Confederacy. Com. by Sir J. Vanbrugh. Acted at the Haymarket, 4to. 1705. This is a very pleafing comedy, and full of bufinefs; the characters are natural, and although there may feem fomewhat improbable in the affair of *Dick* and *Brafs*, yet, as many ftrange things are undoubtedly done in the fortune-hunting fcheme, it can fcarcely be deemed impoffible; the language is pleafing,

ing, and the plot of the two wives againſt their huſbands well conceived and admirably executed. It is not, however, to be regarded as the *chef d'oeuvre* of this witty and ingenious author.

The Confederates. A farce, by Joſeph Gay. 8vo. 1717. This piece is written in rhyme, and although the name put to it is a fictitious one, contains a conſiderable ſhare of humour. It is a very ſevere ſatire on a farce written in confederacy by the three great geniuſes, Pope, Gay, and Arbuthnot, called *Three Hours after Marriage*, which juſtly met with univerſal diſapprobation. The real author of this farce (which was never acted) was Captain John Durant Breval, whom, on this account, Mr. Pope has thought proper to laſh, as he did every one whom he either diſliked or feared, in the *Dunciad*.

The Conflycte of Conſcience. Contaninge a moſt lamentable example of the dolefull deſperation of a miſerable worldlinge, termed by the name of *Philologus*, who forſooke the trueth of God's Goſpel, for feare of the loſſe of lyfe, and worldly goods. By Nathaniel Woodes, miniſter in Norwich. 4to. 1581.

The Connaught Wife. T. of two acts, performed at Smock-Alley, Dublin, 8vo. 1767.

The Connoiſſeur, or *Every Man in his Folly*. A Comedy, by Mr. Conolly. Acted at Drury-Lane, 8vo. 1736. This play is intended to anſwer the ſame kind of purpoſes of ridicule with Shadwell's *Virtuoſo*, and Foote's farce of *Taſte*, but is indifferently executed, and met with little ſucceſs.

The Conqueſt of China by the Tartars. Tragedy, by E. Settle. Acted at the Duke's Theatre, 4to. 1676. This play is written in heroic verſe, and the plot founded on hiſtory.

Conqueſt of Granada. Tragedy, in two parts, by J. Dryden. Acted at the Theatre-Royal, 4to. 1672.— Theſe two plays met with great ſucceſs when performed; on which account, as it ſhould ſeem, Langbaine, who is ever ſtrongly prejudiced againſt this prince of Engliſh poets, has taken amazing pains to point out how much he has borrowed for the forming of theſe pieces from the celebrated romances of Almahide, Grand Cyrus, Ibrahim, and Guzman. Yet ſurely this envy was entirely unneceſſary, ſince, as the plot of the piece is built on hiſtory, it ſhould

should rather be esteemed as a merit, than a blemish in the author, that he has, like an industrious bee, collected his honey from all the choicest flowers which adorned the field he was traversing, whether the more cultivated ones of serious, or the wilder of romantic history. They are, however, written in a manner so different from the present taste, that they have been long laid aside.

The Conquest of Spain. T. 4to. 1705. Acted at the Queen's Theatre in the Haymarket. Scene Spain. It was written by Mrs. Pix.

The Conquest of Canada; or, *The Siege of Quebec.* Historical Tragedy of five acts, by George Cockings, 8vo. 1766.

The Conscious Lovers. C. by Sir Richard Steele. Acted at Drury-Lane, 8vo. 1721. The general design of this celebrated comedy is taken from the *Andria* of Terence; but the author's principal intention in the writing it was, to introduce the very fine scene in the fourth act between young Bevil and Myrtle, which sets forth, in a strong light, the folly of duelling, and the absurdity of what is falsely called the point of honour; and in this particular merit the play would probably

have ever stood foremost, had not that subject been since more amply and completely treated by the admirable author of Sir *Charles Grandison*, in the affair between that truly accomplished gentleman and Sir *Hargrave Pollexfen*. See Sir *Charles Grandison*, vol. I. and II.

The Conspiracy. Tra. by Henry Killigrew, 4to. 1638. This piece was intended for the entertainment of the king and queen at York-House, on occasion of the nuptials of lord Charles Herbert with lady Mary Villiers; and was afterwards acted on the Black-Fryars stage. It was written at seventeen years of age; and the commendation bestowed on it by Ben Jonson and lord Falkland created the author some envy among his contemporaries. The edition above-mentioned is a surreptitious one, published while Killigrew was abroad, and without his knowledge or consent. He afterwards, however, gave the world a more genuine one, in fol. 1653; but was so much ashamed of this first edition, that, to prevent its being known to be the same piece, he altered the name of it to *Pallantus* and *Eudora*, which therefore we would recommend

mend to the reader. The scene lies in Crete.

The Conspiracy ; or, The Change of Government. T. by Whitaker. Acted at the Duke's Theatre, 4to. 1680. Scene Turkey.

Conspiracy and Tragedy of Charles Duke of Byron, Marshal of France. Two Plays, by George Chapman. Acted at Black-Fryars, 4to. 1608. 4to. 1625. These pieces are both founded on history.

The Conspirators. A Tragi-comic Opera, as it was acted in England and Ireland without applause, 8vo. 1749.

The Constant Couple ; or, A Trip to the Jubilee. C. by G. Farquhar. Acted at Drury-Lane, 4to. 1700. This is a very genteel, lively, and entertaining piece ; it met with great success at its first appearance, and is always well received whenever it is represented. It has been said, that the author in his principal character of *Sir Harry Wildair*, meant to present the public with his own portrait : but as the same has also been surmised with regard to his *Captain Plume*, and his young *Mirabel*, we cannot help making one remark on this opinion, which we think must do honour to the author, viz. that such a general belief could arise from nothing but

that resemblance, which must have been apparent to those who knew him, between him and these elegant and pleasing characters. For it is scarcely to be imagined, that a man of the generous, open, familiar, and dissipated cast of character that such a resemblance implies him to have been, could be so much of an egotist as intentionally to make himself the principal in every piece he sent into the world ; and yet it is, perhaps, scarcely possible for any writer, who is to draw characters in real and familiar life, not to throw into that which he intends to render most amiable and important so much of his own principles, opinions, and rules of action, as to render a resemblance apparent to those who are familiar with his complexion of mind and general turn of character. Of this we have numerous instances, in writers of other kinds than the dramatic ; *Joseph Andrews*, *Tom Jones*, and Captain *Booth*, have been ever acknowledged as the characters of their ingenious author ; nor can any one deny a similarity between Sir *Charles Grandison* and his estimable author.

Constantine. Trag. by Phil. Francis, 8vo. 1754. Covent-

Covent - Garden. It met with very bad fuccefs, although not by many degrees the worft of the productions of that feafon.

Conftantine the Great ; or, *The Tragedy of Love*, by N. Lee. Acted at the Theatre Royal, 4to. 1684. The fcene of this play is laid in Rome, and the plot founded on real hiftory.

The Conftant Maid. C. by J. Shirley, 4to. 1640. The greateft part of this play is borrowed from others.

The Conftant Nymph ; or, *The Rambling Shepherd.* A Paftoral. Acted at the Duke's Theatre. Anonym. 4to. 1678. This piece was written by a perfon of quality, who tells us (as moft authors, whofe pieces do not fucceed, are defirous of finding out any other caufe for their failure than want of merit) that it fuffered much through the defects of fetting it off when it came upon the ftage. The fcene is Lucia in Arcadia.

The Contending Brothers. Com. by Henry Brooke, Efq. 8vo. 1778. Not acted.

The Contented Cuckold ; or, *The Woman's Advocate.* Com. by Reuben Bourne, 4to. 1692. Scene London. Was never acted.

The Contention betweene Liberalitie and Prodigalitie. A pleafant comedie play'd

before her Majeftie, 4to. 1602. This piece is anonymous.

The Contention between York and Lancafter, with the tragical Death of the good Duke Humphry, &c. in two parts, 4to. 1600. There is very little difference between this and Shakfpeare's fecond part of Henry VI.

Contentions for Honour and Riches. A Mafque, by J. Shirley, 4to. 1633.

Contention of Ajax and Ulyffes for the Armour of Achilles. An Interlude, 8vo. 1659. The plan taken from the 13th book of Ovid's Metamorphofes.

The Contract. Com. of two acts, by Dr. Thomas Franklin, performed at the Haymarket, 8vo. 1776.— This is a poor performance, and met with no fuccefs.

The Contraft. This play was written by Drs. Benjamin and John Hoadly, and acted at Lincoln's Inn Fields, 1731. It was performed five times in the month of May, but was never printed. The plan of it was a rehearfal of two modern plays, a tragedy and a comedy. and was intended to ridicule the then living poets, among whom we find, by the Grub-ftreet Journal, Mr. Thomfon, author of the *Seafons,* was to be numbered. At the defire

D

fire of bishop Hoadly it was suppressed, and every scrap of paper, copy, and parts, recalled by Mr. Rich, and restored to the authors. Mr. Fielding availed himself afterwards of the same design in his celebrated and popular performance, called *Pasquin*.

The Contretems ; or, *Rival Queens*. A small farce, as it was lately acted with great applause at Heidegger's private Theatre near the Haymarket. Anonymous. 4to. 1727. This piece was never intended for public representation, but was written only in ridicule of the confusion which at that time reigned in the King's Theatre in the Haymarket, in consequence of the contests for superiority between two celebrated Italian singers, Signora Faustina and Signora Cuzzoni.

The Contrivances ; or, *More Ways than One.* Farce, by Harry Carey. Acted at Drury-Lane, 12mo. 1715. This is a very entertaining piece, had good success at its first appearance, and still continues to be well received.

The Convent of Pleasure. Com. by the Duchess of Newcastle, 1668. This is one among many of the pieces of this voluminous female author, which have never been performed, and perhaps very seldom read.

The Cooper. A Musical Entertainment ; acted at the Haymarket, 8vo. 1772.

The Coquet ; or, *The English Chevalier.* Com. by Charles Molloy, 8vo. 1718. Acted at the Theatre in Lincoln's-Inn-Fields, with great applause.

Coriolanus. Tragedy, by W. Shakspeare, fol. 1623. The plot of this play is taken from Plutarch's Life of Coriolanus. Dr. Johnson says, it is one of the most amusing of our author's performances : " The old man's merriment in Menonius ; the lofty lady's dignity in Volumnia ; the bridal modesty in Virgilia ; the patrician and military haughtiness in Coriolanus ; the plebeian malignity and tribunitian insolence in Brutus and Sicinius ; make a very pleasing and interesting variety ; and the various revolutions of the hero's fortune fill the mind with anxious curiosity. There is perhaps too much bustle in the first act, and too little in the last."

Coriolanus. Trag. by J. Thomson. Acted at Covent-Garden, 8vo. 1748. This piece, though it is far from being capital, has some degree of merit. Our pleasing poet's principal merit not lying in the dramatic way ;

C O

way; and this, though the laſt, being far from the beſt of his works, even *in* that way; we cannot pay any very exalted compliments to the piece. The ſtyle of it is, like the reſt of the author's writings, ill calculated to excite the paſſions. Dr. Johnſon obſerves this tragedy was, by the zeal of Sir George Lyttleton, brought upon the ſtage for the benefit of Thomſon's family, and recommended by a prologue, which Quin, who had long lived with him in fond intimacy, ſpoke in ſuch a manner as ſhewed him *to be*, on that occaſion, *no actor*. The commencement of this benevolence is very honourable to Quin; who is reported to have delivered Thomſon, then known to him only for his genius, from an arreſt, by a very confiderable preſent; and its continuance is honourable to both; for friendſhip is not always the ſequel of obligation. By this tragedy a confiderable ſum was raiſed, of which a part diſcharged his debts, and the reſt was remitted to his ſiſters.

Coriolanus; or, *The Roman Matron*. Trag. by T. Sheridan. Acted at Covent-Garden, 8vo. 1755. This piece was compoſed from the two former plays by Shakſpeare and Thom-

C O

ſon, and, being a ſplendid ovation, had ſome ſuccefs.

The Corniſh Comedy. Acted at the Theatre in Dorſet-Gardens, 4to. 1696. Scene Cornwall.

The Corniſh Squire. C. by Sir John Vanburgh, Congreve, and Walſh. Acted at the Haymarket, 1706. This is founded on the Sieur Pourceaugnac of Moliere.

The Coronation. Tr. C. by J. Shirley, 4to. 1640. Scene Epirus.

Corruptions of the Divine Laws. A Dramatic Piece, mentioned by biſhop Bale in the catalogue of his own works.

The Coſtly Whore. A comical Hiſtory, acted by the company of Revels. Anon. 4to. 1633. The ſcene lies in Saxony.

The Cottagers. Opera, by Geo. Savile Carey, 8vo. 1766.

Covent-Garden. C. by Thomas Nabbes, 4to. 1638. This piece was firſt performed in 1632, but was not printed till the time above-mentioned.

Covent - Garden Weeded; or, *The Middleſex Juſtice of Peace*. Com. by R. Broome, 8vo. 1659.

The Covent-Garden Tragedy. Farce, by H. Fielding. Acted at Drury-Lane, 8vo. 1733. This is a burleſque, but not equal to ſome fome other pieces of the fame author.

The Count of Narbonne. Tragedy. by Capt. Jephfon. Acted at Covent-Garden, 1781, and very well received.

The Counterfeit Bridegroom; or, *The Defeated Widow.* Com. 4to. 167-. This is no other than Middleton's *No Wit like a Woman's,* printed with a new title.

The Counterfeits. Com. Acted at the Duke's Theatre, 4to. 1679. J. Leonard has been fuppofed to be the author of this play, which is very far from being a bad one. The fcene lies in Madrid.

Countefs of Salifbury. T. by Hall Hartfon, Efq. 8vo. 1767. This play is taken from Dr. Leland's Romance, called *Longfwerd, Earl of Salifbury.* It was firft acted at Dublin, and afterwards at the Haymarket.

The Country Attorney, C. by Mr. Cumberland. Acted at the Haymarket, 1787. This play has no great fhare of merit.

The Country Captain. C. by the Duke of Newcaftle. Acted at Black-Fryars, and printed at the Hague, 12mo. 1649.

The Country Girl. Com. by A. Brewer, 4to. 1649. Scenes London & Edmonton.

The Country Girl. Com. by David Garrick. Acted at Drury-Lane, 8vo. 1766. This is an alteration of Wycherly's *Country Wife,* and met with fome applaufe.

The Country Houfe. F. by Sir J. Vanbrugh, 12mo. 1715. A tranflation from a French piece.

The Country Election. F. in two acts, 8vo. 1768. This is fuppofed to have been written by Dr. Trufler.

The Country Madcap. Far. Acted at Covent-Garden, 1772. This is only Fielding's *Mifs Lucy in Town,* under a different title.

The Countryman. A play, written in 1653; but probably not printed.

The Country Wife. A Comedy, in two acts, as it is performed at the Theatre Royal, in Drury-Lane, altered from Wycherly, 8vo. 1765.

Country Innocence; or, *The Chambermaid turn'd Quaker.* Com. by John Leonard. Acted at the Theatre Royal, 4to. 1677. This is a moft notorious plagiarifm, being only Brewer's *Country Girl* reprinted.

The Country Laffes; or, *The Cuftom of the Manor.* Com. by Charles Johnfon. Acted at Drury-Lane, 12mo. 1715. This is a very bufy and entertaining comedy, and confifts of two feparate and

and independent plots, one of which is borrowed from Fletcher's *Cuſtom of the Country*; the other from Mrs. Behn's *City Heireſs*, and what ſhe ſtole it from, viz. Middleton's *Mad World my Maſters*. It ſtill ſtands on the liſt of acting plays.

The Country Wake. Com. by Thomas Dogget, 4to. 1696. This play was acted with applauſe at Lincoln's-Inn-Fields; and has ſince been reduced into a ballad-farce, by the name of *Flora*; or, *Hob in the Well.*

The Country Wedding and Skimmington. A Tragi-comi-paſtoral farcical Opera, by Eſſex Hawker, 8vo. 1729, acted at Drury-Lane. This piece is only one long ſcene on a bank near the Thames' ſide at Fulham, with twenty-five airs in it, after the manner of *The Beggar's Opera.*

The Country Wife. Com. by William Wycherly. Acted at the Theatre Royal, 4to. 1675. This comedy contains great wit, high character, and manly nervous language and ſentiment; yet, on account of the looſeneſs in the character of *Horner* and other of the perſonages, it was for ſome time, and had it not been altered, muſt have been totally laid aſide. The laſt performer, who excelled in the charac-

ter of *Pinchwife*, was the late Mr. Quin.

The Couragious Turk; or, *Amurath* I. Tra. by Tho. Goff, 4to. 1632, 8vo. 1656. The plot from the Hiſtories of the Turkiſh Empire, in the reign of Amurath.

The Court Beggar. Com. by Richard Broome. Acted at the Cockpit, 1632, and printed 8vo. 1653.

The Court of Alexander. Opera, by Alex. Stevens. Acted at Covent-Garden, 8vo. 1770.

The Court Lady; or, *Coquet's Surrender.* Comedy. Anonym. 8vo. 1730. This play has very little merit, either in plot, language, or character.

Court Medley; or, *Marriage by Proxy.* A ballad Opera, of three acts, 8vo. 1733.

The Court Secret. Tragi-Com. by James Shirley, 8vo. 1653. This play was never acted. The ſcene lies at Madrid.

Courtſhip-à-la-Mode. C. by David Craufurd. Acted at Drury-Lane, 4to. 1700.

The Coxcomb. Comedy, by Beaumont and Fletcher, fol. 1647. This play has at times been revived and acted with ſucceſs.

The Coxcombs. A Farce, by Francis Gentleman, acted but one night at the Haymarket in 1771.

The

The Cozeners. A Com. in three acts, by Samuel Foote. First acted at the Haymarket in 1774. One character in the piece (that of Mrs. Simony) was designed as a vehicle for satire on the late Dr. Dodd. As some apology for Mr. Foote's stage ridicule, we may observe, that he rarely pointed it at any persons who either met with public respect, or deserved to meet with it.

Craftie Cromwell; or, *Oliver ordering our new state.* Tragi-Com. *Wherein is discovered the traiterous Undertakings and Proceedings of the said* Nol *and his levelling Crew;* written by Mercurius Melancholicus, and printed in 4to. 1648.

The Craft of Rhetoric. Of this piece we shall give the full title as follows; *A newe Commodye in English (in Maner of an Enterlude) ryght elygant and full of Craft of Rethoryk (wherein is shewed and descrybyd as well the bewte and good propertes of Women as their vyces and evyl Condicion) with a moral conclusion and exhortacyon to Vertew.* London, *printed by John Rastell,* 4to. without date. This play is in metre, and in the old black letter.

The Craftsman; or, *Week-ly Journalist.* A Farce, 8vo. 1728. This piece was not intended for the stage, but is a banter on the paper of that title.

Creusa, Queen of Athens. Trag. by W. Whitehead. Acted at Drury-Lane, 8vo. 1754. This play was founded on the *Ion* of Euripides; but the plot is extremely heightened, and admirably conducted by our author; nor has there, perhaps, ever been a more genuine and native simplicity introduced into dramatic writing, than that of the youth Ilyssus, bred up in the service of the Gods, and kept unacquainted with the vices of mankind.

The Critic; or, *A Tragedy Rehearsed.* Farce, by Richard Brinsley Sheridan, Esq. Acted at Drury-Lane, 1779. Not printed. The drift of this performance, which abounds with easy wit, unaffected humour, and judicious satire, is perhaps in general misunderstood It might not have been written with the single view of procuring full houses during its own run, but as a crafty expedient to banish empty ones on future occasions. In short, it is to be regarded in the light of an advertisement published by the manager of Drury-Lane, signifying his wish that no more

more *modern tragedies* may be offered for reprefentation at his theatre. It has already acted as a cauftic on the author of *Zoraida,* whofe piece immediately followed in the fame feafon. We hear indeed that our Cambridge Quixote imputes all his fufferings to the magic of the fell enchantrefs *Tilburina.* Let not however this circumftance difcourage writers of real genius and judgment. Ludicrous parodies or imitations, do no injury to originals of fterling merit. The moft fuccefsful ridicule could never drive our Shakfpeare's phantom from the ftage, though the fpectre raifed by his wouldbe rival Voltaire, is known to have faded long ago at the firft crowing of the cocks of criticifm.

Croefus. Trag. by Wm. Alexander, earl of Sterling, 4to. 1604, and fol. 1639. This is the moft affecting of all our author's pieces. The plot is borrowed from Herodotus, Juftin, and Plutarch, with an epifode in the fifth act from Xenophon's *Cyropaidcia.* The fcene lies in Sardis.

Cromwell, Lord Thomas. Hiftorical Play, 4to. 1613. This drama is in all the Catalogues fet down to Shakfpeare ; but Theobald and other editors of his works

have omitted it, and *The Puritan, Pericles,* Prince of *Tyre,* the Trag. of *Locrine,* the *Yorkfhire* Tra. Sir *John Oldcaftle,* and the *London Prodigal.* Indeed, all thefe, though it is probable from fome beautiful paffages that Shakfpeare may have had a hand in them, are on the whole too indifferent to be received as the genuine and entire works of that inimitable genius.

Crofs Purpofes. Farce, by Mr. Obrien. Acted at Covent-Garden, 8vo. 1772. This piece had confiderable fuccefs.

The Cruel Brother. Tr. by Sir W. Davenant, 4to. 1630. Prefented at Black-Fryars. The fcene Italy.

The Cruel Gift ; or, *The Royal Refentment.* Tra. by Mrs. Centlivre. Acted at Drury-Lane, 12mo. 1717. It was the fecond attempt made by this lady in the tragedy walk, and is far from being a bad one. The defign is founded on the ftory of *Sigifmunda* and *Guifcardo,* which is to be met with in Boccace's novels, and a poetical verfion of it very finely done by Dryden, and publifhed among his fables.

The Cruelty of the Spaniards in Peru. Expreffed by inftrumental and vocal mufic, and by art of perfpective

fpective in fcenes, by Sir William Davenant, &c. reprefented daily at the Cockpit in Drury-Lane, at three in the afternoon punctually, 4to. 1658.

The Crufade. Englifh Opera, by Mr. Reynolds. Acted at Covent-Garden, 1790. Very well received.

The Cuckold in Conceit. Comedy, by Sir John Vanbrugh. It was acted at the Queen's Theatre in the Haymarket, 1706.

Cuckold's Haven; or, *An Alderman no Conjuror*, by N. Tate, Farce. Acted at Dorfet-Gardens, 4to. 1685. The plot of this piece is borrowed partly from *Eaftward Hoe*, and partly from the *Devil's an Afs*, of Ben. Jonfon.

The Cunning Lovers. C. by Robert Broome, 4to. 1654. This piece was acted at Drury-Lane with confiderable applaufe, and was well efteemed. The fcene lies in Verona.

The Cunning Man. A Mufical Entertainment, by Doctor Burney. Acted at Drury-Lane, 8vo. 1766. This is a tranflation of Rouffeau's *Devin de Village*.

Cupid and Death. A Mafque, by James Shirley, 4to. 1653.

Cupid and Hymen. A Mafque, by John Hughes, 8vo. about 1717.

Cupid and Pfyche. A play by Thomas Heywood. Not printed.

Cupid's Revenge. Trag. by Beaumont and Fletcher. Acted by the children of the Revels, 4to. 1615.

Cupid's Revenge. An Arcadian Paftoral, by F. Gentleman. Acted at the Haymarket, 8vo. 1772.

A Cure for a Cuckold. Com. by John Webfter and W. Rowley, 4to. 1661. This play was acted with great applaufe.

A Cure for a Scold, Ballad Opera, by James Worfdale. Acted at London and Dublin, 12mo. 1738. Taken from Shakfpeare's *Taming of the Shrew.*

A Cure for Jealoufy. C. by John Carey, 4to. 1701. Acted at Lincoln's-Inn-Fields.

The Cuftom of the Country. Tragi-Com. by Beaumont and Fletcher. Fol. 1647.

Cutter of Coleman-Street. Com. by Abraham Cowley, 4to. 1663. This play was treated on the ftage with feverity, and afterwards cenfured as a fatire on the king's party.

Cymbeline. Trag. by W. Shakfpeare, fol. 1623. The plot of this play is taken from an old ftory-book, intituled, *Weftward for Smelts*, 4to. 1603. Dr. Johnfon obferves,

obferves, that it "has many juft fentiments, fome natural dialogues, and fome pleafing fcenes, but they are obtained at the expence of much incongruity. To remark the folly of the fiction, the abfurdity of the conduct, the confufion of the names, and manners of the different times, and the impoffibility of the events in any fyftem of life, were to wafte criticifm upon unrefifting imbecility, upon faults too evident for detection, and too grofs for aggravation.

Cymbeline. Trag. altered from Shakfpeare, by W. Hawkins. Acted at Covent-Garden, 8vo. 1759. This is what the title implies, it being only fitted to the Englifh ftage, by removing fome part of the abfurdities in point of time and place, which the rigid rules of dramatic law do not now admit with fo much impunity as at the time when the original author of *Cymbeline* was living. Thus far our predeceffor; but juftice obliges us to add, that the play is entirely ruined by Mr. Hawkins's unpoetical additions and injudicious alterations. It had no fuccefs when performed for a night or two at Covent-Garden, the hand of the reformer having deftroyed all its

powers of entertainment, by difcarding the part of Jachimo, delaying the appearance of Pofthumus till the third act, &c. &c. With a few trivial omiffions, the original piece is ftill a favourite with the public.

Cymbeline. Trag. altered by David Garrick, Efq. Acted at Drury-Lane, 12mo. 1759. This alteration, being lefs violent, is lefs defective than many fimilar attempts on the dramas of Shakfpeare. A material fault, however, occurs in it. By omitting the Phyfician's foliloquy in the firft act, we are utterly unprepared for the recovery of Imogen after fhe had fwallowed the potion prepared by her ftepmother. To fave appearances, this speech was inferted in the printed copy, but was never uttered on the ftage. Ufelefs as it might be to thofe who are intimately acquainted with the piece, it is ftill neceffary toward the information of a common auditor.

Cymbeline, King of Great-Britain. A Tragedy, written by Shakfpeare, with fome alterations by Charles Marfh, 8vo. 1755.

Cymbeline. Tragedy, by Henry Brooke, Efq. 8vo. 1778. Not acted. This is on the fame ftory as Shakfpeare's play.

Cymon

Cymon. Dram. Romance, by David Garrick. Acted at Drury-Lane, 8vo. 1767. It is a wretched production, equally devoid of wit, humour, and poetry.

Cynthia and Endymion; or, *The Loves of the Deities.* Dramatic Op. by T. Durfey, 4to. 1697. This piece was designed to be acted at court before queen Mary II. and after her death was performed at the Theatre Royal, where it met with good success. The story is taken from Ovid's *Metamorphoses,* and *Psyche,* in Apuleius's *Golden Ass.*

Cynthia's Revels; or, *The Fountain of Self-Love.* A Comical Satire, by Ben Jonson. Acted in 1600, by the children of Queen Elizabeth's Chapel.

Cynthia's Revenge; or, *Mænander's Extasy,* by J. Stephens, 4to. 1613. The plot is from Lucan's *Pharsalia* and Ovid's *Metamorphoses.*

Cyrus the Great; or, *The Tragedy of Love.* Trag. by J. Banks. Acted at Lincoln's-Inn-Fields, 4to. 1696. This play was at first forbidden to be acted, but afterwards came on, and met with very good success.

Cyrus. Trag. by John Hoole. Acted at Covent-Garden, 1768, with great success.

Cytherea; or, *The Enamoured Girdle.* Com. by J. Smith, 4to. 1677. This play was never acted.

The Czar of Muscovy. T. by Mrs. Mary Pix, 4to. 1701. The scene Muscovy. It died, in obscurity, and has not been heard of since.

The Czar. Comic Op. by Mr. O'Keeffe. Acted at Covent-Garden, 1790. This piece was considered as a falling-off of this writer's abilities.

D A

DAME DOBSON; or, *The Cunning Woman.* Comedy, by E. Ravenscroft. Acted at the Duke's Theatre, 4to. 1684. Translated from a French comedy, called, *La Divineresse, ou, Les faux Enchantemens.* Damned in its representation on the London Theatre.

D A

Damnation; or, *Hissing-bot.* An Interlude, by C. Stuart. Acted at the Haymarket, for a benefit, 1781.

Damon and Phillida. A Ballad Pastoral, by Colley Cibber, 8vo. 1729. This little Farce is entirely selected out of the *Love in a Riddle* by the same author. Notwithstanding that piece fell

fell to the ground on the second night of its appearance, this entertainment was not only then extremely applauded, but has continued so to be ever since.

Damon and Phillida. Altered from Cibber into a Comic Opera, by C. Dibdin. Acted at Drury-Lane, 12mo. 1768.

The Damoiselle ; or, The New Ordinary. Com. by Richard Broome, 8vo. 1635. Scene London.

The Damoiselles à-la-Mode. Comedy, by R. Flecknoe, 12mo. 1667. The scene of this play is laid in Paris.

Daphne and Amintor. C. Op. by Isaac Bickerstaffe. Acted at Drury-Lane, 8vo. 1765. It is little more than *The Oracle* of Mrs. Cibber, with a few songs interspersed.

Darius. Tr. by the Earl of Sterling, 4to. Edinburgh, 1603. This was one of his lordship's first performances, and was originally written in a mixture of the Scotch and English dialects ; but the author afterwards not only polished the language, but even very considerably altered the play itself.

Darius, King of Persia. Tra. by J. Crowne. Acted by their majesties servants, 4to. 1688.

The Dead Alive. A Farce,

by John Keefe. Acted at the Haymarket, 1781. Not printed. The sketches of character are strongly marked ; and the incidents, though extravagant, are within the limits of possibility.

Deaf Indeed. Farce, by Mr. Topham. Acted at Drury-Lane, 1780. Not printed.

The Deaf Lover. Farce, by F. Pilon. Acted at Covent-Garden, 8vo. 1779.

Death of Dido. A Masque, by R. C. 1621.

The Death of Adam. Tr. translated from the German of Mr. Klopstock, by Robert Lloyd, 12mo. 1763.

The Death of Bucephalus. A Burlesque Trag. by Dr. Ralph Schomberg. Acted at Edinburgh, 8vo. 1775.

The Death of Cæsar. Tr. translated from Voltaire, and published in Dr. Franklin's edition, 12mo.

The Death of Dido. Masque, by Barton Booth. Acted at Drury-Lane, 8vo. 1716.

The Debauchée ; or, The Credulous Cuckold. Com. Acted at the Duke's Theatre, 4to. 1677. Anonym.

The Debauchées ; or, The Jesuit Caught. Com. by H. Fielding. Acted at Drury-Lane, 8vo. 1733. This play is built on the story so recent at that time of

Father

DE

DE

Father Girard and Mifs Cadiere, and in it the author has by no means fpared the characters of the black-hooded gentlemen of that reverend tribe.

The Deceit. Farce, by Henry Norris, 12mo. 1723.

The Deceit ; or, The Old Fox Outwitted. Paftoral Farce, of one act, by J. W. As it was defigned to have been acted, 8vo. 1743. Printed with a collection of Poems, called *The Poplar Grove ; or, The Amufements of a Rural Life.*

The Deceiver Deceived. Com. by Mrs. M. Pix, 4to. 1698. Acted at the Theatre in Lincoln's-Inn-Fields. There are two dialogues in this play, one in the fourth act, by Durfey, and the other in the laft, by Motteux, both fet to mufic by Eccles. Scene Venice.

Deception. Com. acted at Drury-Lane, 1784. This piece appears to be the early and crude production of a man of fome talents, though the fable has no novelty to recommend it.

Decius and Paulina. A Mafque, by L. Theobald, 8vo. 1718.

The Decoy. An Opera, by H. Potter. Acted at Goodman's-Fields, 1733. 8vo.

Demetrius. Opera, tranf-lated from *Metaftafio*, by John Hoole, 8vo. 1768.

Demetrius and Marfina ; or, The Imperial Impofter and unhappy Heroine. Trag. Sold among the books and manufcripts of John Warburton, Efq. about the year 1759. Not printed.

Demophoon. Opera, tranf-lated from *Metaftafio*, by John Hoole, 8vo. 1768.

Deorum Dona. A Mafque, by Robert Baron, 8vo. 1648. Performed before Flaminius and Clorinda, king and queen of Cyprus, at their regal palace in Nicofia. Scene Nicofia.

The Depofing and Death of Queen Gin. An Heroic-Comic-Trag. Farce. Anonymous, 8vo. 1736. Acted at the New Theatre in the Haymarket. The defign of it is founded on an act of Parliament, laying an additional duty on the retailing of fpirituous liquors of any kinds.

The Deferving Favourite. Tragi-Com. by Lodowick Carlell. Scene Spain. This piece met with great applaufe, and was acted feveral times before the king and queen at Whitehall, and at Black-Fryars, 4to. 1629.

The Defert Ifland. A Dramatic Tale, in three acts, by A. Murphy, 8vo. 1760. This little piece, which is allied to tragedy, although the cataftrophe of it is a happy one, was firft

performed

D E

performed at the Theatre
Royal in Drury-Lane, on
the fame night with the *Way
to Keep Him*, a comedy of
the fame number of acts by
the fame author. The plan
of this piece has its original,
according to the author's own
confeffion, in a little drama
of a fingle act, called *L'Ifola
difabitata* ; or, *The Uninhabited Ifland*, written by the
Abbe Metaftafio. Mr.
Murphy has greatly ex-
tended the original, fo that
the language, in which there
is a confiderable fhare both
of poetry and *pathos*, may
properly be called his own.
But the plan being extremely fimple, even for one act,
and that ftretched into three
without the introduction of
a fingle incident or epifode,
renders it fomewhat too
heavy and declamatory to
give much pleafure in a public reprefentation, though
it will bear a clofe examen
and *critique* in the clofet.
The fuccefs of it evinced
the truth of this obfervation,
for notwithftanding the great
approbation fhewn to the
other piece brought on at
the fame time, yet even the
fprightlinefs of that could
not fecure to this a run of
many nights, after which
the *Way to Keep Him* continued an acting piece for
the remainder of that feafon ; and, by the addition
of two new acts afterwards,

D E

ftill ftands on the ftock-lift
of the theatre, while the
Defert Ifland became truly
deferted, and has never fince
been reprefented.
   The Deferter. Mufical
Drama, by C. Dibdin. Acted
at Drury-Lane. 8vo. 1773.
Taken from a French piece,
intituled, *Le Deferteur* ; and
acted with fuccefs.
   *The Deftruction of Jeru-
falem*, by Titus Vefpafian.
Tragedy, in two parts, by
J. Crowne. Acted at the
Theatre Royal 4to. 1677.
   *The Deftruction of Jerufa-
lem.* By Thomas Legge.
Written in the time of queen
Elizabeth, and probably
never printed.
   Deftruction of Troy. Tr.
by J. Banks. Acted at the
Duke's Theatre, 4to. 1679.
This is very far from being
a defpicable piece, although
it met with very indifferent
treatment from the critics.
   The Deuce is in Him. F.
by George Colman. Acted
at Drury-Lane, 8vo. 1763.
The firft hint of this piece
was taken from Marmon-
tel's *Tales*, and that part of
the fable which relates to
Madame Florival, from a
ftory originally publifhed
in *The Britifh Magazine*.
It met with very great and
deferved fuccefs from the
public. The plan on which
this delicate fatire on platonic love is founded, has
been approved by thofe who
are

are the ſtricteſt advocates for morality, in dramatic exhibitions. The piece, though very ſerious in the main, is extremely laughable in many parts.

The Devil is an Aſs. C. by Ben Jonſon. Acted in 1616, printed fol. 1641. Jonſon is certainly but little chargeable with borrowing any part of his plots, yet *Wittipol's* giving his cloak to *Fitz-dotterel* for leave to court his wife for a quarter of an hour, ſeems founded on a circumſtance of Boccace's *Decameron,* Day 3. Nov. 5. Mrs. *Centlivre* has made her Sir *George Airy* do the ſame, only converting the cloak into a purſe of an hundred guineas.

The Devil of a Duke ; or, *Trappolin's Vagaries.* Ballad Farce, by R. Drury, 8vo. 1732. Acted at Drury-Lane.

The Devil's Charter. T. by Barnaby Barnes, 4to. 1607. This tragedy contains the life and death of that moſt execrable of all human beings, pope Alexander VI.

The Devil's Law-Caſe ; or, *When Women go to Law, the Devil is full of Buſineſs.* Tragi-Com. by J. Webſter, 4to. 1623. This is a good play, and met with ſucceſs.

The Devil of a Wife ; or,

A Comical Transformation. Farce, by Thomas Jevon. Acted at the Theatre Dorſet-Garden, 4to. 1686. This little piece Langbaine gives great commendations to, and it met with ſucceſs in the repreſentation.

The Devil to Pay ; or, *The Wives Metamorphoſed.* Ballad Farce, by C. Coffey, 8vo. 1731. This well-known little piece has itſelf, perhaps, gone through as many metamorphoſes, and had as many hands concerned in the fabrication of it, as ever clubbed together in a buſineſs of ſo little importance. The ground work of it, and indeed the beſt part, is ſelected from a farce of three acts, written by Jevon the player. One theatrical anecdote, however, muſt not be omitted in our mention of this piece, which is, to the part of *Nell* the great Mrs. Clive owed the riſe of her juſtly eſtabliſhed reputation, that being the firſt thing ſhe was ever taken any conſiderable notice of in, which occaſioned her ſalary, then but trifling, to be doubled. Harper, who played *Jobſon,* had alſo his ſalary raiſed, from the merit he ſhewed in the performance.

The Devil upon Two Sticks ; or, *The Country Beau.* Ballad Farce, by C. Coffey,

Coffey, 1744. This was acted one night only, at Shepheard's-Wells, May-Fair.

The Devil upon Two Sticks. Com. by Samuel Foote. Acted at the Haymarket, 1768. Printed in 8vo. 1778. This was one of the moſt ſuccefsful of Mr. Foote's performances ; but though fraught with wit, humour, and fatire of the moſt pleaſant and inoffenſive kind, yet feems to have funk into the grave of its ingenious author.

Dido, Queen of Carthage. Trag. by Chriſtopher Marlow and Thom. Nafh. Acted by the children of her majeſty's chapel, 4to. 1594. This play is uncommonly fcarce.

Dido. Trag. in imitation of Shakfpeare's ſtyle, by Jofeph Reed. Acted at Drury-Lane, 1767. Not printed.

Dido. Com. Opera, by Thomas Bridges. Acted at the Haymarket, 8vo. 1771.

Dioclefian ; or, *The Prophetefs.* Dram. Opera, by Tho. Betterton, 4to. 1690.

Dione. Paſtoral, by John Gay, printed in his Poems, 4to. 1720. This piece, fays Dr. Johnfon, is a counterpart to *Amynta* and *Paſtor Fido*, and other trifles of the fame kind, eaſily imitated, and unworthy of imitation. What the Italians call Comedies, from a happy con-

clufion, Gay calls a Tragedy, from a mournful event ; but the ſtyle of the Italians and of Gay is equally tragical. There is fomething in the poetical *Arcadia* fo remote from known reality and ſpeculative poſſibility, that we can never fupport its reprefentation through a long work. A paſtoral of a hundred lines may be endured ; but who will hear of ſheep and goats, and myrtle bowers and purling rivulets, through five acts? Such fcenes pleafe barbarians in the dawn of literature, and children in the dawn of life ; but will be for the moſt part thrown away, as men grow wife, and nations grow learned.

The Difappointed Coxcomb. C. by Bartholomew Bourgeois, 8vo. 1765.

The Difappointment ; or, *The Mother in Faſhion.* C. by Thomas Southerne. Acted at the Theatre Royal, 4to. 1684. The fcene lies in Florence, and part of the plot is taken from the *Curious Impertinent* in Don Quixote.

The Difappointment. Ballad Op. by J. Randal. Acted at the Haymarket, 8vo. 1732.

The Difcovery. A Com. by Mrs. Sheridan, acted at the Theatre Royal, Drury-Lane, 1763, 8vo. This original compoſition was received with uncommon applaufe

plaufe. It is a very moral, fentimental, yet entertaining performance.

The Difcovery. Com. tranflated from Plautus, by R. Warner, 8vo. 1773.

The Difguife. A Dram. Novel, 2 vols. 12mo. 1771.

The Difobedient Child. A pretty and merry Interlude, by Thomas Ingeland, 4to. without date. This author lived in the time of queen Elizabeth; and his piece is written in verfe of ten fyllables, and printed in the old black letter.

The Diffembled Wanton; or, *My Son get Money.* C. by Leonard Welfted. Acted at Lincoln's-Inn-Fields. 8vo. 1726. This is an entertaining comedy, and met with tolerable fuccefs.

Diffipation. Comedy, by M. P. Andrews. Acted at Drury-Lane, 8vo. 1781. This play was borrowed from Garrick's *Bon Ton*, and feveral other pieces; but has nothing very great to recommend it.

The Diftracted State. Tr. by J. Tatham, written in 1641, 4to.

Diftrefs upon Diftrefs; or, *Tragedy in true Tafte.* An Heroi-comi-parodi-tragi-farcical Burlefque, in two acts, by George Alexander Stevens, 8vo. 1752. This piece was never performed nor intended for the ftage, but is only a banter on the bombaft language and inextricable diftrefs aimed at by fome of our tragedy writers.

The Diftreft Mother. T. by Ambrofe Philips. Acted at Drury-Lane, and printed in 4to. 1712. This play is little more than a tranflation from the *Andromaque* of Racine. It is, however, very well tranflated, the poetry pleafing, and the incidents of the ftory fo affecting, that although it is, like all the French tragedies, rather too heavy and declamatory, yet it never fails bringing tears into the eyes of a fenfible audience; and will, perhaps, ever continue to be a ftock play on the lifts of the theatres. The original author, however, has deviated from hiftory, and Philips likewife followed his example, in making *Hermione* kill herfelf on the body of *Pyrrhus*, who had been flain by her inftigation; whereas, on the contrary, fhe not only furvived, but became wife to *Oreftes*, How far the *Licentia poetica* will authorize fuch oppofitions to well-known facts of hiftory, is, however, a point which we have no time at prefent to enter into a difquifition in regard to.

Dr. Johnfon obferves that
fuch

fuch a work requires no un-common powers; but that the friends of Philips exerted every art to pro-mote his intereſt. Be-fore the appearance of the play a whole *Spectator*, none indeed of the beſt, was de-voted to its praiſe; while it yet continued to be acted, another *Spectator* was writ-ten, to tell what impreſſion it made upon Sir Roger de Coverley; and on the firſt night a ſelect audience, ſays Pope, was called together to applaud it.

It was concluded with the moſt ſuccefsful epilogue that was ever yet ſpoken on the Engliſh theatre. The three firſt nights it was received twice; and not only conti-nued to be demanded through the run, as it is termed, of the play, but whenever it is recalled to the ſtage, where by peculiar fortune, though a copy from the French, it yet keeps its place, the epilogue is ſtill ſpoken. It was printed in the name of Budgel, but is known to have been the work of Addiſon.

The Diſtreſt Wiſe. C. by J. Gay, 8vo. 1743. This piece was defigned by its author for the ſtage, and entirely finiſhed before his death. It is, however, far from being equal to the ge-nerality of his writings.

The Diſtreſt Wiſe. Com. altered from Gay. Acted at Covent-Garden, 1772, for the benefit of Mrs. Lef-fingham.

The Diverſions of the Morn-ing. Farce, by Samuel Foote. Acted at Drury-Lane, 1768. Not printed.

The Divine Comedian; or, *The Right of Plays,* im-proved in a ſacred Tragi-Com. by Richard Tuke, 4to. 1672. This play is on a religious ſubject, and we imagine was never acted.

The Divorce. Farce, by Mr. Jackman, acted at Drury-Lane, 1781. This farce afforded much laugh-ter; and, as far as the aim of the ridicule is in queſtion, the author is entitled to ap-plauſe.

The Doating Lovers; or, *The Libertine Tam'd.* Com. by Newburgh Hamilton, 12mo. 1715. Acted at Lin-coln's-Inn-Fields. Scene London.

Doctor Fauſtus's Tragical Hiſtory, by Chriſtopher Marlow, 4to. 1604.

Doctor Fauſtus, Life and Death of, with the Humours of Harlequin and Scaramouch, as they were acted by Mr. Lee and Mr. Jevon. Farce, by W. Mountford; acted at the Queen's Theatre in Dorſet-Gardens, and reviv-ed at the Theatre in Lin-coln's-Inn-fields, 4to. 1697.

Doctor

D O

Doctor Laſt in his Chariot. Com. by Iſaac Bickerſtaffe. Acted at the Haymarket, 8vo. 1769. This is a tranſlation of Moliere's *Malade Imaginaire.*

The Doctor and Apothecary. Muſical Entertainment. Performed at Drury-Lane, 1788. The Songs and Muſic have much merit, and were well received.

Don Carlos, Prince of Spain. Tragedy, by Tho. Otway. Acted at the Duke's Theatre, 4to. 1676.

Don Garcia of Navarre; or, *The Jealous Prince,* a tranſlation from Moliere by Ozell.

The Comical Hiſtory of Don Quixote. By Thomas Durfey; acted at Dorſet Gardens, 4to. 1694.

Don Quixote in England. Com. by. H. Fielding, 8vo. 1733. Acted at the Little Theatre in the Haymarket, with ſuccefs.

Don Sancho; or, *The Student's Whim.* Ballad Op. in three acts, with Minerva's Triumph. A Maſque, by Elizabeth Boyd, 8vo. 1739.

Don Saverio. Muſical Drama; acted at Drury-Lane, 4to. 1750. The muſic by Dr. Arne, who alſo probably wrote the words.

Don Sebaſtian, King of Portugal. T. by J. Dryden.

D O

Acted at the Theatre Royal, 4to. 1690, 4to. 1692. This is commonly (as Dr. Johnſon obſerves) eſteemed either the firſt or ſecond of Dryden's dramatic performances. It is too long to be all acted, and has many characters and many incidents; and though it is not without ſallies of frantic dignity, and more noiſe than meaning, yet as it makes approaches to the poſſibilities of real life, and has ſome ſentiments which beam a ſtrong impreſſion, it continued long to attract attention. Amidſt the diſtreſſes of princes, and the viciſſitudes of empire, are inſerted ſeveral ſcenes which the writer intended for comic; but which, I ſuppoſe, that age did not much commend, and this would not endure. There are, however, paſſages of excellence univerſally acknowledged; the diſpute and the reconciliation of Dorax and Sebaſtian has been always admired.

Dorval; or, *The Teſt of Virtue.* C. tranſlated from Diderot, 8vo. 1767.

The Double Dealer, C. by W. Congreve. Acted at the Theatre Royal, 4to. 1694. This is the ſecond play this author wrote; the characters of it are ſtrongly drawn, the wit genuine and original,

original, the plot finely
laid, and the conduct inimitable,

The Double Deceit ; or, *A
Cure for Jealousy*. Com. by
W. Fopple, 8vo. Acted at
Covent-Garden, 1736.

The Double Deceit ; or,
The Happy Pair. A Comic
Farce, printed 8vo. 1745,
but never acted.

The Double Deception. C.
by Miss Richardson. Act-
ed at Drury-Lane, 1779.
This play was performed
only four nights.

The Double Disappointment.
Farce, 1747. Acted at Co-
vent-Garden. This has no
great share of merit either
as to plot or language.

The Double Disguise. C.
Opera, of two acts. Acted
at Drury-Lane, 1784. Des-
titute of any kind of merit.

The Double Distress. T.
by Mrs. Mary Pix, 4to.
1701. Acted at Lincoln's-
Inn-Fields. Scene Perse-
polis.

The Double Falshood ; or,
The Distrest Lovers. Trag.
by L. Theobald. Acted at
Drury-Lane, 8vo. 1727.
This piece Theobald en-
deavoured to persuade the
world was written by Shakspeare. How true his as-
sertion might be, we cannot
pretend to determine, but
very few perhaps gave any
credit to it. The play,
however, was acted with

considerable success, and
was the last piece in which
Mr. Booth appeared. Dr.
Farmer is of opinion, that
it is a production of Shirley's, or at least not earlier
than his time. Mr. Ma-
lone inclines to believe it
written by Massinger.

The Double Gallant ; or,
The Sick Lady's Cure. C.
by C. Cibber. Acted at
the Haymarket, 4to. 1709.
Part of this play is borrowed from Mrs. Centlivre's
Love at a Venture, and part
from Burnaby's *Visiting
Day*.

The Double Marriage. T.
by Beaumont and Fletcher,
fol. 1647. Scene Naples.
This play is one of their
best plays.

The Double Mistake. C.
by Mrs. Elizabeth Griffiths.
Acted at Covent-Garden,
8vo. 1766.

The Doubtful Heir. Tra.
Com. by James Shirley.
Acted at the private house
in Black-Fryars, 8vo. 1652.

Douglas. Trag. by John
Home. Acted at Covent-
Garden, 8vo. 1757. This
tragedy is founded on the
quarrels of the families of
Douglas and others of the
Scots clans. It has a great
deal of pathos in it, some of
the narratives are pleasingly
affecting, and the descriptions poetically beautiful ;
yet on the whole it appears
rather

rather heavy. The author was a Scotſman, and a clergyman of that church. The piece made its firſt appearance on the Edinburgh theatre, at that time in no unflouriſhing condition. This, however, drew the reſentment of the elders of the kirk, and many other rigid and zealous members of that ſect, not only on the author but the performers, on whom, together with him, they freely denounced their anathemas in pamphlets and public papers. The latter indeed it was out of their power greatly to injure, but their rod was near falling very heavy on the author, &c. whom the aſſembly repudiated and cut-off from his preferments. In England, however, he had the good fortune to meet with friends, and being, through the intereſt of the earl of Bute and ſome other perſons of diſtinction, recommended to the notice of his preſent majeſty, then prince of Wales, his royal highneſs was pleaſed to beſtow a penſion on him, and his piece was brought on the ſtage in London, and met with ſucceſs.

The Dowager. By Tho. Chatterton. Some ſcenes of a play by this extraordinary young man are in M. S.

The Downfall of the Aſſociation. Comic Trag. in five

acts, 8vo. 1771. Printed at Wincheſter.

The Dragon of Wantley. A Burleſque Opera, by H. Carey, 8vo. 1738; acted at Covent-Garden. This piece has a great deal of humour in it, and was a very fine burleſque on the Italian operas, at that time ſo much the paſſion of the town.

The Dramatiſt. Comedy. Acted at Covent-Garden, 1789, for the benefit of Mrs. Wells.

The Drummer; or, *The Haunted Houſe.* Com. by Addiſon, 4to. 1715. Nothing perhaps can give a ſtronger proof of how vague and indeciſive as to real merit the judgment of an audience is to be conſidered, and how frequently that judgment is biaſſed by names alone, than the ſucceſs of this Comedy, coming out at firſt without any known parent, notwithſtanding it had all the advantages of admirable acting, was ſo univerſally diſliked, that the author choſe to keep himſelf concealed till after his death.

The Drunken Newſ-writer. Comic Interlude. Performed at the Haymarket, 8vo. 1771.

The Duel. A Play, by William Obrien. Acted at Drury-Lane, 8vo. 1772.

The Duelliſt. Com. by William

D U

William Kenrick. Acted at Covent-Garden, 8vo. 1773. This was taken from Fielding's *Amelia*. It was acted once only.

The Duenna. Com. Op. by Richard Brinsley Sheridan, Esq. Acted at Covent-Garden, 1775. This piece was received with applause by crowded audiences through a run of sixty-five nights during the first season of its appearance. In the following year it was repeated at least thirty times, and still continues a favourite with the public. It exhibits so happy a mixture of true humour and musical excellence, that it deservedly stands *second* on the list of its kindred performances. The *Beggar's Opera* perhaps will always remain the *first*.

The Duenna. Com. Op. in three acts, 8vo. 1776. This is a parody on Mr. Sheridan's celebrated performance, and is entirely political. The supposed author of the present Grub-street piece (which is not the worst of its kind) was Israel Pottinger.

Duke and no Duke. Farce, by N. Tate. Acted by their majesties' servants, 4to. 1685. The scene of this piece lies in Florence, and the plot is taken from *Trappo lin suppos'd a Prince*.

The Duke of Guise. Tra.

by Dryden and Lee. Acted by their Majesties' servants, 4to. 1683, 4to. 1687. This play met with several enemies at its first appearance upon the stage. Dryden wrote only the first scene, the whole fourth act, and the first half, or somewhat more, of the fifth. All the rest of the play is Lee's.

The Duke of Milan. Tr. by P. Massinger. Acted at Black-Fryars, 4to. 1623, 4to. 1638.

The Duke of Milan. Tr. Com. by Richard Cumberland, Esq. Acted at Covent-Garden, 1779. Not printed.

The Duke's Mistress. Tr. Com. by James Shirley. Acted at the private house, Drury-Lane, 4to. 1638. Scene Parma.

The Dumb Lady; or, *The Farrier made Physician*. C. by John Lacy. Acted at the Theatre Royal, 4to. 1672. The plot and much of the language of this play is from Moliere's *Medecin malgre lui*.

The Dumb Knight. An historical Com. by Lewis Machin. Acted by the children of the Revels, 4to. 1608. The scene of this play lies in Cyprus, and the incidents of the plot are taken from Bandello's novels.

The Dupe. Com. by Mrs.

Mrs. Sheridan, acted at Drury-Lane, 8vo. 1763, was damned on account of a few paſſages which the audience thought too inde-licate.

Duplicity. Com. by Mr. Holcroft. Acted at Covent-Garden, 1781. It was received with great applauſe, and undoubtedly has merit.

The Dutch Courtezan. C. by J. Marſton. Played at Black-Fryars, by the children of the Revels, 4to. 1605.

The Dutch Lover. Com. by Mrs. Behn. Acted at the Duke's Theatre, 4to.

1673. The plot is founded on the ſtories of *Eufemie* and *Theodore,* Don *Jame* and *Frederic,* in a Spaniſh novel.

The Dutchess of Malfey. Trag. by John Wehſter. Acted at Black-Fryars and the Globe, 4to. 1623.

The Dutchess of Malfey. Tragedy. Acted at the Duke's Theatre, 4to. 1678.

The Duchess of Suffolk, her Life. An hiſtorical play by Thomas Drue, 4to. 1631.

The Dutchman. Muſical Entertainment, by Thomas Bridges. Acted at the Haymarket, 8vo. 1775.

E A   E A

THE *Earl of Essex.* T. by H. Jones, 8vo. 1753. Acted at Covent-Garden. This piece, on its firſt appearance, met with great ſucceſs, taking a run for twelve nights, and bringing the author ſome very good benefits ſince in Dublin. It has been ſaid that he was aſſiſted in the writing it by the earl of Cheſterfield, and the late laureat C. Cibber.

The Earl of Essex. Tra. by Hen. Brooke. Acted at Drury-Lane, 8vo. 1761. Brooke ſeems to have varied his conduct, from that of the former plays on the ſubject, ſo much as to give it

ſomewhat the air of novelty; and this piece appears to bid the faireſt for maintaining its ground.

The Earl of Marr marr'd; with the Humours of Jockey the Highlander. Tragicomical Farce, by J. Philips, 8vo. 1716. This piece was never acted, being merely political.

The Earl of Somerset. T. by Henry Lucas, 4to. 1780.

The Earl of Warwick T. by Dr. Thomas Franklin. Acted at Drury-Lane, 8vo. 1767. This play, which was taken, without any acknowledgment, from another on the ſame ſubject, and

and with the fame title, by Monfieur de la Harpe, was acted with applaufe. The performance of Mrs. Yates was truly excellent.

The Earl of Warwick; or. *The King and Subject*. Trag. by Paul Hiffernan, 8vo. 1767.

The Earl of Weftmorland. Trag. by Henry Brooke, Efq. 8vo. 1778. Acted in Ireland, and favourably received.

The Eaft-Indian. Com. acted at the Haymarket, 1782. This play has fome merit, and is capable of improvement.

Eaftward Hoe. Com. by G. Chapman, Ben Jonfon, and John Marfton. Acted by the children of her Majefty's Revels, in the Black-Fryars, 4to. 1605. From this play Hogarth took the plan of his fet of prints, called, *The induftrious and idle Prentices.*

Edgar; or, *The Englifh Monarch.* An heroic Trag. by T. Rymer, 4to. 1678. This play is written in heroic verfe, and the plot is taken from W. of Malmefbury, and other old Englifh Hiftorians.

Edgar and Alfreda. T. C. by E. Ravenfcroft. Acted at the Theatre Royal, 4to. 1677. This play is on the fame ftory as the preceding one, but the plot of it feemingly borrowed from a

Novel, called *The Annals of Love.*

Edgar and Emeline. A Fairy Tale, by J. Hawkfworth. Acted at Drury-Lane, 8vo. 1761. This little piece met with great fuccefs at the reprefentation, and indeed defervedly.

Edward I. An hiftorical play, by Geo. Peele, 4to. 1593. The title at length runs as follows, " The famous Chronicle of King Edward the Firft, furnamed Longfhankes, with his returne from the Holy Land. Alfo the Life of Llcuellen Rebell in Wales. Laftly, the finking of Queene Elinor, who funck at Charing Croffe, and rofe again at Potter's-hith, now named Queenhith.

Edward II. Trag. by C. Marlow. Acted by the Earl of Pembroke's fervants, 4to. 1598. This play contains the fall of Mortimer, and the life and death of Piers Gavefton, earl of Cornwall, and chief favourite of that unfortunate Prince, together with his own death, and the troublefome events of his reign.

Edward III. *his Reign.* An Hiftory, fundry times played about the City of London. Anon. 4to. 1596.

King Edward III. *with the Fall of Mortimer, Earl of March.* Hiftorical Play, 4to. 1691. Anon. The scene lies at Nottingham, and the plot is from the English History, and a Novel called *The Countess of Salisbury*.

Edward IV. An Historical Play, in two parts, by Tho. Heywood, B. L. No date. The 4th edit. 4to. 1626.

Edward and Eleanora. T. by James Thomson. As it was to have been acted at Covent-Garden, 8vo. 1739. This play, after the parts had been cast, and the whole several times rehearsed, was prohibited to be acted by the Lord-Chamberlain. It is suspected from some passages in this play (which are omitted in Murdock's edition) that the author rather wished to have it forbidden, than to avoid that sentence against it. By the favour of the Prince of Wales, who at that time was in opposition to the court, it is supposed the poet sustained no loss by this play being refused stage representation. The plot is built on the affecting circumstance of conjugal love in Eleanora to Edward I. who, when her husband, at that time not king, received a wound with a poisoned arrow in the holy wars, cured the wound by sucking out the venom, although to the apparent hazard of her own life.

Edward and Eleanora. T.

altered from Thomson, by Thomas Hull. Acted at Covent-Garden, 8vo. 1775.

Edward the Black Prince; or, *The Battle of Poictiers.* Hist. Tra. by Wm. Shirley, 8vo. 1750. This tragedy was acted at Drury-Lane.

Edward the Black Prince; or, *The Battle of Poictiers.* Trag. by Mrs. Hoper. This piece was performed at the Play-house in Goodman's Fields, about 1748.

Edwin. Tra. by Geo. Jeffreys, 8vo. 1724. Act in Lincoln's-Inn-Fields, with but little success.

The Elder Brother. C. by John Fletcher. Acted at the Black-Fryars, 4to. 1637,

The Elders. Farce, by Mr. Cobb. Acted at Covent-Garden, April 21st, 1780, for the benefit of Mr. Wilson.

The Election. Com. of three acts, 12mo. 1749.

Electra. Tra. by Tho. Lewis Theobald. Translated from the Greek of *Sophocles*, with notes, 12mo. 1714.

Electra. Trag. translated from Sophocles, by George Adams, 8vo. 1729.

Electra. Tra. translated from Sophocles, by Dr. T. Franklin, 4to. 1759.

Electra. Tra. translated from Voltaire, by Dr. Tho. Franklin, 12mo. 1761.

Electra. Trag. by W. altered

Shirley, 4to. 1765. This piece, after being rehearfed at Covent-Garden in 1763, was denied a licence at the Lord Chamberlain's Office.

Elfrid ; or, The Fair Inconftant. Tra. by Aaron Hill. Acted at Drury-Lane, 4to. No date (1710). The author, diffatisfied with this juvenile production, afterwards entirely new wrote it, and brought it out again at Drury-Lane in 1731, under the title of *Athelwold.* At the end of the preface he fays, he had attempted a tranflation of Godfrey of Boloyn, and that he intended fuddenly to publifh a fpecimen and propofal for printing it by fubfcription.

Elfrida. Dram. Poem, by W. Mafon, 4to. 1752. This piece was not defigned for the ftage, but is written after the manner of the Greek Tragedy.

Elfrida. Dram. Poem, by W. Mafon. Acted at Covent-Garden, 1772, 8vo. By this alteration of Elfrida, in which the lyric parts are both tranfpofed and curtailed, the author is faid to have been much offended, and to have defigned an angry addrefs to Mr. Colman, (then manager of Covent-Garden Theatre) on the fubject. But that gentleman threatening him with the introduction of a chorus

of Grecian wafherwomen in fome future ftage entertainment, the bard was filenced, being perhaps of opinion, that his claffical interlocutors would have fuffered by the comparifon. Elfrida has fince been altered, by the author, new fet by Giardini, and acted at Covent-Garden, 1776.

Elfrid. Trag. by Mr. Jackfon. Acted at the Haymarket, 1775. This play was performed only three nights.

Eliza. Mufical Entertainment, by Richard Rolt, 8vo. 1754. Set to mufic by Dr. Arne, and performed at the Haymarket, where it was prohibited. It was afterwards acted at Drury-Lane with fuccefs.

Ella. A Tragycal Enterlude, or Difcoorfeynge Tragedie. Wroten bie Thomas Rowlie ; plaiedd before Mafter Canyng, atte hys howfe nempte the Rodde Lodge (alfo before the duke of Norfolck, Johan Howard) 8vo. 1777. One of thofe pieces printed as performances of the 15th century, but now generally acknowledged to have been the forgeries of Thomas Chatterton.

Elmerick ; or, Juftice Triumphant. Tra. by George Lillo. Acted at Drury-Lane, 8vo. 1740.

Eloifa.

Eloifa. A Tragedy, by Mr. Reynolds. Acted at Covent - Garden, 1786. This play is founded on the Eloifa of Roufleau.

The Elopement. Farce, by William Havard. Acted at Drury-Lane, 1763, for the benefit of the author. Not printed.

Elvira ; or, The Worſt not always true.. Com. by a perſon of quality (ſuppoſed to be lord Digby) 4to. 1667. The ſcene lies in Valencia.

Elvira. A Trag. by D. Mallet. Acted at Drury-Lane, 8vo. 1763. It is confeffedly an imitation of Mr. De la Motte's tragedy, founded on the ſame melancholy event, viz. a Portugueſe ſtory, taken from that excellent poem, *The Luſiad of Camoëns,* which has been ſo admirably tranſlated by Mr. Mickle.

Emilia. Tragi-Com. 8vo. 1672. Dedicated to *the only few.* In this dedication the anonymous author confeſſes that the hint of his plot was taken from the *Coſtanza di Roſamando of Aurelio Aureli.*

Emilia. Trag. by Mark Anthony Meilian, 8vo. No date (1771.) The man who can keep his eyes open over this and the other dramatic pieces by our author, might

rival the watchfulneſs of Argus, and ſet the ſtrongeſt doſe of opium at defiance.

The Emperor of the Eaſt. Tragi-Com. by P. Maſſinger, Acted at Black-Fryars, and the Globe, 4to. 1632. This is a very good play ; the hiſtory from the life of the younger Theodoſius, and the ſcene laid in Conſtantinople.

The Emperor of the Moon. Farce, by Mrs. Behn. Acted at the Queen's Theatre, 4to. 1687. This piece is taken from *Arlequin Empereur dans le Monde de la Lune,* which was originally tranſlated from the Italian.

The Empreſs of Morocco. Trag. by Elk Settle. Acted at the Duke's Theatre, 4to. 1678. This play is written in heroic verſe, and is the firſt that ever was adorned with cuts. It was in ſuch high eſteem, that it was acted at court, and the lords and ladies of the bedchamber performed in it.

The Empreſs of Morocco. Farce. Acted at the Theatre Royal, 4to. 1674, ſaid to be written by Thomas Duffet.

The Enchanted Lovers. A Paſtoral, by Sir W. Lower, 12mo. 1658.

The Enchanted Caſtle. A Pantomime. Acted at Covent-Garden, 1786.

The

The Enchanter; or, *Love and Magic*, by David Garrick. Mufical Entertainment of two acts. Acted at Drury-Lane, 8vo. 1760.

Endymion. Com. by J. Lilly, 4to. 1592 ; performed before queen Elizabeth, by the children of the chapel and of Paul's. The ftory from Lucian's Dialogue between Venus and the Moon, and other Mythologifts.

England's Glory. Poem, performed in a mufical Entertainment before her majefty (queen Anne) on her happy birth-day. Fol. 1706. Dedicated to the queen, by James Kremberg, who compofed the mufical parts to this poem, made in the form of an Opera.

The English Fryers; or, *The Town Sparks.* Com. by J. Crowne. Acted by their Majefties fervants, 4to. 1690. Scene London.

The English Lawyer. C. by E. Ravenfcroft. Acted at the Theatre Royal, 4to. 1678. This is only a tranflation, with very little change, of Ruggle's Latin comedy, called *Ignoramus*. The fcene Bourdeaux.

The English Merchant. C. by Geo. Colman, Efq. Acted at Drury-Lane, 8vo. 1767. The plot and perfonages of this play are happily adapted from the *Ecof-*

faife of Voltaire. Mr. Colman's imitation, though well received, muft have appeared to greater advantage could an actor like Mr. Quin have been found for the reprefentative of the *Merchant*. There is a fober dignity in this character, that can only be fupported by a performer of weight and confequence. Being allotted, through neceffity, to a comedian not remarkable for his fuccefs in parts that require manlinefs of deportment, gravity, and good-breeding, it loft its chief power on the ftage.

The English Monfieur. C. by J. Howard, 4to. 1674. Acted at the Theatre Royal with good fuccefs.

The English Moor; or, *The Mock Marriage.* C. by Richard Browne, 8vo. 1659. Scene London.

The English Princefs; or, *The Death of Richard* III. Trag. by J. Caryl, 4to. 1667. Acted at the Duke of York's Theatre.

The English Rogue. C. by T. Thomfon, 4to. 1668. Scene Venice.

The English Traveller. Tragi. Com. by Tho. Heywood. Acted at the Cockpit, Drury-Lane, 4to. 1633.

The Englishman in Paris. Com. of two acts, by Sam. Foote. Acted at Covent-Garden, 8vo. 1753. This little piece met with good

EN [76] EN

fuccefs; its firft appearance was for Macklin's benefit, when that performer acted the part of Buck, and Mifs Macklin, Lucinda, which feemed written entirely to give her an opportunity of difplaying her various qua-lifications of mufic, finging, and dancing, in all of which fhe obtained univerfal ap-plaufe. The author him-felf afterwards repeatedly performed the part of Buck; yet it is difficult to fay, which of the two did the character the greateft juftice. The piece feems defigned to expofe the abfurdity of fend-ing our youth abroad to catch the vices and follies of our neighbouring nations; yet there is fomewhat of an inconfiftency in the portrait of the Englifhman, that fcarcely renders the execu-tion anfwerable to the in-tention. This little comedy was imagined to be a bur-lefque on M. de Boiffy's *François à Londres.* On a comparifon, however, there does not appear the flighteft refemblance.

The Englifhman return'd from Paris. Com. of two acts, by Sam. Foote. Act-ed at Covent-Garden, 8vo. 1756. This is a fequel to the foregoing piece, wherein the Englifhman, who before was a brute, is now become a coxcomb; from being ab-

furdly averfe to every thing foreign, is grown into a de-teftation of every thing do-meftic; and rejects the very woman, now poffeffed of every advantage, whom he before was rufhing headlong into marriage with, when deftitute of any. This piece is much more dramatic and compleat than the other, and has a greater variety of characters in it.

The Englifhman from Paris. Farce, by Arthur Murphy. Acted at Drury-Lane, for the benefit of the author, 1756. Not printed. This piece was performed only one night.

The Englifhman in Bour-deaux. Comedy, tranflated from Favart, 8vo. 1764.

Englifhmen for my Money; or, *A Woman will have her Will.* Com. 4to. 1616. Scene Portugal.

Enough's as good as a Feaft. Com. This piece is men-tioned by Kirkman, but without either date or au-thor's name.

Entertainment at K. James the Firft's Coronation. By Ben Jonfon. Fol. 1640. This piece confifts only of congratulatoryfpeechesfpok-en to his Majefty at Fen-church, Temple-Bar, and in the Strand, in his way to the Coronation.

The Entertainment at Rich-mond. A Mafque; pre-fented

E N

fented by the moſt illuſtrious prince Charles to their Majeſties, 1634.

The Entertainment of K. Charles I. coming into Edinburgh, June 15, 1633. 4to.

The Entertainment of K. James and Q. Anne at Theobald's, when the houſe was delivered up with the poſſeſſion to the queen by the earl of Saliſbury, May 22, 1607, the prince Janville, brother to the duke of Guiſe, being then preſent; by Ben Jonſon.

The Entertainment of the King and Queen, on May-Day in the morning, 1604, at Sir William Cornwallis's houſe at Highgate, by Ben Jonſon.

The Entertainment of the Queen and Prince at Lord Spencer's, at Althorpe, on Saturday, June 25, 1603, as they came firſt into the kingdom, by Ben Jonſon.

The Entertainment of the two Kings of Great-Britain and Denmark, at Theobalds, July 24, 1606, by Ben Jonſon.

An Entertainment on the Prince's Birth-Day, by T. Nabbes, 4to. 1638.

An Entertainment deſigned for her Majeſty's Birth-Day, by Robert Dodſley, 8vo. 1732.

An Entertainment deſigned for the Wedding of Governor Lowther and Miſs Pennington, by Robert

E P

Dodſley, 8vo. 1732. Both theſe laſt are printed in a volume of poems, called, A Muſe in Livery; or, The Footman's Miſcellany.

The Ephefian Matron. A Farce of one act, by Charles Johnſon, 8vo. 1730.

The Ephefian Matron. A Comic Serenata, after the manner of the Italian, by Iſaac Bickerſtaffe, performed at Ranelagh-Houſe, 8vo. 1762.

Epicæne; or, *The Silent Woman.* Comedy, by Ben Jonſon. Acted by the King's ſervants, 4to. 1609. This is accounted one of the beſt comedies extant, and is always acted with univerſal applauſe. The ſcene lies in London. The long ſpeeches in the firſt book are tranſlated, verbatim, from *Ovid de Arte Amandi;* and a great deal in other places is borrowed from the 6th ſatire of *Juvenal* againſt women.

Epicæne; or, *The Silent Woman.* Com. written by Ben Jonſon. Acted at Drury-Lane, 8vo. 1776. This alteration, which is a very judicious one, was made by Mr. Colman.

Epidicus. Com. tranſlated from Plautus, by Laur. Echard, with critical remarks; but never intended for the ſtage. The ſcene of this piece lies at Athens.

Eppi-

E 3

E V [78] E V

Epponina. Dram. Effay, by John Carr, addreffed to the ladies, 8vo. 1765.

Epfom Wells. Com. by T. Shadwell. Acted at the Duke's Theatre, 4to. 1676. This piece has fo much of the true *Vis comica* about it, that it was greatly admired even by foreigners.

Erminia; or, *The Chafte Lady.* Tragi-Com. by R. Flecknoe, 8vo. 1667. This play was never acted.

Æfop. Comedy, in two parts, by Sir J. Vanbrugh. Acted at Drury-Lane, 4to. 1697, the fecond part not added until the third edition, 1702, 4to. This play is taken from a comedy of Bourfaut's, and contains a deal of genuine wit, and ufeful fatire.

Æfop. Farce, acted at Drury-Lane, 1778. It was acted only one night, and is not printed.

Efther; or, *Faith Triumphant.* A facred Tragedy, by Tho. Brereton, 12mo. 1715. This is only a tranflation at large of the *Efther* of Racine.

Ethelinda; or, *Love and Duty.* Trag by Matthew Weft, A. B. T. C. D. 12mo. 1769. Dublin.

An Evening's Intrigue. Com. tranflated from the Spanifh; and the fcene removed into England, by Captain John Stevens, 8vo. 1709.

An Evening's Love; or, *The Mock Aftrologer.* Com. by J. Dryden. Acted at the Theatre Royal, 4to. 1671. This play met with good fuccefs, yet it is a mafs of borrowed incidents. The principal plot is built on Corneille's *Feint Aftrologue* (borrowed itfelf from Calderon's *El Aftrologo fingido*), and the reft taken from Moliere's *Depit amoureux,* and *Les precieufes ridicules,* and Quinault's *L'Amant indifcret,* together with fome hints from Shakfpeare. The fcene Madrid, and the time the laft evening of the carnival in the year 1665.

Every Man in his Humour. Com. by Ben Jonfon. Acted by the lord Chamberlain's fervants, 1598. Printed in 4to. 1601. This comedy is, perhaps, in point of the redundance of characters and power of language, not inferior to any of our author's works.

Every Man out of his Humour. Com. Satire, by Ben Jonfon. Acted 1599. This play is compofed of a great variety of characters, interrupted and commented on in the manner of the ancient drama, by a Grex, or company of perfons, who being on the ftage the whole time, have the appearance of of auditors, but are in reality a set of interlocutors, who by their dialogue among themselves explain the author's intention to the real audience. This practice is now almost entirely left off, yet as the characters in this piece are moſt of them perfect originals, all painted in the ſtrongeſt colours and apparent likeneſſes of ſeveral well-known exiſtents in real life, we cannot help thinking that, with very little alteration more than omiſſion of the Grex, this play might be rendered extremely fit for the preſent ſtage.

Every body Miſtaken. F. by Wm. Taverner.

Every Man. b. l. 4to. no date. To this morality is prefixed the following advertiſement: *Here beʒynneth a Treatyſe how the hye Father of Heven ſendeth dethe to ſomon every creature to come and gyve a counte of theyr lyves in this worlde, and is in manner if a moralle play.*

Every Woman in her Humour. C. 1609, 4to. Anonymous.

Every Woman in her Humour. Farce of two acts, 1760. This little piece has never yet appeared in print, but was performed at Drury-Lane Houſe, at the time mentioned above, for Mrs. Clive's benefit.

Eudora. Trag. by Mr.

Hayley. Acted at Covent-Garden, 1790. The language of this piece is elegant and harmonious, and it deſervedly met with applauſe.

Eugenia. Tr. by Philip Francis. Acted at Drury-Lane, 8vo. 1752. This play is little more than a free tranſlation of a French comedy, called *Cenia.*

Eugenia. Tr. by Samuel Carr, 8vo. 1766.

Eunuchus. Com. a tranſlation of one of Terence's Comedies of this name, by Richard Bernard, 4to. 1598.

The Eunuch. Trag. by William Hemmings, 4to. 1687.

The Eunuch; or, *The Darby Captain.* Farce, by T. Cooke, 8vo. No date. (1737.)

The Eunuch. C. tranſlated by George Colman, 4to. 1765.

Euridice. Tr. by David Mallet. Acted at Drury-Lane, 8vo. 1731. *Euridice* was brought on with alterations at Drury-Lane Theatre in the year 1760, and was republiſhed at the ſame period. The ſucceſs of it was never great, though on its revival the principal characters were repreſented by Mr. Garrick and Mrs. Cibber.

Euridice. Farce, by H. E 4   Fielding.

E U

Fielding. As it was d—m'd at the Theatre Royal in Drury-Lane, 8vo. 1735.

Euridice Hifs'd; or, *A Word to the Wife.* Farce, by Henry Fielding, 8vo. 1736. This very little piece is publifhed, and we fuppofe was acted, at the end of *The Hiftorical Regifter.* It feems to be intended as a kind of acquiefcence with the judgment of the public, in its condemnation of the laft-mentioned Farce, at the fame time apologizing for it, as being only a mere *lufus* of his Mufe, and not the employment of any of his more laborious or ftudious hours.

Europe's Revels for the Peace, and his Majefty's

E X

happy Return. A Mufical Interlude, by P. Motteux, 4to. 1697.

The Example. Tragi-Comic, by James Shirley. Acted at Drury-Lane, 4to. 1637.

Excife. A Tragi-Comical Ballad Opera, of three acts, 8vo. 1733. Not intended for the ftage.

The Excommunicated Prince; or, *The Falfe Relick.* Tra. by Capt. Wm. Bedloe, fol. 1679. The fcene lies at Cremen in Georgia.

The Experiment. Com. of two acts, performed at Covent-Garden, April 16, 1777, for Mrs. Leffingham's benefit. Not printed.

F A

THE *Factious Citizen*; or, *The Melancholy Vifioner*, Com. Acted at the Duke's Theatre, 4to. 1685. Scene Moorfields.

The Faggot-Binder; or, *The Mock Doctor.* Com. tranflated from Moliere; printed in Foote's Comic Theatre, vol. 5.

The Fair. A Pantomime Entertainment. Acted at Covent-Garden, 1753.

The Fair American. C. Opera, by Mr. Pilon, acted at Drury-Lane, 1782. Though this piece is very indifferent in many parts, it was however well received by the audience.

F A

The Fair Captive. Tra. by Elizabeth Haywood. Acted at Lincoln's-Inn-Fields, 8vo. 1721. It was acted without fuccefs.

Fair Emm, the Miller's Daughter of Manchefter, with the Love of William the Conqueror. A pleafant Com. Acted by the Lord Strange's fervants, 4to. 1631.

The Fair Example; or, *The Modifh Citizens.* Com. by Richard Eftcourt, 4to. 1706. Acted at Drury-Lane, with applaufe.

The Fair Favorite. T. C. Sir W. Davenant, fol. 1673.

The Fair Circaffian. A Dramatic

F A

Dramatic Performance, by Dr. Samuel Croxal, 4to. 1720. This is merely a verfification of the *Song of Solomon*.

The Fairies. Opera, by David Garrick, 8vo. 1755. This little entertainment was acted at Drury-Lane, with great applaufe, the parts being moftly performed by children.

The Fair Maid of Briftol. Com. 4to. ¹605. In the old black letter.

The Fair Maid of the Exchange, with the merry Humours of the Cripple of Fenchurch. Com. by Thomas Heywood, 4to. 1625.

The Fair Maid of the Inn. Tragi-Com. by Beaumont and Fletcher, fol. 1647. The scene lies in Florence.

The Fair Maid of the Weft; or, *A Girl worth Gold*. Com. in two parts, by Thomas Heywood, 4to. 1631. The scene lies at Plymouth,the plots are original.

The Fair of St. Germain. This is only a tranflation from Bourfault's *Foire de St. Germains*; and was acted at the Theatre in Little Lincoln's-Inn-Fields,by the French company of comedians from Paris, 8vo. 1718.

The Fair Orphan. C. Opera, of three acts, performed at Lynn, 8vo. 1771.

The Fair Parricide. Tr. Anonymous, 8vo. 1752.

F A

This piece was never acted, nor intended for the ftage. It is written in profe, and very indifferently executed.

The Fair Penitent. Tra. by N. Rowe, 4to. 1703. Acted at Lincoln's-Inn-Fields. This, as Dr. Johnfon obferves, is one of the moft pleafing tragedies on the ftage, where it ftill keeps its turns of appearing, and probably will long keep them, for there is fcarcely a work of any poet at once fo interefting by the fable, and fo delightful by the language. The ftory is domeftic, and therefore eafily received by the imagination, and affimilated to common life ; the diction is exquifitely harmonious, and foft or fpritely as occafion requires. The character of *Lothario* feems to have been expanded by Richardfon into *Lovelace*, but he has excelled his original in the moral effect of the fiction. *Lothario*, with gaiety which cannot be hated, and bravery which cannot be defpifed, retains too much of the fpectator's kindnefs. It was in the power of Richardfon alone to teach us at once efteem and deteftation, to make virtuous refentment over-power all the benevolence which wit, elegance, and courage, naturally excite ; and to lofe at

E 5   laft

F A

laſt the hero in the villain. The fifth act is not equal to the former; the events of the drama are exhauſted, and little remains but to talk of what is paſt. It has been obſerved, that the title of the play does not ſufficiently correſpond with the behaviour of *Califta*, who at laſt ſhews no evident ſigns of repentance, but may be reaſonably ſuſpected of feeling pain from detection rather than from guilt, and expreſſes more ſhame than ſorrow, and more rage than ſhame. This play is ſo well known, and is ſo frequently performed, a..d always with the greateſt applauſe, that little need be ſaid of it, more than to hint that the ground-work of it is built on the *Fatal Dowry of Maſſinger.*

The Fair Quaker of Deal; or, *The Humours of the Navy.* Comedy, by Charles Shadwell. Acted at Drury-Lane, 4to. 1710. This play has no extraordinary merit in point of language, yet the plot of it is buſy and entertaining.

The Fair Quaker; or, *The Humours of the Navy.* Com. by Captain Edward Thompſon. Acted at Drury-Lane, 8vo. 1773. The foregoing play very poorly altered.

A Faire Quarrel. Com.

F A

With new additions of Mr. Chaugh's and Trimtram's Roaring, and the Baud's Song. Never before printed. Acted before the King by the Prince's ſervants; written by Thomas Middleton and William Rowley, Gent. 4to. 1617.

The Fairy Court. Interlude, by F. Gentleman. Not printed.

The Fairy Favour. Maſq. 8vo. 1766. This maſque was written by Mr. Thomas Hull, for the entertainment of the prince of Wales. It was acted a few nights at Covent-Garden.

The Fairy Prince. M. by George Colman. Acted at Covent-Garden, 8vo. 1771.

The Fairy Queen. Op. Anonym. Acted at the Haymarket, 4to. 1692.

The Fairy Tale. A Dramatic Performance, by G. Colman Acted at Drury-Lane, 8vo. 1774. Performed with great applauſe.

The Faithful Bride of Granada. A play, by W. Taverner. Acted at Drury-Lane, 4to. 1704. Scene Granada.

The Faithful Friend. C. by Francis Beaumont and John Fletcher. This play was never printed.

The Faithful General. T. by a young lady, who ſigns herſelf M. N. Acted at the Haymarket, 4to. 1706. Scene

Scene the city of Byzantium in Greece.

The Faithful Irishwoman. Farce, by Mrs. Clive. Acted at Drury-Lane, 1765, for her benefit. Not printed.

The Faithful Shepherd. A Pastoral Com. from the Italian, by D. D. Gent.

The Faithful Shepherd. Past. Tragi-Com. 12mo. 1736. Printed in Italian . and Englifh.

The Faithful Shepherdefs. A dramatic Paftoral, by J. Fletcher, 4to. This is the production of Fletcher alone.

The Fall of Bob; or, *The Oracle of Gin.* Tragedy, by John Kelly, Efq. It was occafioned by the gin-act, and was printed in 12mo. 1736.

The Fall of Carthage. An hiftorical Tragedy, by Wm. Shirley. This play was never acted.

The Fall of the Earl of Effex. Tragedy, by J. Ralph, 8vo. 1731. This play is only an alteration from Banks.

The Fall of Public Spirit. Dramatic Satire in two acts, 8vo. 1757.

The Fall of Mortimer. An hiftorical Play. Acted at the Haymarket, 8vo. 1731. This performance is a completion of Ben Jonfon's imperfect play on the fame fubject.

The Fall of Mortimer, An hiftorical Play, dedicated to the right honourable the earl of Bute, 8vo. 1763. This is only a republication of the foregoing by Mr. Wilkes.

The Fall of Saguntum. T. by P. Frowde, 8vo. 1727. Acted at Lincoln's-Inn-Fields with but indifferent fuccefs, notwithftanding it had very confiderable merit.

The Fall of Tarquin. T. by W. Hunt, 12mo. 1713. The name of this play points out its ftory, and the fcene of it lies at Rome. It is a moft wretched performance, and was never acted, or printed any where but at York, where the author was then ftationed as collector of the excife.

Falfe Appearances. Com. by Gen. Conway. Acted at Drury-Lane, 1789. This piece has no great claim to merit.

Falfe Concord. Farce. Acted at Covent-Garden; March 20, 1764, for the benefit of Mr. Woodward. Not printed.

Falfe Delicacy. Com. by Hugh Kelly. Acted at Drury-Lane, 8vo. 1768. This play, which is fuppofed to have received fome improvements from Mr. Garrick, was acted with confiderable fuccefs on its original appearance. The

E 6   fale

fale of it (fays the author of Mr. Kelly's life) was exceedingly rapid and great ; and it was repeatedly performed throughout Britain and Ireland to crowded audiences. Nor was its reputation confined to the British Dominions. It was tranflated into moft of the modern languages, viz. into Portuguefe, by command of the Marquis de Pombal, and acted with great applaufe at the public Theatre at Lifbon ; into French by the celebrated Madame Ricoboni ; into the fame language by another hand at the Hague ; into the Italian at Paris, where it was acted at the *Theatre de la Comedie Italienne* ; and into German.

The Falfe Count ; or, *A New Way to Play an old Game.* Com. by Mrs. Behn. Acted at the Duke's Theatre, 1682.

The Falfe Favorite Difgrac'd, and the Reward of Loyalty. Tragi-Com. by George Gerbier D'Ouvilly, 8vo. 1657. This play was never acted.

The Falfe Friend ; or, *The Fate of Difobedience.* T. by Mary Pix. Acted at Little Lincoln's-Inn-fields, 4to. 1699.

The Falfe Friend. Com. by Sir J. Vanbrugh, 4to. 1702. Acted at Drury-Lane, with very good fuccefs.

The Falfe One. Tra. by Beaumont and Fletcher, fol. 1647. The ftory of this play is founded on the adventures of Julius Cæfar while in Egypt, where the fcene lies.

Falftaff's Wedding. C. *being a Sequel to the Second Part of the Play of King Henry the Fourth. Written in imitation of Shakfpeare,* by Dr. Kenrick, 8vo. 1760.

Falftaff's Wedding. C. by Dr. Kenrick. Acted at Drury-Lane, 8vo. 1766. This is an alteration of the former play, and was acted for Mr. Love's benefit in 1766. When Shakfpeare's Falftaff is forgotten, Dr. Kenrick's imitation of him may be received on the ftage. We fhould add however, that the prefent comedy is no contemptable performance.

The Family Party. Farce, Acted at the Haymarket, 1789, and well received.

The Family of Love. C. by T. Middleton. Acted by the children of the Revels, 4to. 1608. Scene London.

The Fancied Queen. An Opera, Anonymous, 8vo. 1733. Acted at Covent-Garden. This was written by Robert Drury.

Fancy's Feftivals. Mafq. in five acts, by Thomas Jordan, 4to. 1657.

The Farmer's Journey to London. Farce 8vo. 1769.

The

F A

The Farmer's Return from London. Interlude, 4to. 1762. This little piece was written by Mr. Garrick, and is publifhed with a frontifpiece defigned by Hogarth. The plan of it is a humorous defcription in rhyme given by a farmer to his wife and children on his return from London, of what he had feen extraordinary in that great metropolis ; in which, with great humour and fatire, he touches on the generality of the moft temporary interefting topics of converfation, viz. the illuftrious royal pair, the coronation, the entertainments of the theatre, and the noted impofition of the Cock-Lane ghoft. It was originally written to do Mrs. Pritchard a piece of fervice at her benefit, but, meeting with univerfal applaufe, was repeated between play and farce many times during the courfe of the feafon.

The Farmer. Farce, by Mr. O'Keeffe. Acted at Covent-Garden, 1787.

Fafhionable Levities. C. by Mac Nally. Acted at Covent-Garden, 1785. This piece is not deftitute of merit.

The Fafhionable Lover. Com. by Richard Cumberland, Efq. Acted at Drury-Lane, 8vo. 1772. This piece was very coldly received.

F A

Fatal Conftancy. Trag. by Hildebrand Jacob, 8vo. 1723. This play was acted with fome applaufe at Drury-Lane.

Fatal Conftancy ; or, *Love in Tears.* A fketch of a Tragedy in the heroic tafte, by W. Whitehead, printed in 12mo. 1754, in a volume of Poems.

The Fatal Contract. A French Tragedy, by Wm. Hemings, 4to. 1653. This play met with great fuccefs at its firft reprefentations, and was revived twice after the Reftoration under different titles, viz. firft by that of *Love* and *Revenge*, and afterwards in the year 1687, under that of the *Eunuch.* The fcene lies in France ; and the plot is taken from the French hiftory, in the reign of Childeric I. and Clotaire II.

The Fatal Curiefity. Tra. by George Lillo. Acted at the Haymarket, 8vo. 1736. This piece confifts of but three acts. This play is equal, if not fuperior, to any of this author's other works, and met with a very favourable reception.

The Fatal Difcovery ; or, *Love in Ruins.* Trag. Anonym. Acted at Drury-Lane, 4to. 1698. The fcene of this play lies in Venice, but the original defign of the plot feems taken from the

F A

the old ſtory of *Oedipus* and *Jocaſta*.

The Fatal Diſcovery. A Trag. by John Home. Acted at Drury-Lane, 8vo. 1769. This play is a diſgrace to the talents that produced the beautiful tragedy of *Douglas*. It is indeed little better than Fingal in verſe. *The Fatal Diſcovery* ran its nine nights without reputation, and, as it is ſaid, with very inconſiderable emolument to the author.

The Fatal Dowry. Tr. by Ph. Maſſinger and Nathaniel Field. Acted at Black-Fryars, 4to. 1632.

The Fatal Error. Tra. by Benjamin Victor, 4to. 1776. The ſubject of this play is taken from Heywood's *Woman kill'd with Kindneſs*.

The Fatal Extravagance. Trag. by Joſeph Mitchell, 8vo. 1720. This play was originally written in one act, with only four characters, and was performed at the Theatre in Lincoln's-Inn-Fields. It was, however, ſoon afterwards enlarged into five acts, with two additional characters, and preſented at Drury-Lane with conſiderable ſucceſs in 1726.

Fatal Falſhood; or, *Diſtreſſed Innocence*. Tra. in

F A

three acts, by J. Hewett. Acted at Drury-Lane, 8vo. no date.

Fatal Falſhood. Trag. by Miſs Hannah More. Acted at Covent-Garden, 8vo. 1779.

Fatal Friendſhip. Tra. by Catharine Trotter, afterwards Cockburne, 4to. 1698. Acted at Lincoln's-Inn-Fields, with great applauſe.

The Fatal Jealouſy Tr. Acted at the Duke's Theatre, 4to. 1673. Anonymous. It is, however, aſcribed by his contemporaries to Nevil Paine. The ſcene of it is laid in Naples, and the plot borrowed from *The Unfortunate Lovers*, &c.

The Fatal Inconſtancy; or, *The Unhappy Reſcue*. Tra. by Mr. R. Phillips, 4to. 1701. This piece and its author we find only mentioned by Coxeter in his MS. notes, who tells us moreover, that the ſcene of it is laid near London, and that the prologue was written by Mr. Johnſon.

The Fatal Interview. T. Acted at Drury-Lane, 1782. This play is not of that kind that can either give or encreaſe the literary fame of its anonymous author.

Fatal Love; or, *The Forc'd Inconſtancy*. Trag. by Elk. Settle. Acted at the

the Theatre Royal, 4to. 1680.

Fatal Love ; or, *The Degenerate Brother.* Tra. by Ofborne Sidney Wandelford, Efq. 8vo. 1730. This play was acted without fuccefs.

The Fatal Marriage ; or, *The Innocent Adultery.* Tr. by Thomas Southerne Acted at the Theatre Royal, 4to. 1694. This play met with great fuccefs at its firſt coming out, and has been often performed fince with as great approbation, the tragical part of it being extremely fine and very affecting.

A Fatal Miftake ; or, *The Plot fpoil'd.* Tr. by Jofeph Haynes, 4to. 1692.

The Fatal Prophecy. Dra. Poem, by Dr. John Langhorne, printed in his poems, 12mo. 1766.

The Fatal Retirement. Trag. by Anthony Brown. Acted one night at Drury-Lane, 8vo. 1739. A very indifferent piece.

The Fatal Secret. Trag. by Lewis Theobald, 1735. 12mo. Acted at the Theatre Royal in Covent-Garden.

The Fatal Vifion ; or, *The Fall of Siam.* Tra. by A. Hill, 4to. 1716. Acted at Lincoln's-Inn-Fields, with fuccefs. The fcene is fixed in the city of Sofola in Siam ; but the author owns that the fable is fictitious, and the characters imaginary.

The Fate of Capua. Tr. by Thomas Southerne. Acted at Lincoln's-lnn-Fields, 4to. 1700. Scene, Capua. The domeftic fcenes of this tragedy have uncommon power over the tender paffions.

The Fate of Sparta ; or, *The Rival Kings.* Tr. by Mrs. Cowley. Acted at Drury-Lane, 1788. This play, though it has its defects, as well as all other works, was well received.

The Fate of Villainy. A Play, by Thomas Walker, 8vo. 1730. This was acted at Goodman's-Fields with very indifferent fuccefs.

The Father. Com. tranflated from *Diderot*, by the tranflator of *Dorval*, 4to. 1770.

The Fathers ; or, *The Good-natur'd Man.* Com. by Henry Fielding, Efq. Acted at Drury-Lane, 8vo. 1778. This comedy had but indifferent fuccefs in its reprefentation. It was written many years before the author's death, being mentioned by him in the preface to his Mifcellanies publifhed in 1743. The caufe of its not appearing fooner arofe from its being lent to

Sir

Sir Charles Hanbury Williams, who mislaid it. It is said to have received some touches from the elegant pen of Mr. Sheridan, jun. but they are not very conspicuous.

The Father of a Family. Com. in three acts, by C. Goldoni, 8vo. 1757. This is no more than the translation of a piece, intituled, *Il Padre di Famigliar*, represented for the first time at Venice, during the carnival of 1750. But though it is entitled a Comedy, it has nothing of humour, or even an attempt towards wit, shewn throughout the whole of it.

The Favourite. An Historical Tragedy, 8vo. 1770. This is taken from Ben Jonson. It is dedicated to Lord Bute.

The Feign'd Astrologer. Comedy, Anonymous, 4to. 1668. This is translated from Corneille, who borrowed his piece from Calderon's *El Astroligo fingido*.

The Feign'd Courtezans; or, *A Night's Intrigue*. C. by Mrs. Behn. Acted at the Duke's Theatre, 4to. 1679. This play met with very good success, and was generally esteemed the best she had written. The scene lies in Rome, and the play contains a vast deal of business and intrigue.

Feign'd Friendship; or, *The Mad Reformer*. Com.

Anonymous, 4to. without a date. It was, however, about the beginning of this century, acted at Little Lincoln's-Inn-Fields.

The Female Academy. C. by the duchess of Newcastle, fol. 1662.

The Female Advocates; or, *The Frantic Stock-jobbers*. Com. by Wm. Taverner. Acted at Drury-Lane, 4to. 1713.

The Female Captain. F. by Mr. Cobb. Acted at the Haymarket, 1780. This had been once acted at Drury-Lane, April 5, 1779, for Miss Pope's benefit, under the title of *The Contract*.

The Female Chevalier. C. altered from *Taverner*, by George Colman. Acted at the Haymarket, 1778.

The Female Dramatist. Farce, acted at the Haymarket, 1782. This piece just answered the purpose of giving some novelty at a benefit.

The Female Fortune-Teller. Com. by Mr. Johnson, 8vo. 1726.

The Female Gamester. T. by G. Edmund Howard, Esq. 12mo. 1778. Printed at Dublin.

The Female Officer. C. of two acts, by H. Brooke, Esq. 8vo. 1778. Not acted.

The Female Parson; or, *The Beau in the Suds*. A Ballad Opera, by C. Coffey, 1730. This piece was brought

brought on at the Little Theatre in the Haymarket, but was damned the firſt night.

The Female Parricide. T. by Edward Crane, of Manchefter, 8vo. 1751.

The Female Prelate, being the Hiſtory of the Life and Death of Pope Joan. Tra. by Elk Settle. Acted at the Theatre Royal, 4to. 1680.

The Female Rake; or, *Modern Fine Lady.* A Ballad Comedy. Acted at the Haymarket, 8vo. 1736.

The Female Virtuoſoes. Com. by Thomas Wright. Acted at the Queen's Theatre, 4to. 1693. This play was performed with great applauſe, but is no more than an improved tranflation of the *Femmes Scavantes* of Moliere.

The Female Wits; or, *The Triumvirate of Poets at Rehearſal.* Com. 4to. 1697. With the letters W. M. in the title. This piece was acted at the Theatre Royal in Drury-Lane for feveral days fucceffively, and with applauſe.

Ferrex and Porrex. Tr. fet forth without addition or alteration, but altogether as the fame was ſhewed on the ſtage before the Queenes Majeſtie about nine years paſt, viz. the 18th day of January, 1561, by the Gentlemen of the Inner Tem-

ple, B. L. no date. The firſt three acts of this play were written by Thomas Norton; the two laſt by Thomas Sackville, Efq. afterwards Lord Burkhurſt. The plot is from the Engliſh chronicles.

The Fickle Shepherdeſs. A Paſtoral, 4to. 1703. This is only an alteration of Randolph's *Amintas*; it was acted at the New Theatre in Lincoln's-Inn-Fields, and was played entirely by women. The ſcene lies in Arcadia.

Filli de Sciro; or, *Phillis of Scyros.* An excellent Paſtoral, written in Italian by C. Giudubaldo de Bonarelli, and tranflated into Engliſh by J. S. Gent, 4to. 1655.

The Financier. Comedy, of one act, tranflated from St. Foix, 8vo. 1771.

A Fine Companion. C. by Shakerley Marmion, 4to. 1633. Acted before the king and queen at Whitehall, and at the Theatre in Salifbury-Court.

The Fine Ladies Airs. C. by Thomas Baker. No date (1709). It was acted in Drury-Lane, with fuccefs.

Fire and Brimſtone; or, *The Deſtruction of Sodom.* Drama, by George Lefly, 8vo. 1675.

Fire and Water. Ballad Opera, by M. P. Andrews. Acted

Acted at the Haymarket, 8vo. 1780. There is more of the insipid than the aspiring element in this production.

The First Floor. Farce, by Mr. Cobb. Acted at Drury-Lane, 1787, with great applause.

The Floire. Comedy, by Edward Sharpham. Acted at Black-Fryars, by the children of the Revels, 4to. 1615. The scene of this play lies in London, and the plot seems in a great degree to be borrowed from Marston's *Parasitaster.*

The Flitch of Bacon. Ballad Opera, by Henry Bate. Acted at the Haymarket, 1778.

The Floating Island. Tragi-Com. by W. Strode, 4to 1655. This play contained too much morality to suit the taste of the court; yet it pleased the king so well, that he soon after bestowed a canon's dignity on the author.

Flora. Opera. Acted at Lincoln's-Inn-Fields, being *The Country Wake*, altered after the manner of *The Beggar's Opera*, 8vo. 1732.

Flora's Vagaries. Com. by Richard Rhodes. This play was written while the author was a student at Oxford. Acted at the Theatre Royal, and was printed in 4to. 1670.

Florazene ; or, *The Fatal Conquest.* Trag. by James Goodall. Not acted, but printed at Stamford, 8vo. 1754.

Florimene. A Pastoral, presented by the queen's command before the king at Whitehall, 4to. 1635.

Florizel and Perdita ; or, *The Sheepshearing.* Farce, Anon. 8vo. 1754. This piece is no more than an extract from some scenes of Shakspeare's *Winter's Tale*, so far as relates to the loves of *Florizel and Perdita*, formed into two acts. It was first performed at Covent-Garden Theatre for the benefit of Miss Nosfiter.

Florizel and Perdita. Dram. Pastoral, in three acts, altered from *The Winter's Tale* of Shakspeare, by David Garrick. Acted at Drury-Lane, 1756, printed in 8vo. 1758.

The Flying Voice. A play, by Ralph Wood. One of those destroyed by Mr. Warburton's servant.

The Follies of a Day ; or, *The Marriage of Figaro.* Com. by Mr. Holcroft. Acted at Covent-Garden, 1784. This play is translated from *Les Noces de Figaro*, and was well received.

The Fond Husband ; or, *The Plotting Sisters.* Com. by T. Durfey. Acted at Drury-

Drury-Lane, 4to. 1676. This met with very great applaufe, and is looked upon as one of Mr. Durfey's beſt plays.

Fondlewife and Letitia. Com. of two acts, performed at Crow-ſtreet, Dublin, 12mo. 1767.

Fontainbleau; or, *Our Way in France.* A Comic Opera, by Mr. O'Keeffe. Acted at Covent-Garden, 1784. This piece was received with great applaufe, though the pen of the author in compoſing it certainly ran right againſt dramatic laws.

The Fool's Opera; or, *The Taſte of the Age.* Written by Matthew Medley, and performed by his company in Oxford, 8vo. 1731.

A Fool's Preferment; or, *The Three Dukes of Dunſtable.* Com. by T. Durfey. Acted at the Queen's Theatre, Dorſet Garden, 4to. 1688. This play is little more than a tranſcript of Fletcher's *Noble Gentleman*, except one ſcene relating to Baffet, which is taken from a Novel, called *The Humours of Baffet.*

The Fool turn'd Critick. Com. by T. Durfey. Acted at the Theatre Royal, 4to. 1678. This, like moſt of our author's pieces, is full of plagiariſms.

*The Fool would be a Fa-*vourite; or, *The Diſcrete Lover.* Com. by Lodowick Carlell, 8vo. 1657. Acted with great applaufe.

The Footman. An Opera, 8vo. 1734. Performed at Goodman's-Fields.

The Forc'd Marriage; or, *The Jealous Bridegroom.* Tragi-Com. by Mrs. Behn, 4to. 1671. This play was acted at the Queen's Theatre, and is ſuppoſed to be the firſt of this lady's production.

The Forc'd Marriage. Com. by Ozell. This is only a tranſlation of the *Marriage Forcé* of Moliere, and was never intended for the ſtage.

The Forced Marriage. Trag. by Dr. John Armſtrong 8vo. 1770. This was written in 1754, and is printed in the ſecond volume of the author's Miſcellanies. It is a performance which will not add to the reputation of the elegant author of *The Art of preſerving health.* It had been offered to Mr. Garrick, but was refuſed by him.

The Forced Marriage. C. tranſlated from Moliere, printed in Foote's *Comick Theatre,* vol. IV.

The Forc'd Phyſician. C. by Ozell. This piece is only a tranſlation of Moliere's *Medicin malgré lui.*

The Force of Friendship. Trag. by Charles Johnson. Acted at the Haymarket, 4to. 1710. Scene, Verona. At the end of this tragedy is subjoined a small farce, which was acted with it, called *Love in a Chest.*

The Force of Fashion. Comedy. Acted at Covent-Garden, 1789. A laudable attempt to mix mirth with morality.

The Fortitude of Judith. Trag. by Ralph Radcliff. Not printed.

The Fortune Hunters; or, *The Widow Bewitch'd.* F. by Charles Macklin. This has been acted for the author's benefit, but is not printed.

The Fortune-Hunters; or, *Two Fools well met.* Com. by James Carlisle. Acted by his Majesty's servants, 4to. 1689. This play met with success.

The Fortunate Isles and their union, celebrated in a Masque designed for the court on Twelfth Night, 1626, by Ben Jonson.

The Fortunate Peasant; or, *Nature will Prevail.* Comedy, by Benj. Victor, 8vo. 1776.

Fortune by Land and Sea. Tragi-Com. by Thomas Heywood. Acted by the Queen's servants, 4to. 1655.

Fortune in her Wits. C.

by Charles Johnson, 4to. 1705. This is but an indifferent translation of Cowley's *Naufragium joculare,* and was never presented on the stage.

The Foundling. Com. by Edward Moore. Acted at Drury-Lane, 8vo. 1748. This comedy was the first of Moore's dramatic pieces, but is far superior to his second comic attempt. It met with tolerable success during its run, although on the first night of its appearance, the character of *Faddle* (which it is said was intended for one Ruffel) gave great disgust, and was therefore considerably curtailed in all the ensuing representations. It has not, however, since that time been continued as an acting comedy, being generally considered as bearing too near a resemblance to the *Conscious Lovers.*

The Four Prentices of London, with the Conquest of Jerusalem. An Historical Play, by Thomas Heywood. Acted at the Red Bull, 4to. 1615. The plot is founded on the exploits of the famous Godfrey of Bulloigne, who released Jerusalem out of the hands of the Infidels in 1099.

The Four P's. A merry Interlude of a Palmer, a Pardoner, a Potycary, and a Peda Pedlar ; by John Heywood, 4to. no date, and 4to. 1569. This is one of the firſt plays that appeared in the Engliſh language ; it is written in metre, and not divided into acts.

Four Plays in One ; or, *Moral Repreſentations*, by Beaumont and Fletcher, fol. 1647. Theſe four pieces are entitled as follows, viz. I. *The Triumph of Honour.* Scene near Athens, the Roman army lying there. II. *The Triumph of Love.* The ſcene laid in Milan. III. *The Triumph of Death.* The ſcene, Anjou. IV. *The Triumph of Time.* The plot of this ſeems to be entirely the invention of the author. Whether this medley of dramatic pieces was ever performed or not does not plainly appear. The two firſt may properly be called Tragi-Com. the third a Tragedy, and the laſt an Opera.

The Four Seaſons ; or, *Love in every Age.* A Muſical Interlude, by P. M. Motteux, 4to. 1699.

Frederic Duke of Brunſwick Lunenberg. Tra. by Elizabeth Haywood, 8vo. 1729. Acted at Lincoln's-Inn-Fields, with no ſucceſs.

Free Will. Tragedy, by Henry Cheeke, 4to. Black letter, no date. This is one

of the very old moral plays. Its full title runs as follows : A certayne Tragedie wrytten fyrſte in Italian by F. N. B. (Franciſcus Niger Boſſentinus) entituled *Freewyl* ; and tranſlated into Engliſhe by Henry Cheeke, wherein is ſet foorth in manner of a Tragedie the deuyliſh Deuiſe of the Popiſh Religion, &c.

The French Conjurer. C. by T. P. Acted at the Duke of York's Theatre, 4to. 1678.

The French Flogged ; or, *The Britiſh Sailors in America.* Farce of two acts, performed at Covent-Garden, 8vo. 1767. A piece written for, and acted at Bartholomew-Fair. It was alſo once repreſented at Covent-Garden. The author is ſuppoſed to be Geo. Alex. Stevens.

The Frenchified Lady never in Paris. Com. of two acts, by Henry Dell. Acted at Covent-Garden, 8vo. 1757. Taken from Cibber's *Comical Lovers.*

Frenchman in London. A Comedy, dedicated to Mr. Foote, 8vo. 1755.

A Friend in Need is a Friend Indeed. A Comedy, acted at the Haymarket, 1783, and very well received.

The Friends. Trag. by Marc

Marc Anthony Meilan, 8vo. No date (1771).

The Friendly Rivals; or, *Love the beft Contriver*. C. 8vo. 1752.

Friendfhip à la Mode. C. of two acts, performed at Smock-alley, Dublin, 1766. This is an alteration of Vanbrugh's *Falfe Friend*.

Friendfhip Improved; or, *The Female Warrior*. Tr. by Charles Hopkins. Acted at Lincoln's-Inn-Fields, 4to. 1700.

Friendfhip in Fafhion. Com. by T. Otway. Acted at the Duke's Theatre, 4to. 1678. This piece was, as Dr. Johnfon obferves, hiffed off the ftage for immorality and obfcenity.

The Honourable Hiftorie of *Frier Bacon and Frier Bongay*. As it was plaied by her Majeftie's fervants. Made by Robert Greene, maifter of arts, 1594.

Friendfhip of Titus and Gefippus. Com. by Ralph Radcliff. Not printed.

The Fugitive. Mufical Farce. Acted at Covent-Garden, 1790, and well received.

Fun. A parodi-tragi-comical Satire, 8vo. 1752. This little piece is entirely burlefque, and was written by Dr. Kenrick. It contains fome fevere ftrokes of fatire on H. Fielding, Dr.

Hill, &c. and was intended to have been performed by a fet of private perfons at the Caftle Tavern in Paternofter-row. But although it was fcreened under the idea of a concert of mufic, and a ball, Mr. Fielding, who had received fome information of it, found means of putting a ftop to it on the very night of performance, even when the audience were affembled. The piece, however, which is entirely inoffenfive, otherwife than by fatyrizing fome particular works which were then recent, was foon after printed, and delivered gratis to fuch perfons as had taken tickets for the concert.

The Funeral; or, *Grief à la Mode*. Com. by Sir R. Steele. Acted at Drury-Lane, 4to. 1702. This is much the beft of this author's pieces. The conduct of it is ingenious, the characters pointed, the language fprightly, and the fatire ftrong and genuine. There is indeed fomewhat improbable in the affair of conveying Lady Charlotte away in the coffin; yet the reward, which by that means is beftowed on the pious behaviour of young lord Hardy, with refpect to his father's body, make fome amends for it.

GALATHEA

GALATHEA. C. by John Lyly, 4to. 1592. Played before queen Elizabeth at Greenwich, on New-Year's-Day at night.

Gallic Gratitude ; or, *The Frenchman in India.* Com. of two acts, by James Solas Dodd, performed at Covent-Garden, 8vo. 1779.

Galligantus. A Musical Entertainment, 8vo. 1758. This piece was taken from Mr. Brooke's *Jack the Giant Queller.* It was acted at the Haymarket, and once at Drury-Lane, for Mrs. Yates's benefit.

A Game at Chesse, by T. Middleton, 4to. This play was acted at the Globe, on the Bank Side, and, though it has no date, was published about 1625. It is a sort of religious controversy, the game being played between one of the church of England and another of the church of Rome, wherein the former in the end gets the victory, *Ignatius Loyala* fitting by as a spectator. The scene lies in London.

The Gamester. Com. by James Shirley. Acted at Drury-Lane, 4to. 1637. This is very far from being a bad play. The plot of it is intricate, yet natural ; the characters well drawn, and the catastrophe just and moral. It has been twice altered, and brought on the stage un-der different titles ; first by Charles Johnson, who took his play of the *Wife's Relief* almost entirely from it ; and afterwards by Mr. Garrick.

The Gamester. Com. by Mrs. Centlivre. Acted at Lincoln's-Inn-Fields, 4to. 1705. This piece is formed on models not her own, the plot of it being almost entirely borrowed from a French comedy, called *Le Dissipateur.*

The Gamester. Trag. by Edward Moore. Acted at Drury-Lane, 8vo. 1753. This tragedy is written in prose, and is the most capital piece Mr. Moore produced. The language is nervous, and yet pathetic ; the plot is artful, yet clearly conducted ; the characters are highly marked, yet not unnatural ; and the catastrophe is truly tragic, yet not unjust. Still, with all these merits, it met with but midling success, the general cry against it being that the distress was too deep to be borne ; yet we are rather apt to imagine its want of perfect approbation arose in one part, and that no inconsiderable one, of the audience, from a tenderness of another kind than that of compassion ; and that they were less hurt by the distress of *Beverley,* than by finding their darling vice, their fa-vourite

vourite folly, thus vehemently attacked by the strong lance of reason and dramatic execution. As the *Gil Blas* of this author had been forced upon the town several nights after the strongest public disapprobation of it had been expressed, it was thought by his friends, that any piece acted under his name would be treated with vindictive severity. The Rev. Joseph Spence therefore permitted it, for the first four nights, to be imputed to him, but immediately afterwards threw aside the mask, as he supposed the success of the piece to be no longer doubtful; when, strange to tell! some of the very persons, who had applauded it as his work, were among the very foremost to condemn it as the performance of Mr. Moore. Some part of this tragedy was originally composed in blank verse, of which several vestiges remain.

The Gamesters. Com. by David Garrick, Esq. Acted at Drury-Lane, 8vo. 1758. This is the piece mentioned above, as an alteration of Shirley's *Gamester.* In this alteration the affair of the duel between the two friends and the love scenes between them and their mistresses, are very judiciously omitted; yet we cannot help thinking that two very capital scenes, the one between Volatile and Riot, and the other between Riot and Arabella, which stand in the last act of the *Wife's Relief,* have too much both of nature and judgment not to injure the piece by the loss of them; and that therefore the alteration of this play would have done more justice to the original author, had they been suffered to remain in the same situation they before possessed.

Gammer Gurton's Needle. Com. by John Still, afterwards bishop of Bath and Wells, 4to. 1575. It is one of the oldest of our dramatic pieces, and affords an instance of the simplicity which must ever prevail in the early dawnings of genius. The plot of this play, which is written in metre, and spun out into five regular acts, being nothing more than Gammer Gurton's having mislaid the needle with which she was mending her man Hodge's breeches against the ensuing Sunday, and which, by way of catastrophe to the piece, is, after much search, great altercation, and some battles in its cause, at last found sticking in the breeches themselves.

Garrick in the Shades; or, *A Peep into Elysium.* Farce. 8vo. 1779. This seems to be be the production of some disappointed author, whose resentment extended beyond the grave.

Garrick's Vagary ; or, *England run Mad* ; with particulars of the Stratford Jubilee, 8vo. 1769.

Gasconado the Great. A Tragi-comi-political-whimsical Opera, 4to. 1759, This piece was written by James Worsdale, the painter, and is a burlesque on the affairs of the French nation during the war of 1758.

The General Cashier'd. A Play, 4to. 1712. This play was never acted.

The General Lover. Com. by Theophilus Mofs, 8vo. 1749. This comedy was not acted, and is perhaps the worst composition in the dramatic way that was ever attempted, even without any view to the stage.

The Generous Choice. C. by Francis Manning, 4to. 1703. This piece was acted at Little Lincoln's-Inn-Fields.

The Generous Conqueror ; or, *The Timely Discovery.* Trag. by Bevil Higgons. Acted at the Theatre-Royal, 4to. 1702.

The Generous Enemies ; or, *The Ridiculous Lovers.* Com. by J. Corye. Acted at the Theatre-Royal, 4to. 1672. This play is one en-

tire piece of plagiarism from beginning to the end ; the principal defign being borrowed from Quinault's La Genereufe Ingratitude, that of the Ridiculous Lovers from Corneille's Don Bertram de Ciganal. Bertram's telty humour to his servants, in the third act, is partly borrowed from Randolph's Mufe's Looking-Glafs ; and the quarrel between him and Kobatzi, in the fifth, taken wholly and verbatim from the Love Pilgrimage of Beaumont and Fletcher.

The Generous Free Mafon ; or, *The Conftant Lady.* With the Humours of Squire Noodle and his Man Doodle. A Tragi-comi-farcical Ballad Opera, of three acts, by Wm. Rufus Chetwood, 8vo. 1731.

The Generous Husband ; or, *Coffee-Houfe Politician.* Com. by Charles Johnfon, 4to. No date (1713).

The Generous Impoftor. C. by Mr. O'Burne. Acted at Drury-Lane, 8vo. 1781.

The Genii. Pantomime Entertainment, by H. Woodward. Acted at Drury-Lane, 1753.

The Genius of Nonfenfe. Pantomime, Haymarket, 1780.

The Gentleman Cit. C. tranflated from the French

F   of

of Moliere; and printed in Foote's *Comic Theatre*. vol. V.

The Gentleman Dancing-Mafter. Com. by W. Wycherley. Acted at the Duke's Theatre, 4to. 1673.

The Gentleman Gardiner. A Ballad Opera, by James Wilder. Acted at Smock-Alley, Dublin, 12mo. 1751.

The Gentleman of Venice. Tragi Com. by James Shirley. Acted at Salifbury-Court, 4to. 1655.

The Gentleman Ufher. C. by George Chapman, 4to. 16c6. It is doubtful whether this play was ever acted.

Of Gentylnefs and Nobilite, a Dialogue between the Merchaunt, the Knyght, and the Plouman, dyfputyng who is a verey Gentylman and who is a Nobleman, and how Men fhould come to Auctoryte, compilid in Manner of an Enterlude, with divers Toys and geftis addyd thereto to make myri paftyme and difport. This piece is written in metre, and printed in the black letter, by John Raftell, without date.

The Gentle Shepherd. A Paftoral Com. 12mo. 1729. This truly poetical and paftoral piece is written in the Scots dialect, publifhed by the celebrated Allan Ramfay, the Scots poet, and introduced to the world as his.

There are not, however, wanting perfons who deny him the credit of being its author; but as envy will ever purfue merit, and as in upwards of half a century no other perfon has, and it now moft probable never will lay claim to that honour, reafon we think will lead us to grant it to the only perfon who has been named for it. Be this fact, however, as it will, the excellence of the piece itfelf muft ever be acknowledged, and it may, without exaggeration, be allowed to ftand equal, if not fuperior, to either of thofe two celebrated Paftorals, the *Aminta* of Taffo, and the *Paftor fido* of Guarini. It has been reduced into one act, and the Scotch dialect tranflated, with the addition of fome new fongs, by Theophilus Cibber, and was prefented at Drury-Lane in 1731.

George a Greene, the Pindar of Wakefield. Comedy. Anonym. 4to. 1599. The plot of this play is founded on hiftory, and the fcene lies at Wakefield, in Yorkfhire. This comedy is to be met with in Dodfley's Collection of Old Plays.

George Dandin; or, *The Wanton Wife*. Comedy, by Ozell. A tranflation from Moliere's *George Dandin*.

The

The German Hotel. Com. tranflated from the German by Mr. Marfhall. Aɛted at Covent-Garden, 1790, and well received.

Germanicus. Trag. by a gentleman of the Univerfity of Oxford, 8vo. 1775.

The Ghoft ; or, *The Woman wears the Breeches.* C. Anonym. written in 1640, printed, 4to. 1653.

The Ghoft of Moliere. This is only the tranflation of a little piece of fourteen fcenes, called, *L'Ombre de Moliere*, written by M. Brecourt. The fcene lies in the Elyfian Fields.

The Ghoft. Com. Aɛted at Smock-Alley, Dublin, 8vo. 1767. This is taken from Mrs. Centlivre's play of *The Man's bewitched* ; or, *The Devil to do about her.* It has fince been aɛted at Covent-Garden.

The Ghofts. Comedy, by Mr. Holden. Aɛted at the Duke's Theatre between 1662 and 1665. Not printed.

Gibraltar ; or, *The Spanifh Adventure.* C. by J. Dennis, 4to. 1705. Performed at the Theatre - Royal in Drury-Lane, but without fuccefs. The firft day it being well aɛted in moft of its parts, but not fuffered to be heard ; the fecond day for the moft part

faintly and negligently attended, and confequently not feen. The fcene lies at a village in the neighbourhood of Gibraltar.

Gil Blas. C. by Edward Moore. Aɛted at Drury-Lane, 8vo. 1751. This is by much the leaft meritorious of the three dramatic pieces of our author, and indeed, notwithftanding its being very ftrongly fupported in the aɛting, met with the leaft fuccefs. The defign is taken from the ftory of *Aurora*, in the novel of Gil Blas, but bears too near a refemblance to the plot of the *Kind Impoftor* ; and the author has deviated greatly from truth in the manners of his charaɛters, having introduced a Spanifh gentleman drunk on the ftage, which is fo far from being a charaɛteriftic of that nation, that it is well known they had formerly a law fubfifting among them, though now, perhaps, out of force, which decreed that if a gentleman was conviɛted of even a capital offence, he fhould be pardoned in pleading his having been intoxicated at the time he committed it, it being fuppofed that any one who bore the charaɛter of gentility would more readily fuffer death, than confefs himfelf capable

of

of fo beaftly a vice as drun-kennefs.

The Gipfies. Com. Op. by Charles Dibdin. Acted at the Haymarket, 8vo. 1778.

The Gnome. Pantomime. Acted at the Haymarket, 1788. A good perform-ance.

The Glafs of Government. Tragi-Com. by Geo. Gaf-coigne, 4to. 1575.

Gloriana; or, *The Court of Auguftus Cæfar,* by N. Lee. Acted at the The-atre-Royal, 4to. 1676. This is one of the wildeft and moft indifferent of our au-thor's pieces, being made up of little elfe but bombaft and abfurdity.

The Girl in Stilts. Far. Acted at Covent-Garden, 1786. A piece of no great merit.

The Goblins. Tragi-C. by Sir John Suckling. Act-ed at Black-Fryars, 8vo. 1646. The fcene of this play lies in Francelia, and the author, in the execution of his defign, has pretty clofely followed the foot-fteps of Shakfpeare, of whom he was a profeffed ad-mirer, his Reginella being an open imitation of Mi-randa in the Tempeft, and his Goblins, though counter-feits, being only thieves in difguife, yet feem to be co-pied from Ariel in the fame play.

God hys Promifes. A Tragedie or Interlude, ma-nyfeftynge the chyefe Pro-mifes of God unto Man in all Ages, from the begyn-nynge of the Worlde, to the Deathe of Jefus Chrifte, a Myfterie 1538. The In-terlocutors are Pater cœlef-tis, Juftus Noah, Mofes Sanctus, Efaias Propheta, Adam primus Homo, Abra-ham fidelis, David Rex pius, Joannes Baptifta. This play was written by Bifhop Bale, and is one of the firft dra-matic pieces printed in Eng-land. It is reprinted by Dodfley in his Collection.

Goddwyn. Tr. by Tho. Rowleie, 8vo. 1777. This is one of the pieces fuppofed to be written by Thomas Chatterton.

The Golden Age; or, *The Lives of Jupiter and Saturn.* An Hiftorical Play, by T. Heywood. Acted at the Red Bull, 4to. 1611.

The Golden Age Reftor'd, in a Mafque at Court, 1615, by the Lords and Gentle-men, the King's fervants, by Ben Jonfon.

The Golden Pippin. Bur-letta, by Kane O'Hara. Acted at Covent-Garden, 8vo. 1773. It was produ-ced in three acts, as *Midas* had been before, but, like that

that performance, was not very fuccefsful in its original ftate. It was then reduced to an after-piece, and was received with univerfal approbation.

The Golden Rump. This piece was never acted, never appeared in print, nor was it ever known who was the author of it. This piece, being full of fcandal and treafon, gave rife to the act of parliament for all plays to undergo the infpection of the Lord Chamberlain.

Gondibert and Bertha. Trag. by W. Thompfon, M. A. 8vo. 1753. This piece was never acted, nor we believe intended for the ftage, but is publifhed in a volume with fome poems of the fame author.

The Good-natured Man. Com. by Oliver Goldfmith. Acted at Covent-Garden, 8vo. 1768. Many parts of this play exhibit the ftrongeft indications of our author's comic talents. There is perhaps no character on the ftage more happily imagined and more highly finifhed than *Croaker's*; nor do we recollect fo original and fuccefsful an incident as that of the letter which he conceives to be the compofition of an incendiary, and feels a thoufand ridiculous horrors in confequence of his abfurd apprehenfion.

Our audiences, however, having been recently exalted on the fentimental ftilts of *Falfe Delicacy*, a comedy by *Kelly*, regarded a few fcenes in Dr. *Goldfmith's* piece as too low for their entertainment, and therefore treated them with unjuftifiable feverity. Neverthelefs the *Good-natur'd Man* fucceeded, though in a degree inferior to its merit. The prologue to it, which is an excellent one, was written by Dr. Samuel Johnfon.

Gorboduc. Trag. by T. Norton and Thomas Sackville, Lord Buckhurft, B. L. 4to. 1590.

The Gordian Knot Unty'd. Com. 1691. This is not printed, but appears to have been acted in the before-mentioned year.

The Gofpel Shop. Com. of five acts, with a new Prologue and Epilogue, by R. Hill, Efq. of Cambridge, 8vo. 1778.

Gotham Election. F. of one long act, by Mrs. Centlivre, 12mo. 1715. In this piece the fair author has fhewn great knowledge of mankind, and of the different occurrences of life. It was never acted, being looked on as a party affair, but was printed, with a dedication to Secretary Craggs, of whom it is recorded, greatly

ly

ly to his honour on this occasion, that being complimented on his liberality by Mrs. Bracegirdle, to whom he gave twenty guineas for the author, and told that his generosity appeared the more extraordinary as the Farce had not been acted, he replied, that he did not so much consider the merit of the piece, as what was becoming a secretary of state to do.

The Governor of Cyprus. Tra. by J. Oldmixon, 4to. 1703. Acted at the Theatre in Lincoln's-Inn-Fields.

The Grateful Fair. Com. by Christopher Smart. Acted at Pembroke College, Cambridge. Not printed.

The Grateful Servant. Com. by James Shirley. Acted at Drury-Lane, 4to. 1630. This play met with very great applause when acted, and came forth ushered by eight copies of verses in English, and two in Latin, which the author says were " the free vote of his friends, which he could not in civility refuse," and indeed he must have very little of the poetical warmth about him, if he could be desirous so to do. Lodowick's contrivance to have his wife *Ardelia* tempted by *Piero*, in order that he may procure an opportunity of divorcing her, is the same

with *Contarini's* humour and contrivance in *The Humorous Courtier.* Scene, Savoy.

The Great Duke of Florence. A Comical History, by P. Massinger. Acted at the Phoenix Drury-Lane, 4to. 1636. This play met with very good success.

The Great Favorite; or, *The Duke of Lerma.* Trag. by Sir Robert Howard. Acted the Theatre Royal, 4to. 1668. Some scenes of this play are written in blank verse, and some in rhyme.

The Grecian Daughter. Trag. by Arthur Murphey, Esq. Acted at Drury-Lane, 8vo. 1772. In a postscript to this play the author says, " he does not wish to conceal that the subject of his tragedy has been touched in some foreign pieces ; but he thinks it has been only touched. The *Zelmire* of Monsieur Belloy begins after the daughter has delivered her father out of prison. The play, indeed, has many beauties ; and if the sentiments and business of that piece coincided with the design of *The Grecian Daughter*, the author would not have blushed to tread in his steps. But a new fable was absolutely necessary, and perhaps, in the present humour of the times, it is not unlucky that

no

G R

no more than three lines could be adopted from Monfieur Belloy." It met with very great fuccefs, and was excellently performed in the principal characters, by Mr. and Mrs. Barry.

The Grecian Heroine; or, *The Fate of Tyranny.* A Trag. by T. Durfey. This piece was never acted, but was publifhed with a collection of poems in 1721. The title-page fays it was written in 1718; but the preface mentions it as a production of many years earlier; the characters of *Timoleon* and *Belizaria* being intended for Mr. Betterton and Mrs. Barry.

Green's Tu Quoque; or, *The City Gallant.* Com. by John Cooke, 4to. 1614.

Greenwich Park. Com. by W. Mountford, 4to. 1691. This is a tolerable comedy, and met with very good fuccefs. It was acted at Drury-Lane.

Grim the Collier of Croydon; or, *The Devil and his Dame, with the Devil and St. Dunftan.* Com. by J. T. 12mo. 1662.

Gretna-Green. A Mufical After-piece, by Mr. Stuart. Acted at the Haymarket, 1783, and very well received.

Gripus and Hegio; or, *The Paffionate Lovers.* Paftoral, by Robert Baron,

G U

8vo. 1647. This play confifts of no more than three acts, and is moftly borrowed from Waller's Poems, and Webfter's *Duchefs of Malfy.*

The Grove; or, *Love's Paradife.* An Opera, by J. Oldmixon, 4to. 1703, performed at Drury-Lane. The fcene is a province of Italy, near the Gulph of Venice.

The Grub-ftreet Opera, by H. Fielding, 1731, 8vo. Acted at the Little Theatre in the Hay-market.

The Grumbler. Com. of three acts, by Sir Charles Sedley, 12mo. 1719.

The Grumbler. Farce, altered from Sedley, by Dr. Goldfmith. Acted at Covent-Garden, 1772, not printed. This alteration was made to ferve Mr. Quick at his benefit, and acted only on that night.

The Guardian. Comical Hiftory, by P. Maffinger, 8vo. 1655.

The Guardian. Com. by A. Cowley. Acted before Prince Charles at Trinity College, Cambridge, 1641.

The Guardian. Com. of two acts, by David Garrick, Efq. Acted at Drury-Lane, 8vo. 1759. This little piece is taken in great meafure from the celebrated *Pupille* of M. Fagan. It is a pleafing and elegant performance,

F 4

G U

performance, the language eafy and fentimental, the plot fimple and natural, and the characters well fupported.

The Guardian Outwitted. Comic Opera, by Dr. Tho. Auguftine Arne. Acted at Covent-Garden, 8vo. 1764. It was acted only fix nights, being a very contemptible performance.

Guftavus Vofa ; or, *The Deliverer of his Country.* Trag. by H. Brooke, 8vo. 1739. This play has great merit, yet was prohibited to be played, even after it had been rehearfed at Drury-Lane. The author, however, was not injured by the prohibition, for on publifhing the book by fubfcription, Mr. Victor fays he

G U

was certain Mr. B. cleared above 1000*l.*

Guy Earl of Warwick. A Tragical Hiftory, by B. J. 4to. 1661. The plot of this piece is founded on hiftory, and it has been attributed to Ben Jonfon; but this is perhaps only a conjecture formed from the letters prefixed to it, the execution being greatly inferior to the works of that firft-rate genius.

Guzman. Comedy, by Roger, Earl of Orrery, fol. 1693. The fcene of this play lies in Spain, and the plot is from a romance of the fame name. It was acted at the Duke of York's Theatre many years before the time of his publication.

H A

THE *Halfpay Officers.* Farce, of three acts, by Charles Molloy. Acted at the Theatre in Lincoln's-Inn-Fields, 12mo. 1720. The play is founded on Sir W. Davenant's *Love and Honour*, and fome other old plays.

Hamlet, Prince of Denmark. Tr. by Shakfpeare, 4to. 1604. Dr. Johnfon obferves, that if " the dramas of Shakfpeare were to be characterifed, each by the particular excellence which diftinguifhes it from the reft, we muft allow to the trage-

H A

dy of Hamlet the praife of variety. The incidents are fo numerous, that the argument of the play would make a long tale. The fcenes are interchangeably diverfified with merriment and folemnity ; with merriment that includes judicious and inftructive obfervations; and folemnity, not ftrained by poetical violence above the natural fentiments of man. New characters appear from time to time in continual fucceffion, exhibiting various forms of life and

and particular modes of converfation. The pretended madnefs of Hamlet caufes much mirth ; the mournful diſtraction of Ophelia fills the heart with tendernefs ; and every perfonage produces the effect intended, from the apparition that in the firſt act chills the blood with horror, to the fop in the laſt that expofes affectation to juſt contempt. The conduct is perhaps not wholly fecure againſt objections. The action is induced for the moſt part in continual progreſſion ; but there are fome fcenes which neither forward nor retard it. Of the feigned madnefs of Hamlet there appears no adequate caufe, for he does nothing which he might not have done with the reputation of fanity. He plays the madman moſt when he treats Ophelia with fo much rudenefs, which feems to be ufelefs and wanton cruelty. Hamlet is, through the whole piece, rather an inſtrument than an agent. After he has, by the ſtratagem of the play, convicted the king, he makes no attempt to punifh him ; and his death is at laſt effected by an incident which Hamlet had no part in producing. The cataſtrophe is not very happily produced ; the exchange of weapons is ra-

ther an expedient of necefſity, than a ſtroke of art. A fcheme might eafily be formed to kill Hamlet with the dagger, and Laertes with the bowl. The poet is accufed of having ſhewn little · regard to poetical juſtice, and may be charged wi h equal neglect of poetical probability. The apparition left the regions of the dead to little purpofe ; the revenge which he demands is not obtained but by the death of him that was required to take it ; and the gratification, which would arife from the deſtruction of an ufurper and a murderer, is abated by the untimely death of Ophelia, the young, the beautiful, the harmlefs, the pious.'' It is recorded of the author, that although his knowledge and obfervation of nature rendered him the moſt accurate painter of the fenfations of the human mind in his writings, yet fo different are the talents requifite for acting, that the part of the Ghoſt in this play (no very confiderable character) was almoſt the only one in which he was able to make any figure as a performer. Scene Elfinoor.

Hamlet. Altered by Mr. Garrick. Acted at Drury‑Lane, 1771. This alteration is made in the true fpirit

rit of *Bottom the Weaver*, who wishes to play not only the part assigned him, but all the rest in the piece. Mr. Garrick, in short has reduced the consequence of every character but that represented by himself; and thus excluding Ofric, the Grave-diggers, &c. contrived to monopolize the attention of the audience. Our poet had furnished Laertes, with a dying address, which afforded him a local advantage over the Prince of Denmark. This circumstance was no sooner observed, than the speech was taken away from the former, and adopted by the latter. Since the death of the player, the public indeed has vindicated the rights of the poet, by starving the theatres into compliance with their wishes to fee Hamlet as originally meant for exhibition. Mr. Garrick had once designed to publish the changes he had made in it, and (as was usual with him in the course of similar transactions) had accepted a compliment from the booksellers, consisting of a set of Olivet's edition of Tully ; but, on second thoughts, with a laudable regard to his future credit, he returned the acknowledgment, and suppressed the alteration. In short, no

bribe but Mr. Garrick's own imitable performance, could have prevailed on an English audience to sit patiently, and behold the martyrdom of their favourite author.

Hamtstead Heath. Com. by Thomas Baker. Acted at Drury-Lane, 4to. 1706.

Hanging and Marriage ;. or, The Dead Man's Wedding, F. by Henry Carey, 1713 It does not appear that it was ever acted.

Hannibal and Scipio. Historical Trag. by Tho. Nabbes. Acted in 1635, at Drury-Lane. It was acted before women appeared upon the stage. The part of *Sophonisba* being performed by one Ezekiel Fenne.

Hans Beer Pot,, his invisible comedy of *See me, and fee me not,* 4to. 1618. By Drawbridge Count Belchier. This piece is neither comedy nor tragedy, and is said to have been acted by an honest company of health-drinkers.

The Happy Captive. An English Opera, by Lewis Theobald, 8vo. 1741. The plot of this piece is taken from a novel, entitled *The History of a Slave,* which is to be met with in *Don Quixote,* Part I. Book IV.

The Happy Lovers ; or, *The Beau Metamorphosed.*

An

H A

An Opera, by Henry Ward. Acted at Lincoln's-Inn-Fields, 8vo. 1736.

The Happy Marriage; or, *The Turn of Fortune*. Acted at Lincoln's - Inn - Fields. Written by a young gentleman, 12mo. 1727.

Harlequin Doctor Faustus, with the Masque of the Deities. Composed by John Thurmond, dancing-master 8vo. 1724.

Harlequin Freemason. A splendid and succesful Pantomime. Acted at Covent-Garden, 1781.

Harlequin's Frolicks. A Pantomime, performed at Covent-Garden, 1776.

Harlequin Hydaspes; or, *The Greshamite*. A Mock Opera. Acted at Lincoln's-Inn-Fields, 8vo. 1719.

Harlequin's Jacket. A Pantomime, performed at Drury-Lane, 1775.

Harlequin Incendiary; or, *Columbine Cameron*. A Musical Pantomime. Anon. 8vo. 1746. This piece was performed at the Theatre Royal in Drury-Lane, the season after the quelling of the Rebellion in Scotland. The music was composed by Dr. Arne, but it does not appear who was the contriver of the Pantomime, in which, as usual, *Harlequin* is the favoured lover of *Columbine*, who seems by no means to be distinguished as *Jenny*

H A

Cameron, but by some part of the scene being laid in the Highlands of Scotland, and the defeat of the rebel army, which has really no connection with the rest of the piece, though it forms the catastrophe of the whole.

Harlequin's Invasion. A Christmas Gambol, 1759. This Pantomime is still often performed at Drury-Lane. The plan of it is a supposed invasion made by *Harlequin* and his train upon the frontiers and domain of Shakspeare. The characters are made to speak, and the catastrophe is the defeat of *Harlequin*, and the restoration of *King Shakspeare*. Of Harlequin's Invasion, and all the dialogue, &c. was furnished by Mr. Garrick, who originally wrote some part of it to serve the interest of a favourite performer at Bartholomew-Fair, where it passed under a title rendered designedly long and ostentatious, concluding thus—*The Taylor without a Head*; or, *The Battle of the Golden Bridge*.

Harlequin's Jubilee. A Pantomime, performed at Covent-Garden, 1770. This Pantomime was contrived by Mr. Woodward, and was intended to ridicule *The Jubilee*, acted the preceding season at Drury-Lane. It had, however, little effect.

Harlequin

Harlequin Junior; or, *The Magic Geſtus.* A Pantomime. Acted at Drury-Lane, 1784.

Harlequin Ranger. Pantomime, by Henry Woodward, performed at Drury-Lane, 1752.

Harlequin Sheppard. A Night Scene in grotefque charaĉters, by John Thurmond. Acted at Drury-Lane, 8vo. 1724.

Harlequin Sorcerer, with the Loves of Pluto and Proferpine. Pantom. Acted at Lincoln's-Inn-Fields, 8vo. 1725.

Harlequin Student; or, *The Fall of Pantomime, with the Reſtoration of the Drama.* Entertainment. Acted at Goodman's-Fields.

Harlequin Teague; or, *The Giant's Cauſeway.* Pantomime, acted at the Haymarket.

Harlequin's Triumph. A Pantomime, by John Thurmond, 8vo. 1727.

The Harlot's Progreſs; or, *The Ridotto al Freſco.* A Grotefque Pantomime Entertainment, by Theophilus Cibber, performed at Drury-Lane, 4to. 1733.

The Haſty Wedding; or, *The Intriguing Squire.* Com. by Cha. Shadwell. Scene, Dublin, 12mo. 1720.

The Haunted Tower. C. Opera, by Mr. Cobb. Act-

ed at Drury-Lane, 1789, and well received.

Hearts of Oak. An Interlude, 1762. This is indeed nothing more than a fong and a dance of failors, the former of which was written by Mr. G. A. Stevens, and, being a mere temporary affair on the declaration of war with Spain, met with good fuccefs.

Heautontimorumenos. Com. by Terence, tranflated by Richard Bernard, 4to. 1598. This play has been likewife tranflated by Echard, Cook, Patrick, Gordon, and Colman.

The Heathen Martyr; or, *The Death of Socrates.* Hiſt. Trag. By George Adams, 4to. 1746.

Hector. Dram. Poem, by Richard Shepherd, 4to. 1770.

The Hectors; or, *The Falfe Challenge.* Com. Anonym. 4to. 1656.

The Hector of Germaine; or, *The Palfgrave prime Elector.* An Honourable Hiſtory, by W. Smith, 4to. 1615. This play is not divided into acts.

Hecuba. Trag. by R. Weſt, Efq. Lord Chancellor of Ireland. Acted at Drury-Lane, 4to. 1726. This is a tranflation from Euripides, and met with no fuccefs in the reprefentation.

Hecuba.

Hecuba. Trag. tranf- lated from the Greek of *Euripides*, with annotations chiefly relating to antiqui- ty, by Dr. Thomas Morell, 8vo. 1749.

Hecuba. Trag. by Dr. Delap. Aɛ̄ted at Drury- Lane, 8vo. 1762, but met with very indifferent fuccefs, its run continually only long enough to afford the author one fingle benefit. It is not devoid of merit.

The Heir. Comedy, by Thomas May. Aɛ̄ted by the company of Revels, 1620. The plot, language, and conduɛ̄t of this play are all admirable ; it met with great applaufe. It is to be found in Dodfley's collec- tion. Scene, Syracufe.

The Heir of Morocco, with the Death of Gayland. Tr. by Elk Settle. Aɛ̄ted at the Theatre Royal, 4to. 1682. Scene, Algiers.

The Heirefs ; or, The An- tigallican. Farce, by Tho. Mozeen. Aɛ̄ted at Drury- Lane.

The Heirefs. Com. faid to be written by General Burgoyne. Aɛ̄ted at Drury- Lane, 1786. The general charaɛ̄ter of this comedy is fenfe, chaflity, and propriety of fentiment ; though the fable is flight, and rather mechanical than natural.

Hell's higher Court of Juftice ; or, The Tryal of the three Politic Ghofts, (viz. Oliver Cromwell, the King of Sweden, and Cardinal Mazarine), 4to. 1661.

Henry and Emma ; or, The Nut Brown Maid. Muſical Drama taken from Prior. Aɛ̄ted at Covent-Garden, 1749.

Henry and Emma. Paf- toral Interlude, by Henry Bate, altered from Prior, aɛ̄ted at Covent-Garden, April 13, 1774, for Mrs. Hartley's benefit.

Henry and Rofamand. Trag. by W. Hawkins, 8vo. 1749. This play, though never aɛ̄ted, is very far from a bad piece.

Henry II. or, The Fall of Rofamond. Trag. by Tho. Hull. Aɛ̄ted at Covent- Garden, 8vo. 1774.

Henry II. King of Eng- land, with the Death of Ro- famond. Tragedy, by John Bancroft, 4to. 1693. This piece, which was publifhed by Mountfort, the player, is in general tragedy, but with a mixture of comedy : it has not the author's name prefixed to it, yet it met with very good fuccefs, and is indeed truly deferving of it. The ſtory of it may be found in the Englifh hifto- rians, and reprefents chiefly that part of this prince's life which relates to Rofa- mond. The fcene lies in Oxford ;

Oxford; and the epilogue was written by Dryden.

Henry III. of France, stabbed by a Friar, with the fall of the Guises. Trag. by Thomas Shipman. Acted at Drury-Lane, 4to. 1678.

Henry IV. An Historical Play, by W. Shakfpeare, in two parts. The firft containing the Life and Death of *Henry*, furnamed *Hotfpur*, and the fecond the Death of *Henry IV.* and Coronation of *Henry V.* Acted by the Lord Chamberlain's fervants, 4to. 1600. Both of thefe plays are perfect mafter-pieces in this kind of writing, the tragedy and comedy parts of them being fo finely connected with each other, as to render the whole regular and complete, and yet contrafted with fuch boldnefs and propriety, as to make the various beauties of each the moft perfectly confpicuous. The character of *Falftaff* is one of the greateft originals drawn by the pen of even this imitable mafter; and in the character of the Prince of Wa'es, the hero and the libertine are fo finely blended, that the fpectator cannot avoid perceiving, even in the greateft levity of the tavern rake, the moft lively traces of the afterwards illuftrious character of the

conqueror of France. Dr. Johnfon obferves, " None of Shakfpeare's plays are more read than the firft and fecond parts of Henry the Fourth. Perhaps no author has ever in two plays afforded fo much delight. The great events are interefting, for the fate of kingdoms depends upon them; the flighter occurrences are diverting, and, except one or two, fufficiently probable; the incidents are multiplied with wonderful fertility of invention; and the characters diverfified with the utmoft nicety of difcernment, and the profoundeft fkill in the nature of man."

King Henry IV. with the Humours of Sir John Falftaff. Tr. Co. Acted at Lincoln's-Inn-Fields, with alterations by Mr. Betterton, 4to. 1700.

Henry IV. of France. Tr. by Charles Beckingham, 8vo. 1719. The plot of this play is taken from the hiftory of that great prince; the piece was written by the author at the age of nineteen, and acted in Lincoln's-Inn-Fields with good fuccefs.

The Chronicle Hiftory of Henry V. with the Battel fought at Agincourt, in France, together with Antient Piftoll, 4to. 1600. This play has alfo an intermixture

mixture of comedy, and is juftly efteemed an admirable piece.

Henry V. Trag. by the Earl of Orrery, fol. 1672. It was acted at the Duke of York's Theatre with great fuccefs.

The famous Victories of Henry V. containing, *The honourable Battel of Agin-court.* Acted by the king's fervants, 4to. no date.

Henry V. or, *The Conqueft of France by the Englifh.* Tr. by Aaron Hill. Acted at Drury-Lane, 8vo. 1723. This is a very good play. The plot and language are in fome places borrowed from Shakfpeare, yet on the whole it is greatly altered, and a fecond plot is introduced by the addition of a new female character, viz. *Harriet,* a niece to lord *Scroope,* who has been formerly feduced by the king. She appears in men's cloaths throughout, and is made the means of difcovering the confpiracy againft him.

Henry VI. Hiftorical Play in three parts, by William Shakfpeare. Two of thefe plays were printed in 4to. (N. D.) but the whole were not publifhed together until the folio edition of 1623. Thefe three plays contain the whole life and long unhappy reign of this prince. In confequence of which it

is impoffible but that all the unities of time, place, and action, muft be greatly broken in upon; yet has the author made the moft valuable ufe of the incidents of real hiftory, to which he has very ftrictly adhered. " Of thefe three plays" (fays Dr. Johnfon), I think the fecond beft. The truth is, that they have not fufficient variety of action, for the incidents are too often of the fame kind; yet many of the characters are well difcriminated, King Henry and his Queen, King Edward, the Duke of Gloucefter, and the Earl of Warwick, are very ftrongly and diftinctly painted.

Henry VI. the Firft Part, with the Murder of the Duke of Gloucefter. Tragedy by J. Crowne. Acted at the Duke's Theatre, 4to. 1681. This play was at firft reprefented with applaufe; but at length the Romifh faction oppofed it; and by their intereft at court got it fuppreffed.

Henry VI. the Scond Part; or, *The Miferies of Civil War.* Tra. by J. Crowne. Acted at the Duke's Theatre 4to. 1680. This play, like others of the fame ftamp, is, in a great meafure, borrowed from Shakfpeare.

King Henry VII. or, *The Popifh Impofter.* Trag. by

Charles

Charles Macklin. Acted at Drury-Lane, 8vo. 1746. This piece is built on the story of Perkin Warbeck, but it met with general disapprobation; and indeed the very impropriety in the title of mentioning a Popish Impofter in a period of time previous to the introduction of Proteftantifm in thefe kingdoms, had an air of abfurdity, which feemed even before its appearance to ftand as a foretafte of no very elegant or judicious entertainment. When, however, it is confidered, that it was the fix weeks labour only of an actor, who even in that fhort fpace was often called from it by his profeffion, and that the players, for the fake of difpatch, had it to ftudy act by act juft as it was plotted, and that the only revifals it received from the *brouillon* to the prefs were at the rehearfals of it, no perfon will be difappointed in finding fo many imperfections con. tained in it.

Henry VIII. The famous Hiftory of his Life. Hiftorical Play, by Wm. Shakfpeare, fol. 1623. This is the clofing piece of the whole feries of this author's hiftorical dramas; and " is (fays Dr. Johnfon) one of thofe which ftill keeps poffeffion of the ftage by the

fplendour of its pageantry. The coronation, not many years ago, drew the people together in multitudes for a great part of the winter. Yet pomp is not the only merit of this play; the meek forrows and virtuous diftrefs of Katherine have furnifhed fome fcenes which may be juftly numbered among the greateft efforts of tragedy. But the genius of Shakfpeare comes in and goes with Katherine. Every other part may be eafily conceived and eafily written."

Henry VIII. An Hiftorical Play, by Mr. William Shakfpeare, with hiftorical notes by Jofeph Grove, 8vo. 1758.

The Heraclidæ. Trag. tranflated from Euripides, by R. Potter, 4to. 1781.

Heraclius, Emperor of the Eaft. Trag. by Lodowick Carlell, 4to. 1664. This piece is not deftitute of merit.

Hercules. Mufical Dram. by Thomas Broughton; fet to mufic by Mr. Handel, and performed at the Haymarket.

Hercules. Tra. tranflated from Euripides, by R. Potter, 4to. 1781.

Hercules Furens. Trag. by Jafper Heywood, 12mo. 1561, and 4to. 1581. This is only a tranflation from Seneca.

Hercules

H E

Hercules Oetæus. Trag. tranflated from Seneca by J. Studley, 4to. 1581.

The Hermit Converted; or, *The Maid of Bath Married*, 8vo. no date. (1771.) This piece is evidently the effect of a diftempered imagination.

The Hermit; or, *Harlequin at Rhodes.* A wretched Pantomime. Acted at Drury-Lane, 1766.

Herminius and Efpafia. Trag. by Mr. Hart, 8vo. 1754. It met with very little fuccefs.

Hermon, Prince of Chorea; or, *The Extravagant Zealot.* Trag. by Dr. Clancy, 8vo. 1746.

Hero and Leander, The Tragedies of, by Sir Robert Stapylton, 4to. 1669. Whether this play was ever acted or not feems to be a dubious point. The plot is taken from Ovid's Epiftles, and *Mufæus's Erotopaignion.*

Herod and Antipater, with the Death of Fair Mariam. Trag. by Gervafe Markham and William Sampfon. Acted at the Red Bull, 4to. 1622.

Heriod and Mariamne. Trag. by Samuel Pordage, Efq 4to. 1674. Acted at the Duke's Theatre. This play was given by its author to Mr. Settle, to ufe and form as he pleafed; it was, however, many years

H E

before it could be brought upon the ftage, but when it did appear it met with very good fuccefs. The plot is from Jofephus, the ftory of *Tyridates* in *Cleopatra*, and the *Unfortunate Pclitic*; or, *The Life of Herod*, tranflated from the French, 8vo. 1639.

Herod the Great. Trag by the Earl of Orrery. It was never acted, but was printed in fol. 1694.

Herod the Great. Dram. Poem, by Francis Peck, printed with the Life of Milton, 4to. 1740.

Heroic Friendfhip. Tra. 4to. 1719. This is a very paltry and ftupid performance, and was never acted.

Heroic Love; or, *The Cruel Separation* Trag. by Lord Lanfdowne, 4to. 1698. This play was acted at Lincoln's-Inn-Fields with great applaufe, and is indeed one of the beft of the tragedies of that period. The plot is taken from the feparation of Achilles and Bryfeis, in the firft book of Homer; and the fcene lies in the Grecian fleet and camp before Troy. The unities are ftrictly adhered to, and the language fublime, yet eafy, the author feeming to have made it is principal aim to avoid all that fuftian and bombaft wherewith the tragic writers, and more efpecially

pecially thofe of that time, were but too apt to interlard their works. Dr. Johnfon obferves, that this tragedy was written, and prefented on the ftage, before the death of Dryden. It is a mythological tragedy, upon the love of Agamemnon and Chryfeis, and therefore eafily funk into negleft, though praifed in verfe by Dryden, and in profe by Pope.

The Heroic Lover ; or, *The Infanta of Spain.* Tr. by George Cartwright, 8vo. 1661. This play was probably never afted. It is in all the later catalogues (which have copied from one another, and confequently perpetuated inftead of correfting miftakes) intituled *Heroic Love.* The fcene lies in Poland; and the author himfelf calls it a Poem, confifting more of fatal truth than flying fancy : penned many years ago, but not publifhed till now.

The Heroine of the Cave. Trag Afted at Drury-Lane, 8vo. 1775. This play was begun by Henry Jones, under the title of *The Cave of Idra*, from a narrative in the Annual Regifter. On the death of this unfortunate author, it fell into the hands of Mr. Reddifh, for whofe benefit it was performed. Not being

long enough for an evening's entertainment, as originally left by its author, Mr. Reddifh put it into the hands of Dr. Hiffernan, who extended the plan, and added fome new charafters.

He Wou'd if He Cou'd ; or, *An old Fool worfe than any.* Burletta, by Ifaac Bickerftaffe. Afted at Drury-Lane, 8vo. 1771.

He would be a Soldier. Com. Afted at Covent-Garden, 1786. The charafters of this piece have an air of novelty, are drawn with fome judgment, and grouped with dramatic effect.

Hewfon Reduc'd ; or, *The Shoemaker Returned to his Trade*, 4to 1661.

Hey for Honefty, down with Knavery. Com. by Tho. Randolph, 4to. 1651. This is little more than a tranflation from the Plutus of Ariftophanes.

Hibernia free'd. Trag. by Capt. W. Phillips, 8vo. 1722. Afted at the Theatre in Lincoln's-Inn-Fields.

Hic et Ubique ; or, *The Humours of Dublin.* Com. by Rich. Head, 4to. 1663.

Hide and Seek. Mufical Farce. Afted at Covent-Garden, 1789. This Farce is deftitute of fable.

The Highland Fair ; or, *The Union of the Clans.* An Opera, by Jofeph Mitchell, 8vo.

8vo 1731. The plot of this piece is the fatal and bloody confequences which frequently ufed to happen at fome of the highland fairs, from the quarrels which were apt to arife on the meeting of perfons of the feveral clans, whofe family connections and party attachments rendered each clan in fome degree a feparate nation, either in alliance, or in a ftate of warfare, with every other neighbouring one ; but the fubject being too local for the Englifh ftage, when brought on at the Theatre Royal in Drury-Lane, it met with little or no fuccefs.

H gh Life Below Stairs. Farce. Acted at Drury-Lane, 8vo. 1759. This little piece feems to aim at the reformation of morals. The firft to reprefent as in a mirrour to perfons in high life fome of their own follies and fopperies, by cloathing their very fervants in them, and fhewing them to be contemptible and ridiculous even in them. The fecond and more principal aim is to open the eyes of the great, and convince perfons of fortune what impofitions, even to the ravage and ruin of their eftates, they are liable to, from the wattefulnefs and infidelity of their fervants, for want of a proper infpection into their domeftic affairs.

It poffeffefs a confiderable fhare of merit, and met with moft amazing fuccefs in London. This piece has been often afcribed to Mr. Townley, mafter of Merchant-Taylors' fchool ; but we are affured he only allowed his name to be ufed as the reputed parent of it, the real author being Mr. Garrick.

The Highland Reel. Com. Romance, by Mr. O'Keeffe. Acted at Covent-Garden, 1788, and well received.

Hippolitus. Trag. by E. Preftwich, 8vo. 1651. A tranflation from Seneca.

Hippolytus. Trag. tranflated from Euripides, by R. Potter, 4to. 1781.

Hypfipile. Opera, tranflated from Metaftafio by J. Hoole, 8vo. 1768.

The Hiftorical Regifter, for the year 1736. Com. by Henry Fielding. Acted at the Haymarket, 8vo. 1737. To fome reflections on the miniftry thrown out in this piece, and in the Pafquin of the fame author, was owing an act of Parliament for laying a reftraint on the ftage, by limiting the number of theatres, and fubmitting every new dramatic piece to the infpection of the lord chamberlain previous to its appearance on the ftage.

Hob; or, *The Country Wake.* A Farce, by Mr. Cibber. Acted at Drury-Lane, 12mo. 1720. This is is only Dogget's *Country Wake*, reduced to the size of a farce. It has since had the addition of some songs, and was performed under the title of *Flora* ; or, *Hob in the Well*.

Hob's Wedding. Farce, by John Leigh, 8vo. 1721. This is partly taken from the same play with that from which the last-named piece is borrowed.

The Hobby Horse. Farce, by Capt. Edward Thompson. Acted at Drury-Lane, April 16, 1766, for the benefit of Mr. Benfley.

The Tragedy of Hoffman ; or, *A Revenge for a Father.* Acted at the Phœnix, Drury-Lane.

The Hogge hath lost his Pearle. Com. divers Times publicly acted by certain London 'Prentices, 4to. 1614. The part of the plot from which the piece derives its name, is the elopement of the daugh er of one Hogge, an usurer, who is one of the principal characters in the play.

The Hollander. Com. by Henry Glapthorne, acted 1635, at the Cockpit, Drury-Lane, and at Court, and printed in 4to. 1640.

Holland's Leaguer. Com by Shakerley Marmyon. Acted at Salisbury-Court, 4to. 1632.

The Honest Criminal ; or,

Filial Piety. Drama, 8vo. 1778.

The Honest Electors ; or, *The Courtiers sent back with their Bribes.* Ballad Op. of three acts, 8vo. No date (1733).

The Honest Lawyer. Com. by S. S. Acted by the Queens Majesties servants, 4to. 1616.

An Honest Man's Fortune. Tragi-Com. by Beaumont and Fletcher, fol. 1647. The incident of *Lamira's* preferring *Montaigne* to be her husband in the time of his greatest adversity, and when he had the least reason to expect it, seems borrowed from Heywood's *History of Women,* book ix. Scene in Paris.

The Honest Whore. Com. by Thomas Dekker, 4to. 1604. The first part contains *The Humours of the Patient Man and the Longing Wife,* and was acted with applause. The second part contains the humours of *The Patient Man and the Impatient Wife,* the *Honest Whore* persuaded by strong arguments to turn *Courtezan* again ; her bravely refusing these arguments ; and, lastly, the comical passage of an *Italian Bridewell,* where the scene ends. Neither part is divided into acts, and we believe the latter was never acted.

The

The Honest Yorkshireman. See *The Wonder.*

Honest in Distress, but reliev'd by No Party. T. as it is basely acted by her Majesty's subjects upon God's Stage the World, 8vo. 1705. This piece consists of three short acts. The scene laid in London, and was written by Edward Ward, the author of *The London Spy*, but was never intended for the stage.

Honoria and Mammon. Com. 8vo. 1659.

Honour Rewarded; or, *The Generous Fortune-Hunter.* Farce of three acts, by J. Dalton, of Clifton, 8vo. 1775.

Hoops into Spinning-Wheels. Tragi-Com. by J. Blanch, 4to. 1725. It is impossible to conceive any thing more stupid and ridiculous than this performance.

Horace. Trag. by Cha. Cotton, 4to. 1671. This is only a translation of the *Horace* of P. Corneille. The plot of the original piece is taken from the several Roman historians of the story of the *Horatii* and *Curiatii.* It is a very good translation.

Horace. Trag. by Mrs. Cath. Phillips, fol. 1678. This is a translation of the same piece as the foregoing,

and was very justly celebrated.

Horatius. Roman Trag. by Sir William Lower, 4to. 1656. This is also a translation from Corneille, but is not equal to either of the preceding two.

An Hospital for Fools. A Dramatic Fable. Acted at Drury-Lane, 1739, 8vo. This piece, being known to be Miller's, was damned, the disturbance being so great, that not one word of it was heard the whole night. The reason of this partial prejudice against it may be traced under the account already given of *The Coffee-House.*

The Hotel; or, *The Double Valet.* Farce, by Tho. Vaughan, Esq. Acted at Drury-Lane, 8vo. 1776. This trifling piece was performed with more success than it deserved.

An Hour before Marriage. Farce, of two acts. As it was attempted to be acted at Covent-Garden, 8vo. 1772. This piece was not suffered to be heard throughout. What gave so much offence cannot be discovered in the perusal of it, and indeed it seems to have deserved a better fate.

A Pleasant conceited Comedie. Wherein is shewed, *How a Man may chuse a*

Good Wife from a Bad. C. Anonym. 4to. 1602. Acted by the earl of Worcester's servants. The foundation of this play is taken from Cynthio's Novels.

The Humorous Courtier. Comedy, by James Shirley. Acted at Drury-Lane, 4to. 1640. This play was acted with very good success.

Humorous Day's Mirth. by G. Chapman, 4to. 1599.

The Humorous Lieutenant. Tragi-Com. by Beaumont and Fletcher, fol. 1647. This is an exceeding good play. It was the first that was acted, and that for twelve nights successively, at the opening of the Theatre in Drury-Lane, April 8, 1663. The plot in general is taken from Plutarch's Life of Demetrius, and other writers of the Lives of Antigonus and Demetrius; and the incident of the Humorous Lieutenant refusing to fight after he has been cured of his wounds, seems borrowed from the story of Lucullus's soldier, related by Horace in the second book of his Epistles, Ep. 2. Scene, Greece.

The Humorous Lovers. C. by the Duke of Newcastle. Acted at the Duke's Theatre, 4to. 1677. This comedy is said, by Langbaine, to be a very good one.

The Humourist. Com. by Thomas Shadwell. Acted at Drury Lane, 4to. 1671. The scene of this piece is laid in London, and the intention of it was to ridicule some of the vices and follies of the age.

Humour out of Breath. Com. by John Daye, 4to. 1607.

The Humours of a Coffee-House. Com. as it is daily acted at most of the Coffee-houses in London, by Edw. Ward.

The Humours of Court; or, Modern Gallantry. Ballad Opera, 8vo. 1732.

The Humours of an Election. Farce, by F. Pilon, Acted at Covent-Garden, 8vo. 1780.

The Humours of Exchange-Alley. Farce, by W. R. Chetwood, 1720.

The Humours of an Irish Court of Justice. Dram. Satire, 8vo. It was never acted.

The Humours of Oxford. Comedy, by James Miller. Acted at Drury-Lane, 8vo. 1729. This was the first and the most original of all our author's dramatic pieces, and met with middling success.

The Humours of Portsmouth; or, All is Well that ends Well. Farce, of three acts,

acts, 8vo. No date, about 1760.

The Humours of Purgatory. Farce, by Benjamin Griffin. Acted at Lincoln's - Inn - Fields, 12mo. 1716.

The Humours of Whist. A Dramatic Satire, as it is acted every day at White's and other Coffee-houses and Affemblies, 8vo. 1743. Anonym. This piece was never intended for the ftage, but only defigned as a reprefentation of the various characters found among the frequenters of the gaming tables.

The Humours of the Age. Com. by Thomas Barker. Acted at Drury-Lane, 4to. 1701. This play was written in two months, and that when the author was but barely of age.

The Humours of the Army. Com. by Charles Shadwell. Acted at Drury-Lane, 4to. 1713, This play met with very good fuccefs.

The Humours of the Road; or, *A Ramble to Oxford.* Com. Anonym. 8vo. 1738.

Humphry Duke of Gloucefter. Trag. by Ambrofe Phillips. Acted at Drury-Lane, 8vo. 1722. The plot of this play is founded on hiftory; and the piece met with applaufe.

The Huntington Divertifement; or, *An Enterlude for the general Entertainment*

at *the County Feaft, held at Merchant - Taylors' - Hall,* June 20, 1678, 4to.

Hurlo Thumbo. Comedy, by Sam. Johnfon, 8vo. 1729. This piece was performed at the Little Theatre in the Hay-market, and had a run of above thirty nights. The oddity, whimficalnefs, and originality of it was what occafioned this amazing fuccefs, the play itfelf being one of the moft abfurd compages of wild extravagant incidents, incoherent fentiments, and unconnected dialogues. The author himfelf performed the principal part, viz. that of Lord *Flame,* fometimes in one key, fometimes in another ; fometimes fidling, fometimes dancing, and fometimes walking in very high ftilts. The celebrated Dr. Byrom, the inventor of a peculiar kind of fhorthand, wrote a prologue to it, in which his intention was to point out, by a friendly hint to the author, the abfurdity of his play. Mr. Johnfon however, fo far from perceiving the ridicule, looked on it as a compliment, and had it both fpoken and printed to the piece Yet, notwithftanding all that has here been faid, it contains in fome places certain ftrokes both of fentiment and imagination

H Y

gination that would do honour even to the moſt capital genius, and which ſpeak the author, if a madman, at leaſt a madman with more than ordinary abilities.

The Huſband his own Cuckold. Com. by John Dryden, jun. Acted at Lincoln's-Inn-Fields, 4to. 1696. The ſtory on which this play is founded was an accident which happened at Rome.

Hycke-Scorner. 4to. b. l. no date. Emprynted by me Wynkyn de Worde. Very old ; the date and author's name unknown.

Hyde-Park. Comedy, by James Shirley. Acted at Drury-Lane, 4to. 1637.

Hymenæi ; or, *The Solemnities of a Maſque and Barriers at a Marriage,* by Ben Jonſon, 4to. 1606.

Hymen's Triumph. Paſtoral Tragi-Com. by Sam. Daniel, 4to 1623. This piece was preſented at an

H Y

entertainment given to king James I. by his queen at her court in the Strand, on the nuptials of lord Roxborough.

Hypermneſtra; or, *Love in Tears.* Trag. by Rob. Owen, 4to. 1703. 12mo. 1722. The ſcene lies in Argos. It was never acted.

The Hypochondriack. C. by Mr. Ozell. This is only a tranſlation of Moliere's *Malade Imaginaire.*

The Hypochondriack. F. Anonym. borrowed from the foregoing ; but never acted.

The Hypocrite. Com. by Iſaac Bickerſtaffe. Acted at Drury-Lane, 8vo. 1769. This is an alteration of Cibber's Nonjuror. Scarce any thing more than the character of Maw-worm was written by the preſent author.

Hyppolitus. Trag. tranſlated from Seneca, by J. Studley, 4to. 1758.

J A

JACK *Drum's Entertainment* ; or, *The Pleaſant Comedy of Paſquil and Katharine.* Anon. 4to. 1601.

Jack Juggler. This is called a comedy in Jacob, Langbaine, and all the old Catalogues, whoſe authors do not pretend to have ſeen it, or to aſſign any date to it.

J A

Jack Straw's Life and Death, a notable Rebel in England, who was killed in Smithfield, by the Lord-Mayor of London, 4to. 1594.

Jack the Giant Queller. An Operatical Play, by H. Brooke. This ſatirical and ingenious piece was performed

formed at the Theatre in Dublin in 1748; but there being in it two or three satirical songs against bad Governors, Lord Mayors, and Aldermen, it was prohibited after the first night's represpresentation.

Jacob and Esau. An Interlude, 4to. 1568. This is a very early piece. It is written in metre, and printed in the old black letter. Its full title runs as follows: A new, merry and wittie Comedie or Enterlude, newlie imprinted, treating upon the Historie of *Jacob* and *Esau*, taken out of the 27th chapter of the first book of Moses, entituled Genesis.

James IV. *King of Scotland*, by Robert Green, 4to. 1599. The design of this piece is taken from the History of that brave, but cruel king, who lost his life in a battle with the English at Flodden-Hill, in the beginning of the sixteenth century; for further particulars of which, see Buchanan and other Scotch Historians.

Jane Shore. Trag. by N. Rowe. Acted at Drury-Lane, 4to. 1713. This is a very excellent tragedy, and is continually acted with great success. The scene lies in London, and the author in the plot of it has in a great measure followed the

History of this unhappy fair one, as related in a collection of Novels in six volumes, 12mo. which we have elsewhere also quoted. It is said to be written in imitation of Shakspeare's *style*. In what he thought himself an imitator of Shakspeare, it is not (as Dr. Johnson observes) easy to conceive. The numbers, diction, the sentiments, and the conduct, every thing in which imitation can consist, are remote in the utmost degree from the manner of Shakspeare, whose dramas it resembles only as it is an English story, and as some of the persons have their names in history. This play, consisting chiefly of domestic scenes and private distress, lays hold upon the heart. The wife is forgiven because she repents; and her husband is honoured, because he forgives. This therefore is one of those pieces which we still welcome on the stage.

Ibrahim, the Illustrious Bassa. Tragedy, in heroic verse, by Elke Settle. Acted at the Duke's Theatre, 4to. 1677.

Ibrahim XII. Emperor of the Turks. Trag. by Mary Pix, 4to. 1696. The plot is to be found in Sir Paul Ricaut's continuation of the Turkish History.

G   *The*

J E

The Jealous Farmer Out-witted; or, *Harlequin Statue.* Pantomime. Acted at Covent-Garden.

The Jealous Lovers. C. by Thomas Randolph, 4to. 1632, prefented by the Students of Trinity-College, Cambridge. This play, which is efteemed the beft of of our author's works, is commended by no lefs than four copies of Englifh, and fix of Latin verfes, from the moft eminent wits of both Univerfities; and was revived with great fuccefs in 1682.

Jealous Wife. Com. by Geo. Colman, 8vo. 1761. This piece made its appearance at Drury-Lane Theatre with prodigious fuccefs. The ground work of it is taken from Fielding's Hiftory of Tom Jones, at the period of Sophia's taking refuge at Lady Bellafton's houfe. The characters borrowed from that work, however, only ferve as a kind of under plot to introduce Mr. and Mrs. Oakley, viz. The Jealous Wife and her hufband. It muft be confeffed, that the paffions of the lady are here worked up to a very great height, and Mr. Oakley's vexation and domeftic mifery, in confequence of her behaviour, very ftrongly fupported. Yet, perhaps, the author

J E

would have better anfwered his purpofe with refpect to the paffion he intended to expofe the abfurdity of, had he made her appear fomewhat lefs of the virago, and Mr. Oakley not fo much of the hen-pecked hufband; fince fhe now appears rather a lady, who, from a confcioufnefs of her own power, is defirous of fupporting the appearance of jealoufy to procure her an undue influence over her hufband and family, than one, who, feeling the reality of that turbulent, yet fluctuating paffion, becomes equally abfurd in the fuddennefs of forming unjuft fufpicions, and in that haftinefs of being fatisfied, which love, the only true bafis of jealoufy, will conftantly occafion.

Jean Hennuyer, Bifhop of Lizieux; or, *The Maffacre of St. Bartholomew.* Dramatic Entertainment, in three acts, tranflated from the French, 8vo. 1773.

Jehu. Farce. Acted at Drury-Lane, 1779. Not printed. This piece was not fuffered to be reprefented throughout.

Jeronymo; or, *The Spanifh Tragedy, with the Wars of Portugal.* Anonym. 4to. 1605. This play contains the life and death of Don Andrea.

The

The Jerujalem Infirmary; or, *A Journey to the Valley of Jehosaphat*. Farce, as it will be acted next Southwark Fair. Anonym. *Venice*, 8vo. 1749. This piece never was, nor ever is intended to be acted. It is a piece of the most unintelligible and abusive jargon ever seen.

The Jew decoy'd; or, *The Progress of an Harlot*. A Ballad Opera, 8vo. 1733. This piece was never performed.

The Jew of Malta. Tr. by Chrift. Marlowe, 4to. 1633. This play was not publifhed till many years after the author's death.

The Jew of Venice. C. by Lord Lanfdowne. Acted at Lincoln's-Inn-Fields, 4to. 1701. This play is altered from Shakfpeare's Merchant of Venice, and in fome refpects with judgment. The introducing the feaft, more particularly when the Jew is placed at a feparate table, and drinks to his money, as his only miftrefs, is a happy thought; yet, on the whole, his lordfhip has greatly leffened both the beauty and effect of the original, which, notwithftanding this modernized piece, aided by magnificence and mufic, ftill ftands its ground, and will ever continue one of the darling reprefentations of the theatre. The Prologue

was written by Bevil Higgons, in which the ghofts of Shakfpeare and Dryden are made to rife crowned with laurel; and in the fecond act is introduced a mufical mafque, written by his lordfhip, called Peleus and Thetis. In this play, as Rowe remarks, the character of Shylock is made comic, and we are prompted to laughter inftead of deteftation.

The Jew's Tragedy; or, *Their fatal and final Overthrow*, by Vefpafian and Titus his fon. By William Hemmings, 4to. 1662. This play was not printed till fome years after the author's death.

If it be not Good the Devil is in it. A new play, as it hath bin lately acted with great applaufe by the Queenes Majefties fervants at the Red-Bull; written by Tho. Dekker, 4to. 1612.

If you know not me, you know Nobody; or, *The Troubles of Q. Eliz* in two parts, by T. Heywood, part 1ft, 4to. 1606. part 2d, 4to. 1605. The fecond part contains the building of the Royal-Exchange, and the famous victory of queen Elizabeth in the year 1588.

Ignoramus; or, *The English Lawyer*. Com. Acted at Drury-Lane, 12mo. 1736.

The

The Ill-natur'd Man. C. Acted every day in this Metropolis, 8vo. 1773.

I'll Tell You What ! A Play, by Mrs, Inchbald. Acted at the Haymarket, 1785. This piece cannot properly be called either a comedy or a tragedy ; for though it contains many serious scenes, it abounds with humour, pleafantry, and laughable situations.

The Ilumination ; or, *The Glazier's Conspiracy.* A Prelude, by F. Pilon. Acted at Covent-Garden, 8vo, 1779. This trifle was produced by the rejoicings on the acquittal of Admiral Keppel.

The Image of Love. This is one of bifhop Bale's dramatic pieces, mentioned by himfelf in his Catalogue.

The Imaginary Cuckold. Com. by Ozell. This is only a tranflation of Moliere's Cocu Imaginaire.

The Imaginary Obstacle. Com. Tranflated from the French, and printed in Foote's Comic Theatre, vol. II.

Imitation ; or, *The Female Fortune - Hunter.* A Comedy, acted at Drury-Lane, 1783, and written in imitation of the Beaux Stratagem.

The Imperial Captives. Tra. by John Mottley, 8vo. 1720. This piece has merit,

and was acted with fome fuccefs in Lincoln's-Inn-Fields.

Imperiale. Trag. by Sir Ralph Freeman, 4to. 1655. Langbaine gives this play a moft excellent character.

The Imperial. Tragedy. Anonym. Fol. 1669. The greateft part of this play is taken from a Latin one.

The Impertinent Lovers ; or, *The Coquet at her Wit's End.* Com. 8vo. Anonym. 1723.

The Impertinents. Com. by Ozell. Tranflated from the Facheux of Moliere.

The Impostor. Trag. by Henry Brooke, Efq. 8vo. 1771. This tragedy was not acted.

The Impostor Detected ; or, *The Vintner's Triumph over* B[rook]e and H[ellie]r. A Farce, occafioned by a Cafe lately offered to the H——e of C——s, by the faid B—ke and H————r, 4to. 1712. This piece was evidently never intended for the ftage, but was only a political and party affair.

The Impostor. Comedy, by Mr. Cumberland. Acted at Drury-Lane, 1789, with applaufe. This piece confifts of incidents not unlike thofe of the Beaux Stratagem.

The Imposture. Tragi-Com. by J. Shirley. Acted at the private houfe, Black-Fryars, 8vo. 1652.

Impof-

I N

Impofture Defeated; or, *A Trick to cheat the Devil.* Com. by Geo. Powell, 4to. 1698. The author himfelf fays, that this trifle of a comedy was only a flight piece of fcribble for the introduction of a little mufic.

The Impromptu of Verfailles, by Ozell, tranflated from Moliere's Comedy of the fame name.

The Inchanted Lovers. A Dramatic Paftoral, by Sir Wm. Lower, 12mo. 1658.

Incle and Yarico. Trag. of three acts, by the author of *The City Farce,* 8vo. 1742. Not acted; but is faid to have been intended to be performed at Covent-Garden. The ftory from The Spectator.

Incle and Yarico. Opera, in three acts, by Mr. Colman, jun. Acted at the Haymarket, 1787. This, like the former, is taken from the ftory in The Spectator, vol. 1. No. 11.

The Inconfoleables; or, *The Contented Cuckold.* Dramatic Farce, Anonym. 8vo. 1738. This piece was never acted, and is by no means deferving of a reprefentation.

The Inconftant; or, *The Way to win Him.* Com. by Geo. Farquahar. Acted at Drury-Lane, 4to. 1702. This is a very lively and entertaining comedy, although

I N

there are fome incidents in it which fcarcely come within the limits of probability. The author in his preface, and Rowe in the Epilogue, fay the hint of the play only was taken from Beaumont and Fletcher's Wild Goofe Chace, though, in fact, the main plot and whole fcenes were borrowed from thence; but the cataftrophe of the laft act, where young Mirabel is in danger of his life at a courtezan's houfe, and is delivered by the carefulnefs of his miftrefs Oriana, difguifed as his page, owes its origin, it is faid, to an affair, which the author had himfelf fome concern in, when on military duty abroad. The fcene lies in Paris.

The Independent Patriot; or, *Mufical Folly.* Comedy, by Francis Lynch. Acted at Lincoln's-Inn-Fields, 8vo. 1737.

Indian Emperor; or, *The Conqueft of Mexico by the Spaniards.* T.C. by J. Dryden, 4to. 1677 This play is a fequel to the Indian Queen. It is written in heroic verfe, the plot is taken from the feveral hiftorians who have written on this affair, and met with great fuccefs in the reprefentation.

The Indian Emperor; or, *The Conqueft of Peru by the Spaniards.* Tra. by Francis

G 3   Hawling.

Hawling. This was acted in the year 1728.

Indian Queen. Trag. by Sir Robert Howard and Mr. Dryden, fol. 1665.

The Indiscreet Lover. C. by Abraham Portal. Acted at the King's Theatre in the Haymarket, for the benefit of the British Lying-Inn Hospital, in Brownlow-street, 8vo. 1768.

The Inflexible Captive. by Miss Hannah More, 8vo. 1774. This is on the story of *Regulus,* and was acted one night at Bath.

The Informers Outwitted. A Tragi-comical Farce, Anonymous. This piece was never acted, but was printed in 1738, 8vo.

Ingratitude of a Common-wealth; or, *The Fall of Caius Martius Coriolanus.* T. by N. Tate. Acted at the Theatre Royal, 4to. 1682. This play is founded on Shakspeare's *Coriolanus.*

Injur'd Innocence. Trag. by Fettiplace Bellers, 8vo. 1732. Acted at the Theatre Royal in Drury-Lane, with some success.

Injur'd Love; or, *The Cruel Husband.* Trag. by N. Tate, 4to. 1707. This tragedy was prepared for the stage, but was never performed.

Injur'd Lover; or, *The Lady's Satisfaction.* C. Acted at Drury-Lane, 4to. N. D.

The Injur'd Lovers; or, *The Ambitious Father.* Tr. by W. Mountfort. Acted at Drury-Lane, 4to. 1688. This play met with but indifferent success, and indeed seems not to have merited better.

The Injur'd Princess; or, *The Fatal Wager.* Tragi-Com. by T. Durfey. Acted at the Theatre Royal, 4to. 1682. The foundation and some part of the language of this play is taken from Shakspeare's *Cymbeline.*

Injur'd Virtue; or, *The Virgin Martyr.* Trag. by Benj. Griffin, 12mo. 1715. Acted at Richmond by the Duke of Southampton and Cleveland's servants. The scene, Cæsarea.

The Inner Temple Masque; or, *Masque of Heroes,* by Thomas Middleton, 4to. 1619.

The Inner Temple Masque, by Wm. Browne, performed about the year 1620.

Innocence Betray'd; or, *The Royal Imposto,* by Messieurs Daniel Bellamy, sen. and jun. 8vo. 1746. This piece was never acted.

Innocence Distress'd; or, *The Royal Penitent.* Trag. by Mr. Gould, 8vo. 1737. This play was never acted.

The Innocent Mistress. Com. by Mrs. M. Pix, 4to. 1697. This play was acted

at

at the Theatre in Little Lincoln's-Inn-Fields, and in the fummer feafon, yet met with very good fuccefs.

The Innocent Ufurper ; or, *The Death of the Lady Jane Gray.* Trag. by J. Banks, 4to. 1694. This play was prohibited the ftage on account of fome miftaken cenfures and groundlefs infinuations that it reflected on the government. The author in his dedication, however, has vindicated himfelf from that charge, by fetting forth, that it was written ten years before, fo that it could not poffibly have been meant to call a reflection on the prefent government. It is far from being the worft of his dramatic writings ; and although it falls fhort of Mr. Rowe's Tragedy on the fame ftory, yet it excells it with refpect to the *pathos*, and a ftrict adherence to hiftorical fact. The plot is built on the fufferings of that fair unfortunate victim to the ambition of her relations ; and the fcene lies in the Tower.

The Inoculator Com. by George Saville Carey, 8vo. 1766.

The Inquifition. F. by J. Philips, 8vo. 1717. This piece was never performed, but is fuppofed to be acted at Child's Coffee-houfe, and

G 4

the King's Arms Tavern in St. Paul's Church-yard. The fubject of it is the controverfy between the Bifhop of Bangor and Dr. Snape.

The Infatiate Countefs. Trag. by J. Marfton, 4to. 1603.

The Infignificants. Com. of five acts, by Dr. Bacon, 8vo. 1757.

The Infolvent ; or, *Filial Piety.* Trag. by Aaron Hill. Acted at the Haymarket, 8vo. 1758. This play was altered by Mr. Hill from an old manufcript play, called, *The Guiltlefs Adulterefs*, which had long been in the hands of the managers of Drury-Lane, and was fuppofed to have been written by Sir Wm. Davenant.

The Inflitution of the Order of the Garter. Dramatic Poem, by Gilb. Weft, 4to. 1742. This piece was never intended for the ftage, yet is truly dramatic, and has many very good things in it. It is republifhed in Dodfley's Collection of Poems in fix volumes, 12mo. Dr. Johnfon obferves, that this piece is written with fufficient knowledge of the manners that prevailed in the age to which it is referred, and with great elegance of diction ; but for want of a procefs of events, neither knowledge nor elegance

gance

IN

gance preferve the reader from wearinefs.

The Inftitution of the Garter; or, *Arthur's Round Table reftored*. Mafque. Acted at Drury-Lane, 1771. This is partly an alteration by Mr. Garrick of the preceding.

An Interlude between Jupiter, Juno, and Mercury, by Henry Fielding, 1743. This piece was never performed, it being only an introduction to a projected comedy, intituled, *Jupiter upon Earth*.

A New Interlude of Impacyente Poverte, newlye Imprinted. M. V. L. X. (we fuppofe 1560.) 4to. This piece is in metre, and in the old black letter.

An Interlude of Welth and Helth, full of Sport and mery Paftyme. Printed 8vo. in the old black letter, without date.

The Interlude of Youth. 4to. 1565. This is an old, ferious, moral, and inftructive piece, written in verfe, and printed in the black letter.

The Intrigues at Verfailles; or, *A Jilt in all Humours*. Com. by T. Durfey. Acted at Lincoln's-Inn-Fields, 4to. 1697. This play did not meet with fo much fuccefs as the author expected from it, and in his dedication he condems the tafte of

IN

the town for preferring others of his plays before it. It is, however, like moft of his pieces, a complication of plagiarifms. *Tornezre's* difguifing himfelf in women's cloaths, and his miftrefs hufband (Count Brifac) falling in love with him in that habit, is borrowed from a novel, called *The Double Cuckold*; and the character of *Vandofin* appears to be a mixture of Wycherley's *Olivia* in *The Plain Dealer*, and Mrs. Behn's *Myrtilla*, in *The Amorous Jilt*. Scene, Verfailles.

The Intriguing Chambermaid. A Ballad Farce, by H. Fielding, 8vo. 1733. This piece is borrowed almoft entirely from the *Diffipateur*. It was performed at Drury-Lane with good fuccefs.

The Intriguing Courtiers; or, *The Modifh Gallants.* Comedy, Anonymous, 8vo. 1732. It was never performed any where; but feems to have been occafioned by fome pieces of gallantry in the amorous hiftory of the Englifh court at that time.

The Intriguing Milliners; or, *Attorney's Clerks.* Far. 1738. This is merely a burlefque; and although anonymous, was written by Mr. Robinfon, of Kendal.

The

*The Invader of his Coun-
try*; or, *The Fatal Resentment*. Trag. by John Den-
nis. Acted at Drury-Lane,
8vo. 1720. This is an al-
teration of Shakſpeare's *Coriolanus*, and was unſucceſs-
ful in its repreſentation.
The author, in a dedication
to the Duke of Newcaſtle,
makes a formal complaint
againſt the players for not
doing him juſtice. Firſt, in
producing his play on a
Wedneſday, which occaſioned his benefit to fall upon a
Friday. " Now, ſays he,
my Lord, Friday is not
only the very worſt day of
the week for an audience;
but this was the particular
Friday when a hundred perſons, who deſigned to be
there, were either gone to
meet the king, or preparing
here in town to do that
duty which was expected
from them at his arrival."

The Invaſion. Farce, 8vo.
1759. This piece was never
acted, nor intended for the
ſtage, but is only a ridicule
on the unneceſſary appre-
henſions ſome perſons en-
tertained on account of the
threatened invaſion of the
flat-bottomed boats from
France on the coaſt of England in that year.

The Invaſion; or, *A Trip
to Brighthelmſtone*. Farce,
by F. Pilon. Acted at Co-
vent-Garden, 8vo. 1778.

This was performed with
conſiderable ſucceſs.

Ion. Tragedy, tranſlated
from Euripides, by R. Potter, 4to. 1781.

John, King of England.
Dramatic Piece, by Biſhop
Bale.

King John. Trag. by
William Shakſpeare, fol.
1623. This is the genuine
work of our matchleſs bard.
The plot is from the En-
gliſh hiſtorians; and the
ſcene lies in England, and
ſometimes in France. Dr.
Johnſon obſerves, that
though it is not written with
the utmoſt power of Shak-
ſpeare, it is varied with a
very pleaſing interchange
of incidents and characters.
The lady's grief is very affecting; and the character
of the baſtard contains that
mixture of greatneſs and levity, which our author delighted to exhibit.

King John and Matilda.
Trag. by Robert Daven-
port. Acted at the Cock-
pit, Drury-Lane, 4to. 1655.
This play was acted with
great applauſe, and was
publiſhed by one Andrew
Pennycuicke, who himſelf
acted the part of *Matilda*,
no women having at that
time ever appeared on the
ſtage. The plot is taken
from ſome circumſtances in
the ſame reign with the
G 5   foregoing

foregoing play, and the scene laid in England.

John the Baptist. An Interlude, by Bishop Bale, 4to. 1538. This was the second dramatic piece printed in England; it is in metre, and in the old black letter, and the full title is as follows: A brefe Comedie or Interlude of Johan Baptyste's preachyng in the Wyldernesse, openynge the craftye Assaultes of the Hypocrytes, wyth the gloryouse Baptyfme of the Lord Jesus Chrifte.

Jonas. Trag. by Ralph Radcliff. Not printed.

Joseph Andrews. Farce, by Robert Pratt. Acted at Drury-Lane, for Mr. Bensley's benefit, 1788. Not printed.

Jovial Crew; or, The Devil turned Ranter An Interlude full of pleasante myrth. Anonymous 4to. 1598.

The Jovial Crew; or, The Merry Beggars. Com. by Richard Brome. Acted at the Cockpit, Drury-Lane, in the year 1641, 4to. 1652. This play met with great success at its first appearance, and was frequently revived and performed with the same applause; it was afterwards altered into a Ballad Opera, by the addition of several songs by Mr. Roome and Sir William

Young, and brought on the stage with its former title at Drury-Lane Theatre in the year 1732, in which form it was since revived at Covent-Garden, where it took a very successful run for several nights together, and afterwards brought many crowded houses.

A Journey to Briftol; or, The Honeft Welchman. F. by John Hipperfley, 1729. This is but an indifferent piece. It was performed at Lincoln's-Inn-Fields Theatre, but with very little success.

Iphigenia. Trag. by J. Dennis, 4to. 1700. This was brought on at Lincoln's-Inn-Fields, but was damned.

Iphigenia in Aulis. Tra. translated from Euripides, printed in 8vo. 1780, with three other pieces from the same author.

Iphigenia in Tauris. Tr. translated from Euripides, by Gilb. Weft, Efq. 4to. 1749.

Irene; or, The Fair Greek. Trag. by Charles Goring. Acted at Drury-Lane, 4to. 1708. This play is founded on the celebrated story of the Sultan Mahomet, who being reproved by his grandees for giving too indulgent a loose to his passion for a beautiful Greek named *Irene,* who was his favourite

rite miſtreſs, to the neglect of his ſtate affairs and the prejudice of his empire, took off her head with his own hand in their preſence, as an atonement for his fault.

Irene. Trag. by Samuel Johnſon. Act'd at Drury-Lane, 8vo. 1749. This is the only dramatic piece among all the writings of this celebrated author. It is founded on the ſame ſtory with the foregoing; the author, however, has taken ſome trifling liberties with the hiſtory, *Irene* being here made to be ſtrangled by order of the Emperor, inſtead of dying by his own hand. The unities of time, place, and action are moſt rigidly kept up, the whole coming within the time of performance, and the ſcene which is a garden of the Seraglio, remaining unmoved through the whole of the play. The language of it is, like all the reſt of Dr. Johnſon's writings, nervous ſentimental, and poetical. Yet, notwithſtanding theſe perfections, aſſiſted by the united powers of Mr. Garrick, Mr. Barry, Mrs. Pritchard, and Mrs. Cibber, all together in one play, it did not meet with the ſucceſs it merited, and might juſtly have expected.

Ireland Preſerv'd; or,

The Siege of Londonderry. Tragi-Com. Written by a gentleman, who was in the town during the whole ſiege. Printed at Dublin, 8vo. 1738-9. This play was written by John Michelborne, one of the governors of Londonderry during the ſiege of it

Iriſh Hoſpitality; or, *Virtue Rewarded.* Com. by C. Shadwell, 12mo. 1720. This is one of five plays by this author, which were written for the latitude of our ſiſter iſland, and were all performed in Dublin with great applauſe.

The Iriſh Fine Lady. F. by Charles Macklin. Acted at Covent-Garden one night only, Nov. 28, 1767. Not printed.

The Iriſh Maſque at Court. By Ben Jonſon, fol. 1640.

The Iriſh Widow. Com. of two acts, by David Garrick, Eſq. Acted at Drury-Lane, 8vo. 1772. The intention of this piece ſeems to have been merely to introduce Mrs. Barry to the public in a new light, and was very ſucceſsfully executed.

The Iron Age. An Hiſtory, in two parts, by Tho. Heywood, 4to. 1632. The firſt part includes from the rape of *Helen*, to the death of Ajax, &c. The ſecond from the death of Pentheſilea,

I S

Penthesilea, to that of most of the Grecian leaders in that war.

Isabella; or, *The Fatal Marriage*. Play, altered from Southerne, by David Garrick, Esq. 8vo. 1758.

The Island of Slaves. Com. of two acts, 1761. This is little more than a literal translation of the *Isles des Esclaves* of M. Marivaux.

The Island Princess. Tr. Com. by Beaumont and Fletcher, fol. 1647.

The Island Princess. Tr. Com. by Nahum Tate, altered from Beaumont and Fletcher, and acted at the Theatre Royal, 4to. 1687.

The Island Princess; or, *The Generous Portuguese.* Opera, by P. A. Motteux, 4to. 1699. This is only the principal parts of Fletcher's *Island Princess* formed into an Opera, and performed at the Theatre Royal. The scene lies in the Spice Islands; and the music was composed By Mr. Daniel Purcell, Mr. Clarke, and Mr. Leveridge.

The Island Queens; or, *The Death of Mary, Queen of Scotland.* Tragedy, by J. Banks, 4to. 1684. This piece was prohibited the stage, for which reason the author thought proper to publish it, in defence of himself and his tragedy. The story is founded on the

I T

Scotch and English histories, to which the author has closely and impartially adhered, and well preserved that power of affecting the passions which appears through all his works, and sometimes makes ample amends for want of poetry and language. It was reprinted in 1704, with the title of the *Albion Queens*; or, *The Death*, &c. To this edition are the names added of Wilks, Booth, Oldfield, Porter, &c. in the Dramatis Personæ. From which it seems that it was afterwards allowed the liberty of being performed.

The Island of St. Margui-rite. Musical Entertainment. Performed at Drury-Lane, 1789. An indifferent piece.

The Islanders. Comic Opera, by Charles Dibdin. Acted at Covent-Garden, 8vo. 1780.

The Isle of Gulls. Com. by J. Daye. Acted at Black-Fryars, 4to. 1606. This is a very good play, and met with great success. The plot is taken from Sir Ph. Sidney's *Arcadia*.

The Italian Husband. Tr. by Edward Ravenscroft, 4to. 1698. Acted at Lincoln's-Inn-Fields. The story of this play is barbarous and bloody, and the villainy carried on to bring about the catastrophy, deep and horrid;

J U

horrid ; but the piece itfelf has little merit.

The Italian Hufband ; or, *The violated Bed avenged.* A moral drama. By Ed-ward Lewis, M. A. 8vo. 1754. This performance was never acted ; for no theatre paft or prefent would have received it.

The Jubilee. Dramatic Entertainment, by David Garrick, Efq. Acted at Drury-Lane, 1769. Not printed. A fpectacle ren-dered interefting by mute reprefentations of a princi-pal fcene in each of the plays of Shakfpeare. Thefe groups were originally de-figned to form a part of the real Jubilee at Stratford. That attempt, however, having failed ridiculoufly, leaving Mr. Garrick, the fteward and inventor of it, feveral hundred pounds out of pocket, by means of the prefent exhibition (which was Mr. Wilfon the por-trait-painter's contrivance) he at once reimburfed him-felf, and more fuccefsfully entertained the public for upwards of ninety evenings in the firft feafon of the piece.

The Judgment of Paris, A Mafque, by Wm. Con-greve, 4to. 1701. This is a very pretty piece of poe-try, and is now frequently

J U

performed to mufic, by way of an *Oratorio.*

The Judgment of Paris. An Entertainment of five Interludes, by Abraham Langford, 8vo. 1730.

The Judgment of Paris ; or, *The Triumph of Beauty.* Paftoral Ballad Opera of one act, performed at Lin-coln's - Inn - Fields, 8vo. 1731.

The Judgment of Paris. An Englifh Burletta in two acts, by Dr. Ralph Schom-berg. Performed at the Haymarket with that de-gree of fuccefs that com-monly attends our author's literary undertakings, 8vo. 1768.

Julia ; or, *The Italian Lover.* Tra. by Mr. Jeph-fon. Acted at Drury-Lane, 1787. The language and fentiments of this play are elevated, and often fub-lime.

Juliana, Princefs of Po-land. Tragi-Com. by John Crowne, 4to. 1671. Acted at the Duke of York's The-atre.

Julius Cæfar. Trag. by Alexander, earl of Sterling, 4to. 1604. This is much the moft regular dramatic piece of this noble author, at leaft in refpect to the unity of action ; he has run into the very fame fault which Shakfpeare had done before

before him, viz. the not closing the piece with the moft natural and affecting cataftrophe, the death of Cæfar. Shakfpeare, however, has made a noble ufe of his confpirators, and has drawn the characters of *Antony, Brutus,* and *Caffius,* in a manner that gives delight even in defpight of the non-neceffity of continuing the ftory. But this author has rendered them fo cold and languid, that the reader is apt to wifh he had facrificed them all at once to the manes of the murdered emperor. His ftyle is fententious, yet neither pure nor correct, for which however his lordfhip pleads his country.

Julius Cæfar. Trag. by W. Shakfpeare, fol. 1523. The ftory of this tragedy is from hiftory. The fpeeches of *Brutus* and *Anthony* over *Cæfar's* body are perhaps the fineft pieces of oratory in the Englifh language, the firft appearing unanfwerable till the fecond comes to overthrow its effect; nor can there be a finer fcene of refentment and reconciliation between two friends, than that of Brutus and Caffius in the 4th act. The duke of Buckingham, however, aware of the faults we took notice of in regard to the cataftrophe, has divided

the two revolutions in this piece, and formed out of them two plays; the one called Julius Cæfar, the other Marcus Brutus. Under the account of the latter, the reader will find the reafon why neither of them came on the ftage.

Julius Cæfar. Trag. by J. Sheffield, duke of Buckingham, with a prologue and chorus, 4to. 1722.

Jupiter and Alcmena. C. Opera, performed at Covent-Garden, 1781. This child of many authors, which owes its origin to Greece, was adopted by Plautus, and by many other writers fince his time. This piece was well performed, and well received.

The Junto; or, *The interior Cabinet laid open.* A ftate Farce, 8vo. 1770. A defpicable political catchpenny.

The Juror. Farce, by W. B. formerly of St. John's-College-Cambridge, 8vo. 1718. Never acted.

The Juft General. Tra. Com. by Cofmo Manuche, 4to. 1652. This piece was intended for the ftage, but never acted. Yet, although it was a firft attempt of the author's, it is very far from contemptible.

The Juft Italian. Tragi-Com. by Sir W. Davenant. Acted

J U

Acted at Black-Fryars, 4to.
1630.
Juſtice Triumphant ; or,
The Organ in the Suds. F.

J U

of three acts, 8vo. 1747.
This piece relates to ſome
proceedings then tranſacted
-in a village near London.

K I

K I

K *ENSINGTON Gardens*;
or, *The Pretenders*.
Com. by John Leigh, 8vo.
1720. This was acted at
Lincoln's-Inn-Fields play
houſe, with ſome ſuccefs.
The Kentiſh Election. C.
by L. N. 8vo. 1735.
The Kentiſh Barons. Op.
by the Hon. Francis North.
Acted at the Haymarket,
1791. The fable of this
Opera nearly borders upon
tragedy, as it approaches
the provinces of terror and
pity. This play, though it
has many faults, has much
merit, and thefe were difcriminated by the audience.
A Key to the Lock. Com.
of two acts, by Mr. O'Keeffe,
Acted at the Haymarket,
1788, with little applaufe.
The Kind Keeper ; or, *Mr.
Limberh. m.* A Com. by J.
Dryden. Acted at the
Duke's Theatre, 4to. 1680.
This play was intended as
an honeft fatire againft the
crying fin of keeping ; but
in ſhort it expofed the keeping part of the town in fo
juſt a manner, and fet them
in fo ridiculous a light, that
unable to ſtand the laſh of
the poet's pen, aided by
the force of comic reprefen-

tation, they found means to
ſtop the play after a run of
only three nights.
King and no King. Tra.
Com. by Beaumont and
Fletcher, 4to. 1619. This
play was very roughly handled by Rymer ; but, as he
dealt no lefs feverely with
the works of the immortal
Shakſpeare, his cenfures
ought to have but little influence over our opinions ;
and this piece amongſt others
ſtands up in evidence againſt
his judgment, it having always met with fuccefs whenever acted or revived. For
a further account of it, fee a
criticiſm on it by Dryden, in
the preface to his *Troilus*
and *Creſſida*.
*The King, and the Miller
of Manſfield*, Farce, by R.
Dodfley. Acted at Drury-
Lane, 8vo. 1737. The plot
of this little piece is built on
a traditional ſtory in the
reign of our King Henry II.
The author, however, has
made a very pleafing ufe of
it, and wrought it out in a
truly dramatic conclufion.
The dialogue is natural, yet
elegant ; the fatire poignant, yet genteel ; the fentimental parts ſuch as do
honour

honour both to the head and heart of its author, and the cataltrophe though fimple, yet affecting, and perfectly juft.

King Arthur ; or, *The Bri-tifh Worthy*. A Dramatic Opera, by John Dryden. Acted at the Queen's Theatre, 4to. 1691. This play is a kind of fequel to the *Al-bion* and *Albanius* of the fame author, and feems to have been written rather for the fake of the finging and machinery, than with a view to the more intrinfic beauties of the drama, the inci-dents being all extravagant, and many of them very pu-erile. The whole affair of the *Enchanted Wood*, and the other wonders of *Of-mond's* art, are borrowed from Taffo, who has made his *Rinaldo* perform every thing that *Arthur* does in this play. The fabulous hiftory of this prince is to be met within *Geoffrey* of *Monmouth*, as alfo in the firft volume of Tyrrel's *Hif-tory of England*. The fcene lies in Kent. The genius of Dryden, however, ftrug-gles through the puerilities with which the flory of our legendary prince is encum-bered. The contraft of cha-racter between *Philadel*, a genteel aerial fpirit, friend-ly to the Chriftians, and *Grimbald*, a fierce earthy

goblin, engaged on the ad-verfe party, is not only well defigned, but executed with the hand of a mafter.

King Arthur ; or, *The Bri-tifh Worthy*. Dram. Opera, altered by David Garrick. Acted at Drury-Lane, 8vo. 1770.

King Charles I. Trag. by W. Havard, 8vo. 1737. This piece was performed at the Theatre in Lincoln's-Inn-Fields with very good fuccefs ; and indeed there are fome parts of it which feem to approach as near to the ftyle of Shakfpeare, as any of the attempts that have been made to imitate him.

The King's Entertainment at Welbeck in Nottingham-fhire, a feat of the earl of Newcaftle, at his going to Scotland in 1633, by Ben Jonfon, fol. 1640.

Kenfington Gardens ; or, *The Walking Jockey*. Inter-lude, by Mr. Cobb. Acted at the Haymarket, 1781. Not printed.

A Knack how to Knowe an honeft Man. A pleafant conceited Comedie, feveral times acted. Anonym. 4to. 1596.

The Knight of Malta. Tragi-Com. by Beaumont and Fletcher, fol. 1647. Scene, Malta.

The Knight of the Burn-ing Peftle. Com. by Beau-mont

mont and Fletcher, 4to.
1613, 4to. 1635. It ap-
pears to have been written
in 1611, and not well re-
ceived, when acted on the
stage. The names of Beau-
mont and Fletcher are not
on the title-page of the first
publication of it.

The Knights. Com. of
two acts, by Samuel Foote,
8vo. 1754. This piece made
its first appearance at the
Little Theatre in the Haymarket, about the year
1747, and at that time terminated with a droll con-
cert of vocal music between
two cats, in burlesque of the
Italian comic Operas. As
this, however, was only
temporary, the author, to
adapt it more properly to
true dramatic taste, and
render it a more perfect
Farce, has wound up a conclusion for it, which, however, even as it now stands,
is scarcely so conclusive or
so natural as it could be
wished. This fault, how-
ever, is amply made amends
for by its possessing in the
highest degree a much more
essential excellence of comedy, viz. great strength of
character, and the most accurate and lively colouring
of nature. His two knights,
Sir *Penurious Tryfle* and Sir
Gregory Gazette, the first of
which has the strongest passion for perpetually enter-

taining his friends with a
parcel of stale trite insignificant stories, and the latter,
who is possessed with a most
insatiable thirst for news,
without even capacity sufficient to comprehend the full
meaning of the most fami-
liar paragraph in a public
Journal, are very strongly
painted. The first of them
received additional life from
the admirable execution of
the author in his representation of the character, in
which indeed it has been reported, that he mimicked
the manner of a certain gentleman in the West of England ; and the other seems
to have afforded a hint to a
writer since, viz. Mr. Murphy, in his *Upholsterer*, to
expatiate still more largely
on this extravagant and absurd kind of folly. His
other characters of *Tim* and
Miss *Suck*, with the scene of
courtship introduced between
them, though not absolutely new in the first conception, yet are managed after
a new manner, and always
give great entertainment in
the representation. It was
acted at Drury-Lane.

The Knot of Fools. Play,
acted in the year 1613.

Know your own Mind.
Com. by A. Murphy, Esq.
Acted at Covent-Garden,
1777, with considerable success, 8vo. 1778.

L A

LA CONTADINA IN CORTE. Comic Op. acted at the King's Theatre, in the Haymarket, 1782. This piece was formerly brought on the stage as a ballad by Veftris ; but now fresh set to music principally by Sacchini, in a manner worthy of that compofer.

The Ladies Choice. Petite Piece, of two acts, by Paul Hiffernan, performed at Covent-Garden, 8vo. 1759. It was acted a few nights, but with no fuccefs.

The Ladies Frolick. Op. altered from *The Jovial Crew,* by James Love. Acted at Drury-Lane, 1770. Not printed.

The Ladies of the Palace ; or, *The New Court Legacy.* Ballad Opera, of three acts, 8vo. 1735. Court Scandal.

Lady Alimony ; or, *The Alimony Lady.* Com. Anonymous, 4to. 1669. Said in the title-page to be duly authorized, daily acted, and frequently followed.

The Lady Contemplation. Com. in two parts, by the Duchefs of Newcaftle, fol. 1662. Three fcenes in the firft, and two in the fecond part, were written by the Duke.

The Lady Errant. Tragi-Com. by W. Cartwright, 8vo. 1651. This was by fome efteemed an excellent comedy.

Lady Jane Grey. Trag. by N. Rowe. Acted at Drury-Lane, 4to. 1715. This is an admirable play, and frequently performed with fuccefs to this day.

The Lady of May. Mafq. by Sir Philip Sidney. This piece was prefented to Q. Elizabeth in the gardens at Wandftead in Effex, and is printed together with fome poems at the end of the *Arcadia.*

The Lady of the Manor. Com. Op. by Dr. Kenrick. Acted at Covent-Garden, 8vo. 1778.

The Lady of Pleafure. C. by Ja. Shirley. Acted at Drury-Lane, 4to. 1637.

The Lady's laft Stake ; or, *The Wife's Refentment.* C. by C. Cibber. Acted at the Haymarket, 4to. 1707. This is very far from a bad comedy. The manners, the ftyle, and many of the incidents, are original, and do honour to their author.

The Lady's Priviledge. Com. by Hen. Glapthorne. Acted at Drury-Lane, and twice at Whitehall before their Majefties, 4to. 1640.

The Lady's Revenge ; or, *The Rover Reclaim'd.* Com. by Wm. Popple, Efq. Acted at Covent-Garden, 8vo. 1734.

The Lady's Tryal. Tra. Com. by John Ford. Acted at Drury-Lane, 4to. 1639.

1639. The scene lies in Genoa.

The Lady's Triumph. C. Opera, by Elk. Settle, 12mo. 1718. This piece was performed by fubfcription at the Theatre in Lincoln's-Inn-Fields.

The Lady's Vifiting Day. Com. by Charles Barnaby, 4to. 1701. Acted at Lincoln's-Inn-Fields.

The Lame Lover. Com. by Samuel Foote. Acted at the Haymarket, 8vo. 1770. This piece, though little inferior to any performance of the fame writer, did not meet with equal fuccefs.

The Lancafhire Witches. Com. by Thomas Heywood, Acted at the Globe, 4to. 1634. The foundation of this piece in general is an old Englifh novel; but that part of it in which *Whetftone*, through the means of his aunt, revenges himself on *Arthur*, *Shakftone*, and *Bantam*, for having called him *Baftard*, is borrowed from the hiftory of John Teutonicus, a German, who was a known baftard and a noted magician.

The Lancafh re Witches, and Teague O'Divelly the Irifh Prieft. Com. by T. Shadwell. Acted at the Duke's Theatre, 4to. 1682. This play is in fome meafure on the fame foundation with the foregoing one. It

was, however, written in the time of high contefts between the *Whig and Tory* parties, and therefore met with ftrong oppofition from the Papifts, on account of the character of *Teague O'Divelly*.

Landgartha. Tragi-Com. by Henry Burnell, 4to. 1641. Acted at Dublin, with great applaufe. The plot is founded on the Swedifh hiftory, being the conqueft of Fro (or Frollo) king of Sweden, by Regner (or Reyner) king of Denmark, with the repudiation of Regner's Queen Langartha.

The Languifhing Lover; or, *An Invocation to Sleep.* A Mufical Interlude, by D. Bellany, 12mo. 1746.

The Late Revolution; or, *The Happy Chang .* Tr. C. Acted throughout the Englifh dominions, in the year 1688, 4to. 1690. It is faid in the title-page to be written by a perfon of quality. From the time in which this piece was produced, it will readily be concluded to be, as it really is, intirely political.

The Law againft Lovers. Tragi-Com. by Sir Wm. Davenant, fol. 1673. This play is a mixture of the two plots of Shakfpeare's *Meafure for Meafure*, and *Much ado about Nothing*.

The Laws of Candy. Tr. Com.

Com. by Beaumont and Fletcher, fol. 1647. This is one of the moſt indifferent of theſe authors plays, and has not been acted for many years.

The Law of Lombardy. Trag. by Robert Jephſon. Acted at Drury-Lane, 8vo. 1779. This play, which in its plot reſembles *Much ado about Nothing,* was not very ſuccefsful. It was acted nine nights, and then laid aſide.

Law Tricks; or, *Who would have thought it?* C. by John Day. Acted by the children of the Revels, 4to. 1608. This is an admirable play.

The Lawyers Feaſt. Far. by Ja. Ralph, 8vo. 1744. This little piece was performed at the Theatre Royal in Drury-Lane, with ſome ſuccefs.

The Lawyers Fortune; or, *Love in a hollow Tree.* C. by William, lord Viſcount Grimſtone, 4to. 1705. This piece is certainly full of abſurdities; but ſome indulgence ought to be allowed it, when it ſhall be known that the author was but thirteen years of age at the time he wrote it; and ſo conſcious did his modeſty and good ſenſe afterwards render him of its numerous deficiencies, that as far as was in his power he attempted to buy in the impreſſion. In conſequence of an election, however, at St. Alban's, where his lordſhip ſtood for candidate, the old ducheſs of Marlborough, who was a ſtrong opponent to his intereſt, cauſed a new edition of it to be printed at her own expence, and diſperſed among the electors, with a frontiſpiece, in which his lordſhip was repreſented as an elephant dancing on a rope. This edition alſo he bought up as nearly as he was able, but could not ſucceed ſo far as to prevent ſome of the copies from getting into the world. The ſcene lies in a country town.

The Lawyers. Comedy, by Mr. Williamſon. Acted at the Haymarket, 1783. This is a good moral comedy, was well received, and drew tears from every corner of the houſe.

Of Lazarus rais'd from the Dead. A Comedy, by Biſhop Bale.

King Lear. The full title of this play, in the original edition, ſtands thus: " M. William Shakſpeare his true Chronicle Hiſtory of the Life and Death of King Lear and his three daughters; with the unfortunate life of Edgar, Sonne and Heire to the Earle of Glouceſter, and his ſullen and aſſumed affumed humour of *Tom of Bedlam*. As it was played before the King's Majefty, at Whitehall upon St. Stephen's night in Chriftmas hollidaies. By his Majefties fervants, playing ufually at the Globe on the Bankfide." 4to. 1608. This play is founded on the Englifh hiftory, and is one of the Chef d'Oeuvres of this capital mafter. The diftinction drawn between the real madnefs of the king, and the feigned frenzy of *Edgar*, is fuch, as no pen but his own was capable of. The quick, hafty, choleric difpofition of *Lear*, fupported in the midft of tendernefs, diftrefs, and even lunacy, and the general tenor of his whole converfation, which even in all the wild extravagant ramblings of that lunacy ftill tend as towards a centre to the firft great caufe of it, the cruelty of his daughters, is painting only to be reached by Shakfpeare's happy pencil. In a word, to attempt to enumerate all its beauties, would take a larger portion of our work, than the deftined limits of it would permit. The play, however, as it is now acted, is only an alteration of the original piece, made by N. Tate. Dr. Johnfon fays, " this play is defervedly celebra-

ted among the dramas of Shakfpeare. There is perhaps no play which keeps the attention fo ftrongly fixed ; which fo much agitates our paffions and interefts our curiofity. The artful involutions of diftinct interefts, the ftriking oppofition of contrary characters, the fudden changes of fortune, and the quick fucceffion of events, fill the mind with a perpetual tumult of indignation, pity and hope. There is no fcene which does not contribute to the aggravation of the diftrefs or conduct of the action, and fcarce a line which does not conduce to the progrefs of the fcene. So powerful is the current of the poet's imagination, that the mind, which once ventures within it, is hurried irrefiftibly along. On the feeming improbability of Lear's conduct, it may be obferved, that he is reprefented according to hiftories at that time vulgarly received as true. And, perhaps, if we turn our thoughts upon the barbarity and ignorance of the age to which this hiftory is referred, it will appear not fo unlikely as while we eftimate Lear's manners by our own. Such preference of one daughter to another, or refignation of dominion on fuch conditions, would be be yet credible, if told of a petty prince of Guinea or Madagafcar. Shakfpeare, indeed, by the mention of his carls and dukes, has given us the idea of times more civilized; and of life regulated by fofter manners; and the truth is, that though he fo nicely difcriminates, and fo minutely defcribes the characters of men, he commonly neglects and confounds the characters of ages by mingling cuftoms ancient and modern, Englifh and foreign."

King Lear. Tragedy, by N. Tate. Acted at the Duke's Theatre, 4to. 1681. This is only an alteration of Shakfpeare's Lear; but it now ftands forward, and is conftantly acted inftead of the original.

The Hiftory of King Lear. by George Colman. Acted at Covent-Garden, 8vo. 1768. A judicious alteration of the two foregoing pieces.

L'Eroe Cinefe. Serious Opera, performed at the Haymarket, 1782. The words by Metaftafio, and the mufic, which was entirely new and excellent, by Signor Rauzzina.

The Learned Ladies. C. by Ozell. A tranflation only of the Femmes Sçavantes of Moliere.

The Legacy; or, *The Fortune-Hunter.* Com. tranf-lated from the French, and printed in Foote's Comic Theatre.

Lethe. Dramatic Satire, by David Garrick. Acted at Drury-Lane, 8vo. 1748. This piece confifts only of a number of feparate characters, who, coming by Pluto's permiffion to drink of the waters of forgetfulnefs, relate to Æfop, who is appointed the diftributor of thefe waters, the feveral particulars which conftitute the diftinguifhing parts of their feveral difpofitions. In the execution of this defign, there is fcope given for very keen and poignant fatire on the reigning follies of the age. Yet fo true is it, that the ftricken deer will ever weep, and the galled jade wince, that notwithftanding the wit and fenfible manner in which this fatire is conveyed, notwithftanding befides the admirable performance of the piece, in which the author himfelf, during its firft run, acted no lefs than three of the characters, it met with confiderable oppofition; nor was it till fome time after that it made its ftand firmly, and became, as it now is, one of the conftant and regular petite pieces of the Englifh ftage. It is, however, confiderably altered by the drefs it now appears in, in, and, in the latter editions, Mr. Garrick added a new character called Lord Chalkſtone.

The Letter Writers; or, *A New Way to Keep a Wife at Home.* Com. by Henry Fielding, 8vo. 1732. This play was acted at the Little Theatre in the Haymarket with ſome ſucceſs; but, like the reſt of that author's larger dramatic pieces, has never been revived ſince its firſt run. In ſhort, Fielding's happy turn of humour, more eſpecially for ſcenes in lower life, rendered almoſt all his farces ſucceſsful, but was not ſo well adapted to the more elegant parts of genteel and regular comedy.

The Levee. Farce, by John Kelley, Eſq. 8vo. 1741. This piece was never acted, being denied a licence by the inſpector of farces.

The Levellers Levell'd; or, *The Independents' Conſpiracy to rout Monarchy.* An Interlude, written by Mercurius Pragmaticus, 4to. 1647. The author of this piece is unknown; but the very title of it implies him to have been a warm royaliſt.

Leucothëe. Dram Poem, by Iſaac Bickerſtaffe, 8vo. 1756. This little piece, which was never acted, nor ſeems intended by the author for repreſentation, is a kind of tragic opera, founded on the ſtory of Apollo's love for Leucothoë, the daughter of Orchamus, king of Perſia.

The Libertine. Trag. by Thomas Shadwell. Acted by their Majeſties ſervants, 4to. 1676. This play met with great ſucceſs, and is by ſome eſteemed one of the beſt of this author's writings. It is on a ſubject which has employed the pens of the firſt-rate writers in different languages, there being, beſides this, two French plays on the ſtory (one by Corneille, the other by Moliere), one Italian, and one Spaniſh.

The Libertine. Trag. by Ozell. This is only a tranſlation of Moliere's play on the ſame ſubject.

The Libertine; or, *Hidden Treaſure.* Com. tranſlated from the French, and printed in Foote's Comic Theatre.

Liberty Aſſerted. Trag. by J. Dennis, 4to. 1704. This play was acted with great ſucceſs at the Theatre in Lincoln's-Inn-Fields, and is dedicated to Anthony Henley, Eſq. to whom the author owns himſelf indebted for the happy hint upon which it was formed.

Liberty Chaſtiz'd; or, *Patriotiſm in Chains.* Tragi-comi-political Farce, as it was performed by M——s S——ts in the year 1268.

Modern-

Modernifed by Paul Tell-Truth, Efq. 8vo. 1768. This, we believe, is a production of George Saville Carey.

Liberty-Hall. Opera, by Mr. Dibdin. Acted at Drury-Lane, 1785. This piece has great merit.

The Life and Death of Captain Thomas Stukeley, with his Marriage to Alderman Curteis Daughter, and valiant ending of his Life at the Battaile of Alcazar, 1605, 4to. b. l.

Like Mafter like Man. C. of two acts, performed at Smock-Alley, 12mo. 1770. Taken from Vanbrugh's Miftake, and printed at Dublin.

Like Will to like, queth the Devil to the Collier. An Interlude, by Ulpian Fulwell, 4to. 1587. This is entirely a moral piece, printed in the old black letter, the prologue written in alternate verfe, and the whole piece in rhyme.

Lilliput. A Dramatic Entertainment, by David Garrick, Efq. Acted at Drury-Lane, 8vo. 1757. This piece was acted by children.

Lingua; or, *The Combat of the Tongue and the Five Senfes for Superiority.* A ferious comedy. Anon. 4to. 1607.

Lionel and Clariffa. C. Op. by Ifaac Bickerftaffe.

Acted at Covent-Garden, 8vo. 1768. In this Opera, which was well received, the author boafts that he had borrowed nothing. It was afterwards altered, and acted at Drury-Lane with the new title of the School for Fathers.

The Litigants. Com. by Mr. Ozell, 12mo. 1715. This is no more than a tranflation from the Plaideurs of Racine.

The Little French Lawyer. Com. by Beaumont and Fletcher, fol. 1647. The plot of this play is taken from Gufman de Alfarache; or, The Spanifh Rogue.

The Little Orphan of the Houfe of Chao. A Chinefe Trag. Tranflated from the French verfion of P. Du Halde's Defcription de l'Empire de la Chine, by Dr. Percy.

The Liverpool Prize. F. by F. Pilon. Acted at Covent-Garden, 8vo. 1779, with fuccefs.

The Livery Rake and Country Lafs. A Ballad Opera, by Edward Phillips, 8vo. 1733. This was performed at the Haymarket with fome fuccefs.

Locrine, the eldeft Sonne of King Brutus, difcourfing the warres of the Britaines and Hunnes, with their difcomfiture; the Britaines victory, with their accidents;

dents ; and the death of Al-
banact. No leffe pleafant
than profitable. Newly fet
foorth, overfeene, and corrected by W. S. 4to. 1595.
This play is one of thofe
which have by fome been
confidered as the production
of Shakfpeare, but more generally rejected.

*Lodowick Sforza, Duke of
Milan.* Trag. by Robert
Gomerfal, 12mo. 1633.

London Chanticleers. C.
Anonym. 4to. 1659. This
piece is rather an Interlude
than a play, not even being
divided into acts. It is entirely of the Baffe Comedie
of the French, the fcene
lying wholly among perfons
of the loweft rank. Yet it
has a good deal of humour
in it.

The London Cuckolds. C.
by Edw. Ravenfcroft. Act-
ed at the Duke's Theatre,
4to. 1682. This play met
with very great fuccefs, and
has, till within a very few
years paft, been frequently
prefented on our ftages;
particularly on Lord-May-
or's day, in contempt and
to the difgrace of the city.
It feems calculated only to
pleafe the upper galleries,
being of a kind of humour
too low for any thing above
the rank of a chamber-maid
or foot-boy to laugh at, and
intermingled with a feries
of intrigue, libertinifm, and

lafcivioufnefs, that nothing
more virtuous than a com-
mon proftitute could fit to
fee without a blufh. It is,
however, at length totally
banifhed from the ftage.

The London Merchant ; or,
*The Hiftory of George Barn-
well.* Tra. by Geo. Lillo,
8vo. 1730. This play was
acted at the Theatre Royal
in Drury-Lane with great
fuccefs. It is written in
profe, and although the language is confequently not
fo dignified as that of the
bufkin is ufually expected to
be, yet it is well adapted to
the fubject it is written on,
and exalted enough to ex-
prefs the fentiments of the
characters, which are all
thrown into domeftic life.
The plot is ingenious, the
cataftrophe juft, and the
conduct of it affecting. And
no leffon can be furely more
proper, or indeed more neceffary, to inculcate among
that valuable body of youths,
who are trained up to the
branches of mercantile bufinefs, fo eminently eftimable
in a land of commerce, fuch
as England. Mr. Gorges
Edmund Howard fays, that
having communicated his
play of The Female Game-
fter to Dr. Samuel Johnfon,
that gentleman obferved,
that he could hardly confider
a profe tragedy as dramatic ;
that it was difficult for the

H   per-

performers to speak it; that, let it be either in the middling or in low life, it may, though in metre and spirited, be properly familiar and colloquial; that many in the middling rank are not without erudition; that they have the feelings and sensations of nature, and every emotion in consequence thereof, as well as the great; that even the lowest, when impassioned raise their language; and that the writing of prose is generally the plea and excuse of poverty of genius.

The London Prodigal. C. by Wm. Shakspeare, 4to. 1605. Upon this play Mr. Malone observes, that one knows not which most to admire, the impudence of the printer in affixing our great poet's name to a comedy publicly acted at his own theatre, of which it is very improbable that he should have written a single line, or Shakspeare's negligence of fame, in suffering such a piece to be imputed to him, without taking the least notice of it.

Look about You. Comedy. Anony. Acted by the Lord High Admiral's servants, 4to. 1600. This is a very diverting play.

A Looking-Glass for London and England. Tragi-Com. by Thomas Lodge and Robert Green, 4to. 1598.

Lord Blunder's Confession; or, *Guilt makes a Coward.* A Ballad Opera. Anonym. 8vo. 1733. This piece was never acted.

The Lord of the Manor. Comic Opera. Acted at Drury-Lane, 8vo. 1781. The author of this flimzy piece has kept himself concealed. It was, however, well set to music by Mr. Jackson, and met with some success.

Of the Lord's Supper, and Washing the Feet. A Comedy. This is one of the many religious dramas mentioned by bishop Bale as his own.

Lord Mayor's Day; or, *A Flight from Lapland.* A Pantomime, acted at Covent-Garden, 1782, and well received.

Lord Russel. Tragedy, by the Rev. Dr. Stratford. Acted at Drury-Lane, 1784, by a company of volunteers, and met with an indifferent reception.

Lord Russel. Trag. by Mr. Hayley. Acted at the Hay-market, 1784. This piece met with much approbation, and will probably continue to be an acting play.

Lorenzo. Trag. by Mr. Merry. Acted at Covent-Garden,

Garden, 1791, and very well received.

The Loſt Lady. Tragi-Com. by Sir W. Berkley, fol. 1639.

The Loſt Lover ; or, *The Jealous Huſband.* Com. by Mrs. De la Riviere Manley. Acted at the Theatre Royal, 4to. 1696. Though this piece did not fucceed on the ſtage, yet the dialogue of it is very genteel, and the incidents not unintereſting ; and, indeed, if we make proper allowances for the ſex of its author, the time it was written in, and its being a firſt eſſay in that arduous way of writing, it may very juſtly be confeſſed, that it deſerved a much better fate than it met with.

The Loſt Princeſs. Tra. by Murrough Boyle, Lord Viſ. Bleſſington, 8vo. without date, but belongs to the writings of the preſent century.

The Lots. Com. tranſlated from Plautus, by R. Warner, vol. V. 8vo. 1774.

The Lottery. Com. 8vo. 1728. This play was acted at the New Theatre in the Haymarket.

The Lottery. A Ballad Farce, by Henry Fielding, 8vo. 1731. This is a lively and entertaining piece, was acted at Drury-Lane with confiderable fuccefs, and ſtill remains on the liſt

of acting farces, efpecially near the time of drawing the ſtate lotteries, when the ſcene of the wheels, &c. in Guildhall gives great pleaſure to the nightly reſidents of the upper regions of the theatre.

Love-à-la-Mode. Com. Anonym. 4to. 1663. This play, which was acted at Middleſex-houſe with great applaufe, is ſaid in the title-page to have been written by a perſon of honour.

Love-à-la-Mode. F. by C. Macklin, 1760. This farce has never been wholly printed, but was brought on at the Theatre Royal in Drury-Lane, where after ſome ſtruggles between two parties, the one prejudiced for, the other againſt its author, it at length made its footing good, and had a very great run, to the conſiderable emolument of the writer, who, not being paid as an actor, referved to himſelf a portion in the profits of every night it was acted. The piece does not want merit with refpect to character and fatire, yet has the writer's national partiality carried him into ſo devious a path from the manners of the drama, as among four lovers who are addreſſing a young lady of very great fortune, viz. an Iriſh officer, a Scots baronet, a Jew broker,

broker, and an Englifh
country· 'fquire, to have
made the firft of them the
only one who is totally dif-
interefted with refpect to
the pecuniary advantages
apparent from the match.
A character fo different
from what experience has
in general fixed on the gentlemen of that kingdom,
who make their addreffes to
our Englifh ladies of fortune, that although there
are undoubtedly many
among the Irifh gentlemen,
poffeffed of minds capable
of great honour and gene-
rofity, yet this exclufive
compliment to them, in oppofition to received opinion,
feems to convey a degree of
partiality, which every dramatic writer at leaft fhould
be ftudioufly careful to
avoid. The Scotchman,
and the Englifh gentleman
jockey are, however, ad-
mirably drawn; but the
thought of the cataftrophe
is borrowed from Theophi-
lus Cibber's comedy of *The
Lover*; and the character
of the *Irifhman* bears too
much refemblance to She-
ridan's *Capt. O'Blunder*,
to entitle its being looked
on as an entire original.

Love and Ambition. Tr.
by Ja. Darcy, 8vo. 1732.
This play was brought on
the ftage in Dublin, and
met with fome fuccefs.

Love and a Bottle. Com.
by Geo. Farquhar. Acted
at Drury-Lane, 4to. 1699.
This is a very fprightly and
entertaining play; yet on
account of the loofenefs of
the character of *Roebuck*
(which, however, is perhaps
the beft drawn rake we have
ever had on the ftage), and
fome other ftrokes of licentioufnefs that run through
the piece, it has not been
acted for many years paft.
The part of *Mockmode* feems
to be borrowed from the
Bourgeois Gentilhomme of
Moliere.

Love and Duty; or, *The
Diftrefs'd Bride.* Trag. by
John Sturmy, 8vo. 1722.
Performed at the Theatre
Royal, in Lincoln's-Inn-
Fields.

Love and Duty. Trag.
by John Slade, 8vo. 1756.
It was acted one night at the
Haymarket by the author
and his friends.

Love and Folly. Serenata
in three interludes, fet to
mufic by Mr. Galliard.
Acted at the King's Theatre
in the Haymarket, 4to.
1739.

Love and Friendfhip; or,
The Rival Paffions. As it
was acted before the three
mock kings, Phyz, Trunk,
and Ufh, 8vo. 1723. Printed at the end of a pamphlet,
intituled, " To Diabolou-
menon, or, The proceedings
at

L O

L O.

at the Theatre Royal, in Drury-Lane."

Love and Friendſhip. Serenata, ſet to muſic by Mr. W. Defeſch, 4to. 1734.

Love and Friendſhip ; or, *The Lucky Diſcovery.* Com. 8vo. 1754. Never acted.

Love and Glory. Maſq. by T. Philips, gent. ſet to muſic by T. Arne, and acted at Drury-Lane, 8vo. 1734.

Love and Honour. Tragi-Com. By Sir Wm. Davenant. Acted at the Black-Fryars, 4to. 1649. This play met with very good ſucceſs.

Love and Honour. Dram. Poem, by Theodore de la Mayne, 12mo. 1742. This piece was not intended for public repreſentation, nor is even rendered in many particulars conformable to the rules of the Theatre. The deſign of the author is to reduce all the circumſtances of the Æneid, which have a reference to the loves of Dido and Æneas, into the limits of a drama ſomewhat more extenſive than a common tragedy. His piece opens with the landing of Æneas, and the cataſtrophe cloſes with his departure and the death of Dido. In a word, he has formed it into a tragedy, though ſomewhat irregular, under the modeſt title of a Dramatic Poem only.

H 3

Love and Innocence. Paſtoral Serenata, performed at Marybone, 8vo. 1769.

Love and Liberty. Trag. by Charles Johnſon, 4to. 1709. This play was intended for the Theatre Royal in Drury-Lane, but was not acted.

Love and Revenge. Trag. by Elk. Settle. Acted at the Duke's Theatre, 4to. 1675. This play is in great meaſure borrowed from Heming's *Fatal Contract* ; the plot of which, as well as of this piece, is founded on the French chronicles of Mezeray, De Serres, &c.

Love and Revenge ; or, *The Vintner Outwitted.* Ballad Opera. Anonymous, 1729. This is little more than the *Match in Newgate* converted into an Opera, by the addition of ſongs. It was acted with ſucceſs at the Little Theatre in the Hay-Market.

Love and War. Tra. by Thomas Meriton. This is a very middling piece, and was never acted, but printed in 4to. 1658.

Love and Wine, being a ſequel to Love and Friendſhip, a Comedy, 8vo. 1754. By the author of *The Friendly Rivals.*

Love at a Loſs ; or, *Moſt Votes carry it.* Com. by Mrs. C. Trotter, afterwards Cockburne. Acted at Drury-Lane,

LO

Lane, 4to. 1701. This play was printed in so very incorrect and mutilated a manner, that the author wished to call in and suppress the edition. Many years after she reviewed this performance, and made great alterations in it, intending to bring it on the stage under the title of *The Honourable Deceivers* ; or, *All Right at the Last.*

Love at a Venture. Com. by Mrs. Centlivre, 4to. 1706. This play was acted by the Duke of Grafton's servants, at the New Theatre at Bath.

Love at First Sight. C. by David Crawford, 4to. 1704. This play was acted at the Theatre in Little Lincoln's-Inn-Fields, but was not published till the above year, though written four years before.

Love at first Sight ; or, *The Wit of a Woman.* Ballad Opera, of two acts, by Joseph Yarrow, 8vo. 1742. This little piece was never acted any where but in the York company of comedians, in which the author was a performer at the time of its publication.

Love at First Sight. Ballad Farce, by Tho. King. Acted at Drury-Lane, 8vo. 1765.

Love Betray'd ; or, *The Agreeable Disappointment.*

LO

Com. by Mr. Burnaby, 4to. 1703. Acted at Lincoln's-Inn-Fields. The author confesses, that he borrowed part of his plot, and about fifty lines of this comedy, from Shakspeare's play of *Twelfth Night.*

Love crowns the End. A Pastoral, by John Tatham, 12mo. 1640. This was acted by, and, we suppose, written for the scholars of Bingham, in Nottinghamshire, in the year 1632.

Love Dragoon'd. Farce, by Mr. Motteux. Supposed to have been written about the year 1700.

Love for Love. Comedy, by W. Congreve, 4to. 1695. This play is so extremely well known, and so frequently acted with the approbation it justly merits, that it would be unnecessary to say much of it. This comedy (as Dr. Johnson observes) is of nearer alliance to life, and exhibits more real manners, than either the *Old Batchelor* or the *Double Dealer.*

Love for Money ; or, *The Boarding-School.* Com. by Thomas Durfey. Acted at Theatre Royal, 4to. 1691. This play met with some opposition in the first day's representation ; but, getting the better of that, stood its ground, and had tolerable success.

fuccefs. The plot in general is original, yet the piece
on the whole is very far
from a good one.

*Love freed from Ignorance
and Folly.* A Mafque of
her Majefty's, by Ben Jonfon.

Love in a Cheft. See
Force of Friendſhip.

Love in a Foreſt. Com.
by Charles Johnfon, 8vo.
1732. Acted at Drury-
Lane Theatre. The plot
and part of the language of
this play is from Shakfpeare's
As You Like It.

Love in a Hurry. Com.
by Anth. Afton. Acted at
Smock-alley, Dublin. Chetwood fays it was acted with
no fuccefs, and dates it in
1709.

Love in Difguife. Opera,
by Henry Lucas. Acted at
Dublin, about the year 1776,
but probably never printed.

Love in a Maze. Com.
Acted at the King's Theatre
about 1672. Not printed.

Love in a Miſt. A Farce,
by John Cunningham. Act-
ed at Dublin, 12mo. 1 47.

Love in a Puddle. Com.
Anonymous, and without
date, but fince 1700.

Love in a Riddle. A Paftoral, by C. Cibber. Act-
ed at Drury-Lane, 8vo.
1729. This was the firft
piece written in imitation of
The Beggar's Opera, and
came out in the fucceeding

year. It met, however, with
a moft fevere and undeferv-
ed reception, there being a
general difturbance throughout the whole firft reprefentation, excepting while Mifs
Raftor (the late Mrs. Clive)
was finging ; and on the fecond night the riot was ftill
greater, notwithftanding the
late Frederic Prince of
Wales was prefent, and that
for the firft time after his
arrival in thefe kingdoms,
nor would it have been ap-
peafed, had not Mr. Cibber
himfelf come forward, and
affured the audience that if
they would fuffer the performance to go on quietly
for that night, out of refpect
to the royal prefence, he
would not infift on the piece
being acted any more, al-
though the enfuing night
fhould in right have been his
benefit. Which promife he
faithfully kept. Some time
afterwards, the farce of *Damon* and *Phillida,* taken entirely from this play, was
brought on the ftage as a
novelty, and not being
known to be Cibber's, it
was very favourably received, and has ever fince continued to be acted with
great applaufe.

Love in a Suck. Farce,
by Benjamin Griffin, 12mo.
1715. Acted at Lincoln's-
Inn-Fields.

Love in a Veil. Com. by
Richard

Richard Savage. Acted at Drury-Lane, 8vo. 1719. It met with no success.

Love in a Village. Comic Opera, by Isaac Bickerstaffe. Acted at Covent-Garden, 8vo. 1763. This performance, though compiled from other musical pieces, met with so much favour from the town, that it was acted the first season almost as many times as the *Beggar's Opera* had formerly been, and nearly with as much success.

Love in a Wood ; or, *St. James's Park.* Com. by W. Wycherley. Acted at the Theatre Royal, 4to. 1762. This play has been but seldom acted since its first run, and indeed, although there are good things in it, it is not equal to the author of the *Country Wife* and *Plain Dealer.*

Love in a Wood ; or, *The Country 'Squire.* Farce, by Giles Jacob, 12mo. 1714. This piece was never acted, and was composed by the author in three or four days, and at a time when he was wholly unacquainted with the stage or dramatic writings.

Love in its Extasy ; or, *The Large Prerogative.* Dra. Pastoral, by Peaps, 4to. 1649. This piece was composed by the author when a student at Eton, being then only seventeen years of age,

but was never acted, and not printed till many years after.

Love in Several Masques. Com. by H. Fielding, 8vo. 1727. Acted at the Theatre Royal, in Drury-Lane. This play immediately succeeded *The Provok'd Husband*, which continued to be acted 28 nights with great and just applause.

Love in the City. Comic Opera, by Isaac Bickerstaffe. Acted at Covent-Garden, 8vo. 1767. Whether this Opera was disliked on account of its supposed insufficiency in dramatic and musical merit, or whether it was condemned by a party of Cheapside wits, who thought themselves reflected on by its title, &c. we are unable to determine.

Love in the East ; or, *Adventures of Twelve Hours.* Comic Opera, by Mr. Cobb. Acted at Drury-Lane, 1788. It has some merit, and was well received.

Love in the Dark ; or, *The Man of Business.* Com. by Sir Fra. Fane. Acted at the Theatre Royal, 4to. 1675. This is a busy and entertaining comedy, yet is the plot borrowed from various novels.

Love will find out the Way. Comic Opera, by Thomas Hull. Acted at Covent-

Covent-Garden, in 1777. The fongs only printed. An indifferent piece.

Love in a Camp ; or, *Patrick in Pruffia*. A Farce, by Mr. O'Keeffe. Acted at Covent-Garden, 1786, and very well received.

Love with Honour ; or, *The Privateer*. Farce, Anonymous. Never acted. Printed at Ipfwich, 8vo. 1753.

" *The Love of King David and fair Bethfabe. With the Tragedie of Abfalon*. As it hath been divers times plaied on the ftage." Written by George Beale, 4to. 1599.

Love the Leveller ; or, *The Petty Purchafe*, by G. B. Gent. 4to. 1704. It is neither tragedy nor comedy ; the plot, if it deferves that title, is full of the moft unnatural incidents, the characters the moft unmeaning, and the language the moft trifling, bald, and infipid, that was ever met with. The fcene lies in Crete, and it is faid to have been acted at the Theatre Royal in Drury-Lane.

Love makes a Man ; or, *The Fop's Fortune*. Com. by C. Cibber, 4to. 1698. Acted at Drury-Lane with great fuccefs, and continues ftill to give equal pleafure whenever it makes its appearance. The plot

of it is taken partly from Beaumont and Fletcher's *Cuftom of the Country*, and partly from the *Elder Brother* of the fame authors. There are numberlefs abfurdities and even impoffibilities in the conduct of the piece, yet the fprightlinefs in the character of *Clodio*, the manly tendernefs and opennefs of *Carlos*, and the entertaining tellinefs of Don *Choleric*, form fo pleafing a mixture of comic humour as would atone for even greater faults than are to be found in this drama.

The Love Match. Farce, Anonym. 1762. This little piece made its appearance at Covent-Garden Theatre, but without fuccefs. It was indeed greatly deficient in fome of the dramatic requifites, yet the language was far from being bad, and there were fome of the characters not ill drawn, more particularly that of *Lady Bellair*, which in all probability might of itfelf have protected the piece, and even procured it a run, had it not unluckily made its appearance immediately after that of a much more finifhed character of the fame kin, viz. that of *Sophia* in the *Mufical Lady*. It expired after the fecond night's reprefentation.

Love Reftor'd, in a Mafq. at

at Court, acted by gentlemen the King's servants, by
Ben Jonson, fol. 1640.

Love and War. Mufical
Farce, altered from Jeph-
fon's Campaign. Acted at
Covent-Garden, 1787, and
received with applaufe.

The Lover. Com. by T.
Cibber, 8vo. 1730. Acted
at the Theatre in Drury-
Lane with no great fuccefs,
yet is far from being a bad
play.

The Lover his own Rival.
Ballad Opera, by Abraham
Langford. Acted at Good-
man's-Fields, 8vo. 1736.

Lovers Luck. Com. by
Thomas Dilke, 4to. 1696.
This was acted at Little
Lincoln's-Inn-Fields with
general applaufe, though
moft of the characters are
but copies.

The Lover's Melancholy.
Tragi-Com. by John Ford.
Acted at Black-Fryars and
the Globe, 4to. 1629.

The Lover's Opera. F.
by W. R. Chetwood, 8vo.
1730. This piece was per-
formed at the Theatre in
Drury-Lane, and met with
fome fuccefs.

The Lover's Progrefs. Tr.
Com. by Beaumont and
Fletcher, fol. 1647. The
plot of this play is founded
on a French romance, cal-
led *Lifander and Califta,*
written by M. Daudiguier;

and the fcene is laid in
France.

Love's Adventures. Com.
in two parts, by the Duchefs
of Newcaftle, fol. 1662.

Love's Artifice; or, *The
Perplex'd 'Squire.* Farce of
two acts, by John Wignell,
8vo. 1762. This was in-
tended for the compiler's
benefit at York, but never
performed.

Love's a Jeft. Com. by
P. Motteux, 4to. 1696.
This piece was acted with
fuccefs at the Theatre in
Little Lincoln's-Inn-fields.
In the two fcenes in which
love is made a jeft, the author has introduced many
paffages from the Italian
writers.

*Love's the Lottery, and a
Woman a Prize.* Com. by
Jof. Harris. Acted at Lincoln's - Inn - Fields, 4to.
1699. To this piece is annexed a mafque, intituled
Love and Riches reconcil'd,
which was performed with
it at the fame theatre.

Love's Contrivance; or,
Le Medecin malgre lui. C.
by Mrs. Centlivre. Acted
at Drury-Lane, 8vo. 1703.
This is almoft a tranflation
of Moliere's comedy of the
laft of thefe two titles.

Love's Cruelty. Trag. by
James Shirley. Acted at
Drury-Lane, 4to. 1640.

Love's Cure; or, *The Mar-
tial*

tial Maid. Com. by Beaumont and Fletcher, fol. 1647.

Love's Dominion. A Dramatic Piece, by Richard Flecknoe, 8vo. 1654.

The Love-fick Court; or, *The Ambitious Politic.* Com. by Richard Brome, 8vo. 1658. Of this play a diftich in the title fhews us, that the author himfelf had a very modeft and humble opinion.

The Love-fick King. An Englifh Tragical Hiftory, *with the Life and Death of Cartefmunda, the fair Nun of Winchefter,* by A. Brewer, 4to. 1655. The hiftorical part of the plot is founded on the invafion of the Danes in the reigns of King Ethelred and Alfred.

Love's Kingdom. A Paftoral Tragi-Com. by Rich. Flecknoe, 12mo. 1664. Not as it was acted at the Theatre near Lincoln's-Inn-Fields, but as it was written and fince corrected ; with a fhort treatife on the Englifh Stage, &c. It was brought on the ftage, but had the misfortune to mifcarry in the reprefentation.

Love Labour's Loft. Com. by W. Shakfpeare. Acted at the Black-Fryars and the Globe, 4to 1.9.. This is one of thofe pieces, which confift of fuch a mixture of irregularities and beauti.,

fuch a chequerwork of faults and perfections, as have occafioned fome to fufpect it not to be the work of this author. Dr. Johnfon fays, that " in this play, which all the editors have concurred to cenfure, and fome have rejected as unworthy of our poet, it muft be confeffed that there are many paffages mean, childifh, and vulgar, and fome which ought not to have been exhibited, as we are told they were, to a maiden queen. But there are fcattered through the whole many fparks of genius ; nor is there any play that has more evident marks of the hand of Shakfpeare."

Love's Labyrinth ; or, *The Royal Shepherdefs.* Tragi-Comic, by Thomas Forde, 8vo. 1660. It is uncertain whether this play was ever acted or not.

Love's laft Shift ; or, *The Fool in Fafhion.* Com. by C. Cibber. Acted at the Theatre Royal, 4to. 1696. As it was the fi.ft attempt this gentleman made as an author, fo was the performance of the part of Sir Novelty Fafhion in it the means of eftablifhing his reputation as an actor, in both which lights he for many years afterwards continued a glittering ornament to the Englifh ftage. The plot of it

is

is original; yet is there some degree of improbability in *Loveless*'s not knowing his own wife after a very few years abfence from her; however, this little fault is made ample amends for by the beauty of the incident, and the admirable moral deduced from it. The author, in his apology for his life, p. 173, has given a very entertaining account of the difficulties and difcouragements he met with in getting his piece acted, the prejudices he had to overcome, and the fuccefs it met with, which laft fully anfwered his expectations.

Love's Metamorphofes. by John Lyly, 4to. 1601. Firft played by the children of Paul's, and now by the children of the chapel. Entered on the books of the Stationer's Company Nov. 25, 1600.

Love's Metamorphofes. Farce, by Thomas Vaughan, Efq. Acted at Drury-Lane, April 15, 1776, for Mrs. Wrighten's benefit. Not printed.

Love's Miftrefs ; or, *The Queen's Mafque.* By T. Heywood, 4to. 1636. This play was three times prefented before both their Majefties, within the fpace of eight days, in the prefence of feveral foreign Ambaffa-

dors, befides being publicly acted at the Phœnix in Drury-Lane.

The Loves of Emilius and Louifa. Tragedy, by John Maxwell, being blind, 8vo. 1755. Printed by fubfcription at York for the benefit of the author.

Loves of Ergafto. A Paftoral, reprefented at the opening of the Queen's Theatre in the Haymarket. Compofed by Sig. Giacomo Greber, 4to. 1705.

The Loves of Mars and Venus. A Play fet to mufic by P. Motteux. Acted at Little Lincoln's-Inn-fields, in three acts, 4to. 1697.

The Loves of Mars and Venus. Dramatic Entertainment of Dancing, attempted in imitation of the Pantomimes of the ancient Greeks and Romans, by John Weaver. Acted at Drury-Lane, 8vo. 1717.

Love's Pilgrimage. Com. by Beaumont and Fletcher, fol. 1647. The foundation of this play is built on a novel of Cervantes, called *The Two Damfels.*

Love's Revenge. Dram. Paftoral. By Doctor John Hoadley, 8vo. 1745. The fubject is a revenge vowed by *Cupid* for fome flight received from *Pyfche*, which he puts in execution by exciting a fit of jealoufy between two lovers, whom he afterwards

afterwards, however, on a return of *Pfyche's* kindnefs, reconciles to each other.

Love's Riddle. A Paftoral Comedy, by Abraham Cowley, 12mo. 1638. The plot of this play, as well as of all our author's dramatic pieces, is entirely original. and unborrowed; and though perhaps it is not to be looked on as a firft rate performance, yet, when it is confidered that it was written while the author was a king's fcholar at Weftminfterfchool, candour may be allowed not only to let it pafs uncenfured, but even to beftow fome fhare of commendation on it.

Love's Sacrifice. Trag. by John Ford. Afted at the Phœnix, Drury-Lane, 4to. 1633. This play was generally well received.

Love's Triumph ; or, *The Royal Union.* Trag. by E. Cooke, 4to. 1678. This play is written in heroic verfe. The plot is from the celebrated Romance of *Caffandra.* It never appeared on the ftage.

Love's Triumph. Opera, by P. Motteux. Afted at the Haymarket, 4to. 1708.

Love's Triumph through Callipolis. Performed in a Mafque at Court, 1630, by his Majefty King Charles I. with the lords and gentlemen affifting. The words

of this piece were by Ben Jonfon, the decorations of the fcene by Inigo Jones.

Love's Victim ; or, *The Queen of Wales.* Trag. by Charles Gildon, 4to 1701. Afted at the Theatre in Lincoln's-Inn-Fields, but without our fuccefs.

Love's Victory. TragiCom. by William Chamberlaine, 4to. 1658. This play was written during the troubles of the civil wars, and intended by the author to have been afted, had not the powers then in being fuppreffed the ftage, on which account he was obliged to content himfelf with only printing it.

Love's Welcome, by Ben Jonfon, fol. 1641. This is farther intituled, The King and Queen's Entertainment at Bollover, at the earl of Newcaftle's, the 30th of July, 1634.

Love the beft Phyfician. Com. by Ozell. The literal tranflation of Moliere's *L'Amour Medecin ;* no intended for the ftage.

Love the Caufe and Cure of Grief. Tragedy, of three afts, by Thomas Cooke, 8vo. 1744. Afted at Drury-Lane Theatre, but juftly damned.

Love Triumphant ; or, *Nature will Prevail.* Tra. Com. by J. Dryden. Afted at the Theatre Royal, 4to.

4to. 1694. This piece is the laft Dryden wrote for the ftage; and although it did not meet with the fuccefs that moft of his plays had been indulged with, yet it muft be acknowledged, that in feveral parts of it the genius of that great man breaks forth, efpecially in the difcovery of *Alphonfo's* victorious love, and in the very laft fcene, the cataftrophe of which is extremely affecting, notwithftanding that it is brought about contrary to the rules of Ariftotle, by a change of will in *Veramond.* The plot of it appears to be founded on the ftory of Fletcher's *King and no King;* at leaft on the corrections of the fable of that play, made by Rymer in his reflections on the tragedies of the laft age. Thus, as Dr Johnfon obferves, Dryden began and ended his dramatic labours with ill fuccefs.

Love Triumphant; or, *The Rival Goddeffes.* A Paftoral Opera, by D. Bellamy, fen. Acted by the young ladies of Mrs. Bellamy's Boarding-School, fecond edition, 12mo. 1722.

Love will find out the Way. Comedy, by T. B. 4to. 1661. This is Shirley's *Conftant Maid,* with a new title.

Love without Intereft; or,

The Man too hard for the Mafter. Com. 4to. 1699. It met with very little fuccefs on its appearance at the Theatre Royal.

The Loving Enemies. C. by L. Maidwell. Acted at the Duke of York's Theatre, 4to. 1680.

Low Life above Stairs. F. Anonymous, 8vo. 1759. This was never acted, nor intended for the ftage, but only a wretched catch-penny for felling a pennyworth of blotted paper for a fhilling, encouraged by the great fuccefs of *High Life Below Stairs.*

The Loyal Brother; or, *The Perfian Prince.* Trag. by Thomas Southern, 4to. 1682. This was our author's firft play.

The Loyal General. Trag. by N. Tate, 4to. 1680. Acted at the Duke's Theatre.

The Loyal Lovers. Tra. Com. by Cofmo Manucne, 4to. 1652. The author in this play has feverely lafhed the old committee-men and their informers.

The Loyal Shepherds; or, *The Ruftic Heroine.* Dram. Paftoral, by T. Goodwin, 8vo. 1779.

The Loyal Subject. Tra. Com. by Beaumont and Fletcher, fol. 1679. The fcene lies at Mofcow; and fome parts of the plot and characters

characters are ingenious and well supported, yet on the whole we cannot esteem it as one of the best pieces of these authors.

Lucinda. Dramatic Entertainment of three acts, by Richard Johnson. Printed at the end of Letters from *Lothario* to *Penelope,* two volumes, 12mo. 1769.

Lucius, the first Christian King of Britain. Trag. by Mrs. Manley. Acted at Drury-Lane, 4to. 1717. This play is founded on the legendary accounts of this monarch given by the Monkish writers, improved with a considerable share of agreeable fiction of her own. It met with good success.

Lucius Junius Brutus, Father of his Country. Tr. by Nathaniel Lee. Acted at the Duke's Theatre, 4to. 1681. This is a very fine play, being full of manly spirit, force, and vigour, with less of the bombast than frequently runs through this author's works. The plot of it is partly from the real histories of *Florus, Livy, Dionyf. Halic.* &c. and partly from the fictions in the Romance of *Clelia.*

Lucius Junius Brutus. T. by Mr. Duncombe. Acted at Drury-Lane, 8vo. 1735. 12mo. 1747. This play is built upon Voltaire's *Tragedy of Brutus.*

Lucius Junius Brutus ; or, *The Expulsion of the Tarquins.* Historical Play, by Hugh Downham, M. D. 8vo. 1779. This play was never acted, but possesses great merit.

The Lucky Chance ; or, *An Alderman's Bargain,* by Mrs. Behn. Acted by their Majesties servants, 4to. 1687. This play was greatly exclaimed against by the critics of that time, whose objections the author has endeavoured to obviate in her preface. The crime laid to her charge was indecency and an intrigue bordering, both in action and language, on obscenity. From this she has vindicated herself, if retorting the accusation on others, and proving herself only guilty in a lesser degree than others had been before her, may be esteemed a vindication. But, in short, the best excuse that can be made for her, is the fashionable licentiousness of the time she wrote in, when the barefaced intrigue of a court and nation of gallantry rendered those things apparently chaste and decent, which would at this time be hissed off the stage as obscene and immoral. As to the plot, it is for the most part original, excepting only the incident of *Gayman's* enjoying

L U [160] L Y

ing Lady *Fullbank*, and taking her for the devil, which
is copied from *Kickſhaw* and
Aretina in the *Lady of Pleaſure*, by Shirley. The ſcene
London.

The Lucky Diſcovery; or,
The Tanner of York. A Ballad Opera, by J. Arthur.
Acted at Covent-Garden,
8vo. 1738.

The Lucky Eſcape. Mu-
ſical Farce, by Mrs. Ro-
binſon. Acted at Drury-
Lane, 1778, for the benefit
of the authoreſs.

Ludis Filiorum Iſraelis.
Repreſented by the Guild of
Corpus Chriſti, at Cam-
bridge, on that feſtival, in
the year 1355.

Luminalia; or, *The Feſtival of Light*, 4to. 1627.
Preſented in a maſque at
Court, by the Queen's Ma-
jeſty and her ladies, on
Shrove-Tueſday night, 4to.
1637.

Lun's Ghoſt; or, *The New
Year's Gift*. A Pantomime,
acted at Drury-Lane, 1782.
It was not given to the public as entirely new, but as a
compoſition of the moſt admired ſcenes in other Pantomimes.

The Lunatick. Comedy,
Dedicated to the Three Ruling B—s, at the new houſe
in Lincoln's Inn-Fields,
4to. 1705.

Lupone; or, *The Inquiſi-*

tor. By W. Gordon, 8vo.
1731.

Luſt's Dominions; or, *The
Laſcivious Queen*. Tra. by
Chriſtopher Marloe, 12mo.
1657, 12mo. 1661. This
is very far from being a bad
play in itſelf; but afterwards altered by Mrs. Behn,
and acted under the title of
Abdelazar; or, *The Moor's
Revenge*.

An Enterlude called *Luſty
Juventus*, lyvely deſcribing
the Frailtie of Youth: of
Nature prone to Vyce: by
Grace and good Councell
traynable to Vertue, 4to.
b. l. 1561.

The Lyar. Com. of three
acts, by Samuel Foote,
1762. Printed 8vo. 1764.
This piece was originally
intended to have been re-
preſented during the ſummer
partnerſhip between Mr.
Murphy and the author,
but the run of thoſe pieces
they had before brought on
having exhauſted the time
limited for their repreſentation, this was obliged to be
deferred till the enſuing
winter, when it was repreſented for the firſt time at
the Theatre in Covent-Garden. Its ſucceſs was but
very indifferent; and indeed
it muſt be confeſſed, that it
was in itſelf far from equal
to the generality of this
gentleman's works. As to
the

the plot, it is almoſt entirely borrowed from Sir Richard Steele's *Lying Lover*; which was itſelf founded on the *Menteur* of Corneille, which was moreover little more than a tranſlation from a dramatic piece written by Lopez de Vega. It is not much to be wondered, therefore, if the diſh, thus ſerved up at a fourth hand, did not retain the whole of its original reliſh. And though there were here and there ſome ſtrokes of humour, which were not unworthy of their author, and ſome few touches of temporary ſatire, yet the character of the *Lyar* had certainly neither native originality enough in it to pleaſe as a novelty, nor additional beauties enough, either in his dreſs or demeanour, to excite a freſh attention to him as a new acquaintance. And what ſeemed ſtill more extraordinary, the author, who himſelf performed the part, and therefore one would imagine might have had an eye to his own peculiar excellencies in the writing it, had not even aimed, as he has almoſt uſually done, at affording himſelf any opportunity in it for exerting thoſe amazing talents of mimickry which he has ever been remarkable for, and ſo inimitable in. In

ſhort, on the whole, it was rather tedious and unentertaining, having neither enough of the *Vis comica* to keep up the attention of an audience through ſo many acts as a farce, nor a ſufficiency of incident and ſentiment to engage their hearts, if conſidered under the denomination of a comedy. It has ſince been often acted as a Farce.

The Lyar. Com. in three acts, 8vo. 1763. A catchpenny intended to be impoſed on the public for Mr. Foote's play of the ſame name.

Lycidas. Muſical Entertainment, performed at Covent-Garden, 8vo. 1767. The words altered from Milton, and intended as a dirge on the Duke of York's death. It was acted only one night.

The Lying Lovers; or, *The Ladies' Friendſhip*. Comedy, by Sir Richard Steele. Acted at Drury-Lane, 4to. 1704. As this author borrowed part of all his plots from other authors, it is not at all to be wondered at if we find that to be the caſe with this piece among the reſt. It is not by any means equal to any one of his other plays.

The Lying Valet. Com. in two acts, by David Garrick, 8vo. 1740. This little piece

piece made its firſt appearance at the Theatre in Goodman's-Fields ; but the author ſoon quitting that place for the Theatre Royal in Drury-Lane, brought his Farce with him, which was there aɔed with great and deſerved applauſe. Some of the nibblers in criticiſm have charged this piece as being borrowed from ſome French comedy ; but as we have never yet heard the title of the ſuppoſed original mentioned, we cannot avoid, as far as to the extent of our own knowledge, acquitting the author from this accuſation. A charge, however, which, wherever laid, we are ever apt to ſuſpeɔt as rather the effeɔt of envy, than of a love of juſtice or the public, as it has ever been the practice of the very beſt writers in all ages and nations, to make uſe of valuable hints in the works of their neighbours, for the uſe and advantage of thoſe of their countrymen, to whom thoſe works may not be ſo familiar as to themſelves. No man in his ſenſes would, we think, quarrel with a fine *noſegay*, becauſe ſome of the moſt beautiful flowers in it happened to have been gathered in a neighbouring country ; nor is the world much leſs obliged to the perſon who favours it with a good tranſlation of a good author, than to that author himſelf, or one of equal excellence at home. This little dramatic work under conſideration, which, whether original, tranſlation, or copy, has undoubtedly great merit, if charaɔter, plot, incident, and a rank of diɔtion well adapted to thoſe charaɔters, can give it a juſt title to the praiſe we have beſtowed on it. Nor can there be ſtronger evidence borne to i's deſerts, than that approbation which conſtantly attended on it through the numerous repetitions of it at both our Theatres.

M A

THE *Macaroni.* Com. by Mr. Hitchcock, performed at York, 8vo. 1773. It was once aɔted at the Haymarket.

Macbeth. Trag. by W. Shakſpeare, fol. 1623. This play is extremely irregular, every one of the rules of the Drama being entirely and repeatedly broken in upon. Yet, notwithſtanding, it contains an infinity of beauties, both with reſpeɔt to language, charaɔter, paſſion, and incident. The incantations of of the witches are equal, if not superior, to the *Canadia* of Horace. The use this author has made of *Banquo's* ghost towards the heightening the already heated imagination of *Macbeth*, is inimitably fine. Lady *Macbeth*, discovering her own crimes in her sleep, is perfectly original and and admirably conducted. *Macbeth's* soliloquies, both before and after the murder, are master pieces of unmatchable writing; while his readiness of being deluded at first by the witches, and his desperation on the discovery of the fatal ambiguity and loss of all hope from supernatural predictions, produce a catastrophe truly just, and formed with the utmost judgment. In a word, notwithstanding all its irregularities, it is certainly one of the best pieces of the very best master in this kind of writing that the world ever produced. The plot is founded on the Scottish History. " This play, says Dr. Johnson, is deservedly celebrated for the propriety of its fictions, and solemnity, grandeur, and variety of its action, but it has no nice discriminations of character ; the events are too great to admit the influence of particular dispositions, and the course of the

action necessarily determines the conduct of the agents. The danger of ambition is well described ; and I know not whether it may not be said, in defence of some parts which now seem improbable, that in Shakspeare's time it was necessary to warn credulity against vain and illusive predictions. The passions are directed to their true end. Lady *Macbeth* is merely detested ; and though the courage of *Macbeth* preserves some esteem, yet every reader rejoices at his fall.''

Macbeth. T. with all the alterations, amendments, additions, and new songs. Acted at the Duke's Theatre, 4to. 1674. This alteration was made by Sir Wm. Davenant.

Macbeth, the Historical Tragedy of, (written originally by Shakspeare). Newly adapted to the stage with alterations, by J. Lee, as performed at the Theatre in Edinburgh, 8vo. 1753. Language is not strong enough to express our contempt of Mr. Lee's performance. If sense, spirit, and versification, were ever discoverable in Shakspeare's play, so sure has our reformer laid them all in ruins.

Madam Fickle ; or, *The Witty False One*. Com. by Thomas Durfey. Acted at the

the Duke's Theatre, 4to. 1677. This author in regard both of plot and character, was certainly one of the greatest plagiaries that ever exilted.

The Mad Captain. Op. by Robert Drury. Acted at Goodman's - Fields, 8vo. 1733.

The Mad Couple well Match'd. Comedy, by R. Brome, 8vo. 1653. This play met with good fucceſs, and was revived with fome very trivial alterations by Mrs. Behn, under the title of *The Debauchee*; or, *The Credulous Cackold*.

The Mad-Houfe. A Rehearfal of a new Ballad Opera burlefqued, called *The Mad-Houfe*, after the manner of Pafquin, by R. Baker. Acted at Lincoln's-Inn-Fields, 8vo. 1737.

The Mad Lover. Tragi-Com. by Beaumont and Fletcher, fol. 1647. This play is particularly commended by Sir Afton Cockain, in his copy of verfes on Fletcher's plays.

Madrigal and Trulletta. A Mock Tragedy, 8vo. 1758. This piece was written by Mr. Reed. It was performed at the Theatre in Covent-Garden one night only, under the direction of T. Cibber.

A Mad World my Mafters. Com. by Thomas Middle-

ton. Acted by the children of Paul's, 4to. 1608. This is a very good play, and has been fince borrowed from by many writers.

The Magic Cavern. A Pantomime, acted at Covent-Garden, 1784.

The Magic Girdle. Burletta, by George Savile Carey. Acted at Marybone-Gardens, 4to. 1770.

The Magic Picture. A Com. altered from Maſſinger. Acted at Covent-Garden, 1783, and but indifferently received.

The Magician of the Mountain. Pantomine. Acted at Drury-Lane, 1763.

The Magnetic Lady; or, *Humours Reconcil'd.* Com. by Ben Jonfon, fol. 1640. This play is in general efteemed a very good one, yet did not efcape the cenſure of fome critics of that time.

The Magnificent Lovers. Com. by Ozell. This is only a tranflation, intended for the clofet alone, of *Les Amans Magnifiques* of Moliere.

Mahomet, the Impoſtor. Trag. by J. Miller. Acted at Drury-Lane, 8vo. 1744. This is little more than a good tranflation of *The Mahomet* of Voltaire, whofe writings indeed breathe fuch a fpirit of liberty, and have contracted fuch a refemblance to the

manners

manners of the Englifh authors, that they feem better
adapted to fucceed on the
Englifh ftage without much
alteration, than thofe of any
other foreign writer. This
play met with tolerable fuccefs, its merits having fair
play from the ignorance of
the prejudiced part of the
audience with regard to its
author, who unfortunately
did not furvive to reap any
advantage from it, for being unable to put the finifh-
ing hand to it, he received
fome affiftance in the com-
pleting of it from Dr. John
Hoadly. The author died
during its run. This play,
in the year 1753, was the
innocent caufe of a confiderable revolution in the dramatic world, in another
kingdom, viz. that of Ireland, and which finally terminated in the entire abdication of a theatrical monarch, although he had with
great labour and affiduity
brought his domain into a
more flourifhing ftate than
any of his predeceffors
had done : for through
the too great warmth of
party-zeal in a confiderable
part of the audience, which
infifted on a repetition of
certain paffages in this play,
and alfo a too peremptory
manner of. oppofing that
zeal on the fide of Mr. Sheridan, then manager of the
Theatre Royal in Smock-

alley, Dublin, a difturbance
enfued, in confequence of
which Mr. Sheridan was
obliged to quit firft the houfe
for the fecurity of his perfon,
and afterwards the king-
dom, for the fupport of his
fortune.

A Maidenhead well Loft.
Com. by Tho. Heywood,
4to. 1634.

The Maid of Bath. Com.
by Samuel Foote, Efq. Acted at the Haymarket in
1771. Printed in 8vo. 1778.
A tranfaction which happened at Bath, in which a perfon of fortune was faid to
have treated a young lady
celebrated for her mufical
talents in a very cenfurable
manner, afforded the ground
work of this extremely en-
taining performance. The
delinquent is here held up
to ridicule under the name
of Flint, and it will be difficult to point out a character drawn with more truth
and accuracy than the prefent, efpecially in the fecond
act.

The Maid of Honour. Tr.
Com. by Phil. Maffinger.
Acted at the Phœnix,
Drury-Lane, 4to. 1632.
This play met with great
applaufe.

The Maid of Kent. Com.
by Mr. Waldron, 8vo.
1778. This was originally
acted at Drury-Lane, 1773,
for the author's benefit.

The

The Maid in the Mill. C. by Beaumont and Fletcher, fol. 1647. This is a very excellent play, and was one of thofe which after the Reftoration were revived at the Duke of York's Theatre.

The Maid of Honour. C. altered from Maffinger, by Mr. Kemble. Aĉted at Drury-Lane, 1785. An indifferent performance.

The Maid of the Mill. C. Opera, by Ifaac Bickerftaffe. Aĉted at Covent-Garden, 8vo, 1765. This is taken from Richardfon's novel of *Pamela,* and was performed with great fuccefs.

The Maid of the Oaks. Dramatic Entertainment, by John Burgoyne, Efq. Aĉted at Drury-Lane, 8vo. 1774. The ftyle of this performance is lefs offenfively affeĉted than that of certain proclamations, which induced the Americans to ftyle our author *the Chrononhotonthologos of War.* The *Maid of the Oaks,* in fhort, is a piece that confers no honour, and brings no difgrace on its parent. A few bold touches from Mr. Garrick's pen are fuppofed to have fent it with additional force on the ftage. As the works of a patriot, a patriot manager may revive it ; but perhaps few audiences will thank him for his zeal, or (to ufe Burgoynian phrafe) applaud his fcale of talent in the direĉtion of a theatre, and declare that he confults the public inclination *to a charm.*

The Maid's laft Prayer; or, *Any rather than Fail.* Com. by Tho. Southerne. Aĉted at the Theatre Royal, 4to. 1693.

The Maid's Metamorphofes. Com. by John Lyly, 4to. 1600. This play was frequently aĉted by the children of Paul's, and is one of thofe pieces in which the author has attempted to refine the Englifh language.

The Maid's Revenge. T. by James Shirley. Aĉted at Drury-Lane, 4to. 1630. This is faid to be the fecond play Shirley wrote.

The Maid's Tragedy. By Beaumont and Fletcher. Aĉted at the Black-Fryars, 4to. 1622. This play is an exceeding good one, and ever met with univerfal approbation.

The Maid's Tragedy. By Edm. Waller. See the preceding article. In this play the cataftrophe is rendered fortunate.

The Maid the Miftrefs. A Burletta, altered by Mr. O'Keeffe, from the Italian of La Serva Padrona. Aĉted at Covent-Garden, 1783.

Majefty mifled; or, *The Overthrow of Evil Minifters.*

M A

fters. Tragedy, 8vo. 1734. The title-page fays it was intended to be acted at one of the theatres, but was refufed for certain reafons.

Make a Noife Tom. F. 8vo. 1713 This piece feems to be both local and temporary.

The Mal-Content. Tra. Comic, by John Marfton. Acted by the King's fervants, 4to. 1604.

The Male Coquette; or, *Seventeen Hund ed Fifty-Seven*. Farce, by David Garrick, Efq. Acted at Drury-Lane, 8vo. 1758. This little piece was planned, written, and acted, in lefs than a month. It firft appeared at Mr. Woodward's benefit, and is intended to expofe a kind of character no lefs frequent about this town than either the *Flafhes* or *Fribbles*, but much more pernicious than both, and which the author had diftinguifhed by the title of *Daffodils*; a fpecies of men who, without hearts capable of fenfibility, or even manhood enough to relifh, or wifh for enjoyment with the fex, yet, from a defire of being confidered as gallants, make court to every woman indifcriminately; whofe reputation is certain to be ruined from the inftant thefe infects have been obferved to fettle

M A

near her, their fole aim being to obtain the credit of an amour, without ever once reflecting on the fatal confequences that may attend thereon in the deftruction of private peace and domeftic happinefs. This character, although a very common one, feems to be new to the ftage, and is, in the importance to the world of rendering it deteftable to fociety, undoubtedly worthy of an able pen. The author of this farce has taken as broad fteps towards this point as the extent of fo fmall a work would give fcope for, yet his cataftrophe is fomewhat unnatural, and his hero's difgrace not rendered public enough to anfwer the end entirely. As to the fecond title of it, there feems no apparent reafon for the annexing it, unlefs it is to afford occafion for a humourous prologue written and fpoken by Mr. Garrick, the author of this piece.

The Mall; or, *The Modifh Lovers*. Com. by J. D. Acted at the Theatre Royal, 4to. 1674.

Malcolm. Tra. by Mifs Roberts, 8vo. 1779. This tragedy was never acted.

Mamamouchi; or, *The Citizen turn'd Gentleman*. By Edward Ravenfcroft, 4to. 1675. This play is wholly borrowed,

borrowed, and that even without the leaft acknowledgment of theft, from the *Monf. Pourceaugnac* and the *Bourgeois Gentilhomme* of Moliere, 4to. 1672, and was acted at the Duke's Theatre.

Mangora, King of the Timbufians. Trag. by Sir Thomas Moore, 4to. 1718. This play was brought on the ftage at the Theatre in Lincoln's-Inn-Fields, but was very defervedly damned.

The Man Hater, Com. by Ozell. This is only a tranflation from the *Mifanthrope* of Moliere.

The Man Hater. Com. tranflated from the French, and printed in Foote's *Comic Theatre*, vol. V.

The Manager in Diftrefs. Prelude, by G. Colman. Acted at the Haymarket, 8vo. 1780.

Manlius Capitolinus. T. by Ozell, 12mo. 1715. This is a tranflation in blank verfe from the French of Monf. de la Foffe. Probably never intended for the Englifh ftage, but was acted for threefcore nights running, at the time that the earl of Portland was Ambaffador at the French Court.

Man and Wife ; or, *The Shakfpeare Jubilee.* Com. by George Colman. Acted at Covent-Garden, 8vo. 1770. This fhort piece was compofed for the purpofe of introducing a proceffion of Shakfpeare's characters, before Mr. Garrick's *Jubilee* could be prepared for reprefentation at Drury-Lane.

The Man of Bufinefs. C. by George Colman. Acted at Covent-Garden, 8vo. 1774. This performance was acted with moderate fuccefs.

The Man of Family. A Sentimental Comedy, by C. Jenner, 8vo. 1771. Dedicated to Mr. Garrick, and taken from Diderot's *Pere de Famille.*

The Man of Honour. C. by Francis Linch. At what time this play was written or publifhed is not exactly known, but probably it muft have been about 1730, or between that time and 1740.

The Man of the Mill. Burlefque Tragic Op. 8vo. 1765. A parody on *The Maid of the Mill.*

The Man of Mode ; or, *Sir Fopling Flutter.* Com. by George Etheredge. Acted at the Duke's Theatre, 4to. 1676, 4to. 1684. This is an admirable play ; the characters in it are ftrongly marked, the plot agreeably conducted, and the dialogue truly polite and elegant.

The Man of Newmarket. Com.

M A

Com. by Edward Howard. Acted at the Theatre-Royal, 4to. 1678.

The Man of Quality. F. by Mr. Lee. Acted at Drury-Lane, 8vo. 1776. A poor alteration of Vanbrugh's *Relapse.*

The Man of Reason. C. by Hugh Kelly. Performed at Covent-Garden, 1776. This was acted only one night, and is not printed.

The Man of Tafte. Com. by J. Miller, 8vo. 1731. This play was acted at Drury-Lane with considerable success. The plot of it is borrowed partly from the *Ecole des Maris,* and partly from the *Precieufes Ridicules* of Moliere.

The Man of Tafte. Farce, Anonym. 1752. This piece was performed at Drury-Lane, but is nothing more than the foregoing piece cut into a farce by throwing out that part of the plot which is taken from the *Ecole des Maris,* and retaining only that which is borrowed from the *Precieufes Ridicules.*

The Man's Bewitched; or, *The Devil to do about Her.* Com. by Mrs. Centlivre. Acted at the Haymarket, 4to. 1712. This is by no means one of the best, nor is it the worst, of this lady's dramatic pieces. The language is extremely indifferent, and has a very

M A

great deficiency both of wit and fentiment; but the plot is agreeably intricate and bufy.

The Man's the Mafter. Com. by Sir W. Davenant, 4to. 1669. This is the laft play this author wrote, being finifhed not long before his death, which happened in 1668. The plot of it is borrowed from two plays of M. Scarron, viz. *Jodelet;* or, *Le Maitre Valet,* and the *Heritier Ridicule.*

The Man of the World. A Comedy, by Charles Macklin. Acted at Covent-Garden, 1781. Not printed. This play, in refpect to originality, force of mind, and well adapted fatire, may difpute the palm with any dramatic piece that has appeared within the compafs of half a century.

The Man Milliner. Farce, by Mr. O'Keeffe. Acted at Covent-Garden, 1787. Withdrawn on the firft night's performance.

Marcella. Tra. by Mr. Hayley. Acted at Drury-Lane, 1789, and met with a very unfavourable reception.

Marcellia; or, *The Treacherous Friend.* Tragi-Com. by Mrs. Frances Boothby. Acted at the Theatre Royal, 4to. 1670.

The Marches Day. Dram.

I   Enter

•Entertainment, of three acts, 8vo. 1771.

Marciano ; or, *The Disco-very*. Edinburgh, 4to 1663. This piece, it is said in the title-page, was acted with great applause before his majesty's high commissioner and others of the nobility, at the abbey of Holy-rud-House (at Edinburgh) on St. John's night, by a company of gentlemen.

Marcus Brutus. Tr. by John Sheffield, D. of Buckingham, 4to. 1722. To enrich this very poor play, two of the chorusses were furnished by Mr. Pope ; but they had the usual effect of ill-adjusted ornaments, only to make the meanness of the subject the more conspicuous.

Marcus Tullius Cicero, that famous Roman Orator, his Tragedy, 4to. 1651. It is uncertain whether this play was ever acted or not, but it is written in imitation of Ben Jonson's *Catiline*.

Margaret of Anjou. Historical Interlude, by Edw. Jerningham, Esq. Acted at Drury-Lane, 1777, for Miss Younge's benefit. Not printed.

Margery ; or, *A worse Plague than the Dragon*. A Burlesque Opera, by H. Carey, 8vo. 1739. This piece is a sequel or second part of *The Dragon of Want-*

ley, and was acted with great applause at Covent-Garden Theatre.

Mariam, the fair Queen of Jewry. Trag. by Lady E. Carew, 4to. 1613. This piece, it is probable, was never acted. It is written in alternate verse, and with a chorus.

Mariana. Comic Opera. Acted at Covent-Garden, 1788. The music, composed by Mr. Shield, probably saved this piece from destruction.

Mariamne. Tragedy, by Elijah Fenton. Acted at Lincoln's-Inn-Fields, 8vo. 1723. This play is built on the same story with the last-mentioned one. It was acted with great success, and was indeed the means of supporting and reconciling the town to a theatre, which for some time before had been almost totally neglected in favour of Drury-Lane house.

Mariamne. Trag. translated from Voltaire, and printed in Dr. Franklin's edition of that author.

Marina. A Play of three acts, by Mr. Lillo. Acted at Covent-Garden, 8vo. 1738.

Marplot ; or, *The Second Part of the Busy Body*. C. by Mrs. Centlivre. Acted at Drury-Lane, 4to. 1711. This play, like most second parts,

parts, falls greatly short of the merit of the first. At its original appearance, however, it met with considerable approbation.

Marplot in Lisbon. Com. 12mo. 1760. This is nothing more than Mrs. Centlivre's comedy of *Marplot*, or the second part of *The Busy Body*, which, with this title, and some few alterations in the body of the piece by Mr. Henry Woodward, joint manager with Mr. Barry of the Theatre Royal in Crow-street, Dublin, was represented at that theatre.

Marriage à-la-Mode. C. by J. Dryden. Acted at the Theatre Royal, 4to. 1673. Though this piece is called a Comedy in the title-page, yet it might, without any great impropriety, be considered as a Tragi-Comedy, as it consists of two different actions, the one serious and the other comic. The designs of both, however, appear to be borrowed.

Marriage à-la-Mode. F. 1760. This piece was never printed, but was acted in the winter of the abovementioned year for Mr. Yates's benefit at Drury-Lane.

The Marriage Broker; or, *The Pander.* Com. by M. W. 12mo. 1662.

The Marriage Contract. Com. of two acts, by Hen. Brooke, Esq. 8vo. 1778. Not acted.

The Marriage Hater Match'd. Com. by Tho. Durfey. Acted at the Theatre Royal, 4to. 1692. The admirable performance of a part in this play was what first occasioned the afterwards celebrated Mr. Dogget to be taken notice of as an actor of merit.

The Marriage Night. T. by H. Lord Vis. Falkland, 4to. 1664. This play contains a great share of wit and satire, yet it is uncertain whether it was ever acted or not.

The Marriage of Oceanus and Britannia. An Allegorical Fiction, by R. Flecknoe, 12mo. 1659.

The Marriage of Wit and Sciences. An Interlude. Anonymous, 1606.

The Married Beau; or, *The Curious Impertinent.* Com. by J. Crowne. Acted at the Theatre Royal, 4to. 1694. This play was esteemed a good one, and was frequently acted with general approbation. It has, however, been long laid aside. The story of it is taken from Don Quixote, and the scene lies in Covent-Garden.

The Married Coquet. C. by J. Baillie, 8vo. 1746. This

This play was never acted, nor even printed till after the author's death. It is no very contemptible piece, nor has it any extraordinary merit.

The Married Libertine. Com. by Charles Macklin, 1761. This play was brought on the stage at Covent-Garden Theatre, yet after its first run was no more performed, nor has yet appeared in print. A very strong opposition was made to it during every night of its run, which were no more than the nine necessary to entitle the author to his three benefits. Prejudice against the author seemed, however, to have been in a great measure the basis of this opposition, which, although in some measure overborne by a strong party of his countrymen, who were determined to support the play through its destined period, yet shewed itself very forcibly even to the last. We cannot, however, help thinking its fate somewhat hard; for although it must be confessed that there were many faults in the piece, yet it must also be acknowledged that there were several beauties; and we are apt to believe, that had the play made its first appearance on Drury-Lane stage, with the

advantages it might there have received from the acting, and had the author remained concealed till its fate had been determined, it might have met with as favourable a reception as some pieces which have past on the public uncensured.

The Married Man. Com. by Mrs. Inchbald. Acted at the Haymarket, 1789. Translated from the French.

Mary Queen of Scots. Historical Tragedy, by Mr. St. John. Acted at Drury-Lane, 1789. This piece was very well received.

Marie Magdalene. A Mystery, written in 1512. In this piece a Heathen is introduced celebrating the service of *Mahound*, who is called *Saracenorum Fortissimus*; in the midst of which he reads a lesson from the Alcoran, consisting of gibberish, much in the metre and manner of Skelton.

The Married Philosopher. Com. by John Kelly. Acted at Lincoln's-Inn-Fields, 8vo. 1732.

Marry or do Worse. Com. by W. Walker, 4to. 1704. This piece was acted at Lincoln's-Inn-Fields.

The Marshal of Luxembourg, upon his Death-Bed. Tragi-Com. Done out of French 12mo. 1635.

The Martyr'd Soldier. Trag. by Henry Shirley. Act'd

M A

Acted at Drury-Lane, 4to. 1638. This play met with great applaufe, but was not republifhed till after the author's death.

Mary Magdalen, her Life and Repentance. An Interlude, by Lewis Wager, 4to. 1567. The plot is taken, as it is faid in the prologue, from the feventh chapter of St. Luke. The piece is printed in the old black letter.

The Martyrdom of Ignatius. Tra. by John Gambold, 8vo. 1773. This tragedy was written in the year 1740, more than 30 years before it was publifhed.

A Mafque, prefented at Bretbie in Derbyfhire, on Twelfth-Night,1639,by Sir A. Cockain, 12mo. 1659. This piece is printed in the body of this author's poems.

A Mafque, a Defcription of, with the nuptial fongs at, the Lord Vif. Haddington's marriage at Court, on Shrove-Tuefday at night, 16c8, by Ben Jonfon, fol. 1640,

A Mafque prefented at the Houfe of Lord Haye, for the Entertainment of Le Baron de Tour, the French Ambaffador, on Saturjay, Feb. 22, 1617, by Ben Jonfon, fol. 1617-

A Mufque, prefented at Ludlow Caftle, 1634, on Michaelmaffe-night, before

M A

the right honourable John, Earl of Bridgewater, Vifc. Brackly, Lord Prefident of Wales, and one of his Majefty's moft honourable privie council, by John Milton, 4to. 1637.

A Mafque written at Lord Rochefter's requeft for his Tragedy of *Valentinian,* by N. Tate. This is printed in Mr. Tate's Mifcellanies, 8vo, 1685.

The Mafque of Augures, with the feveral Antimafques, prefented on Twelfth-night, 1621, by Ben Jonfon, 4to. 1621.

The Mafque of Flowers. Anonym. 4to. 1614. This mafque was prefented by the gentlemen of Gray's-Inn, at the Court at Whitehall, in the Banquetting-houfe, upon Twelfth-Night, 1613, and was the laft of the folemnities and magnificencies which were performed at the marriage of the Earl of Somerfet with the Lady Frances, daughter to the Earl of Suffolk.

A Mafque of Owls at Kenelworth, prefented by the ghoft of Captain Cox mounted on his hobbyhorfe, 1626, by Ben Jonfon, fol. 1640.

A Mafque in the Opera of the *Prophetefs,* by Tho. Betterton, printed with that piece.

A Mafque of the two honourable

I 3

nourable Houses, or Inns of
Court, the Middle Temple,
and Lincoln's-Inn, presented before the King at Whitehall on Shrove-Monday at
night, Feb. 15, 1613, by
George Chapman, 4to. no
date. This masque was
written and contrived for the
celebration of the nuptials
of the Count Palatine of
the Rhine with the Princefs
Elizabeth.

A Royal Masque of the
four Inns of Court, per-
formed about *Allhollandtide*,
1633. Anonym.

*The Masque of the Inner
Temple and Graye's-Inn,
Graye's-Inn and the Inner
Temple,* presented before his
Majestie, the Queene's Ma-
jeflie, the Prince Count Palatine and the Lady Elizabeth their Highneffes, in
the Banquetting Houfe at
Whitehall, on Saturday the
twentieth day of Februarie,
1612. By Fran. Beaumont,
4to. no date.

The Masquerade. Com.
by Charles Johnson, 8vo.
1723. Acted at the Thea-
tre Royal, Drury-Lane.

The Masquerade; or, *An
Evening's Intrigue.* A Far.
of two acts, by Benj. Griffin, 12mo. 1717. This was
performed at Lincoln's-Inn-
Fields with fome fuccefs.

Masquerade du Ciel. A
Masque, prefented to the
Great Queen of the Little
World.

The Massacre at Paris.
Trag. by Nat. Lee. Acted
at the Theatre Royal, 4to.
1690. The plot of this play
is founded on the bloody
maffacre of the Proteftants,
which was perpetrated at
Paris on St. Bartholomew's
day, 1572, in the reign of
Charles IX.

*The Massacre at Paris,
with the Death of the Duke
of Guife.* Tragedy, by C.
Marlow, 8vo. without date.
This play is upon the fame
ftory with the laft-mentioned one, but takes in a larger
fcope with refpect to time,
beginning with the unfor-
tunate marriage between
the king of Navarre and
Marguerite de Valois, fifter
to Charles IX. which was
the primary occafion of the
maffacre, and ending with
the death of Henry III. of
France. This play is not
divided into acts, yet it is
far from a bad one, and
might probably furnifh the
hint to Mr. Lee.

*The famous Hiftory of the
Rife and Fall of Maffaniello,*
in two parts, by Tho. Durfey, 4to. 1700. fecond part,
1699. This is on the fame
ftory as *The Rebellion of Naples,* and partly borrowed
from it.

*Mafter Tafte, the Poetical
Fop;* or, *The Modes of the
Court.* Com. by the author
of *Vanella,* 8vo. 1734.

Mafter

Master Anthony. Com. by the Earl of Orrery, 4to. 1690. Though this piece bears the above date, yet it appears to have been acted many years before, at the Duke's Theatre in Lincoln's-Inn-Fields, by having the names of Mr. Angel and Mrs. Long in the drama, who had at that time been dead some years.

Master Turbulent ; or, *The Melancholics.* Com. Anonymous, 4to. 1682.

A Match at Midnight. Com. by W. Rowley. Acted by the children of the Revels, 4to. 1633.

The Match-maker Fitted ; or, *The Fortune-hunters rightly served.* Com. 12mo. 1718. This play was intended for the stage, but not accepted by the performers. Nor, if it had, could it have stood a chance of favour with the public. The language, though far from being low or devoid of understanding, yet is heavy, declamatory, and unadapted to comedy ; and the characters shew the author to have made no very strict observations on those distinguishing features of the mind, which mark out the varieties of nature's oddities. Yet there is somewhat in the plot which is original, and capable of being extended on to advantage,

viz. the circumstance of the designing guardian of a woman of no fortune, who, having by the assistance of her own artifices, and the spreading a belief of her being possessed of a large estate, procured considerable sums by selling his consent by turns to several different fortune-hunters, and tricked them all into the just punishment of ridiculous and improper matches, is himself at last entrapped into marriage with the girl herself. Such a design, executed by an able hand, enlivened with justly drawn characters, and adorned with pleasing and dramatic dialogues, might produce a piece not undeserving the approbation of the public. It is dedicated to Mother Wilson, of Wildstreet, Countess of Drury, under the character of *Surly* her chaplain. This Mother Wilson appears to have been a bawd of repute at that time, and probably might have misused the author. Yet there seems to be but very little connection between those private occurrences, and the general design of the piece.

Match me in London. Tragi-Com. by Thomas Dekker. Presented first at the Bull, in St. John's-
                                                           street,

M A

ftreet, and afterwards at the private houfe, in Drury-Lane, called the Phœnix, 4to. 1631. This is efteemed a good play.

Matilda. Trag. by Dr. Thomas Franklin. Acted at Drury-Lane, 8vo. 1775. This is almoft a tranflation from Voltaire's *Duc de Foix.*

Matrimonial Trouble, in two parts, by the Duchefs of Newcaftle, fol. 1662. The firft of thefe is a Comedy, the fecond a Comi-Tragedy.

May Day. Com. by G. Chapman. Acted at Black-Fryars, 8vo. 1611.

May Day. Ballad Op. by David Garrick. Acted at Drury-Lane, 8vo. 1775.

The Mayor of Garratt. A Comedy, of two acts, by S. Foote. Performed at the Theatre in the Haymarket, 1763. Printed in 8vo. 1769. In this very humorous and entertaining piece the character of Major Sturgeon, a city-militia officer, is entirely new, highly wrought up, and was moft inimitably performed by Mr. Foote, with prodigious applaufe.

The Mayor of Quinborough. Com. by Thomas Middleton. Acted at Black-Fryars, 4to. 1661. This play was often performed with great applaufe.

M E

Msafure for Meafure. A Play, by William Shakfpeare, fol. 1623. This is a moft admirable play, as well with refpect to character and conduct, as to the language and fentiment, which are equal to any of this inimitable author's pieces. The play is ftill frequently performed, and always with affured approbation. Dr. Johnfon fays, " Of this play the light or comic part is very natural and pleafing, but the grave fcenes, if a few paffages be excepted, have more labour than elegance. The plot is rather intricate than artful. The time of the action is indefinite ; fome time, we know not how much, muft have elapfed between the recefs of the Duke and the imprifonment of Claudio ; for he muft have learned the ftory of Mariana in his difguife, or he delegated his power to a man already known to be corrupted. The unities of action and place are fufficiently preferved.

Meafure for Meafure ; or, *Beauty the beft Advocate.* Com. by Charles Gildon. Acted at Lincoln's-Inn-Fields, 4to. 1700. An alteration of Shakfpeare's *Meafure for Meafure.*

Medea. Tragedy, by Sir Edw. Sherburne, 8vo. 1648. This

This is only a tranſlation from Seneca, with annotations, but never intended for the ſtage. To it is annexed a tranſlation of Seneca's anſwer to Lucilius's query, Why good men ſuffer miſfortunes?

Medea. Tragedy, by J. Studley, 8vo. 1563. This is the ſame play as the foregoing, only tranſlated by a different hand, and with an alteration of the chorus to the firſt act.

Medea. Trag. by Chas. Johnſon. Acted at Drury-Lane, 8vo. 1731. The preface conſiſts almoſt entirely of complaints of the ill treatment this play met with from a ſet of gentlemen belonging to the Inns of Court, who came determined to condemn it unheard. There are alſo a few ſtrokes at Mr. Pope, who, in the *Dunciad*, had, it is ſaid without provocation, introduced the author into that ſatire. The part of *Medea* was performed by Mrs. Porter; *Jaſon*, by Mr. Wilks.

Medea. Trag. by Rich. Glover, 4to. 1761. This play was not written with a deſign for ſtage-repreſentation, being profeſſedly formed after the model of the ancients, each act terminating with a chorus. The author has indeed ſhewn a

good deal of erudition and a perfect acquaintance with the ancient claſſics. Some parts of his language are poetical, the ſentimental paſſages forcible, and the *Ordo Verborum*, though ſomewhat ſtiff, yet not pedantic or turgid. Nevertheleſs, there is a languid coldneſs that runs through the piece, and robs it of the great eſſence of tragedy, pathetic power. The whole is declamatory, and the author ſeems to have kept the *Medea* of Seneca very conſtantly before his eyes; and it muſt be apparent to every one of but ordinary judgment, that long declamations, pompous invocations of ghoſts, and powers of witchcraft, and choruſſes compoſed in the uncouth meaſure of iambic, dithyrambic, &c. are by no means adapted to the faſhion of the Engliſh ſtage. If it ſhould be urged, that theſe kind of pieces are not written for the Theatre, but for the cloſet, we cannot think even that excuſe obviates the objection, or clears an author who writes in this manner from the charge of affectation of ſingularity, and more than it would avail a man who ſhould dreſs himſelf in the ſhort cloak, trunk-hoſe, &c. of king James the Firſt's times.

times, and though he paid and received vifits in this habit, fhould plead, by way of apology, that he did not chufe to dance in it at an affembly, or go to court on a birth-day. And, indeed, we can perceive no jufter reafon for our cloathing our language, than for the decorating our perfons after the fafhions made ufe of two thoufand years ago. Tafte is periodical and changeable, and though it may not always be abfolutely right, it is very feldom totally wrong; and confequently a compliance with it, in a moderate degree, will ever be lefs blameable than an oppofition to it, which has not fome very peculiar advantages of convenience or pleafure to urge in its excufe. It has been often performed at Drury-Lane and Covent-Garden, for Mrs. Yates's benefit.

Medea. Trag. tranflated from Euripides, by R. Potter, 4to. 1781.

The Meeting of the Company; or, Bayes's Art of Acing. Prelude, by David Garrick, Efq. Acted at Drury-Lane, at the opening of the Theatre in 1774. Not printed.

Melicerta. An heroic Paftoral, by Ozell. This is only a tranflation from a

piece of the fame name by Moliere.

Melite. Com. tranflated from Corneille, 12mo. 1776

Menæchmi. Com. by W. W. 4to. 1595. This is only a loofe tranflation from Plautus. From this play the plot of the *Comedy of Errors* is borrowed.

The Mercantile Lovers. Dramatic Satire, by Geo. Wallis. Acted at York, 8vo. 1775.

The Merchant of Venice. Tragi-Com. by W. Shakfpeare, 4to. 1600. This is an admirable piece, and ftill continues on the lift of acting plays. The ftory is built on a real fact, which happened in fome part of Italy, with this difference indeed, that the intended cruelty was really on the fide of the Chriftian, the Jew being the unhappy delinquent who fell beneath his rigid and barbarous refentment. Popular prejudice however, vindicates our author in the alteration he has made; and the delightful manner in which he has availed himfelf of the general character of the Jews, the very quinteffence of which he has enriched his *Shylock* with, makes more than amends for his deviating from a matter of fact, which he was by no means obliged

obliged to adhere to. The decifion of *Portia's* fate by the choice of the cafkets affords a pleafing fufpence, and gives opportunity for a great many inimitable reflections. The trial fcene in the fourth act is amazingly conducted; the anxiety both of the characters themfelves, and of the audience, being kept up to the very laft moment ; nor can we clofe our mention of that fcene without taking notice of the fpeech, put into *Portia's* mouth, in praife of mercy, which is perhaps the fineft piece of oratory on the fubject (though very fully treated on by many other writers) that has ever appeared in our or any other language. The fcene lies partly at Venice, partly at Belmont, the feat of *Portia* on the Continent. For the alterations which lord Landfdowne has made in this play, fee *Jew of Venice*. " Of the Merchant of Venice," fays Dr. Johnfon, " the ftyle is even and eafy; with few peculiarities of diction, or anomalies of conftruction. The comic part raifes laughter, and the ferious fixes expectation. The probability of either the one or the other ftory cannot be maintained. The union of two actions in one event is in this drama eminently

happy. Dryden was much pleafed with his own addrefs in connecting the two plots of his *Spanifh Fryer*, which yet we believe the critic will find excelled by his play."

The Merchant. Comedy, tranflated from Plautus, by G. Colman. Printed in Thornton's tranflation of that author.

Mercurius Britannicus; or, *The Englifh Intelligencer.* Tragi-Com. By R. Braithwaite. Acted at Paris with great applaufe, 4to. 1641. This piece is wholly political, the fubject of it being entirely on the fhip-money, which was one of the great points that occafioned the troubles of King Charles I. It confifts of only four fhort acts, and of the fifth is faid in the *Epilogue* as follows : " *It is determined by the Ædils, the Miftrefs of publicke Plays, that the next day (by Jove's Permiffion) the fifth Act fhall be acted upon Tyber, I fhould fay Tyburne, by a new Society of Abalamites. Vive le Roy.*" Before the firft act is prefixed this other title, viz. *The Cenfure of the Judges, or The Court Cure.*

Mercury Harlequin. Pantomime, by Henry Woodward, Acted at Drury-Lane, 1756.

Mercury vindicated from Alchymifts at Court, by gentlemen

tlemen the King's fervants, by Ben Jonſon, fol. 1640.

Merlin; or, The Britiſh Inchanter and King Arthur, the Britiſh Worthy. Dram. Opera. Acted at Goodman's-Fields, 8vo. 1736.

Merlin; or, The Devil of Stonehenge, by Lewis Theobald. Acted at Drury-Lane, 8vo. 1734.

Merope. Tragedy, by G. Jefferys. Acted at Lincoln's - Inn - Fields, 8vo. 1731. This is taken from the Italian play.

Merope. Tragedy, by A. Hill. Acted at Drury-Lane, 8vo. 1749. This play was, and ſtill continues to be, acted with great applauſe. It is chiefly borrowed from the Merope of Voltaire, yet has Mr. Hill, whoſe manner and ſtyle are very peculiar and original, made it entirely his own by his manner of tranſlating it. Some critics there are indeed, who have found fault with this gentleman as a turgid and bombaſt writer; to their opinions, however, we cannot ſubſcribe, for although it may be allowed, that a peculiar Ordo Verlorum, and a frequent uſe of compound epithets, which ſeem to be the true characteriſtics of Mr. Hill's writings, may give an apparent ſtiffneſs and obſcurity to a work, yet when once perfectly di-

geſted and properly delivered from the lips of oratory, they certainly add great force and weight to the ſentiment—nor can it ſurely be conſidered as paying this author any very exalted compliment, to rank the Tragedy of Merope as ſuperior to any one which has hitherto appeared ſince; nor can there, perhaps, be a ſtronger evidence in its favour, than the uſe which ſome of the later tragic writers have made of the deſign of this play, having more or leſs adopted the plot as the ground-work of their own pieces, as witneſs the Tragedies of Barbaroſſa, Creuſa, Douglas, &c. The ſtory of Merope is well known in hiſtory; and the ſcene lies at Mycene. Soon after the run of this piece the author died.

Merope. Trag. tranſlated from Voltaire, printed in Dr. Franklin's edition of that author.

Merope. Trag. by M. de Voltaire, tranſlated by Dr. John Theobald, 8vo. 1744. This is a mere tranſlation, and was never brought on the ſtage.

Merope. Trag. by Mr. Ayre. Italian and Engliſh, 8vo. 1740. This is only the literal tranſlation of an Italian Tragedy on the ſame ſubject.

ME

ME

fubject of the foregoing pieces.

The Merry Cobler. A farcial Opera of one act, by Charles Coffey, 1735. This is a fecond part of the *Devil to Pay* ; or, *The Wives Metamorphofed* ; but being in no degree equal to the firft, it was defervedly damned the firft night at the Theatre Royal, Drury-Lane.

The Merry Counterfeit ; or, *The Vifcount à-la-Mode.* Farce, taken from Mrs. Behn. Acted at Covent-Garden, 1762, for the benefit of Mr. Shuter. Not printed.

The Merry Devil of Edmonton. Com. Acted at the Globe. Anonymous, 4to. 1608. The plot is founded on the Hiftory of one Peter Fabal, of whom more particular mention is made in Fuller's *Church Hiftory*, and in the Chronicles of Henry VI.'s reign.

The Merry Mafqueraders; or, *The Humourous Cuckold.* Com. Anon. 8vo. 1732. Not acted.

The Merry Midnight Miftake ; or, *Comfortable Conclufion.* Com. by David Ogborne, 8vo. 1765. Mr. Ogborne dreamed, that he was intended for a comic writer ; and to fhew how little fuch nocturnal vifions are to be trufted, on his awaking, he fat down and

compofed this dramatic performances.

The Merry Miller ; or, *The Countryman's Ramble to London.* Farce, by Thomas Sadler, 8vo. 1766.

The Merry Wives of Windfor. Com. by Wm. Shakfpeare. Acted by the Lord Chamberlain's fervants,4to. 1602. This piece is allowed by the critics to be the mafter piece of our author's writings in the comic way, There is perhaps no comedy, in which fo extenfive a groupe of perfect and highly finifhed characters are fet forth in one view. In the delineation of *Juftice Shallow* he has gratified a very innocent revenge on a certain magiftrate, who, in his adolefcent years, had been unreafonably harfh upon him ; yet he has done it with fo inoffenfive a playfulnefs as bears ftrong teftimony to his own good-nature, having only rendered him laughable, without pointing at him any of the arrows of malevolent or poignant fature. Dryden allows this play to be exactly formed ; and as it was written before the time that Ben Jonfon had introduced the tafte for cold elaborate regularity, it plainly proves, that our immortal bard was by no means incapable of polifhing and regulating his plots to an equal

equal degree of exactnefs, had not his choice of hiſto-ſical plans very frequently compelled him, and the un-bridled ſtrength of his imagination as often induced him, to o'erleap the bounds of thoſe dramatic rules, which were firſt eſtabliſhed by writers who knew not what it was to write, to act, and to think, above all rule. The editions of 1602 and 1619 are of the firſt ſlight ſketch, which the author afterwards altered, enlarged, and improved. Dr. Johnſon ſays, "Of this play there is a tradition preſerved by Mr. Rowe, that it was written at the command of queen Elizabeth, who was ſo delighted with the character of Falſtaff, that ſhe wiſhed it to be diffuſed through more plays; but ſuſpecting that it might pall by continued uniformity, directed the poet to diverſify his manner, by ſhewing him in love. No taſk is harder than that of writing to the ideas of another. Shakſpeare knew what the queen, if the ſtory be true, ſeems not to have known, that by any real paſſion of tenderneſs, the ſelfiſh craft, the careleſs jollity, and the lazy luxury of Falſtaff, muſt have ſuffered ſo much abatement, that little of his former caſt would have remain-

ed. Falſtaff could not love, but by ceaſing to be Falſtaff. He could only counterfeit love; and his profeſſions could be prompted, not by the hope of pleaſure, but of money. Thus the poet approached as near as he could to the work enjoined him; yet, having perhaps in the former plays completed his own idea, ſeems not to have been able to give Falſtaff all his former power of entertainment. This comedy is remarkable for the variety and number of the perſonages, who exhibit more characters appropriated and diſcriminated than perhaps can be found in any other play. Whether Shakſpeare was the firſt that produced upon the Engliſh ſtage the effect of language diſtorted and depraved by provincial or foreign pronunciation, I cannot certainly decide. This mode of forming ridiculous characters can confer praiſe only on him, who originally diſcovered it, for it requires not much of either wit or judgment; its ſucceſs muſt be derived almoſt wholly from the player, but its power in a ſkilful mouth, even he that deſpiſes it, is unable to reſiſt. The conduct of this drama is deficient; the action begins and ends often before the concluſion, clufion, and the different parts might change places without inconvenience; but its general power, that power by which all works of genius fhall finally be tried, is fuch, that perhaps it never yet had reader or fpectator, who did not think it too foon at an end."

Meſſalina, The Roman Empreſs, her Tragedy, by N. Richards, 12mo. 1640. The plot of this play is from Suetonius, Pliny, Juvenal, and other authors, who have written on the vicious character of that infatiate woman.

The Metamorphoſes. A Comic Op. by Mr. Jackfon. Acted at Drury-Lane, 1783. Some parts of this piece were received with great applaufe.

The Metamorphoſes; or, *The Old Lover Outwitted.* Farce, by John Corey, 4to. 1704. It was acted at Theatre in Lincoln's-Inn-Fields.

The Metamorphoſes. Com. Opera, by Charles Dibdin. Acted at the Hay-market, 8vo. 1776.

The Metamorphos'd Gypſies. A Mafque, by Ben Jonfon, fol. 1641. This piece was thrice prefented before King James I.

The Methodiſt. Com. Being a continuation and completion of the plan of the *Minor*, written by Mr

Foote, 8vo. This piece was never acted, nor intended fo to be, and is no more than a moft impudent catchpenny job of Ifrael Pottinger, whom the great fuccefs of Mr. Foote's *Minor* had induced to write this fequel to it, which is contrived in fuch a manner from the arrangement of the title page, as to appear to the unwary purchafer the product of the fame author. But there is fomewhat worfe in this piece than even the impofition on the public, which is the grofs reflection thrown on the private character of the chief of the Methodifts, contrary to the intention of the author of the *Minor*. For although that gentleman has made a very juft and ingenious attack on enthufiafm itfelf, and expofed the fanction which the promoters of vice and venders of lewdnefs lay claim to under the mafk of religion, and the protection of fome miftaken and pernicious tenets, yet he has not endeavoured to caft fo fevere a cenfure on men of any holy profeffion, however mifled by blind zeal or enthufiaftic madnefs to inculcate and propagate thofe tenets, as to hint at their being themfelves either the abettors or encouragers of thofe pefts of fociety, who
screen

fcreen themfelves under their doctrine, or may pretend to enlift them'elves under their banners. This the prefent writer has done, who, by a continuation of the characters and plot of the *Minor*, has made Dr. Squintum and Mrs. Cole, that is to fay, an old bawd and a methodift preacher, coadjutors and joint inftruments in carrying on the purpofes of debauchery, and bringing to perfection all the infamous tranfactions of a common biothel: a charge which, if juft, would not only caft an *opprobrium* on a whole fect of teachers, which it is to be hoped not one among them could poffibly deferve, but alfo be a fevere reflection on the legiflature itfelf, for not having entered into a ftricter inquifition on a neft of vipers, which, lying clofely concealed under the fhadow of religion, are empoifoning and deftroying the very fountain of piety and virtue.

Michaelmas Terme. Com. by Thomas Middleton, 4to. 1607.

Microcofmus. A Moral Mafq. by T. Nabbes. Acted at Salifbury-Court, 4to. 1637.

Midas. An Englifh Burletta. Acted at Covent-Garden, 8vo. 1764. The burlefque in this humourous performance turning chiefly on heathen deities, ridiculous enough in themfelves, and too a' furd for burlefque, the aim of which is to turn *great* things to *farce*, the prefent mock-opera was not altogether fo fuccefsful at firft, as in many refpects it deferved to be.

Midnight Hour. Farce, by Mrs. Inchbald, tranflated from the French. Acted at Covent-Garden, 1787, and met with applaufe.

Midfummer Night's Dream. Com. by Wm. Shakfpeare. Acted by the Lord Chamberlain's fervants, 4to. 1600. This play is one of the wild and irregular over-flowings of this great author's creative imagination. It is now never acted under its original form, yet it contains an infinite number of beauties, and different portions of it have been made ufe of feparately in the formation of more pieces than one. Wild and fantaftical as this play is (fays Dr. Johnfon), all the parts in the various modes are well written, and give the kind of pleafure which the author defigned. Fairies in his time were much in fafhion; common tradition had made them familiar,

familiar, and Spenfer's Poem had made them great. *A Midfummer Night's Dream*, written by Shakfpeare, with alterations an additions, and feveral new fongs. As it is performed at the Theatre Royal, in Drury-Lane. By Mr. Colman, 8vo. 1763. This piece was acted only once, when the fpectators were uncommonly few, and therefore not in the beft humour. Refpect for Shakfpeare, however, kept them filent; but that filence likewife induced them to fympathize with Lyfander and Helena, Demetrius and Hermia, who in one fcene are all lying faft afleep on the ftage. After the reprefentation was over, Mr. Colman, who did not efcape the narcotic qualities of the dofe he had adminiftered, took away a third part of its ingredients, and prevailed on his patients to try the effects of it a fecond time. But in this contracted form it fucceeded lefs, infpiring drowfinefs without the benefit of repofe. We have reafon to think, however, that our theatrical phyfician had ftill further hopes of gaining fomewhat by his prefcription, having, if we are not deceived, compelled thofe under his regimen at the Haymarket to fwallow it once more, though

he could never contrive to make it a popular medicine.

The Milefian. Com. Op. by Mr. Jackfon. Acted at Drury-Lane, 8vo. 1776.

The Miniature Picture. Comedy, by Lady Craven. Acted at Drury-Lane, 1781. Not printed. This piece was firft performed in a private Theatre at Newberry. It was produced very late in the feafon at Drury-Lane, and acted only three or four nights.

The Minor. Comedy of three acts, by Samuel Foote, 8vo. 1760. This piece was firft prefented in the fummer feafon at the Little Theatre in the Haymarket, and though it was performed by an entirely young and unpractifed company, it brought full houfes for 38 nights in that time of the year, and continues ftill one of the ftock piece for the winter alfo. As the principal merit of all this gentleman's writings confifts in the drawing peculiar characters well known in real life, which he heightened by his own manner of perfonating tho originals on the ftage, it will be neceffary to inform pofterity, that in the characters of Mrs. Cole and Mr. Smirk, the author reprefented thofe of the celebrated Mother Douglas, and Mr. Langford, the auctioneer ;

MI

tioneer; and that in the conclufion, or rather epilogue to the piece fpoken by Shift (which the author performed, together with the other two characters), he took off to a great degree of exactnefs the manner and even perfon of that moft noted enthufiaftic preacher, and chief of the methodifts, Mr. George Whitfield. And indeed, fo happy was the fuccefs of this piece in one refpect, that it feemed more effectually to open our eyes (thof of the populace efpecially) in regard to the abfurdities of that pernicious fet of politic enthufiafts, than all the more ferious writings that had ever been publifhed againft them. Mr. Foote has been accufed of borrowing not only the hint, but even the whole of the character of Mrs. Cole, from another piece, which was at that time only in embrio. What juftice there is in this charge, however, we may perhaps canvafs farther in another part of this work, when we come to make mention of that piece. An additional Scene to the Comedy of *The Minor*, 8vo. 1761. In this Mr. Foote is pretty fmartly animadverted upon, for making it his practice to expofe the harmlefs peculiarities of private perfons upon the public ftage.

MI

Minorca. Trag. by H. Dell, 8vo. 1756. This piece was printed juft when the place from which it is named was taken. Nothing can be more contemptible than it is in every point of view.

Miracle Play of St. Katharine. By Geoffery, afterwards Abbot of St. Alban's, a Norman. The above play was, for aught that appears to the contrary, the firft fpectacle of this fort exhibited in thefe kingdoms; and, as M. L'Extant obferves, might have been the firft attempt towards the revival of dramatic entertainments in all Europe.

The Miraculous Cure; or, *The Citizen Outwitted.* F. Compiled by Brownlow Forde, 12mo. 1771.

The Mirror; or, *Harlequin Every where.* Pantomimical Burletta, by Cha. Dibdin. Acted at Covent-Garden, 8vo. 1780.

The Mirrour. Com. in three acts, by Henry Dell, 8vo. 1757 Never acted.

Mirza. Tra. by Robert Baron, 8vo. 1647. This tragedy is founded on real facts which happened not long before, and is illuftrated with hiftorical annotations. The ftory of it is the fame as that which Denham made the ground-work of his *Sophy*, and which

which may be found in Sir Thomas Herbert's Travels. It is a good play, but whether ever acted or not, is uncertain.

The Mifer. Com. by T. Shadwell, 4to. 1672. This play, by the author's own confeffion, is founded on the *Avare* of Moliere, which is itfelf alfo built on the *Aulularia* of Plautus. Shadwell, however, has by no means been a mere tranflator, but has added confiderably to his original.

The Mifer. Com. by H. Fielding, 8vo. 1732. This play was acted with great applaufe at the Theatre Royal in Drury-Lane, and is the piece which now continues to be performed annually.

The Mifer. Com. by J. Ozell, 12mo. 1732. This is nothing more than a literal tranflation of the celebrated French play of Moliere, from which all the above-mentionedpieces have been borrowed.

The Mifer of Moliere, tranflated by Michael de Boiffy, 12mo. 1752.

The Mifer. Com. tranflated from Plautus, by Bonnel Thornton, 8vo. 1767.

The Miferies of Inforced Marriage, by Geo. Wilkins, 4to. 1607. To this comedy Mrs. Behn is indebted for great part of the plot of the

Town Fop ; or, Sir Timothy Tawdry. She has, however, confiderably improved on this play, which is not divided into acts.

Mifs in her Teens ; or, *The Medley of Lovers.* Far. by David Garrick. Acted at Covent - Garden, 8vo. 1747. This farce met with great fuccefs, and indeed defervedly fo, being a laughable diverting piece. The characters of Flafh and Fribble may perhaps be confidered as fomewhat *outré*, and too much on the Caricature, but that has ever been allowed in farce, or what the French call Baffe Comedie, where probability is frequently facrificed to invention, and a ftrict adherence to nature, or humour, and ridicule. And, moreover, the inimitable performances of the author and Mr. Woodward in thefe characters feemed to overbear even the flighteft reflection of this kind that might arife, fince even in the reprefentation of what might itfelf exceed the bounds of nature, the enchanted audience could fcarcely perceive that they were not walking in her very ftraiteft and moft limited paths.

Mifs Lucy in Town. F. by Henry Fielding. Acted at Drury-Lane, 8vo. 1742. This piece, which is a fequel

or

or fecond part of The Virgin Unmafked, was prefented for fome nights, and met with applaufe. But it being hinted, that a particular man of quality was pointed at in one of the charaƈters, an application was made to the Lord Chamberlain, who fent an order to forbid it being performed any more.

The Miffion frem Rcme into Great-Britain in the Caufe of Popery and the Pretender. Scenically reprefented, 4to. No date, about 1746.

The Miftake. Com. by Sir John Vanburgh. Aƈted at the Haymarket, 4to. 1706. This is an admirable play, and always meets with applaufe. The quarrelling fcene between Carlos and Leonora is perhaps as highly touched as any we have in the whole lift of Englifh comedies.

The Miftakes; or, The Happy Refentment. Com. by the late Lord Cornbury, 8vo. 1758. The author of this piece was the learned, ingenious, and witty Lord Cornbury. It was, however, never aƈted, being a very juvenile performance, and unequal to the very deferved reputation his Lordfhip's abilities afterwards acquired.

Mifiaken Beauty; or, The Lyar. Com. Aƈted at the Theatre Royal, 4to. 1685.

Anonymous. This is little more than a tranflation of the Menteur of Corneille.

The Miftaken Hufband. C. by Dryden. Aƈted at the Theatre Royal, 4to. 1675. This play is on the model of Plautus's Menœchmi, and is extremely farcical. It is not, however, Mr. Dryden's, being only adopted by him, and enriched with one good fcene from his hand. The real author unknown.

The Miftakes; or, The Faife Report. Com. by J. Harris, 4to. 1690. This play was written by another perfon, but falling into this gentleman's hands, he made many alterations in it confiderably for the worfe.

Mithridates, King of Pontus. Trag. by Nath. Lee. Aƈted at the Theatre Royal, 4to. 1678.

The Mock Doƈtor; or, The Dumb Lady Cured. Ballad Farce, by Henry Fielding. Aƈted at Drury-Lane, 8vo. 1753. This petite Piece is taken wholly from the Madecin malgré lui of Moliere, excepting the fongs, which are not very numerous. Some other writers have made ufe of that comedy as the ground-work of their pieces, but, by attempting to enlarge on and improve it, have abfolutely fpoiled it. This author, however, whofe natural bent of genius had
the

the fame kind of turn with that of Moliere himfelf, has been contented with only giving a fprightly and happy tranflation of him, varying no mo more from his original with refpect to plot, incident, or conduct, than the different tafle of the two nations rendered abfolutely neceffary; by which means he has introduced the foreigner amongft us pofleffed of all his natural vivacity and humour, and with no other alteration than that which his Pofteffe would necef farily occafion, viz. the being dreffed in the full mode of the country he is vifiting. How far the author was right in the adoption of this method, the fuccefs of the piece fufficiently evinces; it having been received with univerfal approbation at its firft appearance, and continuing to this day one of the conftant ftanding deferts to our moft pleafing dramatic collations.

The Mock Duellift; or, *The French Valet*. Com. by P. B. 4to. 1675. This play was acted at the Theatre Royal with fome fuccefs, and is attributed to one Mr. Peter Belon.

The Mock Lawyer. Ballad Opera, by Ed. Phillips, 8vo. 1733. This was acted at Covent-Garden with fome fuccefs.

The Mock Marriage. C. by Thomas Scot. Acted at Dorfet-Gardens, 4to. 1696. This play was the firft attempt of a young author, in the dramatic way, and was performed in an indifferent part of the feafon; yet it met with confiderable approbation.

The Mock Preacher. A fatyric, comical, allegorical Farce. Acted to a crowded audience at Kennington-Common, and many other Theatres, with the humours of the mob, 8vo. 1739.

The Mock Philofopher. A new, pleafant, and diverting Comedy, reprefenting the humours of the age, by S. Harper, 12mo. 1737.

The Mock Tempeft; or, *The Enchanted Caftle*, by T. Duffet, 4to. 1676. This piece was acted at the Theatre Royal, and written purpofely in a burlefque ftyle. The defign of it was to draw away the audience from the other theatre, to which at that time there was a very great refort, drawn thither in confequence of the applaufe given to Dryden's alteration of The Tempeft, which was then in its full run: but it was intermixed with fo much fcurrility and ribaldry, that though it met with fome little fuccefs at firft, it prefently fell to the ground.

Mock

Mock Thyeftes. Farce, by J. Wright, 12mo. 1674.

Modern Antiques. Farce, by Mr. O'Keeffe. Acted at Covent-Garden, 1791, and well received.

A Modern Character. Introduced into Æfop as acted at the Haymarket, 8vo. 1751.

Modern Courtfhip. Com. in two acts, 8vo. 1768.

The Modern Hufband. C. by Henry Fielding, 8vo. 1734. This play was acted at the Theatre Royal in Drury-Lane with fome fuccefs, but never revived fince.

Modern Poetafters; or, *Directors no Conjurors.* A Farce, Anonymous, 1725, on the famous Ode Writers, Satyrifts, Panegyrifts, &c. of the prefent Times, and their Patrons, &c. It was never acted, and feems by its denomination to be only a piece of perfonal fatire and partial abufe, neither intedned nor fit for the ftage.

The Modern Prophets; or, *New Wit for an Hufband.* Com. by Thomas Durfey. Acted at Drury-Lane, 4to. 1707. This piece is an exceffive bad one, having no kind of merit but the expofing, with fome little humour, a fet of abfurd enthufiafts who made their appearance at that time under the title of The French Prophets.

The Modern Receipt; or, *A Cure for Love.* Com. altered from Shakfpeare, 12mo. 1739.

The Modern Wife; or, *The Virgin her own Rival.* Com. by J. Stevens, 8vo. 1744. This piece was, as the title-page informs us, acted gratis at the Theatre in the Haymarket, by a company of gentlemen for their diverfion.

The Modifh Couple. C. by Captain Bodens. 8vo. 1732. This play was acted at Drury-Lane without any great fuccefs.

The Modern Hufband. C. by Cha. Burnaby, 4to. 1702. This play was performed at Drury - Lane, and was damned.

The Modifh Wife. Com. by Francis Gentleman. Acted at the Haymarket, 8vo 1774.

The Mogul Tale. Farce. Acted at the Haymarket, 1784, and well received.

The Mohocks. A Tragi-Comical Farce, as it is acted (fays the title-page) near the Watch-houfe in Covent-Garden, 8vo. 1712. This piece was never acted. The fubject of it is an expofition of the behaviour of a fet of mifchievous young men, who were diftinguifhed by the title of Mohocks (as thofe of the prefent time are by that of Bucks and Bloods) and

and who ufed, on the pre-
fumption of their being protected by rank or fortune
from punifhment for their
errors, to miftreat every inoffenfive perfon whom they
met abroad, under the idea
of frolicks. Thefe perni-
cious beings have almoft almoft always fubfifted under
one title or other. The modern race, however, feem-
ing to have rather more of
the monkey than the bear in
them, confine themfelves to
lefs favage kinds of mifchief
than thofe hinted at here,
who ufed to ftop at no barbarity, cutting and maim-
ing innocent perfons with
their fwords, &c. and indeed
imitating the unpolifhed
nation whofe name they affumed.

Momus turn'd Fabulift ; or,
Vulcan's Wedding. Opera.
Anonym. 8vo. 1729. This
piece has a confiderable fhare
of merit. It was acted at
Lincoln's-Inn-Fields with
fuccefs.

Monarchical Image ; or,
Nebuchadnezzar's Dream.
Dramatical Poem, by Rob.
Fleming, 8vo. 1691.

Money is an Afs. Com.
Thomas Jordan, 4to. 1663.
This play was acted with
applaufe ; the part of Captain Pennilefs, the principal character in it, having
been performed by the au-
thor.

Money's the Miftrefs. C.
by T. Southerne, 8vo. 1725.
This author's comedies are
by no means equal to his
tragedies, nor is this even
the beft of the former. It
met with no approbation on
its appearance at Lincoln's-
Inn-Fields.

Monfieur de Pourceaugnac;
or, *Squire Trelooby.* Ano.
4to. 1704. This piece was
acted at the Subfcription
Mufic at the Theatre Royal
in Lincoln's - Inn - Fields,
March 20, 1704. by a fe-
lect company from both
houfes.

Monfieur D'Olive. Com.
by George Chapman, 4to.
1606. This play was
efteemed a good one, and
met with fuccefs.

Monfieur Thomas. Com.
by John Fletcher. Acted at
Black-Fryars, 4to. 1639.
In this comedy the author
was unaffifted by his friend
Beaumont (who probably
was dead before the writing
of it) or any other perfon ;
but it was not publifhed till
after his death, by Richard
Broome. It was afterwards
revived on the ftage by T.
Durfey, under the title of
Trick for Trick.

Montezuma. Trag. by
Henry Brooke, Efq. 8vo.
1778. Not acted.

The Monument in Arcadia.
A dramatic Poem, in two
acts, 4to. 1773, by George
Keate,

Keate, Efq. As no writer can be much injured by comparifon with himfelf, we fhall not hefitate to affirm, that the paftoral drama before us is by far the leaft valuable of Mr. Keate's productions.

More Diffemblers befides Women. Com. by Thomas Middleton, 8vo. 1657.

The Moral Quack. Dramatic Satire, by Dr. Bacon, 8vo. 1757.

The Morning Ramble ; or, *The Town Humours* Com. Anonym. 4to. 1673. This is a good play, and by Downes afcribed to Hevil Paine.

Mortimer's Fall. Trag. by Ben Jonfon. This piece is to be found among Jonfon's works, but is no more than a fragment, juft begun, and left imperfect by means of the author's death. What it would have been, however, may in fome meafure, be gathered from the arguments of each feveral act, which are publifhed to it for the reader's fatisfaction. The lofs of it is the more to be regretted, as it is the only plan this author had proceeded on for a dramatic piece, on any ftory from the hiftory of our own domeftic affairs.

Mother Bombie. Comedy, by John Lilly, M. A. 4to. 1594.

'*The Mother in Law* ; or, *The Doctor the Difeafe.* C. by James Miller, 8vo. 1734. This comedy was acted with very great fuccefs at the Theatre in Drury-Lane. The fcene of it is laid in London, and the plot is compounded of thofe two comedies of Moliere, viz. the *Monfieur Pource-augnac,* and the *Malade Imaginaire.*

Mother Shipton, her Life . Com. by Thomas Thomfon, 4to. N. D. This play, it is faid, was acted nineteen days fucceffively with great applaufe, yet what merit it has can by no means be called its own, all the characters, excepting thofe which relate to Mother Shipton, being ftolen from from Maffinger's City Madam, and Middleton's Chafte Maid in Cheapfide.

Mother Shipton. Pantomime. Acted at Covent-Garden, 4to. 1770.

The Mournful Nuptials ; or, *Love the Cure of all Woes.* Trag. by Thomas Cooke. 8vo. 1739. This was afterwards altered, and brought out at Drury-Lane, in 1744, under the title of Love the Caufe and Cure of Grief; or, The Innocent Murderer.

The Mourning Bride. T. by W. Congreve. Acted at Lincoln's - Inn - Fields, 4to.

4to. 1697. This is the only tragedy our author ever wrote, and met with more fuccefs than any of his other pieces, yet it is certainly greatly inferior to the very worft of them ; for although the ftory is a pleafing and affecting one, and well told, yet the language has fo much of the bombaft, and fo little of real nature in it, that it is fcarcely credible it could be the work of an author fo remarkable for the contrary, in the eafy flowing wit of his comedies. Dr. Johnfon however obferves, " that if he were to felect from the whole mafs of Englifh poetry the moft poetical paragraph, he knows not what he could prefer to an exclamation in this tragedy :

Almeria.
It was a fancy'd noife; for all is hufh'd.

Leonora.
It bore the accent of a human voice.

Almeria.
It was thy fear, or elfe fome tranfient wind
Whiftling through hollows of this vaulted ifle :
We'll liften ———

Leonora.
Hark !

Almeria.
No, all is hufh'd, and ftill as death.
——'Tis dreadful !
How reverend is the face of this tall pile ;
Whofe ancient pillars rear their marble heads,
To bear aloft its arch'd and ponderous roof,

By its own weight made ftedfaft and immoveable,
Looking tranquility ! It ftrikes an awe
And terror on my aching fight ; the tombs
And monumental caves of death look cold,
And fhoot a chilnefs to my trembling heart.
Give me thy hand, and let me hear thy voice ;
Nay, quickly fpeak to me, and let me hear
Thy voice—my own affrights me with its echoes."

He who reads thefe lines enjoys for a moment the powers of a poet ; he feels what he remembers to have felt before, but he feels it with great increafe of fenfibility; he recognizes a familiar image, but meets it again amplified and expanded, embellifhed with beauty, and enlarged with majefty."

Mucedorus, the King's Sonne of Valentia, and Amadine, the King's Daughter of Arragon. With the merry Conceits of the Moufe. 4to. 1615. This piece is, in fome of the old catalogues, faid to be Shakfpeare's.

Much Ado About Nothing. Com. by Wm. Shakfpeare. Acted by the Lord Chamberlain's fervants, 4to. 1600. This comedy, tho' not free from faults, has however numberlefs beauties in it, nor is there perhaps

K.   haps

haps in any play fo pleafing a match of wit and lively repartee as is fupported between Benedict and Beatrice in this; and the contrivance of making them fall in love with one another, who had both equally forfworn that paffion, is very pleafingly conducted. The fcene lies in Meffina, and that part of the plot which relates to Claudio and Hero, with the Baftard's fcheme of rendering the former jealous by the affiftance of Margaret the waiting-maid, and Borachio, is borrowed from the fifth book of Ariofto's Orlando Furiofo, in the ftory of Ariodant and Geneura. The like ftory is alfo related in Spenfer's Fairy Queen, book 2. canto 4. Mr. Steevens obferves, that "this play may be juftly faid to contain two of the moft fprightly characters that Shakfpeare ever drew. The wit, the humourift, the gentleman, and the foldier, are combined in Benedict. It is to be lamented, indeed, that the firft and moft fplendid of thefe diftinctions, is difgraced by unneceffary profanenefs; for the goodnefs of his heart is hardly fufficient to atone for the licence of his tongue. The too farcaftic levity, which flafhes out in the converfation of Beatrice, may be excufed on account of the fteadinefs of friendfhip fo apparent in her behaviour, when fhe urges her lover to rifque his life by a challenge to Claudio. In the conduct of the fable, however, there is an imperfection fimilar to that which Dr. Johnfon has pointed out in the Merry Wives of Windfor:—the fecond contrivance is lefs ingenious than the firft; or, to fpeak more plainly, the fame incident is become ftale by repetition. I wifh fome other method had been found to entrap Beatrice, than that very one which before had been fuccefsfully practifed on Benedict."

The Mulberry Garden. C. by Sir Charles Sedley. Acted at Drury-Lane, 4to. 1668. 4to. 1675. This was efteemed a very good comedy.

Muleaffes the Turk. Trag. by John Mafon, 4to. 1610. Whatever merit this play might really poffefs, the author himfelf had a moft exalted opinion of it. This tragedy has fome beautiful lines and fpeeches, which, however, are difgraced by intrufions of the loweft and moft obfcene comedy that has hitherto appeared on the ftage.

The Mufe of Newmarket. 4to. 1681. This is only an affemblage of three drolls acted

acted at Newmarket, and said to be all ftolen from other plays. The names of them are as follows : viz. 1. The Merry Milkmaids of Iflington ; or, The Rambling Gallants Defeated. 2. Love Loft in the Dark ; or, The Drunken Couple. 3. The Politic Whore; or. The Conceited Cuckold.

The Mufes Looking Glafs. Com. by Thomas Randolph, 4to. 1638. This is perhaps one of the moft eftimable and meritorious of all the old pieces extant. It contains an affemblage of characters whofe height of painting would do honour to the pen of Shakfpeare or Jonfon : the language is at the fame time natural and poetical, the fentiments ftrong, the fatire poignant, and the moral both abfolutely chafte and clearly confpicuous. In a word, there is nothing but the difference of the manners, and the want of intricacy in the plot, which could prevent its becoming one of the favourites of the prefent ftage.

The Mufe of Offian. A Dramatic Poem, of three acts. Extracted from the feveral poems of Offian, the fon of Fingal, by David Erfkine Baker. Performed at Edinburgh, 12mo. 1763.

The Mufes in Mourning. Opera, by A. Hill, 8vo.

1760. This little piece was never acted.

The Mufical Lady. Farce, by George Colman. Acted at Drury-Lane, 8vo. 1762. In the piece before us, Mr. Colman has attacked the ladies on the affectation of a paffion for mufic, and a tafte in compofition, without either feeling the one, or poffeffing the other, and thereby becoming dupes to fafhionable abfurdity, and an eafy prey to the interefted views of a fet of foreign fidlers and Italian impoftors, to the neglect of real and fuperior merit, becaufe Britifh, or at the beft imagining thofe qualifications the only title to encouragement, which never thrive perfectly but in a land of luxury and effeminacy, and ought by no means to be fet in competition with thofe manly virtues and generous qualities, which are the diftinguifhing characteriftics of our more hardy countrymen. In this attempt the author has fucceeded better than in his former ; his Sophia is a more finifhed character than his Polly Honeycombe, and the ufe made of her darling folly by Mr. Mafk, much more judicious and conducive to her reformation than the baffled defign of Mr. Scribble. The characters are all finely drawn ;

K 2

nor are thofe of Old Maſk and even the Laundreſs leſs delicately finiſhed, than the more important ones of Young Maſk and Sophy. The language is lively and ſenſible, and the plot, though ſimple, ſufficiently dramatic. In a word, we cannot avoid giving it as our opinion, that, notwithſtanding the ſucceſs of the Jealous Wife, the Muſical Lady ſtill ſtands foremoſt in the point of merit among all Mr. Colman's writings. Yet, though that merit might fully entitle it to the approbation it met with, it would ſcarcely be juſt to omit taking notice, that its ſucceſs was greatly contributed to by the admirable performance of perhaps the moſt promiſing young actreſs that has appeared on this ſtage for many years paſt, viz. Miſs Pope, who ſupported the character of Sophia with a ſprightlineſs tempered with judgment, and an elegance heightened by eaſe, that might have done honour to a performer of three times the experience in life that her years then afforded her an opportunity of acquiring.

Muſtapha, the Son of Solyman the Magnificent. T. by Roger, earl of Orrery, fol. 1672 and 1690. It is eſteemed a good play, and was acted at the Duke of York's Theatre.

Muſtapha. Tragedy, by Fulk Greville, Lord Brooke, fol. 1633.

Mutual Deception. Com. Acted at the Haymarket, 1786, for the benefit of Mr. Palmer, and very well received.

Mydas. Com. by John Lyly, 4to. 1592.

The Myſterious Huſband. Trag. written in proſe by Mr. Cumberland. Acted at Covent-Garden, 1783. The ſituations in this piece are produced with great contrivance, and the progreſſion of the plot is very artful, all the incidents tending in ſucceſſive order to the grand myſtery.

Myrtillo. A Paſtoral Interlude, by Colley Cibber, 8vo. 1716. Performed at Drury - Lane, with no very great ſucceſs.

The Myſterious Mother. Trag. by Horace Walpole, 8vo. 1768. This dramatic piece was printed by our author at Strawberry Hill, and diſtributed among his particular friends, but with ſuch ſtrict injunctions of ſecrecy, that, knowing its merit, we cannot but expreſs our ſurprize that its author ſhould wiſh to withhold it from the public. Mr. Walpole has given the ſtory of

it

it in the following words : "I had heard when very young, that a gentlewoman, under uncommon agonies of mind, had waited on Archbifhop Tillotfon, and befought his counfel. A damfel that ferved her had, many years before, acquainted her that fhe was importuned by the gentlewoman's fon to grant him a private meeting. The mother ordered the maiden to make the affignation, when fhe faid fhe would difcover herfelf, and reprimand him for his criminal paffion ; but being hurried away by a much more criminal paffion herfelf, fhe kept the affignation without difcovering herfelf. The fruit of this horrid artifice was a daugh-

ter, whom the gentlewoman caufed to be educated very privately in the country ; but proving very lovely, and being accidentally met by her father-brother, who never had the flighteft fufpicion of the truth, he had fallen in love with, and actually married her. The wretched guilty mother learning what had happened, and diftracted with the confequence of her crime, had now reforted to the Archbifhop to know in what manner fhe fhould act. The prelate charged her never to let her fon and daughter know what had paffed, as they were innocent of any criminal intention. For herfelf, he bade her almoft defpair."

N A

THE *NABOB*. Com. by Samuel Foote. Acted at the Haymarket, 1772. Printed in 8vo. 1778. A fevere fatire on the greater part of thofe gentlemen who have acquired wealth in the Eaft-Indies. At the time this play was produced, a general odium had been excited againft the members of the Eaft-India Company, which was kept alive by every art which virulence and party could fuggeft. Mr. Foote, ever attentive to avail himfelf of popular fubjects,

N A

feized the prefent occafion to entertain the town at the expence of fome individuals. The character of Sir Matthew Mite was intended for a gentleman who had rifen from the low fituation of a cheefemonger. How far it refembles the original muft be left to the determination of thofe who have an opportunity of making the comparifon.

Nancy ; or, *The Parting Lovers*. A Mufical Interlude, by H. Carey, 8vo. 1739. This piece was acted

K 3 with

with fuccefs at the Theatre Royal in Drury-Lane.

Nanine. Com. tranflated from Voltaire, and printed in Dr. Franklin's edition of that author.

Narciffus ; or, The Self-Admirer. Com. tranflated from J. J. Rouffeau, 12mo. 1767. This was firft acted at Paris, 1752.

National Prejudice. Com. of two acts, performed at Drury-Lane, April the 6th, 1768, for Mrs. Abington's benefit. Not printed.

The Natural Son. Com. by Mr. Cumberland. Acted at Drury-Lane, 1784. The incidents of this piece are borrowed from Fielding's celebrated Tom Jones.

Nature will Prevail. A Dramatic Proverb. Acted at the Haymarket, 1778. Not printed.

Nature's Three Daughters, Beauty, Love and Wit. C. in two parts, by the duchefs of Newcaftle, fol. 1662.

Nautical Prejudice. Com. Acted at Covent-Garden, 1791, for the benefit of Mrs. Wells.

Neck or Nothing. Farce, by David Garrick, Efq. Acted at Drury-Lane, 8vo. 1766. This piece is an imitation of the Crifpin Rival de fon Maitre of Le Sage.

The Necromancer ; or, Harlequin Dr. Fauftus. A

Pantomime. Acted at Lincoln's-Inn-Fields, 8vo. 1731.

Neptune's Triumph for the Return of Albion. Mafque, by Ben Jonfon, performed at Court on Twelfth Night, 1624.

Nero, Emperor of Rome, his Trag. by Nathaniel Lee, Acted at the Theatre Royal, 4to. 1675. This tragedy is written in a mixed ftyle, part being in profe, part in rhyme, and part in blank verfe.

Nero, the Tragedy of. Anonym. 4to. 1624. This play is, in the title-page, called Nero newly written, becaufe it was written after that of Claudius Tiberius Nero, which Kirkman has by miftake called Nero's Life and Death. See Claudius Tiberius Nero. It is on the fame foundation with Lee's play, and the fcene laid in the fame place.

The Neft of Plays, by Hildebrand Jacob. Acted at Covent-Garden, 8vo. 1738. This was the firft Dramatic Entertainment licenfed by the Lord Chamberlain, after paffing the act for reftraining the liberty of the ftage ; which was of itfelf affigned as a reafon for its want of fuccefs. Be that as it will, the work was damned the firft night.

The

N E

The New Academy; or, *The New Exchange* Com. by Richard Broome, 8vo. 1658.

The New Athenian Comedy, by J. S. 4to. 1693, containing the Politics, Oeconomics, Tactics, Cryptics. Apocalyptics, Styptics, Sceptics, Pneumatics, Theologics, Mathematics, Sophistics, Pragmatics, Dogmatics, &c. of that most learned Society. This piece was not intended for the stage; it consists only of three acts, and is a low piece of banter on the Athenian society.

New Brooms! An occasional Prelude, by George Colman. Performed at Drury-Lane, at the opening of the Theatre, 1776. 8vo.

Newe Custome. An Interlude, Anonym. 4to. 1573. The whole title of it is as follows: " A new Enterlude, no less wittie than pleasant, intituled *Newe Custome*; devised of late, and for diverse causes now set forth, never before this tyme imprinted." It is printed in the black letter, and is written in English hexameter rhymes.

New Hippocrates. Farce, 1761. This piece made its appearance for two several benefits on Drury - Lane stage, and is said to have been written by Dr. Hiffernan. The intent of it is to

N E.

expose the folly of persons of fortune confiding the conduct of their health and constitutions to foreign empirics, to the prejudice of deserving regular-bred gentlemen of the faculty, who, possessed of great learning, skill and judgment, are nevertheless often neglected, and denied that encouragement which is at the same time unreasonably lavished on these pernicious beings; to whom, from their absolute deficiency of every one of those qualities, it would be madness to entrust the management of even the most trivial concern in life itself. The design so far, may be good, but the execution of it is puerile, and defective in almost every essential to the drama; character, incident, and probability, being all alike wanting in it; the foreign quack being made an absolute Englishman, and the only attempt at real character, which is that of Miss Griseldine Waponrake, a Yorkshire, galloping, fox-hunting, female rustic, dragged in by head and shoulders without any previous expectation, or subsequent consequence, or, in a word, without any farther connexion to this piece, than it might be made to have equally well to any other.

K 4   The

The fuccefs it met with, which was a kind of cold contemptuous difregard, was furely as much as its merit could demand, and indeed the author feems to have fhewn a confcioufnefs of the fame judgment by not publifhing the piece.

The New Inn ; or, *The Light Heart.* Com. by Ben Jonfon, 8vo. 1631. Nothing perhaps can give a ftronger idea of the felf-opinion, haughtinefs, and infolence of this writer, whofe merit, great as it was, muft be greatly eclipfed by thofe ill qualities, than his behaviour with regard to this play, which not fucceeding according to the exalted idea he had himfelf formed of its worth, he publifhed it with the following title-page, which we fhall here tranfcribe at large : " *The New Inn* ; or, *The Light Heart*, A Comedy, never acted, but moft negligently played by fome of the King's Servants, and more fqueamifhly beheld and cenfured by others the King's fubjects, 1629. Now at laft fet at Liberty to the Readers, his Majefty's Servants and Subjects to be judged." He alfo annexed to the play an ode, in which he openly and infolently arraigns the public for want of tafte, and threatens to quit the ftage.

Such was the refentment fhewn by this opiniated genius, on one fingle flight fhewn to him by an audience from whom he had before received repeated favours. This ode, however, drew upon him an anfwer from Mr. Feltham, which could not fail of feverely wounding a mind fo fufceptible of feeling, and fo avaricious of praife, as Jonfon's. Nor do we hint this by way of cafting any reflection on the memory of this truly great genius, whofe merits in fome refpects are, and ever will remain, unequalled ; but only as a hint, how greatly even the moft exalted merit may degrade itfelf by too apparent a felf-confcioufnefs, and how vaftly more amiable muft have been the private characters of the modeft Shakfpeare and humble Spenfer, who conftantly mention themfelves with the utmoft humility, and others with the higheft refpect, than that of the over-bearing Jonfon ; who, tender as he thus was as to any attack made on himfelf, was neverthelefs perpetually carping and cavilling at the works of others, the due commendations given to which his envious difpofition would not permit him to hear with patience, nor acquiefe to with unreferve or candour.

candour. But fuch is the frailty of human nature, and fuch the errors which perfons of great abilities are perhaps more epidemically liable to than others, whofe confcioufnefs of defect abates and antidotes the pride of nature.

Newmarket; or, *The Humours of the Turf.* Com. of two acts, by Geo. Downing, 12mo. 1763. This piece has been acted at Drury-Lane.

New Market Fayre; or, *A Parliamentary Outcry of State Commodities fet to Sale.* Tragi-Com. 1640.

New Market Fayre; or, *Mrs. Parliament's New Figaries.* Tragi-Com. Part II. Written (as the title fays) by the Man in the Moon, and printed at You may go look. Thefe two fatyrical plays, each of which confifts of little more than one fcene, were written by fome loyalift, to fatirize and expofe the proceedings of the rebels, whofe power was at that time arifen to its greateft height.

A New Rehearfal; or, *Bayes the Younger.* Anon. 8vo. 1714. Containing an examen of The Ambitious Step-mother, Tamerlane, The Biter, Fair Penitent, Royal Convert, Ulyffes, and Jane Shore; all written by N. Rowe, Efq. alfo a word or two upon Mr.

Pope's Rape of the Lock. This piece is written in imitation of the Duke of Buckingham's Rehearfal. Mr. Rowe's plays, however, being rendered in it the fole fubject of examination and criticifm. This piece, although anonymous, was written by C. Gildon.

News from Parnaffus. Prelude, by Arthur Murphy. Acted at Covent-Garden, 1776. Not printed.

News from Plymouth. C. by Sir Wm. Davenant, fol. 1673.

The New Peerage; or, *Our Eyes May Deceive Us.* Com. by Mifs Lee. Acted at Drury-Lane, 1787, and tolerably well received.

News from the New World Difcover'd in the Moon. A Mafque, by Ben Jonfon, fol. 1641. Prefented at Court before king James I. 1620.

New Spain; or *Love in Mexico.* Opera, by Mr. Scawen. Acted at the Haymarket, 1790, and favourably received.

A New Trick to cheat the Devil. Com. by R. Davenport, gent. 4to. 1639. This play met with good fuccefs.

A New Way to Pay Old Debts. Com. by P. Maffinger. Acted at the Phœnix, in Drury-Lane, 4to. 1633. This Play is one of the old comedies, and perhaps

haps the very beſt of this author's writing. The plot is good and well connected, the language dramatic and nervous, and the characters, particularly that of Sir Giles Over-reach, highly and judiciouſly drawn.

A New Wonder, A Woman never Vext. Com. by Wm. Rowley, 4to. 1632. This is a diverting play, and met with ſuccefs.

Next Door Neighbours. Comedy of three acts, by Mrs. Inchbald. Acted at the Haymarket, 1791. The plot of this comedy is borrowed from two French plays; the characters are drawn with confiderable effect, the general tendency of the play is good, and the dialogue is ſprightly and elegant.

The Nice Lady. Com. by G. S. Green, 8vo. 1762. Not acted.

Nice Valour; or, *The Paffionate Madman.* Com. by Beaumont and Fletcher, fol. 1647.

The Nice Wanton. A pleafaunt Comedie, Anon. 1634.

Nicomede. Tragi-Com. by John Dancer. Acted at the Theatre Royal in Dublin, 4to. 1671. This is a tranflation from the French of Corneille.

A Night's Intrigue. Far. Anonymous, 8vo. without date. But written fince 1700.

The Night Walker; or, *The Little Thief.* Com. by John Fletcher. Acted at Drury-Lane, 4to. 1640. This was Fletcher's only, unaffifted by his colleague Beaumont.

The Nigramanſir, a morall Enterlude and a pithie, written by Maiſter Skelton laureat, and plaid before the king and other eſtatys, at Woodſtoke, on Palme Sunday. It was printed by Wynkin de Worde in a thin quarto, in the year 1504.

Noah's Flood; or, *The Deſtruction of the World.* An Opera, by Edward Ecclestone, 4to. 1679. This piece is of the fame nature with Dryden's *State of Innocence*, but falls infinitely ſhort of the merit of that Poem. The firft edition of it not felling off according to the expectations of the bookfeller, they put to it, at different times, two new titlepages, viz. *The Cataclifm;* or, *General Deluge of the World*, 1684, and 2dly, *The Deluge;* or, *The Deſtruction of the World*, 1691, with the addition of feveral ornamental fculptures. Befides this, another edition of it came out in 12mo. 1714, with the title of *Noah's Flood;* or, *The Hiſtory of the general Deluge;* and the names

names of feveral eminent bookfellers, who joined in an impofition upon the world of this piece as a new one, and the parent unknown, as may be feen in the preface.

The Noble Gentleman. C. by Beaumont and Fletcher, fol. 1647. This play was revived with very little alteration by Mr. Durfey, under the title of *The Fool's Preferment* ; or, *The Three Dukes of Dunftable.*

The Noble Ingratitude. A Paftoral Tragi-Com. by Sir Wm. Lower, 12mo. 1659. This is a tranflation from the French of M. Quinault.

The Noble Soldiers ; or, *A Contract broken juftly Revenged.* Trag. by Samuel Rowley, 4to. 1634. This piece was not publifhed till after the author's deceafe, though according to the editor's preface it had met with fuccefs in the reprefentation ; but where it was acted it is not eafy to trace, any more than the foundation of the ftory, the former not being mentioned at all, nor any mention made as to the other, or what king of Spain it was who was guilty of the act of perjury with Onælia, on which the plot of this piece turns.

The Noble Stranger. Com. by Lewis Sharpe. Acted at the private houfe in Salifbury-court, 4to. 1640.

The Nobleman. Com. by Mrs. Cooper. Acted at the Haymarket, about May 1736. Not printed.

The Noble Peafant. Op. by Mr. Holcroft. Acted at the Haymarket, 1784, and well received. Set to mufic by Mr. Shields.

Nobody and Somebody, with the true Chronical Hiftorie of *Elyidure,* who was fortunately three times crowned Kinge of England. Acted by the Queen's fervants, 4to. no date.

No Fools like Wits ; or, *The Female Vertuofoes.* C. Acted at Lincoln's - Inn-Fields, 8vo. 1721. This is only a republication of Wright's *Female Vertuofoes,* by Mr. Gay, and was fet up and acted in oppofition to Mr. Cibber's *Refufal,* which was partly borrowed from the fame play, or at leaft from the fame original, viz. the *Femmes fçavantes* of Moliere.

No One's Enemy but his Own. Com. by Mr. Murphy. Acted at Covent-Garden, 8vo. 1764. Although this play contains a great deal of fpirited dialogue, properly characterifed, and well fupported ; yet the character of Carelefs, whom the author intends for the perfon who is *No One's Enemy but his own,* being that of a worthlefs wretch, without

K 6

out honour or probity, the piece was totally difliked by the public.

No Wit like a Woman's. Farce. Acted at Drury-Lane, 1769.

No Wit, No Help like a Woman's. Com. by Tho. Middleton, 8vo. 1657.

None are fo blind as thofe who won't fee. Farce, by Mr. Dibdin. Acted at the Haymarket, 1782. Very well received by the audience.

The Nonjuror. Com. by Colley Cibber. Acted at Drury-Lane, 8vo. 1717. The general plot of this Comedy is borrowed from the *Tartuffe* of Moliere ; and the principal character in it, viz. that of Doctor Wolfe, is a clofe copy from that great original. The conduct of the piece, however, is fo greatly altered as to render it perfectly Englifh, and the Coquet *Maria* is truly original and moft elegantly fpirited. The principal intention, however, of the author, who was a man warmly attached to the illuftrious family then not long eftablifhed on the Britifh throne, and which had beeñ very lately difturbed in the poffeffion of it by a moft unprovoked rebellion, was by Moliere's *Tartuffe* in a ha-

bit very little different from his own, viz. '' that of an Englifh popifh prieft, lurking under the doctrine of our own church, to raife his fortune upon the ruin of a worthy gentleman, whom his diffembled fanctity had feduced into the treafonable caufe of a Roman Catholic outlaw, (fee Cibber's Apology) to point out the mifchiefs and ruin which were frequently brought into the moft noble families by the felf-interefted machinations of thofe fkulking and pernicious people, who at that troublefome and unfettled period, covering their private views beneath the mark of public zeal and fanctity, acted the part of the great ferpent of old, firft tempting to fin, and then betraying to punifhment. The play met with great fuccefs in the reprefentation, taking a run of eighteen nights, the fubject itfelf being its protection, and its enemies not daring to fhew any more at that time than a few fmiles of filent contempt. The confequence however was what the author forefaw ; that is to fay, that ftirring up a party againft him, who would fcarcely fuffer any thing he wrote afterwards to meet with fair play, and making him the conftant

butt

butt of Mift's *Journal*, and all the *Jacobite* faction.

The Northern Heirefs ; or, *The Humours of York*. Com. by Mrs. Mary Davis. Acted at Lincoln's-Inn-Fields, 12mo. 1716.

The Northern Lafs ; or, *A Nest of Fools*. Com. by R. Brome. Acted at the Globe and Black - Fryars, 4to. 1632. This is one of the beft of this author's pieces ; it met with good applaufe in the reprefentation, and is commended by his contemporary Ben Jonfon.

Northward Hoe. By Tho. Decker and John Webfter, 4to. 1607. A part of the plot is borrowed from Maleipini's \novels, part 1. Nov. 2.

Northumberland. Trag. by Mark Anthony Meilan, 8vo. No date. This is on the fame ftory as Rowe's Lady Jane Gray, and was never acted.

The Norwich Merchant ; or, *The Happy Reconciliation*. Farce, 12mo. no date.

The Note of Hand ; or, *Trip to Newmarket*. Far. by Richard Cumberland, Efq. Acted at Drury-Lane, 1770.

8vo. 1772. This is a good Farce, and met with fuccefs.

Novella. Com. by R. Brome. Acted in 1632, but not printed till 1653, in 8vo.

The Novelty ; or, *Every Act a Play*, by P. Motteux. Acted at Lincoln's--Inn-Fields, 4to. 1697. It confifts of five diftinct fhort dramatic pieces, all of them of different kinds.

The Nuptials. Mafque, on the marriage of his Grace James Duke of Hamilton and Lady Anna Cochran, 8vo. 1723.

The Nuptials of Peleus and Thetis, by James Howel, 4to. 1654. This piece confifts of a Mafque, and a Comedy, from whence the Mafque is taken, and was acted at Paris fix times by the King in perfon, the Dukes of Anjou and York, the Princefs Royal, the Princefs of Conti, and feveral other illuftrious perfonages.

The Nutbrown Maid. C. Op. by G. S. Carey, 12mo. 1770.

O A

THE *Oaks* ; or, *The Beauties of Canterbury*. Com. by Mrs. Burgefs. Acted at the Theatre in Canterbury, 8vo. 1780. This play takes it name from

O A

a place near the cathedral of the city, where it was acted and printed. The author of it was a paftry-cook, a mantua-maker, and wife of a parifh-clerk.

Oberon

O D

Oberon the Fairy Prince.
A Mafq. of Prince Henry's,
by Ben Jonfon, fol. 1640.
The Obftinate Lady. Com.
by Sir Afton Cockain, 4to.
1657. This play is written
in imitation of Maffinger's
Very Woman.

Octavia. Trag. by T.
Nuce, 4to. 1581. This is
only a tranflation of the *Octavia* of Seneca.

The Oculift. Dramatical
Entertainment of two acts,
by Dr. Bacon, 8vo. 1757.

Ode, upon dedicating a
building and erecting a
ftatue to Shakfpeare, at
Stratford upon Avon, 4to.
1769. A performance en-
titled to our notice here, becaufe for a few evenings it
was recited at Drury-Lane
Theatre, in lieu of a dramatic after-piece. Minute
criticifm would be mif-em-
ployed on a work to which
no man will afford a fecond
reading. We fhall there-
fore content ourfelves to obferve, that, however this
ode might be applauded by
a handful of company af-
fembled to fee the puppet-
fhow at Stratford, it met
with colder treatment from
the judicious audiences of
London. To thefe, the art
of the fpeaker, matchlefs as
it was, appeared but a weak
fubftitute for poetic fpirit and
imagination. The fuccefs
of Mr. *Garrick's* attempts

O E

as a comic writer, we have
often acknowledged ; but
in his prefent effort, after
climbing up with confiderable labour into the Pinda-
ric faddle, he ferves only to
remind us of poor *Tom
Thumb,* when he rode the
great horfe for the entertainment of *King Arthur's*
court. Let other unqualified ode-adventures take
warning, and forbear to
imitate a bard by whofe fire
they are untouched, and
with whofe manner and language they have no acquaintance.

Oedipus. Tr. by Alex.
Neville, 4to. 1581. This
is a tranflation from Seneca,
who himfelf borrowed part
of it from Sophocles.

Oedipus Coloneus. Trag.
by George Adams, 8vo.
1729. This is only a very
flat tranflation from Sophocles, with notes, but not intended for the ftage.

Oedipus Coloneus. Trag.
by Thomas Franklin, 4to.
1759.

Oedipus Tyrannus. Tra.
by George Adams, 8vo.
1729.

Oedipus Tyrannus. Trag.
by Thomas Franklin, 4to.
1759. Printed in Doctor
Franklin's edition of So-
phocles.

Oedipus Tyrannus. By
Thomas Maurice, 4to.
1779.

1779. This is a free tranflation of the fame play.

Oedipus King of Thebes.
Trag. by J. Dryden and
N. Lee. Acted at the Duke's
Theatre, 4to. 1679. This
is a very excellent Tragedy, being one of the beft
executed pieces that either
of thofe two celebrated authors were concerned in ;
yet the critics have juftly
found fault with the impropriety of Oedipus's relifhing
an embrace from Jocafta
after he had quitted his
crown, and was gone to fuch
extremity of diftraction, as
to have pulled out his own
eyes. This Tragedy was
performed about twenty-
five years fince, and never
failed to affect the audience
very ftrongly. The firft and
third acts were written by
Dryden, who drew the ma-
chinery of the whole ; the
remainder by Lee.

Oedipus, King of Thebes.
Trag. by Lewis Theobald,
12mo. 1715. A tranflation
from Sophocles, with critical notes by the tranflator.

Oenone. Paftoral, 4to.
No date. Printed with other
pieces, attributed to Robert
Cox, comedian.

Oithona. Dram. Poem,
taken from Offian ; fet to
mufic by Mr. Barthelemon ;
performed once at the Haymarket, 8vo. 1768.

The Old Batchelor. Com.

by W. Congreve. Acted
at the Theatre Royal, 4to.
1693. This was the firft
piece of this juftly admired
author's writings, being
brought on the ftage when
he was only 21 years old.
Such a Comedy, written at
fuch an age (as Dr. Johnfon
obferves) requires fome confideration. As the lighter
fpecies of dramatic poetry
profeffes the imitation of
common life, of real man-
ners, and daily incidents, it
apparently pre-fuppofes a
familiar knowledge of many
characters, and exact obfervation of the paffing world ;
the difficulty therefore is to
conceive how this know-
ledge can be obtained by a
boy. *The Old Batchelor,*
if nearly examined, will be
found to be one of thofe
comedies, which may be
made by a mind vigorous
and acute, and furnifhed
with comic characters by the
perufal of other poets, without much actual commerce
with mankind. The dialo-
gue is one conftant recipro-
cation of conceits, or clafh
of wit, in which nothing
flows neceffarily from the
occafion, or is dictated by
nature. The characters both
of men and women are ei-
ther fictitious and artificial,
or eafy and common, and
the cataftrophe arifes from
a miftake not very probably
produced,

produced, by marrying a woman in a mask.

Old City Manners. Com. by C. Lennox. Acted at Drury-Lane, 8vo. 1773.

The Old Couple. Com. by Thomas May, 4to. 1658. This is a very good play, and the principal design is to point out the folly, absurdity, and detestableness of avarice.

Old Fortunatus. Com. by T. Decker, 4to. 1600. This play is printed in the black letter. The plan of it is founded on the ancient story of *Fortunatus*, and his inexhaustible purse and wishing hat.

The Old Law; or, *A New Way to please ye.* Com. by P. Massinger, Tho. Middleton, and William Rowley. Acted at Salisbury-house, 4to. 1656.

The Old Maid. A Com. of two acts, by A. Murphy, 1761. This *Petite Piece* was performed several times with great approbation at the Theatre Royal in Drury-Lane, during the summer theatrical partnership of the author and Mr. Foote. It has certainly great merit. The subject of it, and part of the fable, were taken from *L'Etourderie* of Monf. Fagan. The ambiguity and perplexity produced by Clerimont's first mistake of the wife for the maiden is na-

tural and well supported, and the conduct and behaviour of that gentleman and the other characters in consequence of this circumstance, which, though kept unknown to them till the absolute period of the *denouement*, is sufficiently discovered to the audience to give them the full enjoyment of their mutual energy, does honour to the skill and judgment of the author. The *Old Maid's* character is admirably kept up, and indeed, to speak of it on the whole, we know not any farce at present extant which seems to lay a juster claim to a countenance of that public favour which which was at first paid it, and which seemed to grow upon the audience in every subsequent representation, than the piece before us.

An Old Man's Lesson, and a Young Man's Love, 4to. 1605. It is only an Interlude, or indeed, a bare dialogue between a father and son, the former of whom is a widower, and the latter a traveller, who, after a long absence, is returned to his father's house.

The Old Man taught Wisdom; or, *The Virgin Unmask'd.* A Farce, by Henry Fielding, 8vo. 1734. This farce was acted with good success at Drury-Lane Theatre,

atre, and continues on the acting lift to this day.

The Old Mode and the New ; or, *Country Mifs with her Furbeloe.* Com. by T. Durfey. Acted at the Theatre Royal, 4to. 1709. This is a very indifferent play.

The Old Troop ; or, *Monfieur Ragout.* Com. by J. Lacy. Acted at the Theatre Royal, 4to. 1672.

Olindo and Sophronia. T. by A. Portal, 8vo. 1758. This play is a very indifferent one.

Oliver Cromwell. An Hiftorical Play, by George Smith Green, 8vo. 1752. Never acted, though probably intended for the ftage by its author, and refufed by the managers for reafons not unobvious.

Olympia. Trag. tranflated from Voltaire, and printed in Doctor Franklin's edition of that author, 12mo.

The Olympiad. Opera, tranflated from Metaftafio, by John Hoole, 8vo. 1768.

Omai ; or, *A Trip Round the World.* Pantomime, acted at Covent-Garden, 1785.

Once a Lover and always a Lover. Com. by Lord Landfdowne. This is no more than an alteration of *The She Gallants*, which had been written when his lordfhip was very young, but which at a maturer time of

life he revifed, and improved by the addition and amendment of feveral fcenes. It is to be found in the third volume of an edition of his Lordfhip's works, in 12mo. 1736.

The Opera of Operas ; or, *Tom Thumb the Great*, by Mr. Hacket and Mrs. Heywood. Acted at the Haymarket, 8vo. 1733. This is no more than Fielding's *Tragedy of Tragedies* tranfformed into an opera, by converting fome paffages of it into fongs, and fetting the whole to mufic.

The Opportunitie. Com. by J. Shirley. Acted at the private houfe in Drury-Lane 4to. 1640.

The Oracle. C. Anony. 8vo. 1741.

The Oracle. Com. of one act, by Mrs. Cibber. Acted at Covent-Garden, 8vo. 1752. This little piece is a tranflation from the French, and was, we believe, only intended as a means of afifting the authorefs in a benefit. It is, however, very prettily executed, and not only gave great pleafure at the firft reprefentation, but even continued, for a confiderable time afterwards a ftanding theatrical collation. The character of Cynthia is fimple and pleafing, and although all thofe kind of characters apparently owe

their

OR

their origin to Shakfpeare's *Miranda*, yet a very little variation in point of circum-ftance or behaviour, will ever beftow on them a no-velty, which, added to the delight we conftantly take in innocence, cannot fail of giving pleafure.

The Orators. Com. of three acts, by Sam. Foote, 8vo. 1762. This piece met with very good fuccefs. It was performed at the Little Theatre in the Haymarket in the middle of the day, during fome part of the fummer of 1762. The bills publifhed for it were under the idea of *Lectures* on *Eng-lifh Oratory*, and indeed part of the firft act is taken up in an ironical kind of lecture on that fubject. The two laft, however, are an il-luftration of fome of the principles laid down in the faid lecture, by examples with regard to the feveral methods of arguing and de-claiming, peculiar to the oratory of the bar, and that of *fome public* affemblies. The former is an imaginary trial of that ideal being, the *Ghoft* of Cock-Lane, and the other is a fuppofed meeting of mechanics and labouring men at the noted *Robinhood Society*. Mr. Foote has thrown into his defign a a great variety of characters, fome of which have been

OR

fuppofed to be drawn from real life, particularly one of an eminent printer of a neighbouring kingdom, who, with all the difadvan-rages of age, perfon, and addrefs, and even the defi-ciency of a leg, was perpetu-ally giving himfelf the airs of the greateft importance, continually repeating ftories of his wit, and, not con-tented with being a moft tirefome egotift in other re-fpects, was even continually talking of his amours, and boafting of being a favourite with the fair fex. Such a character is furely a genuine object of ridicule ; the ftage feems to demand it as a fa-crifice at the fhrine of *Com-mon Senfe* ; nor can we think the dramatic writer juftly chargeable with perfonality, who feeing fo extraordinary a flower growing in nature's garden, does not exclude it from the nofegay he is ga-thering, becaufe it grew in a particular fpot, and that its glaring colours had hap-pened to have been obferv-ed by hundreds befides him-felf.

The Ordinary. Com. by William Cartwright, 8vo. 1651.

Oreftes. Trag. by Tho. Goffe, 4to. 1633, 8vo. 1656. The plot is borrow-ed from the *Oreftes* of Eu-ripides.

O R

ripides, and the *Electra* of Sophocles.

Orestes. Dram. Opera, by Lewis Theobald. Acted at Lincoln's - Inn - Fields, 8vo. 1731.

Orestes. Trag. tranflated from Voltaire, by Dr. Franklin. Acted at Co-vent-Garden, 1769, for Mrs. Yates's benefit, and fince at Drury-Lane.

Orgula; or, *The Fatal Error.* Tr. by L. W. 4to. 1658.

Orlando Furiofo, one of the twelve Pieres of France. As it was plaid before the Queen's Majeftie, 4to. 1594. This play was written by Robert Green. It is a very irregular one, being not divided into acts.

Ormofdes; or, *Love and Friendfhip.* Tragi-Com. by Sir William Killigrew, 8vo. 1664, fol. 1666.

Oroonoko. Tra. by Tho. Southerne. Acted at the Theatre Royal, 4to. 1696. This play met with very great fuccefs when it firft appeared, and has ever fince continued to give pleafure in the tragic parts of it to every fenfible and feeling auditor, the love of Oroc-noko to Imoinda being, per-haps, the tendereft, and at the fame time the moft man-ly, noble, and unpolluted, that we find in any of our dramatic pieces; his firm-

O R

nefs and refolution, alike perfect in action and in fuf-fering, are truly heroic, and perhaps unequalled. But the intermixture of the low, trivial, and loofe comedy of the widow Lackit and her fon Daniel, with the ad-dreffes of Charlotte Weldon in breeches to the former, are fo greatly below, and indeed fo much empoifon the merit of the other parts, that nothing but the cor-rupt tafte of the period in which the author firft im-bibed his ideas of dramatic writing, can ftand in any degree of excufe for his having thus enwrapped a mafs of fterling ore in rags and filthinefs.

Oroonoko. Trag. by J. Hawkfworth, 8vo. 1759. This piece was acted at Drury-Lane Theatre, and is only an alteration of the foregoing play, in which the Augæan ftable is indeed cleanfed, the comic parts being very properly quite omitted. Yet ftill there feems fomewhat more want-ing than fuch a mutilation, to render this play what one would wifh it to be; for as the comedy took up fo con-fiderable a fhare in the length of a drama of no im-moderate extent, the ftory of the tragedy was appa-rently not fufficiently full of bufinefs to make out the ca-taftrophe taſtrophe of an entire piece, without the addition of more incidents. And although Dr. Hawkſworth in his alteration has greatly amended this play in point of omiſſion, yet the little further extent that he has given to the characters of Aboan and Hotman ſeems not ſufficient to fill up the hiatus which thoſe omiſſions have occaſioned, and we cannot help thinking therefore, it is ſtill to be wiſhed, that ſome other writer of ability would conſider it as worth his while once more to reviſe this admirable groundwork of a Tragedy, and by interweaving with its preſent texture ſuch additional incidents as Mrs. Behn's extenſive novel might very amply furniſh, by which means the whole might be rendered equally intereſting, and the piece become entitled to that immortality its merit is entitled to, pay a pleaſing and grateful tribute to the memory of an author, whoſe value ſeems likely to ſink almoſt into oblivion for want of ſome ſuch care.

Oroonoko ; or, *The Royal Slave.* Trag. altered from Southerne, by Francis Gentleman. Acted at Edinburgh, 12mo. 1760.

The Orphan; or, *The Unhappy Marriage.* Trag. by Thomas Otway. Acted at the Duke's Theatre, 4to. 1680. This play, from its frequent repetitions on the theatre, is too well known to need our ſaying much in regard to it. The plot is founded on the Hiſtory of Brandon, in a novel called *Engliſh Adventures.* The language is truly poetical, tender, and ſentimental, the circumſtances affecting, and the cataſtrophe diſtreſsful. Yet there is ſomewhat improbable and bungling in the particular on which all the diſtreſſes are founded. As Dr. Johnſon obſerves, it is one of the few pieces that keep poſſeſſion of the ſtage, and has pleaſed for almoſt a century, through all the viciſſitudes of dramatic faſhion. Of this play nothing new can eaſily be ſaid. It is a domeſtic tragedy drawn from middle life. Its whole power is upon the affections ; for it is not written with much comprehenſion of thought, or elegance of expreſſion. But if the heart is intereſted, many other beauties may be wanting, yet not be miſſed.

The Orphan of China. T. tranſlated from Voltaire, 8vo. 1755. This was the firſt tranſlation of Voltaire's play.

The Orphan of China. T. tranſlated from Voltaire ; printed in Dr. Franklin's edition

edition of that author's works. This play was originally acted at Paris, 1755. *The Orphan of China.* T. by A. Murphy. Acted at Drury-Lane, 8vo, 1759. The subject had before been handled by M. de Voltaire, in his *Orphelin de la Chine.* Mr. Murphy has, however, greatly varied from the French poet in the conduct of his plot, by very properly introducing the orphan, who in that play is an infant and only spoken of as a youth advanced in life, and one of the capital characters in the piece. On a close examination, perhaps, he may be found to have made some use of the *Heraclius* of Corneille ; but whatever assistances he may have had recourse to for the laying his foundation, the superstructure must be allowed his own ; and though this gentleman's genius seems to be more naturally devoted to the comic than the tragic Muse, it would be injustice to him, not to confess, that this is far from standing the last on the list of our modern tragedies ; nor would it be perhaps saying too much, to observe, that, was the whole play, or indeed even at the last act of it, equal to the merit of the fourth, it would stand a very fair chance of being

esteemed the very foremost on that list. The representation of this play gave Mrs. Yates the first opportunity of displaying her theatrical powers, and confirmed her reputation as one of the most excellent tragic actresses who have trod the English stage.

The Orphan of Venice. T. by J. Darcy, 1749. This play was acted at the Theatre Royal in Dublin.

Orpheus. An English Opera, by J. Hill, fol. 1740. This little piece was the first attempt in writing of an author who has since been more voluminous than generally read. For this alone it is remarkable, and for having been the occasion of giving the first vent to that spirit of vindictiveness and abuse, which has since flowed in such abundant torrents from the pen of its author.

Orpheus and Euridice. An Opera set to music, by J. F. Lampe, 8vo. 1740.

Orpheus and Euridice, with the Pantomime Entertainment. As acted at Lincoln's - Inn - Fields, 4to. 1740. By Mr. Henry Somner.

Orpheus and Euridice. A Masque, by M. Bladen, 4to. 1704.

Orpheus and Euridice. A Masque, by J. Dennis.

Orpheus

Orpheus and Euridice. A Dramatic Entertainment of Dancing, attempted in imitation of the ancient Greeks and Romans, by J. Weaver. Acted at Drury-Lane, 8vo. 1718.

Ofman. Trag. by Fran. Gentleman. This piece has never yet appeared in print, although about the year 1751 proposals were published for the printing and acting it by subscription, each subscriber for a ticket at the performance at the Little Theatre in the Haymarket being, by the proposal, entitled to a copy of the play in large or small paper, according to the part of the house for which he chose to take the ticket. This design, however, was laid aside, most probably for want of sufficient encouragement to the subscription. Yet the play did not want merit, and being afterwards brought on the stage at Bath, met with approbation.

Ofman. Trag. by Chrift. Arnold, 4to. 1757. This play was not acted.

Ofmond, the Great Turk, otherwise called *The Noble Servant.* Trag. by Lodowick Carlell, 8vo. 1657. The main action of this play is, in reality, the taking of Conftantinople by Mahomet II. in the year 1453.

Othello, The Moor of Ve- nice. Trag. by W. Shakspeare. Acted at the Globe and Black-Fryars, 4to. 1622. This is generally allowed to be one of 'the *chef d'Oeuvres* of this admirable author, notwithstanding all the several cavils and censures thrown on it by Rymer. Dr. Johnson says, " The beauties of this play imprefs themfelves fo strongly upon the attention of the reader, that they can draw no aid from critical illuftration. The fiery opennefs of Othello, magnanimous, artlefs, and credulous, boundlefs in his confidence, ardent in his affection, inflexible in his refolution, and obdurate in his revenge; the cool malignity of Iago, filent in his refentment. fubtle in his defigns, and ftudious at once of his intereft and his vengeance; the foft fimplicity of Defdemona, confident of merit, and confcious of innocence, her artlefs perfeverance in her fuit, and her flownefs to fufpect that fhe can be fufpected; are fuch proofs of Shakfpeare's fkill in human nature, as, we fuppofe, it is vain to feek in any modern writer. The gradual progrefs which Iago makes in the Moor's conviction, and the circumftances which he employs to inflame him, are fo artfully natural,

natural, that, though it will perhaps not be faid of him as he fays of himfelf, that he is *a man not eafily jealous*, yet we cannot but pity him, when at laft we find him *perplexed in the extreme*. There is always danger, left wickednefs, conjoined with abilities, fhould fteal upon efteem, though it miffes of approbation ; but the character of Iago is fo conducted, that he is from the firft fcene to the laft hated and defpifed. Even the inferior characters of this play would be very confpicuous in any other piece, not only for their juftnefs, but their ftrength. Caffio is brave, benevolent, and honeft, ruined only by his want of ftubbornnefs to refift an infiduous invitation. Roderigo's fufpicious credulity, and impatient fubmiffion to the cheats which he fees practifed upon him, and which by perfuafion he fuffers to be repeated, exhibit a ftrong picture of a weak mind betrayed by unlawful defires to a falfe friend ; and the virtue of Æmilia is fuch as we often find worn loofely, but not caft off eafily, to commit fmall crimes, but quickened and alarmed at atrocious villainies. The fcenes, from the beginning

to the end, are bufy, varied by happy interchanges, and regularly promoting the progreffion of the ftory ; and the narrative in the end, though it tells but what is known already, yet is neceffary to produce the death of Othello.

Ovid's Tragedy, by Sir Afton Cockain, 8vo. 1669. The title of this play is a mifnomer. Ovid having fcarcely any thing to do with the main plot of the piece, which is the jealoufy of Baffane, and the murther of his bride Clorina, and his friend Pyrontus in confequence of it ; not very much unlike that of Alonzo, Carlos, and Leonora, in the *Revenge*.

The Oxford Act. Ballad Op. 8vo. 1733.

The Oxonian in Town. Com. by George Colman. Acted at Covent-Garden, 8vo. 1770. The reprefentation of this piece, after a few nights, was in danger of being interrupted by means of a fet of Irifh fharpers and gamblers, who applied fome paffages in the performance perfonally to themfelves. The good fenfe of the majority, however, interfered, and fruftrated the defigns of a fet of beings who are a difgrace to fociety.

PADLOCK

PADLOCK. Com. Op. by Ifaac Bickerftaffe. Acted at Drury-Lane, 8vo. 1768. This very pleafing entertainment was fet to mufic by Mr. Dibdin, who performed the part of Mungo in it. Few pieces have been more applauded than this was during the firft feafon of its reprefentation.

The Painter's Breakfaft. Dram. Satyr, by Mr. Brenan. This piece does not appear to have been acted or printed.

Palladius and Irene. Drama in three acts, 8vo. 1773.

Palamon and Arcyte. Com. in two parts, by Richard Edwards. Thefe are very old pieces, being publifhed together with the author's fongs, &c. in 1585. The ftory of them is profefledly taken from Chaucer's celebrated poem of *The Knight's Tale.*

Pamela. A Comedy. As it is performed gratis at the late Theatre in Goodman's Fields, 8vo. 1742. The late Mr. Love, of Drury-Lane Theatre, was author of this play, but it does little credit to his memory.

Pamela ; or, *Virtue rewarded.* Com. Anonym. 1742. This play is on the fame plan with the foregoing one, but much worfe executed, and was never acted.

Pamela. Com. by Carlo Goldoni, 8vo. 1757. This piece is founded entirely on the celebrated novel of that title, written by Mr. S. Richardfon.

Pan and Syrinx. Opera, of one act, by Lewis Theobald, 8vo. 1717. Set to mufic by Mr. Galliard, and performed in Lincoln's-Inn-Fields.

Pan's Anniverfarie ; or, *The Shepherd's Holiday.* A Mafque by Ben Jonfon, fol. 1640, prefented at Court before King James, 1625.

Pandora ; or, *The Conquefts.* Tragi-Com. by Sir William Killigrew, 8vo. 1664.

The Pantheonites. Dram. Entertainment, by Francis Gentleman. Acted at the Haymarket, 8vo. 1773.

Papal Tyranny in the reign of King John. Trag. by C. Cibber. Acted at Covent-Garden, 8vo. 1744. This play is not an alteration from Shakfpeare, though founded on the fame portion of the Englifh hiftory as his King John ; nor is it by any means fo good a play as his.

Parafitafter ; or, *The Fawn.* Com. by J. Marfton. Acted at Black-Fryars by the children of the Revels, 4to. 1606. The fcene of this play is laid in Urbino, and part of the plot, is

P A

is borrowed from the ſtory told by Philomena in Boccace's *Decameron.*

The Parricide. Tra. by J. Sterling. Acted at Goodman's-Fields, 8vo. 1736.

The Parricide; or, *Innocence in Diſtreſs.* Trag. by William Shirley, 8vo. 1739. This play was acted at Covent-Garden Theatre.

The Parſon's Wedding. Com. by Thomas Killigrew, fol. 1664. This play was revived with conſiderable ſucceſs at the Theatre in Lincoln's-Inn-Fields, and acted entirely by women. The ſcene lies in London; and the plot, made uſe of by Careleſs and Wild to circumvent Lady Wild and Mrs. Pleaſance into marriage, ſeems borrowed from like circumſtances in the Antiquary and Ram Alley.

Parthenia; or, *The Lſt Shepherdeſs.* An Arcadian Drama, 8vo. 1764.

The Parthian Exile. Tr. by Geo. Downing. Acted at Coventry and Worceſter, 8vo. 1774.

The Parthian Hero. Tra. by Matthew Gardiner, 8vo. 1741.

Paſquin. A Dramatic Satire on the Times, by H. Fielding. Acted at the Haymarket, 8vo. in 1736. This piece contained ſeveral very ſevere ſatirical reflections on the miniſtry, which

P A

being taken notice of, as well as ſome others in a ſucceeding play ot the ſame author, and performed at the ſame houſe, were the occaſion of a bill being brought into the Houſe of Commons for reſtraining the liberty of the ſtage.

Of the Paſſion of Chryſt. Two Comedies. Theſe two pieces are by Biſhop Bale.

The Paſſionate Lovers. Tragi-Com. by Lodowick Carlell, in two parts, 4to. 1655.

Il Paſtor Fido; or, *The Faithful Shepheard*, tranſlated out of Italian into Engliſh, 4to. 1602. By Mr. Dymock.

Il Paſtor Fido; or, *The Faithful Shepherd.* A Paſtoral, by Sir R. Fanſhaw, 4to. 1647. This is only a tranſlation of Guarini's celebrated paſtoral of that name, written originally on occaſion of the young duke of Savoy, Charles Emanuel's marriage with the Infanta of Spain. The ſcene lies in Arcadia. Prefixed to it are verſes by Sir J. Denham.

Paſtor Fido; or, *The Faithful Shepherd.* A Paſtoral, by Elk. Settle, 4to. 1677.

Pathomachia; or, *The Battle of Affections, ſhadowed by a feigned Siege of the Citie of Pathopolis.* C. Anon. 4to. 1630. The running title

L

PA

title of this piece is *Love's Loadstone*. Who the author of it was we know not, but it was not publifhed till fome time after his death, by F. Conftable, one of his friends.

Patie and Peggy ; or, *The Fair Foundling*. A Scotch Ballad Opera, by Theophilus Cibber. Acted at Drury-Lane. 8vo. 1730. This is Ramfey's *Gentle Shepherd* reduced into one act.

Patient Grifele. Com. by Ralph Radcliff. Not printed.

Patiente Grizzele. Com. Anon. 1600.

The Patriot ; or, *The Italian Conspiracy.* Trag. by C. Gildon. Acted at Drury-Lane, 4to. 1703.

The Patriot, being a dramatic hiftory of the Life and Death of William the firft Prince of Orange, founder of the Republic of Holland, 4to. 1740.

The Patriot. Tr. by W. Harrod, 8vo. 1769.

The Patriot King ; or, *The Irish Chief.* Trag. by F. Dobbs. Acted at Smock-Alley, Dublin, 8vo. 1774. This play had been rejected both at Drury-Lane and Covent-Garden.

Patriotifm. Far. Acted by his Majefty's fervants, 8vo. 1763. Defpicable political nonfenfe.

The Patron. A Comedy

PA

of three acts, by Samuel Foote, Efq. performed at the Haymarket, 8vo. 1764. The hint borrowed from one of Marmontel's Tales. The character of the Patron, faid to be Lord Melcombe, is that of a fuperficial pretender to wit and learning, who, being a man of fafhion and fortune, affords his countenance and protection to a fet of contemptible witlings, for the fake of the incenfe offered by them to his vanity. The character of a mere antiquarian, a favourite object of ridicule with Mr. Foote, is here introduced with great pleafantry, Mr. Ruft having fallen in love with a fine young lady, becaufe he thought the tip of her ear refembled that of the Princefs Poppæa. Sir Peter Pepperpot, a rich Weft-India merchant, comes in likewife, with his account of barbecues and turtle-feafts ; and a miferable poet, with a low Moorfields bookfeller, ferve to complete the entertainment. Mr. Foote, in a dedication to Lord Gower, fpeaks of this piece as the beft in his own eftimation that he had then written.

Paul the Spanish Sharper. Farce, of two acts, by Ja. Wetherbey, 8vo. 1730. Never acted.

Paufanias, the Betrayer of his

his Country. Trag. 4to. 1696. We find, by Doctor Garth's *Dispensary*, that Norton was the author of it. The story of it may be found in Plutarch.

The Padler's Prophecie. Com. Anonym. 4to. 1595. This is rather an interlude than a regular play. It is very old, and not divided into acts.

A Peep behind the Curtain ; or, *The New Rehearsal.* Farce, by David Garrick, Esq. Acted at Drury-Lane, 1767. This is a very pleasing entertainment, and received every advantage which it could derive from excellent acting.

Peleus and Thetis. Masq. by Lord Lansdowne. See *Jew of Venice.*

Penelope. A Farce, by Thomas Cooke and John Mottley, 8vo. 1728. Almost the whole first act of this piece was written by the last-named author some years before the other gentleman had any hand in it, or had ever seen it. It is a mock tragedy, and was probably intended as no more than a burlesque drama without any particular aim. But as it was brought on the stage soon after the publication of Mr. Pope's translation of the *Odyssey* of Homer, that gentleman considered it as a ridicule on his work, and has, in conse-

quence of that supposition, treated Mr. Cooke somewhat severely, as the author of it in his notes to the *Dunciad.* The piece, as a burlesque, is not without merit, but met with no success in the representation, from making its first appearance at the Little Theatre in the Haymarket, and being performed by a most contemptible set of actors.

King Pepin's Campaign. Burlesque Opera, by Wm. Shirley. Acted at Drury-Lane, 1745. Printed 8vo. 1755.

Percy. Trag. by Miss Hannah More. Acted at Covent-Garden, 8vo. 1778. This was a successful piece.

The Perfidious Brother. Trag. by Lewis Theobald. Acted at Lincoln's-Inn-Fields, 4to. 1715. The model of this play is somewhat like that of the *Orphan*, the whole scene of it being laid in a private family at Brussels. It appears to have been acted without success.

The Perfidious Brother. Trag. by Henry Meftayer, 12mo. 1716. The author of this play, who was a watch-maker, complains, in a Dedication to Mr. Theobald, of that gentleman's purloining his piece from him, and getting it represented as his own.

Periander, King of Corinth. Trag. by J. Tracy, 8vo. 1713. This tragedy, though very far from a contemptible one, met with but middling fuccefs when performed at the Theatre in Lincoln's-Inn-Fields.

Pericles, Prince of Tyre. Trag. by Wm. Shakfpeare. Acted at the Globe, 4to. 1609. This is one of thofe pieces which the editors of Shakfpeare's works have generally agreed to reject. The laft publifher, however, of this play, Mr. Malone, entertains a more favourable opinion of it, and declares himfelf thoroughly convinced, that if not the whole, at leaft the greater part, of the Drama was written by Shakfpeare, into whofe works he hopes to fee it admitted in fome future publication of them, inftead of *Titus Andronicus.* The ftory on which it is formed is of great antiquity. It is found in a book once very popular intituled, *Gefta Romanorum,* which is fuppofed by the learned editor of *The Canterbury Tales of Chaucer,* 1775, to have been written five hundred years ago. One of the earlieft editions of that work was printed in 1488, and therein the hiftory of *Appollonius, King of Tyre,* makes the 153d chapter.

The Perjur'd Hufband; or, *The Adventures of Venice.* Tra. by Mrs. Centlivre. Acted at Drury-Lane. 4to. 1700. This is the firft of this lady's attempts for the Drama; and though her writings afterwards took the comic turn, yet both this piece and the *Cruel Gift* fhew her very capable of making a figure in the fervice of the tragic Mufe.

The Perjuror. Farce, of one act, by Chrift. Bullock, 8vo. 1717. Acted at Lincoln's-Inn-Fields; a very good performance.

Perkin Warbeck, the chronicle hiftory of. A Strange Truth, by John Ford. Acted at the Phœnix, Drury-Lane, 4to. 1634. This is not a bad play. It is founded on the hiftory of that ftrange Pretender to the crown, who fet himfelf up, and caufed himfelf to be proclaimed king of England, declaring himfelf to be Richard duke of York, brother to Edward V. who loft his life in the Tower.

Perolla and Izadora. Tr. by C. Cibber. Acted at the Theatre Royal, 4to. 1706. As this author's tafte was very far from lying in the tragic ftrain of writing, it is not to be wondered at that this play, together with
some

PE

fome others of his tragedies, have been entirely fet afide.

The Perplex'd Couple; or, *Miftake upon Miftake.* Com. by Charles Molloy. Acted at Lincoln's-Inn-Fields, 12mo. 1715. This play is for the moft part borrowed from Moliere's *Cocu Imaginaire.*

The Perplex'd Lovers. C. by Mrs. Centlivre. Acted at Drury-Lane, 4to 1712. The greateft part of the plot of this play is, by the author's own confeffion, borrowed from a Spanifh play, the name of which however fhe has not informed us of.

The Perplexities. Com. by Thomas Hull. Acted at Covent-Garden, 8vo. 1767. This is only an alteration from Sir Samuel Tuke's *Adventures of Five Hours.*

Perfeverance; or, *The third Time the beft.* Mufical Entertainment. Performed at Covent-Garden, 1789, for the benefit of Mrs. Mountain.

The Perfian Princefs; or, *The Royal Villain.* Trag. by Lewis Theobald. Acted at Drury·Lane, 12mo. 1715. The author, in his preface to this play, afferts it to have been written and acted before he was full nineteen years of age.

The Perfian. Com. tranflated from Plautus by Rich. Warner, and printed in the

PH

fifth volume of that gentleman's edition, 8vo. 1774.

The Perfians. Tr. tranflated from Æfchylus by R. Potter, 4to. 1777.

Perfeus and Andromeda, *with the Rape of Columbine*; or, *The Flying Lovers,* in five Interludes; three ferious, and two comic. Acted at Drury-Lane, 8vo. 1728.

Perfeus and Andromeda. Pantomime. Acted at Lincoln's - Inn - Fields, 4to. 1730.

The Peruvian. A Comic Opera- Acted at Covent-Garden, 1786. This Opera is taken from *l'Amitie à l'Epreuve*; or, The Teft of of Friendfhip, by Marmontel.

The Petticoat Plotter. F. of two acts, by Newburgh Hamilton, 12mo. 1720. performed at the Theatre Royal in Drury-Lane and Lincoln's-Inn-Fields.

The Petticoat Plotter; or, *More Ways than one for a Wife.* A Farce, of two acts, by Henry Ward, performed at York, 8vo. 1746.

Phœbe. Paftoral Opera, by Dr. John Hoadly, fet to mufic by Dr. Greene, 8vo. 1748.

Phædra. Tra. tranflated from Corneille, 8vo. 1776

Phædra aud Hippolitus. Trag. tranflated from Seneca,

L 3

neca, by Sir Edward Sherburne, 8vo. 1701.

Phædra and Hippolitus. Trag. by Edmund Smith. Acted at the Haymarket, 4to. 1707. This play, as Dr. Johnson obferves, pleafed the critics only. It was hardly heard the third night. Addifon, in *The Spectator*, mentions this neglect of it as difgraceful to the nation, and imputes it to the fondnefs for operas then prevailing. The authority of Addifon is great; yet the voice of the people, when to pleafe the people is the purpofe, deferves regard. In this queftion, we cannot but think the people were right. The fable is mythological, a ftory which we are accuftomed to reject as falfe, and the manners are fo diftant from our own, that we know them not by fympathy but by ftudy; the ignorant do not underftand the action, the learned reject it as a fchool-boy's tale; *incredulus odi.* What we cannot for a moment believe, we cannot for a moment behold with intereft or anxiety. The fentiments, thus remote from life, are removed yet further by the diction, which is too luxuriant and fplendid for dialogue, and envelopes the thoughts rather than difplays them. It is a fcholar's play, fuch as may

pleafe the reader rather than the fpectator; the work of a vigorous and elegant mind, accuftomed to pleafe itfelf with its own conceptions, but of little acquaintance with the courfe of life.

Phædra and Hippolitus. Opera, compofed by Mr. Thomas Rofeingrave, 8vo. 1753. Printed at Dublin. This piece (ftrange as it may feem) is no other than the foregoing tragedy by Mr. Smith, turned into an opera by abbreviation, and the additton of fongs. It does not appear to have been acted.

Phænissæ. Trag. tranflated from Euripides; printed with three other pieces of the fame author, 8vo. 1780.

Phaeton; or, *The Fatal Divorce.* Tra. by Charles Gildon, 4to. 1698. This play is written in imitation of the ancients, was acted at the Theatre Royal, and met with good fuccefs. The plot, and a great many of the beauties of it, the author himfelf owns to have been taken from the *Medea* of Euripides, and he has evidently made ufe of many hints from the French play of *Phaeton.*

Pharnaces. Opera, altered from the Italian, by T. Hull.

T. Hull. Acted at Drury-Lane, 8vo. 1765.

The Phœnician Virgins. Trag. tranflated from Euripides, by R. Potter, 4to. 1781.

The . Phœnix. Tragi-Com. by Thomas Middleton. Acted by the children of Paul's, 4to. 1607. This is a good play.

Phœnix in her Flames. Trag. by Sir Wm. Lower, 4to. 1639. Scene, Arabia.

Philander. A Dramatic Paftoral, by Mrs. Lennox, 8vo. 1758. A piece not intended, nor indeed of merit fufficient, for the ftage.

Philafter ; or, *Love lies a Bleeding.* Tragi-Com. by Beaumont and Fletcher, 4to. 1622. This was the firft piece that brought thefe afterwards moft juftly celebrated authors into any confiderable eftimation, and is even now confidered as one - of the moft capital of their plays. It was prefented at the Old Theatre in Lincoln's-Inn-Fields, when the women acted by themfelves; a circumftance recorded by Mr. Dryden, who wrote a prologue for them, which may be found among his *Mifcellany Poems.* The fcene lies in Cilicia.

Philafter ; or, *Love lies a Bleeding.* Tr. C. Acted at the Theatre Royal; revifed, and the two laft acts new-

written, by E. Settle, 4to. 1695.

Philaßer. A Trag. by Beaumont and Fletcher. Acted at Drury-Lane, 8vo. 1763. The revival of this piece was greatly approved by the public ; as Mr. Colman's alterations were extremely judicious. This play has been generally confidered as one of the beft produced by the twin-writers above-named ; but, on account of the indecencies in fome parts of it, hath been deemed unfit to appear before a modern audience. Thefe blemifhes and other improprieties being removed, the tragedy thus new-modelled was brought on, with this additional advantage, that Mr. Powell firft appeared on the ftage in the reprefentation thereof, in the character of Philafter. Mrs. Yates alfo difplayed new graces on this occafion, and the editor's prologue has been both greatly admired and criticifed.

Philip of Macedon. A Tr. by D. Lewis. Acted at Lincoln's-Inn-Fields, 8vo. 1727.

Phillis at Court. Comic Opera, of three acts, performed at Crow-ftreet, Dublin, 8vo. 1767.

Philoclea. Tr. by M'Namara Morgan. Acted at Covent-Garden, 8vo. 1754. This

P H

This play is founded on part of Sir Philip Sidney's celebrated romance of the *Arcadia*. The piece before us is crowded with an immense number of absurdities both in language and plot, the first being alternately bombaſt and puerile, and the other incorrect, imperfect, and contradictory. Yet did this tragedy meet with better ſuccefs than plays of much greater merit that appeared in that and ſome of the enſuing ſeaſons. This ſuccefs, however, may be in great meaſure attributed to the manner in which the more tender and ſenſible parts of the audience could not fail being affected by the paſſionate ſcenes of love in it, which gave ſo fine an opportunity for a diſplay and exertion of fine figure, and tendernefs of expreſſion, in Mr. Barry and Miſs Noſſiter.

Philoctetes. Trag. tranſlated from Sophocles, by Dr. Thomas Sheridan, 8vo. 1725.

Philoctetes. Tra. tranſlated from Sophocles, by G. Adams, 8vo. 1729.

Philoctetes. Tra. tranſlated from Sophocles, by Dr. Thomas Franklin, 4to. 1759.

Philodamus. Trag. by Thomas Bentley, Eſq. 4to. 1767.

P H

The Philoſophic Whim; or, *Aſtronomy.* Farce, by Doctor Hiffernan, 4to. 1774.

Philotas. Tra. by Sam. Daniel, 4to. 1605. This play is eſteemed a good one, but met with ſome oppoſition, not on account of any deficiency in the poetry or in the conduct of the deſign, but from a ſuſpicion propagated by ſome of the author's enemies, that he meant to perſonalize, in the character of Philotas, that unfortunate favourite of queen Elizabeth's, the earl of Eſſex; which obliged him to enter on his vindication from that charge in an apology printed at the end of it.

Philotas. Trag. by Philip Frowde, 8vo. 1731. This tragedy was acted at Lincoln's-Inn-Fields Theatre, with very little ſuccefs; yet we cannot help looking on it as a very admirable play. The characters of Clytus, Alexander, and Philotas, are very finely ſupported; thoſe of Antigone and Cleora beautifully contraſted; the language bold and ſpirited, yet poetical and correct; the plot ingenious, and the cataſtrophe intereſting. The deſign of this, as well as the foregoing play, is taken from Quintus Curtius and Juſtin, and

and the scenes of both are laid in Persia.

Phormio. Com. by R. Bernard, 4to. 1598. This is only a translation from Terence, with some critical and useful notes, and additions for the use of learners. This play has been also translated by Hoole, Patrick, Echard, Cooke, Gordon, and Colman, but never brought on the stage in its own form, although two very celebrated poets, viz. Moliere among the French, and Otway among the English writers, have made great use of the plot in their respective comedies of The Tricks of Scapin.

Physick lies a Bleeding; or, *The Apothecary turned Doctor.* Com. Acted every day in most apothecaries shops in London, by Tho. Brown, 4to. 1698.

The Picture. Tragi-Com. by Ph. Massinger. Acted at the Globe and Black-Fryars, 4to. 1630. This play met with good success, and indeed very deservedly, it having great merit.

The Picture; or, *The Cuckold in Conceit,* A Ballad Opera, 8vo. 1745. This piece was written by James Miller, and was acted at Drury-Lane, after the death of the author.

Piety in Pattins. Farce, by Samuel Foote, Esq.

Acted at the Hay-market, 1773. This piece was first introduced to the stage in an entertainment, called *The Primitive Puppet-shew.*

Pigmy Revels. Pantomime. Acted at Drury-Lane, 1773.

The Pilgrim. Com. by Beaumont and Fletcher, fol. 1647. This is a very good play, and met with approbation on its first appearance; besides which, it was in the year 1700, altered and revived by Sir John Vanbrugh at the Theatre-Royal in Drury-Lane, with a new prologue and epilogue, and a secular masque, by Mr. Dryden, being the last of that great poet's works, and written a very little before his death. Yet do they stand as a proof, with how strong a brilliancy his poetic fires glowed even to the last. The prologue is pointed with great severity against Sir Richard Blackmore, who, though by no means a first-rate poet, yet we cannot help thinking deserving of more immortality, than either the envy or ill-nature of his brother wits have, by their ridicule on his works, permitted the prejudices of mankind, ever easily led aside by what they imagine a superior judgment, to grant him. This comedy,

however,

however, when revived about thirty years ago, together with the secular malque, by the managers of Drury-Lane Theatre, though very well, nay, in some of the characters, very greatly performed, did not meet with the applause it might reasonably have expected. Such is the difference of taste at different periods.

The Pilgrim. Trag. by Thomas Killigrew, Fol. 1664. This play was written at Paris 1651, while the author was on his travels.

The Pilgrims; or, *The Happy Converts.* A Dramatic Entertainment, by W. Harrison, 4to. 1701. This was never acted, yet is very far from being totally devoid of merit.

Piso's Conspiracy. Tra. Anonym. 4to. 1676. Acted at the Duke's Theatre. This is no more than the tragedy of *Nero,* printed with a new title.

The Plague of Riches; or, *L'Embarras des Richesses.* Com. French and English, 8vo. 1735.

The Plain Dealer. Com. by W. Wycherley. Acted at the Theatre Royal, 4to. 1676. This play is looked upon as the most capital of our author's pieces, and indeed Dryden has given it

the character of being the boldest, most general, and most useful satire, that was ever presented on the English stage. The plot, however, and particularly the two most principal characters in it, viz. Manly and Olivia, seem in some measure borrowed from the *Misanthrope* of Moliere, as does also that of Major Oldfox from Scarron's *City Romance.* Yet, notwithstanding, he is scarcely to be condemned for these little thefts, since he has applied them to so noble an use, and so greatly improved on his originals. The character of Lord Plausible is said to have been intended for George Lord Berkeley, who was created Earl of Berkeley by King Charles II. a nobleman of strict virtue and piety, and of the most undistinguished affability to men of all ranks and parties. Scene, London.

The Plain Dealer. Com. by Isaac Bickerstaffe. Acted at Drury-Lane, 8vo. 1766. In this alteration from Wycherley's comedy with the same title, the principal character is wretchedly mutilated. Much of his manly satire is omitted, while all his misanthropy is preserved.

The Platonick Lady. C. by

by Mrs. Centlivre. Acted at the Haymarket, 4to. 1707. This is not one of her beft plays.

The Platonic Lovers. A Tragi-Com. by Sir Wm. Davenant. Acted at Black-Fryars, 4to. 1636.

The Platonit Wife. Com. by Mrs. Griffiths. Acted at Drury-Lane, 8vo. 1765. It met with little fuccefs, being acted only fix nights.

A Play betwene Johan the Hufband, Tyb the Wife. and Sir Johan, the Prieft, by J. Heywood, 4to. *Imprynted at London, by William Ryftall,* 1533. This piece, and fome others of this author's, which we fhall prefently have occafion to fpeak of, are mentioned in *The Mufeum Afhmoleanum.* They are printed in the old black letter, written in metre, and not divided into acts, and are, we believe, fome of the earlieft, if not the very earlieft, dramatic pieces printed in London.

A Play betwene the Pardoner and the Frere, the Curate, and Neybour Pratte. An Interlude, by J. Heywood. *Imprynted by Wyllyam Raftall,* 1533. Black letter, 4to.

A Playhoufe to be Let. A Com. by Sir Wm. Davenant, fol 1673. This piece is only an affemblage of fe-

veral little detached pieces in the dramatic way, written in the time of Oliver Cromwell, and during the prohibition of theatrical reprefentations. Thefe are connected with one another by the addition of a firft act by way of introduction, each act afterwards being a feparate piece.

Plymouth in an Uproar. Com. Op. by Mr. Neville. Acted at Covent-Garden, 8vo. 1779. A temporary trifling performance, occafioned by the alarm excited at Plymouth, on the appearance of the French Fleet before that place in the fummer of 1779.

The Play is the Plot. C. by John Durant Breval. Acted at Drury-Lane, 4to. 1718.

A Play of Love. An Interlude, by John Heywood, 4to. 1533.

A Play of the Weather, called, *A new and very merry Interlude of all Manner of Weathers,* by J. Heywood, fol. 1533.

The Princely Pleafures at Kennelworth Cafle. A Mafque, in profe and rhime by George Gafcoigne, 4to. 1575. This is a relation of the entertainment given to queen Elizabeth at Kenelworth, by R. Dudley, Earl of Leicefter, on the

L 6   9th,

P L

9th, 10th, and 11th of July, 1575.

Pleafure reconcil'd to Virtue. A Mafque, by Ben Jonfon, prefented at Court before King James I. 1619; with an additional mafque *for the honour of Wales,* in which the fcene is changed from the Mountain Atlas as before, to Craig-Eriri.

The Plot. A Pantomimical Entertainment, 8vo. 1735. Acted at Drury-Lane.

A Plot and no Plot. Com. by J. Dennis, Acted at Drury-Lane, 4to. 1697. This play was intended as a fatire upon the credulity of the *Jacobite* party of thofe days.

The Plotting Lovers ; or, *The Difmal Squire.* Farce, by Cha. Shadwell, 12mo. 1720. This piece was acted in Dublin.

Pluto Furens et Vinctus ; or, *The Raging Devil bound.* A Modern Farce, 4to. 1669. The title fays it was printed at Amfterdam.

Plutus ; or, *The World's Idol.* By Lewis Theobald, 12mo. 1715. This is only a tranflation from the Greek of Ariftophanes. It was not intended for the ftage.

Plutus the God of Riches. 8vo. 1742. This is another tranflation of the fame piece executed jointly by Mr. H.

P O

Fielding and the Rev. Mr. Young.

Poetafter ; or, *The Arrangement.* Comical Satyr, by Ben Jonfon. Acted by the children of the Queen's chapel, in 1601. This piece is a fatire on the poets of that age, more particularly Decker, who is feverely lafhed under the title of *Crifpinus,* yet has very fpiritedly returned it in his *Satyromaftix.* It is adorned with many tranflations from Horace, Virgil, Ovid, and others of the antient poets, whom Ben Jonfon was on every occafion fond of fhewing to the world his intimate acquaintance with.

The Polite Gamefter ; or, *The Humours of Whift.* Dra. Satire, 8vo. 1753.

The Political Rehearfal. Harlequin Le Grand ; or, *The Tricks of Pierrot le Premier,* &c. Tragic, comic, pantomimical Performance, of two acts, 12mo. 1742.

The Politic Whore ; or, *The Conceited Cuckold.* Acted at Newmarket, 4to. 1680. See *The Mufe of Newmarket.*

The Politician. Com. by James Shirley. Acted at the private houfe, Salifbury-Court, 4to. 1655.

The Politician Cheated. Com. by Alexander Green, 4to. 1663. This play never made

made its appearance on the ftage.

The Politician Reformed. Drama, in one act, 8vo. 1774.

Polidus; or, *Diftreffed Love.* Tragedy, by Mofes Browne, 8vo. 1723. The author of this play feems to have been a very young gentleman, and indeed fome fuch excufe is neceffary to atone for its deficiencies. It was never acted at any of the regular theatres.

Polly. An Opera, by J. Gay, 4to. 1729. This is a fecond part of *The Beggar's Opera,* in which, according to a hint given in the laft fcene of the firft part, Polly, Macheath, and fome other of the characters, are tranf-ported to America. When every thing was ready, however, for a rehearfal of it at the Theatre Royal in Covent-Garden, a meffage was fent from the Lord Chamberlain, that *it was not allowed to be acted, but commanded to be fuppreffed.* What could be the reafon of fuch a prohibition it is not very eafy to difcover, unlefs we imagine it to have been by way of revenge for the numerous ftrokes of fatire on the courts, &c. which fhone forth in the firft part, or fome private pique to the author himfelf; for the opera before us is fo totally inno-

cent of either fatire, wit, plot, or execution, that, had not Mr. Gay declaredly pub-lifhed it as his, it would have been difficult to have perfuaded the world that their favourite Polly could ever have fo greatly dege-nerated, from thofe charms which firft brought them in-to love with her, or that the author of *The Beggar's Opera* was capable of fo poor a performance as the piece before us. But this is frequently the cafe with fecond parts, undertaken by their authors in confequence of fome extraordinary fuc-cefs of the firft, wherein the writer, having before ex-haufted the whole of his in-tended plan, hazards, and often lofes in a fecond at-tempt, for the fake of pro-fit, all the reputation he had juftly acquired by the firft. Yet notwithftanding this prohibition, the piece turn-ed out very advantageous to Mr. Gay, for being per-fuaded to print it for his own emolument, the fub-fcriptions and prefents he met with on that occafion, from perfons of quality and others, were fo numerous and liberal, that he was ima-gined to make four times as much by it as he could have expected to have cleared by a very tolerable run of it on the ftage.

Polly

P O

Polly Honeycombe. Dramatic Novel, by G. Colman, 8vo. 1760. This little piece was brought on the stage at Drury-Lane house, and met with most amazing success. Its design is to expose the mischiefs which may arise to young girls from the fashionable taste of novel reading; but this is far from being rendered clear in the *denouement*. Its greatest merit appears to be in the portrait of a ridiculous couple, who in the decline of life, and after having been for many years united, not only affect to keep up the fondness of a honeymoon, but are even pepetually shewing before company such a degree of fulsome tenderness to each other, as not only renders them ridiculous in themselves, but disguiling and troublesome to all their friends and acquaintance.

Polly. Opera, altered from Gay, by George Colman. Acted at the Haymarket, 8vo. 1777. At the distance of near fifty years from its original publication, Mr. Colman ventured to produce this piece before the public, when it completely justified all the censures which had been passed upon it, being as insipid and uninteresting a performance as ever appear-

P O

ed on the English stage. After a few nights representation it sunk into its former obscurity.

Polyeuctes; or, *The Martyr.* Trag. by W. Lower, 4to. 1655. The scene lies in Felix's palace at Militene, the capital city of Armenia.

Pompey. Trag. by Mrs. Katherine Philips, 4to. 1663. This play is a translation from the *Pompée* of Corneille. It was frequently presented with great applause.

Pompey the Great. Tra. by Edmund Waller, 4to. 1664. This is a translation of the same play as the foregoing, and was acted by the Duke of York's servants.

Pompey the Great his fair Cornelia's Tragedy, effected by her Father and Husband's Downcast, Death, and Fortune, by Thomas Kyd, 4to. 1595. This is only a translation from an old French author, one Robert Garnier. The translation is in blank verse, with only now and then a couplet, by the way of closing a paragraph or long sentence, and chorusses which are written in various measures of verse, are very long and sententious. It was first published under the title of *Cornelia*, 4to. 1594.

Ponteach; or, *The Savages of America.* Trag. by

P R [231] P R

by Major R. Rogers, 8vo. 1766.

The Poor Man's Comfort. Tragi-Com. by Robert Daborne. Acted at the Cockpit, in Drury-Lane, 1655.

The Poor Scholar. Com. by R. Neville, 4to. 1662. This play was never acted.

The Poor Soldier. Comic Opera, by Mr. O'Keeffe. Acted at Covent - Garden, 1783. This piece, like most of this author's other productions, produces many agreeable incidents.

Poor Vulcan. Burletta, by Charles Dibdin. Acted at Covent-Garden, 8vo. 1778.

Porsenna's Invasion ; or, Rome preserved. Trag. 8vo. 1748. Printed for the author, but never acted.

The Portrait. Burletta, by G. Colman, Esq. Acted at Covent-Garden, 8vo. 1770.

The Portsmouth Heiress ; or, *The Generous Refusal.* Com. Anonym. 4to. 1704. This play was never acted.

The Positive Man. F. by Mr. O'Keeffe. Acted at Covent-Garden, 1782. This piece is destitute of aptness or regularity in the plot.

The Pragmatical Jesuit new Leaven'd. A Com. by Richard Carpenter, 4to. no date. The design of this piece is to expose all the numerous subtilties of the Ro-

mish clergy, for the gaining over of proselytes, and promoting their own religion.

The Preceptor ; or, *The Loves of Abelard and Heloise.* A Ballad Opera, of one act, by Wm. Hammond, 8vo. 1740. The very title of this piece informs us of its subject.

The Preceptor. Com. in two acts, by T. Warboys, 8vo. 1777. Not acted.

The Prejudice of Fashion. Farce, acted at the Haymarket, Feb. 22, 1779. Not printed.

Preludio. By Geo. Colman. Acted at the Haymarket, 1781. In this trifle the characters of *The Beggar's Opera* are reversed.

The Presbyterian Lash ; or, *Noctroffe's Maid Whipp'd.* A Tragi-Comedy, acted in the great Room at the Pye Tavern a 'Aldgate, by Noctroffe the Priest, and several of his Parishoners, at the cutting of a Chine of Beef. Anon. 4to. 1661. This is entirely a personal satire on Zachary Crofton, a violent Presbyterian teacher then living.

The Presence. Com. by the Duchess of Newcastle, fol. 1662. This very voluminous writer had composed twenty-nine additional scenes to this piece, which she intended to have interwoven with the general texture

ture of the comedy, but finding they would render it too long for a fingle drama, fhe omitted them ; but has printed them feparately and publifhed them with the play.

The Prefs-Gang ; or, *Love in Low Life.* Ballad Farce, by Hen. Carey, 8vo. 1755. This piece was performed at Covent-Garden on the profpect of the laft war.

Prefumptuous Love. A Dramatic Mafque. Anon. 4to. 1716. This Mafque was performed at the Tneatre in Lincoln's-Inn-Fields, in a comedy, called, *Every Body Miftaken*, which was never printed, and was only an alteration of Shakfpeare's *Comedy of Errors.*

The Pretenders ; or, *The Town Unmafk'd.* Com. by Thomas Dilkes, 4to. 1698. Scene, Covent-Garden. This piece was acted, but without fuccefs, at the Theatre in Lincoln's-Inn-Fields.

The Pretender's Flight ; or, *A Mock Coronation, with the Humours of the facetious Harry St. John.* Farce, by John Phillips, 8vo. 1716. Of this piece very little feems needful to be faid, fince its date points it out to have been written at the clofe of the rebellion in 1715, when the Chevalier quitted Scotland.

The Prince of Agra. Tr. by Hugh Kelly. Acted at Covent-Garden, April 7, 1774, for Mrs. Leffingham's benefit. It is an alteration of Dryden's *Aurenzebe.*

The Prince of Prigg's Revels ; or, *The Practices of that grand Thief Capt. Ja. Hind.* Written by J. S. 4to. 1658.

The Prince of Tunis. Tr. by Henry Mackenfie. Acted at Edinburgh, 8vo. 1773.

The Princefs ; or, *Love at firft Sight.* Tragi-Com. by Thomas Killegrew, fol. 1663.

The Princefs of Cleve. Tragi-Com. by Nat. Lee. Acted at Dorfet-Gardens, 4to. 1689. This play is founded on a French romance of the fame title.

The Princefs of Elis ; or, *The Pleafures of the Enchanted Ifland.* A Dram. Piece, in three parts, by Mr. Ozell. This only a tranflation from Moliere.

The Princefs of Parma. Trag. by H. Smith, 4to. 1699. This play was acted at the Theatre in Lincoln's-Inn-Fields.

The Princefs of Parma. Trag. by Richard Cumberland, Efq. This play has not yet appeared in print. It was acted in 1778, at the private Theatre of Mr. Hanbury

Hanbury, at Kelmarſh, in Northamptonſhire.

The Priſon Breaker; or, *The Adventures of John Shepherd*. A Farce, Anon. 8vo. 1725.

The Priſoner at Large. Farce, by Mr. O'Keeffe. Acted at the Haymarket, 1788, with much applauſe.

The Priſoners. Tragi-Com. by Tho. Killigrew, Acted at the Phœnix, Drury-Lane, 12mo. 1640.

The Prodigal. Comedy, tranſlated from Voltaire, and printed in Dr. Franklin's edition of that author.

The Prodigal; or, *Recruits for the Queen of Hungary*. Com. by Thomas Odell, 8vo. 1744. This is little more than an alteration of Shadwell's *Woman Captain*. It was acted with ſome ſucceſs at the Little Theatre in the Haymarket.

The Projectors. Com. by J. Wilſon, 4to. 1665. This play met with good ſucceſs on the ſtage.

The Projectors. Com. Anon. 8vo. 1737. This is a very middling piece, and was never acted.

The Projects. Farce, by Mr. Kemble. Acted at Drury-Lane, 1786. The incidents of this farce conſiſt of the projects of young lovers to diſappoint the avaricious or amourous views of age.

Promos and Caſſandra. Com. in two parts, by Geo. Whetſtone, 4to. 1578, black letter. The full title is as follows; " The right excellent and famous Hiſtorye of Promos and Caſſandra ; divided into two comical diſcourſes. In the firſt Part is ſhewne the unſufferable Abuſe of a lewde Magiſtrate ; the virtuous behavious of a chaſte Ladye ; the uncontrowled Lewdeneſs of a favoured Courtiſan ; and the undeſerved eſtimation of a pernicious Paraſyte. In the ſecond Parte is diſcourſed the perfect Magnanimitye of a noble Kinge, in checking vice and favouring Vertue. Wherein is ſhewne, the reigne and overthrow of diſhoneſt practices, with the advauncement of Upright Dealing." Both theſe plays, are written in verſe, for the moſt part alternate.

Prometheus. Pantomime. Acted at Covent-Garden, 1776.

Prometheus chained. Tr. tranſlated from Æſchylus, by R. Potter, 4to. 1777.

Prometheus in Chains. tranſlated from the Greek of Æſchylus, by T. Morell, 8vo. 1773.

The Propheteſs. A Tragical Hiſtory, by Beaumont and Fletcher, fol. 1647. This play is founded on the hiſtory of the Emperor Dioclefian,

clefian, to whom, when in a very low ftation in life, it was foretold by a *Prophetefs* that he fhould become Emperor of Rome, when he fhould have killed a mighty Boar; in confequence of which prediction, he applied himfelf more particularly to the hunting of thofe animals, but in vain. The prophecy, however, was at laft fulfilled by his putting to death Aper, the father-in-law, of the Emperor Numerian whofe many tyrannies and acts of cruelty, and particularly the murder of his fon-in-law, had occafioned a mutiny among the people, which Diocletian heading, immediately mounted the throne he had fo long been waiting for.

The Prophetefs; or, *The Hiftory of Dioclefian*, with alterations and additions, after the manner of an opera, by T. Betterton. Acted at the Queen's Theatre, 4to. 1690. This is the above play altered into the form of an opera by the addition of feveral mufical entertainments, compofed by Mr. Henry Purcell. It has been alfo brought on the ftage again feveral times, and particularly during the theatrical adminiftration of the late Mr. Rich.

The Prophet. Com. Op. Acted at Covent-Garden, 1788. Met with fome applaufe.

Proteus; or, *Harlequin in China*. Pantomime, by Mr. Woodward, 1755. This piece was performed with very great fuccefs.

The Provok'd Hufband; or, *A Journey to London.* Com. by C. Cibber. Acted at Drury-Lane, 8vo. 1727. This comedy was begun by Sir John Vanbrugh, but left by him imperfect at his death, when Mr. Cibber took it in hand, and finifhed it. It met with very great fuccefs; yet fuch is the power of prejudice and perfonal pique in biaffing the judgment, that Mr. Cibber's enemies, ignorant of what fhare he had in the writing of the piece, beftowed the higheft applaufe on the part which related to Lord Townley's provocations from his wife, which was moftly Cibber's, at the fame time that they condemned and oppofed the *Journey to London* part, which was almoft entirely Vanbrugh's, for no other apparent reafon but becaufe they imagined it to be Mr. Cibber's. He foon, however, convinced them of their miftake, by publifhing all the fcenes which Sir John had left behind him, exactly from his own MS. under the

the fingle title of *The Jour-ney to London*.

Provok'd Wife. Com. by Sir John Vanbrugh. Acted at Lincoln's-Inn-Fields, 4to. 1697. This Comedy has a great many very fine fcenes in it, and the character of Sir John Brute is very highly and naturally drawn. Yet it has in the language, as well as the conduct of it, too much loofe wit and libertinifm of fentiment to become the theatres of a moral and virtuous nation ; fince no behaviour of a hufband, however brutal, can vindicate a wife in revenging her caufe upon herfel:, by throwing away the moft valuable jewel fhe poffeffes, her innocence and peace of mind. Lady Brute's conduct, moreover, feems rather to proceed from the warmth of her own inclinations, than a fpirit of refentment againft her hufband ; nay, fhe feems fo far to have loft even the very fenfe of honour, that a little matter appears capable of inducing her to turn pander to her niece Belinda. Had Lady Brute, indeed, appeared to the audience ftrictly virtuous through the whole tranfaction, yet had carried on fuch a deception to her hufband, as to have alarmed all thofe fufpicions which a confcioufnefs of his own behaviour towards her would authorize him in entertaining the belief of, and then reformed him by a perfect clearing up of thofe fufpicions, and, by fhewing him how near he might have been to the brink of a precipice, taught him to avoid for the future the path that was leading him towards it, the moral would have been compleat ; whereas as it now ftands, all that can be deduced from it is, that a brutifh hufband deferves to be made a cuckold, and that there can be no breach of virtue in giving him that defert provided he can afterwards, either by the perfuafions of his wife, or the blufter of her gallant, be foothed or frightened out of her, a maxim of the moft happy tendency to perfons inclinable to gallantry and intrigue ; fince the fame practices may equally anfwer againft the furly and brutal hufband. This play was one of thofe which were feverely cenfured by Mr. Collier, on account of its immorality.

The Prude. Com. tranflated from Voltaire, and printed in Dr. Franklin's edition of that author.

The Prude. Com. Op. by Elizabeth Ryves, 8vo. 1777. Not acted.

Prunella. An Interlude, by Richard Eftcourt, 4to. without date. This piece was

was performed for Mr. Eſtcourt's benefit, between the
acts of Rehearſal, and muſt
have been before the year
1713. It was intended as
a burleſque on the Italian
Operas in general, and particularly on thoſe of *Arſinoe*,
Camilla, and *Thomyris*, at
that time greatly in vogue.

Pſyche. Trag. by Tho.
Shadwell. Acted at the
Duke's Theatre, 4to. 1675.
This is the firſt piece this
author wrote in rhyme, for
which ſome of his contemporary critics were very ſevere
upon him. His intention
in this work was not to produce a perfect regular dramatic piece, but only entertain the town with a variety
of muſic, dancing, ſcenery,
and machinery, rather than
with fine writing or exact-
neſs of poetry.

Pſyche. An Opera, by
Mr. Ozell. This is a literal tranſlation of *The Pſyche*
of Moliere.

Pſyche Debauch'd. Com.
by Thomas Duffet. Acted
at the Theatre Royal, and
printed in 4to. 1678. This
piece is a mock Opera. It
was intended to ridicule
Shadwell's *Pſyche*. It is,
however, nothing but a maſs
of low ſcurrility and abuſe,
without either wit or hu-
mour; and met with the
contempt it merited.

Public Wooing. Com.

by the Ducheſs of New-
caſtle, fol. 1662.

The Puritan; or, *The
Widow of Watling-ſtreet.*
Com. by Wm. Shakſpeare.
Acted by the children of
Paul's, 4to. 1607. This
play is not unentertaining,
yet it is one of the ſeven
which have been rejected by
the editors of Shakſpeare's
works.

Pyrrhus and Demetrius.
Opera, by Owen M'Swiny,
4to. 1709. This is a tranſlation from the Italian of
Scarlatti, and was performed at the Queen's Theatre
in the Haymarket.

Pyrrhus, King of Epirus.
Trag. by Charles Hopkins.
Acted at Lincoln's-Inn-
Fields, 4to. 1695. This is
the leaſt meritorious and
leaſt ſucceſsful of this author's performances, but
has his great youth at the
time he wrote it to plead in
its defence. It has, how-
ever, many ſtrokes in it
which an older writer need
by no means have been
aſhamed of. The ſtory of
it may be found in Livy, in
Plutarch's Life of *Pyrrhus*,
&c. The ſcene is the City
of Argos, beſieged by Pyrrhus, with the camp of the
Epirotes on the one ſide,
and that of the Macedoni-
ans, who came to its relief,
on the other.

Pyramus and Thiſbe. A
Comic

Comic Mafq, 12mo. 1716. This piece was performed at Lincoln's-Inn-Fields. *Pyramus* and *Thifbe*.

Mock Opera, fet to mufic by Mr. Lampe. Acted at Covent-Garden, 8vo. 1745.

Q U

Q U

THE *Quacks*; or, *Love's* the *Phyfician*. Com. by Owen M'Swiny, 4to. 1705. This piece confifts only of three acts, and is a tranflation from the *L'Amour Medecin* of Moliere. It met with little fuccefs.

The Quaker. Comic Op. by Charles Dibdin. Acted at Drury-Lane, 8vo. 1777.

The Quaker's Wedding. Com. by Richard Wilkinfon, gent. printed in 12mo. 1728. It was acted at Drury-Lane, 1703, and is only *Vice Reclaim'd*, &c. with a new title.

Quality Binding. Dram. Proverb. Acted at the Haymarket, 1788. A fatire on the empty promifes of the great.

The Queen; or, *The Excellency of her Sex.* Tragi-Comedy, Anonymous, 4to. 1653. This excellent old play is faid to have been found out by a perfon of honour, and given to the editor Alexander Goughe, to whom three copies of verfes are addreffed on the publication of it. Part of the plot, viz. the affair of Solaffa's fwearing Velafco

not to fight, is taken from Belleforeft's *Hiftoires Tragiques*, novel 13.

The Queen and Concubine. Com. by R. Brome, 8vo. 1659.

Queen Catharine; or, *The Ruins of Love.* T. g. by M. Pix. Acted at Lincoln's-Inn-Fields, 4to. 1698.

Queen Mab. Pantomime by H. Woodward, performed at Drury-Lane, 1752.

The Queen of Arragon. Tragi-Com. by Wm. Habington, fol. 1640.

The Queen of Corinth. Tragi-Com. by Beaumont and Fletcher, fol. 1647.

The Queen of Corfica. Tr. written by Francis Jaques, 1642. This play is yet in manufcript in the library of the earl of Shelburne.

The Queen's Arcadia. A Paftoral Tragi-Com. by S. Daniel, 4to. 1606. This piece was prefented to Queen Anne, wife of James the Firft, and her ladies, by the Univerfity of Oxford, in Chrift-Church, in Aug. 1605, and is dedicated in verfe to her majefty.

The Queen's Exchange. Com. by Rich. Brome, 4to. 1657.

QU

1657. This play was acte 1 at Black-Fryars, with great applaufe.

The Queen's Mafque of Beauty. By Ben Jonfon, fol. 1640. This piece was perfonated at court by Anne queen to king James I. and her ladies, on Twelfth-night, 1605.

The Queen's Mafk of Black-nefs. By Ben Jonfon, fol. 1640. This piece, as well as the foregoing, was pre-fented a' ս ourt by the queen and her ladies.

Queen Tragedy Reftor'd. A Dramatic Entertainment, by Mrs. Hooper, 8vo. 1749. This piece, which is a ftrange incoherent jumble of repeated abfurdities, though intended by its au-thor as a burlefque on the modern writers, and a means of reftoring tragedy to her ancient dignity, was per-formed one night only at the Little Theatre in the Haymarket, by a fet of per-formers of equal merit with

QU

the piece ; the author her-felf, who had never trod a ftage before, appearing in the part of *Queen Tragedy.* As the houfe was almoft en-tirely filled with her own friends, a filent difguft and ennui was all the reception it met with ; but on attempt-ing to bring it on a fecond night, the fame it had ac-quired was apparent, from there not being an audience fufficient even to pay the ex-pences.

Querer per folo Querer. To love only for Love's Sake. A Dramatic Romance, by Sir Rich. Fanfhaw, 4to. 1671. This is only a tranflation, or rather paraphrafe from the Spanifh of Antonio de Mendoza, made by Sir R. during his confinement at Tankerfly Caftle in 1654, when he was taken prifoner by Oliver at the battle of Worcefter.

The Quidnuncs. Moral Interlude, 4to. 1779.

R A

THE *Ragged Uproar* ; or, *The Oxford Rora-tory.* Dramatic Satire, in many fcenes, and in one very long act, in which is introduced the Alamode Syftem of Fortune-telling. Originally planned by fe-veral truly eminent hands

R A

well verfed in the art of de-figning ; the whole con-cluding with an important fcene of witches, gypfies, and fortune-tellers ; a long jumbling dance of politici-ans ; and an epilogue fpo-ken by Mary Squires, &c.

flying

flying on broomſticks, 4to. 1754.

The Raging Turk ; or, *Bajazet II*. Trag. by Tho. Goffe, 4to. 1631. The plot of this play may be found by confulting Knolles' Turkiſh Hiſtory, Calchocondylas, and other writers on that reign. It was not publiſhed till after his death.

Ram Alley ; or, *Merry Tricks*. Com. by Lodowick Barrey. Acted by the children of the Revels, 4to. 1611.

The Rambling Juſtice ; or, *The Jealous Huſbands, with the Humours of John Twyford*. Com. by John Leonard. Acted at Drury-Lane, 4to. 1678. Great part of this play is borrowed from Middleton's *More Diſſemblers beſides Women*.

The Rampant Alderman ; or, *News from the Exchange*. Farce, Anon. 4to. 1685. This Farce is ſtolen from Marmion's *Fine Companion*, and ſeveral other plays.

The Rape ; or, *The Innocent Impoſtors*. Trag. by Doctor Brady. Acted at Drury-Lane, 4to. 1692. This piece was introduced on the ſtage by Mr. Shadwell.

The Rape. Trag. Acted at Lincoln's - Inn - Fields, 8vo. 1730.

The Rape of Europa by

Jupiter. A Maſque. Anon. 4to. 1694.

The Rape of Helen. A Mock Opera, by J. Breval, Eſq. Acted at Covent-Garden, 8vo. 1737.

The Rape of Lucrece. A True Roman Tragedy, by Tho. Heywood, 4to. 1638. The plot is ſelected from Livy, Florus, Valerius Maximus, and other Roman hiſtorians.

The Rape of Proſerpine, by Lewis Theobald, 4to. 1727. Acted at the Theatre Royal in Lincoln's-Inn-Fields. The muſic to this piece was compoſed by Mr. Galliard, and the ſcene lies in Sicily.

Rape upon Rape ; or, *The Juſtice caught in his own Trap*. By this title, Fielding's Coffee-houſe Politician was firſt printed.

The Raree Show ; or, *The Fox trap't*. Opera, by J. Peterſon, comedian, 8vo. 1739. This was printed at York, where it was performed.

The Reapers ; or, *The Engliſhman out of Paris*. Op. 8vo. 1770. A tranſlation of *Les Moiſſonneurs*.

The Rebellion. Trag. by Thomas Rawlins. Acted by the company of Revels, 4to. 1640. Scene, Sevil. This play was acted with great applauſe.

Rebellion

Rebellion Defeated; or, *The Fall of Defmond.* Trag. by John Cutts, 4to. 1745. This tragedy was never acted, yet is not absolutely devoid of merit.

Rebellion of Naples; or, *The Tragedy of Maffinello.* 8vo. 1651. This play is said to have been written by a gentleman who was himself an eye-witnefs to the whole of that wonderful tranfaction, which happened at Naples in 1647.

Recruiting Officer. Com. by George Farquhar. Acted at Drury-Lane, 4to. 1707. This moft entertaining and lively comedy, written on the very fpot where the author has fixed his fcene of action, viz. at Shrewfbury, and at a time when he was himfelf a recruiting officer in that town, and by all accounts of him, the very character he has drawn in that of Captain Plume. His Juftice Ballance was defigned as a compliment to a very worthy country gentleman in that neighbourhood. The characters are natural, the dialogue genteel, and the wit entirely fpirited and genuine.

The Recruiting Serjeant. Mufical Entertainment, by Ifaac Bickerftaffe, Acted at Drury-Lane, 8vo. 1770.

Redowald. Mafque, by Jof. Hazard, 12mo. 1767. Printed at Chelmsford.

The Reformation. Com. 4to. 1673. Acted at the Duke's Theatre. This piece is afcribed to one Mr. Arrowfmith, M. A. of Cambridge.

The Reform'd Wife. C. by Mr. Burnaby. Acted at Drury-Lane, 4to. 1700.

The Refufal; or, *The Ladies Philofophy.* Com. by C. Cibber. Acted at Drury-Lane, 8vo. 1720. The ground-work of that part of this play which relates to the fecond title, is built on the *Femmes Scavantes* of Moliere, which Wright's *Female Virtuofoes* is alfo borrowed from. But Mr. Cibber has introduced a fecond plot into it, by making the circumftances of his cataftrophe depend on the abfurdities of that year of folly and infatuation in which this play made its appearance, when the bubbles of the South-Sea fcheme rendered even men of underftanding fools, and then fubjected them to the defigning views of knaves. His Sir Gilbert Wrangle, whom he has made a South-Sea director, is an admirably drawn, an exceeding natural, and yet, we think an original character; and although the prejudice which the author had raifed againft himfelf on another

another occasion (see *Nonju-ror*) permitted this piece to run for no more than six nights, and that with repeated disturbances at every one of them, yet we cannot help looking on it as one of the most finished of our author's comedies. With the revival of this play, if we do not mistake, Mr. Garrick opened the Theatre Royal at Drury-Lane in the year 1747, being the first of his management; nor can we in justice omit taking notice of the great merit shewn by Mr. Macklin in the performance of the part of Sir Gilbert.

The Regent. Trag. by Mr. Greathead. Acted at Drury-Lane, 1788. This play, though the production of a youg writer, has much merit.

The Regicide; or, *James the First of Scotland.* Tra. by Dr. Smollet, 8vo. 1749. The plot of this piece is founded on the Scottish history of the reign of that monarch, who was basely and barbarously murdered by his uncle Walter Stuart, earl of Athol, in the year 1437. This play was offered to the managers of the theatres, but rejected, a particular account of which the author has given, under feigned characters, in his adventures of *Roderic Random,* in

which he has displayed a great deal of wit and humour, but with how much justice we cannot pretend to determine. It was published afterwards by subscription, very much, we believe, to its author's emolument. As therefore it stands in print, and open to every one's examination, we shall by no means here enter into any particular investigation of its merits, but leave it entirely to the decision of the public, how far the author and managers were or were not in the right in their respective parts of the contest.

The Register Office. Far. of two acts, by Joseph Reed, 8vo. 1761. This little piece which was performed at the Theatre Royal, in Drury-Lane with great applause, is intended to expose the pernicious consequences that may, and probably do, frequently arise from Offices of Intelligence, or, as they are called, *Register Offices,* where the management of them happens to be lodged in the hands of wicked and designing men. This design is surely a laudable one, as the stage ought certainly to be made a vehicle to convey to the public ear and eye, not only the representation of general vice and folly, but also the knowledge of any

M particular

particular evil or abuse, which may occur to a few persons indeed, but those perhaps either too unconsequential or too indolent to attempt a redress of it, and which cannot therefore by any means so readily as by this be brought forth to open day-light, and in consequence to public redress. In the execution of this, the plan of which is rendered as simple as possible, several characters are introduced; the generality of which are well drawn, particularly the provincial ones of an Irish spalpeen, a Scotch pedlar, and Yorkshire servant-maid, as also that of a military male *slip-slop*, whose ignorance leads him into the perpetual use of hard words, whose meaning he does not understand, and consequently mis-pronounces, and whose impudence secures him from a blush on the detection of his absurdity. There is also another character in it, which was omitted in the representation, viz. that of Mrs. Snare, an old puritanical bawd, which treads so close on the heels of the celebrated Mrs. Cole in Mr. Foote's *Minor*, not only in the general portrait, but in the particular features of sentiment and diction, that we should certainly be ready to fly out in exclamation against the author

as the most barefaced and undaunted plagiary, had he not, in an advertisement annexed to the piece, assured us, that the said character was written previous to the appearance of *The Minor*, and even that the MS. had been lodged in Mr. Foote's own hands, under an expectation of that gentleman's bringing it on the stage in the year 1758, two years before he brought out his own piece of *The Minor*.

Regulus. Trag. by John Crowne. Acted by their Majesties servants, 4to. 1694. The title of this play declares what the subject of its plot must be.

Regulus. Trag. by Wm. Havard, 8vo. 1744. This play was presented at the Theatre Royal in Drury-Lane, with some success.

The Rehearsal. Com. by the Duke of Buckingham. Acted at the Theatre Royal, 4to. 1672. This play was acted with universal applause, and is indeed the truest and most judicious piece of satire that ever yet appeared. Its intention was to ridicule and expose the then reigning taste for plays in heroic rhime, as also that fondness for bombast and fustian in the language, and clutter, noise, bustle, and shew in the conduct of dramatic pieces, which then so strongly prevailed

vailed, and which the writers of that time found too greatly their advantage in not to encourage by their practice, to the exclusion of nature and true poetry from the stage. This play was written, and had been several times rehearsed before the plague in 1665, but was put a stop to by that dreadful public calamity. It then, however, wore a very different appearance from what it does at present, the poet having been called Bilboa, and was intended for Sir Robert Howard; afterwards however, when Mr. Dryden, on the death of Sir. W. Davenant, became laureat, and that the evil greatly increased by his example, the duke thought proper to make him the hero of his piece, changing the name of Bilboa into Bayes ; yet still, although Mr. Dryden's plays became now the more particular mark for his satire, those of Sir Robert Howard and Sir W. Davenant by no means escaped the severity of its lash. This play is still repeatedly performed, constantly giving delight to the judicious and critical parts of an audience. Mr. Garrick, however, introduced another degree of merit into the part of Bayes, having rendered it by his inimitable power of mimickry not only

the scourge of poets but of players also, taking off, in the course of his instructions to the performers, the particular manner and style of acting of almost every living performer of any note.

The Rehearsal. A Farce, or, A second part of Mrs. Confusion's Travail and hard Labour she endured in the Birth of her first Monstrous Offspring, the Child of Deformity, the hopeful fruit of seven years Teeming, and a precious Babe of Grace, delivered in the year 1648, by Mercurius Britannicus, printed in the year 1718, 4to. This is one of the pieces produced in the Bangorian controversy, occasioned by Bishop Hoadley's famous sermon before the King.

The Rehearsal; or, *Bays in Petticoats*, by Mrs. Clive. Com. in two acts, performed at Drury-Lane, 8vo. 1753.

The Relapse ; or, *Virtue in Danger.* Being the sequel of *The Fool in Fashion.* Com. by Sir J. Vanbrugh. Acted at Drury-Lane, 4to. 1697. In this continuation of Cibber's *Love's last Shift*, all the principal characters are retailed, and finely supported to the complexion they bore in the first part. It was, however, an hasty performance, being written

RE

in fix weeks time, and fome broken fcenes that there are in it may be deemed an irregularity. There are much wit, great nature, and abundance of fpirit, which run through the whole of it, yet it muſt be acknowledged, there is a redundancy of licentioufnefs and libertinifm mingled with them, and that two or three of the fcenes convey ideas of fo much warmth and indecency, as muſt caſt a very fevere reflection on ſuch audiences as could fit to fee them without being ſtruck with diſguſt and horror.

Religious. Tragi-Com. by the Duchefs of Newcaſtle, fol. 1662.

The Religious Rebel ; or, *The Pilgrim Prince.* Trag. Anon. 4to. 1671.

The Renegado. Tragi-Com. by Phil. Maſſinger. Acted at Druiy-Lane, 4to. 1630. This was eſteemed a good play.

Reparation. Comedy, by Mr. Andrews. Acted at Drury-Lane, 1784. The ſtory of this piece is perhaps better calculated for a Tragedy than a Comedy ; but Mr. Andrews has here relieved pity and indignation with crollery and wit.

The Reprifals ; or, *The Tars of Old England.* Com. of two acts, by Dr. Smollet. Acted at Drury-Lane,

RE

8vo. 1757. It met with good fuccefs in the reprefentation, but not equal to what its merit might have juſtly claimed.

The Reſtoration; or, *Right will take Place.* Tr. Com. without date. This play was never acted ; it is a very paltry performance, yet has been attributed, but injuriouſly, to the Duke of Buckingham.

The Reſtoration of King Charles II. or, *The Life and Death of Oliver Cromwell.* An Hiſtori-Tragi-Comi-Ballad Opera, by W. Alton, 8vo. 1733.

Retaliation. Farce, by Mac Nally. Acted at Covent-Garden, 1782. This piece was received with uncommon applaufe.

The Return from Parnaſſus ; or, *A Scourge for Simony.* Com. Anonym. 4to. 1606. This piece was publicly acted in St. John's College, Cambridge, by the ſtudents.

The Revenge. T. by E. Young Acted at Drury-Lane 8vo. 1721. This play met, and juſtly, with very great fuccefs, as it is undoubtedly the maſter-piece in the dramatic way of that great and valuable author. The defign of it feems to have been borrowed partly from Shakfpeare's *Othello*, and partly from Mrs. Behn's *Abdelazar* ; the plot favouring greatly

greatly of the former, and the principal character, viz. Zanga, bearing a confiderable refemblance to the latter. Yet it will not furely be faying too much, to obferve, that Dr. Young has in fome refpects greatly improved on both. If we com-¹ ⁴ ;e the Iago in one with the Zanga in the other Tragedy, we fhall find the motives of refentment greatly different, and thofe in the latter more juftly as well as more nobly founded than in the former. Iago's caufe of revenge againft Othello is only his having fet a younger officer over his head on a particular and fingle vacancy, notwithftanding he himfelf ftill ftands moft high in his efteem and confidence, and confequently in the faireft light, for being immediately preferred by him to a poft of equal if not greater advantage. To this, indeed, is added a flight fufpicion, which he himfelf declares to be but bare furmife, of the general's having been too great with his wife, a particular which Othello's character and caft of behaviour feems to give no authority to; and on thefe flight motives he involves, in the ruin he intends for the Moor, three innocent perfons befides, viz. Caffio, Defdemona, and Roderigo.

Far different is Zanga's caufe of rage, and differently purfued. A father's affured death, flain by Alonzo, the lofs of a kingdom, in confequence of his fuccefs, and the indignity of a blow beftowed upon himfelf from the fame hand; all thefe accumulated injuries, added to the impoffibility of finding a nobler means of revenge, urge him againft his will to the fubtilties and underhand methods he employs. Othello's jealoufy is raifed by trifles, the lofs of a poor handkerchief, which Defdemona knew not was of value, and only pleading for a man's forgivenefs who had been cafhiered on a moft trivial fault, are all the circumftances he has to corroborate the vile infinuations of Iago. He therefore muft appear too credulous, and forfeits by fuch conduct fome of our pity. Alonzo, on the contrary, long ftruggles againft conviction of this kind, nor will proceed to extremities till, as he fays himfelf, *" Proofs rife on Proofs, and ftill the laft the ftrongeft."* The man his jealoufy ftands fixed on, is one who had for three years been not only his wife's lover but her deftined hufband. He finds a letter (forged indeed, but fo as to deceive him) from

M 3   Carlos

Carlos to his wife in rapturous terms, returning thanks for joys long fince beftowed on him; he finds his picture hid in a private place in his wife's chamber, is told a pofitive and circumftantial ftory by one whofe perfect truth he had long confided in; and laftly is confirmed in all his apprehenfions by that unwillingnefs to footh them, which Leonora's confcious innocence urges her pride to affume. Such are the advantages the piece before us has with refpect to plot over Othello. And, notwithftanding that Abdelazar has been rendered by Mrs. Behn a very fpirited character, yet any one on infpection will eafily perceive how much more highly coloured Zanga is, and what advantages, even in the fubtilty and probability of fuccefs in his machinations, the one has above the other. In a word, we may, with great juftice, affign to this piece a place in the very firft rank of our dramatic writings.

The Revenge; or, A Match in Newgate. Com. Acted at the Duke's Theatre, 4to. 1680. This play is no more than Marfton's *Dutch Courtezan,* revived with fome very trifling alterations.

Revenge for Honour. Tr. by G. Chapman, 4to. 1659.

*The Revenge of Athri-*dates. Englifh Op. Acted at Smock-Alley, Dublin, 8vo. 1765. Anon.

The Revenger's Tragedy. by Cyril Tourneur. Acted by the King's fervants, 4to. 1607.

The Revengeful Queen. Trag. by William Phillips. Acted at Drury-Lane, 4to. 1698. The plot of this play is taken from Machiavel's *Florentine Hiftory.*

The Revolution of Sweden. Trag. by C. Trotter, afterwards Cockburne. Acted at the Hay-Market, 4to. 1706.

The Rewards of Virtue. Com. by J. Fountain, 4to. 1661. This play was not intended for the ftage by its author; but after his death, Mr. Shadwell, who perceived it to have merit, made fome few alterations in it, and revived it under the title of *The Royal Shepherdefs,* in the year 1669.

Rhodon and Iris. A Paftoral, by R. Knevet, 4to. 1631.

King Richard the Second. Trag. by Wm. Shakfpeare. Acted at the Globe, 4to. 1597. This play has not been acted for many years. Dr. Johnfon obferves, that it is extracted from Holinfhed, in which many paffages may be found which Shakfpeare has with very little alteration tranfplanted into his fcenes; particular a fpeech of the Bifhop of Carlifle, life, in defence of King Richard's unalienable right and immunity from human jurisdiction. This play is one of thofe which Shakfpeare has apparently revifed; but as fuccefs in works of invention is not always proportionate to labour, it is not finifhed at laft with the happy force of fome other of his tragedies, nor can be faid much to affect the paffions or enlarge the underftanding.

The Hiftory of King Richard the Second. By N. Tate. Acted at Drury-Lane, under the name of *The Sicilian Ufurper*, 4to. 1681.

The Hiftory of King Richard the Second. Trag. by L. Theobald, 8vo. 1720. This is only an alteration from Shakfpeare. It was acted at the Theatre in Lincoln's-Inn-Fields with fuccefs.

King Richard the Second. T. altered from Shakfpeare, and the ftyle imitated by J. Goodhall, 8vo. 1772.

King Richard the Second. T. altered from Shakfpeare, by Fran. Gentleman. Acted at Bath about the year 1754. Not printed.

King Richard the Third. Trag. by W. Shakfpeare. Acted by the King's fervants, 4to. 1597. Dr. Johnfon fays, " This is one of the moft celebrated of our author's performances;

we yet know not whether it has not happened to him as to others, to be praifed moft when praife is not moft deferved. That this play has fcenes noble in themfelves, and very well contrived to ftrike in the exhibition, cannot be denied. But fome parts are trifling, and others fhocking, and fome improbable." This play originally took in a long feries of events belonging to the reign of Richard the Third, but was very different from the form in which it now makes its appearance on the ftage.

King Richard the Third. Trag. altered from Shakfpeare, by Colley Cibber. Acted at Drury-Lane, 4to. 1700. The compiler of a late critical work has been very lavifh of his praife of this alteration; but as his encomiums do not appear to be well founded, we think it unneceffary to infert them. The flowery defcriptive lines, appropriated to a chorus in *King Henry the Fifth*, are very abfurdly put into the mouth of the anxious Richard, whofe crown and life depended on the battle for which he was then preparing. When this piece was firft introduced to the ftage, the licencer expunged the whole firft act, affigning as his reafon for it, that the diftreffes of King

Henry

Henry the Sixth, who is killed by Richard in that part of the play, would put weak people too much in mind of King James, then living in France. In this mutilated ſtate it was acted ſeveral years before the proſcribed part was admitted. It has always been a very popular and ſucceſsful performance.

Richard Cœur de Lion. Com. tranſlated from the French. Acted at Covent-Garden, 1786. A very indifferent piece.

Richard Cœur de Lion. Hiſtorical Romance, by M. Sedaine. Acted at Drury-Lane, 1786, and much better written than the above.

The Richmond Heireſs; or, A Woman once in the Right. Com. by Thomas Durfey. Acted at the Theatre Royal, 4to. 1693. This play did not meet at firſt with all the ſucceſs the author expected from it, but being revived afterwards, with alterations, was very favourably received.

Richmond Wells; or, Good Luck at Laſt. Com. by J. Williams. Acted at Richmond, 12mo. 1723.

The Rider; or, The Humours of an Inn. Farce, of two acts, 8vo. 1768.

The Ridiculous Guardian. Comic Burletta, acted at the Haymarket, 4to. 1761.

The Rights of Hecate. Pantomime Entertainment. Acted at Drury-Lane 1764.

Rinaldo. Opera, 8vo. 1711. Performed at the Queen's Theatre in the Haymarket.

Rinaldo and Armida. Tr. by J. Dennis. Acted at Lincoln's-Inn-Fields, 4to. 1699. The hint of the chief characters in this, as well as the laſt-mentioned piece, is from Taſſo's *Gieruſalemme.*

Ripe Fruit; or, The Marriage Act. Interlude, by Charles Stuart. Acted at the Haymarket, 1781.

The Rival Brothers. Tr. Anonymous. Acted at Lincoln's-Inn-Fields, 4to. 1704.

The Rival Candidates. Com. Opera, by H. Bate. Acted at Drury-Lane, 8vo. 1775. This was acted with great applauſe.

The Rival Father; or, The Death of Achilles. Tr. by William Hatchett, 8vo. 1730. This play was acted at the New Theatre in the Haymarket. The conduct of the piece in general is borrowed from the *Mort D'Achille* of Corneille, and the author confeſſes his having taken ſome hints from the *Andromache* of Racine, and endeavoured to imitate the ſimplicity of ſtyle which Phillips has preſerved in his *Diſtreſs'd Mother.* He has, however, fallen greatly ſhort of all his originals. Yet, on the whole, there is ſome fome merit in it ; and it will not be faying too much to confefs, that there ha e been many pieces fince its appearance, which have not been fo deferving of approbation that have met with good fuccefs.

The R val Father. .Far. 8vo. 1754. This piece was never acted, no deferved to be fo.

The Rival Fools. Com. by C. Cibber. Afted at Drury-Lane, 4to. 1709. This play is partly borrowed from Fletcher's *Wit at feveral Weapons.* It met, however, with very bad fuccefs. There happened to be a circumftance in it, which, being in itfelf fomewhat ridiculous, gave a part of the audience a favourable opportunity of venting their fpleen on the author ; viz. a man in one of the earlier fcenes on the ftage, with a long angling rod in his hand, going to fifh for Miller's Thumbs ; on which account, fome of the fpectators took occafion whenever Mr. Cibber appeared, who himfelf played the charact r, to cry ou continually Miller's Thumbs.

The Rival Friends. C. by Peter Hauftead, 4to. 1632.

The Rival Generals. Tr. by J. Sterling. Acted at Dublin, 8vo. 1722.

The Rival Kings ; or, The Loves of Oroondates and Statira. Tragedy, by John Banks. Acted at the Theatre Royal, 4to. 1677. This is one of the leaft known of this author's pieces, and bears he ftrong characteriftic of all his writings, viz. the being affecting in its conduct, without having one good line in its compofition. It is written in rhyme, and the plot taken almoft entirely from the romance of Caffandra, excepting what relates to Alexander.

T e R val Knights. A Pantomime, acted at Covent-Garden, 1783.

The Rival Ladies. Tragi-Com. by J. Dryden. Acted at the Theatre Royal, 4to. 1664. The dedication to this play is a kind of preface in defence of blank verfe. The fcene lies in Alicant ; the difpute betwixt Amileo and Hypolito, and Gonfalvo's fighting with the pirates, is borrowed from Encolpius, Giton, Eumolphus, and Tryphena's boarding the veffel of Lycas, in Petronius Arbiter ; and the cataftrophe has a near refemblance to that of Scarron's *Rival Brothers.*

The Rival L vers. Com. in two acts, by Tho. Warboys, 8vo. 1777. Not acted.

The Rival Milliners ; or, The

The Humours of Covent-Garden. A tragi, comic, farcical, operatical, fantaf-tical Farce, by Robert Drury, 8vo. 1735. This is a burlefque or mock trage-dy, and was performed at the Little Theatre in the Haymarket, with fome ap-plaufe.

The Rival Modes. Com. by J. Moore Smyth. Act-ed at Drury-Lane, 8vo. 1727. The reputed genius of this gentleman gave the higheft expectations of this piece for a long time before its appearance, which, how-ever, it was very far from anfwering, and confequent-ly very foon dropt into ob-livion.

The Rival Mother. Com. Anon. 8vo. 1678.

The Rival Queens; or, *The Death of Alexander the Great.* Tra. by Nathaniel Lee. Acted at the Theatre Royal, 4to. 1677. This is looked on as one of the beft of this author's pieces, and is to this day frequently re-prefented on the ftage; but with confiderable alterations from what Mr. Lee left it. It muft be confeffed, that there is much bombaft and extravagance in fome parts of it; yet in others there is fo much real dignity, and fuch beautiful flights of imagina-tion and fancy, as render even the madnefs of the true ge-

nius more enchanting than even the more regular and finifhed works of the cold laborious play-wright of fome periods fince his time. The fcene is in Babylon, and the ftory may be found in the hiftorians of that hero's life.

The Rival Queens, with the Humours of Alexander the Great. A comical Trage-dy, by C. Cibber. Acted at Drury-Lane, 8vo. 1729. This piece is a burlefque on the laft-mentioned play, al-moft every fcene being pa-rodized with a good deal of humour.

The Rival Priefts; or, *The Female Politician.* C. by Meff. Bellamy, 1746. None of the writings of thefe gentlemen were ever acted at the public theatres.

The Rivals. Com. by Richard Brinfley Sheridan, Efq. Acted at Covent-Garden, 8vo. 1775. This was the firft dramatic piece of an author, who has fince reached the higheft point of excellence in the leaft eafy and moft hazardous fpecies of writing. The prefent play is formed on a plot un-borrowed from any former drama, and contains wit, humour, character, inci-dent, and the principal re-quifites to conftitute a per-fect comedy. It notwith-ftanding

ftanding met with very harfh treatment the firft night, and was with difficulty allowed a fecond reprefentation.

The Rival Sifters ; or, *The Violence of Love.* Tr. by Robert Gould. Acted at Drury-Lane, 4to. 1696. The plot is in great meafure borrowed from Shirley's *Maid's Revenge,* but the original ftory is to be found in *God's Revenge againft Murder.*

The Rival Widows ; or, *The Fair Libertine.* Com. by Mrs. E. Cooper, 8vo. 1735. This Piece was acted at the Theatre Royal in Covent-Garden, with fome fuccefs.

The Roaring Girl ; or, *Moll Cutpurfe.* Com. by Tho. Middleton and Tho. Dekkar. Acted at the Fortune Stage by the Prince's Players, 4to. 1611.

Robert Earl of Huntington's Downfall, afterwards called Robin Hood of merry Sherwode ; with his Love to the chafte Matilda, the Lord Fitzwater's daughter, afterwards his Maid Marian. An hiftorical Play, by Tho. Haywood, 4to. 1601.

Robert Earl of Huntington's Death, otherwife called Robin Hood, of merry Sherwode, with the lamentable Tragedy of chafte Matilda, his fair Maid Marian, poi-

foned at Dunmow by the King. An hiftorical Play, by T. Heywood, 4to. 1601. This play and the preceding one are both printed in the old black letter, and are neither of them divided into acts.

Robin Confcience. An Interlude. Anonymous.

Robinhood. A Mufical Entertainment, 8vo. 1751. This Piece was performed at the Theatre Royal in Drury-Lane, but without any great fuccefs, it having little more than mufical merit to recommend it, which was not then quite fo much the idol of public adoration as it feems at prefent to be.

Robinfon Crufoe. Pantomime. Acted at Drury-Lane, 1781.

Rodogune ; or, *The Rival Brothers.* Trag. by S. Afpinwall, 8vo. 1765. This is a tranflation from the French of Corneille.

Roger and Joan ; or, *The Country Wedding.* A comic Mafque. Anonymous. 4to. 1739.

Rollo Duke of Normandy. Trag. by John Fletcher. Acted by his Majefty's fervants, 4to. 1640. This was efteemed an excellent tragedy, and, though now laid afide, ufed to be received with great applaufe.

The Roman Actor. Trag. by Phil. Maffinger. Acted

M 6   at

at Black‑Fryars, in 4to. 1629.

The Roman Bride's Revenge. Trag. by Charles Gildon. Acted at the Theatre Royal, quarto, 1697. This was a very hasty production, having been written in a month, and met with that success that such precipitancy in works, which undoubtedly require the utmost care in composition, revisal, and correction, justly deserves. Yet it is far from being destitute of merit, the first and second acts, written probably while the author's genius and imagination were in their full glow, being very well executed. The moral intended in it, is to set forth, in the punishment of one of the principal characters, that no consideration whatsoever should induce us to neglect or delay the service of our country.

The Roman Empress. Tr. by William Joyner. Acted at the Theatre Royal, 4to. 1671. This play met with great approbation and success, notwithstanding its first appearance laboured under some inconveniencies. The language of it is poetical, spirited, and masculine, and free from what he calls the jingling antitheses of Love and Honour; Terror and Compassion being the alternate sensations he aims at

exciting in his auditors. It is not very apparent for what reason the author should alter the names of the characters from those which they bear in history. Yet he tells us, that by the advice of friends he has done so, and that this Emperor was one of the greatest that ever Rome boasted. Langbaine conjectures, that under the character of Valentius, the author has intended to draw that of Constantine the Great, and that Crispus, and his mother-in-law Faustina, lie concealed under those of Florus and Fulvia.

The Roman Father. Tra. by W. Whitehead. Acted at Drury-Lane, 8vo. 1750. This Play is founded on that celebrated incident of the earliest period of the Roman history, the combat between the Horatii and the Curiatii. The same story had been long ago made the subject of a dramatic piece, by the great French tragic writer, P. Corneille, whose Horace is esteemed amongst his *chef d'oeuvres.* From that tragedy, therefore, Mr. Whitehead confesses, that he has borrowed the idea of two or three of his most interesting scenes. And we must confess we cannot help wishing he had even more closely followed the plan of that
very

very capital writer in the conduct of the piece, since, by confining himself entirely to Rome, and the family of the Horatii, he has deprived himself of the opportunity of throwing in that var ety of incident and contrast of character which Corneille's play is possessed of, in consequence of his having introduced the young Curiatius, whose rugged, hardy valour, though truly heroical, sets off, in the most advantageous manner, the equality and resolution mingled with superior tendernefs and humanity, which shine out in the character of the young Horatius. This tragedy has certainly great merit, and obtained the just approbation of repeated and judicious audiences.

The Roman Generals ; or, *The Diftreffed Ladies.* Trag. by John Dover, 4to. 1667. From the general tenor of the prologue and epilogue, it is not unreasonable to collect, that the piece was never acted, nor intended to be so, they seeming rather addrefled to the reader than the auditor.

The Roman Maid. Trag. by Capt. Robert Hurst, 8vo. 1725. This Play was acted at the Theatre Royal in Lincoln's-Inn-Fields, with very little success.

The Roman Revenge. Tr. by A. Hill, 8vo. 1753. This Play was acted at the Theatre at Bath with some fuccefs, but is not equal to the generality of its author's works. The plot of or it is the death of Julius Cæfar ; and he has heightened the diltrefs by a circumstance, which, however, we know not that he has any authority for in history, viz. the making Bru us find himfelf, after the death of the dictator, to be his natural fon. How far fuch an addition to, or deviation from, recorded facts is warrantable, or comes within the limits of the *Licentia Poetica,* we have neither room nor inclination to enter into a difcuffion of in this place.

The Roman Sacrifice. Tr. by William Shirley. Acted at Drury-Lane, 1776. Not printed. This Piece was performed only four nights, and was very coldly received.

The Roman Victim. Tra. by William Shirley. This Play is promifed in the collection of the author's dramatic works. It appears to have been refufed both by Mr. Garrick and Mr. Harris.

The Roman Virgin ; or, *Unjuft Judge.* Trag. by Thomas Betterton. Acted at the Duke's Theatre, 4to. 1679. This is only an alteration of Webfter's *Appius and Virginia*.

The Romance of an Hour. Com. of two acts, by Hugh Kelly, performed at Covent-Garden, 8vo. 1774. This little Comedy was acted with fuccefs.

Rome Excis'd. A Tragicomi Ballad Opera, 8vo. 1733. This little Piece is entirely political, and was never intended for the ftage.

Rome Preferv'd. Trag. tranflated from Voltaire, 8vo. 1760.

Rome's Follies ; or, *The Amorous Fryars.* Com by N. N. 4to. 1681.

Romeo and Juliet. Trag. by W. Shakfpeare. The complete one, as acted at the Globe, 4vo. 1609. The fable of this now favourite play is built on a real tragedy that happened about the beginning of the fourteenth century. The ftory, with all its circumftances, is given us by Bandello, in one of his novels, vol. II. Nov. 9, and alfo by Girolamo de la Corte, in his Hiftory of Verona. The fcene, in the beginning of the fifth act, is at Mantua ; through all the reft of the piece in or near Verona. As we have mentioned before that this is at prefent a very favourite Play, it will be

neceffary to take notice what various alterations it has gone through from time to time, and in what form it at prefent appears, which is confiderably different from that in which it was originally written. The tragedy in itfelf has very ftriking beauties, yet on the whole is far from being this great author's mafter-piece. An amafing redundance of fancy fhines through the whole diction of the love fcenes ; yet the overflowings of that fancy in fome places rather runs into puerility, and the frequent intervention of rhymes, which appears in the original play, and which feems a kind of wantonnefs in the author, certainly abates of that verifimilitude to natural converfation which ought ever to be maintained in dramatic dialogue, efpecially where the fcene and action fall under the circumftance of domeftic life. The characters are fome of them very highly painted, particularly thofe of the two lovers, which, perhaps, poffefs more of the romantic, giddy, and irrififtible paffion of love, when it makes it firft attack on very young hearts, than all the labours of an hundred poets fince, was all the effence of their love fcenes to be collected into one, could poffibly con-

ney

vey an idea of. Mercutio, too, is a character fo boldly touched, and fo truly fpirited, that it has been a furmife of fome of the critics, that Shakfpeare put him to to death in the third act, from a confciculnefs that it would even exceed the extent of his own powers to fupport the character through the two laft acts, equal to the fample he had given of it in the three former ones. The cataftrophe is affecting, and even as it ftands in the original is fufficiently dramatic. " This play, fays Dr. Johnfon, is one of the moft pleafing of our author's performances. The fcenes are bufy and various, the incidents namerous and important, the cataftrophe irrefiftibly affecting, and the procefs of the action carried on with fuch probability, at leaft with fuch congruity to popular opinion, as tragedy requires. Here is one of the few attempts to exhibit the converfation of gentlemen, to reprefent the airy fprightlinefs of juvenile elegance. Mr. Dryden mentions a tradition, which might eafily reach his time, of a declaration made by Shakfpeare, that *he was obliged to kill Mercutio in the third act, left he fhould have been killed by him.* Yet he thinks

him *no fuch formidable perfon, but that he might have lived through the Play and died in his bed,* without danger to a poet. Dryden well knew, had he been in queft of truth, that, in a pointed fentence, more regard is commonly had to the words than the thought, and that it is very feldom to be rigoroufly underftood. Mercutio's wit, gaiety, and courage, will always procure him friends that wifh him a longer life ; but his death is not precipitated, he has lived out the time allotted him in the conftruction of the play ; nor do we doubt the ability of Shakfpeare to have continued his exiftence, though fome of his fallies are perhaps out of the reach of Dryden, whofe genius was not very fertile of merriment, nor ductile to humour, but accute, argumentative, comprehenfive, and fublime. The Nurfe is one of the characters in which the author delighted : he has, with great fubtilty of diftinction, drawn her at once loquacious and fecret, obfequious and infolent, trufty and difhoneft. His comic fcenes are happily wrought, but his pathetic ftrains are always polluted with fome unexpected depravations. His

perfons,

perfons, however diftreffed, *have a conceit left them in mifery, a miferable conceit.*"

Romeo and Juliet. By Ja. Howard, Eíquire, who, as Downes, in his *Rofcius Anglicanus*, page 22, tells us, altered his tragedy into a tragi-comedy, preferving both Romeo and Juliet alive; fo that, when the play was revived in Sir William Davenant's company, it was played alternately, viz. tragical one day, and tragi-comical another, for feveral days together. This alteration hath never been printed.

Romeo and Juliet. A Tr. revifed and altered from Shakfpeare, by Mr. Theo. Cibber; firft revived (in September, 1744) at the Theatre in the Haymarket; afterwards acted at Drury-Lane, 8vo. no date [1748]. Subjoined to this is a ferio-comic apology for part of the life of the author. Very confiderable alterations and additions were made in this edition; but thefe agree fo ill with the remainder written by Shakfpeare, that it is impoffible to read them with any degree of fatiffaction.

Romeo and Juliet. A Tr. Acted at Drury-Lane, 12mo. 1751. The third of thefe alterations, which is now univerfally and repeatedly performed in all the Britifh Theatres, is the work of Mr. Garrick, whofe perfect acquaintance with the properties of effect, and unqueftionable judgment as to what will pleafe an audience, have fhewn themfelves very confpicuoufly in this piece. For, without doing much more than reftoring Shakfpeare to himfelf, and the ftory to the novel from which it was originally borrowed, he has rendered the whole more uniform, and worked up the cataftrophe to a greater degree of diftrefs than it held in the original; as Juliet's awaking before Romeo's death, and the tranfports of the latter, on feeing her revive, overcoming even the very remembrance of the very lateft act of defperation he had committed, give fcope for that fudden tranfition from rapture to defpair, which makes the recollection, that he *muft* die, infinitely more affecting, and the diftrefs of Juliet, as well as his own, much deeper than it is poffible to be in Shakfpeare's play, where fhe does not awake till after the poifon has taken its full effect in the death of Romeo. There is one alteration, however, in this piece, which, we muft confefs, does not appear to us altogether neceſſary, viz. the introducing Romeo from the beginning as in love with Juliet, whereas Shakſpeare ſeems to have intended, by making him at firſt enamoured with another (Roſalind), to point out his misfortunes in the conſequence of one paſſion, as a piece of poetical juſtice for his inconſtancy and falſhood in regard to a prior attachment, as Juliet's in ſome meaſure are for her breach of filial obedience, and her raſhneſs in the indulgence of a paſſion, ſo oppoſite to the natural intereſts and connections of her family. Beſides theſe, two other managers, viz. Mr. Sheridan of the Dublin, and Mr. Lee of the Edinburgh Theatre, have each, for the uſe of their reſpective companies, made ſome ſuppoſed amendments in this play ; but, as neither of them have appeared in print, we can give no farther account of them : nor of a third alteration by Mr. Marſh, which he has likewiſe had the prudence to conceal from the public.

Romeo and Juliet. Com. written originally in Spaniſh, by that celebrated dramatic poet Lopez de Vega, 8vo. 1770.

Romulus. Trag. by H. Johnſon, from the French

of Monſieur De La Motte, 8vo. 1721.

Romulus and Herſilia ; or, *The Sabine War.* Trag. Anon. Acted at the Duke's Theatre, 4to. 1683. This is a very good play.

Romulus and Herſilia. Tr. by Dr. Ralph Schomberg. Never printed.

Roſamond. Opera, by Joſeph Addiſon, 4to. 1707. The plot of this little Piece is taken from the Engliſh Hiſtory in the reign of Henry II. and it is obſerved that it exceeds, in the beauty of the diction, any Engliſh performance of the kind. It was, however, very ill ſet to muſic, by which means the ſucceſs it met with fell far ſhort of what its merit might juſtly have laid a claim to. In the year 1767 it was entirely new ſet by Dr. Arnold, and performed at Covent - Garden, 8vo. The ſcene is laid in Woodſtock Park. Dr. Johnſon obſerves, that the opera of Roſamond, though it is ſeldom mentioned, is one of the firſt of Addiſon's compoſitions. The ſubject is well choſen, the fiction is pleaſing, and the praiſe of Marlborough, for which the ſcene gives opportunity, is, what perhaps every human excellence muſt be, the product of good luck improved by genius. The thoughts are

ſome-

sometimes great, and sometimes tender; the versification is easy and gay. There is is doubtless some advantage in the shortness of the lines, which there is little tempation to load with expletive epithets. The dialogue seems commonly better than the songs. The two comic characters of Sir Trusty and Grideline, though of no great value, are yet such as the poet intended. Sir Trusty's account of the death of Rosamond is, we think, too grossly absurd. The whole drama is airy and elegant; engaging in its process, and pleasing in its conclusion.

The Rose. Comic Opera, in two acts, performed at Drury-Lane. 8vo. 1773. The music by Dr. Arne, who is supposed to have been the author of the words also. It was represented only one night.

Rose and Colin. Comic Opera, by Charles Dibdin. Acted at Covent-Garden, 8vo. 1778.

Rosina. A Musical Piece of two Acts, by Mrs. Brook. Acted at Covent-Garden Theatre, 1783, and very well received.

Rotheric O'Connor, King of Connaught; or, The Distress'd Princess. Trag. by Charles Shadwell, 12mo. 1720.

*The Rover; or, The Ba-*nish'd Cavaliers. Com. in two parts, by Mrs. Aphra Behn. Acted at the Duke's Theatre, 4to. 1677. These two comedies are both of them very entertaining, and contain much business, bustle, and intrigue, supported with an infinite deal of sprightliness. The basis of them both, however, may be found on a perusal of Killigrew's Don Thomaso; or, The Wanderer. The scene of the first part is laid in Naples during the time of the Carnival, which is the high season for gallantry; and that of the second at Madrid.

The Rover; or, Happiness at Last. A Dramatic Pastoral, designed for the Theatre, but never acted, by Sam. Boyce, 4to. 1752.

The Round Heads; or, The Good Old Cause. Com. by Mrs. Behn. Acted at the Duke's Theatre, 4to. 1682. Great part, both of the plot and language of this play, is borrowed from Tatham's Comedy, called The Rump.

The Rout. Farce of two acts. Acted at Drury-Lane, 8vo. 1758. This very insignificant little piece made its first appearance for the benefit of the Marine Society, and was said to be written by a Person of Quality, and *presented* to that charity, without the least view to private emolument.

In

R O   [259]   R O·

In fome little time after-wards, however, this boaſt-ed perſon of diſtinction, turned out to be no other than the *illuſtrious* Dr. Hill.

The Royal Captives. Tr. Acted at the Haymarket, 8vo. 1729. This Play met with no ſuccefs in the repre-ſentation.

The Royal Convert. Tr. by N. Rowe, 4to. 1707. This Play, though not ſo often acted as ſome others of this author's pieces, is far from falling ſhort of any one of them in point of merit. The ſcene of it is laid in the kingdom of Kent, and the fable ſuppoſed to be in the time of Hengiſt, and about twenty years after the firſt invaſion of Britain by the Saxons. The characters of Rodogune and Ethelinda are very finely contraſted, as are alſo thoſe of Hengiſt and Aribert ; the incidents are intereſting ; the language occaſionally ſpirited and tender, yet every where poetical ; and the cataſtro-phe affecting and truly dra-matic. Nor do we know any reaſon why it ſhould not be as great a favourite as either *Jane Shore* or the *Fair Penitent,* unlefs that its being founded on a re-ligious plan renders it lefs agreable to the general taſte of an audience, than thoſe ſtories where love is in ſome meaſure the baſis of

the diſtrefs. It was acted at the Queen's Theatre in the Haymarket, and with but ſmall ſuccefs, if we may judge from the motto to it, *Laudatur & alget.* Doctor Johnſon obſerves, that the fable of this play is drawn from an obſcure and bar-barous age, to which fic-tions are moſt eaſily and properly adapted ; for when objects are imperfectly ſeen, they eaſily take forms from imagination. The ſcene lies among our anceſtors in our own country, and there-fore very eaſily catches at-tention. Rodogune is a perſonage truly tragical, of high ſpirit, and violent paſſions, great with tem-peſtuous dignity, and wicked with a ſoul that would have been heroic if it had been virtuous. Rowe does not always remember what his characters require. In *Ta-merlane* there is ſome ridi-culous mention of the God of Love ; and Rodogune, a ſavage Saxon, talks of Venus, and the eagle that bears the thunder of Jupiter. This play difcovers its own date, by a prediction of the *Union,* in imitation of Cran-mer's prophetic promiſes to *Henry the Eighth.* The an-ticipated bleſſings of Union are not very naturally in-troduced, nor very happily expreſſed.

The Royal Cuckold; or, *Great*

Great Baſtard. Tragi-Com. 4to. 1693. This was never acted.

The Royal Flight ; or, *The Conqueſt of Ireland.* A Farce, 4to. 1690.

The Royaliſt. Com. by Thomas Durfey. Acted at the Duke's Theatre, 4to. 1682. This Play met with good ſucceſs, but, like moſt of our author's pieces, is collected from novels.

The Royal King and the Loyal Subject. Tragi-Com. by Thomas Heywood, 4to. 1637. This Play was acted with great applauſe. The plot very much reſembles, and is probably borrowed from, Fletcher's *Loyal Subject.*

The Royal Marriage. A Ballad Opera, of three acts. Anonym. 8vo. 1736. This piece was never performed, but written in compliment to the marriage between his late Royal Highneſs Frederick Prince of Wales, and the Princeſs Auguſta, of Saxegotha, the late Princeſs-Dowager of Wales.

The Royal Martyr ; or, *King Charles the Firſt,* by Alexander Fyfe, 4to. 1709. This play was never acted.

The Royal Maſque, preſented at Hampton - Court on the 8th of January, 1604. Anonymous. 4to. 1604.

The Royal Maſter. Tragi-Com. by James Shirley, 4to. 1638. This play was acted at the Theatre in Dublin, and before the Lord Lieutenant at the Caſtle.

The Royal Merchant ; or, *The Beggar's Buſh.* Com. 4to. 1706. by H. N. (probably Henry Norris the Comedian). This Play is only an alteration from Beaumont and Fletcher's *Beggar's Buſh,* and in this altered form has been frequently performed.

The Royal Merchant. Op. by Thomas Hull, founded on Beaumont and Fletcher. Acted at Covent-Garden, 8vo. 1768.

The Royal Miſchief. Tr. by Mrs. De la Riviere Manley. Acted by his Majeſty's ſervants, 4to. 1696. The plot, as the authoreſs herſelf informs us in her preface, is taken from a ſtory in Sir John Chardin's Travels ; but ſhe has improved the cataſtrophe, by puniſhing the criminal characters for their illicit amours, whereas in the original tale they are ſuffered to eſcape. The allegories in it are juſt, the metaphors beautiful, and the Ariſtotelian rules of the drama ſtrictly adhered to.

The Royal Shepherd. Op. by Richard Rolt. Acted at Drury - Lane, 8vo. 1764. Taken from Mataſtatio. It met with no ſucceſs.

The Royal Shepherdeſs. Tragi - Com. by Thomas Shadwell. Acted at the

Duke

Duke of York's Theatre, 4to. 1669. This play is not Shadwell's own, being, as he himself acknowledges, in his epiftle to the reader, taken from a comedy written by M. Fountain, called *The Rewards of Virtue.* It met, however, with confiderable applaufe. The fcene lies in Arcadia.

The Royal Shepherds. Paftoral, of three acts, by Jofias Cunningham, 8vo. 1765.

The Royal Slave. Tragi-Com. by Wm. Cartwright, 4to. 1639. The firft r prefentation of this play was by the ftudents of Chrift-church in Oxford, betore King Charles I. and his Queen, on the 30th of Aug. 1636. And it is very remarkable, that Dr. Bulby (afterwards the very celebrated mafter of Weftminfter-fchool), who acted a principal part in it, fignalized himfelf fo greatly, and the play gave on the whole fuch general fatisfaction to their Majefties and the Court, and that not only for the noblenefs of ftyle in in the piece itfelf, and the ready addrefs and graceful carriage of the performers, but alfo for the pomp of the fcenery, the richnefs of the habits, and the excellency of the fongs, which were fet by that admirable compofer Mr. Henry Lawes, that it was univerfally acknowledg-

ed to exceed every thing of that nature that had been feen before. The Queen in particular, was fo extremely delighted with it, that her curiofity was excited to fee her own fervants, whofe profeffion it was, reprefent the fame piece, in order to be able, from comparifon, to form a juft idea of the real merit of the performance fhe had already been witnefs to. For which purpofe fhe fent for the fcenes and habits to Hampton-Court, and commanded her own regular actors to reprefent the fame, when, by general content of every one prefent, the judgement was given in favour of the literary performers, though nothing was wanting on the fide of the author, to inform the actors as well as the fcholars, in what belonged to the action and delivery of each part; nor can it be imagined that there was any deficiency in point of execution in the former, fince fo much of their reputation muft have been dependent on their fhewing a fuperiority on that occafion. The prologues and epilogues, written for both thefe reprefentations, are printed with the play.

The Royal Suppliants. T. by Doctor Delap. Acted at Drury-Lane, 8vo. 1781.
This

This nine-nights' play is taken from the *Heraclidæ* of Euripides.

The Royal Voyage; or, *The Irish Expedition*. Trag-Com. Acted in the years 1689 and 1690, 4to. 1690. It was never acted.

Rudens. Com. translated from Plautus, by Lawrence Echard, 1694.

Rule a Wife and have a Wife. Comedy, by John Fletcher. Acted by his Majesty's servants, 4to. 1640. This is a very pleasing play, and is frequently acted at this time. The plot of Leon's feigned simplicity, in order to gain Margaretta for a wife, and his immediate return to the exertion of a spirited behaviour for the controul of her, create an agreeable surprize, and are truly dramatical. The characters of Estifania and the Copper Captain are also well drawn and lively supported. In a word, this play, though not perfectly regular, may undoubtedly stand in a rank of merit superior to much the greatest part of those which are daily presented on our stage, and that with repeated tokens of approbation.

The Rump; or, *The Mirrour of the late Times*. Com. by John Tatham. Acted at Dorset-Court, 4to. 1660. This piece was written soon

after the Restoration; and the author, being a steady Royalist, has endeavoured to paint the Puritans in the strongest and most contemptible colours.

" The famous Tragedie of the Life and Death of *Mrs. Rump*. Shewing how she was brought to bed of a monster, with her terrible pangs, bitter teeming, hard labour, and lamentable travell, from Portsmouth to Westminster, and the great misery she hath endured by her ugly, deformed, ill-shapen, base-begotten brat, or imp of reformation, and the great care and wonderful pains taken by Mr. London Midwife, Mrs. Haslerigg, Nurse Gossip Vaine, Gossip Scot, and her man Litesum, Gossip Walton, Gossip Martin, Gossip Nevil, Gossip Lenthal, secluded Gossip's Apprentices. Together with the exceeding great fright she took at a free parliament : and the fatal end of that grand tyrant O. C. the father of all murthers, rebellions, treasons, and treacheries, committed since the year 1648. As it was presented on a burning stage, at Westminster, the 29th of May 1660." This long title is prefixed to a trifling piece of eight pages, which is entirely political, and of no value.

Mrs.

The Runaway. Com. by Mrs. Cowley. Acted at Drury-Lane, 8vo. 1776. This piece is suppofed to have received fome touches from the pen of Mr. Gar-

rick, to which gentleman the authorefs acknowledges her obligations in a Dedication. It was performed with a confiderable degree of fuccefs.

S A

S A

THE *Sacrifice.* Tr. by by Sir Francis Fane, 4to. 1686. This play was never acted, the author having long before devoted himfelf to a country life, and wanting patience to attend the leifure of the ftage.

The Sacrifice ; or, *Cupid's Vagaries.* Mafque, by Benjamin Victor. Never acted, 8vo. 1776.

The Sad One. Tra. by Sir John Suckling, 8vo. 1646. This play was never acted, having been left by the author unfinifhed. In fhort, it is rather a fketch or fkeleton of a play, than an entire piece ; for though it confifts of five acts, and feems to have fomewhat of a cataftrophe, yet none of thofe acts are of more than half the ufual length ; nor is the fubject of any one fcene fo much extended on, as it is apparent it was the author's intention to have done. The fcene lies in Sicily.

The Sad Shepherd ; or, *A Tale of Robin Hood.* A Paftoral, by Ben Jonfon, fol.

1640. This piece is printed among this writer's works, but was never acted, as it was left imperfect by him at his death, on'y two acts and part of a third being finifhed. The fcene is in Sherwood, confifting of a landfcape, of a foreft, hills, valleys, cottages, a caftle, a river, paftures, herds, flocks —all full of country fimplicity. Robin Hood's bower, his well, the Witch's *Dimble*, the Swine'ard's *Oak*, and the Hermit's *Cell.*

The Sailors Farewell ; or, *The Guinea Outfit.* Com. of three acts, by Thomas Boulton, 12mo. 1768.

The Sailor's Opera ; or, *A Trip to Jamaica,* 12mo. 1745.

Saint Cicily ; or, *The Converted Twins.* A Chriftian Tragedy, by E. M. 4to. 1676.

Saint Helena ; or, *The Ifle of Love.* Mufical Entertainment, by Capt. Edward Thompfon. Acted at Richmond, and once at Drury-Lane, 1776. Not printed.

Saint

Saint Patrick for Ireland. Hiſtorical Play, by James Shirley, 4to. 1640. The play is now in print, and common to be met with in Ireland, it having been re-publiſhed there about thirty years ago, by Mr. Chetwood.

Saint Patrick's Day ; or, *The Scheming Lieutenant.* F. by Richard Brinſley Sheridan, Eſq. Acted at Covent-Garden, May 2, 1775. Not printed. This piece waſ originally repreſented at the benefit of Mr. Clinch, who ſeems to have been favoured with it in conſequence of his performance of the Iriſhman in Mr. Sheridan's play of *The Rivals.*

Salmacida Spolia. Maſq. Anonym. 4to. 1639. This Maſque, though printed without any author's name to it, ought to be arranged among the works of Sir William Davenant, ſince whatever was either ſooken or ſung in it was written by that gentleman. It was preſented by the King and Queen's Majeſties at Whitehall on Tueſday the 21ſt of January 1639. The ſcenes and machines, with their deſcriptions and ornaments, we e invented by Inigo Jones, and the muſic compoſed by Mr. Lewis Richard.

The Salopian Squire ; or,

The Joyous Miller. A Dramatic Tale, by E. Dower, 8vo. 1739.

Sampſon Agoniſtes. Dramatic Poem, by John Milton, 8vo. 1670. This piece is written in imitation of the Greek tragic poets, more particularly Æſchylus. The meaſure is not regular, being compoſed of every kind indiſcriminately blended. The ſpeaking ſcenes are relieved and explained by *choruſes*, and all the regular conſtraint of diviſion into acts and ſcenes is totally avoided, the poem having never been intended by the author for the ſtage, who ſtrongly laboured to render it admirable for the cloſet. So noble, ſo juſt, ſo elegant, ſo poetical is the diction of it, that the great Mr. Dryden, whoſe imagination might be ſuppoſed to be equal to that of any man, has transferred many thoughts of this piece into his tragedy of *Aureng-zebe.* The foundation of the ſtory is in holy writ, ſee Judges, ch. xiii. and the ſcene is laid at or near the gates of Gaza. We remember to have ſeen in the poſſeſſion of a gentleman in Dublin (one Mr. Dixon) an alteration of this poem, ſaid by himſelf to be his own, ſo as to render it fit for the ſtage ; and the ſame gentleman alſo ſhewed ed a bill for the intended performance (which was, through some difpute among the proprietors of the theatre, entirely laid afide) in which, from the number of characters, and the apparent ftrength to fupport them, it appeared to have been caft to the greateft advantage poffible, every performer of importance, whether actor, finger, or dancer, having fomewhat allotted to them towards the illuftration of it. This reprefentation, if we miftake not, was intended for the year 1741-2.

Sancho at Court; or, *The Mock Governor*. An Opera Com. by James Ayres, 8vo. 1742. The title of this piece fufficiently points out the plan of it.

Sapho and Phao. Com. by John Lyly, 4to. 1584. This old play was firft prefented before Queen Elizabeth on a Shrove-Tuefday, and afterwards at the Black-Fryars Theatre. The plot is taken from one of Ovid's Epiftles.

Satyromaftix; or, *The Untruffing of the humourous Poet*. Acted publickly by the Lord Chamberlain's fervants, and privately by the children of Paul's, 4to. 1602. By Thomas Dekker.

The Savage; or, *The Force of Nature*, 8vo. 1736.

This piece, which was never acted, is inferted by the author of *The Britifh Theatre* among the writings of Mr. James Miller.

Saul. Trag. by Aaron Hill. Of this intended tragedy the author finifhed no more than one act, which is to be found in the laft volume of his works publifhed in two volumes, 8vo.

King Saul. Trag. written by a deceafed perfon of honour, and now made public at the requeft of feveral men of quality, who have highly approved of it, 4to. 1703. This play is dedicated by the publifher Henry Playford, to the Countefs of Burlington, who is therein faid to be related to the noble perfon who was fuppofed to be the author of it. We know no ton what foundation, but this play has been afcribed to Dr. Trapp.

Saul and Jonathan. Tr. by Edward Crane, of Manchefter, 8vo. 1761.

Sawney the Scot; or, *The Taming of the Shrew*. Com. by John Lacy. Acted at Drury-Lane, 4to. 1698. This is only an alteration, without much amendment, of Shakfpeare's comedy of the laft-mentioned title. It met, however, with very good fuccefs.

Scanderbeg. Trag. by William Havard, 8vo. 1733.

N   This

This play is founded on the fame plan with Lillo's *Chriftian Hero*, being built on the life of the famous George Caftriot, king of Epirus, who, on account of his illuftrious actions, which in great meafure refembled thofe of Alexander the Great, had the title of Scanderbeg (or Lord Alexander) univerfally allowed to him. It was acted at the Theatre in Goodman's-Fields, but with no very good fuccefs.

Scanderbeg ; or, Love and Liberty. By Thomas Whincop, 8vo. 1747. This tragedy was never acted, but was publifhed by fubfcription after the author's death, for the benefit of the widow.

Scaramouch, a Philofopher, Harlequin, a School-Boy, Bravo, Merchant, and Magician. Com. by Edward Ravenfcroft. Acted at the Theatre Royal, 4to. 1677. This comedy confifts of the compounded plots of three plays of Moliere, viz. *The Marriage Forcé ; The Bourgeois Gentilhomme ;* and *The Fourberies de Scapin.*

The Schemers ; or, The City Match. Com. Acted at Drury-Lane, 8vo. 1755. This is Jafper Main's *City Match* altered, and was both acted and printed for the benefit of the Lock-Hofpital. The alterer is faid to

have been Wm. Bromfield, Efq.

The Scholar. Com. by Richard Lovelace. Acted at Gloucefter-hall and Salifbury-Court. Not printed.

The School for Arrogance. Com. by Mr. Marfhall. Acted at Covent-Garden, 1791, and favourably received.

The School-Boy ; or, The Comical Rivals. A Com. Acted at Drury-Lane, 4to. 1707. This comedy is little more than the plot of Major Rakifh and his fon, and the Widow Manlove in *Woman's Wit ; or, The Lady in Fafhion,* a comedy written by the fame author, taken *verbatim,* and thrown by itfelf into the form of a farce, under which appearance it had better fuccefs than the entire comedy, and is now frequently performed; whereas the other has been long thrown entirely afide. The characters of Young Rakifh and the Major are themfelves in great meafure to be confidered as copies, as any one may be convinced who will carefully examine Carlifle's *Fortune Hunters,* the character of Daredevil in Otway's *Soldiers Fortune,* and thofe of Sir Thomas Revel and his fon in in Mountford's *Greenwich Park*.

The School for Action. Com. by Sir Richard Steel, left unfinished by him at his death.

The School for Eloquence. Interlude by Mrs. Cowley. Acted at Drury-Lane, 1780 for Mr. Brereton's benefit. Not printed.

The School for Fathers. Comic Opera, by Isaac Bickerstaffe. Acted at Drury-Lane, 8vo. 1770. This is only *Lionel and Clarissa*, with some slight alterations.

The School for Guardians. Com. by Arthur Murphy, Esq. Acted at Covent-Garden, 8vo. 1767. This comedy lingered on the stage for six nights, and then was laid aside.

A School for Husbands. Com. by J. Ozell.

The School for Lovers. Com. by Wm. Whitehead. Acted at Drury-Lane, 8vo. 1762. This is the last dramatic work but one of that laureat, and his first attempt in the walks of comedy. In an advertisement prefixed to it, he acknowledges it to have received its first foundation in a dramatic piece written, but not intended for the stage, by M. de Fontenelle, to whose memory he dedicates this piece, subscribing himself

a *Lover of Simplicity*. What species of *Drama*, however, it ought to be classed in, is somewhat dificult to determine, since, though it is styled a comedy, the risible faculties have much less opportunity of exertion than the tender feelings of the heart, and the catastrophe, though happy in the main, and suitable to poetical justice, is not completely so, since two amiable characters are left, the one entirely unprovided for, and the other in a situation far from agreeable, viz. that of only being witness to a degree of happiness in the possession of others, which, with respect to herself, she must imagine out of reach, or at least deferred for a considerable period of time. Those who are acquainted with the play will readily conceive, that the characters we mean are Bellmour and Araminta; and as to Modely, though he has, through the course of the piece, appeared to have foibles, yet, as they have not arisen from any badness of heart, and that the open sincerity of his repentance is too apparent to every auditor, not to render him deserving of a restoration to esteem, the author might perhaps have waved some little of his punishment, and restored his

N 2 *Araminta*

Araminta alfo to his arms. What the author, however, feems to have principally aimed at, viz. delicacy, fentiment, and the confequence of inftruction in the conduct of a generous and well-placed paffion, he has undoubtedly moft eminently fucceeded in. His Celia and Sir John Dorilant, and more efpecially the latter, are characters moft perfectly amiable and worthy of imitation ; and to remove at once the great cavil of the critics, who feemed, with refpect to this piece, to be at a lofs where to fix a cenfure, if a dramatic piece has thofe effential good qualities of affording at once a fenfibility to the heart, a leffon to the underftanding, and an agreeable amufement to the fenfes, of what importance is it to look back to what title the author has thought proper to give it?

The School for Rakes. C. by Mrs. Elizabeth Griffiths, Acted at Drury-Lane, 8vo. 1769. This play was performed with confiderable fuccefs.

The School for Scandal. Com. by Richard Brinfley Sheridan, Efq. Acted at Drury-Lane, 1776. Any attempt to be particular in the praife of this comedy, would be at once difficult

and unneceffary. No piece ever equalled it in fuccefs on the ftage, and very few are fuperior to it in point of intrinfic merit. The policy of our earlieft theatres being at prefent revived, *The School for Scandal* is ftill unprinted, and therefore efcapes that minutenefs of criticifm of which in our idea it has no reafon to be afraid.

The School for Sandal fcandalized. Interlude. Acted at Mr. Lewis's benefit at Covent - Garden, March 1780. Not printed.

The School for Vanity. A Com. by Mr. Pratt. Acted at Drury-Lane, 1783. The laudable defign of this comedy is to expofe to public ridicule the very troublefome and often dangerous vice of perfonal vanity in men and women.

The School for Widows. Com. Acted at Covent-Garden, 1789. We apprehend few widows will attend to the leffons here given.

School for Women. Com. by J. Ozell. This is a tranflation of Moliere's *Ecole des Femmes.* As is alfo

The School for Women criticiz'd, of a little piece called the *Critque de l'Eccle des Femmes,* written likewife by Moliere, and englifhed by the fame gentleman. Neither

Neither of thefe pieces was ever intended for the Englifh ftage in their prefent form, being only tranflations calculated for the acquiring an acquaintance with that celebrated French poet in the clofet.

The School for Wives. C. by Hugh Kelly. Acted at Drury-Lane, 8vo. 1774. The hard treatment Mr. Kelly's comedy of *A Word to the Wife* met with from the public, induced him to produce the prefent in the name of Mr. Addington. He afferts, that it is unborrowed from any other writer. The fuccefs of it was fully equal to its merit.

The School of Compliment. Com. by James Shirley. Acted at the private houfe Drury-Lane, 4to. 1631. The author, in a prologue, declares this to be the *Firft Fruits of his Mufes,* and *that he meant not to fwear himfelf a Factor to the Scene.* Yet the fuccefs the firft attempt met with probably induced him to change this intention, and devote himfelf a very induftrious one, as the multitude of plays he afterwards wrote fufficiently evince him to have been.

School Play. An Interlude. Anonym. 8vo. 1664. This little piece, which confifts of only five fcenes, was prepared for, and performed in, a private grammar fchool in Middlefex in the year 1663.

Scipio Africanus. Trag. by Charles Beckingham, 12mo. 1718. This play was acted at the Theatre in Lincoln's-Inn-Fields with confiderable fuccefs, and defervedly. For though the author was not above nineteen years of age when he wrote it, yet he has been happy in his diction, proper in his expreffions, and juft in his fentiments. His plot is founded on hiftorical facts, and thofe fuch as are well fuited to form the fubject of a dramatic piece. His action is uniform and entire, his epifodes judicious, his characters well drawn, and his unities perfectly deferved. So that, on the whole, it may certainly be pronounced an excellent tragedy, conformable to the rules of the drama and the precepts of modern criticifm.

The Scribler. C. 12mo. 1751. Printed at Dublin, but it does not appear to have been acted.

The Scornful Lady. Com. by Beaumont and Fletcher. Acted at Black-Fryars, 4to. 1616. This play was efteemed an exceeding good one, and even within very late years has been performed with great applause.

The Scots Figaries; or, *A Knot of Knaves*. Com. by J. Tatcham, 4to. 1652. This play is great part of it written in the Scotch dialect, and the author, who had the highest detestation for the Scots, has drawn the characters of them and of the *Puritans* in this piece in very contemptible as well as hateful colours.

The Scottish Politic Presbyter slain by an English Independent; or, *The Independent's Victory over the Presbyterian Party*, &c. Tragi-Com. Anonym. 4to. 1647. This is one among the numerous farcastical pieces, which the disturbances and heartburnings both in church and state of that unhappy period gave birth to.

The Scowerers. Com. by Thomas Shadwell. Acted by their Majesties servants, 4to. 1691. This play contains a great deal of low humour; yet, although Langbaine entirely acquits our author of plagiarism with respect to it, the character of Eugenia seems to be pretty closely copied from Harriot, in Sir George Etherege's *Man of Mode*.

The Sea Voyage. Com. by Beaumont and Fletcher, fol. 1647. The design of this play is borrowed from Shakspeare's *Tempest*.

The Search after Happiness. Pastoral Drama, by Miss Hannah Moore, 8vo. 1773. This Pastoral was composed by the authoress at the age of eighteen years, and recited by a party of young ladies, for whose use it was originally written.

Sebastian. Trag. by G. P. Tooley, 8vo. 1772.

Second Thoughts are Best. Com. by Mrs. Cowley. See *The World as it goes*.

Second Thought is Best. Com. Opera, by J. Hough, Esq. Acted at Drury-Lane, March 30, 1778, at Miss Younge's benefit.

The Secret Expedition. Farce, of two acts, 8vo. 1757.

Secret Love; or, *The Maiden Queen*. Tragi-Com. by J. Dryden. Acted at the Theatre Royal, 4to. 1668. The plot of the serious part of this play is founded on a novel, called the History of Cleobuline, Queen of Corinth.

The Secret Plot. Trag. of three acts. Written by Rupert Green, Dec. 30, 1776, aged eight years and eleven months, 12mo. 1777. The printing of this piece is one of the foolish instances of parental vanity, which nothing can justify or excuse.

Seduction.

Seduction. Com. by Mr. Holcroft. Acted at Drury-Lane, 1787. It is a well-written Comedy, and was acted with much applause.

Seeing is Believing. A Dramatic Proverb, by Mr. Joddrell. Acted at the Haymarket, 1783. This piece, on its reprefentation, created laughter in defpight of common fenfe.

Sejanus. Tra. by Fran. Gentleman, 8vo. 1752. This tragedy never made its appearance on either of the London theatres; but it was acted at Bath with fome degree of applaufe.

Sejanus his Fall. Trag. by Ben Jonfon, 4to. 1605. This play was firft acted in 1603, and is ufhered into the world by no lefs than nine copies of commendatory verfes. It has indeed great merit. The plot is founded on hiftory, the ftory being to be feen in the Annals of Tacitus, and Suetonius's Life of Tiberius. The author has difplayed great learning, and made an advantageous ufe of his acquaintance with the antients; yet fearful, as it fhould feem by the preface, of being taxed by the critics with a plagiarifm which he thought himfelf by no means entitled to be afhamed of, he has pointed out all his quotations and authorities.

The Self Rival. Com.

by Mrs. Mary Davys. This piece was never acted, but was intended for the Theatre Royal in Drury-Lane.

The Firft Part of the Tragicall Raigne of *Selimus,* fometime Emperour of the Turkes, and grandfather to him that now raigneth. Wherein is fhowne how he moft unnaturally raifed warres againft his owne father Bajazet, and prevailing therein, in the end caufed him to be poifoned; alfo with the murthering of his two brethren Corcutus and Acomat. Acted by the Queen's players, 4to 1594.

Selima and Azor. Dram. Romance. Acted at Drury-Lane, 1776. The fongs only printed in 8vo. A pompous nothing, pilfered from the French, and faid to be the work of Sir G. Collier.

Selindra. Tragi-Com. by Sir William Killegrew, 8vo. 1664. fol. 1666.

Semele. An Opera, by W. Congreve. This fhort piece was performed and printed in 4to. 1707.

Semiramis. Tr. tranflated from Voltaire, 8vo. 1760.

Semiramis. Tr. tranflated from Voltaire, and printed in Dr. Franklin's edition of that author.

Semiramis. Tra. by G. Edward Ayfcough. Acted at Drury-Lane. 8vo. 1776.

The

The prefent tragedy, as written by, Voltaire, has a confiderable degree of dramatic merit, which is all evaporated through the wretchedneſs of this tranſlation from a tranſlation, and by injudicious changes in the conduct of the fable. The ghoſt of Ninus, on his firſt appearance at Paris, was by no means treated with ſuch civility as might have been expected to be ſhewn by a polite nation to ſo great a ſtranger on their ſtage. The phantom indeed, contrary to the rule his predeceſſors had conſented to obſerve, bolted out at noonday, and in the midſt of all the aſſembled Satraps of the realm. Captain Ayſcough, however, obliged him to entertain his widow and his ſon with only a private exhibition. In this ſcene, the figure and poſt of the Aſſyrian monarch exactly reſembled thoſe of an old Chelſea penſioner employed to watch a churchyard, and burſting from a ſentry-box to catch the perſons who came to ſteal bodies for the ſurgeons. The Captain's play, in ſhort, like himſelf and other paraſites of the late Lord Lyttelton, was every way contemptible; though it is plain that he though differently, as he appeared, during the firſt night of its repreſentation, in various parts of the houſe, thruſting out his head to engage the attention and receive the homage of the ſpectators. The theatre on this occaſion was filled with his brother officers, who were all ſo ſick of their duty under him, that they never returned to it a ſecond time. Our author therefore gained only a few pounds by all his three benefits, being obliged to employ the profits of one to make up deficiences in the other two, when there wasnot money enough in the houſe to defray his night expences. This fool of faſhion has done yet more extenſive miſchief; having made the ſtory of Ninus and Semiramis ſo diſguſting, that ſhould it be undertaken by a more ſkilful hand, it would fail, for ſome years at leaſt, in its power to attract an audience.

Separate Maintenance. Com. by George Colman, Eſq. Acted at the Haymarket, 1779. The characters of genteel life are not ſufficiently diſtinct from each other to afford much entertainment to an Engliſh audience. For this reaſon, we think this performance not the moſt pleaſing of Mr. Colman's Dramatic works.

Of

Of the Sepulture and Re-surrection. Two Comedies, by Bishop Bale. These two pieces stand on the list this right reverend father has given us of his own writings, and which is all the information we have concerning them.

The Sequel of Henry the Fourth, with the Humours of Sir John Falstaffe and Justice Shallow, altered from Shakspeare, by Mr. Betterton. Acted at Drury-Lane, 8vo. 1719.

A Sequel to the Opera of Flora. Acted at Lincoln's-Inn-Fields, 8vo. 1732.

The Seraglio. A Comic Opera, by Capt. Edward Thompson. Acted at Covent-Garden, 8vo. 1776. This writer, by sometimes flattering, and sometimes abusing managers, contrived to get two or three of his pieces on the stage. The present one, like the rest, was commended only by its author in the news-papers.

Sertorius. Tra. by John Bancroft. Acted at the Theatre Royal, 4to. 1679. The plot of this tragedy is founded on Plutarch's Life of Sertorius, Velleius Paterculus, Florus, and other historians. The scene lies in Lusitania, and the epilogue is written by Ravenscroft. The clever Corneille has a play on the same subject, but Mr. Bancroft does not seem to have borrowed any thing from him.

Sesostris; or, *Royalty in Disguise.* Trag. by John Sturmy, 8vo. 1728. This play was acted with some success at the Theatre Royal in Lincoln's-Inn-Fields.

Sethona. Tra. by Alexander Dow. Acted at Drury-Lane, 8vo. 1774. This play may properly be styled a faggot of utter improbabilities, connected by a band of the strongest Northern fustian. Overawed by Scottish influence, Mr. Garrick prevailed on himself to receive it; but though his theatre was apparently full several times during its nine nights' run, it brought so little cash into his treasury, that he would not have lamented its earlier condemnation. It expired on the premises, but hardly left enough behind it to defray the expences of its funeral. Sethona, and its predecessor Zingis, exhibit striking instances of the national partiality with which Scotmen labour for promotion of each other. Mr. Dow has been represented by persons who knew him well during his first residence in the East-Indies, as a man utterly unqualified for the production of any work of learning or fancy, either

either in profe or metre. At his return to England, however, he ftood forwaid as the hiftorian. of Indoftan, and then as the author of Zingis and the drama before us. Thefe phænomena perhaps are to be folved by our recollection of his ftrict intimacy with two of his own countrymen, the one a tranflator, the other a dramatic poet. Though thefe gentlemen were candidates for literary fame, yet between them they contrived to transfer as much of it as would fet up a needy brother in trade, and afford a degree of diftinction and confequence fufficient to befriend in future his profpects of advancement.

The Seven Champions of Chriftendome. By J. Kirke, Acted at the Cockpit, and at the Bull in St. John's-ftreet, 4to. 1638. The plot of this piece is taken from a well-known book in profe which bears the fame title, and from Heylin's Hiftory of St. George. It is written in a mixed ftyle, for which the author himfelf apologizes in his epiftle dedicatory, by obferving that the nature of the work being hiftory, it confifts of many parts, not walking in one direct path of comedy or tragedy, but having a larger field to trace, which fhould

yield more pleafure to the reader; novelty and variety being the only objects thefe our times are taken with. The tragedy may be too dull and folid, the comedy too fharp and bitter; but a well-mixed portion of either, doubtlefs, would make the fweeteft harmony.

The Seven Chiefs againft Theles. Trag. tranflated from Æfchylus, by R. Potter, 4to. 1777.

The Seven Deadly Sins. A play, by Richard Tarlton. This play was never printed.

Seventeen Hundred and Twenty; or, *The Hiftoric, Satiric, Tragi, Comic, Humours of Exchange-Alley.* C. by Francis Hawling. Acted at Drury-Lane, 1723. Not printed.

Seventeen Hundred and Eighty-One. Farce, acted at Covent-Garden, 1781. Not printed.

The Several Affairs. C. by Thomas Meriton. This piece was never acted, nor ever appeared in print, but as the author himfelf informs us in the dedication to another play of his, called *The Wandering Lover,* was only referved as a pocket companion for the amufement of his private friends. The ftupidity of the title, however, affords a moft contemptible idea of
the

S H

the piece, and leaves us some reason to congratulate ourselves on the not having been in the number of Mr. Meriton's friends.

The Several Wits. Com. by the Duchess of Newcastle, fol. 1662.

Shakspeare's Jubilee. Masque, by G. S. Carey, 8vo. 1769.

The Sham Beggar. Com. in two acts. Acted at Dublin, 8vo. 1756.

The Sham Lawyer; or, *The Lucky Extravagant.* Com. by Dr. James Drake. As it was damnably acted at Drury-Lane, says the title-page, 4to. 1697. This play is mostly borrowed from two comedies of Beaumont and Fletcher, viz. *The Spanish Curate,* and *Wit without Money.*

The Sham Prince; or, *News from Nassau.* Com. by Charles Shadwell, 12mo. 1720. This play was written in five days, and acted in Dublin; the design of it being to expose a public cheat who had at that time passed himself on the Irish nation as a person of the first importance, and by that means imposed on many to their great loss and injury.

The Shamrock; or, *The Anniversary of St. Patrick.* A Pastoral Romance, by Mr. O'Keeffe. Acted at Covent - Garden, 1783.

S H

This piece is destitute of plot, incident, or character.

The Sharper. Com. by Michael Clancy. This play was acted at Smock-Alley, Dublin, and printed at the end of the author's life, 8vo. 1750.

The Sharpers. A Ballad Opera, by Mat. Gardiner, 8vo. 1740.

The She Gallants. Com. by Lord Lansdowne. Acted at Lincoln's-Inn-Fields, 4to. 1696. This Comedy was written when the author was extremely young, yet contains an infinite deal of wit, fine satire, and great knowledge of mankind. It was acted with considerable applause, notwithstanding that envy of its merit raised a party against it, who misrepresented it, as designing, in some of the characters, to reflect on particular persons, and more especially on the government; but when it comes to be considered, that it was written above a dozen years before it was performed, and at a time when neither the same government subsisted, nor the persons supposed to be aimed at had been any way noted; and that moreover it was not composed with any design to be made public, but only as a private amusement, any impartial judge must

N 6

surely

furely acquit his lordfhip of the charge laid againft him.

The She Gallant ; or, *Square Tees Outwitted.* C. of two acts, performed at Smock-Alley, Dublin, 8vo. 1767.

The Sheep Shearing ; or, *Florizel and Perdita.* Paft. Com. This is taken from Shakfpeare's *Winter's Tale*, and was firft acted at Mr. Barry's benefit about 1754.

The Sheep Shearing. Dramatic Paftoral in three acts, taken from Shakfpeare, by George Colman. Acted at the Haymarket, 1777, 8vo. This is borrowed from *The Winter's Tale*, and met with fo cold a reception, that it appeared only one night.

The Shepherdefs of the Alps. Comic Opera, by Charles Dibdin. Acted at Covent-Garden, 8vo. 1780. Like the reft of this writer's pieces, it was taken from the French, and was difmiffed from public view after three nights reprefentation.

The Shepherd's Artifice. Dramatic Paftoral, by C. Dibdin. Acted at Covent-Garden, 8vo. 1765. A very trifling infipid performance.

The Shepherd's Courtfhip. Mufical Paftoral of four Interludes, by William Shirley. Not acted, nor yet printed, but is promifed in an edition of the author's dramatic works.

The Shepherd's Holiday. Paft. Tragi-Com. by Jofeph Rutter. Acted before their Majefties at Whitehall, 8vo. 1635. This play has only the initials J. R. in the title page ; but Kirkman, whofe authority in general is a very good one, has afcribed it to this gentleman, and all the other writers have followed his example. The piece is written in blank verfe, and Langbaine ftyles it the nobler fort of paftoral. It is alfo recommended by two copies of verfes, the one from Ben Jonfon, who calls the author *his dear fon* (in the Mufes) *and his right learned friend,* and the other from Thomas May.

The Shepherd's Lottery. A Mufical Entertainment, by Mr. Mendez. Acted at Drury - Lane, 8vo. 1751. There are feveral pretty fongs in it, and the mufical compofition is very pleafing. It met with good fuccefs at firft, but has not been often repeated.

The Shepherd's Paradife. Paftoral, by Walter Montague, 8vo. 1629. This piece was acted privately before king Charles I. by the Queen and her Ladies of Honour, whofe names are fet down in the Dramatis Perfonnæ. It is, however, a very infipid piece.

She Stoops to Conquer ; or,

S H

or, *The Miftakes of a Night*. Com. by Dr. Goldfmith. Acted at Covent - Garden, 8vo. 1773. The prefent dramatic piece is, by fome critics, confidered as a farce, but ftill it muft be ranked among the farces of a man of genius. One of the moft ludicrous circumftances it contains (that of the robbery) is borrowed from *Albamazar*. It met with great fuccefs, and reftored the public tafte to the good opinion of our author.

She Ventures, and he Wins. Com. Acted at Lincoln's-Inn-Fields, 4to. 1696. This play was written by a young lady who figns herfelf Ariadne. The plot is taken from a novel written by Mr. Oldys, called, *The Fair Extravagant*; or, *The Humourous Bride*.

She Wou'd if She Cou'd. Com. by Sir George Etheridge. Acted at the Duke of York's Theatre, 4to. 1671. This play has been for fome time laid afide, yet it is undoubtedly a very good one, and at the time it was written was efteemed as one of the firft rank.

She Wou'd and She Wou'd Not; or, *The Kind Impoftor*. Com. by C. Cibber. Acted at Drury-Lane, 4to. 1703. This is a very bufy, fprightly, and entertaining comedy.

S H

The Shipwreck. Com. tranflated from Plautus, by Bonnel Thornton, printed in his edition, 8vo. 1767.

The Shipwreck. Dramatic Piece, by William Hyland, Farmer in Suffex, 8vo. 1746.

The Shipwreck Trag. Acted at Covent - Garden, 1784. This piece is altered from Lillo's *Fatal Curiofity*, and met with little fuccefs.

A Shoemaker's a Gentleman. Com. by William Rowley. Acted at the Red Bull, 4to. 1638. It confifts of a good deal of low humour, and it appears to have been a great favourite among the ftrolling companies in the country.

The Shoemaker's Holiday; or, *The Gentle Craft, with the humourous Life of Simon Eyre, Shoemaker, and Lord Mayor of London*. Com. Acted before the Queen, by Thomas Earl of Nottingham, Lord High Aftmiral his fervants, on New-year's day at night, 4to. 1600. This play has been attributed to Dr. Barton Holiday. Printed in the black letter, and not divided into acts.

Shuffling, Cutting, and Dealing in a Game of Pickquet, being acted from the year 1653 to 1658. By O. P. and others with great applaufe,

plaufe, By H. Neville, 4to. 1659.

Sicelides. A Pifcatory Drama or Paftoral, by Phineas Fletcher, 4to. 1631. This piece was acted in King's College, Cambridge, and is printed without any author's name. It was intended originally to be performed before King James the Firft on the 13th of March, 1614; but his majefty leaving the univerfity fooner, it was not then reprefented. The ferious parts of it are moftly written in rhyme, with chorufes between the acts. Perianus's telling Armillus the ftory of Glaucus Scylla and Circe, in the firft act, is taken from Ovid's *Metamorphofes,* lib. 12. And Atychus's fighting with and killing the Ork that was to have devoured Olynda, is an imitation of the ftory of Perfeus and Andromeda in Ovid's *Metamorphofes,* book 4. or the deliverance of Angelica from the monfter by Ruggiero, in the *Orlando Furiofo,* cant. 10. The fcene lies in Sicily, the time two hours.

The Sicilian; or, *Love makes a Painter,* by J. Ozell. This is a tranflation for the clofet only of Moliere's *Sicilien, ou, l'Amour Peintre,* not intended for the ftage; but Mr. Crowne, in his *Country Wit,* and Sir Richard Steele, in his *Tender Hufband,* have both borrowed incidents, and indeed wholefcenes, from this play. It confifts of twenty fcenes, not divided into acts; and the general fcene is in Sicily.

The Sicilian Ufurper. Tr. by Nat. Tate, 4to. 1691. This is nothing more than an alteration of Shakfpeare's Richard the Second. It appears to have been acted only once or twice, when it was forbidden by authority.

Sicily and Naples; or, *The Fatal Union.* Trag. by S. Harding, 4to. 1640.

The Siege. Tragi-Com. by Sir Wm. Davenant, fol. 1679.

The Siege; or, *Love's Convert.* Tragi-Com. by Wm. Cartwright, 8vo. 1651. This play is dedicated in verfe to King Charles I.

The Siege of Aleppo. Tr. by William Hawkins, 8vo. 1758. Printed in the fecond volume of Mifcellanies, publifhed by the author in that year.

The Siege of Aquileia. T. by J. Home, 8vo. 1759. This play was performed with fuccefs at the Theatre Royal in Drury-Lane. It is the third dramatic piece produced by this Caledonian bard. It is greatly preferable to the *Agis,* but much inferior to the *Douglas*
of

of the fame author. From the title one would reafonably expect to find in it the feveral circumftances of the fiege whofe title it bears, when the city of Aquileia was held out by the legions of Gordianus againſt the gigantic tyrant Maximin; and fuch, from the firſt fetting out of it, we are permitted to expect; but every incident in this play deviates from the hiſtorical facts which we have on record in regard to that fiege; yet as they all agree with thofe of one much nearer to our own times, and ne rer connected with the hiſtory of the author's own country, viz. the fiege of Berwick, defended by Seton againſt the arms of our Edward III. it is not furely an improbable conjecture to fuppofe, that Mr. Home received his firſt hint from that ſtory; but as by purfuing it under the real characters, he muſt have painted one of our Englifh monarchs (and him indeed one claffed among the heroes of the Britifh Annals) in the light in which in more than this one inftance he appeared to be, viz. a tyrant, and an exerter of brutal power, without any confideration of the feelings of humanity; he chofe, rather than pay fo ill a compliment to an Englifh au-

dience, to preferve the circumſtances only, changing the fcenes of action to one that had fome little kind of analogy with it. The unities are well preferved, and fome of the fentimental parts of the language are fine. But on the whole, the incidents are too few, the diſtrefs too much the fame from beginning to end, and the cataſtrophe too early pointed out to the audience. Befides which, it may be added, that the character of Æmilius bears too ſtrong a refemblance to that of the Old Horatius inWhitehead's *Roman Father*, though it would be paying the laſt-named character a bad compliment to fet this point of execution in any degree of competition with it.

The Siege of Babylon. Tragi-Com. by Sam. Pordage. Acted at the Duke's Theatre, 4to. 1678. This play is founded on the Romance of Caffandra. The fiege lies in Babylon, and the fields adjacent.

The Siege of Belgrade. Opera, by Mr. Cobb. Acted at Drury-Lane, 1791. This Opera abounds with incidents and fituations, which are calculated to intereſt a mingled audience.

The Siege of Calais. Tr. by Charles Denis, tranflated from the French of M.
de

de Belloy, with Hiſtorical notes, 8vo. 1765. Not acted.

The Siege of Conſtantinople Trag. 4to. 1675. Acted at the Duke's Theatre. This play, though publiſhed anonymous, is ſaid to be written by Nevil Paine.

The Siege of Curzola. Comic Opera, by Mr. O'Keeffe. Acted at the Haymarket, 1786, and received with the uſual applauſe given to moſt of this writer's productions.

The Siege of Damaſcus. Trag. by John Hughes. Acted at Drury-Lane, 8vo. 1720. This play was, and ſtill continues to be, acted with general approbation. It is generally allowed, that the characters in this tragedy are finely varied and diſtinguiſhed; that the ſentiments are juſt and well adapted to the characters; that it abounds with beautiful deſcriptions, apt alluſions to the manners and opinions of the times where the ſcene is laid, and with noble morals; that the diction is pure, unaffected, and ſublime, without any meteors of ſtyle or ambitious ornaments; and that the plot is conducted in a ſimple and clear manner. When it was offered to the managers of Drury-Lane houſe in the year 1718, they refuſed to act it, unleſs the author made an alteration in the character of Phocyas, who, in the original, had been prevailed upon to profeſs himſelf a Mahometan, pretending he could not be a hero if he changed his religion, and that the audience would not bear the ſight of him after it, in how lively a manner ſoever his remorſe and repentance might be deſcribed. The author (being then in a very languiſhing condition) finding, if he did not comply, his relations would probably loſe the benefit of the play, conſented, though with reluctance, to new model the character of Phocyas.

The Siege of Derry. Tr. Com. Anony. 1692. This is an exceeding bad play, and was never acted; but as it was written very near the period of the tranſaction which it deſcribes, no bad idea may be formed from it of the diſtreſſes which the garriſon and inhabitants of that city underwent during that famous ſiege. See further under *Piety and Valour.*

The Siege of Gibraltar. Muſical Farce, by F. Pilon. Acted at Covent-Garden, 8vo. 1780. This is a very trifling and contemptible drama.

The Siege of Jeruſalem, by *Titus Veſpaſian.* Trag. by M. Latter, 8vo. 1763.

The

S I

The Siege of Jerusalem, by *Titus Vespasian*. Trag. by Mary Latter, 8vo. 1763.

The Siege of Jerusalem. Trag. 8vo. 1774. Of this piece, which is said to be the production of Lady Strathmore, a few copies only were printed. It has not been published.

The Siege of Memphis; or, *The Ambitious Queen*. Tra. by Thomas Durfey. Acted at the Theatre Royal, 4to. 1676. This play is written in heroic verse, and as Mr. Durfey's genius apparently lay much more to comic humour then tragic power, it is not much to be wondered that he should, in his attempts of the latter kind, run into somewhat of fustian and bombast. However, the judgement of the audience, which on the whole is generally right, pointed out to him his mistake in the indifferent success this piece met with. The plot is in some measure borrowed from history, and the scene is Memphis besieged.

The Siege and Surrender of Mons. Trag-Com. Anonymous, 4to. 1691. The author's intention, as he himself expresses it in the title-page, was to expose the villainy of the priests, and the intrigues of the French.

The Siege of Rhodes. A

S I.

Play in two parts, by Sir William Davenant, 4to. 1656. Both these plays met with great approbation. They were written during the time of civil wars, when the stage lay under a prohibition, and indeed all the *Belles Lettres* were at a stand, and consequently made not their appearance till after the Restoration, at Lincoln's-Inn-Fields, when Sir William himself obtained the management of the theatre. The plot, as far as it has a connection with history, is to be found in the several historians, who have given an account of this remarkable siege in the reign of Solyman the Second, who took this city in the year 1522. The scene, Rhodes, and camp near it.

The Siege of Sinope. Tr. by Mrs. Brooke. Acted at Covent-Garden, 8vo. 1781. Taken from Metastasio.

The Siege of Tamor. Tr. by Gorges Edmond Howard, 12mo. 1773. Printed at Dublin. It does not appear to have been acted.

The Siege of Urbin. Tr. Com. by Sir W. Killigrew, fol. 1666.

The Silver Age. A history, by Thomas Heywood, 4to. 1613. This is the second of a series of historical dramas which this author has pursued, and which contain

tain on the whole the greatest part of the Heathen mythology. This part contains the Loves of Jupiter and Alcmena, the birth of Hercules, and the Rape of Proferpine, concluding with the Arraignment of the Moon. In the purfuance of a plan of this kind, it was impossible to avoid making ufe of the facts which hiftory pointed out to the author, and thofe affiftances which the ancient writers feems to hold forth to his acceptance; nor can he by any means be chargeable with plagiarifm for fo doing. In the intrigue of Jupiter and Alcmena therefore he has borrowed fome paffages from the *Amphitruo* of Plautus; the Rape of *Proferpine* is greatly enriched by taking in the account which Ovid has given of that tranfaction in his *Metamorphofes*; and other parts of the piece are much advantaged by quotations from the legends of the poets.

The Silver Tankard. Mufical Farce, by Lady Craven. Acted at the Haymarket, 1781. Not printed. An infipid trifle.

Sir Anthony Love; or, *The Rambling Lady.* Com. by Tho. Southerne. Acted at the Theatre Royal, 4to. 1691. This play met with very great applaufe.

Sir Barnaby Whigg; or, *No Wit like a Woman's.* C. by Thomas Durfey. Acted at the Theatre Royal, 4to. 1681.

Sir Clyomen, Knight of the Golden Shield, Son to the King of Denmark; and Clamydes the White Knight, Son to the King of Swavia (both valiant Knights), their Hiftory. Acted by her Majefties players. Anonymous. 4to. 1599. This is a very indifferent play, written in verfe, and in the language more obfolete than the date feems to warrant, and is very difagreeable in the reading.

Sir Courtly Nice; or, *It cannot be.* Com. by J. Crowne, 4to. 1685. This play was written at the command of King Charles II. The plot and part of the play is taken from a Spanifh comedy, called *No Pued-effer;* or, *It cannot be,* and from a comedy, called *Tarugo's Wiles.* The fong of *Step-Thief* is a tranflation, or rather paraphrafe of Mafcarille's *Au Voleur* in Moliere's *Precieufes Ridicules.* The character of Crack is admirably kept up; but the chief merit of the play is in the very fine contraft fupported between the two characters of Hothead and Teftimony, characters which even now give pleafure.

Sir

S I

S I

Sir Giddy Whim ; or, *The Lucky Amour.* Com. Anonymous, 4to. 1703. This piece was never acted.

Sir Giles Goofe-Cappe, Knight. Com. Anon. 4to. 1606. This play was prefented by the children of the Chapel.

Sir Harry Gaylove ; or, *Comedy in Embrio.* By the author of Clarinda Cathcart and Alicia Montague, 8vo. 1772. This play was printed in Scotland, but not acted.

Sir Harry Wildair, being the fequel to *The Trip to the Jubilee,* by George Farquhar. Acted at Drury-Lane, 4to. 1701. This comedy is a continuation of *The Conftant Couple,* and has feveral of the fame characters. Yet, although the fuccefs and real merit of the firft part fo much infured fuccefs to this as to afford it a run of nine nights to crouded audiences, yet it was by no means equal in merit to that firft part, nor is it now ever performed, although *The Conftant Couple* ftill remains one of the moft favoured pieces on the lift of acting plays. From a peculiar happinefs in hitting the character of Jubilee Dicky in thefe plays, the celebrated Mr. Henry Norris, the comedian, gained fo much reputation, as

occafioned his own chriftian name to be funk in that of his character, and his being ever after diftinguifhed by the name of Dicky Norris ; under which name, at the head of a play-bill, a benefit for that gentleman was advertifed.

Sir Hercules Buffoon ; or, *The Poetical Squire.* Com. by J. Lacy. Acted at the Duke's Theatre, 4to. 1684. This play was not publifhed, nor brought on the ftage, till about three years after the author's deceafe.

Sir John Cockle at Court. Farce, by Robert Dodfley, 8vo. 1737. This little piece is a fequel to *The King and the Miller of Mansfield,* in which the Miller, newly a knight, comes up to London, with his family, to pay his compliments to the King. It is not, however, equal in merit to the firft part, for though the King's difguifing himfelf in order to put Sir John's integrity to the teft, and the latter refifting every temptation, not only of bribery, but of flattery alfo, is ingenious, and gives an opportunity for many admirable ftrokes both of fentiment and fatire, yet there is a fimplicity ; and fitnefs for the drama, in the ftory of the firft part, that it is

scarcely

scarcely poffible to come up to, in the circumftances which arife from the incidents of the latter.

The firft Part of the true and honourable Hiftory of the Life of Sir John Oldcaftle, the good Lord Cobham. Acted by the Earl of Nottingham, the Lord High Admiral's fervants, 4to. 1600. This is one of the feven plays difcarded from Shakfpeare's works by moft of the editors, yet it was undoubtedly publifhed in his lifetime with his name. Mr. Malone fays, the hand of Shakfpeare is not to be traced in any part of this play; and Dr. Farmer fuppofes it to be the production of Thomas Heywood, whofe manner it refembles.

Sir Martin Mar-all; or, *The Feign'd Innocence.* Com. by J. Dryden. Acted at the Duke's Theatre, 4to. 1668. The plot and great part of the language of Sir Martin and his man Warner, are borrowed from Quinault's *Amant indifcret,* and the *Etourdi* of Moliere. Warner's playing on the lute inftead of his mafter, and being furprifed by his folly, is taken from M. du Parc's *Francion,* book 7. and Old Moody and Sir John being hoifted up in their altitudes, owes its origin to a like incident in Marmion's *Antiquary.* Downes fays the Duke of Newcaftle gave this play to Dryden, who adapted it to the ftage, and it is remarkable, that it is entered on the books of the Stationers Company as the production of that nobleman.

Sir Martin Mar-all. C. by J. Ozell. This is only a literal tranflation of Moliere's *Etourdi,* to which Mr. Ozell gave the above title, from the hint of Dryden's comedy.

Sir Patient Fancy. Com. by Mrs. Behn. Acted at the Duke's Theatre, 4to. 1678. The hint of Sir Patient Fancy is borrowed from Moliere's *Malade Imaginaire;* and thofe of Sir Credulous Eafy and his Groom Curry, from the *M. Pourceaugnac* of the fame author. Thofe laft characters have alfo been made ufe of by Brome in his *Damoifelle.* Mr. Miller alfo, in his comedy of *The Mother-in-Law;* or, *The Doctor the Difeafe,* has availed himfelf of both of thefe plots, and blended them together much after the fame manner that Mrs. Behn has done in this. The fcene lies in two different houfes in London.

Sir Roger de Coverly; or, *The Merry Chriftmas.* A dramatic Entertainment of two

two acts, by Mr. Dorman, 1740, 8vo. This piece was never acted.

Sir Roger De Coverly. C. by James Miller. Not acted or printed. In a preface to this author's Miscellanies, he says that this play was written at the defire of Mrs. Oldfield, who was to have performed the widow ; the part of Will Honeycomb was alfo intended for Wilks, and Sir Roger for Mr. Cibber. The deaths, however, of the two former, and the retirement of the latter from the ftage, prevented its reprefentation ; and probably the copy is now loft.

Sir Roger de Coverly. C. by Dr. Dodd. Not acted or printed.

Sir Salomon ; or, The Cautious Coxcomb. Com. Acted at the Duke of York's Theatre, 4to. 1671. This Play is very little more than a tranflation from the *Ecole des Femmes* of Moliere. It met with fome enemies at firft, but, notwithftanding, made its part good in the reprefentations.

Sir Thomas Overbury. T. by Richard Savage, 8vo. 1724. This Play was acted at the Theatre Royal in Drury-Lane, and the author performed the principal part in it himfelf, but without fuccefs, both his

voice and afpect being very much againft him. -

Sir Walter Raleigh. Tr. by George Sewell, 8vo. 1719. This Play, the title of which points out the plot, was acted at Lincoln's-Fields Theatre with very great fuccefs. It is extremely well written.

Sir William Wallace. Tr. by Mr. Jackfon. Acted at Edinburgh 1780, but not printed.

The Sifters. Com. by Mrs. Charlotte Lenox, 8vo. 1769. This Comedy was taken from the authorefs's own novel, entituled *Henrietta.* Though it was treated feverely, and performed but one night at Covent-Garden, it is written with a confiderable degree of good fenfe and elegance.

The Sifters. Com. by J. Shirley. Acted at the private houfe, Blackfriars, 8vo. 1652.

The Sifters. Com. tranflated from the French, and printed in the fecond volume of Foot's *Comic Theatre.*

Six Day's Adventure ; or, The New Utopia. Com. by Edward Howard. Acted at the Duke of York's Theatre, 4to. 1671. This Play mifcarried in the reprefentation ; and the witty Lord Rochefter

Rochefter wrote a fharp invective againft it.

The Sleep Walker. Com. tranflated from the French of *Pont de Vile*, by Lady Craven, 12mo. 1778. Printed at Strawberry-Hill, but not publifhed.

The Slighted Maid. Com. by Sir Robert Stapylton. Afted at Lincoln's - Inn-Fields, 4to. 1663.

The Slip. Farce, by Chriftopher Bullock, 12mo. 1715. This piece was acted with applaufe at Lincoln's-Inn-Fields.

The Smugglers. A Farce, of three acts, by Thomas Odell, 8vo. 1729. Acted with fome fuccefs at the Little Theatre in the Haymarket.

The Snake in the Grafs. A dramatic entertainment of a new fpecies, being neither tragedy, comedy, pantomime, farce, ballad, or opera, by Aron Hill, 8vo. 1760. This was never acted, but is printed with the author's other works.

The Snuff Box ; or, *A Trip to Bath.* Com. in two acts, by William Heard. Acted at the Haymarket, 8vo. 1775.

The Sociable Companions ; or, *The Female Wits.* Com. by the Duchefs of Newcaftle, fol. 1662.

Socrates. A Dramatic Poem, by Amyas Bufhe,

Efq. A. M. and F. R. S. 4to. 1758.

Socrates. Trag. tranflated from the French of Voltaire, 12mo. 1760.

Socrates. Dramatic Performance, tranflated from Voltaire, and printed in Dr. Franklin's edition of that author.

Socrates Triumphant ; or, *The Danger of being Wife in a Commonwealth of Fools.* Trag. Anonym. 8vo. 1716. This piece was never acted.

The Soldier. Trag. by Richard Lovelace. Never printed.

Soldier's Fortune. Com. by Thomas Otway. Acted at the Duke's Theatre, 4to. 1681. The plot of this play is by no means new, the feveral incidents in it being almoft all of them borrowed. For inftance, Lady Dunce's making her hufband an agent for the conveyance of the ring and letter to her gallant, Capt. Beaugard, is evidently taken from Moliere's *Ecole des Maris*, and had befides been made ufe of in fome Englifh plays before, particularly in *The Fawne*, and in *Flora's Vagaries*. The original ftory from which Moliere himfelf probably borrowed the hint, may be feen in Boccace, dec. 3, nov. 3. Sir Davy's bolting out of his clofet, and furprifing his Lady

S O

Lady and Beaugard kissing, and her behaviour on that occasion, is borrowed from the story of *Millamant*; or, *The Rampant Lady*; in Scarron's *Com ca Romance*. The character of Bloody Bones is much like that of Bravo in *The Antiquary*, and Courtine's conduct under Silvia's balcony has a great resemblance to Monsieur Thomas's carriage to his mistress in Fletcher's comedy of that name. There is a sequel to this play, which is called *The Atheist*; or the second part of *The Soldier's Fortune*, 4to. 1684. The plot of which, so far as relates to the amours of Beaugard and Portia, is founded on Scarron's novel of *The Invisible Mistress*. Both these plays have wit, and a great deal of busy and intricate intrigue, but are so very loose in respect to sentiment and moral, that they are now entirely laid side.

Soliman and Perseda, The Tragedie of (Anonym. 4to. 1599), *wherein is laide open Love's Constancy, Fortune's Inconstancy, and Death's Triumphs*.

Solon; or, *Philosophy no Defence against Love*. Tragi-Com. by Martin Bladen, 4to. 1705. This piece was never acted, and even printed unknown to the author.

The Son-in-Law. Farce,

S O

by J. O'Keefe. Acted at the Haymarket, 1779. The songs only printed. This piece was extremely successful in its representation, and and does no small credit to the talents of its author.

The Song of Solomon. A Drama, by J. Bland, 8vo. 1750.

The Sophister. Comedy, Anonym 4to. 1639. This play was acted at one of the Universities.

Sophomphaneas; or, *Joseph.* Trag. by Francis Goldsmith, 8vo. no date. This is only a translation from Hugo Grotius, with critical remarks and annotations.

Sophonisba; or, *Hannibal's Overthrow*. Trag. by Nath. Lee. Acted at Drury-Lane, 4to. 1676. This tragedy is written in rhyme, yet it met with great applause, especially from the female and more tender part of the audience. The loves of Sophonisba and Masinissa are delicately and affectingly managed; but the author has greatly deviated from the idea history gives us of the characters of Scipio and Hanibal, in the manner he has here represented them, yet, perhaps, he might, in some measure, be drawn into this error by following too closely the example set him by Lord Orrery

SO

SO

rery in his romance of *Parthenissa*, wherein he has made Hannibal as much of a whining lover towards his Izadora, as Lee has done with regard to Rosalinda. The histories of Scipio and Hannibal are to be found by perusing Plutarch and Cornelius Nepos; and the story of Masinissa and Sophinisba is very nearly related by Petrach, in his *Trionfo a' Amore*, c. 2. The scene of the play, Zama.

Sophonisba. Trag. by J. Thomson, 8vo. 1730. This play was acted at Drury-Lane Theatre with very great applause, and is founded on the same story with the foregoing piece. Yet it was not without its enimies, a very severe criticism being published against it; and, to say truth, though the author has in good measure avoided the rants and wild extravagancies which break forth in Lee's tragedy, yet at the same time he falls greatly short of him in poetical beauties and luxuriance of imagination. And on the whole, perhaps, it will not be doing Mr. Thomson any injustice to say, that had he never published his Seasons, and some other Poems, but confined his pen to dramatic writing only, he would not have stood in that rank of poetical fame which he now holds in the annals of Parnassus. Dr. Johnson observes, that every rehearsal of this tragedy was dignified with a splendid audience, collected to anticipate the delight that was preparing for the public. It was observed, however, that nobody was much affected, and that the company rose as from a moral lecture; that it had upon the stage no unusual degree of success. Slight accidents will operate upon the taste of pleasure. There was a feeble line in the play;

O, Sophonisba, Sophonisba, O!

This gave occasion to a waggish parody,

O, Jemmy Thomson, Jemmy Thomson, O!

which for a while was echoed through the town. Dr. Johnson likewise observes he had been told by Savage, that of the prologue to *Sophonisba* the first part was written by Pope, who could not be persuaded to finish it, and that the concluding lines were added by Mallet.

The Sophy. Trag. by Sir John Denham. Acted at Black-Fryars, fol. 1642. This tragedy is built on the same story in Herbert's Travels, on which Baron has constructed his tragedy of *Mirza*. It is, however, very differently handled by the

the two authors. And Baron objects on this account, that Denham has deviated from the truth of history in making Abbas die in his tragedy, whereas he really survived several years after his fon's murder. This, however, is no more than a *Licentia Poetica*, which has ever been confidered warrantable, and which on the prefent occafion is made ufe only for the fake of dramatic juftice.

Sophy Mirfa. Trag. This play is on the fame fubject as Sir John Denham's. It was begun by Mr. Hughes, who wrote two acts of it, and finifhed by his brother-in-law, Mr. William Duncombe, in the hands of whofe fon it now remains in manufcript.

The Sot. Burletta. Acted at the Haymarket, 8vo. 1775.

South Sea; or, *The Biters Bit.* A Farce, by William Rufus Chetwood, 8vo. 1720. This piece was not intended for the ftage, but only defigned as a fatire on the South-Sea project, and the inconceivable bubbles of that æra of folly and credulity.

The South-Briton. Com. of five acts, performed at Smock-alley Theatre, Dublin, 8vo. 1774.

The Spanifh Barber; or,

The Fruitlefs Precaution. Com. by G. Colman. Acted at the Haymarket 1777. This is a very pleafing though farcical performance, and was taken from the *Barbier de Seville* of Monf. Beaumarchais.

The Spanifh Bawd, reprefented in *Celeftina, or the Tragicke Comedy of Califto and Melibea*; wherein is contained, befides the Pleafantnefe and Swectnefe of the Stile, many philofophical Sentences, and profitable Inftructions neciffary for the younger Sort: Shewing the Deceits and Subtilties houfed in the Bofoms of falfe Servants and Cunny-catching Bawds. Fol. 1631. This play is the longeft that was ever publifhed, confifting of 21 acts. It was written originally in Spanifh.

The Spanifh Curate. C. by Beaumont and Fletcher, fol. 1747. This is a good comedy, and although it is not now on the lift of acting plays, it was at many different times after the death of its author revived, and always with fuccefs.

The Spanifh Fryar; or, *The Double Difcovery.* Tr.-Com. by John Dryden. Acted at the Duke's Theatre, 4to. 1681. Langbane charges the author of this play with cafting a reflection on the whole body

O   of

of the clergy in his character of Dominick the Fryar, and seems to imagine it a piece of revenge practised for some opposition he met with in his attempt to take orders. However that might be with respect to Mr. Dryden in particular, we cannot pretend to say, but this one point appears plain to us, viz. that the satire thrown out in it is only general against those amongst the clergy who disgrace their cloth by wicked and unbecoming actions ; and is by no means pointed at, or can any way affect, the sacred function in itself. That there have been such characters as Father Dominick among the Priests of all religions, and more especially those of the Romish Church, to whom the practice of confession affords more frequent opportunities, and uninterrupted scope, for such kind of conduct, no man in his senses will, we believe, attempt to deny ; and if so, how or where can they be more properly exposed than on the stage ? But can that be said to cast a reflection on the much greater number of valuable, well - meaning, and truly religious among the divine professors ? No, surely. Yet the *qui capit ille facit* is a maxim so perfectly founded in truth, that

we are ever apt to suspect some consciousness in themselves of the truth of particular satire in those persons who appear over angry at hints thrown out in general only. This play considered in itself has perhaps as much merit as any that this author has given to the world. The characters of Torrismond and Leonora in the tragic part are tender and poetical, yet there are some ideas and descriptions thrown out by the latter, towards the beginning of the third act, which are rather too warm and luxuriant to bear repetition on a public stage, and are therefore now omitted in the acting. But the whole comedy is natural, lively, entertaining, and highly finished both with respect to plot, character, and language. The scene lies in Arragon, and the plot of the comic parts is founded on a novel, called *The Pilgrim*, written by M. St. Bremond.

The Spanish Gypsie. C. by Thomas Middleton and William Rowley. Acted at Drury-Lane and Salisbury - Court, 4to. 1653. The plot of this play, with respect to the story of Rodeiigo and Clara, if not borrowed from, has at least a very near resemblance to, a novel of Cervantes, called

The

The Force of Blood. The scene lies at Alicant.

The Spanish Lady. Mufical Entertainment, by T. Hill. Acted at Covent-Garden, 8vo. 1769. This piece w s originally written on receiving the news of a fignal conqueft gained in the Spanifh Weft-Indies by the Englifh forces, in 1762.

The Spanish Rivals. A Mufical Farce, acted at Drury-Lane, 1784. In this piece fenfe is facrificed to found.

The Spanish Rogue. Com. by Thomas Duffet, 4to. 1674. This play is written, after the manner of moft of the French comedies, in rhyme. It is the beft of all this Author's dramatic works, yet met with very indifferent fuccefs.

Spanish Tragedy. See Jeronymo.

The Spanish Tragedy; or, *Hieronimo is mad again. Containing the lamentable end of Don Poratio and Belimperia. With the pitifull Death of Hieronimo*; by Thomas Kyd, 4to. 1603. This play was the object of ridicule to almoft every writer of the times.

The Spanish Wives. A Farce of three acts, by Mrs. Mary Pix, 4to. 1696. It was acted at Dorfet-Gardens.

The Sparagus Garden. C.

by Richard Brome. Acted in the year 1635, by the then Company of Revels at Salifbury-Court, 4to. 1640.

The Spartan Dame. Tr. by Tho. Southerne. Acted at Drury-Lane, 8vo. 1719. This play, when it made its firft appearance, was received with univerfal and indeed merited app!aufe. The fubject of it is taken from Plutarch's Life of Agis.

Speeches at Prince Henry's Barriers. By Ben Johnfon, fol. 1640. Thefe fpeeches are not much dramatic, being only fome compliments paid to Prince Henry, the eldeft fon of King James I.

The Spenathrift. Com. by Mathew Draper. Acted at the Haymarket, 8vo. 1731. The hint of this play is taken from Shakfpeare's *London Prodigal.*

The Spendthrift. Com. tranflated from the French, and printed in Foote's *Comic Theatre*, vol. 1,

The Spendthrift; or, *A Chriftmas Gambol.* Farce, by Dr. Kenrick. Acted at Covent-Garden 1758. Not printed. This was taken from Cha. Johnfon's *Country Laffes*, and was acted only two nights.

The Spightful Sifter. C. by Abr. Bailey, 4to. 1667.

The Spirit of Contradiction. Farce, of two acts,

by

by a Gentleman of Cambridge, 8vo. 1760. This farce made its appearance at the Theatre Royal in Covent-Garden, but with very little succefs.

The Spiritual Minor. C. 8vo. 1763. A low and ftupid imitation of Foote's *Minor.*

The Spleen; or, *Iflington Spaw.* A Comic Piece, of two acts, by George Colman, performed at Drury-Lane, 8vo. 1756. A performance which will not leffen the fame of its ingenious author, though it did not meet with equal fuccefs.

The Spouter; or, *The Triple Revenge.* Comic Farce, in two acts, 8vo. 1756. A whimfical production of Mr. Murphy, with the connivance of Mr. Garrick. The chief perfonages in this piece were defigned as reprefentations of living authors and managers. Garrick himfelf, Richard Foote, and young Cibber, are all the objects of its merriment, which is unmixed with the leaft offenfive feverity, as will be fuppofed from the circumftance of their leaders having been privy to the publication.

The Spouter; or, *The Double Revenge.* Com. Farce, in three acts, by H. Dell, 8vo. 1756.

The Spring. Paftoral, by James Harris, Efq. Acted at Drury-Lane, 4to. 1763.

The Squire of Alfatia. Com. by Thomas Shadwell. Acted by their Majeflies fervants, 4to. 1688. This play is founded on the *Adelphi* of Terence, the characters of the two elder Belfonds being exactly thofe of the Micio and Demea, and the two younger Belfonds the Efchinus and Ctefipho of that celebrated Comedy. Mr. Shadwell has however certainly, if not improved on thofe characters in their intrinfic merit, at leaft fo far modernized and moulded them to the prefent tafte, as to render them much more palatable to an audience in general, than they appear to be in their ancient habits. This play met with good fuccefs, and is ftill at times performed to univerfal fatisfaction. The fcene lies in Alfatia, the cant name for White-Fryars; and the author has introduced fo much of the cant or gamblers' language, as to have rendered it neceffary to prefix a gloffary for the leading the reader through a labyrinth of uncommon and unintelligible jargon.

Squire Badger. Burletta, in two parts. Acted at the Haymarket, 8vo. 1772. It is is taken from Fielding's *Don Quixote in England*, and was afterwards brought out under the title of *The Sot*.

The Squire Burlesqued; or, *The Sharpers Outwitted*. C. by Bartholomew Bourgeois, 8vo. 1765.

Squire Old-Sap; or, *The Night Adventures*. Com. by Thomas Durfey. Acted at the Duke's Theatre, 4to. 1679. This play is greatly obliged to several novels and other Dramas for the composition of its plot, which is very intricate and busy. For instance, the character of Squire Old-Sap and the incident of Pimpo's tying him to the tree in the first act, is borrowed from *The Comical History of Francion*. Tricklove's cheating Old Sap with the bell, and Pimpo's standing in Henry's place, is related in Boccace's novels, Dec. 7, Nov. 8, and in Fontaine's Tale of *La Gageure des trois Commeres*; and Tricklove's contrivance with Welford for having Old-Sap beaten in her cloaths in the same act, and which is also an incident in Fletcher's *Woman pleas'd*, Ravenscroft's *London Cuckolds*, and some other Comedies, is evidently taken from Boccace, Dec. 7. Nov. 7.

The Stage Beau toss'd in a Blanket; or, *The Hipocrite*

à-la-Mode. Com. Anony. 4to. 1704. This piece, though without a name, was written by the humourous Tom Brown. It consists of three acts only, and is a satire on Jeremy Collier, who wrote a severe book against the stage and dramatic writers.

The Stage Coach. Farce, by George Farquhar, 4to. 1710. In this little piece he was assisted by Mr. Motteux; yet after all it is nothing more than a plagiarism, the whole plot of it, and some entire scenes, being borrowed from a little French piece, called *Les Caresses d'Orleans*.

The State Farce; or, *They are all come Home*, 8vo. 1757.

The Stage Mutineers; or, *A Playhouse to be Let*. A Tragi-Comi-Farcical Ballad Opera. Acted at Covent-Garden, Anony. 8vo. 1733. This piece is only a burlesque on a contest between the manager of one of the theatres and his performers, at the head of the male-content part of whom Mr. Theophilus Cibber at that time stood in a very conspicuous light, and is in this piece characterized by the name of Ancient Pistol, all the speeches put into his mouth being thrown into the bombastic or mock tragedy

O 3

gedy ſtyle which Shakſpeare has given to that character in his two parts of *Henry IV.* and *The Merry Wives of Windſor.* As in all diſputes of this kind both ſides are generally to blame, we ſhall not here attempt to enter on the merits of the cauſe, but content ourſelves with obſerving, that the Farce under our preſent conſideration ſeems to be written in favour of the performers. The ſcene lies in the playhouſe at the time of rehearſal.

The Staple of News. C. by Ben Jonſon, fol. 1631. This play, though not printed till the above date, was firſt acted in the year 1625. He has introduced in this Comedy four Goſſips, by way of Interlocutors, who remain on the ſtage during the whole repreſentation, and make comments and criticiſms on all the ſeveral incidents of the piece. It, however, is not the only inſtance of this kind of conduct, he having done the very ſame thing in two other plays, viz. *Every Man out of his Humour,* and the *Magnetic Lady;* and Fletcher in his *Knight of the burning Peſtle* has followed the very ſame example. Scene, London. It is entered on the books of the Stationers' Company, Apr. 14, 1626.

The State Juggler; or, *Sir Politic Ribland.* A new Exciſe Opera. Anonym. 8vo. 1733. This is one of thoſe pieces in which Sir Robert Walpole, then prime miniſter, was abuſed, in regard to the jobs which the public imagined were going forwards with reſpect to the exciſe and other branches of the public revenues.

The State of Innocence; or, *The Fall of Man.* An Opera, 4to. 1676. This piece was never performed, the ſubject being too ſolemn and the characters of a nature that would render it almoſt blaſphemy for any perſon to attempt the repreſentation of them. It is written in heroic verſe or rhyme, and the plot is founded on Milton's *Paradiſe Loſt,* from which he has even borrowed many beauties in regard to his language and ſentiments. Some of the nicer and more delicate critics have found fault with this Opera, charging the author with anachroniſm and abſurdity in introducing Lucifer converſing about the world, its form, matter, and viciſſitudes, at a time previous to its creation, or at leaſt to the poſſibility of his knowing any thing concerning it. And indeed Mr. Dryden ſeems himſelf to have been aware of its lying open

open to fuch kind of objections, by his having prefixed to it an apology for *Heroic Poetry*, and for the *Licentia Poetica*, of which he
had indeed made a moft ample ufe in this piece. On
the whole, however, it has
undoubtedly very great
beauties, and is very highly
commended by Nat. Lee,
in a copy of verfes publifhed
with it; nor is it at all de-
tracting from its merit to
own, that we are by no
means blind to fome few
faults that it may have. As
Dr. Johnfon truly obferves,
it is termed by Dryden an
opera; it is rather a tragedy
in heroic rhyme, but of
which the perfonages are
fuch as cannot decently be
reprefented on the ftage. It
is one of Dryden's hafty productions; for the heat of his
imagination raifed it in a
month.

The State of Phyfic. C.
Anon. 8vo. 1742. This
piece was never acted.

The Statefman Foiled. A
Mufical Com. of two acts,
by Robert Dofie; perform-
ed at the Haymarket, 8vo.
1768.

*King Stephen, the Hiftory
of.* A Play, by William
Shakfpeare. Entered on
the books of the Stationers'
Company, June 29, 1660,
but not printed. It cannot
but be a fubject of regret,

that this performance is loft
to the world.

Saint Stephen's Green;
or, *The Generous Lovers.*
Com. by Wm. Philips, Efq.
8vo. 1720. This piece was
never acted.

The Step-Mother. Tragi-
Com. by Sir Robert Stapylton, 4to. 1664. Acted at
Lincoln's-Inn-Fields, by
the Duke of York's fer-
vants.

The Stock-jobbers; or, *The
Humours of Exchange-Alley.*
Com. of three acts, Anony.
8vo. 1720. This is one
more of the pieces written
on the follies of the year
1720, but which, like the
reft of them, was never acted.

The Stolen Heirefs; or,
*The Salamanca Doctor out-
plotted.* Com. by Sufannah
Centlivre. Acted at Lin-
coln's-Inn-Fields, 4to.
1703.

The Strange Difcovery.
Tragi-Com. 4to. 1640.
This play has the letters J.
G. gent. prefixed to it as
the initials of the author's
name, and in fome copies of
this only edition the name
J. Gough at length.

The Stratford Jubilee.
Com. of two acts, by Fran.
Gentleman, as it hath been
lately exhibited at Stratford
upon Avon with great ap-
plaufe.

The Strollers. Farce. Acted at Drury-Lane. This is only an extract of some parcular scenes from a comedy written by John Durant Breval, called *The Play's the Plot*, published in 1718.

The Students. Com. altered from Shakspeare's *Love's Labour Lost,* and adapted to the stage, 8vo. 1762.

The Sturdy Beggars. A New Ballad Opera, 8vo. 1733. This piece was written on occasion of the Excise-bill.

The Successful Pirate. A Play, by Charles Johnson. Acted at Drury-Lane, 4to. 1713. This play is taken from an old one written by Lodowick Carlell, called *Arviragus and Philicia.*

The Successful Strangers. Tragi-Com. by William Mountfort. Acted at Drury-Lane, 4to. 1696. This play is much superior to *The Injured Lovers* of the same author; yet he is by no means clear from the charge of plagiarism with regard to his plot.

Such Things Are. A new Drama, by Mrs. Inchbald. Acted at Covent-Garden, 1787. This was intended as a compliment to Mr. Howard, the Philanthropist.

The Suicide. Com. in four acts, by George Colman. Acted at the Haymarket, 1778. Not print-

ed. Although none of the characters can be spoken of as new, yet the business of the drama is conducted with so much judgement, that we cannot but esteem this very pleasing comedy as little inferior to the best of Mr. Colman's productions.

The Sullen Lovers; or, *Impertinents.* Com. by T. Shadwell. Acted at the Duke of York's Theatre, 4to. 1668. The author owns in his preface, that he had received a hint from the report of Moliere's *Les Fâcheux,* on which he had founded the plot of this comedy; but at the same time declares, that he had pursued that hint in the formation of great part of his own play before the French one ever came into his hands. Be this, however, as it may, he has certainly made very good use of whatever assistances he borrowed, having rendered his own piece extremely regular and entertaining. The place of the scene in London, the time supposed in the month of March in the year 1667-8.

The Sultan; or, *Love and Fame.* Trag. by Francis Gentleman. Acted at the Haymarket, 8vo. 1770. This play was written about the year 1755, and has been frequently acted at Bath, York, and Scarborough.

The

The Sultana. F. Acted at Drury-Lane, 1755. A frivolous raree-show performance, which but for the splendor of its scenery, and the sprightliness of a female performer, would have met with early condemnation.

The Sultaness. Trag. by Cha. Johnson, 8vo. 1717. This is little more than a translation of *The Bajazet* of Racine; a piece which of itself is esteemed the very worst of that author's writings.

Summer Amusement; or, *An Adventure at Margate.* Com. Opera, by Messieurs Andrews and Miles. Acted at the Haymarket, 1779.

The Summer's Tale. Musical Com. of three acts, by Richard Cumberland, Esq. Acted at Covent - Garden, 8vo. 1765. This comedy met with but a cold reception, though it was performed nine nights.

Summer's last Will and Testament. Com. by Thomas Nash, 4to. 1600.

The Sun's Darling. A. Masque, by John Ford and Thomas Dekker. Acted at Whitehall, and afterwards at the Cockpit in Drury-Lane, 4to. 1656. The plan of this masque alludes to the four seasons of the year.

The Superannuated Gallant. Farce, by J. Reed, 12mo. 1746.

The Supplicants. Trag. translated from Æschylus, by R. Potter, 4to. 1781.

The Supposes. Com. by George Gascoigne, 4to. 1566. This is one of the earliest dramatic pieces which can properly be called plays in the English language, and was acted at Gray's-Inn. It is a translation from an Italian comedy, by the celebrated Ariosto.

The Surprisal. Comedy, by Sir Robert Howard, fol. 1665.

The Surrender of Calais. Com. by Mr. Colman, jun. Acted at the Haymarket, 1791. This play is in the manner of Shakspeare's histories, of which it is not a very bad imitation. The scenes, as well as the characters, are contrasted, and the poetic fancy is unrestrained by the common rules of the regular drama.

Susanna. By Tho. Garter, 4to. 1578. The running title of this play is, *The Commody of the moste vertuous and godlye Susanna.* It is written in metre, printed in the old black letter, and not divided into acts, three great tokens of its being a very ancient piece.

Susanna; or, *Innocence Preserv'd.* Musical Drama, by Elizabeth Tollet, 12mo. 1755.

Suspicious

S U

Suspicious Husband. C. by Dr. Benjamin Hoadly, 8vo. 1747. This comedy was first presented at Covent-Garden house, and appears to have one standard proof of merit, which is, that although, on the first night it was performed it seemed threatened with considerable opposition; yet, from the time the curtain rose, it gradually overcame all prejudice against it, met with universal applause, and continues to this day one of the most favourite pieces with the public, being as frequently presented to crowded theatres as any one modern comedy on the list. To speak impartially of it, however, its merit is rather, pleasing than striking, and the busy activity of the plot takes off our attention to the want of design, character, and language, which even its best friends must confess to be discoverable on a more rigid scrutiny. Yet the audience is kept constantly alive; and as the principal intent of comedy is to entertain, and afford the care-tired mind a few hours of dissipation, a piece consisting of a number of lively busy scenes, intermingled with easy sprightly conversation and characters, which, if not glaring, are at least not unnatural, will frequently

S U

answer that purpose more effectually than a comedy of more complete and laboured regularity, and therefore surely lays a very just claim to our approbation and thanks. Yet this play is not entirely devoid of merit with respect to character, since that of Ranger, though not new, is absolutely well drawn, and may, we think, be placed as the most perfect portrait of the lively, honest, and undesigning rake of the present age; nor can Mr. Garrick's inimitable performance of that character, which indeed was in great measure the support of the piece during its first run be ever forgotten, while one person survives who has seen him in it. Clarinda is an amiable, lively, and honest coquet; and Strickland, though evidently copied from Ben Jonson's Kitely in *Every Man in his Humour*, and indeed greatly inferior to that character, has nevertheless some scenes in which the agitations of a weak mind, affected with that most tormenting of all passions, *Jealousy*, are far from being badly expressed; nor can we bring a more convincing argument to prove this assertion, than the universal reputation the performing of that character brought to an actor of no

very

very capital fhare of merit in other parts, viz. Mr. B idgewater, who, during th run of this comedy, obtained fo much of the public approbation by his performance of Mr. Strickland, as even in an advertifement of his benefit to affign that approbation as a reafon for his making choice of this play rather than any other. The fcene lies in London, and the time about thirty-fix-hours.

The Sufpicious Hufband criticized; or, *The Plague of Envy*. Farce, by Charles Macklin, 1747. This piece was acted at the Theatre Royal in Drury-Lane, and is a criticifm on the foregoing play. It has never appeared in print.

The Swaggering Damfel. Com. by Robert Chamberlaine, 4to. 1640. It is uncertain whether this play was ever acted.

Swetnam the Womanhater arraign'd by Women. Com. Acted at the Red-Bull by the late Queen's fervants. Anonymous, 4to. 1620.

The Swindlers. Farce, Acted at Drury-Lane, Apr. 25, 1774, for the benefit of Mr. Baddeley, but not printed.

The Swop. Farce of two acts. Performed at the Hay-Market, 1789, and condemned on the firft reprefentation.

The Sword of Peace; or, *The Voyage of Love.* Com. Acted at the Haymarket, 1788. Tolerably well received.

The Sylph. Com. Piece, in one act, tranflated from Fagan, 8vo. 1771.

Sylla. A Dramatic Entertainment, by Mr. Derrick, 8vo. 1753. This is only a tranflation, not defigned for the ftage, of a kind of Opera, written originally in French by the King of Pruffia.

Sylvia; or, *The Country Burial.* Ballad Opera, by George Lillo, 8vo. 1731. It was performed at Lincoln's-Inn-Fields Theatre, but with no very great fuccefs.

The Syracufan. Tra. by Dr. Dodd. This piece was never either acted or printed.

The Syrens. Mafque, in two acts, by Capt. Edw. Thompfon, performed at Covent-Garden, 8vo. 1776. This piece, after being thrice performed, was difmiffed with contempt.

A *TALE OF A TUB*, Com. by Ben Jonson, fol. 1640. This is not one of our author's beft pieces, being chiefly confined to low humour.

Tamberlane the Great; or, *The Sythian Shepherd*. Tr. in two parts, by Chriftopher Marloe, 4to. 1590. The fcene of both thefe pieces lies in Perfia, and they are both printed in the old black letter. The plot is taken from the Life of Tamerlane.

Tamberlane the Great. Trag. by Charles Saunders. Acted at the Theatre Royal, 4to. 1681. This was efteemed a very good play, and was highly commended by Banks and other his contemporary writers.

Tamerlane. Trag. by N. Rowe. Acted at Lincoln's - Inn - Fields, 4to. 1702. This play was written in compliment to King William III. whofe character the author intended to difplay under that of Tamerlane. It was received with great applaufe at its firft appearance, and ftill continues to be an admired play. In purfuance of Mr. Rowe's intended compliment, it has been a conftant cuftom at all the theatres, both in London and Dublin, to reprefent it on the 4th of November, which was that monarch's birth-day. In Dublin more efpecially it is made one of what is called the *Government Nights* at the Theatre, when the Lord Lieutenant, or in his abfence the Lords Juftices, pay the ladies the compliment of rendering the boxes entirely free to fuch of them as chufe to come to the houfe. Nor has it been unufual in fome theatres to perform this play on the fucceding night alfo, which is the anniverfary of his firft landing on the English coaft. Dr. Johnfon obferves, that the virtues of Tamerlane feem to have been arbitrarily affigned him by his poet, for we know not that hiftory gives him any other qualities than thofe which make a conqueror. The fafhion however of the time was, to accumulate upon Lewis all that can raife horror and deteftation; and whatever good was witheld from him, that it might not be thrown away, was beftowed upon King William. This was the tragedy which Rowe valued moft, and that which probably, by the help of political auxiliaries, excited moft applaufe; but occafional poetry muft often content itfelf with occafional praife. Tamerlane has for a long time been acted only once a year, on the night

T A

night when King William landed. Our quarrel with Lewis has been long over, and it now gratifies neither zeal nor malice to fee him painted with aggravated features, like a Saracen upon a fign.

The Taming of the Shrew. A pleafaunt conceited Hiftorie. As it hath beene fundry times acted by the right honourable the Earle of Pembrooke his fervants, 4to. 1607. This play is a different one from Shakfpeare's, and fuppofed to be prior to it. The merit of it, in any other light than being what our great bard availed himfelf of, is but flender.

The Taming of the Shrew. Com. by William Shakfpeare. Acted at the Black-Fryars and the Globe, fol. 1623. This is very far from being a regular play, yet has many very great beauties in it. The plot of the drunken Tinker's being taken up by the Lord, and made to imagine himfelf a man of quality, is borrowed from Goulart's *Hiftoires admirables.* The fcene, in the latter end of the third and the beginning of the 4th acts, is at Petrucio's houfe in the country; for the reft of the play, at Padua. This Comedy has been the ground work of fome other pieces, particularly *Sawney the Scot,*

T A

The Cobler of Prefton, and *Catharine and Petruchio;* among which the laft is much the moft regular and perfect Drama that has ever been formed from it. Dr. Johnfon fays, " Of this play the two plots are fo well united, that they can hardly be called two without injury to the art with which they are intervowen with all the variety of a double plot, yet is not diftracted by unconnected incidents. The part between Katherine and Petruchio is eminently fpritely and diverting. At the marriage of Bianca, the arrival of the real father perhaps produces more perplexity than pleafure. The whole play is very popular and diverting."

Tancred. Trag. by Sir Henry Wotton, compofed when the author was a young man at Queen's College, but never printed.

Tancred and Sigifmund. Trag. This play was the work of five gentlemen of the Inner Temple, and was performed there before Queen Elizabeth in the year 1653.

Tancred and Sigifmunda. Trag. by James Thomfon. Acted at Drury-Lane, 8vo. 1744. The plot of this play is taken from the novel of *Gil Blas.* It is one of the beft of this author's dramatic

tic pieces, and met with very good fuccefs. The characters are well fupported, yet they are not fufficiently new and ftriking. The loves of Tancred and Sigifmunda are tender, pathetic and affecting; yet there is too little variety of incident or furprize, to preferve the attention of an audience fufficiently to it; and the language in many places poetical and flowery, yet in the general too declamatory and fentimental. On the whole, therefore, the piece, though far from wanting fome fhare of merit, appears heavy and dragging in the reprefentation, and feems therefore better adapted to the clofet than the theatre.

Tantara Rara; or, *Rogues all*. Farce. Acted at Covent-Garden, 1788. This piece is tranflated from the French, and, though it has much merit, was interdicted on the reprefentation.

Tartuffe; or, *The French Puritan*. Com. by Math. Medbourne. Acted at the Theatre Royal, 4to. 1670. This play is an improved tranflation of Moliere's *Tartuffe*, and according to the author's own account met with very great applaufe.

Tartuffe; or, *The Hypocrite*. Com. by J. Ozell.

This is only a literal tranflation from Moliere.

Tarugo's Wiles; or, *The Coffee-houfe*. Com. by Sir Thomas St. Serfe. Acted at the Duke of York's Theatre, 4to. 1668 This piece, if not intitled to the *firft*, may, without prefumption, lay claim to a place in the *fecond* rank of our dramatic writings.

Tafte. Com. of two acts. by Samuel Foote. Acted at Drury-Lane, 8vo. 1752. This piece and its profits were given by its author to Mr. Worfdale the painter, who acted the part of Lady Pentweafle in it with great applaufe. The general intention of it is to point out the numerous impofitions that perfons of fortune and fafhion daily fuffer in the purfuit of what is called *Tafte* or a love of *Vertu*, from the tricks and confederacies of painters, actioneers, *Medal Dealers*. &c. and to fhew the abfurdity of placing an ineftimable value on, and giving immenfe prizes for, a parcel of maimed bufts, erazed pictures, and inexplicable coins, only becaufe they have the mere name and appearance of antiquity, while the more perfect and really valuable performances of the moft capital artifts of our own age and country,

country, if known to be such, are totally defpifed and neglected, and the artifts themfelves fuffered to pafs through life unnoticed and difcouraged; thefe points Mr. Foote has in this Farce fet forth in a very juft, and at the fame time a very humourous light; butwhether the generality of the audience did not relifh, or perhaps did not underftand this confined fatire, or that, underftanding it, they were fo wedded to the infatuation of being impofed on, that they were unwilling to fubfcribe to the juftice of it, we will not pretend to determine; but it met with fome oppofi ion for a night or two, and during the whole run of it, which was not a long one, found at beft but a cold and diftafteful reception.

The Taxes. Dramatic Entertainment, by Dr. Bacon, 8vo. 1757.

The Taylors. Trag. for warm weather. Acted at the Haymarket, 8vo. 1778. This piece was firft acted, 1767, at a time when there had been great difturbances between the mafter Taylors and their journeymen about wages. The author of it hath kept himfelf concealed; but the manner in which it came to the manager is faid to have been as follows : A fhort time before its ap-

pearance, Mr. Foote received the manufcript from Mr. Dodfley's fhop, offering it for his acceptance, with a requeft at the fame time, that if it was not approved, it might be returned in the manner it came to him. Mr. Foote, on perufing it, was much pleafed with the performance, ordered it immediately into rehearfal, and took the principal character himfelf.

Tchoo Chi Cou Ell; or, *The Little Orphan of the Family of Tochoo*. Tr. 8vo. 1737. This is nothing more than a literal tranflation from the Chinefe language of the tragedy in the firft volume of Du Halde's *Hiftory of China*, by Richard Brookes.

Teague's Ramble to London. Interlude. Acted at the Haymarket, 1770. Not printed.

The Tears and Triumphs of Parnaffus. Ode, by Robert Lloyd; performed at Drury-Lane, 4to. 1760.

Texnolamia; or, *The Marriage of the Arts*. Com. by Barton Holiday, 4to. 1618. This piece was acted by the ftudents of Chrift Church, Oxford, before the Univerfity at Shrove-Tide. It is entirely figurative, all the liberal arts being perfonated in it.

Telemachus. Mafque, by George

George Graham, 4to. 1763.

Tempe Reftor'd. Mafq. 4to. 1631. This piece was prefented before K. Charles I. at Whitehall on Shrove-Tuefday, 1631, by the Queen and fourteen of her ladies. It is founded on the ftory of Circe, as related in the 14th book of Ovid's *Metamorphofes.*

The Tempeft. A Com. by William Shakfpeare, fol. 1623. This is a very admirable play, and is one inftance, among many, of our author's creative faculty, who fometimes feems wantonly, as if tired with rummaging in nature's ftorehoufe for his characters, to prefer the forming of fuch as fhe never dreamt of, in order to fhew his own power of making them act and fpeak juft as fhe would have done had fhe thought proper to have given them exiftence. One of thefe characters is Caliban in this play, than which nothing furely can be more *outré*, and at the fame time nothing more perfectly natural. His Ariel is another of thefe inftances, and is the moft amazing contraft to the heavy earth-born clod we have been mentioning; all his defcriptions, and indeed every word he fpeaks, appearing to partake of the properties of that light and invifible element which he is the inhabitant of. Nor is his Miranda lefs deferving of notice, her fimplicity and natural fenfations under the circumftances he has placed her in, being fuch as no one fince, though many writers have attempted an imitation of the character, has ever been able to arrive at. The fcene is at firft on board a veffel in a ftorm at fea; through all the reft of the play, in a defert ifland. Dr. Johnfon fays, " It is obferved of *The Tempeft*, that its plan is regular ; this the author of *The Revifal* thinks, what we think too, an accidental effect of the ftory, not intended or regarded by our author. But whatever might be Shakfpeare's intention in forming or adopting the plot, he has made it inftrumental to the production of many characters, diverfified with boundlefs invention, and preferved with profound fkill in nature, extenfive knowledge of opinions, and accurate obfervation of life. In a fingle drama are exhibited princes, courtiers, and failors, all fpeaking in their real characters. There is the agency of airy fpirits, and of an earthly goblin. The operations of magic, the tumults of a ftorm, the adventures

T E

T E.

tures of a defert ifland, the native effufion of untaught affection, the punifhment of guilt, and the final happinefs of the pair for whom our paffions and reafon are equally interefted.''

The Tempeft ; or, *The Enchanted Ifland.* Com. by J. Dryden. Acted at Dorfet-Gardens, 4to. 1670. The whole ground work of this play is built on the forementioned one of Shakfpeare, the greateft part of the language and fome entire fcenes being copied *verbatim* from it. Mr. Dryden has, however, made a confiderable alteration in the plot and conduct of the play, and introduced three entire new characters, viz. a fifter to Miranda, who, like her, has never feen a man ; a youth who has never beheld a woman ; and a female monfter, fifter and companion to Caliban ; befides which, he has fomewhat enlarged on the characters of the failors, greatly extended the mufical parts, and terminated the whole with a kind of mafque. In fhort, he has, on the whole, rendered it more fhewy, more intricate, and fitter to keep up the general attention of the audience ; and yet to the immortal evidence of Shakfpeare's fuperior abilities over every

other genius, we cannot but obferve that the work of this very great poet Mr. Dryden, interwoven as it is with the very texture of Shakfpeare's play, and fine as it muft be confidered taken fingly, appears here but as patch-work, as a fruit entirely unequal to the noble ftock on which it is engrafed. Mr. Dryden, in his preface, obferves, that Fletcher in his *Sea Voyage*, and Sir John Suckling in his *Goblins*, have borrowed very confiderably from Shakfpeare's *Tempeft*. Sir William Davenant had fome fhare with Dryden in this alteration.

The Tempeft. Opera, 8vo. 1756. By David Garrick, Efq. This is only the principal fcenes of Shakfpeare's *Tempeft*, thrown into the form of an opera, by the addition of many new fongs. It was performed at the Theatre Royal in Drury-Lane with fuccefs.

The Temple Beau. Com. by Henry Fielding. Acted at Goodman's-Fields, 8vo. 1729. This play contains a great deal of fpirit and real humour.

The Temple of Dullnefs, with the humours of Signor Capechio and Signora Dorinna. A Comic Opera. Acted at Drury-Lane, 4to. 1745.

The

The Temple of Love. A Mafque. Prefented by the Queen's Majefty and her ladies at Whitehall on Shrove Tuefday 1634. By Inigo Jones and Wm. Davenant, 4to. 1634.

Temple of Love. Paftoral Opera, englifhed from the Italian. Performed at the Haymarket, 4to. 1706. By Peter Motteux.

The Temple of Peace. Mafque of one act, performed at Dublin, 8vo. 1749.

The Tender Hufband; or, *The Accomplifhed Fool.* C. by Sir Richard Steele. Acted at Drury-Lane, 4to. 1705. Some part of this play is borrowed from Moliere's *Sicilien, ou L'Amour Peintre.*

Teraminta. An Englifh Opera, by Mr. H. Carey, 8vo. 1732. This piece was performed at the Theatre in Lincoln's-Inn-Fields.

Tethy's Feftival; or, *The Queen's Wake,* celebrated at Whitehall, the 5th of June, 1610, devifed by Sam. Daniel, 4to. 1610.

The Theatrical Candidates. Prel. by David Garrick, Efq. Acted at Drury-Lane, 8vo. 1775.

The Theatrical Manager. Dram. Satire, 8vo. 1751. Abufe on Mr. Garrick.

Thebais. Trag. by Tho. Newton, 4to. 1581. This is a tranflation from one of the tragedies publifhed as Seneca's.

Thelypthora; or, *More Wives than One.* Far. by F. Pilon. Acted at Covent-Garden, 1781. The popularity of Mr. Madan's book with the fame title as this piece, and the novelty of its doctrine, feemed to point them out as good fubjects for comic ridicule. His piece was reprefented once, and attempted a fecond time but without fuccefs.

Themiftocles, the Lover of his Country. Trag. 1729. 8vo. by Dr. Sam. Madden. Acted with fome fuccefs at the Theatre in Lincoln's-Inn-Fields.

Theodoric King of Denmark. Trag. by a young gentlewoman, 8vo. 1752.

Theodofius; or, *The Force of Love.* Trag. by Nath. Lee. Acted at the Duke's Theatre, 4to. 1680. This play met with great and deferved fuccefs, and is to this day a very favourite tragedy with moft of the fenfible part of the audience. The paffions are very finely touched in it, and the language in many parts extremely beautiful. Every thing that relates to the loves of Varanes, Athenais, and Theodofius, is uniform, noble, and affecting; yet even all thefe beauties cannot bribe us from remarking how

how very unequal to thefe is the epifode of the loves of Marcian and Pulcheria, which is in itfelf fo trifling, and fo unconnected and unneceffary to the main plot of the play, that, with a very little alteration, thofe two characters, and every thing that relates to them, might be entirely omitted, and the piece rendered the better for the want of them. Marcian's behaviour to Theodofius is not only inconfiftent with probability, but fuch as renders the latter too contemptible for the fufferance of an audience after it, to admit him again on the ftage; and Pulcheria's banifhing the general only to have an opportunity of recalling him, to furprize him by making him her hufband, has fomething in it fo truly ludicrous and puerile, that one fhould imagine it rather the treatment of a fkittifh boardingfchool mifs to fome pretty mafter juft come home to a holiday breaking-up, than that of a princefs, to whom the empire of the world was to devolve, towards a hardy foldier, whofe arms that world had trembled at the found of. It were therefore to be wifhed, that this flight hint might induce fome perfon equal to the tafk, to undertake an alteration of

it, by curtailing thefe fuperfluous excrefcences, and filling up the hiatus they would leave, with fome incidents that might have more uniformity and connection with the general defign of the play.

Therfytes, his Humours and Conceits. An Interlude. Anon. 1598.

Thomas and Sally. A Mufical Entertaiment, 8vo. 1761. This little piece was performed at Covent-Garden Theatre with great fuccefs. It was written by Mr. Ifaac Bickerftaffe. The plot is very fimple, being no more than a country 'fquire's attempting the virtue of a young girl in the neighbourhood, who, after refifting all the perfuafions of an old woman who pleads in the 'fquire's favour, is at laft refcued from intended violence by the timely approach of a youth, for whom fhe had long maintained a pure and unaltered paffion. The fongs are pleafing, and the mufic well adapted to the prefent tafte.

Thomafo; or, *The Wanderer.* Com. in two parts, by Thomas Killigrew, fol. 1664.

Thomyris, Queen of Scythia. An Opera, by P. Motteux, 4to. 1707. This was performed at the Theatre Royal in Drury-Lane, and

and was one of the attempts made at that time for the introduction of Englifh operas after the manner òf the Italian.

Thorney Abbey ; or, *The London Maid*. Tra. by T. W. 12mo. 1662.

The Thracian Wonder. A comical Hiftory, by John Webfter and William Rowley, 4to. 1661. This play was acted with great applaufe.

The Three Conjurors. A political Interlude, ftolen from Shakfpeare, 4to. 1763. A fquib thrown at Lord Bute.

Three Hours after Marriage. Com. of three acts, by Meffrs. Gay, Pope, and Arbuthnot. Acted at Drury-Lane, 8vo. 1717. This little piece, the joint produce of this triumvirate of firft-rate wits, was very defervedly damned. The confequence of which was the giving Mr. Pope fo great a difguft to the ftage, that he never attempted any thing in the dramatic way afterwards ; and, indeed, he feems, through the courfe of his fatirical writings, to have fhewn a more peculiar degree of fpleen againft thofe authors who happened to meet with fuccefs in this walk, in which he had fo confpicuoufly failed. Yet it is far from improbable,

that had he thought it worth his while fingly to have taken the pains of writting a dramatic piece, he might have fucceeded equally, if not fuperior to any of his contemporaries. Though this piece was printed under the name of Gay, his hand is not very difcernible in any part of it. We may however obferve, that the character of Sir Tremendcus, being apparently defigned for Dennis, was in all probability introduced by Pope. Foffile, who was meant as the reprefentative of Dr. Woodward, might likewife have been the production of Arbuthnot, who through the knowledge incident to his profeffion was enabled to furnifh a fufficient train of phyfical terms and obfervations. Phœbe Clinket alfo fhould feem to have been intended as a ridicule on one of the females, whofe petulant attacks had irritated the little bard of Twickenham. Cibber informs us, that his own quarrel with him was occafioned by a joke thrown into the Rehearfal, at the expence of this unfuccefsful performance.

A right excellent and famous Comedy, called, *The Three Ladies of London.* Wherein is notablie declared and fet forth how by meanes

meanes of Lucar, Love and
Confcience is fo corrupted,
that the one is married to
Diffimulation, the other
fraught with all abhomina-
tion. A perfect patterne
for all eftates to looke into,
and a worke right worthie
to be marked. Written by
R. W. as it hath been pub-
liquely plaied.—At London.
Printed by Robert Warde,
dwelling neere Holburne
Conduit, at the figne of the
Talbot, 1584.

*The Three Old Women
Weatherwife.* An Interlude,
by G. S. Carey. Acted
at the Hay-market, 1770.

*Three Weeks after Marri-
age.* Com. of two acts, by
Arthur Murphy, performed
at Covent-Garden, 8vo.
1776. This piece affords a
very ftriking proof of the
capricioufnefs of public
tafte, and the injuftice of
fome public determinations.
It is no other than the
What we muft all come to, of
the fame author, with only
a new title. On its firft appearance it was condemned
almoft without a hearing,
and lay dormant for feveral
years, until Mr. Lewis ventured to produce it again at
his benefit, when it met
with univerfal applaufe, and
ftill continues to be favourably received.

Thierry and Theodoret.

Trag. by Beaumont and
Fletcher. Acted at the
Black-Fryars, 4to. 1621.
The plot of this play may
be feen by confulting De
Serres, Mezeray, and other
of the French writers on the
reign of Clotaire II. and
the fcene lies in France.
In the folio edition of thefe
authors' works in 1679, the
editor, either defignedly,
or from fome careleffnefs of
the compofitor, has omitted
a great part of the laft act,
which contains the King's
behaviour during the ope-
ration of the poifon adminiftered to him by his mother, and which is as affecting as any part of the play.

Thyeftes. Trag. by Jaf-
per Heywood, 8vo. 1560.
This is only a tranflation
from the *Thyeftes* of Seneca.
It was not intended for the
ftage.

Thyeftes. Tra. by John
Wright, 12mo. 1674. This
is another tranflation of the
fame play.

Thyeftes. Trag. by John
Crowne. Acted at the Theatre Royal, 4to. 1681. This
is the only piece on this ftory
that has made its appear-
ance on the Englifh ftage,
where it met with good fuccefs.

*Time vindicated to himfelf
and his Honours.* Mafque,
by Ben Jonfon, prefented
·at

at Court on Twelfth-night, 1623.

Timanthes. Trag. by John Hoole. Acted at Covent-Garden, 8vo. 1770. This second tragedy by the worthy and ingenious Mr. Hoole, like his first, is the child of Metastasio, and indeed has all the features of its parent.

The Times. Comedy, by Mrs. Elizabeth Griffiths. Acted at Drury-Lane, 8vo. 1779. This piece, like most other of the same author's, is taken from the French. It possesses as much merit, but was not acted with equal success to some of her former pieces.

Timoleon. Trag. by B. Martyn, 8vo. 1730. This play was acted at Drury-Lane Theatre with some success.

Timoleon; or, *The Revolution.* Trag-Com. Anon. 1697. The comic parts of this play are intended as a satire on mercenary courtiers, who prefer money to merit.

Timon in Love; or, *The Innocent Theft.* Com. by J. Kelly, 8vo. 1733. This play was acted at Drury-Lane with indifferent success. It is a translation, with but little alteration, of *The Timon Misantrope* of M. De L'Isle.

Timon of Athens. Trag.

by William Shakspeare, fol. 1623. There are some passages in this play equal to any thing this author ever wrote, particularly Timon's grace, and his several curses; nor was there ever perhaps an higher finished character than that of Apemantus. Yet it is not without some faults in point of regularity. The story may be found in Lucian's *Dialogues*, Plutarch's Life of Marc Anthony, &c. The scene lies in Athens and the woods adjaeent. Dr. Johnson observes, this play " is a domestic tragedy, and therefore strongly fastens on the attention of the reader. In the plan there is not much art, but the incidents are natural, and the characters are various and exact. The catastrophe affords a very powerful warning against that ostentatious liberality which scatters bounty, but confers no benefits, and buys flattery, but not friendship."

The History of Timon of Athens, the Manhater, made into a play, as the alterer modestly phrases it, by Thomas Shadwell. Acted at the Duke's Theatre, 4to. 1678. This tragedy is borrowed from the foregoing one, but is not near so good a play, almost every thing that is valuable in it being
what

what the author has taken
verbatim from Shakfpeare.
Timon of Athens. Alter-
ed from Shakfpeare and
Shadwell, by James Love.
Acted at Richmond, 8vo.
1768.
Timon of Athens. Trag.
Altered from Shakfpeare.
by R. Cumberland. Acted
at DruryLane, 8vo. 1771,
but with little fuccefs.
'Tis better than it was.
Com. by George Digby,
Earl of Briftol. This play
is taken from the Spanifh,
and acted at the Duke's
Theatre between 1662 and
1665. Not printed.
'Tis Pity She's a Whore.
Trag. by John Ford. Act-
ed at the Phœnix, Drury-
Lane, 4to. 1633. We can-
not help confidering this
play as the mafter-piece of
this great author's works.
There are fome particulars
in it both with refpect to
conduct, character, fpirit,
and poetry, that would have
done honour to the pen of
the immortal Shakfpeare
himfelf.
'Tis well if it Takes. C.
by William Taverner, 8vo.
1719. This play was acted
with fuccefs at the Theatre
in Lincoln's-Inn-Fields,
yet, like moft of its author's
pieces, quickly funk into
oblivion.
'Tis Well its no Worfe.
Com. by Ifaac Bickerftaffe.

Acted at Drury-Lane, 8vo.
1770. It was not unfuccefs-
fully performed.
Tittle Tattle ; or, *Tafte
à-la-Mode.* F. 8vo. 1749.
This is no other than Ex-
tracts from Swift's *Polite
Converfation.*
Titus. Opera, tranflated
from Metaftafio, by John
Hoole, 8vo. 1768.
Titus Andronicus. Trag.
by Wm. Shakfpeare, 4to.
1594. This play has by
fome been denied to be
Shakfpeare's ; and Raven-
fcroft, in the epiftle to his
alteration of it, too pofitive-
ly afferted that it was not
originally Shakfpeare's, but
brought by a private author
to be acted, and that he
only gave fome mafter-
touches to one or two of the
principal parts or characters.
However, as Theobald ad-
mitted it into his edition of
this author's works, we cannot think ourfelves entitled
to deny it a place. It is true,
there is fomewhat more extravagant in the plot, and
more horrid in the cataftrophe, than in moft of Shakfpeare's Tragedies ; but as
we know that he fometimes
gave an unlimited fcope to
his imagination, and as
there are fome things in the
characters of Aaron, Tamo-
ra, and Titus, which are
fcarcely to be equalled, we
can hardly deny our hom-
age

age to thofe ſtamps of ſterling merit which appear upon it, nor our acquiefcence to the opinion of a critic ſo well acquainted with the manner of our author as Mr. Theobald unqueſtionably was. Later critics of abilities, much ſuperior to Mr. Theobald's, have, however, given very different opinions on this ſubject. See Dr. Johnſon's, Dr. Farmer's, Mr. Steeven's, and Mr. Malone's ſentiments on the fame ſubject at the end of this play, in the laſt edition of Shakſpeare. The ſcene lies in Rome, and the plot borrowed, but very ſlightly, from the Roman hiſtory of the latter empire.

Titus Andronicus ; or, *The Rape of Lavinia.* Tr. by Edward Ravenſcroft. Acted at the Theatre Royal, 4to. 1687.

Titus and Berenice. Tr. by Thomas Otway, 4to. 1677. This is a tranſlation, with ſome few alterations, from a tragedy of the fame name by M. Racine.

Titus Veſpaſian. Tr. by John Cleland, 8vo. 1760. This piece is by no means deſtitute of merit.

The Tobacconiſt. Com. of two acts, by Fra. Gentleman, altered from Ben Jonſon's *Alchymiſt.* Acted at the Haymarket and Edinburgh, 8vo. 1771.

Tombo Chiqui ; or, *The American Savage.* A dramatic Entertainment, in three acts, by John Cleland, 8vo. 1758. This is no more than a tranſlation of the *Arlequin Sauvage* of De L'Iſle.

Tom Eſſence ; or, *The Modiſh Wife.* Com. Acted at the Duke's Theatre, 4to. 1677. One Mr. Rawlins is ſaid to be the author of this play

Tom Jones Com. Opera, by Joſeph Reed. Acted at Covent-Garden, 8vo. 1769. This is taken from Fielding's novel, with the fame title, and was received with conſiderable applauſe.

Tom Thumb. Burletta, by Kane O'Hara. Acted at Covent-Garden, 1780. An alteration of Fielding's *Tom Thumb,* with the addition of ſongs. It met with great ſucceſs.

Tome Tylere and his Wyfe. A paſſing merrie Interlude. Anonymous, 1598. This play has been attributed to William Wayer. The plot of it refembles M. Poifon's *Le Sot vengé,* and the intent of it is to repreſent and humble a ſhrew.

The Ton ; or, *The Follies of Faſhion.* Com. by Lady Wallace. Acted at Covent-Garden, 1788. This play has many defects, and was foon withdrawn.

Tony Lumpkin in Town ; or,

or, *The Dilettanti*. Farce, by J. Keefe. Acted at the Haymarket, 1778, printed 8vo. 1780. A very humorous production, which received the applaufe it deferved.

Too Civil by Half. Far. by Mr. Dent, acted at Drury-Lane, 1782. The dialogue of this piece has feveral good turns in it, and the incidents are laughable. It was very favourably received.

The Touchftone. A Pantomime. Acted at Covent-Garden, 1779.

The Tournament. Interlude, 8vo. 1777. This is one of the pieces publifhed under the name of Thomas Rowley, a Prieft, of the fifteenth century. It is now generally acknowledged to be the production of T. Chatterton.

The Town Fop; or, *Sir Timothy Tawdrey*. Com. by Mrs. Aphra Behn. Acted at the Duke's Theatre, 4to. 1677.

The Town Shifts; or, *Suburb Juftice*. Com. by Edward Revet. Acted at the Duke's Theatre, 4to. 1671. Langbaine fpeaks highly in favour of this play as an inftructive and moral piece; and particularly commends the author for the fignature of one of his characters, viz. Lovewell, who,

though reduced to poverty, not only maintains himfelf by the principles of innate honefty and integrity, but even takes great pains in the perfuading his two friends and comrades, Friendly and Faithful, to the practice of the fame. The whole piece, according to the preface, was begun and finifhed in a fortnight.

The Toy. Com. Acted at Covent-Garden, 1789, with applaufe.

The Toyfhop. Farce, by Robert Dodfley, 8vo. 1735. The hint of this elegant and fenfible little piece feems built on Randolph's *Mufes Looking-glafs*. The author of it, however, has fo perfectly modernized it, and adapted the fatire to the peculiar manner and follies of the times he writes to, that he has made it perfectly his own, and rendered it one of the jufteft, and at the fame time beft-natured rebukes that fafhionable abfurdity perhaps ever met with.

The Tragedy of Tragedies; or, *The Life and Death of Tom Thumb the Great*, 8vo. 1731, with annotations by *Scriblerius Secundus*. This piece firft made its appearance in the Little Theatre in the Haymarket, in the year 1730, in one act only; but in the above-mentioned

P

mentioned year the fuccefs it had met with before induced the author to enlarge it to the extent of three acts, and bring it on the ftage again, firft in the Haymarket, and afterwards in Drury-Lane Theatre. It is perhaps one of the beft burlefques that ever appeared in this or any other language, and may properly be confidered as a fequel to the Duke of Buckingham's *Rehearfal*, as it has taken in the abfurdities of almoft all the writers of tragedy from the period where that piece ftops. In a word, this piece poffeffes in the higheft degree the principal merit of true burlefque, viz. that while it points out the faults of every other writer, it leaves no room for the difcovery of any in itfelf.

Tragopodagra; or, *The Gout*. Trag. tranflated from Lucian, by Dr. Thomas Franklin, 4to. 1781.

Trappolin fuppofed a Prince. Tragi-Com. by Sir Afton Cockain, 12mo. 1658. The author of this piece borrowed his defign from an Italian Tragi-Com. called *Trappoline creduto Principe*. It is a moft abfurd piece of work, every rule of character, probability, and even poffibility, being abfolutely broken through, and very little wit or humour to com-

penfate for fuch irregularity.

The Travels of the Three Englifh Brothers, Sir Thomas, Sir Anthony, and Sir Robert Shirley. An hiftorical Play, by John Daye, 4to. 1607.

The Traytor. Trag. by James Shirley, 4to. 1635. This play was originally written by one Rivers, a Jefuit, but is greatly altered by its prefent author.

The Traytor to Himfelf; or, *Man's Heart his greateft Enemy.* A moral interlude, by William Johns, 4to 1678. This piece is written in rhyme, and was performed by the boys of the public fchool at Evefham, at a breaking-up, and publifhed fo as to render it ufeful on the occafion. It contains many moral and inftructive fentences, well adapted to the capacities of youth.

The Treacherous Hufband. Trag. by Samuel Davey, 8vo. 1737.

The Treafure. Comedy, tranflated from Plautus, by Bonnel Thornton, 8vo. 1767.

Trick for Trick; or, *The Debauch'd Hypocrite.* Com. by Thomas Durfey. Acted at the Theatre Royal, 4to. 1678. This is very little more than a revival of Beaumont and Fletcher's *Monf. Thomas,*

Thomas, though Mr. Durfey has scarcely had candour enough to acknowledge the theft.

A Trick to Catch the Old One. Com. by Thomas Middleton. Acted both at Paul's and Black - Fryars, 4to. 1608. This is an excellent old play, and appears to have been greatly in vogue at the time it was written.

Trick upon Trick; or, *Squire Brainless.* Com. by Aaron Hill. It made its appearance at Drury-Lane, but was damned the very first night.

Trick upon Trick. Com. of two acts, by R. Fabian, 1735, 8vo. This piece made its appearance at Drury-Lane.

The Tripple Marriage. C. translated from the French of *Destouches*; and printed in Foot's *Comic Theatre*, vol. I.

A Trip to Calais. Com. by Sam. Foote, 8vo. 1778. This comedy was intended for representation in 1776, at the Haymarket, but containing a character designed for a Lady of Quality, she had interest enough to prevent its obtaining a licence. It was afterwards altered, and acted under the title of *The Capuchin.*

The Trip to Portsmouth. Sketch of one act, with

songs, by George Alexander Stevens, performed at the Haymarket, 8vo. 1773.

A Trip to Scarborough. Com. by Richard Brinsley Sheridan, Esq. Acted at Drury-Lane, 1776. An alteration of Vanburgh's *Relapse*; but such a one as will add little to the reputation of the gentleman whose name it bears.

A Trip to Scotland. F. by William Whitehead, Esq. Acted at Drury-Lane, 8vo. 1770. One of the best farces of the present times.

Tristram Shandy. A piece of two Acts, by Mr. Macnally. Acted at Covent-Garden, 1783, with much applause.

The Triumph of Mirth; or, *Harlequin's Wedding.* Pantomime, acted at Drury-Lane, 1782.

The Triumphant Widow; or, *The Medley of Humours.* Comedy, by William Duke of Newcastle. Acted at the Duke's Theatre, 4to. 1677. This is esteemed an excellent play, though now never acted.

The Triumph of Beauty. A masque, by James Shirley, 8vo. 1646. This piece is printed together with some poems of the Author's, and esteemed of less consequence than the generality of his dramatic works.

Triumphs of the Gout.

A mock Tragedy, tranflated from the Greek of Lucian, by Gilbert Weft, Efq. 4to. 1749. Printed with his tranflation of Pindar.

The Triumphs of Hymen. Mafque, by J. Wignell, 8vo. 1762.

The Triumphs of Love and Honour. A play, by Thomas Cooke, 8vo. 1731. Acted at the Theatre Royal in Drury-Lane, but without fuccefs.

The Triumph of Peace. A mafque, by James Shirley, 4to. 1633. This mafque was prefented before the King and Queen, at the Banqueting-houfe at Whitehall, by the Gentlemen of the Four Inns of Court, on the 3d of February, 1633.

The Triumph of Peace. A mafque, by Robert Dodfley, 4to. 1749. This was written on occafion of the figning the treaty of peace at Aix-la-Chapelle. It was fet to mufic by Dr. Arne, and performed at Drury-Lane.

The Triumphs of the Prince d'Amour. A mafque, by Sir W. Davenant, 4to. 1635. This mafque was written in three days, at the requeft of the members of the Inner Temple, by whom it was prefented for the entertainment of the Prince Elector, at his Highnefs's palace in the Mid-

dle Temple, on the 24th of February, 1635.

The Triumphs of Virtue. Tragi-Comedy, Anonym. 4to. Acted at the Theatre Royal, 1697.

Troades. Trag. 12mo. 1660. This piece is publifhed with poems upon feveral occafions, and has the letters S. P. which all the writers explain to be Samuel Pondage.

Troades ; or, *The Royal Captives* ; Trag. by Sir Edward Sherbourne, 8vo. 1649. This is a critical tranflation, with remarks, of the fame piece with the foregoing.

Troades. Trag. tranflated from Euripides, 8vo. 1780.

Troas. Trag. by Jafper Heywood, 4to. 1581. This is a tranflation from Seneca, in which, however, the tranflator has taken confiderable liberties with his author.

Troas. Trag. tranflated from Seneca, by J. T. 4to. 1686, None of thefe tranflations were ever intended for the ftage.

Troilus and Creffida. Tr. by Wm. Shakfpeare, 4to. 1609. This is, perhaps, the moft irregular of all Shakfpeare's plays, being not even divided into acts ; yet it contains an infinite number of beauties. The characters of the feveral Greeks

TR

TR·

Greeks and Trojans are finely drawn and nicely diftinguifhed ; and the heroifm of the greateft part of them finely contrafted by the brutifhnefs of Therfites, and the contemptible levity of Pandarus. Creffida's love in the firft part of the play, and her inconftancy in the fequel, befpeak the author perfectly acquainted with the female heart : Troilus's conviction of her falfhcod is admirably conducted ; and his behaviour on the occafion, fuch as a lover of the complexion he at firft appears would naturally full into. The fcene lies in Troy and the Grecian camp, alternately. Dr. Johnfon fays, " This play is more correctly written than moft of Shakfpeare's compofitions, but it is not one of thofe in which either the extent of his views or elevation of his fancy is fully difplayed. As the ftory abounded with materials, he has exerted little invention ; but he has deverfified his characters with great variety, and preferved them with great exactnefs. His vicious characters fometimes difguft, but cannot corrupt, for both Creffida and Pandarus are detefted and contemned. The comic characters feem to have been the favourites of the writer ;

they are of the fuperficial kind, and exhibit more of manners than nature ; but they are copioufly filled and powerfully impreffed. Shakfpeare has in his ftory followed, for the greater part, the old book of Caxton, which was then very popular ; but the character of Therfites, of which it makes no mention, is a proof that this play was written after Chapman had publifhed his verfion of Homer."

The True Born Scotchman. See *The Man of the World.*

The True Widow. Com. by Thomas Shadwell. Acted at the Duke's Theatre, 4to. 1679. The plot of this piece is entirely invention, not having been borrowed from any one. It did not, however, meet with fuccefs in the reprefentation.

Try Again. Acted at the Haymarket, 1790, with applaufe.

The Hiftory of the Tryall of Chevalry. With the Life and Death of Cavaliero Dickc Bowyer. As it hath bin lately acted by the Right Honourable the Earl of Darby his fervants. Winftanley and Philips have afcribed this piece to William Wayer ; but Langbaine imagines it not to be written by that author.

The Tryal of the Time-Killers.

P 3

T U

Killers. Com. of five acts, by Dr. Bacon, 8vo. 1757.

Tryphon. Trag. by R. Earl of Orrery, fol. 1672. It was performed at the Duke of York's Theatre with great succefs.

Tumble down Dick; or, *Phaeton in the Suds.* Farce, by Henry Fielding, 8vo. 1737. This piece was acted at the Little Theatre in the Haymarket, and was written in ridicule of an unfuccefsful Pantomime, performed at Drury-Lane houfe, called, *The Fall of Phaeton.*

Tunbridge-Wells; or, *A Day's Courtfhip.* Comedy. Acted at the Duke's Theatre, 4to. 1678. This play feems intended as a kind of imitation of Shadwell's *Epfom Wells,* but falls greatly fhort of the merit and humour of that comedy.

Turk and no Turk. Mufical Com. by Mr. Colman, jun. Acted at the Haymarket, 1785. This piece was received with applaufe.

Tunbridge Walks; or, *The Yeoman of Kent.* Com. by Thomas Baker, 4to. 1703. This is an entertaining and well conducted play, and contains a great deal of true character and pointed fatire.

Turncoat. A Parody on the Tragedy of *Athelfan,* 8vo. 1756.

The Turkifh Court; or, *The London 'Prentice.* Bur-

T W

lefque Satirical Piece, by Mrs. Latitia Pilkington, 1748. This was performed only at the Little Theatre in Capel-ftreet, Dublin, but was never printed.

The Tufcan Treaty; or, *Tarquin's Overthrow.* Tra. 8vo. 1733. This play was acted at Covent-Garden. It was written by a gentleman then deceafed, and revifed and altered by William Bond, Efq. The ftory of it is founded on the Roman hiftory, foon after the expulfion of the Tarquins.

The Tutor. Farce, acted at Drury-Lane, 1765. This piece was brought out under the patronage of Mr. Colman, but it was acted only two nights.

A Tutor for the Beaus; or, *Love in a Labyrinth.* A Com. by J. Hewitt. Acted at Lincoln's-Inn-Fields, 8vo. 1737. An indifferent piece.

Twelfth-Night; or, *What you Will.* Com. by Wm. Shakfpeare, fol. 1623. This comedy, with refpect to its general plot, is taken from Belleforeft's novels, Tom. 4. Hift. 7. but the miftakes arifing from Viola's change of habit, and true refemblance to her brother Sebaftian, feem to owe their origin to the *Menæchmi* of Plautus, which not only Shakfpeare, but feveral others of our dramatic writers,

ers, have fince borrowed from. There is fomewhat fingularly, ridiculous and pleafant in the character of the fantaftical Steward Malvolio ; and the trick played him by Sir Toby Belch, and Maria, contains great humour and fomewhat of originality in the contrivance, which cannot fail of affording continual entertainment to an audience. This play has at different times, even lately, been revived, particularly on Twelfth-Night, to which period, however, it has no kind of reference in any thing but its name. The fcene lies in a city on the coaft of Illyria. Dr. Johnfon fays, " This play is in the graver part elegant and eafy, and in fome of the lighter fcenes exquifitely humourous. Ague Cheek is drawn with great propriety, but his character is, in a great meafure, that of the natural fatuity, and is therefore not the proper prey of a fatirift. The foliloquy of Malvolio is truly comic ; he is betrayed to ridicule merely by his pride. The marriage of Olivia, and the fucceeding perplexity, though well enough contrived to divert on the ftage, wants credibility, and fails to produce the proper inftruction required in the drama, as

it exhibits no juft picture of life."

The Twin Brothers. C. tranflated from Plautus, by Richard Warner, 8vo. 1773.

Twin Rivals. Com. by George Farquhar. Acted at Drury-Lane, 1703. This play met with very great fuccefs, and is faid by the critics to be the moft regular and compleat of all this author's dramatic works.

The Twins. Tragi-Com. by William Rider. Acted at the private houfe, Salifbury-court, 4to. 1655.

Two Angry Women of Abington. Com. by Henry Porter, 4to. 1599. This play is not divided into acts. The full title runs thus : *A pleafant Hiftory, called. The two angrie Women of Abington ; with the humourous Mirth of Dick Coomes and Nicholas Proverbs, two Serving Men.* Acted by Lord Nottingham, Lord High Admiral's fervants.

The Two Englifh Gentlemen ; or, The Sham Funeral. Com. by James Stewart, 8vo. 1774. This defpicable piece was acted one night at the Haymarket, by a fet of performers every way worthy of the author.

The Two Gentlemen of Verona. Com. by William Shakfpeare, fol. 1623. This is a very fine play, the plot fimple and natural ; the

characters

characters perfectly marked, and the language poetical and affecting.

The Two Gentlemen of Verona. Com. by Shakfpeare; with alterations and additions by Benjamin Victor. Acted at Drury-Lane, 8vo. 1763.

The History of the Two Maids of M.ore Clacke, with the Life and fimple manner of John in the Hofpitall. Played by the children of the King's Majeftie, Revels. Written by Robert Armin, 4to. 1609.

The Two Merry Milk-Maids; or, The beft Words wear the Garland. Com. by J. C. Acted by the company of the Revels, 4to. 1620.

The Two Noble Kinfmen. Tragi-Com. by J. Fletcher and William Shakfpeare. Acted at the Black-Fryars, 4to. 1634. The ftory of this play is taken from Chaucer's *Palamon and Arcite;* or, *The Knight's-Tale.*

The Two Mifers. Mufical Farce, by Kane O'Hara. Acted at Covent-Garden, 8vo. 1775.

Two Plots Difcovered, a Third Pays for All. Com. by G. P. 12mo. 1742. It is fcarcely poffible to conceive any thing more contemptible than this piece.

The Two Queens of Brentford; or, Bayes no Poetafter.

Mufical Farce, or Comical Opera, being the fequel of *The Rehearfal,* by Thomas Durfey, 8vo. 1721.

Two Lamentable Tragedies in One. By Rob. Yarrington, 4to. 1601.

Two to One. A Mufical Comedy, by Mr. Colman, jun. Acted at the Hay-Haymarket, 1784, and very well received.

The Two Connoiffeurs. A Comedy in rhyme, by Mr. Haley. Acted at the Haymarket, 1784, and received with much applaufe.

Two wife Men, and all the reft Fools. A Comical Moral, cenfuring the follies of that age, by Geo. Chapman, 4to. 1619.

Tyranny Triumphant! and Liberty Loft; The Mufes run Mad; Apollo ftruck Dumb; and all Covent-Garden confounded. A Farce, by Fitzcrambo, Efq. Secretary to the Minor Poets, 8vo. 1743.

Tyrannical Government Anatomix'd; or, *A Difcourfe concerning evil Counfellers; being the Life and Death of John the Baptift, and prefented to the King's moft excellent Majefty by the author.* Anonymous, 4to. 1641. This piece, which is only a tranflation from Buchanan, was printed by order of the Houfe of Commons.

Tyrannic Love; or, *The Royal Martyr.* Trag. by J. Dryden,

T Y

J. Dryden. Acted at the Theatre Royal, 4to. 1672. 4to. 1686. This play is written in rhyme, yet has many things in it extremely pleasing. The plot of it is founded on history, and the scene laid in Maximin's camp, under the walls of Aquileia. " This tragedy (as Dr. Johnson obferves) is conspicuous for many paffages of strength and ele-

T Y.

gance, and many of empty noise and ridiculous turbulence. The rants of Maximin have been always the sport of criticism ; and were at length, if Dryden's own confeffion may be trufted, the shame of the writer."
    The Tyrant King of Crete. Trag. by Sir Charles Sedley. This play was never acted.

V A

VALENTIA ; or, *The Birth-Day.* Tr. by T. Stewart, 8vo. 1772.
    Valentine and Orfon. A famous Hiftory, played by her Majefty's players. Not printed.
    Valentine's Day. Mufical Drama, by Wm. Heard. Acted at Drury-Lane, 8vo. 1776. This was acted only one night at Mr. Reddifh's benefit.
    Valentinian. Trag. by Beaumont and Fletcher, fol. 1647. This play was acted at firft with confiderable applaufe.
    Valentinian. Tragedy. Acted at the Theatre Royal, 4to. 1685. Thefe alterations were made by the Earl of Rochefter.
    The Valiant Scot. Play, by J. W. gent. 4to. 1637.
    The Valian Welchman ; or, *The Chronicle Hiftory of the Life and valiant Deeds*

V A

of Caradoc the Great, King of Cambria, now called Wales. Tragi-Com. by R. A. gent. 4to. 1615.
    Vanelia ; or, *The Amours of the Great.* Opera, 8vo. 1732. Court fcandal.
    Vanquifh'd Love ; or, *The Jealous Queen,* by Meffrs. Daniel Bellany, fen. and jun. It was never acted, but is publifhed with the other dramatic and poetical works of this united father and fon, in 2 vols. 8vo. 1746.
    Vanella. T. 8vo. 1736. This piece was never intended for the ftage ; but has a reference to the ftory of Mifs Vane, an unfortunate young lady, who was faid to have had an amorous connection with a certain very great perfonage.
    The Variety. Com. by William Duke of Newcaftle, 12mo. 1649. This play was

V E

was acted with very great applause at Black-Fryars.

Variety. Com. Acted at Drury-Lane, 1782. This play, though it has very little dramatic merit, yet, owing to the sprightliness of the dialogue, it was tolerably well received.

Venice Preserved; or, *A Plot Discovered.* Trag. by Thomas Otway. Acted at the Duke's Theatre, 4to. 1682. This tragedy, which is still a very favourite one with the public, is borrowed from the Abbe de St. Real's *Histoire de la Conjuration de Marquis de Bedcmar.* This tragedy, says Dr. Johnson, still continues to be one of the favourites of the public, notwithstanding the want of morality in the original design, and the despicable scenes of vile comedy with which Otway has diversified his tragic action.

Venus and Adonis; or, *The Maid's Philosophy*, 8vo. 1659. This is one among six pieces supposed to be written by Robert Cox, the comedian, and printed in the second part of *Sport upon Sport.*

Venus and Adonis; or, *The Triumphs of Love.* Mock Opera, by Martin Powell. Acted at Punch's Theatre, in Covent - Garden, 8vo. 1713.

Venus and Adonis. A

V I

Masq. by C. Cibber, 8vo. 1715. This piece was presented at the Theatre Royal in Drury-Lane with no very great success.

Vertumnus and Pomona. Comic Opera. Acted at Covent - Garden, 1782. The fable of this piece is taken from a story in Ovid, under the same title.

A very good Wife. Com. by George Powell. Acted at the Theatre Royal, 4to. 1693.

A very Woman; or, *The Prince of Tarent.* Tragi-Com. by Phil. Massinger, 8vo. 1655.

The Vestal Virgin; or, *The Roman Ladies.* Trag. by Sir Robert Howard, fol. 1665. The scene of this play lies in Rome; and the author has written two fifth acts to it, the one of which ends tragically, and the other successfully.

The Vestal Virgin. Tr. by Henry Brooke, Esq. 8vo. 1773. Not acted.

Vice Reclaim'd; or, *The Passionate Mistress.* Com. by Richard Wilkinson. Acted at the Theatre Royal, 4to. 1703. Though this play made its appearance at a very disadvantageous season of the year, it met with very good success.

The Victim. Trag. by Charles Johnson. Acted at Drury-Lane. 12mo. 1714.

Victorious

Victorious Love. Trag. by William Walker. Act-ed at Drury-Lane, 4to. 1698. This play is a kind of imitation of Southerne's *Oroonoko.* The author wrote it in three weeks time, at nineteen years of age, and acted a part in it himself.

The Village Lawyer. C. Entertainment. Acted at the Haymarket, 1787, for Mr. Edwin's benefit.

The Villagers. Farce, of two acts, taken from *The Village Opera.* Acted at Drury-Lane, for Mrs. Prit-chard's benefit, about the year 1759. Not printed.

The Village Conjuror. Interlude, tranflated from J. J. Rouffeau, 12mo. 1767.

The Village Opera, by Charles Johnfon. Acted at Drury-Lane, 8vo. 1729. This is one of the many imitations of *The Beggar's Opera.* It is far from being devoid of merit, yet met with very indifferent fuc-cefs.

The Village Wedding ; or, *The Faithful Country Maid.* Paftoral Entertainment of Mufic, by James Love. Acted at Richmond, 8vo. 1767.

The Villain. Trag. by Thomas Porter, 4to. 1663. This play was acted at the Duke of York's Theatre for

ten nights fucceffively to crouded audiences, which at that period was meeting with very great fuccefs. It is in itfelf a very good piece.

Vimonda. Tr. Acted at the Haymarket, 1787, and well received.

The Vintner Trick'd. F. by H. Ward, 8vo.

Virginia. Tr. by Mr. Crifp, 8vo. 1754. This tragedy is built on the ce-lebrated ftory of Virgini-us's killing his daughter, to preferve her from the luft of Appius the Decemvir. It was acted at the Theatre Royal in Drury-Lane with fome fuccefs, and indeed not undefervedly.

Virginia. Tr. by Mrs. Frances Brooke, 8vo. 1756. This play, confidering it as written by a lady, is far from being devoid of merit. It was not, however, brought on the ftage.

The Virgin Martyr. Tr. by Phil. Maffinger, and Thomas Dekker. Acted by the fervants of the Re-vels, 4to. 1622. The plot is from the Martyrologies of the Tenth Perfecution in the time of Diocleñan and Maximin.

The Virgin Prophetefs ; or, *The Fate of Troy.* An Op. by Elk. Settle, 4to. 1701. This piece was performed at the Theatre Royal. The plot

plot is on the ſtory of Caſſandra.

The Virgin Queen. Tra. by Richard Barford, 8vo. 1729. Acted at the Theatre Royal in Lincoln's-Inn-Fields.

The Virgin Widow. C. by F. Quarles, 4to. 1649. This piece, which is the only dramatic attempt of our author, is rather an interlude than a regular play, and was not brought on the ſtage at any of the theatres.

Virtue Betray'd; or, *Anna Bullen.* Tragedy, by John Banks. Acted at the Duke's Theatre, 4to. 1682. This play met with great ſuccefs at its firſt repreſentation, more particularly becoming a favourite with the fair ſex.

The Virtuoſo. Com. by Thomas Shadwell. Acted at the Duke's Theatre, 4to. 1676. This play contains an infinite deal of true humour, and a great variety of characters highly drawn, and perfectly original.

The Virtuous Octavia. Tragi-Com. by Sam. Brandon, 12mo. 1598. The plot of this play is taken from Suetonius's Life of Auguſtus and Plutarch's Life of Marc Antony.

The Virtuous Wife; or, *Good Luck at Laſt.* Com. by Tho. Durfey, 4to. 1680. This is as entertaining a

comedy as any which this author has written.

The Viſion of Delight. Maſque, by Ben Jonſon, fol. 1641. Preſented at Court in Chriſtmas, 1617.

The Viſion of the Twelve Goddeſſes. Maſque, by S. Daniel, 4to. 1623. Preſented by the queen and her ladies at Hampton-Court on the 8th of January.

Ulyſſes. Trag. by Nich. Rowe, 4to. 1706. The ſcene of this play is laid in Ithaca, and the plot borrowed from the *Odyſſy.* It was acted at the Queen's Theatre in the Haymarket with ſuccefs; but is not the beſt of this author's pieces.

Ulyſſes. Opera, performed at Lincoln's-Inn-Fields, 4to. 1733. The words by Mr. Humphreys. The muſic by John Chriſt. Smith, jun.

The Uneaſy Man. Com. tranſlated from St. Foix, 8vo. 1771.

The Unfortunate Lovers. Trag. by Sir Wm. Davenant. Acted at the Black-Fryars, 4to. 1643.

The Unfortunate Ducheſs of Malfy; or, *The Unfortunate Brothers.* Tr. Anony. 4to. 1708. This play was acted at the Queen's Theatre in the Haymarket.

The Unfortunate Mother. Tra. by Tho. Nabbes, 4to. 1640.

1640. This play was never acted.

The Unfortunate Shepherd. A Pastoral, by John Tutchin, 8vo. 1685.

The Unfortunate Usurper. Trag. Anonymous. 4to. 1663. The scene lies at Constantinople, and the plot of it is historical, being founded on the story of *Andronicus Comnenius.*

The Ungrateful Favourite. Trag. Anony. 4to. 1664. This play is said to be written by a person of honour, but it was never acted.

The Unhappy Father. Tr. by Mary Leapor, 8vo. 1751.

The Unhappy Fair Irene, The Tragedy of, by Gilbert Swinhoe, 4to. 1658. This play is but an indifferent one.

The Unhappy Favourite ; or, *The Earl of Essex.* Tr. by John Banks. Acted at the Theatre Royal, 4to. 1685. This tragedy is possessed of the same kind of merit with the *Virtue Betray'd* of the same author ; and it met with the same success, having constantly a very strong influence on the tenderer passions of the audience.

The Unhappy Kindness ; or, *A Fruitless Revenge.* Tr. by Thomas Scott. Acted at Drury-Lane, 4to. 1697. This is only an al-

teration of Fletcher's *Wife for a Month.*

The Unhappy Penitent. Tr. by Mrs. Cath. Trotter, afterwards Mrs. Cockburne. Acted at Drury-Lane, 4to. 1701.

The Uninhabited Island. Drama, translated from Metastasio, by Anna Williams, 4to. 1766.

The Universal Gallant ; or, *The Different Husbands.* Com. by Henry Fielding, Esq. Acted at Drury-Lane, 8vo. 1734.

The Universal Passion. Com. by James Miller. Acted at Drury-Lane, 8vo. 1737. This play met with good success, being brought on the stage before the author had incurred that indignation from the town, which some of his later pieces so feelingly experienced the weight of.

The Unnatural Brother. Trag. by Dr. Edw. Filmer. Acted at Lincoln's-Inn-Fields, 4to. 1697. This play is on the whole heavy, cold, and enervate, yet is not without some passages that do great honour to the understanding and sensibility of its author.

The Unnatural Combat. Trag. by Phil. Massinger. Acted at the Globe, 4to. 1639. This tragedy is a very admirable one, and may almost be esteemed the

very

very beſt of this great author's pieces.

The Unnatural Mother.
Tr. Anon. 4to. 1698. This
play was written by a young
lady, and aĉted at Lin-
coln's-Inn-Ficlds.

The Unnatural Tragedy.
by Margaret Duchefs of
Newcaſtle, fol. 1662. There
is nothing very particular in
this play, farther than fome
cenſures which her Grace
has taken occaſion to caſt
on Camden's *Britannia* in
her fecond aĉt.

Volpone ; or, *The Fox.*
Com. by Ben Jonſon. Aĉt-
ed by the King's ſervants,
4to. 1605. This comedy
is joined by the critics with
the *Alchymiſt* and *Silent Woman,* as the Chef d'Oeuvres
of this celebrated poet ; and,
indeed, it is fcarcely poffible
to conceive a piece more
highly finiſhed, both in
point of language and cha-
raĉter, than this comedy.
The plot is perfeĉtly original.

The Volunteers ; or, *The
Stock-jobbers.* Com. by T.
Shadwell. Aĉted by their
Majeſties ſervants, 4to.
1693. This comedy was
not aĉted till after the author's death.

The Volunteers ; or, *Taylors to Arms.* Com. of one
aĉt, by G. Downing. Aĉt-
ed at Covent-Garden, 8vo.
1780. This performance

is in faĉt no more than a trifling prelude, introduced at
the benefit of Mr. Quick.

The Vow-breaker ; or,
*The Fair Maid of Clifton in
Nottinghamſhire.* Trag. by
William Sampſon, 4to.
1636. This play met with
very good fuccefs. The plot
of it feems to be founded on
faĉt.

The Upholſterer ; or, *What
News ?* Farce, of two aĉts,
by A. Murphy, 8vo. 1758.
This piece was firſt aĉted at
Mr. Moffop's benefit at
Drury-Lane, and met with
very good fuccefs, and indeed deſervedly, as it, with
very great humour, expoſes
the abſurdity of that infati-
able appetite for news, fo
prevalent among mankind
in general, and that folly,
which feems in fome mea-
fure peculiar to our own nation, of giving way to an
abfurd anxiety for the concerns of the public, and the
tranſaĉtions of the various
potentates of the world,
even to the negleĉt and ruin
of domeſtic affairs and family intereſt ; and that, in
perſons totally ignorant, not
only of the proceedings of a
miniſtry, but even of any of
thoſe ſprings by which the
wheels of government ought
to be aĉtuated.

The Uſurper. Trag. by
Edward Howard. Aĉted at
the

US

the Theatre Royal, 4to. 1668.

The Ufurper Detected ; or, *Right will prevail.* Comic Tragical Farce, of two acts, 8vo. 1718.

The Ufurpers ; or, *The*

UT.

Coffee-houfe Politicians. A Farce, Anon. 1749.

Ut Pictura Poefis ; or, *The Enraged Mufician.* Mufical Entertainment. Performed at the Haymarket, 1789, and well received.

WA

TIHE *Walking Statue* ; or, *The Devil in the Wine Cellar.* Farce, by A. Hill, 4to. no date. This little farce is printed at the end of *Elfred* ; or, *The Fair Inconftant,* of the fame author. The plot of it is totally farcical, and the incidents beyond the limits of probability ; yet there is fomewhat laughable in the incident of paffing a living man on the father as a ftatue or automaton, and the confequence of it, though fomewhat too low for a dramatic piece of any kind of regularity, may, neverthelefs, be endured, by confidering this as a kind of fpeaking pantomime.

The Walks of Iflington and Hogfdon, with the Humours of Wood-ftreet Compter. C. by Thomas Jordan, 4to. 1657. The title of this play feems to promife nothing more than the very loweft kind of humour, yet its fuccefs was furprifingly great, having taken a run of nine-

WA

teen days together, with extraordinary applaufe.

The Walloons. Comedy, acted at Covent-Garden, 1782. This play poffeffes much humour and variety of characters ; but abounds with glaring abfurdities, and unnatural incidents.

The Wandering Lover. Tragi-Com. by Tho. Meriton, 4to. 1658.

The Wanton Countefs ; or, *Ten Thoufand Pounds for a Pregnancy.* Ballad Opera, 8vo. 1733. This piece was never intended for the ftage, but written for the propagation of fome tale of private fcandal in the court annals of that time.

The Wanton Jefuit ; or, *Innocence feduced.* Ballad Opera. Acted at the Haymarket, 8vo. 1731. This opera was occafioned by the affair of Father Gerard and Mifs Cadiere.

A Warning for Fair Women. Trag. Anonym. 4to. 1599. This is a very old play, which was confiderably

ably in vogue in Queen Elizabeth's time.

The Warres of Cyrus, King of Perfia, againft Antiochus, King of Afyria, with the tragical Ende of Panthæa. Trag. Anonymous, 4to. 1594. This play was acted by the children of her Majelty's chapel.

The Wary Widow; or, *Sir Noify Parrot.* Com. by Henry Higden. Acted at Drury-Lane, 4to. 1693. This is very far from being the worft of our Englifh comedies.

The Waterman; or, *The Firft of Auguft.* Ballad Op. by Charles Dibdin. Acted at the Haymarket, 1774.

The Way of the World. Com. by Wm. Congreve. Acted at Lincoln's - Inn-Fields, 4to. 1700. This is the laft play this author wrote, and perhaps the beft; the language is pure, the wit genuine, the characters natural, and the painting highly finifhed; yet fuch is the ftrange capricioufnefs of public tafte, that notwithitanding the great and deferved reputation this author had acquired by his three former comedies, this before us met with but indifferent fuccefs.

The Way to Keep Him. Com. in three acts, by A. Murphy, 8vo. 1760. This

piece made its firft appearance in this form at Drury-Lane Theatre, as a fubfequent entertainment to *The Deferted Ifland* of the fame author. The intention of it is to point out to the married part of the female fex, how much unhappinefs they frequently create to themfelves, by neglecting, *after* marriage, to make ufe of the fame arts, the fame affiduity to pleafe, the fame. elegance in the decoration of their perfons, and the fame complacency and blandifhments in their temper and behaviour, to *preferve* the *Affections* of the *Hufband* as they had *before* it put in practice to *awaken* the *Paffions* of the *Lover.* Though the language may not abound with the ftudied wit of Congreve or Wycherley, yet it is a natural and eafy dialogue, and is properly adapted to that domeftic life which it is intended to reprefent.

The Way to Keep Him. A Com. by A. Murphy, Efq. Acted at Drury-Lane, 8vo. 1761. This is the foregoing piece enlarged into a regular comedy of five acts, by the addition of two principal characters.

The Weakeft goeth to the Wall. Anony. Acted by the Earl of Oxford, Lord
great

great Chamberlain of England's fervants, 4to 1600.

The Weathercock. Mufical Entertainment, by Th. Foreſt. Acted at Covent-Garden, 8vo. 1775. This piece was performed about three or four times, and then laid aſide. It is a very poor production.

The Wedding. Com. by J. Shirley. Acted at the Phœnix, Drury-Lane, 4to. 1629. This is a very good play.

The Wedding Day. Com. by Henry Fielding. Acted at Drury-Lane, 8vo. 1742. This was the laſt dramatic piece of this author ; and, as if he had exhauſted the whole of his comic humour in his former works, it is by much the dulleſt of them all. Its fuccefs was equal to its merit, being acted only fix nights.

The Wedding Night. Farce, by Mr. Cobb. Acted at the Haymarket, 1780. Not printed.

The Wedding Ring. Com. Opera, in two acts, by Cha. Dibdin, performed at Drury-Lane, 8vo. 1773. The hint of this piece, which met with fome fuccefs, was taken from *Il Filofofo di Campagna.*

The Welch ; or, *Grub-ſtreet Opera.* This piece was written by Henry Fielding, but is one of the moſt indifferent of his works.

Werter. Tr. Acted at Covent-Garden, 1786, for the benefit of Mifs Brunton.

The Weſtminſter School-Boy. Farce, by Capt. Topham. The Weſtminſter-fchool-boys invaded the theatre, and damned this piece unheard.

Weſtward Hoe. Com. by Thomas Decker and John Webſter, 4to. 1607. Many times acted with good fuccefs by the children of St. Paul's.

The Weſt-Indian. Com. by Richard Cumberland, Efq. Acted at Drury-Lane, 8vo. 1771. This comedy may be confidered as one of the beſt which the prefent times have produced. The frequency of its reprefentation renders it fufficiently known. It was performed with very great and deferved fuccefs.

Weſton's Return from the Univerſities of Parnaſſus. Interlude, performed at the Haymarket for that actor's benefit, 1775. Not printed.

Wexford Wells. Com. by Matthew Concanen, 8vo. 1721. This play was never reprefented in London.

The What d'ye call It. A Tragi-Com. Paſtoral Farce, by John Gay. Acted at Drury-Lane, 8vo. 1715. This ingenious and entertaining

taining little piece, which is to this day frequently performed, is an inoffenſive and good-natured burleſque on the abſurdities in ſome of the tragedies then the moſt in favour, particularly *Venice Preſerv'd.*

What you will. Com. by John Marſton, 4to. 1607. Langbaine mentions this comedy as one of the beſt of this author's writing.

What we muſt all come to. Com. in two acts, performed at the Theatre Royal in Covent-Garden, 8vo. 1764. This was introduced as a tail-piece to *No one's Enemy but his own,* and acted at the ſame time ; but ſhared in the condemnation, although it was generally thought to have had merit enough to entitle it to a better fate ; but this comes of keeping bad company.

When you ſee Me, You know Me; or, The famous Chronicle Hiſtorie of King Henry VIII. *with the Birth and virtuous Life of Edward Prince of Wales,* by Samuel Rowley, 4to. 1632.

Which is the Man. Com. by Mrs. Cowley. Acted at Covent-Garden, 1782. This play, though tolerably well received, muſt not be conſidered as one of Mrs. Cowley's beſt productions.

Whig and Tory. Com. by Benjamin Griffin, 8vo.

1720. Acted at the Theatre in Lincoln's-Inn-Fields with no very extraordinary ſucceſs.

The Whim; or, The Miſer's Retreat. A Farce, altered from the French of *La Maiſon Ruſtique.* Acted at Goodman's - Fields, 8vo. 1734.

The Whimſical Lovers ; or, The Double Infidelity. Com. tranſlated from the French, and printed in Foote's *Comic Theatre.*

The White Devil ; or, The Tragedy of Paulo Giordano Urſini, Duke of Brachiano ; with the Life and Death of Vittoria Corombona, the famous Venetian Courtezan. Trag. by John Webſter. Acted by the Queen's ſervants, 4to. 1612.

Who's who. Farce, acted at Drury-Lane, 1785, with great applauſe.

The Whore of Babylon. A Hiſtory, by Tho. Decker, 4to. 1607. This play was never acted, but the general tenor of it is to illuſtrate the virtues of Queen Elizabeth, and, under feigned names, to expoſe the machinations of the Roman Catholics of that time.

The Whore of Babylon. Com. ſaid to be written by King Edward VI. but not printed.

Who'd have Thought It. Farce, by Mr. Cobb. Acted

ed at Covent-Garden, 1781. Not printed.

Who's the Dupe. Farce, by Mrs. Cowley. Acted at Drury-Lane, 8vo. 1779. This piece was acted with confiderable applaufe.

The Widow. Com. by Ben Jonfon, 4to. 1652. Though we have named Jonfon as the author of this play, it was the refult of the joint labours of him, Fletcher, and Middleton, but was not publifhed till after all their deaths.

The Widow of Malabar. Trag. by Mifs Starke. Acted at Covent-Garden, 1791. Not wholly deftitute of merit.

A Widow and no Widow. Com. by Mr. Jodrell. Acted at the Hay-market, 1779.

The Widow Bewitch'd. Comedy, by John Mottley, 8vo. 1730. This play was acted at the Theatre in Goodman's-Fields, and met with very good fuccefs.

The Widow of Delphi. Mufical Com. by Richard Cumberland, Efq. Acted at Covent-Garden, 1780. The fongs only printed. This piece, though great expectations were formed from it, met with little fuccefs.

The Widow Ranter; or, *The Hiftory of Bacon in Virginia.* Tragi-Com. by Mrs. Behn. Acted by their Ma-

jeftics fervants, 4to. 1690. This piece was not publifhed till after the author's deceafe, who died in 1689. The fcene is laid in Bacon's camp in Virginia. The comic part entirely invention.

The Widow of Wallingford. Com. of two acts, 8vo. 1775.

The Widow's Tears. C. by George Chapman. Acted at Black and White-Fryars, 4to. 1612. Some parts of this play are very fine, and the incidents affecting and interefting.

The Widow's Wifh; or, *An Equipage of Lovers.* A Farce, by H. Ward. Acted at York, 8vo. 1746.

The Widowed Wife. C. by Dr. Kenrick. Acted at Drury-Lane, 8vo. 1768. A piece which reached nine nights with little applaufe, and has not fince been heard of.

A Wife and no Wife. F. by Charles Coffey. 8vo. 1732. This piece was never acted.

A Wife for a Month. Tr. Com. by Beaumont and Fletcher, fol. 1647. This play is a very good one. The plot of it, as far as relates to the ftory of Alphonfo, his character, and treatment he meets with from his brother Frederic, is borrowed from the hiftory of of Sancho VIII. King of Leon, which may be feen in *Mariana*, and *Lewis de Mayerne Turquet*. The fcene lies in Naples.

A Wife in the Right. C. by Mrs. Elizabeth Griffiths, 8vo. 1772. This play was performed one night only at Covent-Garden.

The Wife of Bath. Com. by John Gay, 4to. 1713. This piece was acted at the Theatre Royal, in Drury-Lane, but met with very indifferent fuccefs. It was the author's firft dramatic attempt, yet its failure did not difcourage him from purfuing that way of writing in which he was afterwards fo fortunate.

The Wife of Bath. Com. by John Gay. Acted at Lincoln's-Inn-Fields, 8vo. 1730. This is the fame piece, revifed and altered by the author. On this its fecond appearance it met with the very fame, or rather worfe, treatment from the audience, than it had done before, notwithftanding the merit of *The Beggar's Opera* had raifed Mr. Gay's reputation at that time to the moft exalted height. The fcene is laid at an Inn on the road between London and Canterbury, and the time twelve hours, being from nine o'clock at night to nine the next morning.

The Wife's Relief; or, *The Hufband's Cure*. Com. by Charles Johnfon. Acted at Drury-Lane, 4to. 1712. This is a very entertaining play, and ufed to be frequently reprefented.

A Wife to be Let. Com. by Mrs. Elizabeth Haywood, 8vo. 1724. This comedy was acted at Drury-Lane Theatre in the fummer, with but middling fuccefs; which might, however, in fome meafure, be owing to the feafon, and the fmall merit of the performers.

A Wife well managed. Farce, by Mrs. Centlivre. This was acted at Drury-Lane, and printed 12mo. 1715.

The Wild Gallant. Com. Acted at the Theatre Royal, 4to. 1669. This was Mr. Dryden's firft attempt in dramatic writing. He began with no happy auguries; for his performance was fo much difapproved that he was compelled to recall it, and change it from its imperfect ftate to the form in which it now appears, and which is yet fufficiently defective to vindicate the critics.

The Wild Goofe Chace. C. by Beaumont and Fletcher, fol. 1679. This is one of the beft of the writings of thefe united poets. It was
very

·very frequently performed, with univerfal approbation. *Wild Oats*; or, *The Strolling Gentleman.* C. by Mr. O'Keeffe. Acted at Covent-Garden, 1791, for the benefit of Mr. Lewis, and very well received.

A Will or no Will; or, *A New Cafe for the Lawyers.* Farce, by Charles Macklin. This piece has been frequently acted at the author's benefits, but has not yet made its appearance in print.

William and Lucy. Op. An attempt to fuit the ftyle of the Scotch mufic, by Mr. Paton, 8vo. 1780.

William and Nanny. Ballad Farce, in two acts, by R. Goodenough, Efq. Acted at Covent-Garden, 8vo. 1779.

Wiltfhire Tom. An Entertainment at Court, printed in 4to. N. D.

The Winter's Tale. Tr. Com. by William Shakfpeare, fol. 1623. This is one of the moft irregular of this author's pieces, the unities of time and place being fo greatly infringed, that the former extends from being the birth of Perdita till the period of her marriage, and the choice of the latter, for the fcenes of the play, is fixed at fome times in Sicily, and at others in Bithynia. There are, however,

fo many amazing beauties glittering through the different parts of it, as amply make amends for thefe trivial deformities, and ftamp on it the moft indelible marks of its authencity.

The Winter's Tale. A play, altered from Shakfpeare, by C. Marfh, 8vo. 1756.

The Wifdom of Dr. Dodipole. Com. Acted by the children of Paul's, 4to. 1600.

The Wife Woman of Hogfdon. Com. by Tho. Heywood, 4to. 1638. This play met with good fuccefs.

The Wifhes; or, *Harlequin's Mouth opened.* Com. by Mr. Bentley, 1761. This play has not yet made its appearance in print, but was brought on the ftage at Drury-Lane Theatre by the company under the management of Meff. Foote and Murphy. It is written in imitation of the Italian comedy.

The Wifhes of a Free People. A Dramatic Poem, 8vo. 1761. This piece, though publifhed anonymous, is faid to be the work of Dr. Hiffernan. The execution of this piece is fo very undramatic, and contains fo little either of poetry or imagination, that it ftands itfelf as a fufficient anfwer to the charge the au-

thor

thor has, in a poſtſcript to it, thrown on the managers of both the Theatres, for refuſing to bring it on the ſtage.

The Wiſhes. Com. Acted at Covent-Garden, 1782. Withdrawn on the ſecond repreſentation.

The Witch of Edmonton. Tragi-Com. by Wm. Rowley, 4to. 1658. This piece is ſaid, in the title-page, to be founded on a known true ſtory. It met with ſingular applauſe, being often acted at the Cockpit in Drury-Lane, and once at Court.

The Witches. Pantomime. Acted at Drury-Lane, 1765.

Wit at a Pinch; or, *The Lucky Prodigal.* Com. Acted at Lincoln's-Inn-Fields, 12mo. 1715.

Wit at ſeveral Weapons. Comedy, by Beaumont and Fletcher, fol. 1647. This play was eſteemed an entertaining one.

Wit for Money; or, *Poet Stutter.* Anon. 4to. 1691. This is rather a dialogue than a dramatic performance.

Wit in a Conſtable. C. by Henry Glapthorne. Acted at the Cockpit in Drury-Lane, 4to. 1640.

The Wit of a woman. C. Anon. 4to. 1604. This is ſtyled by the author a pleaſant merry comedy, but it by no means deſerves that character.

The Wit of a woman. C. 4to. 1705. By T. Walker. It was performed at the Theatre in Lincoln's-Inn-Fields.

Wit without Money. C. by Beaumont and Fletcher. Acted at Drury-Lane, 4to. 1639. 4to. 1661. This comedy is a very entertaining one, and is among the number of the few pieces written by theſe authors, which are even now repreſented on the London ſtages.

Wit without Money. C. Acted at the Haymarket, 4to. no date.

Wit's laſt Stake. Farce, by Tho. King. Acted at Drury-Lane, 8vo. 1769.

Wit's led by the Noſe; or, *A Poet's Revenge.* Tragi-Com. Acted at the Theatre Royal, 4to. 1678.

The Wits. Com. by Sir Wm. Davenant. Acted at Black-Fryars, 4to. 1636. This was eſteemed a good play, and met with good ſucceſs.

Wits Cabal. Com. in two parts, by the Ducheſs of Newcaſtle, fol. 1662.

A Witty Combat; or, *The Female Victor.* Tragi-Com. by T. P. 4to. 1663. This play was acted by perſons of quality, in the Whitſun-Week, with great applauſe.

The

The Witty Fair One. C. by James Shirley. Acted at the private houfe, Drury-Lane, 4to. 1633.

The Wives Excufe; or, *Cuckolds make themfelves.* Com. by Tho. Southerne. Acted at Drury-Lane, 4to. 1692. There is a great deal of gay, lively converfation in this play, much true wit, and lefs licentioufnefs intermingled with that wit than is to be found in the greateft part of this author's comic writings.

The Wives Revenge. C. Opera, by Charles Dibdin. Acted at Covent-Garden, 8vo. 1778.

The Woer. Com. by G. Puttenham; mentioned in his *Art of Poetry,* but not printed.

Woman Captain. Com. by Thomas Shadwell. Acted at the Duke's Theatre, 4to. 1680. This play met with very good fuccefs in the reprefentation.

The Woman Hater. C. by John Fletcher, 4to. 1607. In the compofition of this piece, Mr. Fletcher had no affiftance. It is a very good comedy, and met with fuccefs.

The Woman in the Moon. Com. by John Lyly, 4to. 1597.

A Woman kill'd with Kindnefs. Trag. by Tho. Heywood. Acted by the

Queen's fervants, 4to. 1617. We cannot help looking on this play as one of the beft of this author's writing. For although there is, perhaps, too much perplexity in it, arifing from the great variety of incidents which are blended together, yet there are fome fcenes and numberlefs fpeeches in it, which would have done no difhonour to the pen of Shakfpeare himfelf.

The Woman made a Juftice. Com. by Tho. Betterton. This comedy was brought on the ftage by its author, but never printed.

The Woman turn'd Bully. Com. Anony. 1675. Acted at the Duke of York's Theatre.

Woman's a Riddle. C. by Chrift. Bullock. Acted at Lincoln's-Inn-Fields Theatre, 4to. 1717.

A Woman is a Weather-Cock. Com. by N. Field. Acted before the King at Whitehall, by the children of her Majefty's Revels, 4to. 1612.

A Woman will have her Will. Com. by W. White, 1601,

The Woman's Prize; or, *The Tamer tam'd.* Com. by John Fletcher, fol. 1647. This piece is a fequel to Shakfpeare's *Taming of the Shrew,* in which Catherine being fuppofed dead, and

Petruchio

Petruchio again married to a young woman of a mild and gentle difpofition, fhe, in combination with two or three more of her female companions, forms a plot to break the violent and tyrannical temper of her hufband, and bring him to the fame degree of fubmiffion to her will, as he had before done with his former wife in her compliance to his; and this defign is at length through a variety of incidents, brought perfectly to bear. The play, in itfelf, is more regular and compact than *The Taming of the Shrew*, yet has not, on the whole, fo many beauties as are to be met with in that comedy.

A Woman's Revenge; or, *A Match in Newgate*. Com. in three acts, by Chriftopher Bullock. Acted at Lincoln's-Inn-Fields, in 12mo. 1715.

The Woman of Tafte; or, *The Yorkfhire Lady*. Ballad Opera, 12mo. 1739.

The Woman's too hard for Him. Com. Acted at Court 1612, but not printed.

Woman's Wit; or, *The Lady in Fafhion*. Com. by Colley Cibber. Acted at the Theatre Royal, 4to. 1697. This is very far from being the beft of this author's comic pieces, nor is he entirely clear from the charge of borrowing in it; the characters of Major Rakifh and his fon, and their courtfhip of the Widow Manlove, being pretty evidently copied from Sir T. Revel and his fon, in Mountford's *Greenwich Park*, and from Carlifle's comedy of *The Fortune-Hunters*.

Women beware Women. Trag. by Thomas Middleton, 8vo. 1657. The plot of this play is founded on a romance called Hippolito and Ifabella.

Woman Pleas'd. Tragi-Com. by Beaumont and Fletcher, fol. 1647. Without any farther alteration than a judicious curtailing of fome particular paffages, or what is underftood in the theatrical language, by *properly cutting* this play, it might be rendered, on a revival, a very agreeable entertainment even to the nice-ftomached audiences of the prefent age.

The Women's Conqueft. Tragi-Com. by Edward Howard. Acted at the Duke of York's Theatre, 4to. 1671. This piece, appears to have been the beft of this gentleman's dramatic works.

The Wonder, a Woman keeps a Secret. Com. by Mrs. Centlivre. Acted at Drury-Lane, 4to. 1714. This comedy had very good

fuccefs

fuccefs at firft, is ftill frequently acted, and is indeed
one of the beft of Mrs.
Centlivre's plays. The
plot is intricate and ingenious, yet clear and diftinct
both in its conduct and cataftrophe ; the language is
in general more correct
than fhe ufually renders it ;
and the characters, particularly thofe of the jealous
Don Felix and Colonel Briton's Highland Servant
Gibby, are juftly drawn,
and very well finifhed.

*The Wonder, an Honeft
Yorkfhireman.* Ballad Op.
by Henry Carey. Acted at
the Theatres, 8vo. 1736.

*The Wonder of Derby-
fhire.* Pantomime. Acted
at Drury-Lane, 1779.

*The Wonders of a King-
dom.* Tragi-Com. by Tho.
Decker, 4to. 1636. Lang-
baine gives this play a good
character.

Wonder of Women ; or,
Sophonifba, her Trag. by
John Marfton. Acted at
the Black - Fryars, 4to.
1606.

Wonders in the Sun ; or,
The Kingdom of Birds. A
Comic Opera, by Thomas
Durfey, 4to. 1706. This
whimfical piece was per-
formed at the Queen's Theatre in th Haymarket.

The Woodman. Comic
Opera, by Mr. Bate Dud-
ley. Acted at Covent-Gar-

den, 1791. A very good
piece, and well received.

A Word to the Wife. C.
by Hugh Kelly. Acted at
Drury-Lane, 8vo. 1770.
This play being produced
at a time when political dif-
putes ran very high, and
the author of it being fufpected to have written on
the unpopular fide, a party
was formed to prevent its
reprefentation. It with difficulty was dragged through
the firft night ; but the fecond proved fatal to it.
The author, however, was
confoled for his difappointment by a very large fub-
fcription to the publication.

The World as it goes ; or,
A Party to Montpelier. Com.
by Mrs. Cowley. Acted
at Covent-Garden, 1781.
The fuccefs of this Lady's
former performance, inftead
of producing caution, feems
to have infpired a degree of
confidence which has been
almoft fatal to her reputation. The prefent hafty,
indecent, and worthlefs
compofition received its
fentence from a very can-
did and impartial audience,
who appeared to condemn
with reluctance what it was
impoffible to applaud. This
play, a little altered, and
not with much advantage to
it, was brought out once
more, under the title of *Second Thoughts are Beft,* and
Q   received

received its final condemnation from an audience equally candid with the former.

The World's Idol; or, *Plutus the God of Wealth*. Com. from the Greek of Ariftophanes, by H. H. B. 1650, 8vo.

Worfe and Worfc. Com. by George Digby, Earl of Briftol. Acted at the Duke's Theatre, between 1662 and 1665. This play feems not to have been printed.

The Wounds of Civil War, lively fet forth in the true Tragedies of Marius and Sylla, by Thomas Lodge. Acted by the Lord Admiral's fervants, 4to. 1594.

The Wrangling Lovers; or, *The Invifible Miftrefs*. Com. by Edward Ravenfcroft. Acted at the Duke's Theatre, 4to. 1677.

The Wrangling Lovers; or, *Like Mafter like Man*. Farce, by Wm. Lyon, comedian, 8vo. 1745. Printed at Edinburgh.

Wyat's Hiftory, 4to. 1607. The whole title of this piece is as follows. The famous Hiftory of Sir Tho. Wyat, with the Coronation of Queen Mary, and the coming in of King Philip, plaied by the Queen's Majefties fervants. Written by Tho. Dickers (Dekker) and John Webfter.

X I

XERXES. Tra. by C. Cibber, 4to. 1699. This tragedy made its firft appearance at Lincoln's-Inn-Fields Houfe, but with no fuccefs, making a ftand of only one night.

Ximena; or, *The Heroic Daughter*. Trag. by Colley Cibber. Acted at Drury-Lane, 8vo. 1719. This play was the production of the fame author with the foregoing; but did not meet with much better fortune. This tragedy, as to the plot and great part of the language, is borrowed from the *Cid* of M. Corneille.

Y O

THE *Young Admiral*. Tragi-Com. by James Shirley. Acted at Drury-Lane, 4to. 1637.

The Young Hypocrite. C. tranflated from the French, by Samuel Foote, and printed in the Comic Theatre, vol. I.

The Young King; or, *The Miftake*. Tragi-Com. by Mrs. Behn. Acted at the Duke's

Duke's Theatre, 4to. 1683. The plot of this play, which is very far from being a bad one, is borrowed from the hiſtory of Alcamenes and Menalippa in M. Calprenade's celebrated romance of *Cleopatra*.

The Young Quaker. Com. by Mr. O'Keeffe. Acted at the Haymarket, 1783. This piece is judiciouſly calculated to pay a compliment to the liberality of the people called Quakers.

The Younger Brother ; or, *The Amorous Jilt*. Com. by Mrs. Behn. Acted at the Theatre Royal, 4to.

1696. This play, though written ten years before her death, was not publiſhed till after that event. It ſeems to have been a favourite of its author, and is indeed not devoid of merit, the two firſt acts particularly abounding with very lively and pleaſing wit. It did not, however, meet with ſuccefs.

The Younger Brother ; or, *The Sham Marquis*. Com. Anony. 8vo. 1719. This piece was acted at Lincoln'-s Inn-Fields Theatre, but without ſuccefs.

Z A

Z *APHIRA.* Trag. by Francis Gentleman, acted at Bath about 1754. Not printed.

Zara. Tr. by A. Hill, 8vo. 1735. This piece is a very good one, although founded on the principles of religious party, which are generally apt to throw an air of enthuſiaſm and bigotry into thoſe dramatic works which are built upon them.

Zara. Trag. tranflated from Voltaire ; and printed in Dr. Franklin's edition of that author.

Z O

Zelmane ; or, *The Corinthian Queen*. Tr. 4to. 1705. This play was acted at the Theatre in Lincoln's-Inn-Fields.

Zenobia. Tr. by Arthur Murphy, Eſq. Acted at Drury Lane, 1768, and received with great applauſe.

Zobeide. Tr. by Joſeph Cradock. Acted at Covent-Garden, 8vo. 1771.

Zoraida. Trag. by W. Hodfon. Acted at Drury-Lane, 8vo. 1780.

ORATORIOS.

THIS species of the drama was introduced into England by Mr. Handel, and carried on during his life with great success. It was borrowed from the *Concert Spirituel* of our volatile neighbours on the Continent, but conducted in a manner more agreeable to the native gravity and solidity of this nation.

A

Acis and Galatea. This was originally set to music by Mr. Handel, for the Duke of Chandos, about the year 1731.

Alexander Balus. Orat. by Dr. Morell, set to music by Handel; acted at Covent-Garden 1748.

Alexander's Feast. Orat. set to music by Handel; acted at Covent - Garden 1736. This excellent ode had formerly been altered for music by Mr. Hughes.

Alfred the Great. Orat. set to music by Dr. Arne, and acted at Drury-Lane about 1761, 4to. This is taken from Mallet's play of *Alfred.*

Allegro ed il Penseroso. Oratorio, taken from Mil-

ton; set by Mr. Handel, acted 1739.

Athaliah. Oratorio, set by Mr. Handel; and performed at Oxford at the time of the Public Act in July 1733. The words by Mr. Humphreys, 4to. 1733.

B

Belshazzar. Oratorio, set by Mr. Handel, 4to. 1745.

C

The Cure of Saul. A sacred Ode, by Dr. Brown, 4to. 1764. This piece was originally composed by the author himself, by selecting different parts of Mr. Handel's works, and adapting them to his own performance. In this state it was first acted at Drury-Lane with but little success. It was afterwards new set (1767) by Dr. Arnold, and performed at the Haymarket.

D

David's Lamentation. O. by John Lockman; performed at Covent-Garden, 4to. 1740.

Deborah. Orat. by Mr. Humphreys; set by Mr. Handel, 1732.

Esther

E S
E

Efther. Orat. by Mr. Humphreys ; fet by Mr. Handel, performed at the Haymarket, 4to. 1732.

F

The Force of Truth. Orat. by Dr. John Hoadly ; fet by Dr. Greene, 8vo. 1764.

H

Hannah. Oratorio, by Chriftopher Smart ; fet by Mr. Worgan, and performed at the Haymarket, 4to. 1764.

I

Jeptha. Orat. by John Hoadly ; fet by Doctor Greene, 8vo. 1737.
Jeptha. Orat. by Dr. Morell ; fet by Mr. Handel, performed at Covent-Garden, 4to. 1751. During the compofition of this Oratorio Mr. Handel became blind.
Jofeph and his Brethren. Orat. by Mr. James Miller; fet by Mr. Handel, and performed at Covent-Garden, 4to. 1744.
Jofhua. Orat. fet by Mr. Handel, performed at Covent-Garden ; in 4to. 1748.
Ifrael in Babylon. Orat. fet by Mr. Handel, performed at Covent-Garden, 4to.
Ifrael in Egypt. Orat.

M E

fet by Mr. Handel, performed at Lincoln's-Innfields, 4to. 1740.
Judas Maccabæus. Orat. by Dr. Morell ; fet by Mr. Handel, performed at Covent-Garden, 4to. 1746. This Oratorio was written at the requeft of Mr. Handel, and by the recommendation of Prince Frederick.
Judith. Orat. by Wm. Huggins, Efq. fet by Wm. Fefch, 8vo. 1733. This piece was performed with fcenes and other decorations, but met with no fuccefs.
Judith. Orat. by Ifaac Bickerftaffe ; fet by Dr. Arne, and performed at the Lock Hofpital Chapel, Feb. 29, 1764, 4to.

M

Meffiah. Orat. fet by Mr. Handel. The words felected by Mr. Jennens. This excellent oratorio was originally performed about the year 1741 ; but by fome unaccountable caprice in the public tafte, met with a very cold reception. The compofer thereupon went over to Dublin, where it was honoured with univerfal applaufe ; and, on his return to England, it found all the approbation it was entitled to, and has ever fince been the favourite of the

the admirers of this fpecies
of Compofition.

N

Nabal. Orat. by Dr.
Morell; fet by Mr. Smith
to the mufic of fome old
genuine performances of
Mr. Handel. It was per-
formed at Covent-Garden,
4to. 1764.

New Occafional Oratorio.
Set by Mr. Handel, and
performed at Covent-Gar-
den, 4to. 1746. This was
brought forward on occafion
of the victory gained at
Culloden by the Duke of
Cumberland.

O

Omnipotence. Orat. 4to.

P

Paradife Loft. Orat. by
Benjamin Stillingfleet; fet
by Mr. Smith, and per-
formed at Covent-Garden,
4to. 1760.

The Prodigal Son. Orat.
by Thomas Hull; fet by
Dr. Arnold, and performed
at Covent-Garden, 4to.
1786.

R

Rebecca. Orat. fet by
Mr. Smith, and performed
at Covent-Garden, 4to.
1761.

Redemption. A facred
Oratorio, felected from the

great and favourite works
of Mr. Handel, by Samuel
Arnold, Mus. Doc. Per-
formed at Drury-Lane 1787.

The Refurrection. A fa-
cred Oratorio, fet to mufic
by Mr. Samuel Arnold,
Mus. Doc. and performed
at Drury-Lane 1787.

Ruth. Orat. fet by Mr.
Smith, and performed at
Covent-Garden, 8vo. 1778.

S

Sampfon. Orat. by New-
burgh Hamilton; fet by
Mr. Handel, and perform-
ed at Covent-Garden, 4to.
1742.

Saul. Orat. fet by Mr.
Handel, and performed at
the Haymarket, 4to. 1738.

Semele. Orat. fet by
Mr. Handel, and perform-
ed at Covent-Garden, 4to.
1743. This is Congreve's
piece of the fame name,
fomething altered.

Solomon. Orat. fet by
Mr. Handel, and perform-
ed at Covent-Garden, 4to.
1748.

Solomon. Serenata. by
Edward Moore; fet by
Dr. Boyce, 4to.

Sufannah. Orat. fet by
Mr. Handel, and perform-
at Covent-Garden, 4to.
1743.

T

Theodora. Orat. by Dr.
Morell;

Z I

Morell; fet by Mr. Handel and performed at Covent-Garden, 4to. 1749. It is faid, that Mr. Handel valued this Oratorio more than any other performance of the fame kind.

The Triumph of Time and Truth. Orat. by Dr. Morell; fet by Mr. Handel, and performed at Covent-Garden, 4to. 1757.

Z

Zimri. An Oratorio, per-

Z I.

formed at Covent-Garden, and fet by Mr. Stanley, 4to. 1760. This piece, was written by Doctor Hawkefworth. Yet, like moft of the pieces compofed for the fake of mufic, found has been too much confidered in it to give fcope for very ftrong teftimonials of that genius which the author has fhewn in many of his other writings.

Q 4   AN ALPHABETICAL

A N

ALPHABETICAL CATALOGUE

_ O F

DRAMATIC WRITERS.

With the Titles of all the Pieces they have written annexed to each Name.

☞ Thofe marked thus * have not been printed.

A R

A DAMS, *George.*—The
Heathen Martyr ; or,
The Death of Socrates.

Addifon, Jofeph, Efq.—
Rofamond. Cato. The
Drummer.

*Alexander, William, Earl
of S.erling.*---Darius. Cræ-
fus. The Alexandrian Tra-
gedie. Julius Cæfar.

Andrews, Miles Peter.—
The Election. The Conju-
rer*. Belphegor ; or, The
Wifhes*. Summer Amufe-
ments ; or, An Adventure
at Margate. Fire and
Water. Diffipation. The
Baron Kinkvervankotfdor-
ftrakengatchdern. Better
late than never. Diffipa-
tion. Reparation.

Armin, Robert.——Two
Maides of More Clacke.

Armftrong, Dr. John.—
The Forced Marriage.

A S

*Arne, Dr. Thomas Auguf-
tine.*——Artaxerxes. The
Guardian Outwitted. The
Rofe.

Arnold Cornelius.—Ofman.

Arrowfmith, Mr.—The
Reformation.

Arthur, J.—The Lucky
Difcovery ; or The Tanner
of York.

Afcough, Charles Edward.
Semiramis.

Afhton, Robert.——The
Battle of Aughrim ; or, The
Fall of Monfieur St. Ruth.

Afpinwall, S. Rodogune;
or, The Rival Brothers.

Afton, Anthony.—Love in
a Hurry.

Afton, Walter.—The Re-
ftoration of King Charles
the Second ; or, The Life
and Death of Oliver Crom-
well.

Averay,

Averay, Robert.—Britannia and the Gods in Council.

Ayre, William.—Amintas.

Merope.

Ayres, James.—Sancho at Court.

B A

B. *W.*—The Juror. *Bacon, Dr.* — The Taxes; The Infignificants; The Tryal of the Time-Killers; The Moral Quack; The Oculift.

Bailey, Abraham.—The Spightful Sifter.

Baillie, Dr. John.—The Married Coquet.

Baker, Thomas.—Humours of the Age; Tunbridge Walks; Act at Oxford; Hampftead Heath; Fine Ladies Airs.

Baker, David Erfkine.—The Mufe of Offian.

Baker, R.——The Mad Houfe.

Bancroft, John.—Sertorius; Henry II.

Banks, John.——Rival Kings; Deftruction of Troy; Virtue Betrayed; Ifland Queens; Unhappy Favourite; Innocent Ufurper; Cyrus the Great.

Barford, Richard.—The Virgin Queen.

Barker, Mr.—Beau defeated; Fidelia and Fortunatus.

Barnes, Barnaby.—The Devil's Charter.

Baron, Robert, Efq.—— Deorum Dona; Gripus and

B E

Hegio; Mirza.

Barry, Lodowick, Efq.—— Ram Alley.

Bafker, Thomas.——The Bloody Banquet.

Bate, Henry.—Henry and Emma; The Rival Candidates; The Blackamoor Wafh'd White; The Flitch of Bacon.

Beaumont, Francis, and John Fletcher.—The Woman Hater; Mafque of the Inner Temple and Gray's-Inn; Knight of the Burning Peftle; Cupid's Revenge; The Scornful Lady; The King and no King; The Maid's Tragedy; Thierry and Theodoret; Philafter. The Faithful Shepherdefs. The Two Noble Kinfmen; The Elder Brother; Monf. Thomas; Wit without Money; Rollo; Rule a Wife and have a Wife; The Night Walker.

The following Plays were firft publifhed together in fol. 1647. Mad Lover; Spanifh Curate; Little French Lawyer; Cuftom of the Country; Noble Gentleman; The Captain; Beggar's Bufh; The Coxcomb; The Falfe One; The

The Chances ; Loyal Subject ; Laws of Candy ; Lover's Progrefs ; Ifland Princefs ; Humorous Lieutenant ; Nice Valour ; Maid in the Mill ; The Prophetefs ; Bonduca ; Sea Voyage ; Double Marriage ; The Pilgrim ; Knight of Malta ; Woman's Prize ; Love's Cure ; Honeft Man's Fortune ; Queen of Corinth; Women Pleafed ; A Wife for a Month ; Wit at feveral Weapons ; Valentinian ; Fair Maid of the Inn ; Love's Pilgrimage ; Four Plays in One ; Wild Goofe Chace ; The Widow ; The Jeweller of Amfterdam ; or, The Hague* ; Faithful Friend* ; A Right Woman* Hiftory of Mador, King of Britain*.

Beckingham, Charles.— Scipio Africanus ; Hen. IV. of France.

Bedloe, Capt. Wm.—The Excommunicated Prince.

Behn, Aphara, or Aphra. —Forced Marriage ; Amorous Prince ; Dutch Lover ; Abdelazar ; Town Fop ; The Rover ; Sir Patient Fancy ; Feigned Courtezans ; The Rover ; City Heirefs ; Falfe Count ; The Roundheads ; The Young King ; Lucky Chance ; Emperor of the Moon ; The Widow Ranter ; Younger Brother.

Belchier. Drawbridge-

Court.—Hans Beer Pot's Invifible Comedy.

Bellamy, Daniel, fen. and jun.—Innocence Betray'd ; Languifhing Lover ; Love Triumphant ; Perjured Devotee ; Rival Nymphs ; Rival Priefts ; Vanquifhed Love.

Bellers, Fettiplace.—Injured Innocence.

Belon, Peter.—The Mock Duellift ; or, The French Vallet.

Bennet, Philip, Efq.—— Beau Philofopher ; The Beau's Adventures.

Bentley, Thomas.——The Wifhes* ; Philodamus.

Berkley, Sir Wm.—Loft Lady.

Betterton, Thomas.—The Roman Virgin ; or, Unjuft Judge ; The Revenge ; or, A Match in Newgate ; The Prophetefs ; or, The Hiftory of Dioclefian ; King Henry the Fourth, with the Humours of Sir John Falftaff ; The Amorous Widow ; or, The Wanton Wife ; Sequel of Henry the Fourth ; The Bondman ; or, Love and Liberty ; The Woman made a Juftice*.

Bickerftaffe, Ifaac.—— Leucothoe ; Thomas and Sally ; or, The Sailor's Return ; Maid of the Mill ; Daphne and Amintor ; The Plain Dealer ; Love in the City ; Lionel and Clariffa ; Abfent Man ; The Padlock ;
The

The Hypocrite; Ephefian Matron; Dr. Laft in his Chariot; The Captive; A School for Fathers; 'Tis Well it's no Worfe; Recruiting Serjeant; He would if he could; or, An old Fool worfe than any.

Bladen, Martin, Efq.—Orpheus and Eurydice; Solon.

Blanch, J.—The Beau Merchant; Swords into Anchors; Hoops into Spinning-wheels.

Bland, J.—The Song of Solomon.

Bodens, Charles.——The Modifh Couple; Marriage á-la-Mode.

Boiffy, Michael.——The Mifer of Moliere.

Bond, William.——The Tufcan Treaty; or, Tarquin's Overthrow.

Booth, Barton.——The Death of Dido.

Boothby, Frances.—Marcellia.

Boulton, Thomas.——The Sailors Farewell; or, The Guinea out fit.

Bourgeois, Benjamin.—The Squire Burlefqued; or, The Sharpers Out-witted; TheDifappointedCoxcomb.

Bourne, Reuben.——The Contented Cuckold.

Boyce, Samuel.—The Rover; or, Happinefs at Laft.

Boyd, Elizabeth.—Don Sancho; or, The Student's

Whim; Minerva's Triumph.

Boyer, Abel.—Achilles in Aulis.

Boyle, Charles, Earl of Orrery.—As you find it.

Boyle, Murrough, Lord Vifcount Bleffington.—The Loft Princefs.

Boyle, Roger, Earl of Orrery.——Muftapha; Henry Fifth; The Black Prince; Tryphon; Mr. Anthony; Guzman; Herod; Altemira.

Brady, Dr. Nicholas.—The Rape; or, The Innocent Impofters.

Brandon, Samuel.—The Virtuous Octavia.

Brenan, Mr.—The Painter's Breakfaft.

Brereton, Thomas.—Efther; Sir John Oldcaftle, loft; Athaliah, unfinifhed; The Oxford Ladies; or, The Nobleman, unfinifhed.

Breval, John Durant.—The Confederates; The Play is the Plot; The Strollers; The Rape of Helen.

Brewer, Anthony. Country Girl; Love-fick King.

Bridges, Thomas.—Dido, The Dutchman.

Brome, Alex.——The Cunning Lovers

Brome, Richard.—Northern Lafs; The Sparagus Garden; The Antipodes; Jovial Crew; or, The Merry Beggars; A Mad Couple well Match'd; Novel.

Q 6   la

la; The Court Beggar; City Wit; or, The Woman wears the Breeches; The Damoifelle; or, The new Ordinary; The Queen's Exchange; The Englifh Moor; or, The Mock Marriage; The Love-fick Court or, The Ambitious Politic; Covent-Garden Weeded; or, The Middiefex Juftice of Peace; New Academy; or, The New Exchange; Queen and Concubine; Chriftianetta; Witt in a Madnes; The Jewifh Gentleman; The Love fick Maid; or, The Honour of young Ladies; The Life and Death of Sir Martyn Skink, with the Warres of the Low Countries*; The Apprentices Prize.

Brooke, Henry, Efq.—— Guftavus Vafa; Earl of Weftmoreland; Little John and the Giants; Earl of Effex; Anthony and Cleopatra; The Impofter; Cymbeline; Montezuma; Veftal Virgin; Contending Brothers; Charitable Affociation; Female Officer; Marriage Contract; Ruth.

Brooke, Frances. Virginia; Siege of Sinope; Rofina.

Brookes, R.—Tchao Chi Cou Ell; or, The Little Orphan of the Family of Tchao.

Broughton, Thomas.—— Hercules.

Brown, Anthony, Efq.— The Fatal Retirement.

Browne, Thomas. Phyfick lyes a Bleeding; or, The Apothecary turned Doctor; The Stage Beau toffed in a Blanket; or, Hypocrific à-la-oMde; The Difpenfary.

Browne, Dr. John.—— Barbaroffa; Athelftan; The Cure of Saul.

Browe, Mofes.—Polidus; All bedevilled.

Browne, William.—The Inner Temple Mafque.

Bullock Chriftopher.—Woman's Revenge; Slip; Adventures of Half an Hour; Cobler of Prefton; Perjuror; Woman's a Riddle; The Traytor.

Burgefs, Mrs.——The Oaks; or, The Beauties of Canterbury.

Burgoyne, John, Efq.— The Maid of the Oaks; Bon Ton.

Burkhead, Henry.—Cola's Fury.

Burnaby, Charles, Efq.— Reformed Wife; Ladies Vifiting Day; Modifh Hufband; Love Betray'd.

Burnel, Henry, Efq.—— Landgartha,

Burney, Dr Charles.— The Cunning Man.

Burton, Philippina.—— Fafhion Difplayed*.

Bufhe, Amyas, Efq. M. A. F. R. S.—Socrates.

                CAPELL,

CAPELL, EDWARD.
—Anthony and Cleo-
patra.
    Carew, Lady Elizabeth.
—Marian, the fair Queen
of Jewry.
    Carew, Thomas, Esq.—
Cœlum Britannicum.
    Carey, Henry.—Hanging
and Marriage; or, The
Dead Man's Wedding; The
Contrivances; Amelia;
Teraminta; Chrononhoton-
thologos; Honeſt Yorkſhire
Man; Dragon of Wantley;
Margery; or, A worſe Pla-
gue than the Dragon; Bet-
ty; or, The Country Bump-
kins; Nancy; or, The Parting Lovers.
    Carey, Henry Lucius,
Lord Viſcount Falkland.—
The Marriage Night.
    Carey, George Savile.---
The Inoculator; The Cot-
tagers; Liberty chaſtiſed;
or, Patriotiſm in Chains;
Shakſpeare's Jubilee; The
Three old Women weather-
wife; The Magic Girdle;
The Nutbrown Maid.
    Carlell, Lodowic, Esq.—
Deſerving Favourite; Ar-
viragus and Philicia; Paſſionate Lover; Fool would
be a Favourite; Oſmond
the Great Turk; Heracli-
tus; Spartan Ladies*.
    Carliſle, James.——The
Fortune Hunters.
    Carr, John.—Epponina.
    Carr, Samuel.—Eugenia.
    Carpenter, Richard.—The
Pragmatical Jeſuit.

    Cartwright, George.——
The Heroic Lover.
    Cartwright, William.—
Royal Slave; Lady Errant;
Ordinary; Siege.
    Caryl, John.—The Eng-
liſh Princeſs; or, The
Death of Richard the Third;
Sir Salomon; or, The Cau-
tious Coxcomb.
    Cavendiſh, William, Duke
of Newcaſtle.—The Coun-
try Captain; Variety;
Triumphant Widow; Hu-
mourous Lovers.
    Cavendiſh, Margaret,
Dutcheſs of Newcaſtle.—
Two volumes of plays were
written by this Lady, but
none of them acted.
    Celiſia, Mrs.—Almida.
    Centlivre, Suſanna.——
Perjur'd Huſband; Love's
Contrivances; Beau's Duel;
Stolen Heireſs; Gameſter;
Baſſet Table; Love at a
Venture; Platonic Lady;
Buſy Body; Man's Bewitch-
ed; Bickerſtaffe's Burying;
Marplot; Perplex'd Lovers;
Wonder; Gotham Election;
Wife well Managed; Cruel
Gift; Bold Stroke for a
Wife; Artifice.
    Chamberlaine, Robert.—
The Swaggering Damſel.
    Chamberlaine, Dr. Wil-
liam.—Love's Victory.
    Chapman, George.—Blind
Beggar of Alexandria; Hu-
mours Day's Mirth; All
Fools; Eaſtward Hoe; Gen-
tleman Uſher; M. D'Olive;
Buſſy

Buſſy D'Ambois; Cæſar and Pompey; Conſpiracy of Biron; May Day; Widow's Tears; Buſſy D'Ambois's Revenge; Maſque of the Middle Temple and Lincoln's-Inn; Two Wiſe Men and all the reſt Fools; Alphonſus Emperor of Germany; Revenge for Honour.

Chapman, Mr.——Fatal Love; Yorkſhire Gentlewoman and her Son; Second Maiden's Tragedy;

Charke, Charlotte.—The Art of Management.

Chatterton, Thomas.—— The Tournament; Æ:la; Goddwyn, unfiniſhed; The Dowager, unfiniſhed.

Chaves, A.—The Cares of Love.

Cheeke, Henry.——Free Will.

Chetwood, William Rufus.—The Stock-Jobbers; or, The Humours of Exchange-Alley; South-Sea; Lover's Opera; Generous Free Maſon.

Cibley, Colley, Eſq.—— Love's laſt Shift; Woman's Wit; Xerxes; Love makes a Man; King Richard the Third; She wou'd and She wou'd not; Careleſs Huſband; Perolla and Izadora; School-boy; Comical Lovers; DoubleGallant; Lady's laſt Stake; Rival Fools; Venus and Adonis; Myrtillo; Nonjuror; Ximena;

Refuſal; Hob; or, The Country Wake; Cæſar in Egypt; Provoked Huſband; Rival Queans; Love in a Riddle; Damon and Phillida; Papal Tyranny in the Reign of King John.

Cibber, Suſannah-Maria. —The Oracle.

Cibber, Theophilus.—Hen. the Sixth; The Lover; Patie and Peggy; The Harlot's Progreſs; or, The Ridotto Al Freſco; Romeo and Juliet; The Auction,

Clancy, Michael. M. D. —Hermon, Prince of Choræa; The Sharper.

Cleland, John.—Tombo-Chiqui; Titus Veſpaſian; The Ladies Subſcription.

Clive, Catharine.—Bayes in Petticoats; Every Woman in her Humour*; The Faithful Iriſhwoman; Iſland of Slaves*.

Cobb, Mr.—The Elders* The Wedding Night*; Contract; or, Female Captain; Who'd have thought It; Kenſington-Gardens, or, Walking Jockey; The Firſt Floor; Haunted Tower Love in the Eaſt; or, Adventures of twelve Hours; Siege of Belgrade.

Cockain, Sir Aſton.—— Obſtinate Lady; Trappolin ſuppoſed a Prince; Maſque for Twelfth-Night; Ovid's Tragedy.

Cockings, George.—The Conqueſt

CO

[351]

C O

Conqueſt of Canada; or, The Siege of Quebec.

Coffey, Charles.—Southwark Fair; or, The Sheepſhearing; The Beggar's Wedding; Phebe; or, The Beggar; Female Parſon; or, The Beau in the Suds; The Devil to pay; or, The Wives Metamorphoſed; A Wife and no Wife; the Boarding-School; or, The Sham Captain; The Merry Cobler; or, Second Part of Devil to Pay; The Devil upon two Sticks; or, Country Beau.

Collier, Sir George.—Selima and Azor.

Colman, George.—Polly Honeycombe; Jealous Wife; Muſical Lady; Philaſter; The Deuce is in Him; A Midſummer's Night Dream; A Fairy Tale; Clandeſtine Marriage; Engliſh Merchant; King Lear; Oxonian in Town; Man and Wife; The Portrait; The Fairy Prince; Comus; Achilles in Petticoats; Man of Buſineſs; Epicœne; or, The Silent Woman; The Spleen; or, Iſlington Spa; Occaſional Prelude; New Brooms; The Spaniſh Barber*; Female Chevalier*; Bonduca; The Suicide*; The Separate Maintenance* The Manager in Diſtreſs; Preludio; The Merchant; Fairy Tale.

Colman, George, jun.—— Battle of Hexham; or, Days

C O

of Old; Incle and Yarico; Turk and no Turk; Two to One; The Surrender of Calais.

Concanen, Matthew, Eſq. —Wexford Wells.

Congreve, William, Eſq. —Old Batchelor; Double Dealer; Love for Love; Mourning Bride; Way of the World; Judgment of Paris; Semele.

Conolly, Mr.—The Connoiſſeur.

Conway, Gen.——Falſe Appearances.

Cook, John.—Green's Tu Quoque.

Cooke, Adam Moſes Emanuel.——The King cannot Err; The Hermit converted; or, The Maid of Bath Married.

Cooke, Edward, Eſq.— Love's Triumph.

Cooke, Thomas.—Albion; The Battle of the Poets; The Triumphs of Love and Honour; The Eunuch; The Mournful Nuptials; Love the Cauſe and Cure of Grief; Amphytryon.

Cooper, Elizabeth.—Rival Widows; The Nobleman*.

Corey, John.—The Generous Enemies.

Corey, John,——A Cure for Jealouſy; The Metamorphoſis.

Cotton, Charles, Eſq.— Horace.

Cowley, Abraham.—— Love's Riddle; Naufragium

um Joculare; Guardian; Cutter of Coleman-ſtreet.

Cowley, Mrs. H.——The Runaway; Who's the Dupe? Albina; The Belle's Stratagem*; The World as it Goes; Second Thought is beſt; Bold Stroke for a Huſband; Fate of Sparta; or, Rival Kings; Which is the Man?

Cox, Robert.—Actæon & Diana; The Black Man; Venus and Adonis; or, The Maid's Philoſophy; Philetis and Conſtantia; King Ahaſuerus and Queen Eſther; King Solomon's Wiſdom; Diphilo and Granida; Wiltſhire; Oenone; Bottom the Weaver; The Cheater Cheated.

Cradock, Joſeph.——Zobeide.

Crane, Edward.—The Female Parricide; Saul and Jonathan.

Craven, Lady Elizabeth. ---The Sleep-walker; The Miniature Picture*; The Silver Tankard.

Craufurd, David, Eſq.-- Courtſhip à-la-Mode; Love at firſt Sight.

Criſp, Henry.---Virginia.

Crowne, John.---Juliana;

Charles VIIIth of France; The Country Wit; Andromache; Califto; City Politics; The Deſtruction of Jeruſalem; The Ambitious Stateſman; The Miſery of Civil War; Henry the Sixth; Thyeſtes; Sir Courtly Nice; Darius; The Engliſh Fryar; Regulus; The Married Beau; Caligula; Juſtice Buſy*.

Croxall, Dr. Samuel.---- The Fair Circaſſian.

Cumberland, Richard.--- The Baniſhment of Cicero; Summer's Tale; Amelia; The Brothers; The Weſt-Indian; Timon of Athens; Faſhionable Lover; The Note of Hand; Choleric Man; Battle of Haſtings; Calypſo; The Bondman*; The Duke of Milan*; The Widow of Delphi*; The Arab; The Carmelite; The Country Attorney; The Impoſtor; Myſterious Huſband; Natural Son.

Cunningham, John.—— Love in a Miſt.

Cunningham, Joſias.--- The Royal Shepherds.

Cutts, John.---Rebellion Defeated.

D A

DALTON, John.---Comus.

Dalton, John.---Honour Rewarded; or, The Generous Fortune Hunter.

D A

Dance, James.---See *Love James.*

Dancer, John.----Amynta; Nicomede; Agrippa, king of Alba.

Daniel,

D A

Daniel, Samuel.----Cleopatra ; Philotas ; Queen's Arcadia ; Tethys' Feſtival ; or, The Queen's Wake ; Hymen's Triumph ; Viſion of the twelve Goddeſſes.

Darcy, James.------Love and Ambition ; Orphan of Venice.

Dauborn, alias Daborn, Robert.----Chriſtian turned Turk ; Poor Man's Comfort.

D'Avenant, Charles, LL. D.---Circe.

Davenant, Sir William, Knt.----Albovine, King of the Lombards ; Cruel Brother ; Juſt Italian ; Temple of Love ; Triumphs of the Prince D'Amour ; Platonic Lovers ; Wits ; Britannia Triumphant ; Salmacida Spolia; Unfortunate Lovers; Love and Honour ; Entertainment at Rutland-houſe ; Siege of Rhodes; The Cruelty of the Spaniards in Peru; The Hiſtory of Sir Francis Drake ; Siege of Rhodes ; Rivals ; Man's the Maſter ; Fair Favourite ; Law againſt Lovers ; News from Plymouth ; Playhouſe to be lett ; Siege ; Diſtreſſes ; Macbeth ; The Colonel*.

Davenport, Robert.----A New Trick to cheat the Devil ; King John and Matilda ; The City Night Cap ; or, Crede quod habes et habes ; The Pedler* ; The Pirate* ; The Fatal Bro-

D E

thers* ; The Politic Queen ; or, Murther will out* ; The Woman's miſtaken ; Henry I. and Henry II.

Dauncey. See *Dancer.*

Davy, Samuel.------The Treacherous Huſband.

Davys, Mary.------The Northern Heirefs ; Self Rival.

Day, John.---Iſle of Gulls; Travels of Three Engliſh Brothers ; Humour out of Breath ; Law Tricks ; Parliament of Bees ; Blind Beggar of Bethnal Green.

Dekker, Thomas.---Old Fortunatus ; Satyromaſtix ; Honeſt Whore ; Weſtward Hoe ; Northward Hoe ; Wyat's Hiſtory ; Whore of Babylon ; If this ben't a good Play, the Devil's in't ; Match me in London ; Wonder of a Kingdom ; Guy Earl of Warwick* ; The Jew of Venice* ; Guſtavus King of Swithland* ; Tale of Jocondo and Aſtolfo ;* The Spaniſh Soldier*.

Delap, Mr.-----Hecuba ; Royal Suppliants ; The Captives.

Dell, Henry.---The Spouter ; or, Double Revenge ; Minorca ; The Mirrour ; The Frenchified Lady Fever in Paris.

Denham, Sir John.---The Sophy.

Denis, Charles.------The Siege of Calais.

Dennis, John.---Plot and

no Plot ; Rinaldo and Armida ; Iphigenia ; Comical Gallant ; Liberty Afferted ; Gibraltar ; Orpheus and Euridice ; Appius and Virginia ; Coriolanus.

Dent, Mr. ---The Candidate ; Too civil by Half.

Derrick, Samuel.---Sylla.

Dibden, Charles.---Shepherd's Artifice ; Damon and Phillida ; Wedding Ring ; The Deferter ; The Waterman ; or, The Firft of Auguft ; The Cobler ; or, A Wife of ten Thoufand ; The Metamorphofis ; The Quaker ; Poor Vulcan ; The Gipfies ; Rofe and Collin ; The Wives revenged : Annette and Lubin : Chelfea Penfioner ; The Mirror ; or, Harlequin every Where ; The Shepherdefs of the Alps ; The Iflanders ; Liberty-hall ; None fo blind as thofe who won't fee.

Digby, George, Earl of Briftol.---Elvira ; 'Tis better than it was* ; Worfe and Worfe*.

Dilke, Thomas, Efq.---- Lover's Luck ; City Lady ; Pretenders.

Dobbes, Francis.------The Patriot King ; or, Irifh Chief.

Dodd, James Solas.------ Gallic Gratitude ; or, The Frenchman in India.

Dodd, William, the unfortunate Clergyman.----The Syracufan* ; Sir Roger de Coverly*.

Dodfley, Robert.----The Toyfhop ; The King and the Miller of Mansfield ; Sir John Cockle at Court ; The Blind Beggar of Bethnal Green ; Rex et Pontifex ; Triumph of Peace ; Cleone.

Dogget, Thomas.—The Country Wake.

Dorman, Mr.----Sir Roger de Coverley.

Doffie, Robert.-------The Statefman fo'led.

Dover, John.---The Roman Generals.

Dow, Alexander.---Zingis ; Sethono.

Dower, E.---The Salopian Squire.

Downham, Hugh.----Lucius Junius Brutus.

Downing, George.---Newmarket ; or, The Humours of the Turf ; Parthian Exile ; Volunteers ; or, Taylors to Arms.

Drake, Dr. James.------ The Sham Lawyer ; or, The Lucky Extravagant.

Draper, Matthew.---The Spendthrift.

Drury, Robert.---Devil of a Duke ; Mad Captain ; Fancy'd Queen ; Rival Milliners.

Dryden, John.-------The Wild Gallant ; Rival Ladies ; Indian Emperour ; Secret Love ; or, The Maiden Queen ; Sir Martin Marall ; Tempeft ; An Evening's Love's ; or, The Mock Aftrologer ; Tyrannick Love ; or,

D U

ar, The Royal Martyr; Conqueſt of Grenada; Almanzor and Almabide; or, The Conqueſt of Grenada; Marrriage Alamode; Aſſignation; or, Love in a Nunnery; Amboyna; State of Innocence and Fall of Man; Aurengzebe; All for Love; Oedipus; Troilus and Creſſida; Kind Keeper; or, Mr. Limberham; Spaniſh Fryar; Duke of Guife; Albion and Albianus; Don Sebaſtian; Amphitryon; King Arthur; Cleomenes the Spartan Hero; Love Triumphant.

Dryden, John.----The Huſband his own Cuckold.

Dudley, Bate.------The Woodman.

Duffet, Thomas.----Amorous Old Woman; Spaniſh Rogue; Emprefs of Morocco; Mock Tempeſt; Beauty's Triumph; Pſyche Debauch'd.

D U

Duncombe, William.----- Athaliah; Lucius Junius Brutus.

D'Urfey, Thomas.------- Siege of Memphis; Fond Huſband; Madam Fickle; Fool turn'd Critic; Trick for Trick; Squire Old-Sap; Virtuous Wife; Sir Barnaby Whig; Royaliſt; Iajur'd Princefs; Commonwealth of Women; Banditti; Fool's Preferment; Buſy D'Ambois; Love for Money; Marriage-hater match'd; Richmond Heirefs; Don Quixote, in three parts; Cynthia and Endymion; Intrigues of Verſailles; Campaigners; Maſſaniello; Bath; Wonders in the Sun; Modern Prophets; Old Mode and the New; Two Queens of Brentford; Grecian Heroine; Ariadne.

ES

EDWARDS, *Richard.*-- Damon and Pythias; Palamon and Arcyte.

Eſtcourt, Richard.---Fair Example; Prunella.

E T

Etherege, Sir George, Knt. ---Comical Revenge; She wou'd if She Cou'd; Man of Mode.

F A

FANE, *Sir Francis, jun.* Knight of the Bath,--- Love in the Dark; Sacrifice; Maſque for Lord Rocheſter's Valentinian.

Farqrhar, George.----Love

F A

and a Bottle; Coſtant Couple; Sir Harry Wildair; Inconſtant; Stage Coach; Recruiting Officer; Twin Rivals; Beaux' Stratagem.

Fenton,

Fenton, Elijah.----Mari-
amme.

Field, Nathaniel.---Wo-
~man is a Weather-cock;
Amends for Ladies.

Fielding, Henry.----Love
in several Masques; Temple
Beau; Author's Farce;
Tragedy of Tragedies;
Coffee-house Politician;
Letter Writers; Grubstreet
Opera; Lottery; Modern
Husband; Mock Doctor;
Debauchees; Covent-Gar-
den Tragedy; Miser; In-
triguing Chambermaid;
Don Quixote in England;
Old Man taught Wisdom;
Pasquin; Historical Re-
gister; Euridice; Euridice
Hiss'd; Tumble-down Dick;
Miss Lucy in Town; Plutus
the God of Riches; Wed-
ding Day; Interlude be-
tween Jupiter, Juno, and
Mercury; The Fathers; or,
The Good-natured Man.

Filmer, Edward.---Un-
natural Brother.

Flecknoe, Richard.------
Love's Dominion; Marri-
age of Oceanus and Britannia; Erminia; Damoiselles
à-la-Mode; Love's King-
dom.

*Fletcher, John. See Beau-
mont, Francis.*

Fletcher, Phineas.---Sice-
lides.

Foote, Samuel, Esq.------
Taste; Englishman in Paris;
The Knights; Englishman

returned from Paris; The
Author; Diversions of the
Morning*; Minor; The
Lyar; Orators; Mayor of
Garratt; The Patron; Com-
missary; Devil upon Two
Sticks; Lame Lover; Maid
of Bath; The Nabob; Pie-
ty in Pattens*; The Bank-
rupt; The Cozeners; The
Capuchin; A Trip to Ca-
lais.

Ford, John.------Lovers
Melancholy; Love's Sacri-
fice; 'Tis Pity She's a
Whore; Broken Heart;
Perkin Warbeck; Fancies
Chaste and Noble; Ladies
Tryal; Sun's Darling;
Beauty in a Trance*; Royal
Combat*; An ill beginning
as a good end, and a bad
beginning may have a good
end*; The London Mer-
chant*.

Ford, Thomas.----Love's
Labyrinth.

Forde, Brownlow.---Mi-
raculous Cure; or, The Citizen Outwitted.

Forest, Theophilus.---Wea-
ther Cock.

Fountain, John.----Re-
wards of Virtue.

Francis, Philip.---Euge-
nia; Constantine.

Franklin, Dr. Thomas.---
The Earl of Warwick;
Orestes; Electra; Matilda;
The Contract; Tragopo-
dagra; or, The Gout.

Fraunce,

Fraunce, Abraham.—— Amyntas.
Freeman, Ralph.---Imperiale.
Frowde, Philip.---Fall of Saguntum; Philotas.

Fulwell, Ulpian.---Like Will to Like, quothe the Devil to Collier.
Fyfe, Alex.---The Royal Martyr King Charles I.

G A

GAGER, *Wm LL D.* ------Meleager; Rivals; Ulyſſes redax.
Gambold, John.——The Martyrdom of Ignatius.
Gardiner, Matthew.---- Parthian Hero; Sharpers.
Gardiner, Mrs.——The Advertiſement; or, A Bold Stroke for a Huſband*.
Garrick, David, born Feb. 29, 1716; *died Jan.* 20, 1779.---The Lying Valet; Miſs in her Teens; or, The Medley of Lovers; Lethe; Romeo and Juliet; Every Man in his Humour; The Fairies; The Tempeſt; Florizel and Perdita; Catherine and Petruchio; Lilliput; The Male Coquet; or, Seventeen Hundred and Fifty-ſeven; Gameſters: Iſabella; or, The Fatal Marriage; The Guardian; High Life Below Stairs; The Enchanter; or, Love and Muſic; Harlequin's Invaſion*; Cymbeline; The Farmer's Return from London; The Clandeſtine Marriage; The Country Girl; Neck or Nothing; Cymon; A Peep Behind the Curtain;

G E

or, The New Rehearſal; The Jubile*; King Arthur; or, The Briiſh Worthy; Hamlet; The Inſtitution of the O er of the Garter; The Iriſh W low; The Chances; Albu.. zar; Alfred; A Chriſtmas Tale; The Meeting of the Company*; Bon Ton; or High Life Above Stairs; May Day; Theatrical Candidates.
Garter, Thomas.-----Suſannah.
Gaſcoigne, George, Eſq. ---Jocaſta; The Suppoſes; The Glaſs of Government; The Pleaſures at Kennelworth.
Gay, John.---The Mohocks; The Wife of Bath; The What D'ye Call It; Three Hours After Marriage; Dione; The Captives; The Beggar's Opera; Polly; The Wife of Bath; Acis and Galatea; Achilles; The Diſtreſs'd Wife; The Rehearſal at Gotham.
Gay, Joſeph.---The Confederates.
Gentleman, Francis.——
Se-

Sejanus; The Stratford Jubilee; The Sultan; or, Love and Fame; The Tobacconist; Cupid's Revenge; The Pantheonites; The Modish Wife; Oroonoko; or, Royal Slave; The Coxcombs; King Richard the Second; Zaphira; The Mentalist*; The Fairy Court*.

Gildon, Charles.----The Roman Bride's Revenge; Phaëton; or, The Fatal Divorce; Measure for Measure; or, Beauty the Best Advocate; Love's Victim; or, The Queen of Wales; The Patriot; or, the Italian Revenge; A Comparison between the Two Stages; A New Rehearsal; or, Bayes the Younger.

Glapthorne, Henry.---Argalus and Parthenia; Albertus Wallenstein; The Ladies Privilege; The Hollander; Wit in a Constable; The Parraside; or, Revenge for Honour*; The Vestal*; The Noble Trial*; The Duchess of Fernandina*.

Glover, Richard, Esq.— Boadicia; Medea.

Goff, Thomas.----Raging Turk; Couragious Turk; Orestes; Careless Shepherdess.

Goldsmith, Francis, Esq. Sophonpaneas.

Goldsmith, Oliver.---The Good-natured Man; She Stoops to Conquer; or, The Mistakes of the Night; The Grumbler*.

Gomersal, Robert.----Lodowick Sforza, Duke of Milan.

Goodenough, Mr.---William and Nanny.

Goodhall, James.—Florazene; or, The Fatal Conquest; King Richard II.

Goodwin T.---The Loyal Shepherds; or, the Rustic Heroine

Gordon, William.----Lupone; or, The Inquisitor.

Goring, Charles, Esq.---- Irene; or, The Fair Greek.

Gosson, Stephen.----Catalin's Conspiracies*; The Comedy of Captain Mario*; Praise at Parting*.

Gough, J. Gent.---The Strange Discovery.

Gould, Robert.—The Rival Sisters; Innocence Distressed; or, the Royal Penitents.

Graham George.—Telemachus.

Granville, George, Lord Lansdowne.—The She Gallants; Heroic Love; The Jew of Venice; Peleus and Thetis; The British Enchanters; or, No Magic Like Love; Once a Lover and always a Lover.

Greathead, Mr.-----The Regent.

Green, Alexander.—The Politician Cheated.

Green,

G R

Green, George Smith.---- Oliver Cromwell ; the Nice Lady.

Green, Robert.—The Hiftory of Fryar Bacon and Fryar Bungay ; The Hiftory of Orlando Furiofo, one of the Twelve Peers of France ; The Comical Hiftory of Alphonfus King of Arragon ; The Scottifhe Story of James the Fourthe flaine at Flodd·on, intermixed with a pleafant Comedie, prefented by Oberon, King of the Fairies ; The Hiftory of Jobe*.

Green, Rupert.—The Secret Plot.

G W.

Greville, Sir Fulk, Lord Brook.— Alaham ; Muftapha.

Griffin, Benjamin.·----Injur'd Virtue ; Love in a Sack ; Humours of Purgatory ; Mafquerade ; Whig and Tory.

Griffith, Elizabeth.—The Platonic Wife ; Amana ; The Double Miftake ; The School for Rakes ; A Wife in the Right ; The Times.

Grimfton, William, Lord Vifcount.----The Lawyer's Fortune.

Gwinne, Matthew.—Nero ; Vertumnus five Annus recurrens.

H A

HAbington, *William.*— The Queen of Arragon.

Haines, Jofeph (commonly called Count Haines).— The Fatal Miftake.

Hamilton, Newburgh.— Doating Lovers ; Petticoat Plotter.

Hammond, William.----- Preceptor.

Harding, Samuel.—Sicily and Naples ; or, The Fatal Union.

Harris, Jofeph.---- The Miftakes ; The City Bride ; Love's a Lottery, and a Woman the Prize ; Love and Riches Reconciled.

Harris, James.——The Spring.

Harrifon William.—The Pilgrims.

H A

Harrifon, Thomas.—Belfehazzar ; or, The Heroic Jew.

Harper, Samuel.——The Mock Philofopher.

Harrod, W.—Patriot.

Hart, Mr.---·Herminius and Efpafia.

Hartfon, Hall.------The Countefs of Salifbury.

Hatchet William.—The Rival Father ; or, The Death of Achilles ; The Chinefe Orphan.

Havard, William.------ Scanderberg ; King Charles the Firft ; Regulus ; The Elopement*.

Haufted, Peter.----The Rival Friends ; Senile Odium.

Hawkins, William.---- Henry

Henry and Rofamond; The Siege of Aleppo; Cymbeline.

Hawkins, William.------ Apollo fhroving.

*Hawling, Francis.----*The Impertinent Lovers; It fhould have come Sooner*.

*Hawkefworth, John, LL. D.----*Amphytryon; Oroonoko; Edgar and Emmeline; Zimri.

*Hayley, Mr----.*Eudora; Lord Ruffel; Marian; Two Connoiffeurs.

*Hazard, Jofeph.----*Redowald.

*Heard, Wm.- -*The Snuff-Box; or, a Trip to Bath; Valentine's Day.

*Hemings, William.----*The Fatal Contract; The Jew's Tragedy; The Eunuch.

Henderfou, Andrew.---- Arfinoe.

*Hewitt, J.-----*A Tutor for the Beaus; or, Love in a Labyrinth; Fatal Falfhood, or, Diftrefs'd Innocence.

Heywood, Mrs. Eliza.---- Fair Captive; Wife to be Let; Frederick Duke of Brunfwick; Opera of Operas.

*Heywood. John.--*A Play between Johan the Hufband; Tyb the Wife, and Sir Johan the Prieft; A merry Play between the Pardoner and the Friar, the Curate and Neighbour Prat; The Play called the Four PP. A newe and a very mery In-

terlude of a Palmer, a Pardoner, a Potycary, a Pedlar; A Play of Genteelnefs and Nobility; A Play of Love; A Play of the Weather, called, A new and a very merry Interlude of Weathers.

*Heywood, Thomas.----*Robert Earl of Huntingdon's Downfall; Robert Earl of Huntingdon's Death; Edward IV Hift. Play; If you know not me, you know Nobody; Fair Maid of the Exchange; Golden Age; Silver Age; Brazen Age; Four 'Preatices of London; Woman killed with Kindnefs; Rape of Lucrece; Fair Maid of the Weft; Iron Age; Englifh Traveller; Maidenhead well Loft; Lancafhire Witches; Love's Miftrefs; Ch llenge fcr Beauty; Royal King and Loyal Subject; Wife Woman oi Hogfdon; Fortune by Land and Sea.

*Hiffernan, Paul.---*The Lady's Choice; Wifhes of a Free People; New Hippocrates; Earl of Warwick; Philofphic Whim; or, Aftronomy.

*Higden, Henry.----*The Wary Widow.

*Higgons, Bevil.-----*The Generous Conqueror; or, The Timely Difcovery.

*Hill, Aaron.----*Elfrid; or, The Fair Inconftant; The Walking

H O

Walking Statue; or, The Devil in the Wine Cellar; Trick upon Trick; or, Squire Brainlefs*; Rinaldo; The Fatal Vifion; or, The Fall of Siam; King Henry V; or, The Conqueft of France by the Englifh; Athelwold; Zara; Alzira; Merope; Roman Revenge; The Infolvent; or, Filial Piety; Merlin in Love; The Mufes in Mourning; The Snake in the Grafs; Saul; Daraxes, unfinifhed.

Hill, Sir John.---Orpheus; The Critical Minute*; The Rout.

Hill, Richard, Efq.---The Gofpel Shop.

Hippefley, John.---Journey to Briftol; or, The Honeft Welfhman.

Hitchcock, Mr.------The Macaroni; The Coquet; or, The Miftakes of the Heart.

Hoadly, Dr. Benjamin.--- The Sufpicious Hufband.

Hoadly, Dr. John.---The Contraft*; Jephtha; Love's Revenge; Phœbe; The Force of Truth.

Hodfon, Wm.—Arfaces; Zoraida.

Holcraft, Thomas.—The Crifis; or, Love and Fear*; CholoricFather; Duplicity; Follies of a Day; or, The Marriage of Figaro; The Noble Peafant; Seduction.

Holden, Mr.--The Ghofts.

R

H O

Holland, Samuel, Gent.--- Venus and Adonis.

Hoole, John.-----Cyrus; Timanthes; Cleonice Princefs of Bithynia.

Home, John.---Douglas; Agis; The Siege of Aquileia; The Fatal Difcovery; Alonzo; Alfred.

Hoper, Mrs.-----Edward the Black Prince*; Queen Tragedy reftored.

Hopkins, Charles.---Pyrrhus, king of Epirus; Boadicea, Queen of Britain; Friendfhip Improv'd.

Hough, J.-------Second Thought is Beft.

Howard, The Hon. Edward.--Ufurper; Six Day's Adventure; Woman's Conqueft; Man of Newmarket; The Change of Crownes, a play*; The London Gentleman*; The United Kingdoms*.

Howard, The Hon. James. ---All Miftaken; The Englifh Monfieur; Romeo and Juliet*.

Howard, Sir Robert, Knt. ---Blind Lady; Surprizal; Committee; Veftal Virgin; Indian Queen; Great Favourite; The Conqueft of China by the Tartars, now loft.

Howard, Gorges Edmund. ---Almeyda; or, The Rival Kings; The Siege of Tamor.

Howell, James, Efq.---- Nuptials

Nuptials of Peleus and Thetis.

Hughes, John.-----The Mifanthrope; Calypfo and Telemachus; Apollo and Daphne; The Siege of Damafcus; Oreftes, unfinifhed; The Mifer; Cupid and Hymen; Amalafont, Queen of the Goths*; Sophy Mirza*.

Hull, Thomas.---The Abfent Man*; Pharnaces; The Spanifh Lady; All in the Right*; The Perplexities; The Fairy Favour; The Royal Merchant; The Pro-

digal Son; Henry the Second; or, The Fall of Rofamond; Edward and Eleonora; The Comedy of Errors*; Love will Find out the Way.

Humphrys, Mr.---Ulyffes.

Hunt, Wm.---The Fall of Tarquin.

Hurft, Robert.----The Roman Maid.

Hyde, Henry, Lord Hyde and Cornbury.-----The Miftakes; or, The Happy Refentment.

Hyland, Wm.----The Shipwreck.

J E

JACOB *Giles.*---Love in a Wood; Soldier's laft Stake.

Jacob, Sir Hildebrand.---The Fatal Conftancy; The Neft of Plays; The Prodigal Reform'd; The Happy Conftancy; The Tryal of Conjugal Love.

Jackman, Mr.------The Milefian; All the World's a Stage.

Jackman, Mr.---The Divorce.

Jockfon, Mr.---Elfrid*; The Britifh Heroine*; Sir Wm. Wallace*.

Jackfon, Mr.---The Metamorphofes.

Jaques, T.---The Queen of Corfica.

Jefferys, George.---Ed-

I N

win; Merope; Triumph of Truth.

Jenner, Charles.-----The Man of Family.

Jephfon, Robert.---Braganza; The Law of Lombardy; The Campaign; or, Love in the Eaft-Indies; Count of Narbonne; Julia; or, The Italian Lover.

Jerningham, Edward.---Margaret of Anjou*.

Jevon, Thomas.-----The Devil of a Wife.

Inchbald, Mrs.---Appearance is againft Them; Child of Nature; I'll tell you What; The Married Man; Midnight Hour; Such Things Are; Next Door Neighbours.

Ingeland,

J O

J O

Ingeland, Thomas.----The Difobedient Child.

Joddrel, Paul.---Widow and no Widow; Seeing is Believing.

Johnfon, Charles.----The Gentleman Cully; Fortune in her Wits; Love and Liberty; The Force of Friendfhip; Love in a Cheft; The Wife's Relief; or, The Hufband's Cure; The Succefsful Pirate; The Generous Hufband; or, The Coffee-houfe Politician; The Victim; The Country Laffes; or, The Cuftom of the Manor; The Cobler of Prefton; The Sultancfs; The Mafquerade; Love in a Foreft; The Female Fortuneteller; The Village Opera; The Ephefian Matron; Medea; Cælia; or, The Perjured Lover.

Johnfon, Dr. Samuel.---Hurlothrumbo; or, The Supernatural; Chefhire Comics; The Blazing Comet, The Mad Lovers; or, The Beauties of the Poets; All Alive and Merry*.

Johnfon, Richard.---Lucinda.

Jones, Henry.---Earl of Effex; The Cave of Idra, unfinifhed.

Jones, John.---Adrafta.

Jonfon, Ben.------Every Man in his Humour; Every man out of his Humour; Cynthia's Revels; or, The Fountain of Love; Poe-

tafter; or, His Arraignment; Sejanus, his Fall;. Part of King James's Entertainment in pafling to his Coronation; A particular Entertainment of Queen and Prince at Althorpe, June 25, 1603; A private Entertainment of the King and Queen on May-Day in the Morning, at Sir William Cornwallis's Houfe at Highgate; Volpone; or, The Fox; The Queen's Mafque of Blackneis; The Entertainment of the two Kings of Great Britain and Denmark, at Theobald's, July 24, 1606; Hymenæi; or, The Solemnities of Mafque and Barriers at Court, on the marriage of the Earl of Effex and Lady Frances, fecond daughter to the Earl of Suffolk; An Entertainment of King James and Queen Anne at Theobald's, 22d of May 1607; The Mafque of Beauty prefented at Whitehall on Twelfth-Night, 1608; A Mafque with Nuptial Songs at Lord Vifcount Haddington's marriage at Court, on Shrove-Tuefday at night, 1608; The Mafque of Queens celebrated at Whitehall, Feb. 2, 1609; Epicœne; or, The Silent Woman; The Cafe is Altered; The Speeches at Prince Henry's Barriers; Oberon, the Fairy Prince; The Alchymift;

chymift; Love freed from Ignorance and Folly; Love Reftored; A Challenge at Tilt at a Marriage; Catiline, his Confpiracy; The Irifh Mafque at Court; Mercury vindicated from the Alchemifts at Court; Bartholomew Fair; The Golden Age reftored; Chriftmas, his Mafque; The Devil is an Afs; A Mafque at Lord Hay's, for the Entertainment of Monfieur Le Baron de Tour, Ambaffador Extraordinary from the French King, Feb. 22, 1617; The Vifion of Delight; Pleafure reconciled to Virtue; For the Honour of Wales; News from the new World difcovered in the Moon; The Metamorphofed Gipfies; The Mafque of Augurs, with the feveral Anti-mafques prefented on Twelfth-Night, 1623; Time vindicated to himfelf and to his Honours; M. prefented on Twelfth-Night, 1623; Neptune's Triumph for the Return of Albion, M. prefented Twelfth-night, 1624;

Pan's Anniverfary; or, The Shepherd's Holiday; The Staple of News; Mafque of Owls at Kenelworth; The Fortunate Ifles and their Union; New Inn; or, The Light Heart; Love's Triumph through Callipolis; Chloridia, Rites to Chloris and her Nymphs; The King's Entertainment at Welbeck, in Nottinghamfhire, at his going to Scotland, 1633; Love's Welcome. The King and Queen's Entertainment at Bolfover, at the Earl of Newcaftle's, the 30th of July 1654; Magnetic Lady; or, Humours reconciled; A Tale of a Tub; The Sad Shepherd; or, A Tale of Robin Hood, unfinifhed; Mortimer's Fall, unfinifhed.

Jordan, Thomas.——The Walks of Iflington and Hogfdon, with the Humours of Wood-ftreet Compter; Fancy's Feftivals; Money is an Afs; Love hath found out his Eyes*.

Joyner, Wm.——Roman Emprefs.

K E   K E

KEATE. *George, Efq.*--- The Monument in Arcadia.

Keefe, John.——Tony Lumkin in Town, or, The Dilettanti; The Son-in-

Law*; The Dead Alive; Agreeable Surprife; Banditti; or, Love's Labyrinth; The Beggar on Horfeback; Blackfmith of Antwerp; The Czar; The Farmer;

Counterfeits ; Country Innocence ; Rambling Justice.

Leapor, Mary.---The Unhappy Father.

Lediard, Thomas.----Britannia.

Lee, Nathaniel.---Nero, Emperor of Rome ; Sophonisba ; or, Hannibal's Overthrow ; Gloriana ; or, The Court of Augustus ; The Rival Queens ; er, Alexander the Great ; Mithridates, King of Pontus ; Theodosius ; or, The Force of Love ; Cæsar Borgia ; Lucius Junius Brutus ; Constantine the Great ; The Princefs of Cleve ; The Maffacre of Paris.

Lee, John.----Macbeth ; The Country Wife ; The Man of Quality.

Lee, Miss.---The Chapter of Accidents ; The New Peerage ; or, Our Eyes may Deceive Us.

Legg, Thomas.------The Deftruction of Jerufalem* ; The Life of King Richard the Third*.

Leigh, John.---Kenfington-Gardens ; Hob's Wedding.

Lennox, Mrs. Arabella.---Philander ; The Sifter ; Old City Manners.

Lefley, George.---Dives's Doom ; or, The Rich Man's Mifery ; Fire and Brimftone ; or, The Deftruction

of Sodom ; Abraham's Faith.

Lewis, David.----Philip of Macedon.

Lewis, Edward, M. A. ----The Italian Hufband ; or, The Violated Bed Avenged.

Lillo, George.----Sylvia, or, The Country Burial ; The London Merchant ; or, The Hiftory of George Barnwell ; The Chriftian Hero ; The Fatal Curiofity ; Marina ; Britannia and Batavia ; Elmerick ; or, Juftice Triumphant. Arden of Feverfham.

Lloyd, Robert. —— The Tears and Triumphs of Parnaffus ; Arcadia ; or, The The Shepherd's Wedding ; The New School for Women ; The Death of Adam ; The Capricious Lovers.

Lockman, John.---Rofalinda ; David's Lamentations.

Lodge, Thomas, M. D.---- Wounds of Civil War ; Looking-Glafs for London and England ; Lady Alimony ; Laws of Nature ; Liberalitie and Prodigalitie ; Luminalia.

Love, James.---Pamela ; The Village Wedding ; Timon of Athens ; The Ladies Frolick ; City Madam*.

Lovelace, Richard.---The Scholar * ; The Soldier*.

Lower,

Lower, Sir William, Knt.
---Phœnix in her Flames ;
Polyeuctes ; or, The Mar-
tyr ; Horatius ; Inchanted
Lovers ; Noble Ingrati-
tude ; Amorous Phantafm.

Lucas, Henry.--The Earl
of Somerfet ; Love in Difguife.

Lylly, or Lilly John.----
Alexander and Campafpe ;
Endimion ; Sappho and

Phaon ; Galatea ; Mydas ;
Mother Bombie ; Woman
in the Moon ; Maid her
Metamorphofis ; Love his
Metamorphofis.

Lynch, Francis, Efq.----
The Independent Patriot ;
The Man·of Honour.

Lyon, William.------The
Wrangling Lovers ; or, Like
Mafter Like Man.

M A

MACHIN, Lewis.---
The Dumb Knight.
Mackenfie, H.------The
Prince of Tunis.

Macklin, Charles.---King
Henry the Seventh ; or, The
Popifh Impoftor ; A Will
and no Will ; or, A New
Cafe for the Lawyers* ;
The Sufpicious Hufband
Criticized ; or, The Plague
of Envy* ; The Fortune
Hunters ; or, The Widow
Bewitched* ; Love-à-la-
Mode* ; The Married Li-
bertine* ; The Irifh Fine
Lady* ; The True-born
Scotchman* ; fince afted at
Covent Garden, under the
title of the Man of the
World.

M'Nally.---April Fool ;
Fafhionable Levities ; Retaliation ; Triftram Shandy.

Madden, Dr. Samuel.---
Themiftocles, the Lover of
his Country.

Maidwell, L.---The Lov-

M A

ing Enemies.

Mallet, David.---Eury-
dice ; Muftapha ; Alfred ;
Britannia ; Elvira.

Manley, De la Reviere.---
The Royal Mifchief ; The
Loft Lovers ; or, The Jealous Hufband ; Almyna ;·
or, The Arabian Vow ; Lu-
cius, the Firft Chriftian
King of Britain.

Manning, Francis.--The
Generous Choice ; All for
the Better ; or, The Infallible Cure.

Manuche, Major Cofmo.--
The Juft General ; The
Loyal Lovers ; The Baf-
tard.

Markham, Gervafe, Efq.
---Herod and Antipater.

Marloe, Chriftopher.----
Tamberlaine the Great ;
Edward II. ; The Maffacre
of Paris ; The Tragical
Hiftory of Dr. Fauftus ;
The Jew of Malta ; Luft's

M A

Dominion; or, The Lascivious Queen.

Marmion, Shakerley.-,--
Holland's Leaguer; Fine
Companion; Antiquary;
The Crafty Merchant; or,
The Souldier'd Citizen*.

Marsh, Charles.- -Amasis King of Egypt; Cymbeline; The Winter's Tale;
Romeo and Juliet*.

Marshall, Mr.---German
Hotel; School for Arrogance.

Marston, John.----Antonio and Mellida; Antonio's
Revenge; Infatiate Countess; Malecontent; Dutch
Courtezan; Parafitalter;
Sophonifba; What you Will.

Martyn Benjamin, Esq.--
Timoleon.

Mason, William.------Elfrida; Caractacus.

Massinger, Philip.---Virgin Martyr; Duke of Milan; Bondman; Roman
Actor; Renegado; Picture;
Emperor of the East; Maid
of Honour; Fatal Dowry;
New Way -to pay Old
Debts; Great Duke of Florence; Unnatural Combat;
Bashful Lover; Guardian;
Very Woman; Old Law;
City Madam; The Noble
Choice; or, The Orator*;
The Wandering Lovers;
or, the Painter*; The Italian Night-piece; or, The
Unfortunate Piety*; The
Judge; or, Believe as you
List*; The Prisoner; or,
The Fair Anchoress*; The

M I

Spanish Viceroy; or, The
Honour of Woman*; Minerva's Sacrifice; or, The
Forc'd Lady*; The Tyrant*; Philenzo and Hippolita*; Antonio and Vallia*; Fast and Welcome*.

Maxwel·, John.-----The
Royal Captive; The Loves
of Princee Emelia and Louifa; The Diftreffed Virgin.

May, Thomas, Esq.—Antigone; The Heir; Agrippina, Emprefs of Rome;
Cleopatra, Queen of Egypt;
Old Couple.

Mayne, Jasper, D. D.—
The City Match; Amorous
War.

Mead, Robert, M. D.—
The Combat of Love and
Friendship.

Meilan, Mark Antony.—
Emilia; Northumberland;
The Friends.

*Melmouth, Courtney. See
Pratt Robert.*

Mendez, Mofes, Esq.——
Chaplet; Shepherd's Lottery; The Double Difappointment.

Meriton, Thomas.—Love
and War; Wandering Lovers.

Merry, Mr.—Lorenzo.

Meftayer, Henry.—Perfidious Brother.

Michelborne, John.—Ireland Preferved; or, Siege of
Londonderry.

Middleton, Thomas.——
Blurt, Mr. Conftable; Phœnix;

MO

nix; Michaelmas Term; Your Five Gallants; Family of Love; Mad World my Mafters; Trick to catch the Old One; Roaring Girl; Fair Quarrel; Inner Temple mafque; World tofs'd at Tennis; Game at Cheffe; Chafte Maid in Cheapfide; Widow; Changeling; Spanifh Gypfie; Old Law; No Wit, no help like a Woman's; More Diffemblers befides Women; Women beware Women; Mayor of Quinborough; Any Thing for a quiet Life; The Puritan Maid, Modeft Wife, and Wanton Widow*.

Miles, Wm. Auguftus.— Summer Amufements; or, An Adventure at Margate; The Artifice.

Miller, James.—The Humours of Oxford; Mother-in-Law; or, The Doctor the Difeafe; The Man of Tafte; Univerfal Paffion; The Coffee-houfe; Art and Nature; An Hofpital for Fools; Mahomet the Impofter; Jofeph and his Brethren; The Picture; or, The Cuckold in Conceit.

Milton, John.—Comus; Sampfon Agoniftes.

Mitchell, Jofeph.—Fatal Extravagance; The Highland Fair.

Molloy, Charles, Efq.— Perplexed Couple; Coquet; Half-pay Officers.

MO

Moncrief, John.----Appius.

Montague, Walter.—The Shepherd's Paradife.

More, Hannah.---Search after Happinefs; The Inflexible Captive; Percy; Fatal Falfhood.

Morell, Thomas.---Hecuba; Prometheus in Chains.

Moore, Edw.------Foundling; Gil Blas; Gamefter.

Moore, Sir Thomas.------ Mangora, King of the Timbufians.

Morgan, McNamara, Efq. ---Philoclea.

Mofs, Theophilus.----The General Lover.

Motteux, Peter Anthony. —Love's a Jeft; Loves of Mars and Venus; Novelty; Europe's Revels; Beauty in Diftrefs; Ifland Princefs; Four Seafons; Acis and Galatea; Britain's Happinefs; Arfinoe, Queen of Cyprus; Amorous Mifer; Temple of Love; Thomyris, Queen of Scythia; Love's Triumph; Love Dragoon'd.

Motley, John, Efq.------ Imperial Captives; Antiochus; Penelope; Craftfman; Widow bewitch'd.

Mountfort, Wm.—Injured Lovers; Edward the Third; Greenwich Park; Succefsful Strangers; Life and Death of Dr. Fauftus; Zelmane,

Mozeen, Wm.—The Heirefs; or, The Antigallican.

Murphy,

M U

Murphy, Arthur.—The Apprentice; The Spouter; or, The Triple Revenge; The Englishman from Paris*; The Upholsterer; or, What News; The Orphan of China; The Desert Island; The Way to keep Him; All in the Wrong; The Old Maid; The Citizen; No one's Enemy but his own; What we must all come to; The School for Guardians; Zenobia; The Grecian Daughter; Alzuma; News from Parnassus*; Know your own Mind.

N E

NABBES, *Thomas.*—Microcofmus; Hannibal and Scipio; Covent-Garden; Spring's Glory; Entertainment on the Prince's Birth Day; Tottenham Court; Unfortunate Mother; Bride.

Nash, Thomas.——Dido, Queen of Carthage; Summer's last Will and Testament; The Isle of Dogs*.

Nevil, Robert.—The Poor Scholar.

N O

Nevill, Alexander.—Oedipus.

Newman, Thomas.—Andria; Eunuch.

Newton, Thomas.—Thebais.

Newton, James.—Alexis's Paradife; or, A Trip to the Garden of Love at Vauxhall.

Norris, Henry.——Royal Merchant; The Deceit.

North, Hon. Francis.—The Kentish Barons.

O G

OBRIEN, *William.*----Crofs Purpofes; The Duel.

Odell, Thomas, Efq.——Chimera; Patron; Smugglers; Prodigal.

Odingfells, Gabriel.——The Bath unmasked; The Capricious Lovers; Bayes's Opera.

Ozborne, David.—The Merry Midnight Mistake; or, Comfortable Conclafion.

O T

Ohara, Kane.—Midas; The Golden Pippin; The Two Mifers; April Day; Tom Thumb.

Oldmixon, John.—Amyntas; Grove; or, Love's Paradife; Governor of Cyprus.

Otway, Thomas.—Alcibiades; Don Carlos Prince of Spain; Titus and Berenice; The Cheats of Scapin; Friendship in Fafhion; Caius Marius; The Orphan;

phan; The Soldier's For-
tune; Venice Preferved;
The Atheift; or the fecond
part of the Soldier's Fortune.
D'Ouville, Geo. Gerbier.
—The Falfe Favourite Dif-
graced.
Owen, Rob. Efq.—Hy-

permneftra.
Ozell, John.—The Cid;
or, The Heroic Daughter;
Alexander the Great; Bri-
tannicus; The Litigants;
Manlius Capitolinus; Ca-
to; The Fair of St. Ger-
mains; The Mifer; The
Plague of Riches.

P E

PALSGRAVE, *John.*—
Accolaftus.
Parfre, Ihan.—Candle-
mas Day; or, The Killing
of the Children of Ifrael.
Paterfon, William.—Ar-
minius.
Paton Mr.—William
and Lucy.
Payne, Nevil.——The
Fatal Jealoufy; The Morn-
ing Ramble; or, The Town
Humours; The Siege of
Conftantinople.
Peaps, Wm.—Love in its
Extafy.
Peck, Francis.—Herod
the Great.
Peele, George, M. A.——
The Arrangement of Paris;
Edward the Firft; King
David and Fair Bethfabe;
The Turkifh Mahomet and
Hyren the Fair Greek*.
Percy, Thomas, D. D.—
The Little Orphan of
China; or, The Houfe of
Chao.
Peterfon, Jofeph.——The
Raree Show; or, The Fox
trapt.

P I

Phillips, Ambrofe.—Dif-
treft Mother; The Briton;
Humphry Duke of Glou-
cefter.
Phillips, Edward.—The
Chambermaid; Mock Law-
yer; Livery Rake and
Country Lafs; Royal
Chace; or, Merlin's Cave;
Britons ftrike Home; or,
The Sailors Rehearfal.
Phillips, John.—Earl of
Mar marr'd; Pretender's
Flight; Inquifition.
Phillips, R.—Fatal In-
conftancy.
Philips, William, Efq.—
The Revengeful Queen;
Hibernia Freed; St. Ste-
phen's Green; Belifarius.
Phillips, T.—Love and
Glory.
Phillips, Catherine.——
Pompey; Horace.
Pilkington, Mrs. Lætitia.
—The Turkifh Court; or,
The London 'Prentice*.
Pilon, F.—The Invafion;
or, A Trip to Brighthelm-
ftone; The Liverpool Prize;
The Illumination; or, The
Glaziers

Glaziers Confpiracy ; The Device ; or, The Deaf Doctor* ; The Deaf Lover ; The Siege of Gibraltar ; The Humours of an Election ; Thelypthora : Aeroftation ; or, Templar's Stratagem ; Barataria ; or, Sancho turned Governor ; Fair American.

Pitcairne, Dr. Archibald. ---The Affembly.

Pix, Mrs. Mary.—The Spanifh Wives ; Abrahim the Thirteenth, Emperor of the Turks ; The Innocent Miftrefs ; The Deceiver deceived ; Queen Catherine ; or, The Ruins of Love ; The Falfe Friend ; or, The Fate of Difobedience : The Czar of Mufcovy ; The Double Diftrefs ; The Conqueft of Spain ; The Beau Defeated ; or, The Lucky Younger Brother.

Popple, William.-----The Lady's Revenge ; or, The Rover Reclaimed ; The Double Deceit ; or, A Cure for Jealoufy.

Pordage, Samuel.——— Troades ; Herod and Mariamne ; Siege of Babylon.

Portal, Abraham.---Olindo and Sophronia ; The Indifcreet Lover ; The Cady of Bagdad.

Porter, Henry.——The Two angry Women of Abington.

Porter, Thomas.---Villain ; Carnival.

Potter, Henry.---The Decoy.

Potter, R.---Prometheus chain'd ; The Supplicants ; The feven Chiefs againft Thebes ; Agamemnon ; The Choephoræ ; The Furies ; The Perfians ; Alceftis ; The Bacchæ.

Pottinger, Ifrael.----The Methodift ; The Humourous Quarrel ; or, The Battle of the Greybeards.

Powell, George.——Alphonfo King of Naples ; A very Good Wife ; Treacherous Brothers ; The Impofture defeated ; or, A Trick to cheat the Devil ; The Cornifh Comedy ; Bonduca ; or, The Britifh Heroine ; A new Opera called Brutus of Alba ; or, Augufta's Triumph.

Pratt, Robert.-----Jofeph Andrews* ; School for Vanity.

Preftwich, Edmund.----- Hippolitus.

Puttenham, Mr.---Luftie London ; The Wocr ; Ginecocratia*.

Q U

QUARLES, FRANCIS, Efq.-----The Virgin Widow.

RADCLIFF,

R*ADCLIFF, RALPH.* ---Dives and Lazarus* ; Patient Grifeld; Friendfhip of Titus and Gefippus ; Chaucer's Melebec* ; Job's Afflictions ; The Burning of Sodom* ; The Delivery of Sufannah ; The Burning of John Hufs ; Jonas ; Fortitude of Judith*.

Ralph, James, Efq.----- Fafhionable Lady ; or, Harlequin's Opera ; Fall of the Earl of Effex ; Lawyer's Feaft ; Aftrologer.

Ramfay, Allan.----The Nuptials ; The Gentle Shepherd.

Randolph, Thomas.----- Ariftippus ; Conceited Pedlar ; Jealous Lovers ; Mufes Looking-Glafs ; Amyntas ; Hey for Honefty, Down with Knavery.

Ravenfcroft, Edward.--- Mamamouchi ; Carelefs Lovers ; Scaramouch, a Philofopher, &c. ; Wrang-,ling Lovers ; King Edgar and Alfreda ; Englifh Lawyer ; London Cuckolds ; Dame Dobfon ; Titus Andronicus ; The Canterbury Guefts ; Anatomift ; Italian Hufband.

Rawlins, Thomas, Efq.--- Rebellion ; Tom Effence ; Tunbridge-Wells.

Reed, Jofeph.--- The Superannuated Gallant ; Madrigal and Tulletta ; The

Regifter Office ; Dido* ; Tom Jones.

Revet, Edward.---The Town Shifts.

Reynolds, John.---The Crufade ; Eloifa.

Rhodes, Richard, M. D. ---Flora's Vagaries.

Richard, Nathaniel.----- Meffalina, the Roman Emprefs.

Richardfon, Elizabeth.--- The Double Deception.

Rider, Wm. M. A.---The Twins.

Ridley, Dr. Glofler.------ Jugurtha* ; The Fruitlefs Redrefs*.

Roberts, Mifs.-----Malcolm.

Robinfon, Maria.----The Lucky Efcape.

Rogers, Richard.---Ponteach ; or, The Savages of America.

Rolt, Richard.---Eliza ; The Royal Shepherd ; Almena.

Roome, Edward.---Jovial Crew.

Rowe, Nicholas, Efq.---- The Ambitious Step-Mother ; Tamerlane ; Fair Penitent ; The Biter ; Ulyffes; Royal Convert ; Jane Shore; Lady Jane Grey.

Rowley, Samuel.---When You fee me You know me ; Noble Spanifh Soldier.

Rowley, William.----New Wonder, a Woman never vext ; All's loft by Luft ;
Match

Match at Midnight ; Shoe-
maker is a Gentleman ;
Birth of Merlin ; Witch of
Edmonton ; The Fool with-
out Book* ; A Knave in
print ; or, One for another* ;
The None Such* ; Book of
the four honourable Loves* ;

The Parliament of Love*.

Rutter, Joseph.---Shep-
herd's Holiday ; Cid.

Rymer, Thomas.----Ed-
gar.

Ryves, Elizabeth.---The
Prude.

S E

*SACKVILLE, Thomas,
Lord Buckhurst.*---Fer-
rex and Porrex.

Sadler, Thomas.------The
Merry Miller ; or, Countryman's Ramble.

Sampson, William.---The
Vow Breaker ; Widow's
Prize*.

Savage, Richard.---Love
in a Veil ; Sir Tho. Overbury.

Saunders, Charles.---Ta-
merlane the Great.

Scawen, Mr.------New
Spain ; or, Love in Mexi-
co.

Schomberg, Ralph, M. D.
---The Death of Bucepha-
lus ; Judgment of Paris ;
Romulus and Hersilia.

Scott, Thomas.----Mock
Marriage ; Unhappy Kind-
ness.

Sedaine, Monf.---Richard
Coeur de Lion.

Sedley, Sir Charles, Bart.
---The Mulberry Garden ;
Anthony and Cleopatra ;
Bellamira ; or, The Mif-
trefs ; Beauty the Conquer-
or ; or, The Death of Mark

S E

Anthony ; The Grumbler ;
Tyrant King of Crete.

Settle, Elkanah.--Camby-
fes, King of Perfia ; Emprefs
of Morocco ; Love and Re-
venge ; The Conqueft of
China by the Tartars ; Ibrahim, the Illuftrious Baffa ;
Paftor Fido ; or, The Faithful Shepherd ; Fatal Love ;
or, The Forced Inconftan-
cy ; The Female Prelate ;
The Heir of Morocco ;
Diftreffed Innocence ; or,
The Princefs of Perfia ;
Ambitious Slave ; or, A
generous Revenge ; Phi-
lafter ; or, Love lies a bleeding ; The World in the
Moon ; The Virgin Prophe-
tefs ; or, The Fate of Troy ;
City-Ramble ; or, Play-
houfe Wedding ; The Siege
of Troy ; The Ladies Tri-
umph.

Sewell, Dr. George.---Sir
Walter Raleigh ; K. Rich-
ard the Firft, unfinifhed.

Shadwell, Charles.---Fair
Quaker of Deal ; Humours
of the Army ; Hafty Wed-
ding ; Sham Prince ; Rotheric

ric O'Conner ; Plotting Lovers ; Irifh Hofpitality.

Shadwell, Thomas.—— The Sullen Lovers ; or, The Impertinent ; Royal Shepherdefs ; The Humourift ; The Mifer ; Epfom Wells ; Pfyche ; The Libertine ; The Virtuofo ; Hiftory of Timon of Athens, the Manhater ; A true Widow ; The Woman Captain ; The Lancafhire Witches, and Teague O'Divelly, the Irifh Prieft ; Squire of Alfatia ; Bury Fair ; Amorous Bigot, with the fecond part of Teague O'Divelly ; The Scowerers ; The Volunteers ; or, The Stock-Jobbers.

Shakfpeare, William, born April, 16, 1564, and died April 23, 1616.——Titus Andronicus ; Love's Labour Loft ; Firft part of King Henry VI. ; Second part of King Henry VI. ; Third part of King Henry VI. ; Pericles ; Locrine ; Two Gentlemen of Verona ; Winter's Tale ; A Midfummer's Night's Dream ; Romeo and Juliet ; The Comedy of Errors ; Hamlet ; King John ; King Richard II. ; King Richard III. ; Firft part of King Henry IV. ; The Merchant of Venice ; All's well that ends Well ; Sir John Oldcaftle ; Second part of King Henry IV. ; King Henry V. ; The

Puritan ; Much ado about Nothing ; As you Like It ; Merry Wives of Windfor ; King Henry the Eighth ; Life and Death of Lord Cromwell ; Troilus and Creffida ; Meafure for Meafure ; Cymbeline ; London Prodigal ; King Lear ; Macbeth ; The Taming of the Shrew ; Julius Cæfar ; A Yorkfhire Tragedy ; Antony and Cleopatra ; Coriolanus ; Timon of Athens ; Othello ; Tempeft ; Twelfth Night.

Sharp, Lewis.——The Noble Stranger.

Sharpman, Edward.—— The Fleire.

Sheffield, John, Duke of Buckingham.---Julius Cæfar ; Marcus Brutus.

Shepherd, Richard.—Hector ; Bianca.

Sheppard, S.—Committee Man curried.

Sherburne, Sir Edward, Knt.—Medea ; Troades ; Phædra and Hippolitus.

Sheridan, Dr. Tho.—Philoftetes.

Sheridan, Thomas, M. A.—Captain O'Blunder ; Coriolanus ; Loyal Subjeft ; Romeo and Juliet.

Sheridan, Richard Brinfley.—The Rivals ; St. Patrick's Day ; or, The Scheming Lieutenant* ; Duenna* ; A Trip to Scarborough* ; The School for Scandal* ; The Camp* ; The

The Critic; or, A Tragedy rehearfed*.

Sheridan, Frances.—The Difcovery; Dupe.

Sheridan, Miss.—Ambiguous Lover.

Shipman, Thomas.—Hen. III. of France.

Shirley, Henry.——The Martyr'd Soldier; Spanifh Duke of Lerma*; Duke of Guize*; The Dumb Bawd*; Giraldo the Conftant, Lover*.

Shirley, James.——The Wedding; The Grateful Servant; School of Compliments; The Changes; or, Love in a Maze; Contention for Honour and Riches; Witty Fair-One; Triumphs of Peace; Bird in a Cage; The Traytor; Lady of Pleafure; Young Admiral; The Example; Hyde Park; The Gamefter; The Royal Mafter; Duke's Miftrefs; Maid's Revenge; Chabot, Admiral of France; The Ball; Arcadia; Humorous Courtier; The Opportunity; St. Patrick for Ireland; Love's Cruelty; The Conftant Maid; The Coronation; The Triumph of Beauty; The Brothers; The Sifters; The Doubtful Heir; The Impofter; The Cardinal; The Court Secret; Cupid and Death; The Politician; The Gentleman of Venice; The Contention of Ajax and Ulyffes for

Achilles' Armour; Honoria and Mammon; Andromana; or, The Merchant's Wife; St. Albons*; Looke to the Ladie*; Rofania; or, Love's Victory*.

Shirley, William.—The Parricide; King Pepin's Campaign; Edward the Black Prince; Electra; The Birth of Hercules; Roman Sacrifice*; The Roman Victim*; Alcibiades*; The Firft part of King Henry the Second*; Second part of King Henry the Second*; The Fall of Carthage*; All miftaken*; The Good Englifhman*; Fafhionable Friendfhip*; The Shepherds Courtfhip*.

Shuckborough, Charles.—Antiochus.

Skelton, John.—The Nigramanfir; Magnificence; The Comedy of Virtue*; The Comedy of Good Order*.

Slade, John.—Love and Duty.

Stuart, Chriftopher.—The Grateful Fair; Judgment of Midas; Hannah.

Smith, Edmund.—Phædra and Hippolitus.

Smith, Henry.—The Princefs of Parma.

Smith, John.——Cytherea.

Smith, William.—Hector of Germany; Freeman's Honour*; St. George for England*.

Smollet,

S T

Smollet, Tobias, M. D.-- The Regicide; The Reprisal; or, The Tars of Old England.

Smith, James Mooie, Esq. ---The Rival Modes.

Somervile, William.----- Elzira*.

Somner, Henry.---Orpheus and Euridice.

Southern, Thomas.--The Loyal Brother; The Disappointment; Sir Anthony Love; or, The Rambling Lady; The Wives' Excuse; or, Cuckolds make Themselves; The Maid's Last Prayer; or, Any Thing rather than Fail; The Fatal Marriage; or, The Innocent Adultery; Oroonoko; The Fate of Capua; The Spartan Dame; Money's the Mistress.

Stanley, Thomas.----The Clouds.

Stapleton, Sir Robert.--- The Slighted Maid; The Step-mother; Hero and Leander; The Royal Choice*.

Starke, Miss.---The Widow of Malabar.

Steele, Sir Richard.--The Funeral; or, Grief Alamode; The Tender Husband; or, The Accomplished Fools; The Lying Lover; or, The Ladies' Friendship; The Conscious Lovers; The Gentleman, unfinished; The School of

S U

Action, unfinished; Cynthia's Revenge.

Sterling, J.---The Rival Generals; The Parricide.

Stevens George Alexander. ---Distress upon Distress; or, Tragedy in true Taste; The French Flogged; or, The British Sailors in America; The Court of Alexander; The Trip to Portsmouth.

Stevens, John.-----The Modern Wife.

Stevens, Captain John.-- En Evening's Intrigue.

Stewart, Charles.--Cobler of Castlebury; Ripe Fruit; or, The Marriage Act; Damnation; or, Hissing Hot.

St. John, Mr.----Mary Queen of Scots.

Still, John.----Gammer Gurton's Needle.

Stockdale, Percival.----- Amyntas.

Stratford, Rev. Dr.--- Lord Ruffel.

Strode, Dr. William.--- The Floating Island.

Studly, John.--Agamemnon; Medea; Hercules Oetæus; Hippolitus.

Sturmy, John.--Love and Duty; The Compromise; Sefostris.

Suckling, Sir John.---- Discontented Colonel; Aglaura; The Goblins; The Sad One, unfinished; Brenoralt.

. Swiney,

S W

Swiney, Mac Owen.----
The Quack ; or, Love's the
Physician ; Camilla ; Pyr-
rhus and Demet. iu .

S Y

Swinhoe, Gilbert, Esq.--
The Unhappy Fair Irene ;
Sydney, Sir Philip.----The
Lady of May.

T A

TARLTON, Richard.--
The Seven deadly Sins.
Tate, Nahum.----Brutus
of Alba ; The Loyal Gene-
ral ; King Lear ; Richard
II. ; or, The Sicilian U-
surper ; The Ingratitude of
a Commonwealth ; or,
The Fall of Coriolanus ;
Cuckold's Haven ; or, an
Alderman no Conjurer ; A
Duke and No Duke ; The
Island Princess ; Injured
Love ; or, The Cruel Hus-
band.
Tatham, John.----Love
Crowns the End ; The Dif-
tracted State ; Scots Va-
garies ; or, a Knot of
Knaves ; The Rump, or,
The Mirror of late Times.
Taverner, William.----
The Faithful Bride of Gra-
nada ; The Maid the Mif-
trefs ; The Female Advo-
cates ; or, The Frantick
Stock-Jobbers ; The Art-
ful Husband ; The Artful
Wife ; 'Tis well if it
Takes ; Ixion * ; Every
Body Mistaken*.
Taylor, John.--The Scul-
ler* ; Fair and Foul Wea-
ther*.

T H

Theobald, Lewis.----Elec-
tra ; The Perfian Princefs ;
or, Royal Villain ; The
Perfidious Brother ; Oedi-
pus, King of Thebes ; Plu-
tus ; or, The World's Idol ;
The Clouds ; Pan and Sy-
rinx ; The Lady's Tri-
umph ; Decius and Pauli-
na ; Richard the Second ;
The Rape of Proferpine ;
Harlequin a Sorcerer ; A-
pollo and Daphne ; The
Double Falfhood ; or, The
Diftreft Lovers ; Oreftes ;
The Fatal Secret ; Orpheus
and Euridice ; The Happy
Captive ; Merlin ; or, The
Devil of Stonehenge ; Death
of Hannibal*.
Theobald, John.----Me-
rope.
Thompfon, Thomas.--The
Englifh Rogue ; Mother
Shipton.
Thompfon, Edward.-----
Hobby Horfe* ; The Fair
Quaker ; or, The Humours
of the Navy ; The Syrens ;
Saint Helena ; or, The Ifle
of Love*.
Thomfon, William.------
Gondibert and Birtha.
Thompfon, James.----So-
phonifba ;

T O

phonifba ; Agamemnon ; Edward and Eleonora ; Alfred ; Tancred and Sigifmunda ; Coriolanus.

Thornton, Bonnel.---Amphitrion ; Braggart Captain ; The Treafure ; The Mifer ; The Shipwreck.

Thurmond, John.—Harlequin Sheppard ; Apollo and Daphne ; or, Harlequin Mercury ; Harlequin Doctor Fauftus, with the Mafque of the Deities ; Apollo and Daphne ; or, Harlequin's Metamorphofes ; Harlequin's Triumph, &c,

Tollet, Elizabeth.----Sufannah ; or, Innocence Preferved.

Tomkis,Mr.--Albumazar.

Toms, Mr.—The Accomplifhed Maid.

Topham, Capt.----Weftminfter School-boy.

T U

Toofey, G. P.—Sebaftian.

Tourneur, Cyril.----The Revenger's Tragedy ; The Atheift's Tragedy ; The Nobleman.

Tracy, John.----Periander, King of Corinth.

Trapp, Dr. Jofeph.— Abramule ; or, Love and Empire.

Trotter, Catharine.--Agnes de Caftro ; Fatal Friendfhip ; The Unhappy Penitent ; Love at a Lofs ; or, Moft Votes carry It ; The Honourable Deceivers ; or, All Right at Laft* ; The Revolution of Sweden.

Tuke, Richard.--The Divine Comedian ; or The Right Ufe of Plays.

Tuke, Sir Samuel.—The Adventures of Five Hours ;

Tutchin, John.--The Unfortunate Shepherd.

V A

VANBRUGH, Sir John. —The Relapfe ; or, Virtue in Danger ; The Provoked Wife ; Æfop ; The Pilgrim ; The Falfe Friend ; The Confederacy ; The Miftake ; The Cuckold in Conceit* ; 'Squire Trelooby* ; The Country-houfe ; A journey to London, unfinifhed.

Vaughan, Tho.----Love's Metamorphofis ; The Hotel.

V I

Victor, Benjamin.—Two Gentlemen of Verona ; Altemira ; The Fatal Error ; The Fortunate Peafant ; or, Nature will Prevail ; The Sacrifice ; or, Cupid's Vagaries.

Villiers, George, Duke of Buckingham.--The Rehearfal ; The Chances ; The Battle of Sedgemore ; The Reftoration.

WA-

WAGER *Lewis.*—— Mary Magdalene, her Lyfe and Repentance.

Waldron, Mr.--The Maid of Kent ; The Contraſt* ; The Richmond Heireſs*.

Walker, Thomas.—The Fate of Villainy.

Walker, William.—Victorious Love ; Mary ; or, Do Worſe.

Walker, T.—The Wit of a Woman.

Wallace, Lady.------The Ton ; or, Follies of Faſhion.

Waller, Edmund, Eſq.—Pompey the Great ; The Maid's Tragedy.

Wallis, George.------The Mercantile Lovers.

Walpole, Horace.-----The Myſterious Mother.

Warboys, Thomas.---The Preceptor ; The Rival Lovers.

Ward, Edward.-----The Humours of a Coffee-houſe.

Ward, Henry.--The Happy Lovers ; or, The Beau Metamorphoſed ; The Petticoat Plotter ; or, More Ways than one for a Wife ; The Widow's Wiſh ; or, An Equipage of Lovers.

Weaver John.——The Loves of Mars and Venus ; Orpheus and Euridice ; Perſeus and Andromeda ; The Judgment of Paris.

Webſter, John.-----The White Devil; or, Tragedie

of P. Giordano Urſini, Duke of Brachiano, with the Life and Death of Victoria Corombona, the famous Venetian Courtezan ; The Devil's Law-Caſe ; or, When Women go to Law, the Devil is full of Buſineſs ; The Ducheſs of Malfey ; Appius and Virginia ; The Thracian Wonder; A Cure for a Cuckold.

Welſted, Leonard.—The Diſſembled Wanton, or, My Son get Money.

Weſt, Gilbert.—The Inſtitution of the Order of the Garter ; Iphigenia in Tauris ; The Triumphs of the Gout.

Weſt, Matthew.---Ethelinda ; or, Love and Duty.

Weſt, Richard.—Hecuba.

Weſton, John, Eſq.--The Amazonian Queen ; or, The Amours of Thaleſtris and Alexander.

Weſtbury, James.--Paul, the Spaniſh Sharper.

Whincop, Thomas, Eſq.—Scanderbeg ; or, Love and Liberty.

Whitaker, William.—The Conſpiracy ; or, Change of Government.

Whitehead, William.—The Roman Father ; Fatal Conſtancy ; Creuſa, Queen of Athens; The School for Lovers ; A Trip to Scotland.

Wignell,

A SHORT

A

SHORT SKETCH

OF THE

RISE AND PROGRESS

OF THE

ENGLISH STAGE.

THE learned are well acquainted at what expence the
Athenians supported their Theatres, and how often,
from among their Poets, they chose Governors of their
Provinces, Generals of their Armies, and Guardians of
their Liberties.---Who were more jealous of their liberties
than the Athenians? Who better knew that Corruption
and Debauchery are the greatest foes to Liberty? Who
better knew, than they, that the freedom of the Theatre
(next to that of the Senate) was the best support of Liberty, against all the undermining arts of those who wickedly
might seek to sap its foundation?-----The divine Socrates
assisted Euripides in his compositions. The wise Solon
frequented Plays, even in his decline of life; and Plutarch
informs us, he thought plays useful to polish the manners,
and instil the principles of virtue.

As Arts and Sciences increased in Rome, when Learning, Eloquence and Poetry flourished, Lælius improved
his social hours with Terence; and Scipio thought it not
beneath him to make one in so agreeable a party. Cæfar, who was an excellent Poet as well as Orator, thought
the former title an addition to his honour; and ever mentioned Terence and Menander with great respect. Auguftus found it easier to make himself Sovereign of the
world, than to write a good Tragedy: he began a Play
called Ajax, but could not finish it. Brutus, the virtuous,
the moral Brutus, thought his time not mis-employed in a
journey

journey from Rome to Naples, only to fee an excellent troop of Comedians; and was fo pleafed with their performance, that he fent them to Rome, with letters of recommendation to Cicero, to take them under his patronage :---The truly pious and learned Archbifhop Tillotfon, fpeaking of Plays, gives this teftimony in their fa. vour, that " they might be fo framed, and governed by " fuch rules, as not only to be innocently diverting, but " inftructive and ufeful, to put fome follies and vices out " of countenance, wh'ch cannot perhaps be fo decently " reproved, nor fo effectually expofed and corrected any. " other way."

It is generally imagined, that the Englifh Stage rofe later than the reft of its neighbours. Thofe who hold this opinion, will, perhaps, wonder to hear of Theatrical Entertainments almoft as early as the Conqueft ; and yet nothing is more certain, if you will believe an honeft Monk, one William Stephanides, or Fitz Stephen, in his *Defcriptio Nobiliffimæ Civitatis Londoniæ*, who writes thus : " London, inftead of common Interludes belonging " to the Theatre, has lays of a more holy fubject ; re- " prefentations of thofe Miracles which the holy Con- " feffors wrought, or of the fufferings wherein the glori- " ous conftancy of the Martyrs did appear." This Author was a Monk of Canterbury, who wrote in the reign of Henry II. and died in that of Richard I. 1191 ; and as he does not mention thefe reprefentations as Novelties to the people (for he is defcribing all the common diverfions in ufe at that time) we can hardly fix them lower than the Conqueft ; and this, we believe, is an earlier date than any other nation of Europe can produce for their Theatrical reprefentations. About 140 years after this, in the reign of Edward III. it was ordained by act of parliament, that a company of men called Vagrants, who had made Mafquerades through the whole City, fhould be whipt out of London, becaufe they reprefented fcandalous things in the little alehoufes, and other places where the populace affembled. What the nature of thefe fcandalous things were, we are not told ; whether lewd and obfcene, or impious and profane ; but we fhould rather think the former, for the word Mafquerade has an ill found, and, we believe, they were no better in their infancy than at prefent.

The

The year 1378 is the earlieft date we can find, in which
exprefs mention is made of the reprefentation of Myfteries
in England. In this year the Scholars of Paul's School
prefented a petition to Richard II. praying his Majefty,
" to prohibit fome unexpert people from prefenting the
" Hiftory of the Old Teftament, to the great prejudice
" of the faid Clergy, who have been at great expence in
" order to reprefent it publicly at Chriftmas." About
twelve years afterwards, viz. in 1390, the Parifh Clerks
of London are faid to have played Interludes at Skinner's
Well, July 18, 19, and 20. And again, in 1409, the
tenth year of Henry IV. they acted at Clerkenwell
(which took its name from this cuftom of the Parifh-clerks
acting plays there) for eight days fucceffively, a Play
concerning the creation of the World ; at which were prefent moft of the Nobility and Gentry of the Kingdom.
Thefe inftances are fufficient to prove that we had the
Myfteries here very early. How long they continued to
be exhibited amongft us cannot be exactly determined.
This period one might call the dead fleep of the Mufes.
And when this was over, they did not prefently awake,
but, in a kind of morning dream, produced the moralities
that followed. However, thefe jumbled ideas had fome
fhadow of meaning. The Myfteries only reprefented, in
a fenfelefs manner, fome miraculous Hiftory of the Old or
New Teftament ; but in thefe Moralities fomething of defign appeared, a Fable and a Moral ; fomething alfo of
Poetry, the virtues, vices, and other affections of the
mind being frequently perfonified. But the Moralities
were alfo very often concerned wholly in religious matters.
For Religion then was every one's concern, and it was no
wonder if each party employed all arts to promote it. The
Mufe might now be faid to be juft awake when fhe began
to trifle in the old interludes, and aimed at fomething like
wit and humour. And for thefe John Heywood the Epi-
grammift undoubtedly claims the earlieft, if not the foremoft place. He was Jefter to King Henry VIII. but lived till the beginning of Queen's Elizabeth's reign. *Gammer Gurton's Needle*, which is generally called our firft Comedy, and not undefervedly, appeared foon after the Interludes ; it is indeed altogether of a comic caft, and wants
not humour, though of a low and fordid kind. And now
Dramatic Writers, properly fo called, began to appear,
                                                        and

and turn their talents to the Stage. Henry Parker, fon of Sir Wm. Parker, is faid to have written feveral Tragedies and Comedies in the reign of Henry VIII. and one John Hoker, in 1535, wrote a Comedy called *Pifcator*; or, *The Fifher caught*. Mr. Richard Edwards, who was born in 1523 (and in the beginning of Queen Elizabeth's reign was made one of the Gentlemen of her Majefty's Chapel, and Mafter of the Children there) being both an excellent Mufician, and a good Poet, wrote two Comedies, one called *Palæmon and Arcite*, in which a cry of hounds in hunting was fo well imitated, that the Queen and the audience were extremely delighted; the other, called *Damon and Pithias, the two faithfulleft Friends in the World*. About the fame time came Thomas Sackville, Lord Buckhurft, and Thomas Norton, the writers of *Gorboduc*, the firft dramatic Piece of any confideration in the Englifh language.

Though Tragedy and Comedy began now to lift up their heads, yet they could do no more for fome time than blufter and quibble; and how imperfect they were in all Dramatic Art, appears from an excellent criticifm, by Sir Philip Sidney, on the writers of that time. Yet all at once (as it happened in France, though in a much later period) the true Drama received birth and perfection from the creative genius of Shakfpeare, Fletcher, and Jonfon.

Having thus traced the Dramatic Mufe through all her characters and transformations, till fhe had acquired a reafonable figure, let us now return and take a more particular view of the Stage and the Actors. The firft Company of Players we have any acconnt of, is from a patent granted, in 1574, to James Burbage, and others, fervants to the earl of Leicefter. In 1578, the Children of Paul's appear to have been performers of Dramatic Entertainments. About twelve years afterwards the Parifh Clerks of London are faid to have acted the Myfteries at Skinner's Well. Which of thefe two Companies may have been the earlieft, is not certain; but as the Children of Paul's are firft mentioned, we muft in juftice give priority to them. It is certain, the Myfteries and Moralities were acted by thefe two Societies many years before any other regular Companies appeared. And the children of Paul's continued to act long after Tragedies

S and

and Comedies came in vogue. It is believed, the next Company regularly eftablifhed was, the Children of the Royal Chapel, in the beginning of Queen Elizabeth's reign ; and fome few years afterwards, as the fubject of the Stage became more ludicrous, a Company was formed under the denomination of *The Children of the Revels.* The Children of the Chapel and of the Revels became very famous ; and all Lillie's Plays, and many of Jonfon's and others, were firft acted by them. Indeed, fo great was their eftimation, that the common players grew jealous of them. However, they ferved as an excellent nurfery for the Theatres ; many, who afterwards became approved Actors, being educated among them.

It is furprizing to confider what a number of Playhoufes were fupported in London about this time. From the year 1750 to the year 1629, when the Play-houfe in White-Friars was finifhed, no lefs than feventeen Playhoufes had been built. The names of moft of them may be collected from the title pages of Old Plays. And as the Theatres were fo numerous, the Companies of Players were in proportion. Befides the Children of the Chapel, and of the Revels, we are told that Queen Elizabeth, at the requeft of Sir Francis Walfingham, eftablifhed in handfome falaries twelve of the principal players of that time, who went under the name of her Majefty's Comedians and Servants. But, exclufive of thefe, many Noblemen retained Companies of Players, who acted not only privately in their Lords houfes, but publicly under their licence and protection. Agreeable to this is the account which Stow gives us--" Players in former times," fays he, " were retainers to Noblemen, and none had the
" privilege to act Plays but fuch. So in Queen Eliza-
" beth's time, many of the Nobility had fervants and
" Retainers who were Players, and went about getting
" their livelihood that way. The Lord Admiral had
" Players, fo had Lord Strange, that played in the City
" of London. And it was ufual on any Gentleman's
" complaint of them for indecent reflections in their
" Plays, to have them put down." And in another part of
" his Survey of London, fpeaking of the Stage, he fays,
" This, which was once a recreation, and ufed therefore
" now and then occafionally, afterwards by abufe became
" a trade and calling, and fo remains to this day. In
          " thofe

" thofe former days, ingenious Tradefmen, and Gentle-
" mens Servants, would fometimes gather a Company
" of themfelves, and learn Interludes, to expofe vice, or
" to reprefent the noble actions of our anceftors. Thefe
" they played at feftivals, in private houfes, at weddings,
" or other entertainments, but in procefs of time it be-
" came an occupation; and thefe Plays being commonly
" acted on Sundays and Feftivals, the Churches were
" forfaken, and the Play-houfes thronged. Great Inns
" were ufed for this purpofe, which had fecret chambers
" and places, as well as open ftages and galleries. Here
" maids and good Citizens Children were inveigled
" and allured to private and unmeet contracts; here
" were publicly uttered popular and feditious matters,
" unchaite, uncomely and fhameful fpeeches, and
" many other enormities. The confideration of thefe
" things occafioned, in 1574, Sir James Hawes
" being Mayor, an act of Common Council, wherein
" it was ordained, That no play fhould be openly
" acted within the liberty of the City, wherein
" fhould be uttered any words, examples, or doings of
" any unchaftity, fedition, or fuch like unfit and uncome-
" ly matter, under the penalty of five Pounds, and 14
" days imprifonment. That no play fhould be acted till
" firft perufed and allowed by the Lord Mayor and Court
" of Aldermen; with many other reftrictions. But thefe
" orders were not fo well obferved as they fhould be; the
" lewd matters of Plays increafed, and they were thought
" dangerous to Religion, the State, Honefty and Man-
" ners, and alfo for infection in the time of ficknefs.
" Wherefore they were afterwards for fome time totally
" fuppreffed. But upon application to the Queen and
" Council, they were again tolerated under the following
" reftrictions. That no Plays be acted on Sundays at all,
" nor on any Holidays till after Evening Prayer. That
" no playing being in the dark, and that it be all over be-
" fore funfet. That the Queen's Players only be tolerat-
" ed, and of them their number and certain names to be
" notified in the Lord Treafurer's letters to the Lord
" Mayor, and to the Juftices of Middlefex and Surry.
" And thofe her Players not to divide themfelves in fe-
" veral cempanies. And that, for breaking any of
" thefe orders, their toleration ceafe. But all thefe pre-

fcriptions,

" scriptions were not sufficient to keep them within due
" bounds; but their plays, so abusive oftentimes of
" virtue, or particular persons, gave great offence, and
" occasioned many disturbances: when they were now
" and then stopped and prohibited." This shews the
the customs of the Stage at that time, and the early
depravity of it.

The Stage soon after recovered its credit, and rose to
a higher pitch than ever. In 1603, the first year of King
James's Reign, a licence was granted under the Privy
Seal to Shakspeare, Fletcher, Burbage, Hemmings,
Condel, and others, authorizing them to act Plays, not
only at their usual House, the Globe on the Bankside,
but in any other part of the Kingdom, during his Majesty's pleasure. And now, there lived together at this time
many eminent players, concerning whom we cannot but
lament such imperfect accounts are transmitted to us.
The little, however, which is known, the Reader will
find collected together, with great accuracy, by Mr. Malone, in his " Supplement to Shakspeare," to which
work we refer our readers for further information.

At this period, the Theatre seems to have been at its
height of glory and reputation. Dramatic Authors
abounded, and every year produced a number of new
Plays: Indeed, so great was the passion at this time for
shew or representation, that it was the fashion for the
nobility to celebrate their weddings, birth-days, and
other occasions of rejoicing, with Masques and Interludes,
which were exhibited with surprising expence; that great
Architect Inigo Jones being frequently employed to fur-
nish decorations with all the magnificence of his invention. The King and his Lords, the Queen and her Ladies, frequently performed in these Masques at Court, and
all the nobility in their own private houses: in short, no
public entertainment was thought compleat without them;
and to this humour it is we owe, and perhaps it is all we
owe it, the inimitable Masque at Ludlow-Castle. For
the same universal eagerness after Theatrical diversions
continued during the reign of King James, and great part
of Charles the First, till Puritanism, which had now gathered great strength, openly opposed them as wicked and
diabolical. But Puritanism, from a thousand concurrent
causes every day increasing, in a little time overturned the
constitution; and, amongst their many reformations this

was

was one, the total fuppreffion of all Plays and Play-houfes.

This event took place on the 11th day of February, 1647, at which time an Ordinance was iffued by the Lords and Commons, whereby all Stage Players, and Players of Interludes and common Plays, were declared to be Rogues, and liable to be punifhed according to the Statutes of the Thirty-ninth of Queen Elizabeth, and Seventh of King James the Firft. The Lord Mayor, Juftices of the Peace, and Sheriffs of the City of London and Weftminfter, and of the counties of Middlefex and Surrey, were likewife authorifed and required to pull down and demolifh all Playhoufes within their jurifdiction, and apprehend any perfons convicted of acting, who were to be publickly whipt; after which they were to be bound in a recognizance to act no more; and in cafe of a refufal to enter into fuch obligation, the parties were to be committed until they found fuch fecurity. If, after conviction, they offended again, they were thereby declared incorrigible rogues, and to be punifhed and dealt with as fuch. It was alfo declared, that all money collected at Play-houfes fhould be forfeited to the poor; and a penalty of 5s. was impofed on every perfon who fhould be prefent at any Dramatic Entertainment.

Before the promulgation of this fevere ordinance, the performances of the Stage had been frequently interrupted, even from the commencement of hoftilities between the King and his Parliament. Of the feveral Actors at that time employed in the Theatres, the greater part, who were not prevented by age, went immediately into the Army, and as it might be expected, took part with their Sovereign, whofe affection for their profeffion had been fhewn in many inftances previous to the open rupture bebetween him and his people. The event of war was alike fatal to Monarchy and the Stage. After a violent and bloody conteft, both fell together; the King loft his life by the hands of an Executioner; the Theatres were abandoned and deftroyed, and thofe by whom they ufed to be occupied were either killed in the wars, worn out with old age, or difperfed in different places, fearful of affembling, left they fhould fubject themfelves to the penalty of the Ordinance, and give offence to the ruling powers.

The

The fate of their Royal Mafter being determined, the furviving dependants on the drama were obliged again to return to the exercife of their former profeflion. In the winter of the year 1648, they ventured to act fome Plays at the Cockpit, but were foon interrupted and filenced by the foldiers, who took them into cuftody in the midft of one of their performances, and committed them to prifon. After this ineffectual attempt to fettle at their former quarters, we hear no more of any public exhibition for fome time. They ftill, however, kept together, and, by connivance of the commanding officer at White-hall, fometimes reprefented privately a few plays at a fhort diftance from town. They alfo were permitted to entertain fome of the Nobility at their country houfes, where they were paid by thofe under whofe protection they acted. They alfo obtained leave at particular fefti-vals to divert the public at the Red-Bull, but this was not always without interruption.

The avidity of the public for Theatrical Entertain-ments fufficiently recompenfed, for a confiderable time, the affiduity of the performers, and the expectations of the Managers and Proprietors. Their fuccefs was, how-ever, foon interrupted by national calamities. In 1665, the plague broke out in London with great violence; and in the fucceeding year, the fire which deftroyed the me-tropolis put a ftop to the further progrefs of Stage per-formances.

After a difcontinuance of eighteen months, both houfes were again opened at Chriftmas 1666. The miferies oc-cafioned by the plague and fire were forgotten, and pub-lic diverfions were again followed with as much eagernefs as they had been before their interruption. In January, 1671-2, the play-houfe in Drury-Lane took fire, and was entirely demolifhed. The violence of the conflagration was fo great, that between fifty and fixty adjoining houfes were burnt or blown up. The Proprietors of the Old Play-houfe, after they had recovered the confterna-tion which this accident had thrown them into, refolved to rebuild their Theatre with fuch improvement as might be fuggefted; and for that purpofe employed Sir Chriftopher Wren, the moft celebrated architect of his time, to draw the defign, and fuperintend the execution of it. The plan which he produced, in the opinion of thofe who were well able to judge of it, was fuch a one as

was

was alike calculated for the advantage of the Performers and Spectators ; and the several alterations afterwards made in it, so far from being improvements, contributed only to defeat the intention of the Architect, and to spoil the building.

The new Theatre, being finished, was opened on the 26th of March, 1674. On this occasion a Prologue and Epilogue were delivered, both written by Mr. Dryden. The new Theatre in Lincoln's-Inn-Fields was opened, on the 30th of April, 1695, with the new Comedy of *Love for Love*, which was acted with extraordinary success during the remainder of the season ; but the prosperity of the new House was of no long continuance. After one or two years success the audiences began to decline, and it was found that two rival Theatres were more than the town was able to support.

From the time that Mr. Rich got possession of Drury-Lane Theatre, he had paid no regard to the properties of any of the parties who had joint interests with him, but proceeded as though he was sole Proprietor of it. Whatever he received he kept to himself, without accounting to any of his Partners ; and he had continued this mode of conduct so long, that those who had any claims on the Theatre abandoned them in despair of ever receiving any advantage from them. The concerns of the Play-house were thought of so little worth, that about this time Sir Thomas Skipwith, who Cibber says had an equal right with Rich, in a frolic, made a present of his share to Colonel Brett, a gentleman of fortune, who soon after forced himself into the management, much against the inclination of his Partner. The ill effect of two Play-houses being open at once, in point of profit, appeared so evident to Mr. Brett, that the first object he dedicated his attention to, was a re-union of the two Companies, and, through the interposition of the Lord Chamberlain, he effected it in the year 1708. It was then resolved, that the Theatre in the Hay-Market should be appropriated to Italian Operas ; and that in Drury-Lane to Plays. The one was given to Swiney, and the other continued with Rich and Brett ; the latter of whom, conducting the business of it in a different manner from what it had heretofore been, brought it once more into so good a state, that Sir Thomas Skipwith repented of his generosity, and applied to the Court of Chancery to have the property he

S 4   had

had given away reſtored him. Colonel Brett, offended at this treatment, relinquiſhed his claim; and Mr. Rich again poſſeſſed himſelf of all the powers of the patent.

Inſtead of being warned, by the experience of paſt times, to avoid the difficulties which a tyrannical and oppreſſive behaviour to the Performers had created, the acting Manager reſumed his former conduct, without fearing or apprehending any reſiſtance to his meaſures.

William Collier, Eſq; a lawyer of an enterpriſing head and a jovial heart, obſerving the ſituation of theatrical affairs to be deſperate in the hands of Mr. Rich, applied for and obtained a licence to take the management of the Company left at Drury-Lane. The late Patentee, who ſtill continued in the Theatre, though without the power of uſing it, was not to be removed without compulſion. Mr. Collier, therefore, procured a leaſe of the houſe from the landlords of it, and, armed with this authority, took the advantage of a rejoicing night, the 22d of November, when, with a hired rabble, he broke into the premiſes, and turned the former owner out of poſſeſſion.

Here ended the power of Mr. Rich over the Theatres. After his expulſion from Drury-Lane, he employed the remainder of his life in re-building the Play-houſe in Lincoln's-Inn-Fields, which was opened about ſix weeks after his death by his ſon, in the year 1714, with the Comedy of *The Recruiting Officer*.

The ſcheme which Mr. Collier had engaged in did not proſper according to his wiſhes ; the profits of the ſeaſon were very ſmall, and by no means a compenſation for the trouble, riſk, and expence, which he had been at in ſeating himſelf on the theatrical throne. The joint-ſharers at the Hay-Market had acquired both fame and money ; he therefore meditated an exchange of Theatres with them, and, by again employing his influence at Court, ſoon effected it. By the agreement which was then entered into between the rival Managers, the ſole licence for acting Plays was veſted in Swiney and his partners ; and the performance of Operas was to be confined to the Hay-Market under the direction of Collier.

In the year 1714 Queen Anne died ; and, amongſt the changes which that event brought about, the management of Drury-Lane Theatre was not too inconſiderable to attract the notice of the Court. At the deſire of the acting

Manager

Managers, Sir Richard Steele procured his name to be inferted inftead of Collier's in a new licence jointly with
them ; and this connection lafted many years equally to the
advantage of all the parties. In this year the prohibition,
which the patent had been long under, was removed, and
Lincoln's-Inn-Fields Theatre opened under the direction
of the late Mr. John Rich.

No fooner were dramatic performances permitted at two
Theatres, than the Manager of the weaker Company was
obliged to have recourfe to foreign aid, and to oppofe his
antagonifts with other weapons than the merits of his actors, or the excellence of the pieces reprefented by them
The performers who were under Mr. Rich's direction were
fo much inferior to thofe at Drury-Lane, that the latter
carried away all the applaufe and favour of the town. In
this diftrefs, the genius of the new Manager fuggefted to
him a fpecies of entertainment, which hath always been
confidered as contemptible, but which at the fame time
hath been ever followed and encouraged. Pantomimes
were now brought forwards ; and, as found and fhew had
in the laft century obtained a victory over fenfe and reafon, the fame event would have followed again, if the
Company at Drury-Lane had not, from the experience of
paft times, thought it advifeable to adopt the fame mea-
fures. The fertility of Mr. Rich's invention in thefe
exotic entertainments, and the excellence of his own performance in them, muft be ever acknowledged. By
means of thefe only, he kept the Managers of the other
Houfe at all times from relaxing their diligence ; and, to
the difgrace of public tafte, frequently obtained more
money by fuch ridiculous and paltry performances than
all the fterling merit of the rival Theatre was able to acquire.

The bufinefs of the Stage was carried on fuccefsfully,
and without interruption, until about the year 1720, when
on a difguft which the Duke of Newcaftle, then Lord Chamberlain, had received from Mr. Cibber, that gentleman
was for fome time forbidden to perform ; and foon after
a difference arifing between the fame nobleman and Sir
Richard Steele, the power, which had been often exer-
cifed by the perfons who had held his Grace's office, was
exerted, and an order of filence was enforced againft the
Managers. On this occafion a controverfy fucceeded ; but
how

how long the prohibition lasted, or in what manner the difference was adjusted, no where appears. //

In this year, 1720, a new Play-house was erected in the Hay-Market, by one Mr. Potter, a carpenter. It was not built for any particular person or Company, but seems to have been intended as a mere speculation by the architect, who relied on its being occasionally hired for dramatic exhibitions.

The number of Theatres in London was this year [1729] increased by the addition of one in Goodman's-Fields, which met with great opposition from many respectable merchants and grave citizens, who apprehended much mischief from the introduction of these kind of diversions so near to their own habitations. Mr. Odell, however, the Proprietor, was not deterred from pursuing his design; he completed the building, and, having collected a Company, began to perform in it. It is asserted, that for some time he got not less than one hundred pounds a week by this undertaking; but the clamour against it continuing, he was obliged to abandon the further prosecution of his scheme; by which means he sustained a considerable loss. It was afterwards revived by Mr. Giffard with some degree of success./

/ The patent for Drury-Lane being renewed, Mr. Booth, who found his disorder increase, began to think it was time to dispose of his share and interest in the Theatre. The person upon whom he fixed for a purchaser was John Highmore, Esq; a gentleman of fortune, who unhappily had contracted an attachment to the Stage, from having performed the part of *Lothario* one night for a wager. A treaty between them was set on foot soon after Mr. Wilks's death, and was concluded by Mr. Highmore's agreeing to purchase one half of Mr. Booth's share, with the whole of his power in the management, for the sum of two thousand five hundred pounds. Mr. Highmore, however, proved unequal to the task, and was at last obliged to give up the management with considerable loss.

The person who next succeeded to the patent of Drury-Lane Play-house was Charles Fleetwood, a gentleman who at one period of his life had possessed a very large fortune, of which at this time a small portion only remained. He purchased not only the share belonging to Mr. Highmore,

but

but thofe of all the other Partners; and fo little value
was then fet upon the Theatre, that the whole fum which
he difburfed for it hardly more than exceeded the half of
what Mr. Highmore had before paid.

Although dramatic entertainments were not at this time
fupported by the abilities of any actors of extraordinary
merit, yet this period feems to have been particularly
marked by a fpirit of enterprize which prevailed in theatrical affairs. In 1733, the houfe in Covent-Garden was
to be finifhed, and Mr. Rich's Company immediately removed thither, which occafioned the old building in Lincoln's-Inn-Fields to be deferted. Mr. Giffard was then
advifed that it would be more to his advantage to quit
Goodman's Fields, and take the vacant edifice. He ac-
cordingly agreed for it in 1735, and acted there during
the two enfuing years.

Soon afterwards, though at a time when fo many
Theatres were employed to divert the public, and when
none of them were in a flourifhing ftate, the imprudence
and extravagance of a gentleman, who poffeffed genius,
wit, and humour in a high degree, obliged him to ftrike
out a new fpecies of entertainment, which in the end produced an extraordinary change in the conftitution of the
dramatic fyftem. To extricate himfelf out of difficulties
in which he was involved, and probably to revenge fome
indignities which had been thrown upon him by people in
power, that admirable painter and acurate obferver of life,
the late Henry Fielding, determined to amufe the town
at the expence of fome perfons in high rank, and of great
influence in the political world. For this purpofe he got
together a company of Performers, who exhibited at the
Theatre in the Hay-Market, under the whimfical title of
the Great Mogul's Company of Comedians. The piece
he reprefented was Pafquin, which was acted to crowded
audiences for fifty fucceffive nights. Encouraged by the
favourable reception this performance met with, he determined to continue at the fame place the next feafon, when
he produced feveral new plays, fome of which were applauded, and the reft condemned. As foon as the novelty
of the defign was over, a vifible difference appeared between the audiences of the two years. The Company,
which as the play-bils faid, dropped from the clouds,
were difbanded; and the manager not having attended

to

to the voice of œconomy in his prosperity, was left no richer nor more independent than when he first engaged in the project.

The severity of Mr. Fielding's satire in these pieces had galled the Minister to that degree, that the impression was not erased from his mind when the cause of it had lost all effect. He meditated therefore a severe revenge on the Stage, and determined to prevent any attacks of the like kind for the future. In the execution of this plan he steadily persisted ; and at last had the satisfaction of seeing the enemy, which had given him so much uneasiness, effectually restrained from any power of annoying him on the public Theatres. An act of Parliament passed in the year 1737, which forbad the representation of any performance not previously licensed by the Lord Chamberlain, or in any place, except the city of Westminster and the liberties thereof, or where the Royal Family should at any time reside. It also took from the Crown the power of licensing any more Theatres, and inflicted heavy penalties on those who should hereafter perform in defiance of the regulation in the statute. This unpopular act did not pass without opposition. It called forth the eloquence of Lord Chesterfield, in a speech wherein all the arguments in favour of this obnoxious law were answered, the dangers which might ensue from it were pointed out, and the little necessity for such hostilities against the Stage clearly demonstrated. It also excited an alarm in the people at large, as tending to introduce restraints on the liberty of the press. Many pamphlets were published against the principle of the act ; and it was combated in every shape which wit, ridicule, or argument, could oppose it in. All these, however, availed nothing ; the Minister had resolved, and the Parliament was too compliant to slight a bill which came recommended from so powerful a quarter. It therefore passed into a law, and freed the then, and all future Ministers, from any apprehensions of mischief from the wit or malice of dramatic writers.

The year 1741 was rendered remarkable in the theatrical world by the appearance of an actor, whose genius seemed intended to adorn, and whose abilities were destined to support the stage. This was the late Mr. Garrick, who, after experiencing some slights from the Managers

of

of Drury-Lane and Covent-Garden, determined to make trial of his theatrical qualifications at the Play-houſe in Goodman's-Fields, under the direction of Mr. Giffard, who was at that time permitted to perform there without moleſtation. The part he choſe for his firſt appearance was that of Richard the Third, in which he diſplayed ſo clear a conception of the character, ſuch power of execution, and a union of talents ſo varied, extenſive, and unexpected, as ſoon fixed his reputation as the firſt actor of his own or any former time. His fame ſpread through every part of the town with the greateſt rapidity; and Goodman's-Fields Theatre, which had been confined to the inhabitants of the City, became the reſort of the polite, and was honoured with the notice of all ranks and orders of people.

At Goodmans-Fields Mr. Garrick remained but one ſeaſon; after which he removed to Drury-Lane, where he continued to increaſe his reputation, and, by a prudent attention to the dictates of frugality and diſcretion, acquired a character, which pointed him out as a proper perſon to ſucceed to the management of the Theatre a few years after; and a fortune which enabled him to accompliſh that point when the opportunity offered.

The affairs of Drury-Lane Theatre ſuffered all the miſchiefs which could ariſe from the imprudence or inability of the Manager. That gentleman had embarraſſed his domeſtic concerns by almoſt every ſpecies of miſconduct, and involved himſelf in ſuch difficulties, that there remained no other means of extricating himſelf from them than by abandoning his country, and retiring abroad. About the year 1745, the whole of his property in the Theatre was either mortgaged or ſold; and the patent, which had been aſſigned to ſome creditors, was advertiſed to be diſpoſed of by public auction. Two Bankers became the purchaſers, and they received into the management the late Mr. Lacey, to whom the conduct of the Theatre was relinquiſhed. The calamities of the times affected the credit of many perſons at this juncture; and amongſt the reſt of the new Managers, who found themſelves obliged to ſtop payment. Their misfortunes occaſioned the patent again to become the object of a ſale. It was offered to ſeveral perſons, but few appeared to have courage enough to venture upon it even at the very low

price

price then afked for it. At length it was propofed by Mr. Lacey, that he and Mr. Garrick fhould become joint-purchafers. The offer was accepted. A renewal of the patent was folicited and obtained. All the preliminaries were in a fhort time fettled, and, in the year 1747, the houfe was opened with a Prologue written by Dr. Johnfon, and fpoken by Mr. Garrick.

From this period may be dated the flourifhing ftate of the Theatre. The new partners were furnifhed with abilities to make their purchafe advantageous to themfelves, and ufeful to the public. Mr. Garrick's admirable performances infured them great audiences; and the induftry and attention of Mr. Lacey were employed in rendering the houfe convenient to the frequenters of it. They both exerted their endeavours to acquire the favour of the town; and the preference which was given to them over their rivals at the other Theatre fufficiently proved the fuperior eftimation they were held in. The harmony which fubfifted between them contributed to the fuccefs of their undertaking, and their efforts in the end procured them both riches and refpect.

The month of December, 1761, was marked with the death of Mr. Rich, who had been manager under the patents granted by Charles the Second almoft 50 years. His peculiar excellence in the compofition of thofe performances which demanded fhew and expence enabled him, with an indifferent company of actors, to make a ftand againft the greateft performers of his time: he was unrivalled in the reprefentation of his favourite character Harlequin, and poffeffed with many foibles fome qualities which commanded the efteem of his friends and acquaintance. On his deceafe, the bufinefs of Covent-Garden Theatre was conducted by his fon-in-law Mr. Beard

The Theatre in the Hay-market had for fome years been occupied in the fummer time by virtue of licences from the Lord Chamberlain. In the month of July, 1766, it was advanced to the dignity of a Theatre Royal; a patent being then made out to Mr. Foote, authorizing him to build a Theatre in the city and liberties of Weftminfter, and to exhibit dramatic performances, &c. therein, from the 14th day of May to the 14th day of Sept. during his life. Mr. Foote very fuccefsfully managed this Theatre until the feafon before his death.

From

From the deceafe of Mr. Rich, Covent-Garden Theatre had been intrufted to the direction of his fon-in-law, Mr. Beard, who introduced feveral mufical pieces to the Stage, which were received with much applaufe, and brought confiderable profits to thofe concerned in the houfe. The tafte of the public inclined very much to this fpecies of performance for feveral feafons; but about the year 1766, the audiences beginning to leffen, and the acting manager finding no relief for a deafnefs which he had long been afflicted with, he became defirous of retiring from the buftle of a Theatre to the quiet of private life. In the fummer of 1767, a negotiation was fet on foot by Meffieurs Harris and Rutherford, for the purchafe of all the property in the Playhoufe which belonged to the then proprietors; but the advantage of having a capital performer as one of the fharers being fuggefted, Mr. Powell was invited to join with them, and he recommended Mr. Colman as a perfon from whom the undertaking would receive great benefit. The propofal being affented to by the feveral parties, the property of the Theatre was affigned in Auguft, 1767, the conduct of the Stage was intrufted to Mr. Colman, and the houfe opened on the 14th of September with the Comedy of *The Rehearfal*; and a Prologue written by Paul Whitehead, and fpoken by Mr. Powell.

Mr. Foote, who, after he had obtained the Patent of the Theatre Royal in the Haymarket, conducted the affairs of his houfe with confiderable fuccefs, and annually acquired a large income as Proprietor and Manager, was induced to transfer his Theatre to Mr. Colman, in confideration of an annuity, and fome particular advantages as a Performer. The reafons which prompted him to take this ftep, were fuppofed to have arifen from an infamous profecution which had been malicioufly (as was generally believed) inftituted againft him. The event of his trial freed him from the charge; but the vexation of mind which it occafioned fo much injured his health, that it probably contributed to fhorten his life. He died the 21ft day of October, 1777.

Notwithftanding Mr. Garrick had quitted the Theatre as Manager and Performer, he did not entirely relinquifh his attention to the Stage; he continued to affift fome authors and actors, and promoted the advantage of
the

the new Patentees occafionally with his advice and affift-ance. The lofs of a man who had taken fo confiderable a part in the dramatic line for fuch a number of years, cannot but be efteemed as an epocha in the annals of the Stage. He died on the 20th January, 1779; and went to the grave with the univerfal admiration of the public at large, and with the particular concern of his numerous friends and connections.

From this period to the prefent time, the hiftory of our Theatres admit of no occurrences that can induce us to lengthen this fhort fketch. We fhall therefore conclude with obferving, that the old Theatre of Drury-Lane, be-ing now fhut up, in order to be taken down and re-built, the company is removed to the new Opera-Houfe, in the Hay-Market, where they meet with tolerable fuccefs, though at advanced prices, which at firft met with fome oppofition from the public.

ADDENDA.

In the Alphabetical Catalogue of Dramatic Writers, to the Plays written by John Burgoyne, Efq. add *The Heirefs*.

Dec. 3, 1791, a Comedy, with Songs, called *A Day in Turkey*, was performed, for the firft time, at the Theatre in Covent-Garden. This comedy is written by Mrs. Cowley; and, though the fable is not unex-ceptionable, and the characters and manners not fuffi-ciently Eaftern, the play on the whole has confiderable merit. The incidents are numerous, and often in-terefting, and the dialogue is fpirited and generally characteriftic.

THE END.

www.ingramcontent.com/pod-product-compliance
Lightning Source LLC
Chambersburg PA
CBHW020239110726

47898CB00004B/1314